PROPHECY
UNFULFILLED

BY THE SAME AUTHOR

Science:

The Dawkins Deficiency: Why Evolution is Not the Greatest Show on Earth, Deep River Books, Sisters, OR, 2011
Information, Knowledge, Evolution, and Self: a question of origins, Xlibris, Bloomington, IN, 2016

Fiction:

Finding the Shepherd - A Tale of Two Loves, Westbow Press, Bloomington, IN, 2016

Theology:

The New Covenant on Trial: Examining the Evidence for a Replacement Covenant, Xlibris, Bloomington, IN, 2016
Once A Christian: How the Bible Convinced Me to Walk Away, Xlibris, Bloomington, IN, 2017
Christians Too, Must Obey: Putting A Fence Around Torah, Xlibris, Bloomington, IN, 2017

From the Back Pew: (series published by Peshat Books)

Volume 1 - *If Not God What?* On Being an Intellectually Fulfilled Theist
Volume 2 - *Choosing to Know God*: Understanding God's Presence in the World
Volume 3 - *Bible Inerrancy: Fact or Fiction?* The Inerrancy of God's Word versus the Fallibility of Human Interpretation
Volume 4 - *Our Shepherd His Flock*: Following the Jewish Messiah on the Path Less Travelled
Volume 5 - *What New Covenant?* Rethinking the Implications of the First Coming of Jesus
Volume 6 - *God's Only Law Book*: What Christianity Fails to Tell You About Your Duty to God
Volume 7 - *Defending God's Sabbath*: Obeying God's Commandment to Safeguard the Sabbath
Volume 8 - *From Sin to Salvation*: A Fresh Perspective on God's Plan for Mankind
Volume 9 - *A Biblical Discourse - Volume 1*: For Those Prepared to Risk Their Orthodox Theology

PROPHECY UNFULFILLED

*The New Testament Examined
by the Rules of Evidence*

WAYNE TALBOT

Library of Congress Control Number:		2018910009
ISBN:	Hardcover	978-1-9845-0168-4
	Softcover	978-1-9845-0167-7
	eBook	978-1-9845-0166-0

Print information available on the last page.

Rev. date: 08/30/2018

To order additional copies of this book, contact:
Xlibris
1-800-455-039
www.Xlibris.com.au
Orders@Xlibris.com.au
773089

DEDICATION

*"Christianity does not profess to convince the perverse and headstrong,
to bring irresistible evidence to the daring and profane, to vanquish the
proud scorner, and afford evidences from which the careless and perverse
cannot possibly escape. This might go to destroy man's responsibility.
All that Christianity professes is to propose such evidences as may
satisfy the meek, the tractable, the candid, the serious enquirer."[1]*
~ Simon Greenleaf (1783-1853) American lawyer and jurist ~

This book is dedicated to all those who, like me, have accepted the
burden of the *serious enquirer*. Whilst Greenleaf rightly warns us of *man's
responsibility*, I am not confident that on a subject as important as this book
addresses, that we should seek merely *to satisfy the meek and the tractable*.
The meek and the tractable are easily fooled, especially by eminent jurists,
and it will not do to lower the standard of evidence to a level which would
not be acceptable in a court of law.

Rather, the standard of evidence should be sufficient to satisfy
the *candid* (truthful and straightforward) and *serious* (demanding, or
characterized by careful consideration) enquirer. I am confident that God
demands no less. If I am to place my faith in an entity, who is said to have
fulfilled the prophecies of the Jewish *mashiach* some two thousand years

ago, I want to be quite certain that I am not succumbing to idolatry. If Jesus was not the promised Messiah, he was not the Son, the Third Person of the Trinity, and Christianity is not a religion of the One True God. There is nothing in the Hebrew Scriptures that can plausibly be taken to mean that the *mashiach* would be "God made flesh". In Christian theology, the concepts of Messiah and Trinity are inextricably bound together, and if the first is found to be false, then so too must the second.

So, dear readers, and others who have pondered this enigma, this book is dedicated to you; to my Orthodox Jewish brothers who have assisted in this study; and to my first loyalty: the God in whom I believe.

However, a note of caution. After publishing an earlier volume, *Once a Christian*[2], I have noticed a marked change in some Christians whom I count as friends, or at least, friendly acquaintants. They are finding it difficult to accept my renouncement of Christianity, and have rationalised, to me, that:

a. I was never truly a Christian.
b. I have not been born again; and/or
c. I do not have the Holy Spirit within.

Some have even distanced themselves from me. So, my warning to you: If you find truth in my writings, there are people who will reconsider their relationship with you, for apostasy is not well accepted in any religion. On that subject, you may consider the plight of a Mormon woman who chose to walk away from her religion[3].

REFERENCES:

1. Greenleaf, Simon, *The Testimony of the Evangelists*, Kregel Classics, Grand Rapids, MI, 1995, p. 12
2. Talbot, Wayne, *Once a Christian*: How the Bible Convinced Me to Walk Away, Xlibris, Bloomington, IN, 2017
3. Naylor, Carma, *A Mormon's Unexpected Journey - Volumes I & 2*, WinePress Publishing, Enumclaw, WA, 2006

AUTHOR'S NOTE

"I have learned a great deal from scholars, as often as not,
more of what thoughts to reject than to accept."
~ My Own Conclusion ~

Curious as it may seem, I wish to thank Simon Greenleaf for his inspiring book, *The Testimony of the Evangelists*[1]. The sub-title of my book, I have purloined from his, for encouraged by his approach, I decided to follow his example. That said, the scope of my study extends beyond just the Gospels, to the entire New Testament, using the New King James Version (NKJV) as my primary source of the Jesus narrative. I recoiled at the thought of comparing more than one Christian version, being already aware of the lack of verbal agreement across the Gospels alone: *"typically less than 40 percent, and more like 20 percent or less in some cases."*[2]. The task is daunting enough as it is. However, I believed it necessary to cross-check the NKJV wording of the Old Testament, with the TJB (The Jewish Bible, translated from the Hebrew), in an endeavour to understand the likelihood of the Greek versions misleading the Evangelists in their understanding. We discuss the limitations of the Greek Septuagint in Chapter 2-1.

I first read Greenleaf's work whilst still a Christian. I must confess that despite often warning others of the dangers lurking thereabouts, I had, myself, succumbed to the *Cult of Authority*: I had accepted the author's assertions because I had accepted his credentials.

Simon Greenleaf (1783 – 1853) was Emeritus Professor of Law, and at one time, the Dane Professor of Law at Harvard University. He is well known for his three-volume *Treatise on the Law of Evidence*, for many years a standard reference work in legal circles. He is described in The Dictionary of American Biography as *"the greatest single authority on evidence in the entire literature of legal procedure"*. I was impressed – who could dispute Simon Greenleaf's credentials as an expert on the laws of evidence, and their application? There are articles that claim that Greenleaf did not believe in the truth of the Gospels, and setting out to discount them, he found the opposite: he found that the writers were indeed trustworthy witnesses, and that their accounts should be accepted as reliable evidence. I have been unable to authenticate his reasons for analysing the New Testament; nor have I been able to find any statement to that effect by Greenleaf himself, only unsupported assertions by others. Nevertheless, I remain unconvinced, for he stated:

> "The proof that God has revealed himself to man by special and express communications, and that Christianity constitutes that revelation, is no part of these inquiries. This has already been shown in the most satisfactory manner, by others, who have written expressly upon this subject."[3]

This suggests, to me, that Greenleaf started with the presupposition of the divine origin of the New Testament, contrary to his advice, that we should start with *"a mind, freed, as far as possible, from existing prejudice"*[4]. That notwithstanding, he did write this book on his findings in which he declared:

> "Let (the Gospel's) testimony be sifted, as it were given in a court of justice on the side of the adverse party, the witness being subjected to a rigorous cross-examination. The result, it is confidently believed, will be an undoubting conviction of their integrity, ability, and truth."[5]

I have accepted that challenge, and this book records my sifting of evidence, my rigorous cross-examination of the witnesses (as far as that is possible), and my conviction regarding their integrity, ability, and truth. I will periodically refer to the fallacy, so prevalent in Christian thought, that the Bible, that being whichever version one prefers, is the inerrant Word of God.

If that is your belief, and you choose to not have it challenged, this book is not for you.

Wayne Talbot
Kelso NSW Australia
August, 2018

REFERENCES:

1. Greenleaf, Simon, *The Testimony of the Evangelists*, Kregel Classics, Grand Rapids, MI, 1995
2. Dunn, James D.G., *Jesus, Paul, and the Gospels*, Wm. B. Eerdmans Publishing Co., Grand Rapids, MI, 2011, p. 34
3. Greenleaf, *Ibid*, p. 13, referencing Hopkins, *Lowell Lectures*, particularly Lect. 2. Wilson, *Evidences* 1.45-61. Horne, *Introduction to the Study of Holy Scriptures* 1.1-39.
4. *Ibid*, p. 11
5. *Ibid*, back cover

CONTENTS

My Approach

Intentions of the Author

In Part 8, we will review an intriguingly named book, *The Right Doctrine from the Wrong Texts*? On encountering this work, my mind went into overdrive pondering the implications of this title. One of the discussions therein concerns the intentions of the authors of the numerous books in the Bible: should we take the texts at face value; should exegesis discern more meanings than the author intended; did the author, being divinely inspired, not fully understand the meaning of the words he wrote; did God have intentions not revealed to His Prophets; and/or are the words as recorded those of the author, those of God, or a combination? Truly, more questions than answers it would appear, but as I later discovered, there were far more varied answers that questions.

So, you might ask, what is my point?

As I have stated in all previous works, I research for my own purposes: I must know the truth of God. I do not expect to find it, at least, not completely, but if nothing else, I should be able to eliminate the untruths that permeate religions. I write to document my findings, and give myself the opportunity to review, appraise, and otherwise criticise my own conclusions. I publish these writings for two reasons. Firstly, much as an artist on completing an arduous work, a masterpiece even, seeks to frame the painting with a sense of fulfillment, I like to see my words in print, masterpiece or no, to bring closure to the project. With no false humility, I take a certain pride in the work. Secondly, I publish to give others the opportunity to reflect on my work. Whether they ever do or not is inconsequential in the overall scheme of things. I would enjoy debate on the contents, but I am not disappointed if such does not happen – my primary goal has been achieved. This study is a continuation of that intriguing mission: revealing the truths and untruths of religions, and in this case, the prophecy fulfillment claims of Christianity.

Whilst not an archaeologist, my methods are somewhat similar. I believe that something of value is hidden beneath, and I am more than curious to know what it is. But first, the essential task of marking out the area to be searched, lest my curiosity be piqued by areas irrelevant to the matter at hand. This is why I have written more than one book examining the Scriptures, for the Scriptures are multi-faceted, and it is far too easy to be distracted by the multitude of themes. Then begins the painstaking task: carefully brushing away the centuries of accumulated literary and theological debris. I must carefully examine each artefact or fragment *in situ*, as it were, lest I attribute it to a specific period or place, unintentionally affirming the consequent. *In situ*, in this context, is to be cognisant of the cultural-historical context, the idioms of languages long dead, what can be learned from extra-biblical sources, and comparing contrary views on each and every subject.

I must not allow presuppositions or preferences to colour my judgement, nor must I jump to conclusions, but slowly, and carefully, accumulate data, until I have sufficient upon which to arrive at a conclusion.

Similarly, I am not a lawyer, but during my service as an officer in the Royal Australian Air Force, I was required to study and pass examinations in Air Force Law, not dissimilar to civil law, being based upon the same principles. The *Rules of Evidence*, especially, closely follow those in civil law, and it is those rules which I will apply in this study.

In my task of clearing away the theological layers of Christian history, I have already written of my conclusions regarding the claimed inerrancy of Scripture[1], a New Covenant[2], why I am no longer a Christian[3], and why I believe that God's Law, as expressed to the Children of Israel, is as relevant today as it ever was[4]. Each of those studies provide part of the framework of this book, and inevitably, I shall repeat some parts, and at other times, refer the reader to those studies for more detail, should the reader be so interested.

What is also inevitable, is that I would already have come to some conclusions, which quite naturally, become presuppositions in this book. Where that occurs, I will not simply make bald assertions, but provide the evidence and reasoning behind them.

So, let the case begin, examining the evidence for the Christian claim that Jesus fulfilled Old Testament prophecies, anywhere from 44 to 400 in number, depending on who is asserting the claim.

Scope of this Study

This study is not just a review of these claimed prophecy fulfillments by Jesus, although that is the goal. Before we can accept the prophecies themselves, we need to understand what they were, and who made them. Before we can accept that prophecies were fulfilled, we need to understand who is making that claim, and their authority to do so. As the only evidence we have is written, we need to call expert witnesses, in this case, New Testament scholars, to testify as to the authenticity and authority of not only the documents in evidence, but the writers themselves. Christian apologists and commentators invariably accept attribution of authorship by the Christian Church, but there is far too much evidence to do so without question. All experience is coloured by culture, knowledge, expectations, emotion, desire, intent, and other human factors, and any writings that ensue contain some elements of all of these. None of us is immune, including those who wrote, edited, interpreted, and translated the documentary evidence that we shall examine, i.e., bible versions. If the disciples of Jesus believed something, we should attempt to understand why, and whether they held shared beliefs based on their common, or individual experiences. We have substantive evidence that some accounts were based on firsthand witness, some hearsay, and some not witnessed at all.

One must undertake due diligence on numerous background issues before attempting to evaluate the truth of prophecy fulfillment. Thus, the first hundred pages or so are spent on what I believe to be, essentials of which the reader should be cognizant. I would apologise for this preamble, except that no apology is warranted – this is essential reading.

Biblical Warnings Concerning Prophecies

"If there arises among you a prophet or a dreamer of dreams, and he gives you a sign or a wonder, and the sign or the wonder comes to pass, of which he spoke to you, saying, 'Let us go after other gods' – which you have not known – 'and let us serve them', you shall not listen to the words of that prophet or that dreamer of dreams, for the Lord your God is testing you to know whether you love the Lord your God with all your heart and with all your soul. You shall walk after the Lord your God and fear Him, and keep His commandments and obey His voice; you shall serve Him and hold fast to Him.

But that prophet or that dreamer of dreams shall be put to death, because he has spoken in order to turn you away from the Lord your God who brought you out of the land of Egypt and redeemed you from the house of bondage, to entice you from the way in which the Lord your God commanded you to walk. So, you shall put away the evil from your midst." (Deuteronomy 13:1-5)

The *Trinity* – Father, Son, and Holy Spirit, is a god "*which you have not known*" - well at least, I have not, and certainly, the Jews of Second Temple Judaism did not. The religion of Christianity tells its followers that they need *not* follow the commandments of God. The *dreamers* who misinterpret the oracles of God and the prophecies, *"entice you from the way in which the Lord your God commanded you to walk"*, as God told the Children of Israel. Will you *"put away the evil from your midst"*?

> "Therefore, say to the house of Israel: Thus, says the Lord God: Repent, turn away from your idols, and turn your faces away from all your abominations. For anyone of the house of Israel, or of the strangers who dwell in Israel, who separates himself from Me and sets up his idols in his heart and puts before him what causes him to stumble into iniquity, then comes to a prophet to inquire of him concerning Me, I the Lord will answer him by Myself.
>
> I will set My face against that man and make him a sign and a proverb, and I will cut him off from the midst of My people. Then you shall know that I am the Lord. And if the prophet is induced to speak anything, I the Lord have induced that prophet, and I will stretch out My hand against him from among My people Israel.
>
> And they shall bear their iniquity; the punishment of the prophet shall be the same as the punishment of the one who inquired." (Ezekiel 14:6-10)

Do you not see how well this prophecy could fit Jesus and his followers? If, and I stress IF, Jesus did not fulfill the ancient prophecies concerning the Messiah, and thus was not the Messiah, then quite likely, he was a false prophet who sought to lead God's people astray, to worship an idol (the Trinity), and suffered the consequences, just as did some of his followers: *"I will cut him off from the midst of My people"*.

God's warnings in the Hebrew Scriptures are clear, concerning false prophets and idol worship. This is why, to my mind, I must be very certain that Jesus was the prophesied Messiah, fulfilling the prophecies as claimed, lest I too be guilty of that which God has forbidden.

REFERENCES:

1. *Bible Inerrancy: Fact or Fiction?* The Inerrancy of God's Word versus the Fallibility of Human Interpretation, Peshat Books, Kelso, NSW, 2012
2. *The New Covenant on Trial*: Examining the Evidence for a Replacement Covenant, Xlibris, Bloomington, IN, 2016
3. Talbot, Wayne, *Once a Christian*: How the Bible Convinced Me to Walk Away, Xlibris, Bloomington, IN, 2017
4. Talbot, Wayne, *Christians Too, Must Obey*: Putting a Fence Around Torah, Xlibris, Bloomington, IN, 2017

PART 1

UNDERSTANDING EVIDENCE

*"You have to take Bible prophecy literally, just
like everything else in the Bible."*
~ Tim LaHaye, American evangelical Christian
minister, speaker, and author (1926-2016) ~

To take the Bible literally, means to take it in the literary sense that it
was written, not just how the words read to you. One must first learn to
recognise the figures of speech: metaphors, allegory, irony, personification,
anthropomorphisms, and so forth. That is not as easy as it may sound,
for we are dealing with contributions from multiple ancient cultures, each
with their own thought patterns, figures of speech, and colloquialisms.
Exegesis also demands that verses should be interpreted in context, not
extracted, and placed in an entirely different context, to have them mean
whatever one wants them to mean. This, I would contend, represents the
most egregious error: but whether committed by the original authors;

later editors, scribes and translators; or by interpreters and readers, is often difficult to discern. We will see many such examples as we proceed.

I believe it worthwhile to spend a few pages reviewing some basic concepts regarding the nature of evidence, and how it should be evaluated in the context of ancient writings.

Before doing so, however, we should understand the nature, and burden, of *proof.*

Proof – What Is It?

Proof is any evidence or argument that convinces one that a proposition is true. It is generally asserted that the burden of proof lies upon the proponent of that proposition, but although that is true philosophically, it is not true in practice. If it were true, then everybody would be convinced by the same evidence, which we know, is untrue. In reality, people do not convince us - we convince ourselves. The evidence or argument offered by the proponent does not represent the totality of that which is evaluated: we all have our own rules of evidence; our own understanding of logic; we evaluate plausibility differently; and each of us has knowledge, learnings, and/or experience which we individually bring to the table. This is as true in theology, as it is in the jurisdictions of law and science.

In matters of philosophy, including theology, or any matters of the heart, however, logic is often disregarded entirely, especially when fear is present.

Perhaps the greatest difficulty of all is whether one wants to be convinced. If you are already convinced of an alternate proposition, no evidence or argument is likely to convince you to change your mind. For example, many noted atheists have expressed their desire that there not be a god. Thomas Nagel, Professor of Philosophy at New York University and a self-confessed atheist wrote: "I want atheism to be true and am made uneasy by the fact that some of the most intelligent and well informed people I know are religious believers. It isn't just that I don't believe in God and naturally, hope there is no God! I don't want there to be a God; I don't want the universe to be like that."[1] Anti-theist Christopher Hitchens stated, "It is to me an appalling thought that anyone could wish for a supreme and absolute and unalterable ruler, whose reign was eternal and unchallengeable"[2] It is unlikely that any evidence or logic would convince these atheists of the existence of God: their minds are just not open to such notions.

If you have engaged in debates with atheists, you would have noticed that commonly, they will take a legal or scientific stance, and assert that the burden of proof of God is upon the proponents. However, in matters of philosophy, law and science are irrelevant, for there can be no substantive legal or scientific evidence to hand. Philosophy must be adjudicated using different rules.

On the other hand, there are many people who seem to want there to be a god, or in the case of Christians, they fear that if they do not believe, they will be condemned to eternal punishment. Thus, the evaluation of evidence, in pursuit of the truth of a proposition, becomes problematic. If truth is your goal, then emotion, preference, and former beliefs must be set aside, to enable new light to be shed.

Proof of a proposition, except in very limited exceptions, is never objective, but always subjective, most especially in matters of philosophy and theology, or matters of the heart. The burden of proof lies with the individual, not with the proponent who may be seeking to convince you. I am not one of the latter; rather, I am laying out the evidence that has convinced me – the rest is up to you.

REFERENCES:

1.   Nagel, T., *The Last Word*, Oxford University Press, New York, 1997, p. 130
2.   Hitchens, Christopher and Wilson, Douglas, *Is Christianity Good for the World*, Canon Press, Moscow, Indiana, 2009, p. 12

CHAPTER 1-1

EVIDENCE OF PROPHECY

"With prophecies the commentator is often a more important man than the prophet."
~ Georg Christoph Lichtenberg (1742-1799)
German scientist and satirist ~

I would suggest paraphrasing this observation as: "later interpretations are given more credence than the original words of the prophet".

I believe it fair to contend that if Jesus of Nazareth fulfilled the messianic prophecies, then we can accept him as the Messiah; but if he did not, then he was not. If Jesus was not the Messiah, then the natural corollary is that any religion founded on the belief that he was, is clearly a religion of man, not of God. Christian apologetics has Jesus fulfilling an implausible number of Old Testament prophecies. My preferred Christian reference, the NKJV (New King James Version) of the bible notes: "an *Outline Star* ☆ is used to indicate that the text contains a prophecy that at the time of the action had yet to be fulfilled. A *Solid Star* ★ indicates that the text contains the fulfillment of a prophecy". In later chapters, we will deal with the prophecies that, according to the NKJV editors, were fulfilled by Jesus. Fortunately for me, and probably for you as well, the count in the NKJV is considerably less than the 400 quoted elsewhere, and I shall largely restrict my enquiries to just that bible translation.

Before we start, I would comment on a failure of logic that I often encounter in Christian apologetics' literature and conversations.

To wit: when Christians are offered evidence that a prophecy was not fulfilled as claimed, they will often contend that, well, yes, but it will be in the Second Coming. If the prophecy was not fulfilled in the First Coming, it cannot be offered as evidence of Jesus being the Messiah. Anybody and everybody can <u>fail</u> to fulfill a prophecy, and such failure can only be evidence that the person was not the one prophesied. Reference to a Second Coming is circular logic: that much should be obvious. If Jesus was not the Messiah in his first coming, there will be no second coming. A second coming assumes the truth of the first, and thus begs the question.

Evaluating Evidence of Prophecy Fulfillment

In writing his book, "*The Testimony of the Evangelists*", Simon Greenleaf sought to demonstrate that the Gospels could be accepted as truth. He addressed his fellow members of the legal profession with these words:

> "If a close examination of the evidences of Christianity may be expected of one class of men more than another, it would seem incumbent on us, who make the law of evidence one of our peculiar studies. Our profession leads us to explore the maze of falsehood, to detect its artifices, to pierce its thickest veils, to follow and expose its sophistries, to compare the statements of different witnesses with severity, to discover truth and separate it from error."[1]

As I confessed, I am not a member of the legal profession, but I do have some understanding of rules of evidence, especially how written evidence, in contrast to oral evidence, should be evaluated. Greenleaf's book is short on the detail of how he approached his analysis, but I suspect that he started with the presupposition that the Gospels, as he had them, were written in their entirety by the people to whom they are attributed, namely: Matthew, Mark, Luke, and John. Accepting them as honest and reliable men, he accepted their testimony, as he would have in a court of law, but with too little, if any, cross-examination. Using his own words, he failed *"to pierce its thickest veils, to follow and expose its sophistries, to compare the statements of different witnesses with severity, to discover truth and separate it from error."*

I do not start with his presuppositions, and thus, am very much concerned about who wrote these accounts, and when, and who may have redacted them over time. We need to ascertain whether the events were witnessed by the evangelists as claimed. There is sufficient internal evidence to demonstrate, irrefutably, that some events were not witnessed by the evangelists themselves, and some events were not witnessed by anybody at all. This all goes to the credibility of the witnesses, whom Simon Greenleaf did not properly investigate in his own study; in short, he failed *to compare the statements of different witnesses with severity, to discover truth and separate it from error.* Likewise, Greenleaf offers no evidence that he called witnesses who could refute the written evidence of the evangelists. Effectively, he conducted his case, with no cross-examination of the witnesses for his case, and ignored witnesses against it. In my view, he failed to do what he said was incumbent upon himself and his peers.

If I am to be offered Scripture verses as proof of prophecy fulfillment, I believe it my duty to evaluate the evidence using every tool available to me. Thus, in the following chapters, I put the case for prophecy fulfillment on trial, using both the Old and New Testaments as my chief witnesses, but also calling expert witnesses for their opinions on significant issues. A reader can cross-examine my evidence at their leisure.

Claims of prophecy fulfillment, if we are to take Simon Greenleaf's lead, should be subjected to the very same rules of evidence as would be used in a court of law. This, we shall do.

Rules of Evidence

Evidence, in its broadest sense, includes everything that is used to determine or demonstrate the truth of an assertion. There are four categories we should identify, and understand their weight in the context of proving prophecy fulfillment:

1. Substantive, or Direct Evidence.
2. Corroborating Evidence.
3. Circumstantial Evidence; and
4. Correlating Evidence.

Every discipline and jurisdiction have rules of evidence, formulated to ensure that only properly obtained, and relevant evidence, is accepted for consideration. For example, evolution is a scientific theory, and only evidence which is derived via the scientific method, should be accepted in determining whether the theory is scientifically proven. Essentially, all arguments toward proof must be based on substantive scientific evidence. Speculation, or even philosophy, can be used to formulate hypotheses, but by themselves, these are inadequate as proof. Other forms of evidence such as corroborating, circumstantial, or correlating can be used in support, but not in place of, substantive evidence. They could be *necessary* in understanding the complete picture, but in and of themselves, cannot be *sufficient*.

There are implications for each of these categories of evidence, especially in the context of written, versus oral, testimony. We will come back to those.

Regarding *substantive* evidence: that some data or fact is *consistent* with the proposition in question, should not in itself be taken as convincing evidence, let alone *proof*, of that proposition, unless it can be shown that such data is *inconsistent* with any other proposition. If the data is consistent exclusively with that proposition, that proposition alone and none other, then we have good reason to accept it as substantive evidence. However, if evidence is consistent with more than one proposition, it is then *circumstantial*, not substantive. For example, that Jesus was born in Bethlehem is of that nature. Christian apologetics quote: "*But you, Bethlehem … out of you shall come forth to Me the One to be Ruler in Israel*" (Micah 5:1), as a prophecy fulfilled by Jesus, but many have come out of Bethlehem, so that is but circumstantial evidence. In passing, the next part of the prophecy is subject to controversy due to the differences in translation from the Greek and Hebrew, and the Christian use of theological annotations, in the form of initial capitals, to subliminally influence understanding. The NKJV renders the next sentence as: "*Whose goings forth are from old, from everlasting*", which is then interpreted as meaning that this ruler of Israel must be divine. However, the translation from the Hebrew is: "*his origins will be from early times, from days of old*", which has no divine connotation whatsoever – it simply refers to the ruler being a descendant of David. This example demonstrates the complexity of understanding evidence.

Circumstantial evidence should carry little weight in a case of such gravity as this one, and like corroborating evidence, can be used as additional support, but not as the foundation of the case.

Circumstantial evidence exists where the data is consistent with the proposition in question, but may or may not itself directly contribute to the proof. At best, it shows that the proposition *may* be true because it is not inconsistent with the proposition. In our case, possibility is a long way from probability. In popular detective stories, it is the evidence category to which the trilogy of *motive*, *means*, and *opportunity* belongs. Having a motive to commit a crime is not direct evidence, but it is circumstantial in that it is not inconsistent with the accused having committed the crime; the same may be said of means and opportunity: one could have all three, but still be entirely innocent. These three should only be used to identify suspects, not as sufficient proof of guilt. Circumstantial evidence may also be consistent with one or more competing theories and thus, substantive evidence is required before circumstantial evidence can be considered as contributing to the proof of the proposition. Admittedly, some jurisdictions allow judgement based on circumstantial evidence alone, but such is unsafe in a case as critical as the one we are presented with here.

Corroborating evidence on the other hand, is evidence of an incident or fact *related* to the primary case, but not directly to that case itself. It can be of any evidence type that directly supports some other evidence independently obtained, though it may still be shown to be consistent with an alternate theory. For example, where a person is accused of arson using an accelerant such as petrol, evidence may be presented that he was seen purchasing petrol in a plastic container the day before the crime. This is corroborating evidence, but not substantive, for he may have purchased the petrol for his lawn mower. Again, in our case with such far-reaching consequences, corroborating evidence can have no weight, without substantive evidence to corroborate. This type of evidence is often misused by Christian apologists. For example, archaeological evidence can corroborate narratives regarding the existence of places, contemporary customs, and even people and times. However, it cannot corroborate what individuals said, the very basis of doctrine and theology. It can sometimes corroborate an individual's actions, but not the reasons for those actions. Thus, whilst to some extent, archaeology can be used as evidence of bible accuracy, it can only do so in an historical sense – it offers no useful evidence to support theology, and is largely irrelevant in the context of such studies.

Remember that contemporary fiction novels narrate many verifiable facts of the type that archaeological evidence offers, but the stories are nevertheless fiction. I have written a similar fiction[2], one that I described as pseudo-biographical, because the places where events occurred do exist, some of the people not central to the story are real, and the events themselves are based on true experiences in my own life. I did a better job than I anticipated, because one close friend believed a particular episode to have been true, even though it was entirely fictional. To him it was plausible, knowing me and some of the experiences of my life, and the way that I described it. This should be a warning for bible students: just because a narrative appears plausible because it is consistent with what is known to be true, or with other narratives, is not sufficient evidence that it is true.

Correlation is often mistaken for causation. That two facts appear related does not argue that one caused the other; the causal link must be demonstrated. As we will later discuss, there are bible verses which correlate, but when examined closely, have been used to beg the question, each verse being used as a proof text of the other. Such circular reasoning is not acceptable as evidence. In the same vein, by the rules of evidence, no document can attest to its own truth. For example, when 2 Timothy 3:16 speaks of "all Scripture", it cannot be referring to itself. It only became Scripture when the Church decided it was. Self-affirmation is not acceptable as evidence, unless corroborated by other reliable evidence.

One should not confuse *evidence* and *proof*; they are categorically different. Proof is the argument or evidence that convinces one that a proposition is true. But the evidence itself can be true or false, fact or fiction. People can be convinced by faulty logic, incompetence in evaluating evidence, implausible stories, presuppositions, and even outright falsehoods. Without the required level of discernment, such evidence is proof to them nonetheless, demonstrating that the burden of proof truly lies with the individual, not with the proponent.

On the other hand, evidence can be factual and true, but unconvincing and thus, not proof (to the enquirer, at least). In legal domains, certain evidence can be ruled inadmissible, irrespective of whether it is true or not. In the same way, some people rule certain types of evidence inadmissible to them personally, perhaps even unconsciously. If we are to genuinely seek after truth, we should carefully evaluate our own *rules of evidence*, being certain that we are not accepting evidence without substantiation, and equally certain that we are not ignoring evidence that we should consider.

Many analysts and investigators will claim *inference to best explanation*. Sadly though, too few apply the appropriate level of rigour to their evidence evaluation. An inference may be logically valid, but nevertheless untrue, especially if the explanation is limited to their preferred paradigm or worldview: evolutionists are particularly susceptible to this error, and theologians are not exempt.

And just one last issue before moving on: Begging the question, or affirming the consequence (Latin: *Petition Principii*). This is a form of logical fallacy in which a statement, or claim, is assumed to be true, without evidence other than the statement or claim itself. Perhaps the best evidence of this fallacy, in Christian theology, is as mentioned before. It can be found by logically evaluating 2 Timothy 3:16. This says that all Scripture is given by the inspiration of God; this letter is Scripture; therefore, this letter is given by the inspiration of God; therefore, what it says is inerrant. Truly, people do believe this way, but cross-examination reveals their error.

I shall be using my understanding of evidence and logic, as described above, to evaluate the claims of prophecy fulfillment in the Gospels. I will give less credence to the Epistles, as for the most part, they are hearsay. Paul's claim of personal, divine instruction lacks corroboration, and some of the internal evidence suggests that his claim is not credible. Even so, the Gospels themselves provide sufficient evidence for me, at least, to render a well-considered, safe verdict.

Authenticity

Something is said to be authentic, if its origin is not in dispute. Christian doctrine is based on many writings whose authenticity has been long disputed. For example, Christianity attributes First and Second Timothy to Paul. However, since the 1700's, New Testament scholars, both Christian and secular, generally agree that these letters addressed to Timothy are not authentic Pauline. They are believed to have been written by one of Paul's students, circa 90-140 CE, as "they reflect a church hierarchy that is more organized and defined than the church was in Paul's time"[3]. The question becomes: Why would Christians place so much credence on the writings of some unknown person, perhaps a student of Paul, but writing long after the time of both Jesus and Paul? More importantly, what was the motivation of the Church of Rome in attributing these works to Paul?

As noted earlier, the Christian doctrine on scriptural inerrancy is, to some extent, based on the words in 2 Timothy, but if we are unsure of the authorship, Christians should give this text, no more credence than writings which are excluded from the canon. Another Christian doctrine is based on these verses: "For the priesthood being changed, of necessity there is also a change in the law" (Heb 7:12), and "Now this is the main point of the things we are saying: We have such a High Priest … in that he says, 'a new covenant', he has made the first obsolete" (Heb 8:1, 13). If, as many scholars assert, Paul was not the author of Hebrews, how can we be confident of the real author's knowledge, understanding, and intentions? The traditional Christian view is that it was written by Paul, yet increasingly, scholars disagree[4].

Now consider that many writings in the New Testament were not truly written by those to whom they are traditionally attributed, then wonder why the Church Fathers thought it necessary that they be attributed to persons of authority; i.e., men who were closely associated with Jesus, or who were appointed by Jesus, or their appointees. They understood that for these writings to have authority, they had to be authentic. Given that the authenticity is much disputed, then so too, their authority must be in doubt.

Authority

Who was authorised to speak for God?

If we are to believe the Hebrew Scriptures, Moses and all the Prophets were. If we are to believe the Gospels, Jesus was. If we are to have the audacity to speak for God, we must first ensure that we have heard authentic voices, speaking with authority. If we read or hear words that are not corroborated by persons at the first level of authority, then it is incumbent upon us to verify the authority behind such words, and the source of the inspiration. As we saw above, many words which Christianity use as proof texts for doctrine, are of dubious authenticity and thus, of suspect authority.

But even when we accept the authority of an author, we must be certain that we are hearing them in their own voice, lest we misunderstand. As Bernard Lee has noted: "To interpret another voice accurately requires that we let it speak out of its own world. For historical reasons that are not hard to indicate, the voice of Jesus has rarely spoken to his followers across the centuries out of his own thoroughgoing Jewishness."[5] Far too often, Jesus' words are interpreted through an Hellenic mindset, not Hebraic,

Written versus Oral Evidence

In his book, *The Testimony of the Evangelists*, Simon Greenleaf provided references to legal precedents on evidence. If you have read his book, without researching the footnotes, you will not have noticed that many were documented in Stanford University texts. What Greenleaf achieved by doing so, was to authenticate his own writings, and this is paramount when evaluating written evidence, in this case, his. I attempt to do similarly, so that if any reader wishes to challenge my sources, they can verify the authenticity of them, and thus their authority. Challenging my personal opinions, or conclusions, is another matter entirely.

This is where written testimony differs from oral testimony. When a witness is called to the witness box, the first question asked is for the person to identify him/her self. In earlier times, this offered the opportunity to challenge the identity of the witness, for often, the law court was not in the same location of the crime or the accused, and public communication was practically non-existent; thus, verification of the identity of a witness was problematic. Today, it is a mere formality, as a rigorous process of identification preceded the appearance of the witness in court. When written evidence is submitted in court, it must be authenticated, and this is where the written evidence of the evangelists needs to be challenged. In Greenleaf's book, he fails to do so. This is an egregious error from a professional jurist, and opens the author's credibility to question.

Chain of Custody

To accept documents being introduced as evidence, we must ensure that they have been handled in a manner which precluded tampering or contamination: in this case, editing or redacting by later, unidentified scribes. In legal contexts, the *chain of custody* refers to the chronological documentation, or paper trail, that records the sequence of custody, control, transfer, analysis, and disposition of the physical evidence. In that context, how do we evaluate whatever bible version we prefer to use? How many Christians have a comprehensive understanding of the documentary process, from the time of the events recorded, their first recording (the autographs), and the subsequent editing, redactions, translations, and interpretations, that culminated in what people erroneously describe as, THE bible?

For example:

"Autographs (original copies) of Luke and the other Gospels have not been preserved, as is typical for ancient documents; the texts that survive are third-generation copies, with no two completely identical. The earliest witnesses (the technical term for written manuscripts) for Luke's gospel fall into two "families" with considerable differences between them, the Western and the Alexandrian, and the dominant view is that the Western text represents a process of deliberate revision, as the variations seem to form specific patterns. The oldest witness is a fragment dating from the late 2nd century, while the oldest complete texts are the 4th century *Codex Sinaiticus* and *Vaticanus*, both from the

Alexandrian family; *Codex Bezae*, a 5th- or 6th-century Western text-type manuscript that contains Luke in Greek and Latin versions on facing pages, appears to have descended from an offshoot of the main manuscript tradition, departing from more familiar readings at many points."[6]

Yes, I acknowledge that the entry is from Wikipedia, but if you examined the references contained therein, you will see that we have every reason to accept it. What is true of Luke's writings is also true of other New Testament texts. Thus, in short, there is no authenticated or reliable *chain of custody* of these documents. Whilst Simon Greenleaf, an eminent scholar, and acknowledged expert in the laws of evidence is satisfied with their authenticity, I cannot agree with him. Again, referring to the *Book of Hebrews*, there is a consensus amongst modern New Testament scholars that this letter was not written by Paul, but perhaps by an unknown follower of Paul, or at least, someone influenced by Paul's letters. As the author's identity cannot be confirmed, then the document cannot be authenticated, and it carries no authoritative, evidentiary weight.

I am entirely confident that no civil court would accept any modern version of the bible as authenticated, and authoritative, written evidence of events in Israel some two thousand years ago. That Western courts require witnesses to swear on the bible, is a curiosity in itself. That notwithstanding, if we are asked to use the rules of evidence in evaluating the claim that Jesus fulfilled the prophecies recorded in the Hebrew Scriptures, we fail in our endeavours if we lend more credence to our bible versions than is justified, knowing that the chain of evidence and custody cannot be satisfactorily authenticated.

Tradition

It is important to understand that the Gospels were not written, as I and other modern authors do; yet, in another way, they were. When I write studies such as this, I research authors whom I believe to be authoritative, and quote their observations and conclusions. In a sense, I am creating my own tradition. In the time of Jesus, this type of writing was uncommon, expensive, and generally conducted by scholars only. The Jesus narratives were primarily conveyed orally, community to community, both by his immediate disciples and their disciples, and by community members themselves. That was why Paul found it necessary to write pastoral letters in correction.

In the decades between the death of Jesus, and the penning of the Gospel autographs, how were the activities and sayings of Jesus retained? Quite simply: orally, and likely, some short, written notes. Oral transmissions lose fidelity, as do written notes, depending on the time between the events recorded, and the recording itself. It is logical to assume that some written notes were based on oral narratives. When the Gospels, as we have them today, are compared, the degree of agreement in both words spoken, and events recorded, is unsurprisingly low. Christianity explains this by asserting that the Holy Spirit guided the evangelists individually, such that the entirety of the Gospel accounts was both complementary and comprehensive. However, that would attribute a poor memory to the Holy Spirit, as many events are recorded in a different sequence, and some sayings are phrased substantially differently. I thus must disagree with this Christian apologetic.

Scholar, James Dunn, conducted a comparison of the Synoptics, and advised: "I draw your attention to the Synoptic material where there is *not* close verbal agreement, and in **a number of cases hardly any verbal agreement although the subject matter is evidently the same.**"[7] [emphasis in original] Either the Holy Spirit was having a bad day, the evangelists were not hearing correctly, or the guidance of the Holy Spirit is a myth, one intended to convince Christians of the Gospels' authenticity. I am persuaded of the latter. James Dunn continued: "What is striking about all these examples is *the lack of verbal agreement* – typically less than 40 percent, and more like 20 percent or less in some cases."[8] [italics in original] Without examining these cases in detail, what should be obvious is that such contradictions cannot represent the *inerrant* Word of God.

As a personal exercise, tabulate the details, given in the four individual Gospels, of the burial of Jesus, the subsequent finding of the tomb being empty, and to where the Apostles went. You will find, as I have, that there are very few points of agreement, which should suggest to any enquirer that the narratives do not represent first-hand accounts. We discuss this in detail in Chapter 9-3.

However, what this lack of verbal agreement does evidence, is oral tradition. A bit like gossip, the story changes with the telling. I am not condemning those communities long ago, merely contending that such is how oral tradition works, and often, embellishments and private interpretation will diminish the authenticity of the narrative. What is also evident is that there were four separate traditions, resulting in four different Gospel accounts, even though there is some cross-fertilisation of them. The essence of the narratives remains the same, but not the details, and it is the details that become doctrine, and the later traditions morphing into theology.

James Dunn, Professor Emeritus of Divinity, explains it this way:

> "In *oral* tradition, each performance is not related to its predecessors or successors ... in oral tradition, as Albert Lord particularly observed, *each* performance is, properly speaking, an 'original'. The point as it applies to the Jesus tradition is not that there was no originating impulse which gave birth to the tradition. On the contrary, in many cases we can be wholly confident that there were things which Jesus said and did which made an *impact*, and a *lasting* impact on his disciples. But properly speaking, the *tradition* of the event is not the *event* itself. And the *tradition* of the saying is not the *saying* itself. The tradition is at best the *witness* of the event, and as there were presumably several witnesses, so there may well have been several traditions, or versions of the tradition, *from the first*. Of an originating *event* we can speak; but we should certainly hesitate before speaking of an original *tradition* of the event. The same is true of a saying of Jesus. The tradition of the saying attests the impact made by the saying on one or more of the original audience. But it may well have been heard slightly differently by others of that audience, and so told and retold in different versions *from the first*. Moreover ... who can doubt that Jesus did indeed teach the same message in different ways and words on many occasions ... If apostles and teachers had no qualms in repeating stories about Jesus and the teachings of Jesus in their own words, neither, it is evident, did they have any qualms about interpreting some teaching of Jesus in a way which brought out its relevance more forcibly to their own situation, or any qualms about drawing a conclusion from their account."[9] [italics in original]

I acknowledge that this is a lengthy quote, but I wanted to highlight the quite significant gulf between what pastors orate from their pulpits, and what scholars write about the authenticity of the Gospels. James Dunn is a British New Testament scholar, a highly regarded theologian working within the Protestant tradition. He has no qualms about revealing his understanding of the Gospels: they are NOT the inerrant Word of God, but the result of four separate traditions, each influenced by the communities in which they developed, and containing private interpretations and conclusions of the participants. In Part 8, we examine the evidence from a number of New Testament scholars concerning how the evangelists used the Old Testament in writing the New.

I leave this choice to the reader: Whom do you believe, and is your belief based on a genuine search for God?

Jewish Tradition

"The Hebrew Bible is not a book, but a whole literature comprising history, myth, lyric poetry, and impassioned ideology."[10]

As we will encounter whilst reviewing the evidence, there is a disparity between how Judaism, the NT writers, and Christianity, view the Scriptures. The Christian Old Testament has discarded the three divisions of the Hebrew Scriptures: *Torah* (Law), *Neviim* (Prophets), and *Kesuvim* (Writings), and re-sequenced the individual books into a single compendium. In the Jewish tradition, these divisions signify differences in authority and reliability, as the above quotation attests. Christianity has decided for itself that ALL Scripture is the inerrant Word of God, contrary to the teachings in Judaism. This issue is particularly significant where the writings of King David (Psalms) and Daniel (dreams) are taken as prophetic, even though in Judaism, neither David nor Daniel are recognised as prophets.

In short, Christianity has created its own traditions, contrary to the traditions that gave them birth. Under the rules of evidence, this must be treated with some suspicion.

Historical Evidence

I have left this to last, due to my, and presumably others', lack of familiarity with how historians approach their task, and what presuppositions that their discipline allows them to employ. The first point to note, is as summarised by historian, Professor Bart Ehrman: "History, for historians, is not the same as 'the past'. The past is everything that has happened before; history is what we can establish as having happened before."[11] In the context of biblical enquiry, this means that an historian must put aside any presuppositions that have a theological basis. All enquiry must start with some presuppositions, but as Ehrman notes: "The question, though, is always this: What are the appropriate presuppositions for the task at hand?"[12] One cannot seek a scientific approach, where experiments can be repeated, for the past cannot be repeated, only reconstructed from other forms of evidence. The only recourse for historians, is to presuppose that it is possible to establish, with some degree of probability, that what is claimed to have happened, did in fact happen.

As in other professions, historians have developed techniques for testing the accuracy and authenticity of written records, such as the *criterion of dissimilarity* and the *criterion of contextual credibility*. I will leave the reader to research such issues for themselves, but here I will simply offer that as an analyst myself, I recognise the value of such disciplined techniques in overriding bias as much as humanly possible. That said, there are some things that can be known from historical evidence, and some things that cannot: these can only be accepted on faith, based on our presuppositions. What we must also appreciate is that presuppositions can be influenced by education, and I would contend, more frequently by ignorance.

For example: If one is ignorant of the writings of the Church Fathers of Catholicism, one is unlikely to believe in the systemic anti-Jewishness of the Roman Church. If one is ignorant of the character of Pontius Pilate, as narrated in extra-biblical sources, one will likely accept, uncritically, the story of his kindness, in allowing the body of Jesus to be taken down from the cross. In passing, Eastern Orthodox Churches became so enamoured by the claimed compassion of Pilate, that they have declared both he, and his wife Claudia Procula, to be saints! However, compare that understanding with that of a contemporary, the great Jewish philosopher,

Philo of Alexandria (20 BCE – 50 CE): "He was cruel by nature and hard-hearted and entirely lacking in remorse." Pilate's rule in Judaea he described as: "… bribes, vainglorious and insolent conduct, robbery, oppression, humiliations, men often sent to death untried, and incessant and unmitigated cruelty."[13] Hyam MacCoby, after a lengthy review of the history of the time, including that recorded by Josephus, summarised "[Pilate's] general conduct of the Roman administration was brutal and corrupt."[14] How then should we believe the Gospel account of Pilate's compassion?

If one has not subjected the Gospel narratives to scrutiny in the light of extra-biblical evidence, one is unlikely to be aware of misrepresentation. If one has not rigorously tested the degree of agreement across the Gospels, one will succumb to the Christian doctrine of inerrancy, and accept that the Synoptics are truly in agreement. Just as likely, if the doctrine of inerrancy, and that every word is that of God, is one's presupposition, then no evidence of contradiction will ever be accepted. I have encountered Christian apologetics where, in attempting to resolve discrepancies across the four Gospels, a fifth narrative is proposed, one which is hardly in accordance with any of them! Yet, the doctrine of inerrancy continues to be espoused. We encounter an example of this, well, many examples really, in Part 8.

Attribution of the Written Evidence

Using the page count in the NKJV as indicative, rather than definitive, I derived the following summary by author:

a. Matthew 13%
b. Mark 8%
c. Luke 28%
d. John 18%
e. Paul 31%
f. Peter 2%
g. Jude 0.26%
h. James 1%

If we sum the writings by the Apostles, we have 33%, or 41% if we accept Mark's account as being dictated by Peter. Luke, being a disciple of Paul, and being heavily influenced by him, we can consider his to be substantially Pauline: thus, 59%. As we discuss later, even Mark's account is said to have been heavily influenced by Paul. From the perspective of evidentiary weight, those numbers are not promising: just a third of the submitted evidence is by the hand of those whom we can consider to be witnesses of the events recorded. Two thirds are hearsay. When we cross-examine the written testimonies of just the Apostles, we find significant portions that were not witnessed by them, and is thus hearsay at best, and quite possibly, fiction to embellish the narrative.

Overall, using the rules of evidence as advocated by Simon Greenleaf, I do not find the written evidence for Jesus as Messiah, to carry much weight in a court of law.

Summary

Let me acknowledge from the outset that opinions, from both experts and others, are just that: opinions. Thus, they generally fall into the category of circumstantial evidence regarding the primary proposition, but can also be corroborating evidence of other opinions. What evidentiary weight is placed upon them is up to the person evaluating the evidence, but sight should never be lost that such evidence is not substantive. On the other hand, neither should sight be lost of on whom the burden of proof is laid. In this case, the burden of proof for prophecy fulfillment lies with Christianity, and ultimately the individual Christian: opinions which question that proposition are evidence of doubt, though how reasonable is again up to those evaluating that evidence.

In a trial where a false verdict will have such dire consequences, as this one surely does, we should ensure that we have credible, substantive evidence for the proposition, before considering any circumstantial evidence that may support it. If the latter is all we have, then the verdict will be unsafe.

I, for one, am not willing to place my faith in such a verdict.

REFERENCES:

1. Greenleaf, Simon, *The Testimony of the Evangelists*, Kregel Classics, Grand Rapids, MI, 1995, p. 9
2. Talbot, Wayne, *Finding the Shepherd - A Tale of Two Loves*, Westbow Press, Bloomington, IN, 2016
3. Levine, Amy-Jill, and Brettler, Marc Zvi, *The Jewish Annotated New Testament*, Oxford University Press, New York, NY 2011, p.406
4. Dewey, Arthur J., *The Authentic Letters of Paul*, Polebridge Press, Salem, OR, 2010 (additional authors Roy W. Hoover, Lane C. McGaughy, Daryl D. Schmidt)
5. Lee, Bernard J., *The Galilean Jewishness of Jesus*, Paulist Press, Mahwah, NJ, 1988, p. 49
6. https://en.wikipedia.org/wiki/Gospel_of_Luke
7. Dunn, James D.G., *Jesus, Paul, and the Gospels*, Wm. B. Eerdmans Publishing Co., Grand Rapids, MI, 2011, p. 28
8. *Ibid*, p. 34
9. Ibid, pp. 39-41
10. MacCoby, Hyam, *Revolution in Judaea: Jesus & The Jewish Resistance*, Ocean Books, London, UK, 1973, p. 64
11. Ehrman, Bart D., *How Jesus Became God: The Exaltation of a Jewish Preacher from Galilee*, Harper One, New York, NY, 2014, p. 150
12. *Ibid*, p. 144
13. Philo, *De Legatione ad Caium*, sec. 38
14. MacCoby, *Ibid*, p. 59

CHAPTER 1-2

PRESUPPOSITIONS

"...you cannot enter into an investigation with a philosophy that dictates the outcome. Objectivity is paramount; this is the first principle of detective work that each of us must learn. It sounds simple, but our presuppositions are sometimes hidden in a way that makes them hard to uncover and recognize."
~ J. Warner Wallace - American homicide
detective and Christian apologist ~

Lest you think me ignorant of my own presuppositions, I shall attempt to convince you otherwise. Some years back, growing ever more sceptical in my old age, I began to question my Catholic, and other Christian beliefs, and burrowed back further to the existence of God: Why did I believe in God at all? One precept that I attempt to live by, is that to properly appreciate truth, one must own it for oneself, and to do that, one must validate, or falsify, a belief, through research and analysis. Thus, as best I can, I put on my detective hat to ensure that my thoughts and writings are not based on ill-considered or false beliefs. Likewise, in all my writings, I try to remember to declare my presuppositions, where I consider them to be relevant.

My Presupposition of God

I thought about the reality of God for some time, researched contrary opinions, but eventually concluded for God, documenting my reasons in an earlier book, "*If Not God, What?*"[1]. In brief, my reasoning followed two lines of enquiry: Philosophy and Science. I had developed my own philosophical hypotheses, but consonant with those perceptive words of Oswald Chambers: "The author who benefits you most is not the one who tells you something you did not know before, but the one who gives expression to the truth that has been dumbly struggling in you for utterance"[2], I found numerous authors who gave expression in a way that I could finally grasp. One of note is Edgar Andrews; his book, "*Who Made God?*"[3] is a very erudite and entertaining study. More recently, I have found a treatise of a more wide-ranging nature, edited by Edward Feser: "*Five Proofs of the Existence of God*"[4].

From science, I had concluded that contrary to the opinion of some, that we are simply illusions of our own mind, that I, and the Universe, do exist as physical realities, and are capable of enquiry by the scientific method, well, up to a point at least. I offer the following as axiomatic: no finite existence can explain itself – all explanations must lie outside itself. You can explore that at your leisure, but applying that axiom to the finite, material existence of the Universe, I asked the obvious question: Where and how did it all begin, or did it not have a beginning at all?

Obviously, that is something we cannot know, but we can attempt to theorize the possibilities. To my mind, the reasoning is as follows. Either:

A. Material existence had a beginning; or
B. Material existence is eternal, i.e. always was and always will be.

If (A), material existence had a beginning, then either

C. Material existence created itself out of nothing; or
D. A non-material, eternal something created material existence.

If (B), material existence is eternal, then we have the conundrum of how an inanimate material existence can be so orderly in terms of constructs and rules. Those holding to philosophical materialism answer this by asserting that ours is just one of an infinite number of possible universes, and thus by chance, we experience our universe as we do – in other universes, the experience would be different. This is a very convenient hypothesis, but entirely lacking in scientific evidence, so I shall just put that aside as wishful thinking. Beyond that, our thinking cannot proceed much further: we simply accept that this incredibly complex and rules-based material existence always was, and always will be. But there remains a problem – the philosophy of materialism. If the material is all there is, then everything must be material, but some things such as laws, rules, patterns, mathematics, and so on, are clearly not material as we understand it. So, what are they? These entities exist independent of the material that is subject to them, and gives them expression, so where are they embodied? Although recent scientific endeavours, based on quantum theory, claim to have answers, this conundrum is unanswerable within philosophical materialism. For this and other reasons, I do not accept (B) as a probable explanation.

If (A), material had a beginning, what created material existence? I outright reject Stephen Hawking's *Something out of Nothing* hypothesis, because when studied closely, his logic is seen to be self-contradictory, for his explanation contains the words: "in the presence of". Even he should understand that these words express something rather than nothing. It is inconceivable to my mind, and it most certainly is not science, to claim that our material existence spontaneously arose uncaused out of nothing at all. You may choose to believe it, but you can have no logic or reason to support such beliefs, other than a preference to believe, or perhaps rejection of alternative explanations. Consider that if there was no cause, we can have no reason, or logic, to argue that it happened only once, or that it is not continuing to happen even now. Similarly, there can be no reason, or logic, to argue that material does not spontaneously *disappear* uncaused back into nothing – rather unfortunate if that material happens to be you.

Time out: I am aware of the claimed mathematical proof that something could indeed come from nothing, this reference[5] being just one example, but I struggle to accept the notion of *something-nothings* that appear and disappear at will, and remain something whilst being in their "nothing" state. No doubt it works mathematically, but I am unconvinced that it works in reality. If it truly does, I would be more inclined to see God's Hand in this magical conjuring of particles which *are*, even when they are *not*. But back to my more relevant thoughts.

To accept (C) is to reject the fundamental scientific premise of cause and effect, and anything becomes possible, just as it is with imagination. You may like that idea, but what you cannot claim is that it is within the realms of conventional science. So, we are back to (A), that material existence had a beginning and that (D), a non-material, eternal something created it. At this point, no other alternatives occur to me; I would offer this as *an inference to best explanation.*

Thus, my continuing presupposition of God's existence is based on my own research and analysis, and is a truth which I own, not vicariously through others, but through my own efforts. There remains a minor flaw in that logic, but it is the best that I can do for now.

A Self-Contradictory Presupposition

One of my favourite reads is *Touchstone*[6], a conservative Christian magazine, subtitled *A Journal of Mere Christianity* (borrowing, no doubt, from the title of a book by C.S. Lewis). I am not a Christian, but am very much aligned with Christian values, which, incidentally, were Jewish before they were Christian. The articles in this journal are informative, thought-provoking, and in a way comforting, because they evidence that even in today's secular world of liberalism, traditional values are still closely held by some. Christian essays inevitably conflate Jesus and God, as they must, and use the terms interchangeably. From time to time, however, this blinds the authors to errors caused by this presupposition of divine equivalence.

Concluding his otherwise excellent essay, "Fatal Instinct: The Thousand-Year Gap in Nietzsche's Education & Our Modern Sickness", author Craig Payne wrote:

> "What, then, is one to say of Nietzsche's repeated contentions that Christianity manifests a 'hatred' of this world, that it thinks of nature and the body as 'evil'? One counters them by pointing out that, in world history, Christianity is one of the truly great *affirmers* of the goodness of life, nature, and the values of the individual. In fact, Christianity believes this to the extent, that

it teaches that God himself took on a physical body and became part of the natural world. If Christians believe the body is 'evil', would that not make Christ a partaker in evil?"[7]

What if I were to answer: YES, although for an entirely different reason?

From the Hebrew Scriptures (*Tanakh*, Old Testament), we learn that God hates and proscribes the spilling of innocent blood, and prohibits human sacrifice. That is one of the reasons why He kept the Children of Israel separate from other cultures during Israel's formative years: God did not want them corrupted by the pagans until their new, monotheistic, culture was well and truly established in their hearts and minds. Thus, we have no choice but to conclude: human sacrifice and the spilling of innocent blood are EVIL. But what does Christianity teach? That God required a human sacrifice and the spilling of innocent blood! Irrespective of the reasons given, the plain facts remain: either God is immutable and infinitely good, or He is not. If God proclaims an act to be evil, but then He Himself requires it of Himself, does that not say that God is a partaker in evil?

The doctrine of *substitutionary atonement* by human sacrifice, and the spilling of innocent blood, is antithetical to the earlier teachings of God. Thus, when Christian authors use this presupposition in contending with other philosophies concerning evil, they seem unaware of the inherent contradiction.

Here is another oddity, also from an article in Touchstone: "*The psalms themselves were written in a Hebrew that nobody at the time spoke.*"[8] Think about it, and no, I did not take it out of context.

Summary

A tricky business, evidence, and our understanding of it. Even worse are our presuppositions of truth. Our evaluation of evidence, in the search for truth, is fraught with dangers and pitfalls, of which most are seemingly unaware. One cannot guarantee to always find truth, but it would seem logical to presume that those who persistently, and rigorously, search, are more likely to find it, than those who do not make the effort.

That is my presupposition, at least.

REFERENCES:

1. Talbot, Wayne, *If Not God, What?* On Being an Intellectually Fulfilled Theist, Peshat Books, Kelso, NSW, 2011
2. Chambers, Oswald, *My Utmost For His Highest*, Barbour Publishing Inc., Uhrichville, OH, 1963, 15th December
3. Andrews, Professor E.H., *Who Made God? Searching for a Theory of Everything*, EP Books, Darlington, England, 2009
4. Feser, Edward, *Five Proofs of the Existence of God*, Ignatius Press, San Francisco, CA, 2017
5. https://science.slashdot.org/story/14/11/07/1451218/mathematical-proof-that-the-universe-could-come-from-nothing
6. www.touchstonemag.com
7. Touchstone, November / December 2017, p. 46
8. Touchstone, November / December 2017, p. 60

CHAPTER 1-3

EPISTEMOLOGY

*"Reading furnishes the mind only with materials of knowledge;
it is thinking that makes what we read ours."*
~ John Locke (1632-1704) English philosopher and physician ~

Epistemology – "Defined narrowly, epistemology is the study of knowledge and justified belief. As the study of knowledge, epistemology is concerned with the following questions: What are the necessary and sufficient conditions of knowledge? What are its sources? What is its structure, and what are its limits? As the study of justified belief, epistemology aims to answer questions such as: How we are to understand the concept of justification? What makes justified beliefs justified? Is justification internal or external to one's own mind? Understood more broadly, epistemology is about issues having to do with the creation and dissemination of knowledge in particular areas of inquiry."[1]

In short: How do we know what we know, and are we justified in believing that what we believe we know is true?

As one who has rejected his former Christian beliefs, I have been told that I no longer "have the Holy Spirit within me" - if I ever did. Christians believe this way, because they have been taught to believe this way. Further, they have been warned: "And do not grieve the Holy Spirit of God, by whom you were sealed for the day of redemption" (Ephesians 4:30). The fear is instilled: grieve the Holy Spirit and you risk losing redemption. An even harsher warning is found in the Gospels: "Whoever speaks against the Holy Spirit, it will not be forgiven him, either in this age or in the age to come" (Matthew 12:32). The question becomes, however: Is denying the Christian doctrine synonymous with speaking against the Holy Spirit? After all, the same passage states: "Anyone who speaks a word against the Son of Man, it will be forgiven him."

Why do Christians believe that they are guided by the Holy Spirit, whereas Orthodox Jews and others including myself are not? The answer is found in John 14:1-31, especially verses 16-17: "And I will pray the Father and He will give you another Helper, that He may abide with you forever – the Spirit of truth, whom the world cannot receive, because it neither sees Him nor knows Him; but you know Him, for He dwells with you, and will be in you." The Apostles being filled with the Holy Spirit (Acts 2:4) is said to be the evidence of fulfillment of that promise. However, consider these words of the Prophet Isaiah:

> "A redeemer will come to Zion, and to those of Jacob who repent from willful sin – the word of Hashem. And as for Me, this is My covenant with them, said Hashem: My spirit which is upon you and My words that I have placed in your mouth will not be withdrawn from your mouth nor from the mouth of your offspring nor from the mouth of your offspring's offspring, said Hashem, from this moment and forever." (Isaiah 59:20-21)

That is a very loaded passage, which we will discuss later in the context of answering the question: Does God require a redeemer from sin? However, if the God's spirit is upon the Children of Israel, and His words that He placed in Isaiah's mouth will not be withdrawn, ever, from of all *of Jacob who repent from willful sin*, why should we believe that the spirit of God only came upon the Apostles and the followers of Jesus? Most especially, why should we believe that those who teach contrary to the word of God, as written in the Hebrew Scriptures, are guided by the spirit of God?

In the broader context of my study, if Jesus was not whom Christianity claimed him to be, these words in John's Gospel carry no evidentiary weight, although the episode in Acts is subject to a separate enquiry. However, let us go back to John 14:17 for a possible alternate interpretation: "whom the world cannot receive". Was Jesus speaking of those who had not accepted him, or of those who had not accepted the God of Israel? Was he including the Jews who had rejected him, as people of the world not receiving the Spirit of truth?

As John Locke long ago observed, we must do more than read, we must also seek to understand.

Sources of Knowledge

In a sense, the Christian belief in the source of their knowledge, is the exact opposite of the scientists' belief in their source of knowledge, at least, those scientists holding to philosophical materialism. Scientists, generally speaking, believe that science is the best, if not the only, source of knowledge; all other knowledge is metaphysical at best. Responding to this philosophy, one commentator observed that such people seem to believe that: "metaphysical assumptions are what you make when you are so unfortunate as not to have the support of scientific data based on observations and experiments."[2] In that sense, God too is a metaphysical assumption by those of us who believe in Him. Continuing, "In her (Maienschein's) view, along with two kinds of people, there seem to be only two kinds of things that pass for knowledge: scientific knowledge confirmed by experiments or observations, and metaphysical assumptions, which are either unfalsifiable in principle or are held by wilfully ignorant people who refuse to look at the scientific evidence that will destroy their cherished beliefs." The irony is, of course, that scientists' belief in philosophical materialism is, itself, a metaphysical assumption, and has no scientific data to support it.

Turning that around, I would offer that in defence of their Scripture interpretations, Christians turn to the metaphysical, in the form of Spirit guidance. Paraphrasing the above: "In the Christian view, there are two types of biblical interpreters: those who are guided by the Holy Spirit, and can see what is meant irrespective of the what the words might seem to say, and those who, unaided by the Holy Spirit, dumbly follow the literal interpretation of the text, and the guidance of those to whom the word of God was initially given". Where the scientist denies the truth of whatever is not directly observed by the five senses, the Christian denies the truth of what is derived through intelligent research and study, unless, of course, they are guided by the Holy Spirit, demonstrated by acceptance of Jesus as Lord and Saviour.

Again, that is begging the question, and has no more evidential validity than Islam's Mohammedan claim of being the recipient of guidance directly from Allah (God).

In the Image of God

What does it mean to say that humans are made in the image of God, but nothing else was created that way? What differentiates humans from apes, chimpanzees, dolphins, kangaroos, turtles, magpies, and other living creatures? One commentary reads: Having the "image" or "likeness" of God means, in the simplest terms, that we were made to resemble God. Adam did not resemble God in the sense of God's having flesh and blood. Scripture says that "God is spirit" (John 4:24) and therefore exists without a body. However, Adam's body did mirror the life of God insofar as it was created in perfect health and was not subject to death."[3] Not particularly helpful in this discussion, apart from which, I reject the latter assertion as a theological assumption. Why have a *Tree of Life* in the Garden if it was not there as a foil against death? There is no statement that Adam and Eve were not subject to death, just a Christological interpretation of Genesis 1:31. If you should be so interested, I have offered an alternative explanation in a previous work[4], one which is far more plausible to my mind because it accords with the omniscience of God, whereas the Christian interpretation does not.

The same article continues: "The image of God (Latin: *imago dei*) refers to the immaterial part of humanity. It sets human beings apart from the animal world, fits them for the dominion God intended them to have over the earth (Genesis 1:28), and enables them to commune with their Maker. It is a likeness mentally, morally, and socially. Mentally, humanity was created as a rational, volitional agent. In other words, human beings can reason and choose. This is a reflection of God's intellect and freedom. Anytime someone invents a machine, writes a book, paints a landscape, enjoys a symphony, calculates a sum, or names a pet, he or she is proclaiming the fact that we are made in God's image."

This is more useful in our context here: we are rational and can choose, but then we have the dilemma: how do we know when we are being *rational*? Can we really be like God *mentally*, when we are not *omniscient*? I would think not: alike in some ways, but not the same.

Truth, Logic, & Opinion

Empirical science aside, and maybe not even then, truth can be very difficult to determine. Even when a rigorous approach is taken, the finding of truth is not guaranteed. Belief is not necessarily coincident with truth, as we all know. For example, some Christian apologists will quote the number of Christian believers down through the ages as evidence of its truth, but that is to ignore the number of Buddhists, Hindus, Muslims and members of other religions. All religions, including Christianity and Judaism, are fragmented into sects, with each holding to different, and at times, contrary beliefs, as did the Pharisees and Sadducees on the question of a life after death. Clearly, the contention by these apologists is *opinion*, devoid of evidence and logic.

I encountered another example of opinion, asserted as truth, but without substantiation, as here. In correspondence with a Christian, I was informed: "We should put stock in the words of scripture over the interpretations and traditions of men". What my correspondent seemingly failed to consider was that the determination of what is, and what is not, scripture, is itself subject to *the interpretations and traditions of men*. Here are just a few interesting facts:

a.   The Catholic Douay-Rheims Bible consists of 73 books.

b.   The Protestant Authorised King James Bible consists of 66 books.

c.   The King James Bible originally had 81 books until the 15 books of the Apocrypha were removed in the nineteenth century.

d.   It is believed that up to 600 books were in existence prior to the Church of Rome, in association with Emperor Constantine, reducing that to just 80 in the then, Catholic canon.

e.   There are 28 other books mentioned in Scripture which are not included in some (any?) canons.

Over the centuries, there has been considerable debate over the identification of Scripture, holy or otherwise. For example, in the 18th century, the Catholic Church considered 73 books were God-breathed and thus inerrant. Protestants believed this applied to 81, but then later the Archbishop of Canterbury ruled that 15 books were not inspired after all. Martin Luther is said to have tried to remove the books of Hebrews, James, Jude, and Revelation because he perceived them to go against certain Protestant Doctrines. During the early days of Christianity, there were intense debates concerning the ongoing authority of the Old Testament, especially regarding some OT laws. For example, Paul wrote that "circumcision is nothing, and uncircumcision is nothing, but keeping the command of God is what counts" (1 Corinthians 7:19). Given that circumcision is a command of God, some were unable to deal with this paradox:

> "Marcion repudiated the God of the Old Testament as the creator of evil and sought to separate Christianity from anything Jewish. Consequently, he accepted as canonical only Paul's epistles (excluding the Pastorals) and the Gospel of Luke. In addition, he expurgated sections of these books that he felt were influenced too much by the Old Testament. Unfortunately, there are still those around who are essentially Marcionite in their approach."[5]

I know of ten Christian traditions with different ideas on what should be in or out. When it comes to the "bible" as scripture, we must also consider that all versions differ on numerous points, some minor, and some major, and as we will discuss later in Chapter 2-1, Christianity has rejected many aspects of what the Apostle Paul described as the *advantage of the Jew*: to them were given the oracles of God (Romans 3:1-2).

What, then, is Scripture, even within Christian traditions? Nobody can agree.

The same correspondent offered: "God is not omniscient in the pagan sense of the Calvinist", which I thought was a bit harsh – I had not previously heard of Calvinists being described as pagan. I realised, from the reference to Calvinism, that he was equating omniscience with predestination. I am not sure why people believe that if God knows what will happen in our future, then it must be predestined to happen; that there is nothing we can do about it; and thus, our free will is somewhat less than free. To my mind, that is woolly thinking. I cannot know, but my thinking is as follows. God is *infinite*, and without having a clear idea of what that means, I can only offer that God's existence is not *finite* as is our existence, and thus is not limited in any sense that we are, including our existence in time and space. God, being outside our finite, physical realm, our past, presence, and future are as one dimension to God. God cannot see what we might do, or what we do not do – His *omnipresence* only allows Him to see what each of us has done, is doing, or will eventually do. We are not predestined to do what we do, but what we do do in the future, is happening in God's infinite *present*. Thus, God's *omnipresence* is not an attribute per se, but a function of His *infinitude*. Similarly, God's *omniscience* is not an attribute per se, but a function of His *omnipresence*, which is a consequence of His infinitude.

In my thinking, there is no contradiction in God's omniscience and our having free will.

In a debate with an atheist friend, over origins and the plausibility of God existing, I opened my argument with the contention that material existence either had a beginning, or it did not. My friend, wary of where the argument was going, suggested that such was not true: there might be a third alternative that we have yet to consider. Unable to process this idea, I abandoned the discussion: "How is your mother doing lately?" Sometimes, our perception of logic can vary, person to person, and I know not how to deal with that.

Summary

The question posed earlier was: How do we know what we know, and are we justified in believing that what we think we know is true?

I believe there to be no unequivocal answer to that question.

I do believe, with all my heart, that God answers those who diligently seek Him, but the way He answers continues to be a mystery to me. If I have come to one conclusion, it is this: it is our attitude, more than our intellect, that determines our grasp of the truth. That is not to suggest other significant influences are not at work, they most certainly are, but in the context of bible study, it is what we bring to the table that determines the outcome. Our sources of "knowledge" are twofold: what we are learning, and what we already believe to be true knowledge - the latter influencing the former. If we encounter the bible from the perspective of what we already believe, some passages will act to reinforce those beliefs, and others will be adjudged as irrelevant.

We should approach bible study with the attitude of knowing nothing, starting with the Book of Genesis. To understand Genesis, and the books that follow, we should defer to those to whom "were committed the oracles of God" (Romans 3:1). God being omniscient, would He have erred in entrusting His Word to people who would not understand, or would twist it for their own purposes? I believe not. In meditating on the Hebrew Scriptures, we should seek to form our own expectations of the promises of God, and His intent in speaking through His Prophets. On that foundation, we can evaluate subsequent events in the light of God's Word. In passing, I do not wholly accept any of the opinions of the Jewish Sages concerning Creation, but that is for another time.

A study of epistemology assists us in understanding our own understanding and beliefs, illuminating the errors in our presuppositions. If we are to be intellectually honest, in the sight of God, we should seek every opportunity, and explore every avenue, to validate, or invalidate, the knowledge that we believe that we have. There is no guarantee of absolute truth, but we can at least, in conscience, declare that we have done our best.

It is my belief that such is all that God requires of us, but with the rider that He does so subject to our individual creation, and the circumstances in which He has placed us. Let me finish with a verse from the Book of Proverbs:

"*I love those who love me, and those who search for me shall find me*" (Prov 8:17).

It is our searching, in my *opinion*, that God values most.

REFERENCES:

1. https://plato.stanford.edu/entries/epistemology/
2. Stephan, Karl D., reviewing *Embryos Under the Microscope: The Diverging Meanings of Life* by Jane Maienschein, Touchstone, Jan/Feb 2018, p. 52
3. https://www.gotquestions.org/image-of-God.html
4. Talbot, Wayne, *Once A Christian, How the Bible Convinced Me to Walk Away*, Xlibris, Bloomington, IN, 2017, Chapter 9-1: Original Sin
5. Beale, G.K., *The Right Doctrine from the Wrong Texts? Essays on the Use of the Old Testament in the New*, Baker Academic, Grand Rapids, MI, 1994, p. 32

CHAPTER 1-4

DISCUSSING PROPHECY

"Knowing this first, that no prophecy of Scripture
is of any private interpretation"
(2 Peter 1:20, NKJV)

Like me, you have probably heard this quoted quite often, and in my experience, just as often, those who quote this verse take it to mean that none of us is entitled to a personal interpretation of prophecy. However, consider these translations:

    a. "no prophecy of Scripture came about by the prophet's own interpretation of things" (NIV); and

    b. "no prophecy in Scripture ever came from the prophet's own understanding" (NLT).

These translations offer the correct meaning, referring not to our interpretation, but to that of the Prophets themselves. The subsequent verse confirms that meaning: "for prophecy never came by the will of man, but holy men of God spoke as they themselves were moved by the

Holy Spirit (aka the Spirit of God)." We are often given to thinking of prophecy as a definitive statement of future events, but as Rabbi Tzvi Freeman describes it: "a prophecy is the state of matters in a higher realm, before it has reached our earthly plane. There, it is amorphous, not fully defined and can materialize in more than one way."[1] That being so, we should be wary of our interpretation of any prophecy, especially where there is considerable doubt as to it having been fulfilled in the way we have been taught. However, there is also a warning here for people like me, who reject a claimed prophecy fulfillment because events did not transpire in the way that I understood them - I have placed my own interpretation of what it would look like, and I could well be in error. I am ever conscious of that intellectual trap, and so I always attempt to view such events in the wider context.

The next question we must ask is: How do we recognise a prophetic utterance? In studies on evolution and related matters, I often make the point that not everything said by a scientist is scientific, even when uttered in a scientific context, and even non-scientists can speak authoritatively on individual scientific issues. Thus, in the same vein, is everything written by a Prophet, *prophetic*, and how is it decided who was a Prophet of God, and who was not? Could an Old Testament writer, one not recognised as a prophet, have written something which God intended to be a prophecy, and how would we know? Whose word should we accept as authoritative on these questions? Christians will readily answer: "Jesus", but that is begging the question: our goal here is to understand whether Jesus was the prophesied Jewish *mashiach*, and self-affirmation is not acceptable evidence. If it were, then Christianity offers no better validation that any other religion such as Islam, Mormonism, Jehovah's Witnesses, or even Scientology. That notwithstanding, I suspect that Jesus saw himself as a prophet, at least at some stage in his life, and others saw him similarly.

Accepting Jesus as Jewish, possibly considered a rabbi[2] in his time, and learned at the feet of the Pharisees since the age of twelve (Luke 2:42-46), it is reasonable to assume that Jesus' view of prophets, and prophecy, accorded with that of his teachers. We cannot be certain of what that was, but I contend that the best sources we could have would be those of Judaism, not Christianity. Nevertheless, there are some useful Christian expositions on the subject.

What IS Prophecy?

Amongst the many definitions that I have found, this one is representative:

> "The broadest meaning [of *prophecy*] is that of *forthtelling*; the narrower meaning is that of *foretelling*. In the process of proclaiming God's message, the prophet would sometimes reveal that which pertained to the future, but, contrary to popular opinion, this was only a small part of the prophets' message. Forthtelling involved insight into the will of God; it was exhortative, challenging men to obey. On the other hand, foretelling entailed foresight into the plan of God; it was predictive, either encouraging the righteous in view of God's promises or warning in view of coming judgment."[3]

The important point here is to differentiate between *forthtelling*, and *foretelling*, and this, I believe, is where many Christian interpretations have it wrong. Far too often, in my opinion, forthtelling has been interpreted as foretelling, especially in the Book of Isaiah. I do not discount the premise that a forthtelling is of a type, that is repeated in the future, but whether God intended it as such is open to conjecture. We find this often in the Christian interpretation of the Psalms, where events narrated about the life of King David are said to have been prophetic of the life of Jesus, as the prophesied Messiah of the royal line of David. In the context of the rules of evidence, this is more likely *correlative* evidence, rather than *substantive*. We must distinguish between insights into the will of God (forthtelling), such as we find in Torah and Proverbs, and foresight into the plan of God (foretelling).

The primary role of the Prophets was as expressed here:

> "Yet the Lord testified against Israel and against Judah, by all His prophets, every seer, saying, 'Turn from your evil ways, and keep My commandments and My statutes, according to all the law which I commanded your fathers, and which I sent to you by My servants the prophets'." (2 Kings 17:13)

The question arises: On what basis are just some of King David's activities seen as prophetic, in the sense of future fulfillment, and others not? Is it the case that scholars have trawled the Psalms for verses that seem to fit their agenda, and ignored those that do not? In Part 4, we examine this question more closely, but for now, reread the role of the Prophets, noting especially commandments, statutes, and laws.

We must be diligent in separately identifying prophecies (foretellings) relating to Israel, the world, in general, and those related specifically to the Messiah. When Jesus did, or said, something that is claimed as the fulfillment of a messianic prophecy, on what basis can we be confident that such was foretold of the life of the Messiah? Does the context in the Hebrew Scriptures allow that interpretation? Most especially, when the prophecy unambiguously relates to the *End of Days*, is it valid to attribute it to Jesus in his claimed First Coming? I have noticed a tendency, in many Christian apologetics, to spiritualise Jesus as Israel, and thus to transfer attribution of prophecies pertaining to Israel, to pertain to Jesus. I suspect Christian justification after the fact, although I can find in the Gospels, evidence that Jesus may well have thought of himself that way also, and certainly, some of John's writings may allude to that idea. However, it is fair to characterise John's Gospel as developed theology, written as it was some sixty years after the death of Jesus.

I can offer no authoritative path, to solving the problem of how to identify a prophecy in the common usage of the word: an event to be fulfilled in the future. My preference is to rely on Jewish literature, for the meaning of the words written by those identified as Prophets, which brings us to the next question.

Promise or Prophecy

In my mind, there is a subtle difference between a *promise* and a *prophecy*, but try as I may, I am unable to articulate the difference in a way that satisfies even myself. All prophecies are promises of God, but not all promises of God are necessarily prophecies, even though some may seem to be. If anything, I would differentiate them this way: a promise is what God says Himself, directly, whereas a prophecy is something that God has spoken through His Prophets. This perhaps, is nothing more than semantics, because the outcomes should be the same. Now, you may wonder why I bring this up, and my answer is that in reviewing the NKJV Old Testament, I find many promises of God not flagged as prophecy, whilst others are. For example, *"I will bless those who bless you, and I will curse him who curses you; and in you all the families of the earth shall be blessed"* (Genesis 12:3). This is flagged as a prophecy, but it is a promise of God in perpetuity, its fulfillment is ongoing, and often not apparent. The fulfillment of a prophecy, I would offer, must be apparent – a milestone if you like. That aside, if Christianity considers Genesis 12:3 to be an enduring prophecy, then woe betide those who have cursed the Children of Israel and their descendants, the Jews, as the Catholic Church has done. If the latter piques your curiosity, I would recommend reading *The Teaching of Contempt*[4] by Jules Isaac.

What was in the minds of the NKJV editors when they selected some "promises" as prophecies, and others not? Could it be that they chose only those that could be attributed to the life of Jesus, even though in some cases, there is no sense of them being messianic? In these cases, they are but circumstantial evidence, being capable of fulfillment by numerous people, and thus of no evidential weight when considering the claim of Jesus as Messiah.

Who Were the Prophets?

Again, there is little consensus on this question, most especially across Judaism and Christianity. Christianity uses the writings of David and Daniel as prophetic, but Judaism does not accept either of these men as Prophets. That is not to assert that neither foretold of future events, but to encourage caution when interpreting their words, most especially in relation to a Messiah who, contrary to expectations of many, including his immediate disciples, did not delay his coming until to the End of Days. Some Jewish commentators do accept David as a prophet, even though his revelations came through dreams, rather than through God speaking directly. Given the choice, I am, as ever, inclined to accept the word of the Jewish Sages. Did Paul not say that this was the advantage of the Jew: that they were entrusted with the oracles of God (Romans 3:1)? Did God entrust the Jew, foreknowing that they would not understand that of which they were entrusted? Did God speak to His anointed in secret (Isaiah 45:19)? If, as Christianity teaches, both the writings in the Old Testament, and their inclusion in the canon of Scripture, were divinely inspired or ordained, why not the Jewish organization of the canon into the three sections of Law, Prophets, and Writings, excluding David and Daniel from the Prophets? If the Jews were inspired to compile the canon of the Hebrew Scriptures, were they not also inspired regarding the organisation of the canon as documented?

Quoting from Unger regarding the ministry, or calling, of those described as prophets:

> According to I Samuel 9:9 the prophet was in earlier Israel commonly called a *ro'eh*, that is one who perceives that which does not lie in the realm of natural sight or hearing. Another early designation of similar etymology was a *hozeh* "one who sees supernaturally" (II Samuel 24:11). Later the Hebrew seer was more commonly called a *nabhi'* (I Samuel 9:9). This popular name is to be related the Accadian *nabu*, "to call or announce," either passively, as Albright (*From the Stone Age to Christianity*, 1940, pp. 231 ff.), "one who is called" (by God), or actively with Koenig (*Hebraeisches and Aramaeisches Woerterbuch zum Alten Testament*, 1936, p. 260), "an announcer" (for), or preferably with Guillaume (*Prophecy and Divination*, 1938, pp. 112f), who construes the term to mean that the prophet is the passive recipient of a message manifest in his condition as well as in his speech, and is "one who is in the state of announcing a message which has been given to him" (by God)."[5]

Given that the Christian Old Testament has erased the Jewish identification of Prophets, the following are listed as being the prophetic books of the Hebrew Scriptures. Firstly, the major prophetic works:

- Joshua
- Judges
- Samuel
- Kings
- Isaiah

- Jeremiah
- Ezekiel

Then, the works of the twelve other prophets:
- Hosea
- Joel
- Amos
- Obadiah
- Jonah
- Micah
- Nahum
- Habakkuk
- Zephaniah
- Haggai
- Zechariah
- Malachi

In all, according to the editors of The Jewish Bible (TJB), there were forty-eight Prophets, and seven Prophetesses[6]. But understand again, that most were of the seer type, *forthtelling* rather than *foretelling*, the latter being the more common understanding of prophecy.

I am more influenced by the Jewish, rather than later Christian, interpretation of prophetic writings. A study of these writings reveals that each of the authors wrote both *forthtellings* and *foretellings*, and I have concluded that Jewish commentary offers the more reliable understanding of which is which. Christianity has interpreted the former as being the latter, most especially in the Psalms of King David, but I find little justification for that.

Thus, my presuppositions on this issue.

REFERENCES:

1. http://www.chabad.org/library/article_cdo/aid/489751/jewish/Is-the-Book-of-Daniel-authentic.htm
2. Spangler, Ann, and Tverberg, Lois, *Sitting at the Feet of Rabbi Yeshua*, Zondervan, Grand Rapids, MI, 2009

3. https://bible.org/seriespage/6-major-prophets
4. Isaac, Jules, *The Teaching of Contempt: Christian Roots of Anti-Semitism*, Holt, Rinehart and Winston, Inc., New York, NY, 1964
5. Unger, Merrill F., *Unger's Commentary on the Old Testament*, Vol. 1, Moody Press, Chicago, 1981, pp. 306-307
6. Scherman, Rabbi Nosson, *The Tanach*, Mesorah Publications, ArtScroll English Edition, Brooklyn, NY, 2011, p. 1331

CHAPTER 1-5

UNDERSTANDING THE EVANGELISTS

"Had it been the object or the intention of Jesus Christ to establish a new religion, he would undoubtedly have written the system himself, or procured it to be written in his life time. But there is no publication extant authenticated with his name. All the books called the New Testament were written after his death. He was a Jew by birth and by profession."
~ Thomas Paine in "The Age of Reason" ~

Let me confess from the outset, that my understanding of the Evangelists is likely no better than that of any other commentator. I would offer, however, that not being bound by Christian doctrine, or the belief that both the Old and New Testaments are inerrant, with whatever caveat or qualification, I may well be in a better position to objectively evaluate the evidence. Thomas Paine was not the first to object to the notion that Jesus intended founding a new religion, and no doubt, will not be the last.

Catholic scholar, Bernard J. Lee, S.M., noted:

"Most christological interpretation has been 'supersessionist', that is, it has interpreted Jesus as initiating a new Covenant that supersedes Judaism. Historically, it is quite improbable that Jesus had any such thing in mind. There is little likelihood that Jesus had any conscious intention of founding a new religious institution either superseding Judaism or alongside it."[1]

When Jesus spoke of building his "church" (Matthew 16:18), most likely he was referring to a congregation within Judaism that accepted him as Messiah – such as were the Nazarenes. I strongly doubt that he had any intention of founding a church that entirely rejected the Jews, Torah, the Sabbath, and other God-ordained commemorations, and then compromised with the sun-worshipping, pagan emperor, Constantine.

How, then, should we understand the Evangelists? What were they trying to say, and to whom? Were they writing for posterity, much as ancient historians such as Josephus or Herodotus did, or was their intention to encourage and bolster the faith of those waiting for the Second Coming? Did they ever contemplate that two thousand years into the future, their writings would continue to be amongst the most controversial in human history, and that significantly, there was still no sign of the Second Coming? Was it in their minds to demonstrate that Jesus was the Divine Son of God, Second Person of the Trinity, or more realistically, that he was the long-awaited Jewish *mashiach* who would redeem them from the oppression of the Romans, just as the Maccabees had liberated Judea from the tyranny of the Syrian king, Antiochus Epiphanes?

When the Evangelists quoted the Psalms of King David, was their intention to show the similarities between their former king, and the man they expected to be their new king? Were they affirming the history of the Children of Israel, to show, not prophecy fulfilled, but continuation of the destiny of their people? In the same way that excerpts from *Ecclesiastes* and *Proverbs* were quoted, were the *Psalms* quoted more in a pastoral, than prophetic sense, much as a minister will quote Scripture from the pulpit?

One commentator asks: "In view of the fact that the New Testament writers use Old Testament passages in ways that we find surprising, should we interpret the Old Testament in the same way that they did? In other words, can we use their technique to find Christian significance in the Old

Testament texts, or were they operating from a revelatory stance in ways that we cannot?"[2] That is a very good question, and goes to the heart of the evaluating the evidence of the New Testament. Another question is this: If the evangelists somehow knew that Jesus wasn't coming back any time soon, or even much later, and that the Nation of Israel would continue to be persecuted, even by the Church formed in the name of Jesus, would they have written as they did?

Consider this: What if, for whatever reason, the NT writers were convinced that Jesus was the Messiah, and in consequence, sought a Christological interpretation of the Old Testament texts, to validate their beliefs?

Continuing the above quotation: "This question is crucial, for the abuse of the Old Testament message is all too common in Christian history."[3] I agree entirely, especially regarding the anti-Jewish writings of the Church Fathers. My own analysis suggests that they were not the recipients of divine revelation, so I am inclined to answer my own question in the affirmative, most especially because even Christian commentators have recognised that *abuse of the Old Testament message is all too common in Christian history.*

Hindsight is a valuable tool, but *justification after the fact* should not be offered as hindsight. As we shall see in a later chapter, the Evangelists seldom quoted the Psalms in an explicitly prophetic sense, such as occurs in Matthew 13:35, concerning speaking in parables (Psalm 78:2): "that it might be fulfilled which was spoken by the prophet". What is particularly interesting about this occurrence is that it is not specifically Messianic – speaking in parables was the custom of the time, so as evidence of messianic prophecy fulfillment, it carries no weight. Nevertheless, the editors of the NKJV were at great pains to annotate this, and other references to the Psalms, as prophecy fulfillment. Even more curious, however, is the assertion in the previous verse: "and without a parable He did not speak to them." (v. 13:34) Was this true, not so much that he *only* spoke in parables, which he did not, but that he never spoke to the people without including a parable? You can adjudge that for yourselves.

The question we must ask is: Was that the intention of the Evangelists?

REFERENCES:

1. Lee, Bernard J., *The Galilean Jewishness of Jesus*, Paulist Press, Mahwah, NJ, 1988, p. 17
2. Beale, G.K., *The Right Doctrine from the Wrong Texts*? Essays on the Use of the Old Testament in the New, Baker Academic, Grand Rapids, MI, 1994, p. 49
3. *Ibid*

CHAPTER 1-6

JEWISH HERMENEUTICS

"The theory and methodology of interpretation, especially the interpretation of biblical texts, wisdom literature, and philosophical texts."

I make no claim of expertise in this subject, but offer some thoughts of those who likely are experts, and some observations of my own. My issue here is not just how we, today, interpret biblical texts, but how the writers of the New Testament interpreted whatever texts they used as their authoritative sources. In the next section, we discuss some issues surrounding the reliability of the Greek translations, but I shall put that aside for now. Unsurprisingly, we have little evidentiary guidance on how the New Testament writers did interpret the Scriptures, Greek or Hebrew. In Chapter 2-5, we review what is known about the authors of the New Testament texts. The point to note here is this: it is unlikely that any were bible scholars, schooled in the rigours of biblical exegesis. Thus, whilst scholars may offer their rules of exegesis, we have little reason to believe that the New Testament writers would have even known of such rules, let alone followed them.

In Part 8, we review an interesting, and more than challenging series of essays on this subject in a study entitled, *"The Right Doctrine from the Wrong Texts?"*[1]. The *Introduction* by G.K. Beale states, in part:

> "There is no book which addresses the crucial issues revolving around the use of the Old Testament in the New in the manner in which this book does. The uniqueness of the book especially lies in its unswerving focus on exegetical methodology rather than theology, as this pertains to the use of the Old Testament in the New. In this respect, the presuppositions and assumptions which underlie Jesus' and the apostles' exegetical method will be examined and compared with the presuppositions underlying typical twentieth-century methods of exegesis."[2]

If you are interested in pursuing the subject, you may care to review this reference to what appears to be a Messianic Jewish view[3], and this one on the hermeneutics of the Talmud[4]. A brief perusal shows that these methodologies are exceedingly complex, and according to the first reference, there are prerequisite qualifications for the varying levels of interpretation. The Torah is understood and interpreted according to the level being discussed. According to Jewish scholars, the Torah can be understood on four levels, while other writings may be confined to only one level. For example, *Bereishis* (the book of Genesis) can be understood on all four levels, while the *Midrash* and *sefer Matitiyahu* (Gospel of Matthew) can only be understood on the *drash* level. The following chart details these four levels.

פרדס	פשאת	רמס	דרש	סוד
PaRDeS	Pshat	Remez	Derash	Sod
Definition	Simple	Hint	Explore - Ask	Secret
Literary level	Grammatical	Allegory	Parabolic	Mystical
Audience level	Common People	Noble (Lawyers, Judges, Scientists)	Kingly (civil servants, political scientists)	Mystic (psychologists)
Hermeneutic level [1]	7 Hillel Laws	13 Ishmael Laws	32 Ben Gallil Laws	42 Zohar Laws
Rabbinic level	Mishna	Gemara	Midrash	Zohar
Gospel	Marqos (Mark), 1 & 2 Peter	I and II Luqas (Luke)	Matityahu (Matthew)	Yochanan (John) 1, 2, 3, and Revelation
Presentation	HaShem's Servant	Son of Man	The King	Son of G-D
Principle Concern	What do we have to do?	What is the meaning behind what we have to do?	How do we go about establishing HaShem's Kingdom on earth?	What metaphysical meaning is there to what is happening?
World	Asiyah	Yetzirah	Beriyah	Atzilut
Symbol	Man	Ox/Bull	Lion	Eagle
Mazzaroth	Deli	Shaur	Aryeh	Aqurav
Tribe	Reuben	Ephraim	Judah	Dan
Temple	Outside Chatzer	Chatzer	Kodesh	Kodesh Kodashim
Purim	Mikrah Megillah	Matanot L'Evyonim	Mishloach Manot	Seudas Purim

It is not my intention to review this subject any further here, other than to point out that it is highly unlikely that the twelve chosen by Jesus as his Apostles has any appreciation of such issues, and as I opine in Chapter 2-6, I strongly doubt that Paul did either. However, there are some scholarly comments on the New Testament authors' usage of the Old Testament which are worth noting. The following samples are taken from the book previously referenced, edited by Beale, with the page numbers shown at the end of the texts:

a. "Most [early] Christians sought to extend the interpretive practices of the New Testament writers and appropriate the Old Testament for Christian purposes in new ways. The Old Testament was combed for passages that could be understood of Christ and his church." (pp. 32-33) [Ed. *In other words, first came the belief in Jesus as Messiah, and then came the attempted substantiation from the Scriptures.*]

b. "The main problem for modern readers in the New Testament use of the Old Testament is the tendency of the New Testament writers to use Old Testament texts in ways different from their original intention." (p. 34)

c. "A third presupposition of the early church is that they lived in the days of eschatological fulfillment. They believed that the end time had dawned upon them (1 Cor. 10:11)." (pp. 38-39) [Ed. *We address this further in Chapter 6-2.*]

d. "The use of the Old Testament – whether in direct quotation, in allusions, or in the employment of biblical themes – is primarily a mode of expression for early Christian thought, arising from a contemporary understanding of the meaning of Scripture." (p. 143)

e. "The New Testament writers do not take an Old Testament book or passage, and sit down and ask, 'What does this mean?' They are concerned with the *kerygma* [preaching], which they need to teach and to defend and to understand for themselves. Believing that Christ is the fulfillment of the promises of God, and that they are living in the age to which all the Scriptures refer [Ed. *clearly they were wrong*], they employ the Old Testament in an ad hoc way, making recourse to it just when and how they find it helpful for their purposes. But they do this is a highly creative situation, because the Christ-event breaks through conventional expectations, and demands new patterns of exegesis for its elucidation." (p. 143) [Ed. *in other words, Jesus did not fulfill the prophecies as they were then understood.*]

f. "The prophecy in Zechariah 12:10 is quoted in John 19:37 as a prediction of the piercing of Jesus' side after his death; Revelation uses the same passage as a prediction of the second coming (cf. Matt. 24:30). The variation of exegesis in these passages suggests that, while the early church was convinced that the Old Testament contained predictions about Jesus and the church, there did not exist at the time of the composition of the New Testament books an established tradition of exegesis for Old Testament passages which the New Testament writers accepted and adopted." (p. 192) In a different context, another essayist asks: "But did the early church go to the Scriptures to find evidence that he died 'for our sins' or was it the study of the Scriptures that led to the realisation that he died 'for our sins'?" (p.198) The first quotation would affirm that the early church went to the Scriptures to find evidence of what they had come to believe, or at least, sought to preach.

The sense that I gain from these and similar comments is that the Apostles and early disciples believed in Jesus, not because they saw him fulfilling prophecy, but for other reasons, no doubt in the hope of the Messiah, encouraged by the eschatological temper of the times, and the despair over being under Roman rule. They felt that the time was right, and here was a person who seemed right, and so they accepted him. The New Testament writers then combed the Scriptures for passages that best fit their understanding, even though there was not an explicit match with the intentions of the original authors.

If this be true, then it is circumstantial evidence that Jesus did not fulfill OT prophecies in the way expected.

Fulfill or Match?

My primary point here is to question the Christian interpretation of the Greek word, *plirow* or *pliroo* (Strongs Greek 4137). Having encountered this issue, I have researched as best I can, and have been able to find just a few other supporting articles for what follows, most quite equivocal. My reason for presenting the argument is that it does seem to explain why the evangelists claimed prophecy fulfillment, when my reading of the Hebrew Scriptures convinces me that there was no such prophecy. Though later editing of the Gospels may well have been biased, I am inclined to believe that the evangelists themselves were generally honest, with the exception of Luke in the Book of Acts, and likely Paul who was given to imagining. I accept that they believed what they wrote in the autographs, noting that we do not have copies of such writings, and so rather than accuse them of dishonesty, I am open to alternate explanations for this conundrum.

Here I would like to introduce an expert witness: "Dr. Joel Manuel Hoffman … is an American scholar, writer, speaker, and novelist known for his criticism of the Christian fundamentalism's style of Biblical interpretation. He has served as a translator for the ten volume series of *My People's Prayer* Book"[5]. Of particular interest, in the context of evaluating claimed prophecy fulfillments, is his belief that in many cases where the Greek has been translated as *fulfill*, it should really be rendered as *match*.

A case in point is James 2:23, which incidentally, the NKJV does <u>not</u> flag as prophecy fulfilled, even though the text would suggest otherwise: "And the Scripture was fulfilled which says, '*Abraham believed God, and it was accounted to him for righteousness*'. And he was called the friend of God", quoting Genesis 15:6. Dr. Hoffman explains:

> "We should be clear. Genesis 15:6 is not a prophecy. It describes the past. So it cannot come true in the future any more than "it rained yesterday" can come true in the future. Yet we find the Greek word *plirow* here. And most translations therefore blindly translate "scripture was fulfilled," even though this is not a case of a prophecy being fulfilled at all. Rather, this is a case of using the OT more generally to demonstrate a point, as if to say, "our current point matches a text in the OT."

> ### "Proof Text"

> Using a text in this way was so common that it now has a technical name: **proof text.**

> A proof text is a text that is used to demonstrate a point. This isn't "proof" in the modern, scientific sense, though. The proof text doesn't have to prove anything. And the proof text doesn't even have to mean the same thing as what it's demonstrating. The point of using a proof text was that it was considered better to use words of Scripture than to invent new ones — even if the words of Scripture were taken out of context. The whole notion of text

matching and of a proof text is generally foreign to our modern way of thinking. But it was central to how texts were understood 2,000 years ago.

In James 2, the proof text is Genesis 15:6. But, quite clearly, this doesn't mean that Genesis 15:6 predicts James 2, or even that James meant to indicate that Genesis 15:6 was a prophecy that came true. We know because Genesis 15:6 isn't a prophecy at all. Rather, James is using a passage in the OT to demonstrate a point. He's using a proof text. And this proof text is introduced with the Greek word *plirow*.

So better translations might be, 'this *matches* Scripture' or 'this *accords* with Scripture' or even 'this *complements* Scripture'."[6]

I have provided the above online reference for ease of access, but for those who wish to explore further, and examine even more examples, the texts can be found in Dr. Hoffman's book, *The Bible Doesn't Say That*[7]. There is much food for thought in this book, and I highly recommend its study.

The author makes a good point, which helps to clarify what has long been a mystery to me: Why would the Evangelists claim prophecy fulfillment when the case can be so easily refuted? The answer would appear to be simple, if not obvious: the evangelists were not necessarily claiming prophecy fulfillment; rather, they were saying that contemporary events matched, or were similar to, past events narrated in the Scriptures. As will be discovered in the analyses which follow in later chapters, the Evangelists made far fewer Scripture fulfillment claims, than the editors of the NKJV have done. If, and I would emphasise "if", on each of the occasions where the Evangelists have been interpreted as explicitly claiming prophecy fulfillment, they were in truth merely comparing current with past events, then the Christian edifice of Jesus fulfilling prophecy is a figment of theologians' imagination, or more likely, just something that they have wanted to be true. Like all edifices built on sand, they will likely crumble when subjected to the winds of time.

When examining in detail, each of the NT verses which the editors have flagged as prophecy fulfilled, I will not reintroduce this argument – hopefully, the reader will keep it in mind anyway. However, when examining the verses where the Evangelists have been interpreted as explicitly claiming prophecy fulfillment, and there are very few of them, I will review this issue to determine the likelihood of the Evangelists meaning what Dr. Hoffman suggests.

REFERENCES:

1. Beale, G.K., *The Right Doctrine from the Wrong Texts*? Essays on the Use of the Old Testament in the New, Baker Academic, Grand Rapids, MI, 1994
2. *Ibid*, p. 9
3. http://www.betemunah.org/rules.html
4. http://www.jewishencyclopedia.com/articles/14215-talmud-hermeneutics
5. https://en.wikipedia.org/wiki/Joel_Manuel_Hoffman
6. https://goddidntsaythat.com/2010/10/19/what-happens-to-prophecies-in-the-new-testament/
7. Hoffman, Joel M., *The Bible Doesn't Say That: 40 Biblical Mistranslations, Misconceptions, and Other Misunderstandings*, Thomas Dunne Books, New York, NY, 2016

CHAPTER 1-7

THE TRAJECTORY
OF PROPHECY

"There was barely any concept of life after death
in most of the Old Testament"
~ The Bible Doesn't Say That – Dr. Joel M. Hoffman[1] ~

Introduction

Let me propose that the Christian approach to prophecy fulfillment places the cart before the horse, so to speak. Having studied Christian apologetics on the subject, I find that in every case, the authors start with the belief that Jesus fulfilled prophecy, and then mine the Old Testament to find verses that would justify their claim. The bible is complex, and with little difficulty, I could find verses in support of practically any theological proposition. Atheists do exactly that, in seeking to disprove the existence of God, or to prove that the God of the bible is not one that any sensible or moral person would want to follow. Contending with them is difficult, because just like Christians justifying prophecy fulfillment, they take verses out of context, and in isolation, such verses do appear to support their case.

The proper way to understand prophecy is to begin at the beginning, and absorb the trajectory of prophecy, through the approximately eleven hundred years of the Prophets, circa 1500-400 BCE. I have no idea of why the period of revelation stopped with Malachi, but that is what the Hebrew Scriptures tell us. Now, whatever Jesus is reported to have done, whether true of not, if his actions were not prophesied, then he was not the prophesied Messiah. He may well have been a messiah, I will not here argue that, but he could not have been the one prophesied. So, let us briefly review what we can learn from the Prophets themselves.

We should keep in the back, or maybe the forefront of our minds, that before the creation of the world, God had a plan, a perfect plan, one which would never require revision. God being omnipresent, and thus omniscient about future events, He foreknew everything of consequence that would ever happen, and He foreknew His own ongoing involvement with His Creation. Christians might contend that such was precisely what occurred when "the Word became flesh and dwelt amongst us" (John 1:14), or as written elsewhere: "He indeed was foreordained before the foundation of the world, and was made manifest in these last times for you" (1 Peter 1:20). Keep hold of that last thought – *in these last times*. Many commentators have noted the eschatological temper of the Jews in the first century, and it would appear that the author of the quoted text believed similarly. We will regularly revisit that perception in reviewing prophecy fulfillment claims.

This Christian contention would be plausible, if, and only if, such *was* the trajectory of prophecy, and there were no statements by God to the contrary. If God asserted certain promises or conditions to be **everlasting**, we cannot assert God's omniscience, and simultaneously claim that He changed His mind. This is pivotal to understanding the Jesus narrative: the Christian claims of a *New Israel*, and a *Replacement Covenant*, because the Jews failed to keep their covenant, are contrary to the trajectory of prophecy as found in the Hebrew Scriptures, and contrary to God's expressed reason for selecting Israel as His First Born Son.

Let us examine some relevant statements concerning the Children of Israel, the Land of Israel, and the reasons for God doing what He did. We start with the promises to Abraham, likely the first person in recorded history to accept monotheism. Before doing so, however, we should reflect on one point: Why is the story of Abraham in the Book of Genesis?

Genesis

The word *genesis* is defined as: the origin or mode of formation of something. The Hebrew word for this book is *Bereishis*, meaning "in the beginning", taken from the first verse of Genesis 1. Though Christian translations of verse 1 are consistent: "In the beginning, God created ...", Jewish translations vary: "In the beginning of God's creating"; "For the sake of the beginning [Torah and Israel] did God create"; and "In the beginning of all things, God created". As Rashi, Ramban, and other Jewish Sages had their own opinions on the meaning of this opening verse, I shall offer my own, more prosaic understanding. In the more modern way of formatting text, much as I do in this book, the words: *in the beginning*, could be set as a paragraph or chapter heading. Consider the implications of this formatting:

In The Beginning

God created the heavens and the earth. The earth was without form, and void; and darkness was on the face of the deep, and the Spirit of God was hovering over the face of the waters.

Notice how this dramatically changes the sense of the narrative. Instead of "in the beginning" referring to a time within the narrative, it refers to the narrative itself, much as headings such a *Prologue* or *Introduction* would do. This is not an unreasonable interpretation, for there is a very intriguing issue that has scholars still debating without consensus, as far as I can ascertain, but I thought it worth mentioning in support of my suggestion above. I will keep this brief but here are some key words in case you are interested to pursue the subject further: *toledoth, colophon, anaphora,* and *cataphora*. I am going to use these terms very (very) loosely so if you are already familiar with them, I would ask your indulgence for my lack of precision.

Referring to Genesis 5:1, "This is the account of the descendants of Adam", does the word "this" refer back (*anaphoric*) to the previous verses, or forward (*cataphoric*) to the subsequent verses? In English particularly, both constructs are valid and in this example, we could understand the "genealogy of Adam" to be as narrated in verses 4:25-26. Recent archaeological discoveries have found clay tablets where the subscript or reference (colophon) of the author or owner appears at the end, and there is no heading at the beginning. The Hebrew word *toledoth* translates to *generations* and appears 13 times in Genesis, but the question is: are they colophons? In modern usage, a colophon is a publisher's emblem or imprint, usually on the title page of a book. What I am suggesting here is that the words, *in the beginning*, may well have been intended as an early form of *colophon*.

Torah (Pentateuch) is a volume comprising five books. The first book is Genesis, which covers the period from God creating the heavens and the earth, to Joseph being in Egypt and dying there. Viewing the text this way, and I would offer this is as a plausible perspective, arguments concerning the six days of creation, and even evolution, should be subject to rethinking.

Now, back to the main theme. Rather than seeing Creation as a single event spread over six days, Judaism offers this perspective:

> "There are two kinds of creation. There is the creation of mountains and valleys, of solar systems and brain cells – and there is the creation of the people who give meaning and purpose to the universe they inhabit. The commentators refer to Genesis as the 'Book of Creation', but the events of the six days, when heaven and earth and all their fullness were brought into being, occupy but a small fraction of the Book. Rather, the primary emphasis of the Book of Creation is how the Patriarchs fashioned a family into the nation that became the Chosen People. It is noteworthy that the Sages juxtapose three historical phenomena: 'With ten utterances the world was created … '; 'There were ten generations

from Adam to Noah … '; 'There were ten generations from Noah
to Abraham … until our forefather Abraham came and received
the reward of them all' (Avos 5:1-3). The implication is plain – that
although the physical work of creation had been completed with
the ten utterances, it was not until Abraham that its human heir
had come forward.

As Ramban and others point out in their commentaries on Genesis,
the events in the lives of the Patriarchs were portents for the future
history of their descendants. Consequently, when this Book tells
how the seeds of man's spiritual were sown, it is no less the story
of Creation than it is the terse narrative of the first six days."[2]

I would stress: *"the primary emphasis of the Book of Creation is how
the Patriarchs fashioned a family into the nation that became the Chosen
People"*. That was God's doing, and if we accept that God is capable of
implementing a perfect plan, we should accept that here, we are seeing the
beginning of God's process of appointing the nation that would be His
first-born son. Did He choose wrongly? We shall see, so back to Abraham.

In passing, I quote from the Hebrew Scriptures, the English translation
of which use the term, *Hashem*, for God meaning simply, *the Name*. That
is because the name of God is unpronounceable. In Hebrew, it is formed
from four letters indicating that God is timeless and infinite; the four
letters chosen are from three Hebrew words meaning: *He was, He is, and
He will be.* If you go to this website[3], you will find 98 bible verses affirming
that truth.

As an aside, names are given to things to differentiate them. If
something is unique, it does not require a "name" *per se*, just an identifier.
Hashem is an identifier of God, just as is my favourite: *Ein Sof,* meaning the
Infinite and Unknowable One. When God instructed His Chosen People
on how they should live (Torah), He did not call it a religion, nor give it
a name. The term Judaism arose later to identify the religious practices of
the people of Judea.

Abraham

"I will make you a great nation; I will bless you, and make
your name great, and you shall be a blessing. I will bless those
who bless you, and him who curses you I will curse; and all
the families of the earth shall bless themselves by you."
(Genesis 12:2-3, TJB).

All the families of the earth! Which families would those be: just those
on the earth at that time, or all families for all time? I assume that God
meant the latter, but before these blessing could come about, Abraham had
to pass ten tests. There is some debate as to the nature of these tests, but
for our purposes here, this list[4] will suffice:
1. God tells him to leave his homeland to be a stranger in the land
   of Canaan.
2. Immediately after his arrival in the Promised Land, he encounters
   a famine.
3. The Egyptians seize his beloved wife, Sarah, and bring her to
   Pharaoh.
4. Abraham faces incredible odds in the battle of the four and five
   kings.
5. He marries Hagar after not being able to have children with Sarah.
6. God tells him to circumcise himself at an advanced age.
7. The king of Gerar captures Sarah, intending to take her for
   himself.
8. God tells him to send Hagar away after having a child with her.
9. His son, Ishmael, becomes estranged.
10. God tells him to sacrifice his dear son Isaac upon an altar.

Note that before this time, their names were Abram and Sarai, but
after Ishmael was born, their names were changed to Abraham and Sarah.

> "I will set My covenant between Me and you, and I will increase
> you most exceedingly … As for Me, this is My covenant with you:
> You shall be a father of a multitude of nations; your name shall
> no longer be called Abram, but your name shall be Abraham, for

I have made you the father of a multitude of nations. I will make you most exceedingly fruitful and make nations of you; and kings shall descend from you. I will ratify My covenant between Me and you, and between your offspring after you, throughout their generations, as an **everlasting covenant**, to be a God to you and to your offspring after you; and I will give to you and to your offspring after you the land of your sojourns – the whole of the land of Canaan – as an **everlasting possession**; and I shall be a God to them." (Genesis 17:2-8, TJB) [emphasis mine]

This latter promise is the basis of the Christian Evangelical support for Israel as an independent Jewish nation, and should be a warning to those who support the BDS (Boycott, Divestment, and Sanctions) movement, or otherwise fail to bless Israel. I would stress the word, *everlasting*: if God shall always be a God to them, then He would never abandon them, nor would He ever revoke His covenant with His Chosen People. God's promise is unconditional. Nevertheless, individual males can invalidate the covenant and be cut off from the people, if they fail to be circumcised (Gen 17:14), despite what Paul said.

The Nation of Israel

Skipping forward to the rescue of the people from slavery in Egypt, God offered yet another covenant at Sinai, one which the people accepted. This covenant contained the essence of the Abrahamic, but with additional conditions. Throughout these early years, the words of Scripture were consistent: obey God and you will be rewarded in this life: there is no suggestion of reward in an afterlife, or even of an afterlife itself. See, for example, Exodus 3:8-12, 23; 6:4; 20:24; 31:16-17 regarding a perpetual covenant and promises forever; 32:13 regarding the land forever; and Leviticus 26:3-46 for God's promises regarding the consequences of obedience and disobedience. These are all earthly matters, and the theme continues throughout Torah. The warnings were of what would happen if the Children of Israel abandoned Torah and the Covenant, and the consequences would all occur in the lives of the people on this Earth. The story of Moses ends with him being prevented from entering the Promised Land: "Then the Lord said to him, 'this is the land which I swore to give Abraham, Isaac, and Jacob', saying 'I will give it to your descendants." (Deuteronomy 34:4). The leadership is then handed over to Joshua.

God then says to Joshua, "No man shall be able to stand before you all the days of your life ... I will not leave you nor forsake you" (Joshua 1:5) – prophecy and promise. In Judges we read that "the children of Israel did evil in the sight of the Lord, and served the Baals ... and the anger of the Lord was hot against Israel, so He delivered them into the hands of plunderers who despoiled them, and He sold them into the hands of their enemies" (Judges 2:11-14). This was as promised in Leviticus 26, with further condemnation from God in Judges 2:20-22, informing the Israelites that the promises made to now dead Joshua would no longer apply to them. Without going into further detail, the Book of Judges describes how God raised up deliverers for them, e.g. Ehud, but time and again, they fall back into idolatry and cease to observe the Covenant.

1 Samuel tells of more strife for the people of Israel if they do not esteem God (vv. 2:30-33), but again promises to raise up a *faithful priest* to guide them (v. 2:35) – this was Samuel. Samuel's understanding of his special role as a prophet begins in verse 3:10, confirmed in verse 3:20. Note that "the iniquity of Eli's house shall not be atoned for by sacrifice or offering forever" (v. 14), which questions the claimed role of Jesus. It is interesting to note God's view of the Ark of the Covenant (and thus the Law), for when the Philistines stole it, they suffered greatly, and were defeated in battle (vv. 4:1 – 7:13). Note also: "Then the temple of God was opened in heaven, and the ark of His covenant was seen in His Temple" (Revelation 11:19). I read that as an affirmation of the covenant made at Sinai, which bodes ill for those who say it was superseded by Jesus. As Samuel grew old, he appointed his sons as judges in his place, but the people complained and wanted a king to rule them, like other nations had. Samuel warned what would happen under a king, but the people insisted, and when Samuel consulted God, he was told to "crown a king for them" (8:22). Later, we find God sending Saul to Samuel, and Samuel being told to anoint him as ruler (9:16). Saul would save God's people, Israel, from the hand of the Philistines. It is worthwhile to review God's historic kindness to the Children of Israel, as narrated by Samuel (1 Samuel

12:6-15). It reveals the constant cycle of Israel's forgetting God and the Covenant, but God rescuing them. That cycle was to repeat many times over, but note that God's redemption was always concerning their earthly existence, just as He had promised. However, *"But if you act wickedly, both you and your king shall perish"* (v. 12:25). Sadly, Saul did not do as God commanded him, and despite his many victories, his kingdom did not endure (vv. 13:13-14; 15:24).

Note here that God's repeated redemption of Israel was not just because God loved His Chosen People – *"Hashem shall not forsake His people for the sake of His great Name; for Hashem has sworn to make you for a people unto Him"* (1 Samuel 12:22). This is a point that Christian apologetics misses: the Covenant was not for the sake of the Israelites, but for the sake of God's Name, and therefore nothing that the Israelites, did, or did not do, could change God's purpose and accomplishment. In the context of the trajectory of prophecy, this is the very essence of the Hebrew Scriptures – to claim that Jesus fulfilled prophecy to implement a *New Covenant*, and anoint a *New Israel*, is entirely false and antithetical. It is saying that God retracted His oath, and changed His mind.

The story continues with God rejecting Saul and anointing his successor, one David, son of Jesse. We discuss some aspects of David's life in a later chapter, but for now, there is nothing further in 1 & 2 Samuel that varies from the theme as discussed above. Saul, and then David, are guided by the Prophet Samuel, who is instructed by God on various issues. The prophecies of Samuel relate to the lives of these kings, not to a life hereafter. It is worth mentioning, however, that the Psalms written by David should be studied in conjunction with 1 & 2 Samuel, which provide the contemporary setting for these writings. You should also note that the text of 2 Samuel 22 is repeated as Psalm 18, with minor differences. The sentiments in David's final words in 2 Samuel 23 can also be found throughout his Psalms.

1 & 2 Kings, unsurprisingly, tell the story of the Kings of Israel, from the early days of Solomon, through a period of increasing spiritual deterioration, as some kings attempted to institutionalise idolatry. There were kings loyal to God, like Hezekiah and Josiah in Judah, and disloyal kings in the competing kingdom, like Jeroboam and Ahab. The important point here, is that the Prophets Isaiah, Hosea, Jeremiah, and Ezekiel, should be read

in conjunction with 1 & 2 Kings, for they were active during that era. For example, the text of 2 Kings 18:13 – 20:19 appears with minor differences in Isaiah 36:1–38:8, 39:1-8. The prophecies narrated by these aforementioned Prophets largely relate to this period of the kings, and can only be properly interpreted in that context. Without that context, the prophecies can be ascribed any meaning one chooses, which is what we will find in our later analysis, leading to false claims of prophecy fulfillment by Jesus.

The Major Prophets

I am not here attempting a lengthy dissertation on the Prophets: my goal is simply to emphasise their goals and achievements in the context of their times. Most of the prophecies were of the nature of both *forthtellings* (will of God) and *foretellings* (plan of God) related to contemporary events, but some were *foretellings* of a future beyond even our time, i.e., the End of Days. In the following review, I wish to evidence that distinction, and where appropriate, point out some Christian prophecy fulfillment fallacies. Unless otherwise stated, all quotations are from the Hebrew Scriptures.

Isaiah

As Jewish commentators are more conversant with such matters, I will start by the following commentary from the TJB:

> "Isaiah was a member of the Judean aristocracy and his long career as a prophet spanned eighty-six years (619-533 BCE) … Isaiah lashes out at the wicked among his people and warns them of dire destruction, but he also consoles and comforts. Interestingly, this Book is the source both of the chilling 'Vision of Isaiah' that is read on the Sabbath before the Ninth of Av, and of the seven prophecies of consolation that follow it. He foretold the exile that took place during his lifetime, as the powerful Assyrian army under Sennacherib conquered the Northern Kingdom … then the seemingly invincible ruler moved against Judah, but Isaiah prophesied that this time the army would be wiped out."[5]

Isaiah prophesied to the Kingdom of Judah, whilst his contemporary, Hosea, prophesied to the Northern Kingdom at the time, the House of Israel.

Regarding the Sennacherib's defeat, read the prophecy in Isaiah 10:20-27. In Chapter 11, Isaiah changes the subject to prophesy concerning the future Messiah. We can recognise this as such from the words in verses 6-9, which could only refer to a future time of perfect harmony. That alone dismisses any claim that Jesus fulfilled the prophecy in Isaiah 11:1. It is illogical to identify Jesus as the prophesied Messiah based on what he might do in his claimed Second Coming: only what was achieved during his time on earth, over two thousand years ago, can be offered as evidence.

As we read through Isaiah, we find prophesies concerning Babylonia (Ch. 13), Moab (Ch. 15), Damascus (Ch. 17), Egypt (Ch. 19), and the Wilderness of the West (Ch. 21), specifically Duma and Arabia. The narration in Chapter 22 of the *key to the House of David*, given to Eliakim: "he will open and no-one will close, he will close and no-one will open" (v. 22), is echoed in Revelation 3:7, in the letter to the church at Philadelphia. The NKJV editors have flagged the latter as prophecy fulfillment, but given a lack of consensus on the purpose of "the key", and the prophecy in Isaiah's text being quite specific to a time, place, and person, I find that improbable. After prophesying concerning Tyre (Ch. 23), Isaiah again returns to the theme of the *End of Days* (Ch. 24). He prophesies that "the land will become unfaithful because of its inhabitants, for they have transgressed commandments and violated laws: they have abrogated the **everlasting Covenant**" (v. 5) [emphasis mine]. Remember, however, that God made the Covenant for **His Name's sake**, which is why it is everlasting, irrespective of the behaviour of the Israelites. Chapter 24 ends with God reigning "in Mount Zion and in Jerusalem", leading Isaiah to praise God for Israel's eventual redemption (Ch. 25-27).

Chapters 28-31 continue with Isaiah's warnings to both the Northern kingdom and Judea, that in failing to obey God's decrees, misery and defeat will be upon them. He also conveys the message from God, that had they heeded his word, they would have had no need to seek the assistance of Egypt in defeating the Assyrians. Verse 30:19 begins another prophecy of the End of Days, when God will defeat His enemies, and the Israelites will heed His Word spoken through His Prophets. In Chapter

32, Isaiah refers of an issue which contradicts Christian interpretations of prophecy fulfillment. In verse 32:1, he mentions Hezekiah, the son of Ahaz prophesied in Isaiah 7:14: "Behold, the king will rule for the sake of righteousness and the officers will govern for justice": compare that with Isaiah 9:5 where he praises God: "For a child has been born to us ... the dominion will rest on his shoulder ... and Mighty God, Eternal Father, called his name Sar-shalom (Prince of Peace)." In Chapter 35, Isaiah prophesies about the return to Jerusalem, speaking of the wilderness and the desert, and the path there called The Road To Holiness. This is the same as the prophecy in Isaiah 40:3, mistakenly interpreted as referring to John the Baptist.

Verses 36:1 – 38:8 are restatements of 2 Kings 18:30 – 20:9, with the expected minor differences. There is an interesting passage which may shed light on Isaiah's view of an after-life, although equally, it may not: "For the Grace cannot thank You nor can Death laud You; those who descend to the pit cannot hope for Your truth. A living person, a living person, he shall thank you, as I do today!" (Isaiah 38:18-19). Perhaps here, Isaiah is only concerned with physical welfare in the context of being able to live to raise children.

According to the Jewish commentary of Isaiah 40:1:

> "God speaks to the prophets of Israel, commanding them to comfort the suffering people (*Targum*). Until this point, many of Isaiah's prophesies have been visions of retribution and destruction. From here through to the end of Isaiah, the prophecies speak words of consolation and assurances of the future Messianic redemption. This passage serves as a divider between the two types of prophecy (Rashi)."[6]

These next chapters, then, deserve particular attention in the context of whether Jesus fulfilled any messianic prophecies. The chapter begins:

> "*Comfort, comfort My people, says your God. Speak consolingly of Jerusalem and proclaim to her that her period [of exile] has been completed, that her iniquity has been forgiven her; for she has received double for all her sins from the hand of Hashem.*"

What should be obvious is that this cannot refer to the time of Jesus, for whilst this prophecy speaks of an imminent return TO Jerusalem, Jesus' life and death heralded a new period of exile FROM Jerusalem. Note too that Israel's iniquity will be forgiven her, not because someone would die in substitutionary atonement, but because God considered that Israel had already atoned sufficiently, having *received double for all her sins*. The following chapters expound on the topic of why the Israelites should not lose hope, for as it is written: "But you, O Israel, My servant, Jacob, you whom I have chosen, offspring of Abraham who loved Me – you whom I shall grasp from the ends of the earth and shall summon from among all its noblemen, and to whom I shall say, 'You are My servant' – I have chosen you and not rejected you. Fear not for I am with you, be not dismayed, for I am your God." (Isaiah 41:8-10) In his letters, Paul contends that those who follow Jesus are the true offspring of Abraham, but nothing in the Hebrew Scriptures supports that contention.

"I have inspired someone from the north, and he has come; he calls out in My Name from where the sun rises (v. 41:2). The tense of the verbs allow the interpretation that this was Cyrus, the benevolent king of Persia, who initiated the return to Zion in the days of Ezra. "Behold My servant, whom I shall uphold … I have placed My spirit upon him so that he can bring forth justice to the nations … he will not slacken nor tire until he sets justice in the land and islands will long for his teaching." (vv. 42:1-4) This is perceived as a messianic prophecy, but Jesus did not accomplish what is stated here. Rather than continue with this level of detail throughout the rest of Isaiah, let me just state that the remaining chapters follow the same theme, with nothing in the prophecies having been fulfilled by Jesus during his time some two thousand years ago. It may be contended that he will do so in his Second Coming, but that is begging the question – it offers no evidence that he was the promised messiah in his first coming. We shall finish with these words:

> "It shall be that at every New Moon and on every Sabbath, all mankind will come to prostrate themselves before Me, says Hashem. And they will go out and see the corpses of the men who rebelled against Me, for their decay will not cease and their fire will not be extinguished, and they will lie in disgrace before all mankind." (Isaiah 66:23-24)

On every Sabbath – could it be said that those who have rejected the Sabbath have indeed rebelled against God?

Jeremiah

Jeremiah had a difficult life, being chosen from a young age to be God's servant, a prophet for his time. He began under Josiah, one of the most righteous kings of Judah, who restored the Temple to its previous glory. But Jeremiah prophesied of the doom to follow due to the idolatry and unrighteousness of the people, but they rejected him, threatening to kill him as they had put to death, the prophet Uriah. King Jehoiakim also rejected him, burned the scrolls of his prophecies, and had him thrown into a dungeon when Jeremiah refused to be silenced. Jeremiah wept, not just because the word of God was ignored, but because he lived during the period when his prophecies came to pass with Jerusalem being destroyed. That he was vindicated gave him no comfort. However, Jeremiah also prophesied that there would be redemption seventy years later, and so the people in exile should accept their fate, building houses and settle, planting gardens and eating the produce. Jeremiah did not live to see the day of redemption, but his prophecy gave great comfort and hope to those who were living in exile. Remember that in the contemporary Jewish literature, a period of seventy years represented two new generations.

This synopsis provides the context of the Book of Jeremiah. Our task is to determine whether he was guided to prophesy of a future messiah, beyond this historical context. The first twenty-nine chapters concerned the people of Judah, but in Chapter 30, God instructed Jeremiah about a future redemption for the people of both Judah and Israel. Here, we are reminded of the error of the author of Hebrews, or perhaps just the Christian interpretation of Hebrews 8 and the quoting of Jeremiah 31. The opening verses set the context, especially:

> "But as for you, do not fear, My servant Jacob, the word of Hashem, and do not be afraid, Israel; for behold, I am saving you from distant places, and your descendants from the land of their captivity, and Jacob will return and be at peace and tranquil, and

none will make [him] afraid. For I am with you – the word of Hashem – to save you; for I will bring annihilation upon all the nations among whom I have dispersed you, but upon you I will not bring annihilation; I will chastise you with justice, but I will never eliminate you completely." (Jeremiah 30:10-11)

In the context of *annihilation*, *save* can only relate to the physical, not the spiritual; thus, the redemption in Jeremiah's messianic prophecy has nothing to do with substitutionary atonement for the forgiveness of sin. With that in mind, I will leave the reader to review Jeremiah chapters 30-31 for themselves, paying particular attention to verses 31:34-39. Chapter 32 returns to contemporary events in the life of Jeremiah, starting with prophecies concerning the purchasing of property in *Eretz* Israel, and continuing with prophecies concerning the fate of Judah. He also conveys God's word to the remnant of Judah, to not go to Egypt, and warns the Jews living in Egypt concerning their idolatrous ways.

As in Isaiah, Jeremiah prophesies to specific groups: the Philistines (Ch. 47); Moab (Ch. 48); Ammon, Edom, Damascus, and Kedar (Ch. 49); Babylonia and the Chaldeans (Ch. 50); and so forth. Jeremiah's narrative ends with his release from prison. These last verses, 52:31-34, are largely identical to 2 Kings 25:27-30, reminding us to always read the Prophets in the context of Kings and Chronicles, lest we misunderstand their historical significance, most especially the events foretold in their prophecies.

Ezekiel

Ezekiel was a contemporary of Jeremiah, their prophecies overlapping in many areas. Jeremiah's initial focus was on the people of Judah, and the fate that would befall them. On the other hand:

"His (Ezekiel's) primary mission was directed not to the Jews of a dying Land Of Israel, but to the Jews of Babylon, the exiled Jews who thought that they had lost their share in the God of Israel. They reasoned: Does a husband have a claim to his wife's loyalty after he divorced her? Does a master have a claim to his slave's services after he sent him away? And can God still claim us as His people after abandoning us to Nebuchadnezzar? To these forlorn Jews, Ezekiel was a prophet of hope, as well as rebuke."[7]

The first chapter of Ezekiel is referred to by the Jewish Sages as "The Account of the Chariot", but they found it so far beyond their comprehension that they felt inadequate to interpret it. Beginning in the second chapter, God refers to Ezekiel as *Son of Man* (curiously in initial capitals in the TJB translation), doing so 93 times throughout the book which bears his name. The TJB commentary reads:

> "Throughout this Book, God addresses Ezekiel as 'Son of Adam', i.e., of Man, and speaks of Israel collectively as 'Adam' (34:31, 36:10). The reference is to Adam, the first man, and the mission for which he was created. By use of these names, God suggests to Ezekiel that he and his nation, despite their severe shortcomings, are still expected to live up to God's hopes for humanity, the mission that was originally given to Adam, and then transferred to Abraham and his offspring (*R' M. Eisemann*)."[8]

We later discuss this form of address concerning where Jesus applied it to himself. Ezekiel's primary mission was to the Jews in exile, the Children of Israel, the ten tribes that Jesus later described as lost. In that sense, Jesus saw his own mission as similar to that of Ezekiel, as described in Ezekiel chapters 2-3. Beginning in Chapter 4, Ezekiel's prophecy describes the siege of Jerusalem, and the destruction and exile that would follow. Ezekiel's theme was much the same as that of Isaiah and Jeremiah: the people were warned about their corruption and idolatry, and the consequences that would surely follow, but they would not listen, and continued their rebellion against God.

In Chapter 33, we find an interesting exposition on righteousness, sin, and forgiveness. This has a direct bearing on the question of whether there was any requirement for Jesus to die to atone for the sins of all:

> "Now you, Son of Man, say to the children of your people: … If I say of a righteous person that he shall surely live, and he relies on his righteousness yet practices corruption, all his righteousness

will not be recalled, rather because of his corruption that he practiced, for that he will die. And if I say to a wicked person, 'You shall surely die', and he repents from his sin and acts with justice and righteousness – the wicked person returns a pledge, repays for his theft, follows the life-giving decrees, without practicing corruption – he will surely live; he will not die. All his sins that he had committed will not be remembered for him; he has practiced justice and righteousness, he shall surely live ... If a righteous person turns back from his righteousness and practices corruption, he shall die for [his acts]; and if a wicked person turns back from his wickedness and acts with justice and righteousness, he shall live for [his acts]. Yet you say, 'The way of the Lord is not proper!' I shall judge you, each man according to his ways, O House of Israel." (Ezekiel 33:12-20)

It really could not be clearer than that: God judges each person according to his ways, and if one lives righteously, bearing in mind that none is perfectly righteous, God will forgive and remember his sins no more. We have two confirmations of the contemporary understanding of righteousness: (1), "For there is no man so highly righteous on earth that he [always] does good and never sins" (Ecclesiastes 7:20); and (2), "For though the righteous one may fall seven times, he will arise, but the wicked one will stumble through evil" (Proverbs 24:14). Let me restate that: *practising righteousness* (or *practicing* if you are a North American reader), does not suggest perfect righteousness – it simply means *actively pursuing* righteousness whilst nonetheless, periodically failing. If that was true in the time of Ezekiel, why would it not be true forever? Did God ever revoke that promise? There is a challenge for modern Christian clergy in Chapter 34, as it was for the leaders of Israel when God warned: "Woe to the shepherds of Israel who have tended themselves! Is it not the flock that the shepherds should tend?" (v. 34:2). In recent years, especially over the issue of child pornography and the sexual abuse of children in their care, Christian churches have sought to protect the shepherds rather than the flock, presumably in the mistaken belief that the congregation would lose faith in the clergy should such abominations become publicly known. Such loss of faith could be well justified, but seems to have happened anyway.

In Chapter 35, Ezekiel was directed to prophesy against Seir, the home of Esau/Edom, Israel's archenemy. Concerning the *End of Days*, God will repay Seir in kind for its hatred and vengefulness against Israel, so that all, Israel and Edom, will know that He is God (vv. 35:11-15). Modern commentary equates Esau with Islam, and the Arab nations that seek the destruction of Israel. If that be true, then the supporters of the BDS (Boycott, Divestments, and Sanctions) movement, and others with bias and prejudice against Israel, as is commonly displayed in the United Nations, the European Union, and the liberal progressives in the USA, may well rue their choices.

In Chapter 37, we find the first suggestion of life after death, when God said to Ezekiel: "Prophesy over these bones! Say to them ... Behold, I bring a spirit into you, and you will come to life. I will put sinews upon you, I will bring flesh upon you, and I will coat you with skin; then I will put a spirit into you and you will come to life; then you will know that I am Hashem." (vv. 37:4-6) Two points of view are presented in the Talmud, as to whether this prophecy is a parable, or whether the bones in the valley will actually come to life. In later years, the Sadducees believed the former, whilst the Pharisees believed the latter. Continuing: God told Ezekiel to prophesy of the two houses, Israel and Judah, becoming one nation (vv. 37:15-28). Again, God's purpose is explicit, as it has been throughout all the previous prophecies: so that "the nations will know that I am Hashem Who sanctifies Israel, when My sanctuary will be among them forever" (v. 37:28). No mention of a *New Israel*, just the same original Israel and its people whom God rescued from Egypt.

The prophecy concerning the *End of Days* continues in Chapter 38, with God singling out Gog and Magog. We are not concerned with the details here, other than to note that God refers to Himself as performing the various actions, not a messiah. Importantly, God confirms that he will not abandon Israel. He did hide His countenance from them, because of their sin, but: "Then they will know that I am Hashem, their God, for I have exiled them to the nations, and I will bring them to their land, and will not leave any of them there. Then I will not hide My countenance from them again, for I will pour out My spirit upon the House of Israel – the word of the Lord Hashem/Elohim." (Ezekiel 39:28-29). The *New Israel* of Christianity was not exiled to the nations, and therefore cannot be the Israel redeemed back to the land that God gave to them. No Son,

Second Person of the Trinity, no Holy Spirit, Third Person of the Trinity - just Hashem/Elohim, the God of Israel, pouring out His spirit upon His chosen people, His First-Born Son (Exodus 4:22).

Returning to the commentary in The Jewish Bible (TJB):

> "Chapters 40-48 are unique in Scripture. At the very moment when Jerusalem lay in ruin and the nation was weeping in its Babylonian exile, Ezekiel proclaimed a very detailed plan for the construction of a future Temple, the laws that would govern it, and the respective roles of the *Kohanim* (Priests), king, and the people in the renewed Temple service. Thus Ezekiel ends his dirges with concrete chapters of consolation."[9]

A question I would ask is this: Given all that had happened to the Children of Israel up to this point, with their rebellion against God, their exiles, their promised returns to the land, and the promise of rebuilding the Temple, why would yet another rebellion change the mind of God concerning their future, especially when all along, God has made His purposes clear: it was for His Name's sake – so that all would know that He is God. Did God not foresee the actions of His chosen people, eventually giving up due to the unforeseen futility of His original plan? If so, how could He be God? If not, then the Christian narrative of a *New Israel* under a *New Covenant* must be false.

The Book of Ezekiel ends with: "And the name of the city from that day shall be 'Hashem-Is-There'!" Not Rome, but Jerusalem, is where God shall be.

The Twelve Prophets

This section reviews the Prophets: Hosea, Joel, Amos, Obadiah, Jonah, Micah, Nahum, Habakkuk, Zephaniah, Haggai, Zechariah, and Malachi. Their writings span a period of over three hundred and fifty years, beginning circa 700 BCE. They begin at the time when there were two Jewish kingdoms, with the Ten Tribes of the north (Israel) seemingly far more powerful than the two tribes to the south: Judah and Benjamin (Judah). As with Isaiah, Jeremiah, and Ezekiel, this period was characterised by:

"strife and disappointment, as prophet after prophet begged and warned, foretold and chastised about the impending doom – all in vain. The Book of Hosea is perhaps the starkest of the twelve. In admonishing his people, he called them God's 'estranged wife'. For his harshness, he incurred God's wrath. To demonstrate the eternal truth that Israel remains His Chosen People despite its major shortcoming, God commanded Hosea to undergo one of Scriptures most difficult ordeals, a personal torture that mirrored God's own anguish and loyalty. Fittingly and inspiringly, The Twelve Prophets ends the era of prophecy with the exhortation:

Remember the Torah of Moses My servant, which I commanded him at Horeb for all of Israel – [its] decrees and [its] statutes. Behold, I send you Elijah the prophet before the coming of the great and awesome day of Hashem. And he will turn back [to God] the hearts of fathers with [their] sons and the hearts of sons with their fathers ... "[10]

According to the New Testament, people questioned whether John the Baptist was Elijah, come to herald the *great and awesome day of Hashem* (End of Days). Clearly, he was not – we are still waiting. Importantly for Christians, the turning back to God entails remembering *the Torah of Moses My servant, which I commanded him at Horeb for all of Israel – [its] decrees and [its] statutes*. One should not believe that Torah is for Israel only, or alternatively, if people believe themselves to be part of the *New Israel*, they might need to explain to God why Torah does not apply to them.

In this review of The Twelve Prophets, I will not proceed as I did with Isaiah, Jeremiah, and Ezekiel, but will just highlight any texts or prophecies which I consider significant in the context of whether Jesus fulfilled any of them. As an aside, the meaning of the Hebrew word *yom* is much debated in the context of the Creation days in Genesis; Hosea 6:2 is an opportunity to contemplate: "He will heal us after two days; on the third day He will raise us up and we will live before Him." In this context, *yom* refers to *a long period of time*, in this case, the two days are the two exiles in Egypt and Babylonia, both of which were *healed* in the form of the First and Second Temples, but at the end of the third day, following the destruction of the Second Temple in 70 CE, God will raise up the people of Israel with the final redemption and the Third Temple. Again I would emphasise the meaning of "redemption" in the Hebrew Scriptures: it refers to the people of Israel being forgiven their sins and returned to the land that God gave them in perpetuity. No more, no less.

There is a suggestion of a messiah here: "For many days, the Children of Israel will sit with no king, no officer, no sacrifice, no pillar, and no *ephod* or *teraphim*. Afterward the Children of Israel will return and seek out Hashem their God, and David their king, and they will tremble for Hashem and for His goodness in the end of days." (Hosea 3:4-5) *Ephod* usually refers to a priestly garment, whilst *teraphim* refers to images of human shape, sometimes associated with idolatry. That aside, mention of *David their king* in the same sentence as *in the end of days*, is interpreted as there being a new King Messiah leading to the messianic age.

Joel chapters 3-4 prophesy concerning the *End of Days*, and gives a warning to those who curse Israel. All Israel will be returned, and all nations will be brought to the Valley of Jehoshaphat (Valley of God's judgement) to be judged. Note that it is God doing the judging, with no suggestion of a Mediator. "Hashem will roar from Zion and will emit His voice from Jerusalem (Ed. *not Rome*); and the heavens and the earth will tremble. But Hashem will be a shelter for His people and a stronghold for the Children of Israel. Thus you will know that I am Hashem your God, Who dwells in Zion, My holy mountain; Jerusalem will be holy, and aliens will no longer pass through her." (Joel 4:16-17). Further, "Judah will exist forever, and Jerusalem from generation to generation. Though I cleanse, their bloodshed I will not cleanse, when Hashem dwells in Zion." (vv. 4:20-21). The TJB commentary reads: "Though I will cleanse the nations by forgiving many of their sins, I will not forgive them for the bloodshed they perpetrated against Israel. When *Hashem dwells in Zion*, i.e., at the End of Days, they will be punished."[11]

In Obadiah 1:21, there is an allusion to the Messiah: "And saviours will ascend Mount Zion to judge the Mountain of Esau, and the kingdom will be Hashem's." One commentary reads, in part: "Messiah and his colleagues will exact retribution from the Edomites for their cruelty", which can have no relevance to the life of Jesus.

Jonah's experience of three days and nights in the fish (v. 2:1) is recalled in Matthew 12:40, with Jesus saying that he would spend three days and nights in the heart of the earth. The purpose of Jesus' analogy is unclear, to me at least, despite the many Christian commentaries to the contrary, but at least few commentators have claimed Jonah's experience as a prophecy, as so many have done with the experiences of King David as narrated in the Psalms.

Micah's prophecy concerning the *End of Days* reveals the error of the Church of Rome in rejecting Torah: "It will be in the end of days that the mountain of the Temple of Hashem will be firmly established as the most prominent of the mountains, and it will be exalted up above the hills, and the peoples will stream to it. Many nations will go and say, 'Come, let us go up to the Mountain of Hashem and to the Temple of the God of Jacob, and He will teach us of His ways and we will walk in His paths'. For **from Zion shall go forth the Torah**, and the word of Hashem from Jerusalem." (Micah 4:1-2) [emphasis mine] Christian doctrine has Torah suspended during Jesus' First and Second Comings, at least if they understand Micah's prophecy. I believe that they have it sadly wrong, to the spiritual detriment of all Christians.

From the TJB notes on Zechariah: "His prophecies deal with the entire period from his own day until the End of Days. The commentaries agree that Zechariah's prophetic visions are so esoteric that many will not be fully understood until the coming of Elijah the Prophet."[12] One prophecy that Jesus is said to have fulfilled is this: "For behold, your king will come to you, righteous and victorious is he, a humble man riding upon a donkey" (Zechariah 9:9). Taken in isolation, it could almost be true, but as we discuss in a later chapter, the context disallows such a claim. In what sense was Jesus victorious when he rode into Jerusalem? Were war horses eliminated from Jerusalem, or did the war horses (metaphorically) invade Jerusalem? Were the Children of Israel returned from exile, or were they driven out to endure an even longer exile than they had ever experienced before? Did God "bend Judah as a bow" to defeat His enemies, or did His enemies defeat Judah?

Mention of thirty pieces of silver in Zechariah 11:12-13 has also been treated as prophecy in relation to the betrayal of Jesus by Judas, but such is demonstrably false. We discuss this in detail in the section on Matthew's Gospel. Zechariah Chapter 12 reveals a prophecy from God concerning Israel, and again, this relates to the End of Days. Nations will besiege

Jerusalem, with even some Jews being forced to join, but the enemies will be destroyed: "Behold, I am making Jerusalem a cup of poison for all the peoples all around" (v. 12:2). Of interest also is that whilst the early Church of Rome forbade the practice of all Jewish commemorations, even the God-ordained festivals, Scripture contends otherwise: "It shall be that all who are left over from all the nations who had invaded Jerusalem will come up every year to worship the King, Hashem, Master of Legions, and to celebrate the festival of Succos" (v. 14:16). Succos (*Sukkot*), the Feast of Tabernacles, was decreed by God in Leviticus 23:34.

And finally, "Malachi, a contemporary of Haggai and Zechariah, and the last prophet, prophesied during the Second Temple era. His name means *My (God's) messenger*. He has been associated with Ezra the Scribe or Mordechai (uncle of Queen Esther). In his concluding admonition he urges the Jews to *remember the Torah of Moses My servant*, implying there would be no further prophets to chastise Israel to observe the Torah. From Malachi forward, scribes and rabbinic sages would be the guardians of the written and oral transmission of the word of God."[13] As to that last statement, Jesus confirmed this when he stated: "The Scribes and Pharisees sit in Moses' seat" (Matthew 23:2). In Malachi 3:1 we read: "Behold, I am sending My messenger, and he will clear a path before Me; suddenly the Lord Whom you seek will come to His Sanctuary, and the messenger of the covenant for whom you yearn, behold, he comes, says Hashem, Master of Legions." This is another prophecy that Christianity claims was fulfilled in the time of Jesus, by John the Baptist. However, the next verse reads: "Who can bear the day of his coming, and who can survive when he appears?" As it turned out, it was Jesus and John who did not survive, whilst practically everyone else did, so this prophecy cannot have been fulfilled. Similarly, though John preached repentance, he could hardly have been said to have eliminated the wickedness of the land in preparation for the Messianic era. Certainly, he may well have seen himself in that role, and others might have thought similarly, but events soon proved him wrong.

Malachi 3:6-7 is thought provoking in the context of God's mercy and forgiveness, refuting the claimed need for substitutionary atonement. I will let you read and contemplate at your leisure. The final verses of Malachi speak to the End of Days, reminding the people to *remember the Torah of Moses My servant* (v. 3:22).

Daniel

Christianity places great store by some of the writings of Daniel, and thus we must review what he had to say. Though in Judaism, he is not recognised as a Prophet, nevertheless:

> "In the concluding chapters of the book, Daniel saw visions that remain the subject of intense speculation, for he was shown prophetic scenes of the 'Four Beasts' representing the 'Four Monarchies' that will dominate Israel during its long series of exiles. And he was shown the calculations of the 'End of Days', when Israel will be redeemed and the world will finally achieve the Divine goal for which it was created. What did the numbers mean? When and how will the events come about? These visions remain clothed in mysteries that will not be stripped away until the time of the final Redemption is at hand. Then we will know how God's seeds will sprout into the glorious fulfillment of the Scriptural prophecies."[14]

The *Four Monarchies* are generally accepted as the Babylonian, Medo-Persian, Greek, and Roman Empires. Daniel 2:41 says that the fourth will be a divided empire, with later commentators offering that it is dominated by Edom and Ishmael, represented by Christianity and Islam. "Then, in the days of these kingdoms, the God of Heaven will establish a kingdom that will never be destroyed nor will its sovereignty be left to another people; it will crumble and consume all these kingdoms, and it will stand forever." (v. 2:44) It is interesting to consider that <u>if</u> Christianity is indeed one of the kingdoms of the divided Roman Empire, then its days are numbered also, its fate being to crumble and be consumed. In an earlier work, *Once a Christian*[15], I explained that one of my primary reasons for rejecting Christianity was the pagan influence of the sun-worshipping Roman Emperor, Constantine, and the degree to which the 4th century Church of Rome compromised with paganism, whilst ostracising Judaism. The truth is embedded in the term that arose in Europe in the 13th century: the *Holy Roman Empire*. If Daniel 2:44 has been interpreted correctly, then likely I was right in walking away from Christianity.

Daniel's vision, verses 7:1-12, covers the period of the four kingdoms and their destruction, which brings us to the controversial "one like a (son of) man" in verse 13, the wording differing in the Hebrew and Greek sources. We discuss this later in detail (Chapter 3-3) so I won't cover it here, other than to note that in both Judaism and Christianity, this entity is accepted as King Messiah, but importantly, it relates to his appearance during the Messianic Era at the End of Days. One might construe this as a prophecy to be fulfilled by Jesus in his Second Coming, but it can offer no evidence of prophecy fulfillment in his First Coming, which is the primary focus of this study. Whilst some Christian commentary places the beginning of the Messianic Era concurrent with the resurrection of Jesus, him now being seated at the right hand of God, this again is begging the question: first believing that Jesus is the Messiah, and thus the Messianic Era must have begun some two thousand years ago. However, only the greatest of literary gymnastics can reconcile the Scriptural description of this era with history as we know it.

Daniel 9 contains the prophecies of the 70 weeks, which some Christian commentators have used in an attempt to prove that Jesus was the prophesied Messiah. Again, a full discussion of this is later given in Chapter 3-4. A curious aspect of this prophecy is how some interpret verse 9:27 as being as yet future, referring to a seven-year treaty broken halfway through. Daniel's prophecies are chronological, as we see in verses 11:16-21, where Antiochus persecutes the Jews, God punishes Antiochus, the Hasmonean dynasty succeeds Antiochus, but is diminished when the two brothers, Aristobulus and Hyrcanus battle for succession. The Hasmoneans sign a "holy covenant" of friendship (vv. 28, 30) with Rome, but this enables Rome to conquer the lands surrounding Israel without fear of Hasmonean influence. Having done so, Rome also conquers Israel itself. This is the world into which Jesus enters.

Daniel 10-12 introduce us to the prophecies of the End Times, with Daniel being given a glimpse of the timing: "From the time the daily offering was removed and the mute abomination put in place, one thousand two hundred and ninety years. Praiseworthy is he who awaits and reaches one thousand three hundred and thirty-five years." (vv. 12:11-12) A little research uncovers dozens of interpretations of these calculations, with some degree of consensus, notably that the *mute abomination* is the Islamic

Dome of the Rock erected over the site of the destroyed Temple. I am content to accept that "the matters are obscured and sealed until the time of the End" (v. 12:9), for likely I have no need to know, unless THE End arrives before mine does. That is looking less and less likely as I age.

Finally, we have another indication of life after death: "As for you, go to [your] end; you will rest – then arise for your portion at the End of Days." (v.12:13) Taking that advice seriously, I shall do likewise, and hopefully, I am among *the wise who understand* (v. 10), and shall arise to inherit some portion when others arise.

Messiah as Redeemer?

It is interesting that there is not a single explicit reference to "a" or "the" messiah in the Hebrew Scriptures. There are seventeen references to the *Redeemer*, almost all in Isaiah, but in the majority of cases, it is clearly identified as God:

- "the word of Hashem and your Redeemer, the Holy One of Israel" (Isaiah 41:14).
- "Thus said Hashem, King of Israel and its Redeemer, Hashem, Master of Legions" (Isaiah 44:6).
- "Our Redeemer, Whose Name is Hashem, Master of Legions, the Holy One of Israel!" (Isaiah 47:4)
- "then all flesh will know that I am Hashem, your Saviour and your Redeemer, the Mighty One of Jacob." (Isaiah 49:26, 60:16)
- "You, Hashem, are our Father, 'our Eternal Redeemer' is Your Name" (Isaiah 63:16)

Redeemer in Jeremiah 50:34 is similarly identified. This raises the question: how, when, and where did the idea of a Jewish *mashiach* (messiah) arise, if the Prophets seemed not to have been told about him by God? It is indisputable that **if** the Prophets did not prophesy concerning a messiah, then Jesus could not have fulfilled messianic prophecies. There are verses which have been interpreted in Judaism as referring to a messiah, but within Judaism, there is no consensus on when he will come, what signs will herald his arrival, or what he will accomplish. Reflecting the understanding of

Redemption, and mentions of King David or a descendant, have some scholars seeing the messiah as a bold leader who will defeat Israel's enemies in the last days. Others respond to the verse, as does Christianity, of him arriving on a donkey, thus a much milder messiah. In his intriguing book, *The Real Messiah*, Aryeh Kaplan noted the following points[16]:

1. In a world prepared to receive him, the Messiah will then be born.

2. He will be a mortal human being, born normally of human parents. Tradition states that he will be a direct descendant of King David.

3. The Rambam (Maimonides) writes: "If there arises a ruler from the House of David, who is immersed in Torah and *Mitzvos* like David his ancestor, following both the Written and Oral law, who leads Israel back to the Torah, strengthening its laws and fighting G-d's battles, then we may assume that he is the Messiah. If he is further successful in rebuilding the Temple on its original site and gathering the dispersed of Israel, then his identity as the Messiah is a certainty."[17]

4. It is very important to note that these accomplishments are a minimum for our acceptance of an individual as the Messiah. There have been numerous people who have claimed to be the Messiah, but the fact that they did not achieve these minimal goals proved them to be false.

5. Although the Messiah will influence and teach all mankind, his main mission will be to bring the Jews back to G-d. Thus the prophet said (Joshua 3:5), "For the children of Israel shall sit many days without a king or prince … Afterward shall the children of Israel return and seek the Lord their G-d and David their king … in the end of days." Similarly (Ezekiel 37:24), "And My servant David shall be king over them, and they shall all have one shepherd, and they shall also walk in My ordinances and observe My Laws."

6. As society reaches toward perfection and the world becomes increasingly G-dly, men will begin to explore the transcendental more and more. As the prophet said (Isaiah 11:9), "For all the earth shall be full of knowledge of G-d, as the waters cover the sea." More and more people will achieve the mystical union of prophecy, as foretold (Joel 3:1), "And it shall come to pass afterward, that I will pour out My spirit on all flesh, and your sons and your daughters shall prophesy."

Note how point (5) effectively summarises the message of all the Prophets: repent and return to God. Isaiah 11:9 prophesies the same message as Jeremiah 31:33. As for *the world becomes increasingly G-dly*, I fear that the arrival of the Messiah must be some time away, for as I see modern society, it is becoming increasing more **un-Godly**. Let us review what Isaiah prophesied:

> "It will happen in the end of days: The mountain of the Temple of Hashem will be firmly established as the head of the mountains, and it will be exalted above the hills, and all the nations will stream to it. Many peoples will go and say, 'Come, let us go up to the Mountain of Hashem, to the Temple of the God of Jacob, and He will teach us of His ways and we will walk in His paths.' For from Zion will the Torah come forth, and the word of Hashem from Jerusalem. He will judge among the nations, and will settle the arguments of many peoples. They shall beat their swords into plowshares and their spears into pruning hooks; nations will not lift sword against nation and they will no longer study warfare." (Isaiah 2:2-4)

This conveys the meaning of Redemption in the Hebrew Scripture prophecies: it is about peace in this world here on Earth, the Children of Israel regathered in *Eretz* Israel, with God reigning in the Temple in Jerusalem, and Torah coming forth from Zion. Whilst Christianity insists on claiming that Jesus abrogated Torah, its people may be denied participation in the world to come. That is the message of prophecy.

Summary

Throughout my journey through the Prophets, I have found only two types of prophecy:
1. Prophecies concerning contemporary or near-term circumstances, where the Prophets warned the people of the consequences of departing from Torah and the Covenant. In each case, what followed was strife and exile, with a later return to *Eretz* Israel; and
2. Prophecies concerning the End of Days.

What I did **not** find were any prophecies even suggestive of the assertion by the author of Hebrews: "So Christ was offered once to bear the sins of many. To those who eagerly wait for him he will appear a second time apart from salvation" (Hebrews 9:28) Christian theology claims that Jesus fulfilled a prophecy in Isaiah 53:10-12, but when read in context, it was Israel that bore the burden.

I contend, without equivocation, that had I read the Hebrew Scriptures, accurately translated into English, absent of any theological annotations, without having read the New Testament, I would never have envisaged an interim era as narrated in the Gospels and Epistles. On encountering the New Testament, I would have wondered what relevance this later testament had to the original Scripture, for I could see no continuity with the prophecies of old, only discontinuity. Jesus was not at all like the messiah that I was expecting, although in truth, I share the uncertainty of Judaism as to the nature and mission of this messiah. Yes, there are mentions, hints really, but according to the Prophets, the messiah does not appear until the End of Days, and his role is unclear – it is still God who is front and centre of all activities. Yes, there is likely to be a messiah, but his role is as a man, doing the bidding of God.

Notice the repeated description of God: *Hashem, Master of Legions*, one *Who dwells in Mount Zion*. No mention of a second-in-command; no mention of a mediator; no mention of someone sitting at His right hand to do His bidding. I will not claim to understand how the messiah will interact with God in those final days, but on one aspect I am utterly convinced: the messiah was (is) not destined to die in substitutionary atonement for our sins. Apart from a suggestion in Isaiah 53:10-12, there is not a single mention anywhere in prophecy to support that idea. Given that all of the prophets had something to say about Israel's redemption and the End of Days, is it not odd that God did not inspire or direct any of them to prophesy of an interim messiah dying for our sins? God gave us His Word to advise, guide, inspire, warn, and to give us hope: why would He choose to be silent on an issue as significant as Christianity claims it to be? Why did God repeatedly state that forgiveness was available to all those who repent, if in fact, that is not true? If God intended His people to accept Jesus as Messiah, why did He not tell His Prophets about it, so that His people would be prepared when the time came? The Christian narrative is most un-God-like, at least, not at all like the God of the Hebrew Scriptures as I understand Him.

On a personal note, perhaps the biggest problem that I have with Christianity is the rejection of Torah and the Sabbath, when throughout the Hebrew Scriptures, it is repeatedly emphasised that God has never repealed His Word on these issues, and in the last days, Torah, especially, will again be prominent in the hearts and minds of all people (see Isaiah 2:3, Jeremiah 31:33, and Malachi 3:22). In the Book of Ezekiel, we find repeated warnings against profaning the Sabbath, and the consequences thereof, yet Christianity, supposedly the New Israel, has chosen to abandon it. Nearly a hundred years ago, Carlyle Haynes wrote: "The Bible in its entirety, both Old and New Testaments, commands, upholds, defends, and teaches the observance of the seventh day as the Sabbath"[18]. Taking to heart: "*Safeguard the Sabbath day to sanctify it, as HASHEM, your God, has commanded you*" (Deuteronomy 5:12); and encouraged by a book by Samuel Bacchiocchi[19] on the subject, I undertook my own study, publishing it under the title, *Defending God's Sabbath*[20]. I do not understand how Christian scholars can be so diligent, furtive even, in scouring the Scriptures seeking morsels to justify the belief that Jesus fulfilled Old Testament prophecies, yet totally ignore the most explicit statements concerning Torah and the Sabbath.

In the context of prophecy, if indeed Jesus did declare the end of Torah, because he fulfilled it, then he was certainly not fulfilling an overarching theme of Old Testament prophecy. If that be true, then he could not have been fulfilling any prophecy, for a messiah could not at one and the same time, fulfill one prophecy but countermand another. That would make no sense at all. If we are to accept the prophecies in the Hebrew Scriptures at all, we must believe in their integrity in their entirety.

History has proven many prophecies to have come to pass, most notably concerning the fate of Israel. Beyond that, we have the prophecies concerning the end times, but no prophecies of an interim messiah. Whatever else Jesus may have been, his life and claimed accomplishments were not prophesied in the Hebrew Scriptures, unless of course, his demise was a fulfillment of this warning:

"But that prophet or that dreamer of dreams shall be put to death, because he has spoken in order to turn you away from the Lord your God who brought you out of the land of Egypt and redeemed you from the house of bondage, to entice you from the way in which the Lord your God commanded you to walk. So, you shall put away the evil from your midst." (Deuteronomy 13:1-5)

REFERENCES:

1. Hoffman, Joel M., *The Bible Doesn't Say That: 40 Biblical Mistranslations, Misconceptions, and Other Misunderstandings*, Thomas Dunne Books, New York, NY, 2016, p. 112

2. Scherman, Rabbi Nosson, *The Tanach*, Mesorah Publications, ArtScroll English Edition, Brooklyn, NY, 2011, p. 2

3. https://www.openbible.info/topics/god_always_was_always_will_be

4. https://www.chabad.org/library/article_cdo/aid/1324268/jewish/What-Were-Abrahams-10-Tests.htm

5. Scherman, *Ibid*, p. 601

6. *Ibid*, p. 650

7. *Ibid*, p. 773

8. *Ibid*, p. 776

9. *Ibid*, p. 838

10. *Ibid*, p.855

11. *Ibid*, p. 874

12. *Ibid*, p. 910

13. *Ibid*, p. 926

14. *Ibid*, p. 1165

15. Talbot, Wayne, *Once a Christian: How the Bible Convinced Me to Walk Away*, Xlibris, Bloomington, IN, 2017

16. Kaplan, Aryek, *The Real Messiah - A Jewish Response to Missionaries*, National Conference of Synagogue Youth, New York, 1995, pp. 91-97

17. *Yad, Melachim* 11:4

18. Haynes, Carlyle B., *From Sabbath to Sunday*, Review and Herald Publishing Association, Washington, D.C., 1928, p. 7

19. Bacchiocchi, Samuel, *From Sabbath to Sunday*, The Pontifical Gregorian University Press, Rome, Italy, 1977

20. Talbot, Wayne, *Defending God's Sabbath*, Peshat Books, Kelso, NSW, 2012

CHAPTER 1-8

SOME RELATED MATTERS

Christianity versus Judaism

There is an interesting, and perhaps for Christians, a very challenging passage in Daniel: "In those times, many will rise up against the king of the South; and sons of the lawless men of your people will exalt themselves to establish a vision, but they will stumble." (Daniel 11:14). The TJB commentary reads:

> "*Rashi* and *Ramban* take this as an allusion to the Nazarene and his disciples. For is there a greater stumbling block than this? All the prophets foretold that the Messiah would redeem the Jews, help them, gather in the exiles, and support their observance of the commandments. But he caused Jewry to be put to the sword, to be scattered, and to be degraded; he tampered with the Torah and its laws; and he misled most of the world to serve something other than God. (*Hil. Melachim* 11:4)"[1]

Whilst I do not agree that Jesus and the Nazarenes were the cause of *Jewry being put to the sword, scattered, and degraded* (unless God so decreed), Roman Christianity certainly played its part, and *tampered with the Torah and its laws*. I would offer that *Rashi* and *Ramban* have to a degree, conflated cause and consequence, especially in view of the Nazarenes being eventually persecuted by Christianity. However, the general tone of their commentary contains much truth, and it is worth considering that if we are to consider the words of Daniel as prophetic, then verse 11:14 can easily be matched to the Jesus narrative, at least as rendered by the Church of Rome. For centuries, encouraged by the Church Fathers, it taught contempt of the Jew, and persecuted those who practiced Judaism (see *The Teaching of Contempt* by Jules Isaac[2]).

Without doubt, the Catholic Church exalted itself above all other religions, with the Pope becoming the head of the Holy Roman Empire. For a time, the Catholic Church decreed that Protestants could not go to heaven, largely because they did not practise the Sacraments. Even today, many Christians believe that only Christians go to heaven – people of all other religions are destined for eternal damnation. In claiming that Jesus abrogated Torah, the term *sons of lawless men* can reasonably be applied to Christians. Jesus and his followers did establish a vision, one, despite Christian claims to the contrary, that does not conform with the Hebrew Scriptures. As for *they will stumble*, well perhaps that remains future, although in the developed Western world, the signs are already there.

The Lord is my Shepherd

The relevance of this to the trajectory of prophecy may not be immediately obvious, but I hope to persuade you that it is indeed relevant to the subject of Jesus fulfilling prophecy. You have no doubt seen the paintings of Jesus, the Good Shepherd, kind and gentle, holding a lamb to signify just how gentle and caring he is with his flock. Often, we see the words: "*I am the good shepherd*" (John 10:11) written underneath, to reinforce the message; or from Psalm 23, "*The Lord is my shepherd*". Unfortunately, such a shepherd is not the shepherd of the Hebrew Scriptures, nor of the times of King David.

Whilst modern shepherding of sheep relates mainly to rounding them up for crutching, drenching, shearing, or shipping off to market, the role of the shepherd of ancient days was to protect the sheep from marauding animals and thieves. Whilst Psalm 23 has the shepherd (Lord) having him (David) lie down in green pastures, leading him to still waters, and restoring his soul, that was not the task of the shepherds of his day, although they may have done that as well. To understand this, we turn to the story of David and Goliath in 1 Samuel 17:31-37. Saul was concerned for the fate of the youth, David, should he go out to fight the Philistines, but David replied, boasted even:

> "Your servant was a shepherd for his father among the flocks; the lion or the bear would come and carry off a sheep of the flock, and I would go after it, strike it down, and rescue the sheep from its mouth. If it would attack me, I would grab onto its beard and strike it and kill it. Your servant has slain even lion and bear; and the uncircumcised Philistine shall be like one of them." (vv. 34-36)

This is how David became so proficient with slingshot and sword – he was a warrior. That is hardly the image we have of Jesus, and so Jesus cannot be the shepherd of David's psalms, for David would have thought of shepherds in the same sense as his own experience. The second part of John 10:11 better conveys the intent: *"The good shepherd gives his life for his sheep"*, but in the Old Testament sense, that was not to die in substitutionary atonement for sin, but to protect life and limb. This is an example of where an Old Testament verse is quoted to *match*, rather than *prophesy*, although the match is clearly something less than Christianity understands.

Heart and Soul

In the modern vernacular, the *heart* is the centre of affection, but in the early Hebrew (*levav*), and even the Greek (*kardia*), it was more than that: it included bit emotion *and* intellect.

"In Hebrew, the heart (*lev* or *levav*) is the center of human thought and spiritual life. We tend to think that the heart refers mainly to our emotions, but in Hebrew it also refers to one's mind and thoughts as well.

Many cultures assumed that the heart was the seat of intelligence, and without an advanced understanding of physiology, it makes sense. The heart is the only moving organ in the body, and strong emotions cause the heartbeat to race. When the heart stops beating, a person is dead. Because the Hebrews were a concrete people who used physical things to express abstract concepts, the heart was the metaphor of the mind and all mental and emotional activity."[3]

Let us look at some examples to illustrate a point:

a. "Hear, O Israel; Hashem is our God, Hashem is the One and Only. You shall love Hashem, your God, with all your heart, with all your soul, and with all your resources." (Deuteronomy 6:4-5, TJB).

b. "And these matters that I command you today shall be on your heart. You shall teach them thoroughly to your children." (Deuteronomy 6:6, TJB)

c. "I will place My Torah within them and will write it onto their heart." (Jeremiah 31:32)

d. "You shall love the Lord your God with all your heart, and with all your soul, and with all your mind." (Matthew 22:37); and

e. "And you shall love the Lord your God with all your heart, with all your soul, with all your mind, and with all your strength." (Mark 12:30)

Notice that in the Hebrew Scriptures, God instructs His people that His commandments are to be upon their hearts, and that He will, under a renewed covenant, write it on their hearts so that they will no longer sin. Obviously, He must also have meant on their *minds*, for how else could they remember, and teach them to their children? However, note that in the Gospels, this concept has been lost, with someone appending *mind* to *heart*, as if they were separate. We should allow this as a translation, to convey the proper sense to those who might otherwise not understand, but in doing so, readers of the bible are misled when reading the Old Testament where only the *heart* is mentioned. I sense, without really knowing, that this is part of the reason for Christians denying the authority of Torah – they accept the *spirit* (heart) but not the *letter* (mind) of the Law. As one scholar puts it, "So the English translation 'heart' starts of by rejecting rational thought in favour of emotion, whilst the original starts off by specifically including both."[4]

Another modern understanding is that the *soul* is the incorporeal or immortal essence of a living thing. Again, In the early Hebrew, this was not so. In days gone by, when a ship sank or an aircraft crashed, the news outlets would report some number of souls lost. This was not a comment on the spiritual fate of the victims, but a more tactful way of saying that people died. Unsurprisingly, the distress signal SOS was understood by many to mean *Save Our Souls*. The quotation at the beginning of this chapter states: "*There was barely any concept of life after death in most of the Old Testament*", which brings us to the ancient understanding of the soul.

The Hebrew *nefesh*, usually translated as *soul*, was also used to refer to a person, just as soul has been for centuries. However,

> "Surprisingly, the original Hebrew word in Deuteronomy 6:5 (*nefesh*) doesn't mean soul at all. It's a general term that includes 'flesh', 'blood', and 'breath'. In other words, the Hebrew word that we usually translate as 'soul' is just the opposite of 'soul'. It's the body and the blood and the breath and everything else about being alive that is tangible."[5]

By now you probably think that I have lost the plot: what has all this to do with prophecy fulfillment? Simply this: "Because you will not abandon my soul to the **grave**" (Psalm 16:10, TJB), whereas the NKJV renders this verse as: "For you will not leave my soul in **Sheol**" [emphasis mine]. In the Hebrew Bible, Sheol is a place of darkness to which all the dead go, both the righteous and the unrighteous, regardless of the moral choices made in life, a place of stillness and darkness cut off from life and from the Hebrew God. Psalm 16:10 is referenced in Acts 2:25, 2:31, 13:35; Romans 1:4; 1 Corinthians 15:4; and Hebrews 13:20, in support of the resurrection, conveying the meaning that after Jesus was crucified, he would be resurrected, rather than his soul (immortal) being left until the Final Judgement. However, that is not what David was saying in his psalm. Let us compare the Jewish and Christian versions:

a. "For this reason my heart rejoices and my soul is elated; my flesh too rests in confidence, because You will not abandon my soul to the grave, you will not allow Your devout one to witness destruction." (Psalm 16:9-10, TJB)

b. "Therefore my heart is glad, and my glory rejoices; my flesh will also rest in hope, for You will not leave my soul in Sheol, nor will you allow Your Holy One to see corruption." (NKJV)

David is clear: his flesh rests in confidence because God will not allow him to be killed (his soul, i.e., blood, flesh, and bone, abandoned to the grave). However, the Christian version twists this in a number of ways. It refers to *Your Holy One* (implying Jesus); has his flesh resting in hope of not seeing corruption (implying bodily resurrection); and the immortal soul not being left in Sheol (implying not waiting until the End of Days).

You can see now how this misunderstanding of heart and soul, and especially the latter, gives credence to prophecy fulfillment, but the correct understanding, as per the original Hebrew Scriptures, lends no support whatsoever.

Immortal Soul

If "*There was barely any concept of life after death in most of the Old Testament*", then it is unlikely that there would be any prophecy on this subject. Remember that the Sadducees, the priestly class, did not believe in life after death. Atheists deny the immortal soul as part of their argument against the existence of God, but clearly, that was not the thinking of the Sadducees – they believed in God, and performed the ceremonies in the Temple just as God instructed. Thus, there is no logical link between a belief in the existence of God, and a belief in the immortal soul, as an *incorporeal or immortal essence of a living thing*, except perhaps in the minds of Christians. Life after death is an essential tenet of Christian belief, yet we know that in Second Temple Judaism, such was not so. It is not my purpose here to explore the development of this theology, for that I would refer you to this online article[6], but in the context of prophecy, my intention is to use the Hebrew Scriptures to raise doubts as to whether the Resurrection of Jesus was in fulfillment of any Old Testament prophecy. I have concluded, as have others, that *the afterlife concept in Judaism does not arise from the word of God directly*[7]. Think about that: if Scripture is the Word of God, and the Prophets spoke as guided by God, how could there be any God-inspired prophecy of the Resurrection?

I am not here contending that there is no life after death. I am simply stating that if the concept does not arise from the word of God directly, and the only word of God that we have handed down to us is what we read in the Hebrew Scriptures, then the logical conclusion must be that God has not spoken through His Prophets on the issue, and thus there is no prophecy of Jesus being resurrected from the dead.

On this, if nothing else, I rest my case.

REFERENCES:

1. *The Tanach*, Scherman, Rabbi Nosson, Mesorah Publications, ArtScroll English Edition, Brooklyn, NY, 2011, p. 1186
2. Isaac, Jules, *The Teaching of Contempt: Christian Roots of Anti-Semitism*, Holt, Rinehart and Winston, Inc., New York, NY, 1964
3. http://www.egrc.net/articles/Rock/HebrewWords/levav.html
4. Hoffman, *Ibid*, p. 111
5. Ibid, p. 112
6. http://www.sptimmortalityproject.com/background/the-cultural-and-historical-development-and-decline-of-immortality-in-judaism/
7. Ibid

CHAPTER 1-9

JEWISH MESSIANIC EXPECTATIONS

"O foolish ones, and slow of heart to believe in
all that the prophets have spoken!"
(Luke 24:25)

"And beginning at Moses and all the Prophets, he expounded to them in all the Scriptures the things concerning himself" (Luke 24:27). I wonder whether Luke knew of what he wrote, for in my own studies, and especially those of numerous biblical scholars, the Scriptures had little specific to say about Jesus at all. Let us firstly acknowledge the Jewish understanding of the term "Messiah":

> "The title 'Messiah' (Greek – 'Christos') was not a divine title amongst Jews. It simply means 'anointed'. It was given to two Jewish officials, the King and the High Priest, who were both anointed with oil at their inauguration ceremony. When David was anointed by Samuel he became a Messiah, or Christ. Every

Jewish king of the House of David was known as Messiah, or
Christ, and a regular way of referring to the High Priest was 'the
Priest Messiah', i.e. the Priest Christ; even the corrupt Roman
appointees of Jesus' day had this title. It is necessary to labour the
point because the word 'Christ' has become so imbued with the
idea of a deity that it is very hard for a non-Jew to appreciate what
these words meant to the average Jew in the time of Jesus."[1]

Into Second Temple times, the concept of a *mashiach* (messiah) grew
to mean not just a king, but a redeemer, one who would accomplish the
redemption of the Jews from their subjection to the power of Rome, just
as had been prophesied. It should be noted, however, that the Hebrew
Scriptures speak more of God accomplishing that redemption, rather than
a messiah. To be *in accordance with the Scriptures*, the messiah needed
to have been preceded by the Prophet Elijah (Malachi 3:23, 4:5 in the
OT), but it would be in the last days, "before the coming of the great and
awesome day of Hashem". You can understand that if the Jews thought
that John the Baptist was Elijah, then they would have believed that the
End of Days was imminent, and would have been ready to accept Jesus as
the redeeming messiah, the one who would rescue them from the power
of the Romans. The significance of Elijah was that the Jews had been
without a prophet since Malachi, some 400 years previously, and were
eagerly awaiting a prophet to herald their redemption.

"These beliefs about the Messiah and Elijah the prophet were
widespread, especially among the Pharisees and consequently
among the mass of the people. However, many other doctrines
were also current. Some believed in a Messiah son of Joseph,
others in a Messiah son of Aaron, others in various combinations
of these with the Messiah, Son of David. Some believed that the
deliverance of Israel would come at the hands of God Himself
without the intervention of a Messiah figure; others that God
would send an angel called the Son of Man, to accomplish the
deliverance (see particularly the Book of Enoch). The Son of Man
was not a Messiah. He was an angel identified with the Guardian
Angel of Israel, with Metatron, with the angel who guided the

Children of Israel in the wilderness, and with Enoch himself who, like Elijah, never died. (It was only after the advent of Christianity that the figure of the Messiah and the figure of the Son of Man were fused into one, with the additional ingredient of the Son of God derived from Gnosticism and from the mystery cults). The prophecies of Scripture about the Last Days were extremely vague and could be reconciled with any or all of the beliefs current at the time."[2]

My intent in quoting the above is to illustrate that beliefs concerning the messiah, and the redemption of Israel, varied significantly, demonstrating the truth that *the prophecies of Scripture about the Last Days were extremely vague*, and subject to personal interpretation. There were many who claimed to be the Messiah, but none accomplished the mission of redeeming and restoring Israel. Judas of Galilee, claimed to be the Messiah at the time of the Jewish War in 66 CE. Simon bar Kokhba was recognised by Rabbi Akiva as Messiah, despite there being no evidence that he was of the kingly line of David. The Romans soon proved that he was not the Messiah, defeating him in battle. Opinions varied then, as they do today, some believing that there would be many messiahs on different missions, not necessarily connected to Israel's final redemption in the last days.

In brief, there were, and are, so many varied expectations of a messiah that to claim that anybody, to date, has accomplished them, is to express preference for what those expectations should be. There is insufficient detail in Hebrew Scripture prophecies to be dogmatic concerning what has, or will be, accomplished by a, or the, Messiah. Note also how at least one Jewish author has accepted the interpretation of "one like the son of man" in Daniel 7, whereas many others believe it should be rendered more simply as, "one like a man".

A more comprehensive Jewish study of the messiah is "Mashiach: Who? What? Why? How? Where? And When?"[3] by Chaim Kramer, founder of the Breslov Research Institute, which translates and publishes many ancient Jewish writings. Of the texts that I have studied, I would highly recommend this as accessing the widest possible sources. The Guide to the Book states:

"This book is based on material drawn from the Bible, Talmud, Midrash and Kabbalah and their commentaries, and on the teachings of Rebbe Nachman of Breslov (1772-1810) and his major disciple, Reb Noson (1780-1844). Because of the enormous volume of material about Mashiach, it has been necessary to be selective.

The messianic ideal includes a variety of components: revelation of the unity of God on all levels, good health, immense wealth, universal peace and the rectification of all humanity, even the worst sinners. Various aspects of the messianic mosaic are discussed in detail in the earlier sections of the book. Inevitably there is some overlap and repetition at certain points, because each aspect is ultimately bound up with all the others. Part VI shows how all parts of the mosaic fit together into the whole.

A number of kabbalistic concepts are crucial to the understanding of how Mashiach will be able to rectify the world. While these concepts appear in various places throughout the book, they are discussed in detail in Part V. This book is not intended as a kabbalah primer, but those unfamiliar with kabbalistic concepts will find everything necessary to understand our discussions. Additional explanatory charts and diagrams are provided in Appendix B."

I recount this so that in the event that the reader, on finishing reading my study, has doubts about Jesus as Messiah, and wants to investigate further, he/she will have a starting point. I have found that book to be both revealing and confusing, leaving me hardly better off than before, in understanding the messiah, if he is to exist at all.

Considering what is known about the Essenes, especially their extremes of cleanliness, forbidding to marry, and not eating meat of any kind, it is not surprising that the notion of a savior from sin should arise in that sect.

Summary

It was not my intention here to provide a detailed explanation of Jewish messianic expectations, of that I would not be competent anyway, but to expose the reader to the diversity of scholarly opinions. Jewish thoughts on the subject are more mystical than pragmatic, no doubt due to the fact that the Hebrew Scriptures leave much to the imagination. I have no personal opinion on the matter, one way or another, for as usual, whom am I to believe? My point, however, is to argue that any claim of Jesus, or anyone, of fulfilling messianic prophecy, is doubtful in the extreme. There is no authoritative consensus on the identity or mission of the Messiah, or even if there is to be one, so I will leave it there for you to consider.

In Chapter 9-1, we will discuss the implications found in this study[4].

REFERENCES:

1. MacCoby, Hyam, *Revolution in Judaea: Jesus & The Jewish Resistance*, Ocean Books, London, UK, 1973, p. 101
2. Ibid, pp. 101-102
3. Kramer, Chaim, *Mashiach: Who, What, Why, How, Where and When?* Breslov Research Institute, Jerusalem, Israel, 2013
4. Knohl, Israel, *The Messiah Before Jesus: The Suffering Servant of the Dead Sea Scrolls*, University of California Press, Berkeley, CA, 2000

PART 2

CROSS-EXAMINING THE WITNESSES

"In trials of fact, by oral testimony, the proper inquiry is not whether it is possible that the testimony may be false, but whether there is sufficient probability that it is true."
~ Simon Greenleaf[1] ~

"In trials ... by oral testimony": This is a disingenuous statement by Greenleaf in this context, for we cannot conduct a trial of the New Testament by *oral testimony* – the witnesses are long dead. We can only conduct the trial based on *written evidence*, and the first step is to evaluate the authenticity of the documents themselves, as discussed earlier. We will delve further into this issue as we proceed.

Greenleaf publicly examined the evidence contained in the Gospels, and according to him, found the narratives to be truthful. He claims to have used the accepted rules of evidence, to examine the veracity of the testimony of the attributed authors, Matthew, Mark, Luke, and John, subsequently concluding that their testimony should be accepted as reliable. But as discussed earlier, and evidenced above, he used the rules associated with *oral* testimony, not *written*.

In examining the evidence for myself, my first question was: Were the Gospels written by the people to whom they are attributed? Turns out, yes, sort of, but Matthew probably dictated his to someone competent in Greek, and no-one is sure of the identity of Mark. When were they written? Well, no-one can be certain, but some time from 25 to 90 years after the events attested, depending on the Gospel. Some scholars push the dates well beyond the conservative dates as above. Were the authors eye-witnesses? Yes, and no. Matthew and John likely were, but the other authors were not, in which case their evidence should be classified as "hearsay". Can we be confident that Matthew and John, for instance, did witness the events recorded? No, not entirely, for some events were not witnessed by the evangelists, and their accounts of them are of dubious accuracy. In at least two incidents, it is highly improbable that the evangelists could have been told by anyone, for there were no witnesses at all, and the person involved was unlikely to have recounted his experiences to them, or anyone else.

In short, we have reason to question the reliability of the writings of these witnesses. Much of the material was obtained from others, over a period of decades, and the degree of agreement in episodes recorded, the detail of episodes commonly recorded, and words spoken, is quite low. This suggests the likelihood that each of the four Gospels represent separate traditions developed over time, in different communities. Such lack of agreement is typical of oral traditions. In a later section, we will review the varied opinions of a number of Christian scholars regarding how the Old Testament was used in the New, and how faithful they were to the intent of the original authors.

Let is continue our cross-examination from various perspectives, attempting to follow the rules of evidence, but far better than Simon Greenleaf appears to have done.

REFERENCES:

1. Greenleaf, Simon, *The Testimony of the Evangelists*, Kregel Classics, Grand Rapids, MI, 1995, p. 28

CHAPTER 2-1

CHOICE OF SOURCE LANGUAGE

"Be as careful of the books you read, as of the company you keep; for your habits and character will be as much influenced by the former as the latter."
~ Paxton Hood, (1820-1885) English nonconformist and author ~

There are numerous books written on the subject of choosing a bible, but all that I have encountered make the same presupposition: choose from amongst *Christian* bibles. I used to do that, until I understood the implications of the New Testament having been written in Greek: viz., the authors used the Greek Septuagint for their Old Testament quotations, not the authentic Hebrew Bible. Now maybe you think that is not such a bad thing, but my intent, in this chapter, is to convince you otherwise.

Given that at one time, I did not understand the implications of this, I cannot condemn anyone else for thinking as I did, but what is quite clear, is that even some supposedly scholarly endeavours evidence the same lack of understanding. For example, *Jews For Jesus*, an organisation identifying as Messianic Jewish, offers: *"We invite you to explore these passages from the Jewish Scriptures and their fulfillments in the life of Jesus.*"[1] The senior researcher, Rich Robinson, claimed to prove Jesus' credentials from the Jewish *Tanakh*, but the trouble is, the Scriptures he quotes are not Jewish at all, but Hellenic Christian, taken from some unidentified version of the Greek Septuagint. When I was undertaking research to validate, or falsify, these claimed prophecy fulfillments, I compared the translations from the Hebrew, and the translations from the Greek, and found numerous discrepancies. These were of such significance that they disproved many claimed prophecy fulfillments. It is incomprehensible to my mind, that someone would offer to explore from the Jewish Scriptures (Hebrew), and then quote from the Septuagint (Greek).

Not being a language scholar, I must rely on the on the scholarship of others, and so present the following evidence, that has convinced me of the necessity to study Scripture from its earliest sources, i.e., from the Hebrew.

Hebrew in the 1st Century

I have found two common answers as to why the New Testament was written in Greek, one entirely plausible, the other entirely false. Firstly, "The basic reason why this language was chosen instead of Aramaic or Hebrew was that the writers wished to reach a broad, Gentile (non-Israelite) audience, not just a Jewish audience."[2] I would confirm that the Jewish audience in the Diaspora, especially centres such as Alexandria and Antioch, did speak Greek, and had been subjected to Greek influence for centuries, ever since Alexander the Great had conquered all and sundry. So, this contention is perfectly reasonable.

Secondly, in reference to the original version of the Gospel attributed to Matthew:

> "To my knowledge, it is almost universally accepted that Jesus and His disciples spoke in Aramaic. The theory that the New Testament was written in Hebrew is without basis, though I believe that I have heard some suggest that some of the sources may have been in Aramaic. The simple fact is that **the Jews lost their facility in Hebrew**. That is why the Old Testament had to

be translated into the Greek language (this translation is known as the Septuagint)."[3] [emphasis mine]

It is simply untrue that the "*Jews lost their facility in Hebrew*". Certainly, in the Diaspora, where Greek influence reigned, Greek was the *lingua franca*, but fluency in Hebrew remained in Judea, especially amongst the Pharisees and likely some Sadducees, the priestly clan: there, the Septuagint was considered an *abomination*. We need a little history to understand this, and I shall insert such in its proper place, but I would pre-empt that discussion with this opinion of Epiphanius, concerning the Nazarenes in the 4th century: "*They are very learned in the Hebrew language*".

In any discussion on the teachings of Jesus, we must adhere to the cultural context, which was <u>not</u> the Hellenic Judaism of the Diaspora. That the Jews had lost their facility in Hebrew may well be universally accepted amongst Christians, but that, I would contend, is because for centuries, that is what they have been taught. It is, nevertheless, untrue. I suspect that this myth arose in order to support the legitimacy of the Septuagint, but that myth has been well and truly dispelled by competent scholars, both Christian and secular. In recent years, the discovery of the Qumran scrolls testifies to the common usage of the Hebrew language in Second Temple Judaism, especially amongst the Essenes.

The Peshitta

I suspect that most Christians are as ignorant of Eastern Christianity as I was, and have given no thought to the history of those religions, nor the sources of their Scriptures. Without debating the legitimacy of various claims, I will simply present them as evidence. I will leave the reader to ponder their significance, and to what extent they support the notion that the bible is the inerrant Word of God. One of the Patriarchs of the Church of the East had this to say:

> "With reference to ... the originality of the Peshitta text, as the Patriarch and Head of the Holy Apostolic Church of the East, we wish to state, that the Church of the East received the scriptures from the hands of the blessed Apostles themselves in the Aramaic

original, the language spoken by our Master Y'Shua Mashiyach Himself, and that the Peshitta is the text of the Church of the East which has come down from Biblical times **without any change or revision**." (Patriarch Mar Eshai Shimun, April 5, 1957)[4] [emphasis in original]

So, the Church of the West says that the New Testament was written in Greek, and the Church of the East says, no, the autographs were written in Aramaic. One can easily understand the friction between the Eastern and Western churches, and why the East does not accept the authority of the Pope in Rome. As an aside, there was, for a while, a Pope in Rome, and one in Avignon (France), both asserting their authority. Did God sort that out? Continuing:

> "And so, this is the core of the matter. These ancient traditions have come down from the First Century, lovingly maintained by this body of believers in an unbroken chain of authority that started with Keefa (Peter) himself. The end result: 360 manuscripts from the Fourth to the Ninth Centuries that are, for all intents and purposes, virtually identical to one another*. They are far more consistent than the 'families' which comprised the Greek New Testament.
>
> Footnote: *This is not to say that more ancient manuscripts do not exist. Many manuscripts were left behind in the Middle east when Muslim invaders banished Aramaic Christians from their own lands. In some cases, manuscripts found their way into private hands, only to be made public when the circumstances of their owners changed."[5]

Sometimes I am prone to remark: *Out of the mouths of babes*! Do you not see the problem: "360 manuscripts from the Fourth to the Ninth Centuries"? How can one claim an unbroken chain of authority, when there is a gap of over two hundred years in the documentary evidence? We spoke earlier of the necessity for a chain of custody to verify the integrity, and thus authority, of written evidence. The Patriarchs of the Church of the East were not thinking in those terms.

It is claimed, by the editors of this New Testament version, that converts to Christianity were ten times more numerous to the east of Jerusalem, than to the west, in the early decades after the resurrection. Peter is said to have spent a great deal of his time in Babylon, Thomas with him, and Thomas continued eastward reaching India in 52 CE. Two different narratives on the provenance of the New Testament, but which is right, if either?

The Septuagint (LXX)

May I offer that Christianity has been, for centuries, perpetrating an untruth regarding this copy of scripture. That is not to accuse Christians of being dishonest: they have simply been repeating what they have been told as truth, and have accepted it, as I once did, but it is well overdue that we set the record straight.

Christians insist that the impetus for the Septuagint was the decline in usage of Hebrew, particularly in the Diaspora, the expanding usage of Greek, and the need to present God's Word in a contemporary language. That is true to an extent, in those areas that had succumbed to Hellenism, but Jewish scholars argue a little differently - that the original Greek translation was either simply a desire by King Ptolemy to have in his Alexandrian library, a version he could read and proudly display, or an effort to delegitimise Judaism by discouraging usage of the original Hebraic texts (or both). Remember that for many years, the Jews were forbidden to practice Judaism. This article[6] and many similar, provide a history that support the Jewish view to some degree, but what seems evident is that the development of the Septuagint would have lacked the rigour and discipline of, for example, the Jewish maintenance of the Hebrew Scriptures. Thus, I am not inclined to believe that these Greek versions were God inspired. That said, there is clear evidence that apart from the desires of Ptolemy, the Hellenist Jews, particularly in Alexandria and Antioch, did begin their own translations of the Hebrew Scriptures, but without any scholarly consensus across the multiple versions. As best as I can discern, most of these translations were fragmentary to suit the needs of the translators, without any concerted effort to translate the entire

Tanakh as a single work, until sometime in the 1ˢᵗ century CE, or more likely, even later. Even then, what did result was most likely a compilation from multiple authors and sources.

Concerning the name, *Septuagint*, the full title in Ancient Greek: Ἡ τῶν Ἑβδομήκοντα μετάφρασις, literally "The Translation of the Seventy", derives from the traditional story recorded in the Letter of Aristeas that the Septuagint was translated at the request of Ptolemy II by 70 or 72 Jewish scholars (6 from each of the 12 tribes of Israel) who independently translated identical versions of the entire Hebrew canon, i.e., Torah. What was this "letter"?

"In the guise of a letter to a brother Philokrates, "Aristeas" writes:

Contents of the Letter.

"By the advice of Demetrius Phalereus, chief librarian of Ptolemy Philadelphus, the king decided to include in his library a translation of the Jewish Lawbook. To secure the cooperation of the high priest Eleazar at Jerusalem, Aristeas advises him to purchase and set free the numerous Jews who had been sold into slavery after his father's campaign against them (312). He sends Andreas, a captain of his body-guard, and Aristeas, laden with rich presents, and entrusted with a letter, asking Eleazar to send him seventy-two elders to undertake the translation. The envoys see Jerusalem, inspect the Temple and the citadel, and admire the high priest and his assistants at their service in the sanctuary; they are instructed, moreover, by Eleazar in the deeper moral meaning of the dietary laws, and return, with the seventy-two elders, to Alexandria. The king receives the Jewish sages with distinction, and holds a seven-day banquet, at which he addresses searching questions to them daily, always receiving appropriate answers. The wisdom of their replies, though it seems to the modern reader rather trivial, arouses general astonishment. Three days after the feast, Demetrius conducts the sages to the island of Pharos, where in seventy-two days of joint labor they complete their work. Demetrius reads the translation aloud in a solemn assembly of the Jewish congregation; it is accepted and sanctioned by them, and any change therein officially forbidden. The king, to whom the translation is also read, admires the spirit of the Law-giver, and dismisses the translators with costly gifts."[7]

The referenced article then proceeds to discuss the errors in the letter. Continuing the discussion:

"The Christian Church received the Septuagint from the Jews as a divine revelation, and quite innocently employed it as a basis for Scriptural interpretation. Only when Jewish polemics assailed it was the Church compelled to investigate the true relationship of the translation to the original. Origen perceived the insufficiency of the Septuagint, and, in his "Hexapla," collected material for a thorough revision of it. But the legend long adhered closely to the Septuagint and was further embellished by the Church. Not only were "the Seventy" (the usual expression instead of Seventy-two) credited with having translated all the Sacred Scriptures instead of the Law only (according to Epiphanius, a whole mass of Apocrypha besides), but the miraculous element increased. At one time we are told the translators were shut up in seventy cells in strictest seclusion (pseudo-Justin and others); at another, in thirty-six cells, in couples."

On this evidence, the authority of the Septuagint came into question very early in the days of Christianity.

"The legend became a weapon in the battle which was waged around the Bible of the Church; the "inspired" Septuagint was not easily surrendered. The rigid orthodoxy of the fourth century, which resulted in the ruin of all knowledge in the Church, did not scruple to set this legend in its crassest form in opposition to the promising beginnings by Origen of a proper Biblical text criticism, and so to arrest the latter completely at the start. Only Jerome, who as a philologist understood the value of Origen's work, made use of his material, and in the Vulgate preserved for the Western

Church this most precious legacy, exercising, consistently with his usage, a rational criticism upon the legend.

Thus Aristeas plays a great, even a fateful, role in the Church. The varying opinions as to this legend very often reflect dogmatic views about the Bible in general, and the understanding, or the misunderstanding, of his critics concerning textual questions."

Well, that certainly puts the cat amongst the pigeons: *the ruin of all knowledge in the Church* indeed! This is likely an exaggeration, but contains sufficient truth for us to doubt that the Gentile Church of Rome, aka Catholicism, rightly followed the teachings of the Jew, Jesus. The Gospels reveal Jesus to be a devout Jewish man, who practised the Judaism of his time, although he clearly lost the plot at some stage. Christianity wrote its own version of the plot, entirely eradicating everything Jewish. Christian dogma, doctrine, and theology, cannot be true.

After much research, I am reasonably satisfied that the Jewish priests and scribes, as best they could, accurately transmitted the Hebrew Bible (*Tanakh* or Old Testament) through the centuries to the time of Jesus. Christianity affirms this, and I have no reason to disagree. The written Hebrew language evolved over this period, and the teaching of the language was oral, generation to generation, so I think it reasonable to assume that some oral interpretation likely accompanied the written version. As with any rational analysis, presumptions and presuppositions must be established, and in this case, I accept the historical authenticity of these texts. I have no confidence regarding the Greek Septuagint.

For those who argue that Hebrew was not a common language in Jerusalem in Jesus' time, ponder this verse: "*it was written in Hebrew, Greek, and Latin*" (John 19:20). Why would Pilate have inscribed the words, Jesus of Nazareth King of the Jews, in Hebrew, if it was not a language spoken or read at the time? We also have the opinion of Epiphanius (315-403 CE) that "They [the Nazarenes] are very learned in the Hebrew language"[8] in his time, so it is highly unlikely that Hebrew was ever lost amongst the Jews in Judea.

From amongst the many articles and books that I have studied on the subject, I have selected this online article[9], *An Historical Account of the*

Septuagint Version, as an exemplar, and readily accessible. I would highly recommend that you read the article in full, as it is reproduced from Lancelot Brenton's English edition of the Septuagint, first published as *The Septuagint Version of the Old Testament, according to the Vatican Text, Translated into English* (London: Samuel Bagster, 1844). However, to give you a sense of what I consider to be the salient issues in the context of my purposes, herewith some quotations:

- In estimating the general character of the version, it must be remembered that the translators were Jews, full of traditional thoughts of their own as to the meaning of Scripture; and thus, nothing short of a miracle could have prevented them from infusing into their version, the thoughts which were current in their own minds. They could only translate passages as they themselves understood them. This is evidently the case when their work is examined.

- It would be, however, too much to say that they translated with dishonest intention; for it cannot be doubted that they wished to express their Scriptures truly in Greek, and that their deviations from accuracy may be simply attributed to the incompetency of some of the interpreters, and the tone of mental and spiritual feeling which was common to them all.

- One difficulty which they had to overcome was that of introducing theological ideas, which till then had only their proper terms in Hebrew, into a language of Gentiles, which till then had terms for no religious notions except those of heathens. Hence the necessity of using many words and phrases in new and appropriated senses.

- These remarks are not intended as depreciatory of the Septuagint version: their object is rather to show what difficulties the translators had to encounter, and why in some respects they failed; as well as to meet the thought which has occupied the minds of some, who would extol this version as though it possessed something resembling co-ordinate authority with the Hebrew text itself. One of the earliest of those writers who mention the Greek translation of the Scriptures, speaks also of the version as not fully adequate.

- At Alexandria, the Hellenistic Jews used the version, and gradually attached to it the greatest possible authority: from Alexandria, it spread amongst the Jews of the dispersion, so that at the time of our Lord's birth it was the common form in which the Old Testament Scriptures had become diffused.

- The Septuagint version having been current for about three centuries before the time when the books of the New Testament were written, it is not surprising that the Apostles should have used it more often than not in making citations from the Old Testament. They used it as an honestly-made version in pretty general use at the time when they wrote. They did not on every occasion give an authoritative translation of each passage *de novo*, but they used what was already familiar to the ears of converted Hellenists, when it was sufficiently accurate to suit the matter in hand. In fact, they used it as did their contemporary Jewish writers, Philo and Josephus, but not, however, with the blind implicitness of the former.

- Thus, whatever may be our estimate of the defects found in the Septuagint — its inadequate renderings, its departures from the sense of the Hebrew, its doctrinal deficiencies owing to the limited apprehensions of the translators — there is no reason whatever for our neglecting the version, or not being fully alive to its real value and importance. After the diffusion of Christianity, copies of the Septuagint became widely dispersed amongst the new communities that were formed; so that before many years had elapsed this version must have been as much in the hands of Gentiles as of Jews.

- In the course of the second century, three other complete versions of the Old Testament into Greek were executed: these are of importance in this place, because of the manner in which they were afterwards connected with the Septuagint.

Please note: "their **deviations** from accuracy, its **inadequate** renderings, its **departures** from the sense of the Hebrew, its **doctrinal deficiencies** owing to the **limited apprehensions** of the translators" [emphasis mine]. Whilst Christianity affirms the accuracy of the Scriptures whilst in the care of the Jews, on what basis can anyone claim that these later Greek versions are authentic renderings? What are we to think of those *who would extol* *this version as though it possessed something resembling co-ordinate authority with the Hebrew text itself?* Consider the implications of this, where the writers of the Gospels are said to have quoted from the Septuagint – can we really trust the claims of Jesus fulfilling Old Testament prophecies? Consider also that "they did not on every occasion give an authoritative translation of each passage *de novo*, but they used what was already familiar to the ears of converted Hellenists, when it was sufficiently accurate to suit the matter in hand." How do we know what was already familiar to the converted Hellenists, and from where did they learn it?

And as for the *three other complete versions* of the Old Testament into Greek, which were *afterwards connected with the Septuagint*, how much faith can we place in their commonality of interpretation? When a final version was compiled by the Christian Church, on what basis were the various interpretations selected? We have no evidentiary trail, at least, none that I can find, of how, when, or by whom, the final canonised version of the Greek Septuagint came about. In legal terms, there is no *chain of custody*.

Let us ponder the context, much of it unstated. There is great debate amongst scholars, and little consensus, of the timing of writing, and the breadth of the Septuagint, at any one point in history. It appears to have started under the orders of King Ptolemy, but this was simply the first five books of the Hebrew Bible: the *Torah* or *Pentateuch*. This original copy was lost to fire in the library of Alexandria, by most accounts, in 48 BCE during Caesar's conquest. It is unknown what copies may have been made of the original, if any, and whether subsequent versions were new translations, by whom, and when. Most of what is taught by Christianity on this subject is pure speculation, other than that the translations into Greek occurred primarily amongst the Hellenist Jews in Alexandria, Antioch, and other areas subject to Greek influence, and later by Gentile Christians. So even if seventy Jewish scholar collectively produced the Greek version of Torah for King Ptolemy, how can we adjudge what influence they had on later translations after this original version was destroyed? Appealing to the authority of these scholars is invalid from an evidentiary perspective.

Recent scholarship on the question of the then, contemporary usage of Hebrew is offered here. Referring to the statement by the Bishop of Hierapolis, Papias (circa 70-130 CE), that "Matthew collected the oracles in the Hebrew language":

"Since the time of Widmanstadt, it had been commonplace to suppose that by 'Hebrew" Papias meant 'Aramaic'. This supposition is due *inter alia* to the long-standing belief that Hebrew in the days of Jesus was no longer used as the vernacular in Palestine, but had been replaced by Aramaic. From the end of the nineteenth century through the twentieth, an Aramaic background to the Gospel tradition has been investigated and supported by … [Ed. *long reference list omitted*]. Since the discovery of the Dead Sea Scrolls, many of which are Hebrew compositions, and the discovery of other Hebrew documents from the Judaean Desert, it is now confirmed that Hebrew was used as a written medium in first century Palestine … In light of these investigations, it may now be concluded, with some finality, that there is no *a priori* reason to assume that Papias meant Aramaic by his reference to 'Hebrew'."[10]

I can find no evidence that the Greek version was in wide use by the Jews in Judaea, but some opinions that it may have been used by the school of Hillel in the Galilee, but for political reasons primarily. I think it reasonable to assume that scholars, even Torah-observant Jewish ones, would nevertheless study Greek for the pure sake of it – scholars are like that, but it is doubtful that the Greek scriptures were studied with any belief in their authenticity. In Talmudic times, some observed *Tevet 8* as a day of fasting, because they feared that this Greek translation would be harmful: it was said that with the translation into the Greek, there were then *two Torahs*. We should not forget that when the Syrian king, Antiochus, ruled Israel (BCE 175-163), he attempted to wipe out Judaism. The Jews were forced to speak Greek and worship Greek gods, and it was forbidden to practice Judaism, celebrate Jewish holidays, or study Torah (reintroduced by Rome circa CE 137 onward). It was only after the Maccabees defeated the Syrians that the proper Jewish order was restored, later celebrated as the holiday of *Hanukkah*. We can be confident that at that time, no copies of the Septuagint existed in the possession of the rabbis. It is said that Hillel the Elder was asked when it was proper to study Greek: he replied that one should study Torah in Hebrew during the day, and at night, and at other times one could study Greek.

This antipathy toward Hellenism by the Jews in Judaea cannot be understated. When Jesus said: *"I was not sent except to the lost sheep of the house of Israel"* (Matt 15:24), could it be that the "lost sheep", to whom Jesus was referring, were those who had turned to Hellenism, accepting the Greek version of Scripture, one known to depart from the Hebrew in significant ways? When Jesus said: *"Do not think that I came to destroy the Law and the Prophets, I did not come to destroy* [misinterpret] *but to fulfill* [interpret correctly]" (Matt 5:17) (using the vernacular of the rabbis of the time), was this a veiled reference to the lost tribes misunderstanding the Law and the Prophets, because they were using the inauthentic Greek versions? This would make sense, given what we know of the deficiencies in the Greek translation of the Hebrew.

In what ways were the ten tribes of Israel lost, but the two tribes of Judah were not? There is no doubting that the Septuagint was in wide use even before the times of Jesus, but considerable doubt that it was accepted as an authentic rendering of Scripture by the Pharisees in Judaea, and perhaps even in Galilee. When Jesus affirmed: "the teachers of the Law and the Pharisees sit in Moses' seat" (Matt 23:2), we can be confident that he was referring to the authenticated Hebrew version, not the later Greek translation.

Why is this important? The earlier referenced article goes on to state:

> "One of the earliest of those writers who mention the Greek translation of the Scriptures, speaks also of the version as not fully adequate. The Prologue of Jesus the son of Sirach (written as many suppose B.C. 130) to his Greek version of his grandfather's work, states: ... 'For the same things expressed in Hebrew have not an equal force when translated into another language. Not only so, but even the Law and the prophecies and the rest of the books differ not a little as to the things said in them.'"[11]

The Law and the Prophecies differ not a little: herein the essence of the matter. As I amply demonstrate in another work[12], and I will do in this as well, the New Testament authors consistently misquoted prophecies, some might unkindly offer, deliberately, to validate their developing theology. We can be kind and contend that they were simply misled by the poor Greek translations, if indeed, it was the Septuagint that was used in crafting the Gospels and Epistles. On the evidence, and in the opinion of many New Testament scholars, this was so. That the *Law and the Prophecies differ not a little* adds weight to my contention regarding Jesus' meaning when he said "*Do not think that I came to destroy the Law and the Prophets, I did not come to destroy* [misinterpret] *but to fulfill* [interpret correctly]".

My point concerning the Septuagint, the Greek translation of the original Hebrew, is simply this: as an authoritative version of Scripture, it was and is, unreliable. If the advantage of the Jew was that to them were given the *oracles of God* (Romans 3:1), and they preserved the writings of these oracles in Hebrew, then an inadequate translation into Greek should carry no weight for the serious bible scholar seeking God's truth, other than to evidence how easily His truth can be distorted.

In discussing the claimed prophecy in Daniel, the author noted: "The official Greek translation of Daniel used in ancient times was that of Theodotion, an Ephesian (ca. 180 AD)"[13]. However, "Around 400 AD Jerome ventured the opinion that the Septuagint 'differs widely from the original [Hebrew], and is rightly rejected'."[14] How curious then, that the Greek version of Daniel 7, which differs from the Hebrew, is used by Christianity to assert that Jesus was the "one like the son of man", even though most Hebrew translations have more simply: "one like a man".

Another opinion is offered here: "The Septuagint came into being in the diaspora, created by the diaspora Jews in order to meet their own religious needs, both liturgical and apologetic. Gradually, however, it became discredited as the Christians took it over and used it in their anti-Jewish polemic."[15] Note that the anti-Jewish polemic was not so much against the Hellenic Jews of the diaspora, but against the Hebraic Jewish Nazarenes, who insisted that whilst being "Christians", they must nevertheless continue with the traditions of Judaism. The Church of Rome eventually declared them to be heretics, for continuing the practices that Jesus and his apostles followed, which should tell you something about the authenticity of Christianity.

For a wider discussion on the religion of the early disciples of Jesus, the Followers of the Way, or Nazarenes, I would recommend *They Loved The Torah*[16] by David Friedman; *Nazarene Jewish Christianity*[17] by Ray Pritz; *Messianic Judaism*[18] by David Stern; and *Nazarene Israel*[19] by Norman Willis

If you haven't already twigged to this outrage, note that in condemning the Nazarenes as heretics, the Church of Rome also unwittingly condemned Paul, *"a ringleader of the sect of the Nazarenes"* [Ed. if he was] (Acts 24:5) as a heretic, the congregation in Jerusalem under the Apostle James, and all the early disciples who were *"all zealous for the law"* (Acts 21:20) equally guilty. There can be no stronger evidence than this, that the early leaders of the Catholic Church were not genuine followers of the Apostles at all, and most certainly, the Pope could not have been a legitimate successor to the Apostle Peter. If for no other reason than this, I agree with the Eastern Orthodox churches that the Pope is not a legitimate authority on the teachings of Jesus.

But back to the issue at hand. I would conclude on the evidence, that the Greek Septuagint, of whatever version or source, cannot be considered a reliable witness, most especially where it conflicts with the Hebrew Scriptures, from which it is said to have derived.

The Latin Vulgate

Prior to, during, and after the life of Jesus, Hellenic Jews as they were known, the large Jewish population living in the Diaspora outside Judah, are known to have used vernacular translations of the Hebrew Bible, including the Targum in Aramaic, and various versions of the Greek. During the early years of Christianity in Rome, some of these texts were translated into Latin, but as one scholar has noted: "they vary widely in readability and quality, and contain many solecisms [grammatical mistakes] in idiom, some by the translators themselves, others from literally translating Greek language idioms into Latin."[20] Given what has been noted above regarding the accuracy of Hebrew into Greek, any subsequent translation from the Greek to the Latin must surely be of dubious quality, accuracy, and authenticity.

These earlier translations were made obsolete by Jerome's compilation of the Latin *Vulgate* (Common Bible) in the late 4th century, which became the official version of the Catholic Bible, to which the laity were never given access (partially the cause of the Reformation beginning in 1517). There were later revisions in the 16th and 19th centuries. It is claimed that Jerome was conversant with the Hebrew language, but there must be considerable doubt as to his competency. As best as we can discern from historical records, only the Jews in Judah, who later fled to Pella, were truly conversant with the Hebrew language, and one must question from whom, and how well, Jerome would have learned Hebrew. We know that Jerome did travel to Syria and surrounding regions, and had contact with the Jews, but that is about all we know on that score. Even so, not all Catholic scholars are convinced by some of Jerome's reporting; for example, that he saw a copy of Matthew's Gospel in Hebrew.

I believe it reasonable to conclude, that the Latin version of Scripture cannot be considered a reliable witness, most especially where it conflicts with the Hebrew Scriptures, from which it is said to have derived, albeit via a very tortuous and contentious pathway.

Old English to New

Perhaps the most influential English translations of the bible is the King James Version, first printed in 1611. Ignoring the issues surrounding translation accuracy, the point to note is that the meaning and import of many English words has changed over the past four hundred years. Where later translations, such as the NKJV, are largely based on the KJV wording, misunderstanding is inevitable. For example, "For God so loved the world, that He gave His only begotten son" (John 3:16). In the modern vernacular, "so loved" describes *how much* God loved the world. However, in earlier times, "so" as an adverb meant "in this way".

In the Greek, the word that has been translated as "so" is *houtous* (Strongs Concordance 3779), meaning *thus, so,* or *in this manner.* The KJV translators got it right, and it is only the change in English usage that has led Christians to misunderstand what was originally written. John was not describing *how much* God loved the world, but *in what manner* God showed His love for the world. In this instance, the difference is perhaps unimportant, but in other cases, the difference is vastly significant.

The translation trail, from proto-Hebrew, to later Hebrew, to Old Greek, to Koine Greek, to Latin, and then to English is fraught with possible error, but we should also understand that similar errors occur in translations from Old English to Modern English. Very little is what it seems – most requiring a deeper level of investigation.

Does THE Bible Exist?

On the surface, this may seem a silly question, but I can confidently answer it by proclaiming: NO! There is no such tome as "THE" Bible. What we do have are numerous translations, based on Latin, Greek, Syriac, and Hebrew sources, which are all inconsistent with, or contradict, each other in various ways. This should surprise no-one, for all translations are interpretations. Many important words in each source language have a semantic range, and likewise, the target language has a semantic range. Thus, each translation requires an interpretation of a word, in context, in the source language, and selection of the most appropriate word in the target language. We should bear in mind that colloquialisms are often not translated correctly, witness Matthew 5:17, and that in other instances, there is no word in the target language which adequately expresses the meaning in the source language: *"For the same things expressed in Hebrew have not an equal force when translated into another language"*.

Let me give an example from Matthew 26:28.

In a brief survey regarding the covenant, the word "new" is not in the Greek, and of the English versions reviewed, 6 have "new covenant", 4 have "new testament", and 8 omit the word "new" altogether. In the New Testament, the Greek word transliterated as *diatheke* can be translated as "will", "covenant" or "testament", each of these words conveying a different connotation, to me at least, but which is right? Comparing these English translations, I find that the older versions, like the King James and Douay-Rheims, render the word as *testament*, not *covenant*. In other contexts where *diatheke* appears in the Greek, an even higher percentage of translations favour testament, not covenant. In a biblical context, what would testament mean? For this we could turn to Hebrews 9:16-18, where we can see that *testament*, as used therein, is of the form: *Last Will and Testament*. You may never have considered this before, but this meaning does fit perfectly in the context of the <u>Last</u> Supper.

If your preferred bible version is the NLT (New Living Translation), you would note this verse in Matthew being rendered as: "for this is my blood, which **confirms** the covenant between God and his people." [emphasis mine] To which covenant was Jesus referring: the covenant made at Sinai with the Children of Israel, or a new covenant? If you study further, you will note that the Apostles gave no indications of seeing covenantal significance in the words of Jesus, simply singing a hymn and going out to the Mount of Olives. Why would they do that? Could it be that they understood Jesus as rendered in the NLT: that Jesus was confirming the covenant of old, rather than announcing a new, replacement covenant? The reaction of the Apostles is circumstantial evidence that such was the reality of the situation.

Jesus had not previously even hinted at a new covenant, and the Gospel of John, said to be of the highest Christology, mentions this covenant, new or otherwise, not at all. Why was that? We have no record of the Apostles preaching a New Covenant, and even if they did, the Sanhedrin did not notice, because they allowed the Followers of the Way, the Nazarenes, i.e. James and his congregation, to continue worshipping in the Synagogue in Jerusalem. It is not my intention herein to start a debate on the New Covenant, I have detailed my analysis in another work[21]: my intention here is to demonstrate that bible translations do vary, and those variations have significance for the doctrines and theology derived therefrom.

Depending on the subject, I cross-check up to 30 bible translations, quite easily done in some cases using these websites listed below[22-24]. In addition, I have copies of Catholic, Protestant, Messianic Jewish, and Aramaic translations of the New Testament, and both Christian and Jewish copies of the Old (*Tanakh*). What is very obvious to me, and should be to you by now, is that there is no such extant work which can be described as "THE" Bible. There are numerous translations which, based on the beliefs of the translators, and other reasons such as noted below, may well represent theological dissertations, rather than an objective rendering of the truth.

Here is another perspective worthy of consideration: "Nearly every Christian church on Earth boasts that they are 'Bible based' even though they are well aware that their bibles are published according to copyright laws that demand 'substantive changes' to the text! In other words, translators (theologians) must change the text to make it different enough from other translations in order to obtain copyright protection."[25] You see the point? How far can one vary a translation to sufficiently abide by copyright laws, yet still maintain the same meaning?

Words matter, and synonyms, despite being described as "having the same sense as one another", often convey nuances, which may or may not be conveyed to the reader, depending on their literacy and background.

Summary

When Gentile Christianity began the fiction that the Jews had lost their facility in Hebrew, was this an honest mistake, or was there a more sinister motive afoot? We have substantive evidence of the Christian antipathy toward the Jew, descending to outright hatred in some quarters, and the prohibition of any religious activity of Judaism, including observance of the traditional Sabbath. We have multiple attestations that in truth, the Jews had not lost their facility in Hebrew. Is it likely, or even possible, that in their quest to have the Greek scriptures accepted as authentic, because the New Testament was both written in Greek, and used the Greek version of the Hebrew Scriptures for their Old Testament quotation sources, that the Gentile Church in Rome understood that they had to entirely discredit anything written in Hebrew? I believe that not only is such possible, but highly likely, as it would have been entirely in character of what the Church in Rome had become.

As much as some scholars choose to make light of the variations in bible translations, some to the extent of contradicting one another. "As any writer knows, a word, a coma, or a period, can dramatically change the intended meaning of a verse ... because of the nature of the text being used to build theological models, **every word matters**."[26] [emphasis mine] I concur, especially where, for example, a translator inserts the conjunction "but", putting the preceding and subsequent sentences, or phrases, in opposition to one another. A classic example is this: *"For the law was given through Moses, but grace and truth came through Jesus Christ"* (John 1:17, NKJV) Many Christian commentators use this rendering in support of their belief that Jesus repealed the law, replacing it with grace, but if one puts law and grace in opposition, the same must be said of law and truth, which is, of course, absurd. Another interpretation is that Judaism was a religion of works, as opposed to Christianity being a religion of grace and the Spirit. I reject both interpretations, explaining why in other studies.

Just as importantly, and perhaps even more so, punctuation matters; after all, the very purpose of punctuation is to disambiguate prose. If you are not convinced, obtain a copy of *"Eats, Shoots & Leaves"*[27] by Lynne Truss. In very short order, you *will* become convinced of the significance that punctuation conveys in written texts. To add a little levity, here is the description on the back cover:

> A panda walks into a café. He orders a sandwich, eats it, then draws a gun and fires two shots in the air.
>
> "Why?" asks the confused waiter, as the panda makes towards the exit. The panda produces a badly punctuated wildlife manual and tosses it over his shoulder.
>
> "I'm a panda," he says at the door, "Look it up."
>
> The waiter turns to the relevant entry, and sure enough, finds an explanation.
>
> "Panda. Large black-and-white bear-like mammal, native to China. Eats, shoots, and leaves."

Theological annotations, used to convey the translators desired understanding, evidence that whatever bible version one uses, it cannot be described as the inerrant Word of God. Even if we allow that the autographs were divinely inspired, we have no warrant to claim the same for subsequent translations. Once again, we have no *chain of custody*, and from the perspective of written evidence in a court of law, whatever version we do have should carry minimal evidentiary weight, except where consistent agreement can be demonstrated.

When I started serious bible study some ten years ago, I had not even a glimpse of the complexity of the task that I had set for myself. I thought that it was as simple as choosing the NLT, NKJV, NIV, or some other popular version.

How little I knew.

And to finish on a lighter note: Michelangelo's Moses has two horns on his head because Michelangelo's Bible, the Latin Vulgate, mistranslated

Exodus 34:29 as "Moses had horns" instead of "Moses' face shone". You can see his sculpture here[28], showing Moses more like a Greek god.

We must be careful with our choice of bible, based on its source language.

REFERENCES:

1. https://jewsforjesus.org/answers/top-40-most-helpful-messianic-prophecies/
2. http://www.biblestudy.org/basicart/why-is-new-testament-written-greek.html
3. http://www.biblestudy.org/basicart/why-is-new-testament-written-greek.html
4. Roth, Andrew Gabriel, *Aramaic English New Testament*, Netzari Press, Jerusalem, Israel, 2012, p. xi
5. *Ibid*
6. *The History of the Septuagint*, http://www.kalvesmaki.com/lxx/
7. http://jewishencyclopedia.com/articles/1765-aristeas-letter-of
8. Epiphanius, *Adversus haereses* 29,7, pp. 42, 402
9. Brenton, Sir Lancelot Charles Lee (1807-1862), *An Historical Account of the Septuagint Version*, http://www.bible-researcher.com/brenton1.html
10. Howard, George, *Hebrew Gospel of Matthew*, Mercer University Press, Macon, GA, 2002, pp. 155-157
11. Brenton, *Ibid*
12. Talbot, Wayne, *Once A Christian – How the Bible Convinced Me to Walk Away*, Xlibris, Bloomington, IN, 2017, (Part 5 – Prophecy Fulfillment)
13. http://www.biblearchaeology.org/post/2012/07/31/New-Light-on-the-Book-of-Daniel-from-the-Dead-Sea-Scrolls.aspx
14. Simon, Marcel, *Verus Israel: A Study of the Relations between Christian and Jews in the Roman Empire AD 135-425*, Schoen Books, South Deerfield, MA, 1986, p. 59
15. *Ibid*
16. Friedman, David, *They Loved the Torah – What Jesus' First Followers Really Thought About the Law*, Lederer Books, Clarksville, MD, 2001
17. Pritz, Ray A., *Nazarene Jewish Christianity: From the End of the New Testament Period until Its Disappearance in the Fourth Century*, Magnes Press, Hebrew University, 1992
18. Stern, David H., *Messianic Judaism - A Modern Movement with an Ancient Past*, Lederer Books, Clarksville, MD, 2007
19. Willis, Norman B., *Nazarene Israel: The Original Faith of the Apostles*, Custom Book Publishing, 2012
20. Helmut Köster Introduction to the New Testament 2 2000 p34 "An early witness for the African text of the Vetus Latina is Codex Palatinus 1 1 85 (siglum "e") from the 5th century, a gospel codex with readings closely related to the quotations in Cyprian and Augustine."

21. Talbot, Wayne, *The New Covenant on Trial*: Examining the Evidence for a Replacement Covenant, Xlibris, Bloomington, IN, 2016
22. http://www.biblecc.com/
23. http://www.hebrewoldtestament.com/
24. http://biblehub.com/interlinear/
25. Roth, *Ibid*, p. vii
26. *Ibid*, pp. vi-vii
27. Truss, Lynne, *Eats, Shoots & Leaves: The Zero Tolerance Approach to Punctuation*, Gotham Books, New York, NY, 2003
28. https://www.michelangelo-gallery.com/michelangelo-moses.aspx

CHAPTER 2-2

PERSPECTIVES ON THE BIBLE

"The Bible is the greatest of all books; to study it is the noblest
of all pursuits; to understand it is the highest of all goals."
~ Charles C. Ryrie (1925-2016) Dean of doctoral
studies, Dallas Theological Seminary ~

Whilst I entirely agree with the sentiments above, I am also cautious of about accepting without question, the words of theologians from the Dallas Theological Seminary. In an earlier study, *"Bible Inerrancy: Fact or Fiction?"*[1], I had cause to evaluate the *Chicago Statement on Biblical Inerrancy* published by that seminary, and available online here[2]. I found it unconvincing, for it failed to deal with the major issues that I raised in my own study. Putting that aside, perhaps we should allow George Bernard Shaw to voice a warning to us all: "No man ever believes that the Bible means what it says: He is always convinced that it says what he means".

We are given to thinking of two volumes: the Old Testament, and the New Testament. The Old, in the form of the Hebrew Scriptures (*Tanakh*, or Tanach), is divided into three sections:

1. Torah (Law).
2. Neviim (Prophets); and
3. Kesuvim (Writings).

The word *Tanakh* is an acronym derived from the first letter of each of these sections. It should be noted that the breaking of Samuel, Kings, and Chronicles into two parts is strictly an artefact of the Christian printers who first issued the books. According to some sources, they were too big to be issued as single volumes, circa 1450. This became the de facto standard. Note also that the divisions of the Tanakh in chapters and verses was also done by medieval Christians, and only later adopted by the Jews – the Hebrew scrolls had no such divisions. Further, many Christian bibles have expanded versions of several books of the *Tanakh* (Esther, Ezra, Daniel, Jeremiah, and Chronicles) including extra material that is not accepted as canonical in Judaism. This extra material was part of the ancient Greek translation of the Tanakh (note previous comments on the Septuagint), but was never a part of the official Hebrew Scriptures. Jews regard this additional material as apocryphal. There is a difference of opinion amongst Christian denominations on these additions. Catholics consider the additional material to be canonical, whilst many Protestants have put it to one side as Apocrypha. Just what is, and what is not, canonical and apocryphal, varies across Christian traditions, and thus, we are back to the question: what is THE bible?

So, how would Jesus have understood the Scriptures? Inference to best explanation would favour the Jewish understanding, and here I will repeat an earlier observation: *"The Hebrew Bible is not a book, but a whole literature comprising history, myth, lyric poetry, and impassioned ideology."*[3]

A Christian View

That notwithstanding, later theological development in Christianity presents us with a perspective entirely different to that of Judaism. The following text (reformatted), is taken from here[4]:

"The Bible may be divided into eight basic sections: four for the Old Testament and four for the New, but it should be noted that in each of these, Christ is the hope and underlying theme of all the books of the Bible. On several occasions, Christ claimed that He is the theme of all of Scripture. The Old Testament in its four-fold division lays the foundation for the coming of the Messiah Savior anticipating Him as Prophet, Priest, and King and as the suffering Savior who must die for man's sin before He reigns.

1. Law – the *Foundation* for Christ.
2. History – *Preparation* for Christ.
3. Poetry – *Aspiration* for Christ; and
4. Prophecy – *Expectation* of Christ.

The New Testament (four-fold division):

5. Gospels – *Manifestation* – Tells the story of the coming of the long-anticipated Savior and His person and work.
6. Acts – *Propagation* – Through the work of the Holy Spirit, Acts proclaims the message of the Savior who has come.
7. Epistles – *Explanation & Application* – Develops the full significance of the person and work of Christ and how this should impact the walk of the Christian as Christ's ambassador in the world; and
8. Revelation – *Consummation* – Anticipates the end time events and the return of the Lord, His end time reign, and the eternal state.

Effectively, this is a *Christological* reinterpretation of the Scriptures, but I am not confident that it is either authentic, or authoritative. Most obviously, as will later be demonstrated, the *long-anticipated Savior* was not someone who would save the whole world from sin, but one who would redeem God's Chosen People, the Jews, from the oppression of other nations. If the Jewish Sages could not see a *two-stage* messianic mission in the prophecies, I am doubtful that God had any such plan in mind, or sought to convey it through His Prophets. Consider what was later written: "Christ was offered once to bear the sins of many. To those who eagerly wait for him, he will appear a second time, apart from sin, for salvation" (Hebrews 9:28). The NKJV annotates this verse as fulfillment of Isaiah 53:10, but consider these two translations:

a.   TJB - "Hashem desired to oppress him, and He afflicted him; if his soul would acknowledge guilt, he would see offspring and live long days, and the desire of Hashem would succeed in his hand"; and

b.   NKJV - "Yet it pleased the Lord to bruise Him; He has put *Him* to grief. When you make His soul an offering for sin, He shall see *His* seed, He shall prolong *His* days, and the pleasure of the Lord shall prosper in His hand." [italics in original]

How did we get from "*if his soul would acknowledge guilt*", to "*when you make his soul an offering for sin*"? This is reminiscent of ignoring the phrase "when he sins" in 2 Samuel 7:12-14, when attempting to make that passage a prophecy of the sinless Jesus as Messiah. To my mind, this is a very clumsy attempt to have Isaiah's account about Israel, to be about Jesus. Clumsy? Did Jesus have offspring (seed), and were his days prolonged? Neither of these were true of Jesus, so how could his crucifixion be fulfillment of a prophecy in Isaiah?

In a one of the essays in a volume entitled, "The Right Doctrine from the Wrong Text?", Klyne Snodgrass warns:

> "We must resist superimposing Christian theology on Old Testament texts and should feel no compulsion to give every Old Testament text, or even most of them, a christological conclusion. But we will have failed if we do not ask how Old Testament texts function in the whole context of Scripture. Without allegorizing the Old Testament, we must seek to understand God's overall purpose with his people. I am not impressed with the concept of *sensus plenior* [fuller sense or meaning], but neither am I willing to isolate texts from God's overall purpose."[5]

What we saw above, items 1-4, is an example of people doing the opposite of this advice, in attempting to make the entire Scripture about Christ. I contend that *none* of the Hebrew Scriptures are about Jesus, because he was not the prophesied Messiah. One should also note that Luke's Acts of the Apostles, is more truly, Acts of Paul; we discuss that later. One final note: "Poetry – *Aspiration* for Christ". Can we really equate *poetry as aspiration* with *statement of prophecy*, as Christianity does so often with the Psalms?

A Jewish View

"Tanach – Textbook of the Soul"
~ Rabbi Nosson Scherman[6] ~

The following texts have been extracted from Rabbi Scherman's exposition on the Tanach[7], with a view to emphasizing his major points, as I understand them. I particularly want to emphasize the Jewish perspective on the three sections: *Torah*, *Prophets*, and *Writings*, contrasting them with the four sections from the Christian perspective as recounted above. I cannot ignore that it was Christianity that reordered the Books of the Hebrew Scriptures, into the Old Testament, erasing the Jewishness from them, not surprising given the anti-Jewishness of the early Church of Rome.

1. TORAH

"The Creator's Code

It was only logical for the Creator of the Universe to provide man with a code of conduct; otherwise man would be like a helpless creature thrashing about in an impenetrable maze. The best proof of this, unfortunately, is found in history books and daily newspapers. The earth is filled with creeds – religious, political, economic, philosophical, and intellectual; and oceans of blood have been spilled, and mountains of treasure expended, in the name of those beliefs. After all these centuries, man is still trapped in the maze, lashing out against those who stand in his directionless path. Surely God's plan of Creation would have helped man answer the essential questions of existence. Where should he turn? For what should he strive? How should he behave? What will help him achieve his goal? What will hinder him? What does God expect, desire, demand, of him?

Although the commandments contained in the Five Books of Moses are the Jew's code of conduct, God wants more than strict adherence to the letter of His laws. The *Torah* is meant to shape people, as well as deeds, because it is only human beings who are God's standard bearers, and whose personal example can inspire others to serve him.

The Books of the Tanach are replete with both certainty and subtlety. The Five Books of Moses emphasize that virtue brings blessing, and sin brings curse. On the other hand, other Books show that God is often patient, and that His ways are often hidden … This is a major principle in the understanding of history – God may *seem* to slumber, but He never abandons His master plan for Creation."

2.   PROPHETS

"Essential to an understanding of Tanach is the concept of prophecy. Colloquially, people think of prophets as predictors of the future, or as spokesmen for an ideal. However, although prophecy may perform these functions, they are not essential to prophecy. As defined by the classic Renaissance commentator, Rabbi Moshe Chaim Luzzatto:

> *Part of a prophet's function may include being sent on a mission by God, but this in itself is not the essence of prophecy, nor is it necessary that a prophet be sent on a mission to others … The essence of prophecy is that the one be attached to God, and that he experience His revelation (Derech Hashem 3:4:6)* [The Way of God].

By definition, prophets are people who had refined their minds and conduct sufficiently to deserve that God's spirit could rest upon them … The prophets elevated the nation simply by being role models of holiness, scholarship, and closeness to God. Until Samuel's time, the prophets tended to be only 'seers' rather than leaders. Since the political leaders of the nation failed to be its spiritual leaders, the Jewish people needed prophets who would lead and admonish, tasks that had once belonged exclusively to the judges.

In later years, the nation split into two kingdoms and the spiritual standing of the people began to erode. The nature of the prophecies began to turn from providing perspective and guidance, to admonitions that tragedy and exile from their land would be inevitable unless the people repented and relearned the lessons of their past. Such were the courageous public demonstrations of Elijah and Elisha, the stirring poetry of Isaiah, the terrible personal ordeals of Hosea and Ezekiel, the dirges of Jeremiah. Other prophecies were encouraging. They came to Israel during times of catastrophic downfall, when the people feared that their bright future was forever behind them, that they had forfeited their right to consider themselves God's Chosen People. At such times, God sent prophets to inspire the downtrodden people and assure them that the sun would shine again. As the Sages put it: 'Had I not fallen, I could not have arisen; had I not sat in the darkness, God would not have been a light for me' (*Midrash Tehillim* 22). This, too, was a message of the prophets.

The Hebrew word *navi*, 'prophet', comes from the term *niv sephesayim*, 'fruit or expression of the lips'. This very title implies the mission of the prophet: he was given a message by God and commanded to express it, to speak to the people, and tell them what God had revealed to them. For this reason, the Books containing such revelations are called Prophets, and, as the Sages explain, 'Only such prophecy as was needed for future generations was written [in Scripture]' (*Yoma* 9b)."

3. WRITINGS

"Not all sacred teachings were meant as Divine messages to be conveyed to the people. Those are the Writings – so-called because they were to be written, rather than proclaimed as 'prophecies', but God ordained that they be preserved as part of Scripture. The reasons vary. It may have been to provide perspective on history, such as the Books of *Chronicles*, *Ruth*, and *Esther*. It may have been to provide wise perspective on the meaning and conduct of life, such as King Solomon's *Proverbs* and *Ecclesiastes*. It may have been to allude to the future Redemption, such as the Book of *Daniel*. Or it may have been to shed light on the eternally perplexing question of why the righteous may suffer, while the wicked prosper, such as the heated disputations of the Book of Job.

Perhaps the best example of a non-prophetic work that has a profound effect on countless millions of people is the Book of *Psalms*. King David is more than the 'Sweet Singer of Israel'. He is a musician of the soul, who plucks at the heartstrings of every Jew, and makes sacred music of every life experience. Whatever a Jew needs, he finds in his Book of Psalms – gratitude, hope, prayer, aspiration, courage, insight. Millions of *Tehillin'lech* (i.e., little Books of *Psalms*) have soaked up infinite numbers of tears – tears that God treasures in His own treasury."

Summary

*"What advantage then has the Jew? Chiefly because
to them were committed the oracles of God."*
(Romans 3:1-2)

How very different: the Jewish perspective on the *Tanach*, and the Christian perspective on the Old Testament. Note, especially, that King David is not considered a prophet, and his Psalms are not considered prophecies. Note too that Daniel's writings are about future Redemption, but not redemption from sin, as Christianity asserts, but redemption from oppression. Redemption, throughout the Hebrew Scriptures, refers to being rescued in this life, not the next, just as certain prophecies were encouraging: "They came to Israel during times of catastrophic downfall, when the people feared that their bright future was forever behind them, that they had forfeited their right to consider themselves God's Chosen People".

Finally, we should never forget that God chose the Children of Israel, instructing Moses to tell Pharaoh, "Thus says the Lord: Israel is My son,

My first-born son" (Exodus 4:22), not for their sake, but for **His Name's** sake. Consider too, that the Land of Israel was not given to the Israelites for their sake, but for God's sake. In the context of the Covenant, as they did not *earn* it, nor was it given for their sake, they could not *un-earn* it, irrespective of what they did, or did not, do. Consider these verses taken from the Hebrew Bible (TJB), emphases mine:

a. "But I acted for **the sake of My Name**, that it not be desecrated in the eyes of the nations in whose midst they were" (Ezekiel 20:9).

b. "Then you will know that I am Hashem, when I act *with you* **for My Name's sake**, and not in accord with your evil ways and your corrupt deeds" (Ezekiel 20:44).

c. "Thus, said the Lord Hashem/Elohim: It is not for your sake that I act, O House of Israel, but **for My holy Name**, that you have desecrated among the nations where you came. I will **sanctify My great Name** that is desecrated among the nations, that *you* have desecrate among them; then the nations will know that I am Hashem – the word of Lord Hashem/Elohim – when I become sanctified through *you* before their eyes." (Ezekiel 36:22-23)

d. "I, only I, am He Who wipes away your wilful sins **for My Sake**, and I shall not recall your sins" (Isaiah 43:25).

See also Deuteronomy 7:7-8 and 9:4-6. The point is that the decisions God made, regarding the election of the Children of Israel and *Eretz Israel* (Land of Israel), were not for their sake, but for **His Sake**, and God being omniscient, He would never change His mind concerning such things. In the context of the need for *substitutionary atonement* by a saviour, ponder Isaiah 43:25 - "I, only I, am He Who wipes away your wilful sins **for My Sake**, and I shall not recall your sins".

The Bible is many things to many people, but accepting the view of Paul, that the advantage of the Jew was that to them were entrusted the oracles of God (Romans 3:1), it is logical, to my mind, to accept the Jewish view over the Christian.

REFERENCES:

1. Talbot, Wayne, *Bible Inerrancy: Fact or Fiction*? The Inerrancy of God's Word versus the Fallibility of Human Interpretation, Peshat Books, Kelso, NSW, 2012
2. http://library.dts.edu/Pages/TL/Special/ICBI_1.pdf
3. MacCoby, Hyam, *Revolution in Judaea: Jesus & The Jewish Resistance*, Ocean Books, London, UK, 1973, p. 64
4. https://bible.org/seriespage/2-comparing-old-and-new-testaments
5. Beale, G.K., *The Right Doctrine from the Wrong Texts*? Essays on the Use of the Old Testament in the New, Baker Academic, Grand Rapids, MI, 1994, p. 49
6. Scherman, Rabbi Nosson, *The Tanach*, Mesorah Publications, ArtScroll English Edition, Brooklyn, NY, 2011, p. xv
7. Ibid, pp. xv - xxi

CHAPTER 2-3

AN ASIDE - A QUICK QUIZ

"For this is My blood of the new covenant, which
is shed for many for the remission of sin."
(Matthew 26:28)

QUESTION: Do you believe that Jesus announced a New Covenant at the Last Supper, one replacing the covenant agreed with the Children of Israel at Sinai?

I apologise for again revisiting this question, but the context is this: If Jesus did fulfill messianic prophecies, has the Christian Church really followed through on those prophecies, or has it diverged from the intent as expressed in the Hebrew Scriptures? If Jesus is the Messiah, has Christianity given him a role that is different to that expressed by the Prophets?

As a Christian, you would, no doubt, answer the opening question with: "Of course, everybody knows that Jesus announced a New Covenant!", referring to the unambiguous statement as quoted above. *Covenant* Theology, as distinct from *Dispensational* Theology, is represented by many views, from there being just one covenant, the *Creation* Covenant; to two, expressed as here: "The two main covenants are the covenant of works in the Old Testament made between God and Adam, and the Covenant of Grace between the Father and the Son where the Father promised to give the Son the elect and the Son must redeem them"[1], to even many more. I wonder why *Covenant of Grace* is deserving of initial capitals, but *covenant of works* is not? I am ever suspicious of theological annotations.

Incidentally, there was NO covenant *between* God and Adam: a covenant, in the biblical sense, is a formal alliance, or agreement, between God and His people. We have no evidence that Adam agreed to his fate: he just accepted it. There was a Creation Covenant of a sort, between God and His Creation, but not with Adam specifically.

But back to the main theme. Christian *Replacement Theology* (Supersessionism) is founded on the belief that Jesus did announce a new, replacement, covenant, even though no details were given. That idea was taken up in the Book of Hebrews, Chapter 8, with a quotation of the covenant stated in Jeremiah 31:31-34. The traditional Christian view is that Hebrews was written by the Apostle Paul, yet: "Although pre-modern commentators assumed that Paul wrote Hebrews, virtually all scholars today agree that Paul was not the author"[2]. I can neither verify nor refute the claim of "virtually all", so you can decide that point for yourselves. Continuing this quotation: "The document was circulated anonymously in antiquity, and the title 'To the Hebrews' was added when it was collected together with Paul's letters ... Although it has traditionally been considered a letter, 13:22 identifies the work as a 'word of exhortation', implying that it was a sermon". In the 3rd century, Origen wrote of the letter, "Men of old have handed it down as Paul's, but who wrote the Epistle God only knows."[3] History records Jerome and Augustine of Hippo as both supporting Paul's authorship, with the Church agreeing in the 4th century to include it as one of Paul's letters.

As evidence in support of the "new covenant" case, I would contend that the Book of Hebrews is not even admissible, as the writings cannot be authenticated.

The opening quotation of the Gospel of Matthew is from the New King James Version (NKJV), just one of many Christian interpretations of the Greek, remembering that all translations are interpretations, and subject to theological bias. How do other translations render this verse? Let us start with a transliteration of the Greek:

"this indeed is the blood of me of the covenant for many being poured out for forgiveness of sins"

Note: no mention of the word "new", but perhaps it can be inferred, as the Hebrew Scriptures contain no reference to a covenant, where the blood of an innocent man is to be spilled for the forgiveness of sins. In truth, the Hebrew Scriptures have God *condemning* the spilling of innocent blood, but we will let that pass for now. The Greek word, *diathēkēs* (Strong's Greek 1242), can be translated as *covenant, will,* or *testament.* Strongs Concordance gives this definition: (a) a covenant between two parties, (b) (the ordinary, everyday sense [found a countless number of times in papyri]) a will, testament. The translators task is to understand which word, from the semantic range, best fits the intent, and context, of the source document. Comparing translations from here[4] [emphases mine]:

a. NKJV - "For this is My blood of the **new covenant**, which is shed for many for the remission of sin."
b. KJB – "For this is my blood of the **new testament**, which is shed for many for the remission of sins."
c. American Standard – "for this is my blood of the **covenant**, which is poured out for many unto remission of sins."
d. GOD's Word – "This is my blood, the blood of the **promise**. It is poured out for many people so that sins are forgiven."
e. Weymouth NT – "for this is my blood which is to be poured out for many for the remission of sins--the blood which **ratifies** the **Covenant**."
f. Holman – "For this is My blood that **establishes** the **covenant**; it is shed for many for the forgiveness of sins."
g. NLT – "for this is my blood, which **confirms** the **covenant** between God and his people. It is poured out as a sacrifice to forgive the sins of many."

If we accept Strongs Concordance definition, "testament" (as in Will & Testament) is the most common usage in the Greek. Analysing the variations, "promise" is acceptable, in that it accords with the sense of a Will & Testament. Some translations have *covenant*, unspecified, and some have *new covenant*, which Jesus had not previously mentioned, and does not further explain. One translation has the blood of Jesus *establishing the covenant*, and another *ratifying the covenant*, although again, we have no evidence to explain which covenant that would be. The NLT renders the verse as *confirming the covenant*, which I assume, can only be an earlier covenant between God and His people, because no other covenant has been mentioned anywhere in the preceding narratives.

The question becomes: If a *covenant* is the issue, as opposed to a will or testament, to which covenant was Jesus referring? According to the Greek, Jesus did not use the word "new". If this is the truth of the matter, then we are entitled to consider earlier covenants. Apart from the claims of prophecy fulfillment, with which we will deal in detail later, there is no prophecy in the Hebrew Scriptures which accords with the spilling of innocent, human blood. I accept that earlier covenants, such as that made with Abraham, do mention blood, but always of animals, never of humans. Apart from the problematic text in Hebrews 8, we have nothing from Jesus on the conditions of this new covenant, whether it replaces the old, and with whom it was agreed. Remember: covenants are agreements. Perhaps we could assume an agreement between Jesus and his Father, but that is supposition only. Even if that were true, in what way would it invalidate, or abrogate, the existing covenant between God and His Chosen People? We should not ignore that God unconditionally promised to Abraham: "I will ratify My covenant between Me and You and between your offspring after you, throughout their generations, as an **everlasting** covenant" (Genesis 17:7) [emphasis mine]. As evidence, that nullifies any argument that God subsequently replaced His covenant with another.

From the Gospels themselves, we have no evidence of a new, *replacement*, covenant, only suggestion of confirmation of an existing covenant. Basically, all we have are variations of translation (interpretation), with many conflicting with each other. So, how else could we solve this dilemma? In a court of law, the actions of witnesses to an event, are taken as circumstantial evidence of the circumstances of the event. If a witness, or even two or three, claimed that there was a large explosion, with a sudden wave of heat and debris, but other people nearby at the time had no recollection of the disturbance, the latter is circumstantial evidence that the explosion did not happen. Accordingly, one way to evaluate the evidence of a new, replacement covenant, would be to gauge the reaction of those present at the Last Supper. As Christianity uses this claimed new covenant as the rationale for its very existence, it would be fair to characterise the event as a "disturbance", particularly before a group brought up to be faithful to the Sinaitic Covenant. Let us start with the Apostles, as a group:

> *"And when they had sung a hymn, they went out to the Mount of Olives"* (Matthew and Mark).

What was in their minds when they did that? Why did they not question the substance of this covenant? To my mind, the narrative suggests that the covenant, if that is what was mentioned, was one with which they were already familiar, due to their lack of response. There is no prior mention in the Gospel accounts of a new covenant, and there is no covenant in the Hebrew Scriptures which they could reconcile with Jesus dying. Luke's account does include the word "new", but the rest of the narrative is substantially different to that of Matthew and Mark.

According to Matthew's account, Judas was identified as the traitor *before* the event in question. Mark's account just identifies "one of the twelve". Luke agrees with Mark, but then, rather than sing a hymn and go out to the Mount of Olives, Luke has the Apostles questioning amongst themselves as to who the traitor was, and then disputing amongst themselves as to who would be the greatest. He follows with a lengthy discourse, the Apostles picking up two swords, and off they went to the Mount of Olives … *as he was accustomed* (Luke 22:38-39). The interesting point about this is that if Jesus was so accustomed, then there would have been no need of Judas betraying Jesus's whereabouts. As an avid reader of detective stories, I tend to notice such discrepancies.

What does the Apostle John record? Well, nothing at all: not a single mention, allusion, or reference. Not only does John not see significance in the announcement, if it really happened, he adds to the confusion by totally ignoring it in his Gospel. John gives us no details of the Last Supper: makes no mention of body, blood, sacrifice for forgiveness of sin, or a covenant, new or old. Instead, he skips to the end of the supper, mentions Judas as the betrayer, narrates Jesus washing the feet of the Apostles, and then a longish discourse (John 13:12 to 17:26) which none of the Synoptics mention.

If the New (Replacement) Covenant be central to Christian doctrine and theology, how is it that the Gospel of John, said to represent the highest Christology, considers it not even worthy of mention? One cannot say: "Oh, John does not mention it because it is already covered by the other Gospels." That is just nonsense.

Summary

If we are to do as Simon Greenleaf entreats, that we should start with *"a mind, freed, as far as possible, from existing prejudice"*[5], and also proceed with our biblical exegesis, as he instructs:

> "Let (the Gospel's) testimony be sifted, as it were given in a court of justice on the side of the adverse party, the witness being subjected to a rigorous cross-examination"[6]

… then I would contend that all is not right with Christian doctrine regarding *Replacement* Theology, based on Jesus proclaiming a new covenant. If you are interested in pursuing this issue further, I have published further thoughts in my book, *"The New Covenant on Trial"*[7].

REFERENCES:

1. https://carm.org/dictionary-covenant-theology
2. Levine, Amy-Jill, and Brettler, Marc Zvi, *The Jewish Annotated New Testament*, Oxford University Press, New York, NY 2011, p.406
3. Eusebius, *Church History Book*, VI Ch. 25 v14
4. http://biblehub.com/matthew/26-28.htm
5. Greenleaf, Simon, *The Testimony of the Evangelists*, Kregel Classics, Grand Rapids, MI, 1995, p.11
6. *Ibid*, back cover
7. Talbot, Wayne, *The New Covenant on Trial: Examining the Evidence for a Replacement Covenant*, Xlibris, Bloomington, IN, 2016

CHAPTER 2-4

BIBLE ORDERING
& SEQUENCE

"I do not feel obliged to believe that the same God who has endowed us
with sense, reason, and intellect, has intended to forego their use."
~ Galileo Galilei, Letter to the Grand Duchess Christina ~

Indeed, we should not.

As we noted in Chapter 2-2, the compilers of the Christian Old Testament chose to re-order the books from the sequence in the Hebrew Scriptures, removing the significance of the three quite distinct sections: *Torah*, *Prophets*, and *Writings*. I believe that this was done purposely, though that purpose is open to conjecture. As an aside, this presents somewhat of a challenge when switching between the Christian and the Jewish versions, in an attempt to compare them. Curiously, I find a similarity between the New Testament and the Islamic Quran: the sequence of books does not match the sequence of writing and/or revelation.

Islam's Quran is a collection of instructions for life, said to have been revealed by the Angel Gabriel to Mohammed over 23 years, subsequently being delivered orally by Mohammed to his followers. As Mohammed was illiterate, the written version was completed 19 years after his death, but the identity of the authors is subject to contention, as it is with the New Testament. The Quran is divided into 114 *suras* (or surahs), i.e. chapters, assigned to two broad categories: the earlier revelations at Mecca which tend to be shorter, and the later revelations at Medina which are generally longer. With some exceptions, the *suras* are arranged in the Quran in descending order of length, the longest at the beginning and the shortest at the end, which fundamentally, puts them in inverse chronological order. The practices of Mohammed were recorded in the *Sunnah*, and the traditions in the *Hadith*. A proper understanding of Islam can only come from a study of all three sources. My point here is that when reading the Quran, one is reading later revelations earlier, and the earlier later, which can lead to misunderstanding, especially as later revelations sometimes contradicted those earlier, a process that Islam justifies as *abrogation*.

For similar reasons, misconception is ever the bane of readers of the New Testament. The sequence of books, beginning with Matthew, does not align chronologically with their authorship. You are no doubt aware of the contention over both the authorship and the dating, with no-one truly knowing. There is evidence that in some cases, the dating is chosen to be within the lifetime of the person to whom the writing is attributed, lest the authenticity and authority of the writings is called into question. As this study is being conducted under the *rules of evidence*, we must ever be cognisant of this factor. I cannot be dogmatic about what follows, but I have accepted it as probable, based on the evidence and scholarly opinions that I have studied.

Dating of New Testament Autographs

Date	Book	Author	Comment
50	James	James	The Just, brother of Jesus
52-53	1 Thessalonians	Paul	
52-53	2 Thessalonians	?	Disciple of Paul?
55	Galatians	Paul	
57	1 Corinthians	Paul	With later editing

57	2 Corinthians	Paul	
57-58	Romans	Paul	With later editing
62-63	Philippians	Paul	
62-63	Colossians	?	Disciple of Paul?
62-63	Philemon	Paul	
62-63	Ephesians	?	Disciple of Paul?
65	1 Timothy	?	Disciple of Paul?
65	Titus	?	Disciple of Paul?
66	2 Timothy	?	Disciple of Paul?
66	Mark	?	"a" Mark, but which?
67	Matthew	?	Canonical, not original
67	Hebrews	?	Truly unknown
67-68	1 Peter	?	Jude on behalf of Peter
68	2 Peter	?	Jude on behalf of Peter
68	Jude	Jude	Brother of James the Just
81-96	Revelation	?	John of Patmos, an elder?
c. 85	John	John	With later editing
90-95	Luke	Luke	Much later?
90-95	Acts	Luke	Much later?
90-95	1-3 John	?	uncertain

Let me offer that Christians read the New Testament backwards, very much as one does when reading the Quran. Read in the sequence given here, an entirely different story emerges. The first Gospel attributed to an Apostle is that of Mark, but the authorship is disputed, and no-one can be entirely confident. Of importance, however, is that at the earliest, it was written over 30 years after the death of Jesus. In between, we have the writings of James, and then of Paul, and likely his disciples, which apart from James, set the doctrine for Christianity, especially for the Gentiles.

I find that numerous scholars agree with my observation, although evidencing differing opinions on the dating of the works. For example:

"A chronological New Testament sequences the documents very differently. Its order is based on contemporary mainstream biblical scholarship. Though there is uncertainty about dating some of the documents, there is a scholarly consensus about the basic framework.

It begins with seven letters attributed to Paul, all from the 50s. The first Gospel is Mark (not Matthew), written around 70. Revelation is not last, but almost in the middle, written in the 90s. Twelve documents follow Revelation, with II Peter the last, written as late as near the middle of the second century.

A chronological New Testament is not only about sequence, but also about chronological context — the context-in-time, the historical context in which each document was written. Words have their meaning within their temporal contexts, in the New Testament and the Bible as a whole."[1]

The author of this article goes on to conclude:

"Seeing and reading the New Testament in chronological sequence matters for historical reasons. It illuminates Christian origins. Much becomes apparent:
- Beginning with seven of Paul's letters illustrates that there were vibrant Christian communities spread throughout the Roman Empire before there were written Gospels. His letters provide a "window" into the life of very early Christian communities.
- Placing the Gospels after Paul makes it clear that as written documents they are not the source of early Christianity but its product. The Gospel — the good news — of and about Jesus existed before the Gospels. They are the products of early Christian communities several decades after Jesus' historical life and tell us how those communities saw his significance in their historical context.
- Reading the Gospels in chronological order beginning with Mark demonstrates that early Christian understandings of Jesus and his significance developed. As Matthew and Luke

used Mark as a source, they not only added to Mark but often modified Mark.

- Seeing John separated from the other Gospels and relatively late in the New Testament makes it clear how different his Gospel is. In consistently metaphorical and symbolic language, it is primarily "witness" or "testimony" to what Jesus had become in the life and thought of John's community.

- Realizing that many of the documents are from the late first and early second centuries allows us to glimpse developments in early Christianity in its third and fourth generations. In general, they reflect a trajectory that moves from the radicalism of Jesus and Paul to increasing accommodation with the cultural conventions of the time."[1]

To my mind, the most important conclusion given above is this one: *Placing the Gospels after Paul makes it clear that as written documents they are not the source of early Christianity but its product.* In the context of evaluating evidence, we should, if this is true, consider the Gospels as hearsay, rather than first-hand accounts witnessed by their authors. This substantially diminishes their credibility, and thus authority.

As aside, following on from the previous chapter, note the comment regarding the Gospel of John: "it is primarily "witness" or "testimony" to what Jesus had become in the life and thought of John's community." John's Gospel makes no mention of a *new covenant*: should we assume from this that John's community did not believe in one, but instead, continued is their obedience to the earlier covenant?

Before the Gospels

We know little of the activities of the early church in Jerusalem, headed by James the Just, brother of Jesus, other than that the community were called Nazarenes, or in modern parlance, Messianic Jews. They practised Judaism in a Messianic context, but we do not truly know what that meant to them. There was a Jesus-following in Judea and in Galilee, which preceded that of Paul, and if we are to accept the motifs in the writings of

James, the gospel they received was likely very different to that preached by Paul. In a later chapter, I will offer evidence that the resurrection as perceived by Paul, differed from the perspective that we gain from other accounts, and has been accepted as Christian doctrine. One might also note here that the religion of the Nazarenes was later declared heretical by Rome, an affront no doubt to James, Jude, and likely Jesus himself. Should you be so interested, New Testament scholar, James Tabor, has devoted a chapter to *Christianity Before Paul* in his book, *Paul and Jesus*[2].

This brings us to the question of the source of Paul's theology, and most importantly, its authenticity. Paul claims to have received it directly from the risen Jesus, or from God, depending on how one interprets the relevant texts. But as I have highlighted in other published studies, Paul preached a separate gospel which was not consonant with that of James, nor with the essence of the Gospels. This has long been recognised, with even Martin Luther attempting to have the Epistle of James, among others, removed from the Christian canon, as it effectively refutes his own theology based on the writings of Paul; specifically, that we are justified by faith alone. Whilst Paul is sometimes referred to as the 13th Apostle, in a spiritual sense he considered himself as the first; for example: "But I make known to you, brethren, that the gospel which was preached by me is not according to man, nor was I taught it, but it came through the revelation of Jesus Christ" (Galatians 1:11-12).

Now, if one combines that with: "For I delivered to you first of all that which I received: that Christ died for our sins according to the Scriptures, and that he was buried, and that he rose again the third day according to the Scriptures", one has to question where Paul obtained his resurrection narrative. If he claimed to have learned of it from Jesus directly, not from the claimed witnesses, and if the Gospels are the product of Christian beliefs, not their source, could it be that the resurrection event was written into the Gospels based on what Paul had earlier written? This would certainly explain the lack of coherence across the four Gospel narratives of discovering the empty tomb (see Chapter 9-3). Paul was entirely wrong when he claimed that Jesus dying for our sins, and then being resurrected, was according to the Scriptures. Even the NKJV editors failed to annotate any Old Testament prophecy to that effect. This raises the question: if Paul did not hear of the resurrection from human witnesses, and if he could not have heard of it from the risen Jesus because it did not happen, then where did he get that idea? Archaeologists have found a clue in an ancient stone tablet containing eighty-seven lines of Hebrew text, which came to light in 2000, and is claimed to have been originally discovered in Jordan, near the eastern shore of the Dead Sea. We discuss the implications of this in Chapter 9-4.

I hope that, from this brief discussion, you can accept that there are valid reasons for questioning the authenticity of some texts in the New Testament. It is well to be aware of the chronology of development of Christian theology, lest we are misled by how that theology is presented to us. If the New Testament was written in the sequence presented in the Christian bible, we are entitled to take one view, but if the chronology was entirely different, we should seek to verify its truth.

To assist with understanding Paul's writings, which even the author of 2 Peter admitted were "hard to understand" (v. 3:16) this website offers a reading program[3]. Another timeline can be found here[4], but as the author states: "While no arrangement of these books can be made with absolute confidence, the following dates are sufficiently reliable to serve the purpose of the Bible student."

Summary

Without belabouring the point, the issue is simply this: the sequencing of the books in the New Testament is a thinly disguised attempt at a theological treatise, not an honest statement of history. Christian publishers have removed theological context from the Old Testament, in the resequencing of the Hebrew Scriptures, and have conspired to promote theology in the sequence of the New. Discussing what he describes as the mythology that "Both Jew and Gentile were united in the one Christian Church, with *one single unified gospel message*" (italics in original), James Tabor commented: "Historians of early Christianity question such a harmonizing view linking Jesus, his first apostles, and Paul. It serves theological dogma more than historical truth."[5]

Serious bible students should understand what is being presented to them, and take steps to defeat this subliminal influencing of their understanding.

<u>REFERENCES</u>:

1. https://www.huffingtonpost.com/marcus-borg/a-chronological-new-testament_b_1823018.html
2. Tabor, James D., *Paul and Jesus: How the Apostle Paul Transformed Christianity*, Simon & Schuster Paperbacks, New York, NY, 2012, pp. 23-47
3. https://www.westarinstitute.org/blog/how-to-read-pauls-letters-chronologically/
4. https://www.biblestudytools.com/resources/guide-to-bible-study/order-books-new-testament.html
5. Tabor, *Ibid*, p. 5

CHAPTER 2-5

NEW TESTAMENT AUTHORS

*"The Bible's power rests upon the fact that it is the
reliable, errorless, and infallible Word of God"*
~ Chuck Colson (1931-2012), Evangelical Christian Leader ~

Based on the discussions in Chapters 1-1 and 2-1, I wonder which version of the Bible Chuck Colson had in mind? No matter, whilst Scripture records God, Himself, inscribing the Ten Words (Commandments) on the tablets given to Moses, we know that the writers of the New Testament were human, and that we have ample reason to doubt that their words represent the *"reliable, errorless, and infallible Word of God"*.

Reiterating Chapter 1-1 regarding the study by James Dunn on the Gospels (I'm sure that you hadn't forgotten), he concluded that in "the Synoptic material … there is not close verbal agreement, and in **a number of cases hardly any verbal agreement although the subject matter is evidently the same.**" (emphasis in the original)[1] The author further commented, "What is striking about all these examples is *the lack of verbal agreement* – typically less than 40 percent, and more like 20 percent or less in some cases" (italics in the original)[2]. Now I am not going to argue that God *would not* use different words through different authors, I do not know Him well enough, but it would seem strange that He would deliberately choose different words to describe the same events, and even have the evangelists record the sayings of Jesus using different words. If it is true that "what Scripture says, God says", then there is another level of mystery in the Bible that is so far unexplained – why would God, the epitome of truth, deliver His message that way?

One might argue that the sense of the sayings does not alter, just because different words are used. I contend strenuously with that suggestion, for words matter, and different meanings are derived from different words. God knows that, and if He intended His words to be considered *reliable, errorless, and infallible*, He would not have introduced such variation, and promoted ambiguity (at least, I hope not).

So now let us review what is known about the human authors.

Matthew

To begin with, we do not know the author of *canonical* Matthew. I will let you research that for yourself, but in brief, many claim that Matthew's *autograph* was in Hebrew, and others that Matthew dictated his original Gospel to some unknown scribe, who was literate in Greek. Another opinion is that the canonical version we have today, was a translation from the Hebrew by Church Father, Jerome. If that be true, we should be rightly suspicious of its accuracy, as Jerome was not known to be overly competent in Hebrew (note earlier arguments), and may well have sprinkled the text with his own theological annotations and redactions, as can be shown for the other Gospels. The significant point, however, is that Jerome aside, any Old Testament quotations in this Gospel, and any interpretations of the Law and Prophets, were most likely taken from the Greek Septuagint, rather than the Hebrew. Further, it is unlikely that the author(s) sought validation of their interpretations from Jewish scholars.

Consider this opinion of the Gospel attributed to the Apostle, Matthew:

"Most scholars believe it was composed between AD 80 and 90, with a range of possibility between AD 70 to 110 (a pre-70 date remains a minority view). The anonymous author was probably a male Jew, standing on the margin between traditional and non-traditional Jewish values, and familiar with technical legal aspects of scripture being debated in his time. Writing in a polished Semitic "synagogue Greek", he drew on three main sources: the Gospel of Mark, the hypothetical collection of sayings known as the Q source, and material unique to his own community, called the M source or 'Special Matthew'."[3]

Simon Greenleaf offers an opinion with which I disagree: "He [Matthew] is generally allowed to have written first of all the evangelists; but whether in the Hebrew or the Greek language, on in both, the learned are not agreed, nor is it material to our purpose to inquire; the genuineness of our present Greek Gospel being sustained by satisfactory evidence"[4]. Not *material to our purpose to enquire*? What happened to *a mind, freed, as far as possible, from existing prejudice*? I have not examined this evidence, but the evidence that I have examined, as presented in previous chapters, is sufficient for me to distrust the genuineness of any Greek scriptures, and derivatives therefrom.

A Wikipedia entry can be found here[5], providing a wider discussion of the subject of who authored the Gospel, and when. That aside, in relation to prophecy fulfillments, we can judge the Gospel of Matthew on its own merits, irrespective of its authorship. We are not concerned, in this study at least, with the overall veracity of this Gospel, just what it has to say regarding prophecies, and how well the author understood the prophets of old.

Mark

The Gospel attributed to Mark, said to be a disciple of Peter, was written in Greek, although its authorship is also disputed. That notwithstanding, no-one seems to know who Mark was. One opinion, within Christianity, is that he was born in Cyrene (Libya), and met Peter on one of his travels.

Another opinion is that he was from Jerusalem, the son of Mary, a pious sister of Barnabas, and amongst the original disciples who followed Jesus. Some have him travelling with Paul and Barnabas, but all agree that he later founded the church of Alexandria. If he was Jewish, and again, that is uncertain, because his identity is uncertain, he would likely have been Hellenic, rather than Hebrew, to have written competently in Greek, his intended readership being culturally Greek disciples. Once again, that takes us back to a Gospel written using the Greek Septuagint as a reference, rather than the Hebrew Scriptures.

Mark is said to have written his account in Rome, at the dictation of Peter, but I am forced to wonder about the language of their conversations. Peter likely spoke Aramaic, with a smattering of Greek, but as best as we can discern, he was not an educated man. Where Mark has included Old Testament references, was that at the dictation of Peter, or was that Mark's editing? How much of this Gospel is Mark, rather than Peter (or even Paul)? In what language did they converse, and if it was Aramaic, how well could Mark convey Peter's intentions in Greek? I believe that on the evidence, we can conclude that Mark was not an eyewitness to many, if not any, of the events narrated in his Gospel: thus, much it is largely hearsay.

According to some scholars whom I have read, Mark was heavily influenced by Paul[6]. That may sound surprising at first, but as we discuss in the next chapter, Mark's Gospel is generally accepted as being the first, following some years after the writings of Paul, and if Mark did travel with Paul and Barnabas, this proposition is plausible. I will let you read the evidence for yourself in the referenced work, but I find it more plausible than the traditional Christian understanding, which again, I believe, was motivated by the need to establish authenticity and authority.

As with the Gospel of Matthew, the internal evidence is sufficient here for our purposes, but we should never ignore the issues of authenticity and authority.

Luke

Luke's Gospel is clearly second generation, as is evidenced by his opening lines. We know little about Luke, other than that he was a physician, a follower of Paul, was fluent in Greek, and may have had some association with Judaism. On that basis, his entire evidence must be classed as *hearsay*. His statement: "just as those who from the beginning were eyewitnesses and ministers of the word delivered them to us" (Luke 1:2) is a little intriguing, as we have no evidence of who these eyewitnesses were, or how these eyewitnesses delivered the word to him: had he met any, or had he read the writings of these eyewitnesses? If we accept even the conservative dating of the Gospels of Matthew and Mark, let alone the liberal, we can have little confidence that Luke had read them in the form that they are accepted today as the autographs. We know that Luke was a follower of Paul, and that Paul in his initial years as the Apostle to the Gentiles, had little or no contact with those whom Jesus appointed as his Apostles. It would be reasonable to conclude that much of Luke's theology derived from Paul's teachings.

Luke's Gospel is very different to the other Synoptics; records many events not found in them; and evidences theological development. A comment worthy of note:

> "Luke is often viewed as the historian of the apostolic age, yet many do not fully recognize him as a theologian as well. The author develops many themes in his Gospel. One of the most notable themes is of Redemption History by which he views the world in three major time periods. First, the time of the "Law and the Prophets" was in effect until John the Baptist (16:16a). After that came the time period of Jesus, when "the gospel of the kingdom of God has been preached" (16:16b). The last time period begins after the ascension of Christ and continues until his return. This is the period of the church.

> The idea of salvation is also prevalent in Luke's Gospel. The words "salvation/deliverance" and "salvation/saving power" are used by Luke, but are not found in Matthew and Mark. Not only is the theme of salvation evident, but Luke also demonstrates Jesus as being sympathetic towards Samaritans and Gentiles (e.g. Good Samaritan 10:30-37; Centurion 7:2-10, see also 2:32)."[7]

Two issues are of note. Firstly, how well did Luke understand the Hebrew Scriptures? Did he understand that prophecies regarding Israel's redemption had nothing to do with *substitutionary atonement*, but were about Israel's rescue from foreign domination? Secondly, what I find of interest here is Jesus' claimed sympathy toward Samaritans and Gentiles, contrasted with his stated mission: "I was not sent except to the lost sheep of the house of Israel" (Matt 15:24). The latter does not suggest that Jesus would lack sympathy for these people, but Luke's Gospel has nothing to say about Jesus fulfilling the mission as he, himself, stated it. One could offer that Luke, a non-Jew, and a theologian to boot, was starting to reflect some of the anti-Jewishness found in the writings of his mentor, Paul.

By way of an example, let us consider what many historians have to say about the relationship between the Jews and Samaritans, the following being but one example of the consensus:

> "In order to enforce their rule the Romans had troops stationed in Judaea … In Jerusalem the Roman garrison consisted of 500 soldiers. It is probable that a large proportion of these soldiers consisted of Samaritans, i.e., men from the Palestinian district of Samaria where a variant of Judaism was practised with a dissident Temple on Mount Gerizim … The Samaritans were much disliked by the Judeans, not only because they belonged to a heretical sect, but also because they habitually robbed and killed Jews who entered their territory. It must have been very galling to the Jews to be under the authority of a Roman occupying force in which the hostile Samaritans were given a prominent place."[8]

When Jesus told his disciples: "do not enter a city of the Samaritans" (Matthew 10:5), was it because the Samaritans *habitually robbed and killed Jews who entered their territory*? Yet, in John's Gospel, Jesus "needed to go through Samaria" (John 4:4), and had no qualms about meeting with the Samarians, even staying with them for two days (John 4:40). As mentioned before, we need to evaluate the Gospel narratives against what is known from extra-biblical sources, which in this instance, gives doubt to the narratives of John 4. If the Samaritans were anti-Jewish, there is a subliminal suggestion in John's account of Jesus communing with them. If the Samaritans were a heretical sect, with their own dissident Temple on Mount Gerizim, whilst the Hebrew Scriptures repeatedly stress the importance of Jerusalem, why would the Samaritans accept Jesus as Messiah, especially as later, he supposedly had a triumphant entry into Jerusalem? You see, the two narratives contradict one another.

Luke's "second" Gospel, the Book of Acts, stands alone as an historical record of the early years, post-Jesus. There is no corroboration of many of his narratives, and there is tension between Luke's portrayal of Paul, and Paul's portrayal of himself. Just how much of Luke's account was witnessed by him is unknown. We do not know from whom he received his accounts, nor to what degree he may have embellished them to reflect his developing theology. One scholar was moved to contend: *"This account owes more to Luke's ability to compose an engagingly plausible tale, than to his access to historically reliable information about Paul's missionary experience … Luke gives us historical fiction rather than an historical report."*[9]

Simon Greenleaf, to his credit, also questions the source of Luke's knowledge. He wrote:

> "He [Luke] does not affirm himself to have been an eye-witness; though his personal knowledge of some of the transactions may well be inferred from the 'perfect understanding' which he says he possessed. Some of the learned seem to have drawn this inference as to them all, and to have placed him in the class of original witnesses, but this opinion, though maintained on strong and plausible grounds, is not generally adopted. If, then, he did not write from his own personal knowledge, the question is, what is the legal character of his testimony?"[10]

Legal character indeed! In answering his own question, Greenleaf states:

> "If it were 'the result of inquiries, made under competent public authority, concerning matters in which the public are concerned'[11], it would possess every legal attribute of an inquisition, and as such, would be legally admissible in evidence, in a court of justice. To entitle such results, however, to our full confidence, it is not

necessary that they should be obtained under a legal commission; it is sufficient if the inquiry is gravely undertaken and pursued, by a person of competent intelligence, sagacity, and integrity."[12]

I do not have the legal standing of Simon Greenleaf, or of anyone for that matter, but I would point out what he has ignored. We have no independent testimony to the character, *competent intelligence, sagacity, and integrity*, of Luke, and no possibility of interrogating him. I cannot know, but I suspect that Greenleaf has referred to precedents in courts of law, where witnesses can be cross-examined, and their testimonies subjected to the utmost scrutiny. This is not the case here, and thus I contend that quoting from legal precedents is irrelevant in this instance, and that Greenleaf's testimony, with the utmost respect for his legal competence, should carry little weight. To my knowledge, courts do not accept written testimony where the author's knowledge of the contents cannot be satisfactorily verified, and the authorship itself of the document version, as presented, cannot be verified. Such is the case here.

What, then, are we to conclude about the witness of Luke, and in the context of this study, how we should view his claims of prophecy fulfillment? Whilst he may have had some knowledge of Judaism, it was likely Hellenic Judaism in the Diaspora, and any familiarity he would have had with the Scriptures, would have been of the Greek versions.

John

As with the other Gospels, the authorship of that attributed to John, one of the original twelve Apostles, and *the one whom Jesus loved*, is much disputed. This Gospel is identified by Christianity as having the "highest Christology", which may be paraphrased, perhaps unkindly, as having the greatest degree of theological development. It contains a significant number of events, sayings, and themes, which are not found in the Synoptics. However, I do not intend to enter the debate on authorship, other than to note from an evidentiary perspective, that the writings of this witness may not be as reliable as others claim. The Gospel is in Greek, written within an Hellenic culture, and as I have discovered by comparing the relevant texts, his Old Testament quotations are from a version of the Greek, not the Hebrew Scriptures. As that is our primary focus here, the author's source adds further doubt to the accuracy of prophecy fulfillments.

Simon Greenleaf's testimony, concerning the witness of John, contains some debatable assertions. He states: "he had the privilege of being present in his [the high priest's] palace at the examination of his Master, and of introducing also Peter, his friend … he was present at several scenes … and at the agony of our Saviour in the Garden of Gethsemane."[13] The Synoptics do not place John at Jesus' trial, only Peter. According to Matthew (26:58), "Peter followed him (Jesus) at a distance to the high priest's courtyard. And he went in and sat with the servants to see the end." Mark 14:66 agrees, noting "below in the courtyard" - archaeological evidence has verified that the courtyard was below the high priest's chambers, and quite separate, so that servants and others there present could not overhear proceedings. Luke 22:55 has the servants kindling "a fire in the midst of the courtyard" with Peter present, corroborating the narratives of Matthew and Mark.

John (18:15-16) tells a different story, "And Simon Peter followed Jesus, and so did another disciple. Now that disciple was known to the high priest, and went with Jesus into the courtyard of the high priest. But Peter stood at the door outside. Then the other disciple, who was known to the high priest, went out and spoke to her who kept the door, and brought Peter in." Even if we were to accept this narrative as the true version of events, all we can know is that the disciples went into the courtyard, not the high priest's chambers, and thus could not have been witness to the trial: archaeological evidence confirms this. Why the Gospel fails to identify this "other disciple" is a mystery, even suggesting that the Apostle John was not the author of the account. From an evidentiary perspective, such an anonymous presence, without corroboration, would not be accepted. Thus, Simon Greenleaf's testimony concerning the authorship of the Gospel of John carries no weight.

I would also question the relationship of John and the High Priest – something is not quite right here. Traditionally, the High Priest was a descendant of Aaron, of the tribe of Levi, but the priesthood had long ago lost their spiritual and moral authority to the Pharisees. In their endeavour to control Judah, without overtly interfering with the religion of the Jews, the role of High Priest became a Roman appointment. According to one commentator:

"More important was the fact that the Romans now actually appointed and dismissed High Priests at will. Valerius Gratus, the Procurator immediately before Pontius Pilate, deposed and appointed four High Priests, His last appointment was Caiaphas, the High Priest who was concerned in the arrest of Jesus."[14]

We have a degree of corroboration of this high turnover of High Priests in John's Gospel: "Caiaphas who was high priest **that year**" (John 18:14) [emphasis mine]. By all accounts, Caiaphas was not at all a good chap, so why would John and he be friends, to the extent that "he had the privilege of being present in his [the high priest's] palace at the examination of his Master, and of introducing also Peter, his friend"? Was it not Caiaphas who declared: "that it is expedient for us that one man should die for the people, and not that the whole nation should perish" (John 11:50)? Would John, the Apostle whom Jesus loved, have been ok with that? That the same author wrote both verses 11:50 and 18:15-16, suggests to me that the Apostle John could not be that author, unless he did not know of the event recorded in verse 11:50 until after the event in 18:15. Why would he still be friends with a High Priest, a Roman political appointee, who had pronounced a death sentence on his Master?

As to John being present at Jesus' agony in Gethsemane, we know from the Gospel accounts that the Apostles were not "present", but nearby and asleep! Three times Jesus went back, and remonstrated with them for their lack of support. Greenleaf is disingenuous in his support of John's Gospel, and has obviously accepted John's account, and perhaps the opinions of others, to interpret that John *had the privilege of being present in the high priest's palace*. As none of the Synoptics corroborate John's account, and John cannot be cross-examined on his witness, we cannot give any weight to Greenleaf's assertions, especially as he misrepresented John's presence during Jesus' claimed agony in the garden. As no-one witnessed this event, even the event itself would not be considered plausible evidence of Jesus' plight.

Greenleaf notes: "In the absence of circumstances which generate suspicion, every witness is to be presumed credible, until the contrary is shown: the burden of impeaching his credibility lying on the objector."[15] As the objector, I accept that burden, and believe that I have provided the evidence, that generates sufficient suspicion to question the credibility of John's witness. On archaeological evidence, and the evidence of the Gospels, John could not have been an eye-witness to the events referred to above.

Finally, John 21:24 lends support to the argument that the Gospel, as we have it, was not entirely of the hand of the Apostle John: "This is the disciple who testifies of these things, and wrote these things; and we know that his testimony is true." A poorly constructed sentence, or a Freudian slip?

Paul

See next chapter.

Peter

This is an extract from Wikipedia, and I commend a thorough reading of that entry:

> "The author of the First Epistle of Peter identifies himself in the opening verse as "Peter, an apostle of Jesus", and the view that the epistle was written by St. Peter is attested to by a number of Church Fathers: Irenaeus (140–203), Tertullian (150–222), Clement of Alexandria (155–215) and Origen of Alexandria (185–253). If Polycarp, who was martyred in 156, and Papias alluded to this letter, then it must have been written before the mid-2nd century. However, the Muratorian Canon of *c.* 170 did not contain this, and a number of other General epistles, suggesting they were not yet being read in the Western churches. Unlike the Second Epistle of Peter, the authorship of which was debated in antiquity (see also Antilegomena), there was little debate about Peter's authorship of The First Epistle of Peter until the advent of biblical criticism in the 18th century. Assuming the letter is authentic and written by Peter, who was martyred *c.* 64, the date of this epistle is probably between 60 and 64."[16]

I cannot know better than the opinions of scholars who have studied these works, but there does seem to be some doubt over the authorship. That notwithstanding, of interest is that I find no sense of the Trinity in these two letters. There is only one sentence that could be interpreted as Jesus being God, depending on how the verse is rendered and/or punctuated. Consider these variations on 2 Peter 1:1,

a.   "through the righteousness of God and our Savior Jesus Christ" (American King James).

b.   "Through the righteousness of God and our Savior Jesus Christ" (King James 2000).

c.   "through the righteousness of our God and of our Saviour Jesus Christ" (Weymouth New Testament).

d.   "the righteousness of our God and Saviour Jesus Christ" (Jubilee Bible 2000).

e.   "by the righteousness of our God and Savior, Jesus Christ" (New American Standard 1977).

f.   "the righteousness of our God and Savior, Jesus the Messiah" (ISV).

g.   "by the righteousness of our God and Savior, Jesus Christ" (NKJV); and

h.   "by the righteousness of our God, and Savior Jesus Christ" (my adding punctuation to the NKJV).

Notice how having a comma after "God", or the addition of "our" before Savior (Weymouth New Testament), subtly alters the meaning to identify two entities, not one, as the later examples do. Given that Koine Greek does not have punctuation and lost many of the nuances available in Classical Greek, translators are left to interpret as they choose. Can we know what the author of 2 Peter meant? Maybe, maybe not, but we do know what some translators meant, but as they were probably guided by their theological presuppositions, they may have been wrong.

Quoting from James Dunn's, *Jesus, Law, and the Gospels*:

> "No one with knowledge of Israel's Scriptures could fail to recognise here a major motif of Israel's theology and understanding of how God conducts his dealings with his creation and his chosen people (Israel). For 'righteousness' in Hebrew thought refers to the *meeting*

of obligations which arise out of a relationship. So the phrase 'the righteousness of God' refers to *God's enactment of the obligation he had accepted in so creating the world and in so choosing Israel to be his people.* His righteousness was his obligation he had taken upon himself to sustain and save both creation and people. For Jews the phrase had an inescapably covenant connotation: it denotes God's *saving* righteousness – which is why the Hebrew term *tsedhaqah* (righteousness) is often better translated 'deliverance' or 'vindication', as we see in modern translations."[17] [italics in original]

Slightly off topic, perhaps, but the natural corollary to God's righteousness being the *enactment of his obligations to his creation*, is that our righteousness is the *enactment of our obligation to God.* What is that? As the Hebrew Scriptures define it, and as Jesus stated as being the first commandment: we are to love God. How do we do that? By keeping His commandments (John 14:15, 21, 23-24, 15:10, 1 John 2:3-5, 5:3, 2 John 1:6).

James

Again, there is debate on the authorship, but the majority opinion seems to favour James, the brother of Jesus. Whether the authorship is significant, in the context of evidence, is dependent upon the content. Does it corroborate other writings, and if so, in what way? We shall examine that in its proper place. We need also consider the date of writing. If, as many scholars contend, this letter preceded all others, including those of Paul, we have a glimpse of the earliest Christianity in Jerusalem, one which differs from the Pauline Christianity in significant ways. Try reading James, absent of Paul: what does it tell you?

Summary

We must not forget that up until the death of Jesus, this was an entirely Jewish story. The Law was explained to the Children of Israel, and committed for safekeeping to the people who settled in Judaea, to be later known as the Jews. The Prophets were anointed by God to call His people to repentance, and the words they wrote were mostly in Hebrew, some in Aramaic, but always from an Hebraic mindset. Throughout the centuries, from Moses to Jesus, the Jewish Sages debated the meaning of both the Law and Prophets, and whilst not as dogmatic as Christians in their pronouncements, their wisdom was conveyed, generation to generation. They were ever conscious of their duty, to hear the Word of God, and to teach it to their children (Deuteronomy 11:13-20).

If we are to understand the Prophets, we must learn as Jesus did, from the Jewish Sages, eschewing the unreliable Greek. That is what I have done, and I hope to be able to convince you to do similarly.

REFERENCES:

1. Dunn, James D.G., *Jesus, Paul, and the Gospels*, Wm. B. Eerdmans Publishing Co., Grand Rapids, MI, 2011, p. 28
2. *Ibid*, p. 34
3. Burkett, Delbert, *An introduction to the New Testament and the origins of Christianity*, Cambridge University Press, 2002.
4. Greenleaf, Simon, *The Testimony of the Evangelists*, Kregel Classics, Grand Rapids, MI, 1995, p. 19 (stating: The authorities on this subject are collected in Horne, Introduction 4.234-238, part 2 chap. 2 Sec. 2.)
5. https://en.wikipedia.org/wiki/Gospel_of_Matthew
6. Tabor, James D., *Paul and Jesus: How the Apostle Transformed Christianity*, Simon & Schuster Paperbacks, New York, NY, 2012, p. 4
7. https://www.blueletterbible.org/study/intros/luke.cfm
8. MacCoby, Hyam, *Revolution in Judaea: Jesus & The Jewish Resistance*, Ocean Books, London, UK, 1973, pp. 53-54
9. Dewey, Arthur J., *The Authentic Letters of Paul*, Polebridge Press, Salem, OR, 2010, p. 166
10. Greenleaf, Ibid, p. 25
11. *Ibid*, quoting 2 *Phil.* on Ev. p. 95 (9th edition), which as best as I can determine, is a reference to a Stanford Law Library publication on legal precedence, related to acceptable evidence.
12. *Ibid*
13. *Ibid*, p. 26
14. MacCoby, *Ibid*, p. 56
15. Greenleaf, Ibid, p. 29, quoting 1 *Stark.* on Evidence. pp.16, 480, 521.
16. https://en.wikipedia.org/wiki/Authorship_of_the_Petrine_epistles
17. Dunn, James D.G., *Jesus, Paul, and the Gospels*, p. 155

CHAPTER 2-6

UNDERSTANDING PAUL

"Paul's triumph is almost wholly a literary victory, reinforced by an emerging theological orthodoxy backed by Roman political power after the time of the emperor Constantine (A.D. 306-37)"[1]
~ James D. Tabor, *Paul and Jesus* ~

I beg your indulgence for what is about to be, a rather lengthy discussion on Paul, self-styled apostle to the Gentiles. Numerous books have been written, providing evidence and the opinions of many, that Paul was the true founder of the Christianity that developed in Rome, a religion that had little to do with the teachings of Jesus, or with the path that he and his disciples had walked. That is a bitter pill to swallow for most Christians – they are followers not of the authentic Jesus, but a Jesus of Paul's imagination. Earlier we spoke of the need to evaluate evidence in terms of authenticity and authority, and as Paul has been, without doubt, the most influential writer of the New Testament, we need to take a very close look at his credentials. Was he whom he claimed himself to be, or more truly, was he as one scholar described him: *"a Hellenistic adventurer whose acquaintance with Judaism was recent and shallow"*[2].

If a witness is found to be not credible, then we should reject all his written evidence, and that of those who wrote in his name. A New Testament without Paul, and without the later editing that was undertaken to support his position, would be a very different testament indeed.

New Testament scholar, James Dunn, wrote:

> "There were three absolutely crucial figures in the first generation of Christianity – Peter, Paul, and James the brother of Jesus[3]. Of these, Paul probably played the most significant role in shaping Christianity. Prior to Paul what we now call 'Christianity' was no more than a messianic sect within first-century Judaism, or better, within Second Temple Judaism – 'the sect of the Nazarenes' (Acts 24:5), the followers of 'the Way' (that is, presumably, the way shown by Jesus)[4]. Without Paul this messianic sect might have remained a renewal movement with Second Temple Judaism and never become anything more than that … Paul's mission and the teaching transmitted through his letters did more than anything else to transform embryonic Christianity from a messianic sect, quite at home within Second Temple Judaism, into a religion hospitable to the Greeks, increasingly Gentile in composition, and less and less comfortable with the kind of Judaism which was to survive the ruinous failure of the two Jewish revolts against Rome (66-73, 132-135 CE)."[5]

This for me, a Christian at the time of reading, was a watershed moment. Here was a scholar saying what I had come to recognise. The Nazarenes were followers of The Way shown by Jesus, a path within Judaism, yet the Church of Rome condemned these followers as heretics, and outlawed the practices of Judaism. For example, even Ignatius of Antioch wrote: "It is outrageous to utter the name of Jesus Christ and live in Judaism!" SAINT Ignatius: really? How then could Christianity be a religion founded on the teachings and example of Jesus? There could be but one answer: it was not, and was itself heretical. Christianity was a religion founded on a strange compromise of Jesus' teachings, Paul's preaching,

Hellenic thought patterns, accommodation with the pagans, and whatever else expediency demanded.

Almost from the beginnings of my studies of the New Testament, I sensed something very wrong, sufficient for me to describe Christian theology as incoherent. Christian interpretation of some events in the Gospels appeared forced, unnatural, and even illogical, and seemed to derive from an attempt to read Paul back into them. Without such eisegesis, Paul told a different story to the *earthly* Jesus, even though Paul claimed to have been instructed by the *risen* Jesus, which raised my suspicions: God was not like that. To my mind, Paul was the most enigmatic of the writers of the New Testament. Who was he really? Numerous scholars have commented that the portrayal of Paul, by Luke, in the Book of Acts, versus how Paul portrays himself in his own writings, evidence significant differences. One aspect of which I am very sceptical, is that Paul was truly a trained Pharisee – his writings and theology give no sign of that being so, especially as I find his theology to be at variance with Judaism of the time, and his interpretation of Jesus' teachings differ from that of many scholars, and of course, mine as well.

Many scholars contend that Paul was the primary influencer of the direction that Christianity took in the decades after the death of Jesus, but James Tabor opined:

> "I go much further. Not only do I believe Paul should be seen as the 'founder' of the Christianity that we know today, rather than Jesus and his original apostles, but I argue he made a decisive bitter break with those first apostles, promoting and preaching views they found to be utterly reprehensible. And conversely, I think the evidence shows that James, the brother of Jesus and leader of the Jerusalem church, as well as Peter and the other apostles, held to a Jewish version of the Christian faith that faded away and was forgotten due to the total triumph of Paul's version of Christianity. Paul's own letters contain bitter sarcastic language directed even against the Jerusalem apostles. He puts forth a starkly different understanding of the message of Jesus – including a complete break from Judaism."[6]

I am not sure that "faded" is a word that I would choose to describe the demise of the Nazarenes: they were persecuted and declared as heretics. Another study offers that Luke, in writing Acts, attempted to smooth over these differences:

> "Why this recasting of Paul in Acts? What had changed by the time Luke composed the Acts of the Apostles? Westar's Acts Seminar has concluded that Acts best fits the historical context of the early second century battle between proto-orthodox and gnostic Christians over the legacy of Paul[7]. In this context, the author of Acts portrays Paul as an obedient Christian Pharisee and the hero of a unified and rapidly spreading religious movement over against Marcion's portrait of Paul as a radical who was hostile to the Hebrew scriptures and the world of the flesh, and who introduced an alien god that is distinct from the earthly creator of Genesis. Though the author of Acts likely knew the letters of Paul and bases some of his narratives on information Paul provides, he does not refer to Paul's letters directly and ignores the major themes in the letters in order to enlist Paul in the ranks of the proto-orthodox cause."[8]

These views of New Testament scholars are significant: they should cause seekers after truth to re-assess the veracity of traditional Christian teachings. Without the Book of Acts, the teachings of Paul would be seen in complete contrast to those of Jesus in the Gospels, but Luke's efforts *to enlist Paul in the ranks of the proto-orthodox cause* have resulted in the Gospels being interpreted in a Pauline sense.

Aside from Paul Dunn's *"Jesus, Paul and the Gospels"*[9], and *"Jesus, Paul and the Law"*[10], which describe many differences between the teachings of Jesus and Paul, other authors have not just noted these discrepancies, but have expressed concern at how Paul has misled Christianity, labelling him as a heretic. For example, J.D. Sheppard has published a short booklet entitled: *"Jesus vs. Paul: Christianity's Greatest Lies Exposed"*[11], and a longer study by James D. Tabor, *"Paul and Jesus: How the Apostle Transformed Christianity"*[12], is of particular interest. I would urge you to study *"The Mythmaker: Paul and the Invention of Christianity"*[13] by Talmudic scholar, Hyam MacCoby, which questions, as I do, whether Paul was truly a Pharisee. We need to study this issue in detail, as it holds the key to understanding how, and why, Pauline Christianity developed as it did. Both of these latter two books have provided most of the arguments in what follows. These, and many similar studies, highlight how far Paul's teachings departed from the Messianic Judaism of the Nazarenes. I do not entirely agree with all the conclusions in these books, as I believe that in some cases, Paul's words have been taken out of context or otherwise misinterpreted, but then again, more than likely, I am the one guilty of misinterpretation. That aside, there is ample evidence that there is no theological continuity from Jesus to the Catholic Church established in Rome

Here are some examples from Sheppard's booklet:

> "Yahushua said he didn't come to abolish the law, but to fulfill it (Matthew 5:17). However, Paul said that Yahushua ended the law (Romans 10:4), and the law was nailed to the cross (Colossians 2:14), and that it is done away with (Ephesians 2:15). But Yahushua said: *'And it is easier for heaven and earth to pass, than one tittle of the law to fail'* (Luke 16:17). If you are still reading this, then I am going to guess that heaven and earth have not passed."[14]

> "'For whosoever shall call upon the name of the Lord shall be saved.' (Romans 10:13) That sure sounds very nice. The only thing I have to do is believe? That's easy! But wait a minute, does Satan not also 'believe' in the Lord? 'Thou believest that there is one God; thous doest well: the devils also believe, and tremble.' (James 2:19) Obviously, there must be more to it than a mere 'belief'."[15]

I find these a tad simplistic, but nevertheless, they illustrate the thinking.

Paul, a Pharisee?

"A Hebrew of the Hebrews, concerning the law, a Pharisee."
(Philippians 3:5)

Paul wanted people to believe that he was a Pharisee, but the question arises: Why would he do so if he truly was not? Why do we find so much in Luke that Paul himself never mentions? Paul never wrote that he came from Tarsus, and it was only Luke who said that Paul was the son of a Pharisee, trained at the feet of Gamaliel in Jerusalem (Acts 22:3). We have sound reasons for rejecting that claim. Consider: "Gamaliel was himself a Pharisee in the tradition of the great Hillel. A generation before Christ there were two great rabbis, Hillel and Shammai. While this is a generalization, many of the rabbinic debates of the first century come down to the opinion of Hillel versus Shammai. With respect to Hellenism, Hillel was more open to Hellenism than Shammai and was therefore more open to cooperation with the Romans."[16] In saying that *Hillel was more open to Hellenism*, the author was not suggesting that Hillel was open to the Greek scriptures. In modern terms, Shammai could be described as ultra-orthodox, and was adamant that only Jews, and those who had fully converted to Judaism (*Ger Tzedek*), could share in the world to come. Hillel was more liberal, and accepted that even Gentile God-fearers who abided by the Noahide laws (*Ger Toshav*) were also welcomed by God. Not everything associated in Hellenism was an afront to Hillel, whereas Shammai was totally opposed. Gamaliel did converse in Greek when necessary, but that was due to his position, and his necessity to converse with the Romans and other officials. A study of Hillel's rulings show that his openness to Hellenism was in respect of leniency regarding some aspects of the law, not to Hellenism itself.

Paul's writing provide little if any evidence that he understood the Hebrew Scriptures, and thus it is unlikely that he did study under Gamaliel, a scholar of Bet Hillel, who eschewed the Greek Scriptures. When asked when one should study the Greek, Hillel replied that one should study in Hebrew during the day, and at night, and at other times they could study in Greek. I strongly doubt that Gamaliel would have rejected that advice of his grandfather, from one so esteemed as Hillel the Elder. The suggestion then is that Paul might have been a Pharisee of the more radical Shammaite party. It is possible, given that Paul is said to have persecuted the early followers of Jesus, such actions being consistent with a hard-line approach to Torah observance. The approach of the Pharisees of Bet Hillel were more tolerant, as Gamaliel demonstrated (Acts 5:34-39). However, we have no independent witness of the Shammaites ever persecuting Nazarenes.

There is also an issue of timing, and here I have encountered two opinions, based on historical evidence that Gamaliel taught between 22-55 CE. The first is: if Paul studied under Gamaliel, beginning say, at age 16, the earliest he could have been born would be circa 6 CE, yet many Christian scholars place his birth some ten years earlier, at the same time as Jesus, no later than 4 BCE. This would make him too old to have studied under Gamaliel. Some Christian texts date Paul's birth to circa 5 CE, which is where the second opinion comes into play. According to a Jewish opinion: *"Gamaliel was a teacher of advanced studies, not a teacher of children"*[17]. Paul would have needed to have been an adult to have studied under Gamaliel, which would accord with an earlier year of birth, but raises another important question: Where did Paul receive his rabbinic training to qualify to undertake advanced studies under Gamaliel? The conundrum:

a. If Paul was born circa 5 CE as Christianity attests, he was too young to study under Gamaliel, if Gamaliel was a teacher of advanced studies, but the right age if Gamaliel taught primary studies; and

b. If Paul was born much earlier, circa 5 BCE, he was the right age to study under Gamaliel, if Gamaliel was a teacher of advanced studies, but we have no evidence of Paul having received the prerequisite rabbinical studies.

I am forced to wonder whether, with inadequate knowledge of Gamaliel's position as the most influential scholar of *Bet Hillel* of his time, the Christian belief in a later year of birth is an attempt to align with Luke's account in Acts? There is no way of knowing, but on the preponderance of evidence, including Luke's propensity to embellish his narratives in support of Paul, we have every reason to doubt the claims of Pharisaic involvement. But we can go further. Acts 5 relates the story of Peter being brought before the Sanhedrin, and Gamaliel, "a teacher of the law held in high respect by all the people" urged restraint (Acts 5:34-39), with all the council agreeing that Peter be released. If that be so, why would the very same council, with Gamaliel present, accede to persecuting Christians in Jerusalem? One scholar asks, quite reasonably:

"What kind of Pharisee was Paul, if he took an attitude towards the early Christians which, on the evidence of the same book of Acts, was untypical of the Pharisees? And how is it that this book of Acts is so inconsistent within itself that it describes Paul as violently opposed to Christianity because of his deep attachment to Pharisaism, and yet also describes the Pharisees as being friendly towards the early Christians, standing up for them and saving lives?"[18]

The answer might surprise you, as it did me, although it should have been obvious. Firstly, some more background. When the High Priest and the Sadducees arrested Peter and other Apostles (Acts 5:17), they "were furious and plotted to kill them" (v. 5:33). Gamaliel, perhaps the most highly respected Pharisee of his time, and the alleged teacher of Paul, stood up and advised against persecuting these followers of Jesus, counselling as follows:

"Men of Israel, take heed to yourselves what you intend to do regarding these men. For some time ago, Theudas rose up, claiming to be somebody. A number of men, about four hundred, joined him. He was slain, and all who obeyed him were scattered and came to nothing. After this man, Judas of Galilee rose up in the days of the census, and drew away many people after him. He also perished, and all who obeyed him were dispersed. And now I say to you, keep away from these men and let them alone; for if this plan or this work is of men, it will come to nothing; but if it is of God, you cannot overthrow it – lest you even be found to fight against God." (Acts 5:35-39)

Christian apologetics often take Gamaliel's words to mean that he suspected that Jesus was the promised Messiah, the preaching of Peter and the others being "of God". However, the political atmosphere of the time would suggest otherwise. Theudas rebelled against Rome, circa 44-46 CE, his followers believing him to be the Messiah. According to Josephus[19], Judas of Galilee, along with a Pharisee named Zadok, founded the sect of the Zealots with the intention of overthrowing Rome. As with Theudas, and later Simon bar Kokhba, his followers considered him the Messiah because, as they understood the Prophets, he would restore Israel to its former glory. As these efforts had come to nought, as these men were not supported by God. Gamaliel was advising similarly regarding the Nazarenes: if God was with them, they would succeed, but if not, they would fail, and fail they eventually did. Gamaliel was urging restraint to avoid any unnecessary violence. Further on we read: "many of the saints I shut up in prison, having received authority from the chief priests; and when they were put to death, I cast my vote against them." (Acts 26:10) The obvious question is: Why would Paul, a supposed disciple of Gamaliel, vote to kill Christians when Gamaliel had already convinced the Sanhedrin that they should not? Admittedly, the Sanhedrin did command "that they should not speak in the name of Jesus" (Acts 5:40), a command that Peter and the others ignored, but I remain unconvinced that if Paul was a true disciple of Gamaliel, that he would ignore the wisdom of his rabbi. Either that, or Paul was not whom Luke claimed him to be.

This does, however, suggest a resolution to a long-standing question of mine: Why would a member of the Pharisees, a sect known to be merciful and tolerant, approach the high priest of the time, a Roman appointee and a Sadducee to boot, for permission to persecute Christians in Tarsus, when he already was busy persecuting them in Judea and Galilee: why the urgency? The obvious answer was that Paul was not a Pharisee, but quite possibly a Sadducee. This raises another question, the final one to be dealt with here: Why would Paul, possibly a Sadducee, masquerade as a Pharisee?

> "It should be noted (in advance of a full discussion of the subject) that modern scholarship has shown that, at this time, the Pharisees were held in high repute throughout the Roman and Parthian empires as a dedicated group who upheld religious ideals in the face of tyranny, supported leniency and mercy in the application of laws, and championed the rights of the poor against the oppression of the rich."[20]

Let me add a little more background. The Sadducees were the upper, rich, priestly class at the time; the Pharisees were a sect of lay teachers.

After the sacking of Jerusalem in 70 CE, and the flight to Yavneh, where modern Judaism was born, the teachings of Shammai were rejected in favour of those of Hillel, and there were numerous incidents of leading rabbis negotiating with the Romans. Hyam MacCoby continued: "Paul's desire to be thought of as a person of Pharisee upbringing should thus be understood in the light of the actual reputation of the Pharisees in Paul's lifetime; Paul was claiming a high honour, which would much enhance his status in the eyes of his correspondents."[21] Remember that Christianity has long sought to demonise the Pharisees, misinterpreting the disputes between Jesus and some Judean Pharisees as a refutation of Judaism, when in truth, it was nothing but an internal dispute over details, a practice in Judaism that continues to this day.

Returning to the Book of Acts: "This I also did in Jerusalem, and many of the saints I shut up in prison, having received authority from the chief priests; and when they were put to death, I cast my vote against them." (Acts 26:10) We will return to the issue of Paul persecuting "Christians" in a bit later, but for now, think about the likelihood of a Pharisee asking permission of the chief priest, a Sadducee, when it was already stated in the case of Peter that such was contrary to Pharisaic doctrine. But then: "I cast my vote against them". Only members of the Sanhedrin had the authority to vote, so here Luke, on behalf of Paul, is implying that Paul was a member of the Sanhedrin! There is considerably more evidence to review, but let me cut to the bottom line with this opinion:

> "Why, therefore, is Paul always so concerned to stress that he came from a Pharisee background? A great many motives can be discerned, but there is one that needs to be singled out here: the desire to stress the alleged continuity between Judaism and Pauline Christianity. Paul wishes to say that whereas, when he was a Pharisee, he mistakenly regarded the early Christians as heretics who had departed from true Judaism, after his conversion he took the opposite view, that Christianity was the true Judaism. All his training as a Pharisee, he wishes to say – all his study of scripture and tradition – really leads to the acceptance of **Jesus as the Messiah prophesied in the Old Testament**. So when Paul declares his Pharisee past, he is not merely proclaiming his own

sins – 'See how I have changed, from being a Pharisee persecutor to being a devoted follower of Jesus!' – he is also proclaiming his credentials – 'If someone as learned as I can believe that **Jesus was the fulfillment of Torah**, who is there fearless enough to disagree?'"[22] [emphasis mine]

I have emphasised the above words to return to the focus of my study: prophecy fulfillment. Very much like many consultants and presenters that I have encountered during my business life, who invariably started with their academic qualifications and other credentials to establish credibility with their audience, Paul, ably and abetted by Luke, sought by usurping the identity of a Pharisee, to establish his credentials as an authority on Scripture. His reason? Paul could not be seen as starting a new religion in the name of Jesus, as no Jew with any knowledge of the teachings of Jesus would accept him. As explained here:

> "So Paul's claim to expert Pharisee learning is relevant to a very important and central issue – whether Christianity, in the form given to it by Paul, is really continuous with Judaism, but deriving, in so far as it has an historical background, from pagan myths of dying and resurrected gods and Gnostic myths of heavenly-descended redeemers. Did Paul truly stand in the Jewish tradition, or was he a person of basically Hellenistic religious type, but seeking to give a colouring of Judaism to a salvation cult that was really opposed to everything that Judaism stood for?"[23]

Hyam MacCoby, questions the narrative of Paul persecuting Christians, based on the words of Gamaliel in Acts 5:34-39. He comments:

> "The historical importance of this passage has not been adequately appreciated by scholars. It contradicts completely some of the leading assumptions of the Gospels and indeed of Acts. On the principle that passages which go against the grain of the narrative should be given particular attention, we should regard this passage as giving us a valuable glimpse into the real historical situation of the time. The first point to notice is that Gamaliel does not

in any way condemn the apostles as heretics or rebels against the Jewish religion. He regards them instead as members of a Messianic movement *directed against Rome.* The proof of this is the comparison he makes between them and other movements of the time … Josephus confirms that both movements mentioned were Messianic movements against Rome; neither of them was in any way directed against the Jewish religion."[24] (italics in original)

This doesn't shed light on Paul's movements, but it does raise serious questions about the authenticity of Luke's account. MacCoby continues:

"If Jesus, as the Gospels represent, had actually been a rebel against the Jewish religion, declaring the Torah abrogated and himself able to cancel its provisions at will, why did Gamaliel the Pharisee, leader of a religious party whose loyalty to the Torah was renowned, have nothing to say about this when giving his opinion about what should be done to Jesus' immediate followers? If the Pharisees had really been Jesus' deadly enemies during his lifetime, why should their leader suddenly forget all about this shortly after Jesus' death and give his support to the very men with whom Jesus had consorted, including Peter, his right-hand man?"[25]

I reiterate my question: why would Paul persecute the rank and file, and not cut off the head of the serpent, if that is what he thought it was? If Paul was truly trained at the feet of Gamaliel, how was it that he had a view of the "Christians" entirely opposite to that of Gamaliel? On the evidence, I cannot accept Luke's narrative as true, although just which part of the contradictory stories IS true, is difficult to determine. From other sources, I am inclined to accept the Gamaliel account over the persecution account.

Some years before encountering MacCoby's book, I had come to a parallel conclusion: that Christianity had so departed from the Jewish, Torah-observant Jesus, that I could not believe that it was a religion of which Jesus, or God, would approve. I published my evidence in *"Once a Christian: How the Bible Convinced Me to Walk Away"*[26]. Recent further studies have confirmed the righteousness of that decision.

Who Were the Pharisees?

To begin this short review, the Pharisees were not the sanctimonious, self-righteous, hypocrites as portrayed in the Gospels as we have them: that was the propaganda of Paul. On the contrary, it was the Sadducees who were most deserving of that acrimony. The Pharisees, trained rabbis, were the lay teachers of the Law, just as Jesus acknowledged (Matthew 23:2). They were not a religious group *per se*, as we understand orders of priests, brothers, and nuns today, but men from a wide variety of backgrounds, all contributing their views on how the law should be applied in specific circumstances of their times. Judaism was not a religion of dogma, but of open and respectful discussion (mostly), where determinations were made very much in the way they should be made in a democracy, based on a consensus of those participating in the elected governing body. Once a decision was made, all were expected to abide by it.

Whereas Christianity claims to be always right in matters of doctrine and theology, with the Catholic Church going so far as to proclaim that the Pope is inerrant when he speaks *ex Cathedra* (which he has rarely done), Judaism accepts that it can be wrong, but that God having given Torah as a framework for the Law, he also gave mankind free will in determining just how it should be interpreted. They "acknowledged a human element in religious teaching - an element for which no divine inspiration could be claimed – they acknowledged also the right to disagreement or difference of opinion."[25] There is a wonderful story which will give you a sense of this:

> "Among the Pharisees, a majority vote was regarded with such seriousness that there was a legend amongst them that God had once attempted to intervene to reverse one of these majority decisions (by telling them through a 'voice from Heaven' that the minority opinion was correct), but had been told that He was out of order, since He Himself had given the sages the power of decision by vote, and He Himself had said in His Torah that 'it [the Torah] is not in Heaven' (Deuteronomy 30:12), by which the sages understood that the Torah was to be applied and administered by the processes of human intellect, not by miracles or divine

intervention. God's reaction to this, the legend continues, was to laugh, and say, 'My children have defeated Me!'"[28]

If you have the chance to read the Talmud, you will note that it bears no resemblance to Christian works, for it contains the often contradictory opinions of multiple sages, as do the Jewish bible commentaries that I have studied. When we read of Jesus' interactions with the Pharisees, we should see them in the light of Jesus himself being a Pharisee, doing what Pharisees always did – disputing with each other on issues of law. The acrimony that we sense in some of these events, I would offer, results from later editing. I would remind readers of the earlier comment by Hyam MacCoby, that Gamaliel, the chief Pharisee of the time, and a highly respected member of the Sanhedrin, held no animosity toward Peter, and expressed no theological opposition to their preaching. If that be so, on what basis can it be claimed that the Judean Pharisees were enemies of Jesus?

I cannot stress enough, the distance between the Pharisees and Sadducees, the latter being the rich, priestly class, and the former everyday Jews of their time, but of special learning. The Sadducees had no say on the religious law; the high priest was a Roman appointee who served at the pleasure of the Roman governor (remember how John's Gospel put it: "Caiaphas who was high priest **that year**" (John 18:13) [emphasis mine]? As politicians are wont to do, even to this day, they seek to protect their own interests, and the Sadducees of Second Temple Judaism were no different. The primary dispute between the two groups concerned the validity of the Oral Law, with sects such as the Karaites continuing the dispute to this day. The Sadducees were beholden to the authority of the priests, whilst the Pharisees, those truly learned in the Law, were led by personalities, as we note from the variety of people regarded as the Sages. Trying to keep this short, the Pharisees were the guardians of Mosaic Law, whilst the Sadducees, through the high priest and the Sanhedrin, were the guardians of secular law.

You will recall from the Gospels that when Jesus was brought before the high priest, Pilate, and even Herod according to one account, there was no religious condemnation by the Pharisees. The reason is simple: Jesus was being tried according to secular law, for crimes against the State, in this case, claiming to be king, as Pilate inscribed on the cross (John 19:19). I would like to write more on this subject, but I do not want to wander too far from my primary theme. Hopefully, I have whetted your appetite sufficiently for you to pursue your own research into the subject. If you do, I am confident that you will conclude as I have done: that Paul was not a Pharisee, and the Pharisees were not the evil people as portrayed in Christian narratives.

Hebrew or Hellenist?

The more I study the writings of Paul, the more I become convinced that unlike Jesus and possibly his earliest disciples, Paul had an Hellenic mindset, rather than Hebraic, further evidence, albeit circumstantial, that he could not have been a trained Pharisee. He quoted from a version of the Septuagint, then extant, rather than the Hebrew Scriptures, and quoted the works of Greek poets.

In a chapter entitled, *"Were Paul's Teachings Divinely Inspired?"*[29], Rabbi Tovia commented: "there is no existing evidence that he [Paul] possessed more than a perfunctory knowledge of the Hebrew language. He virtually never used it, and when he used the Greek text he misquoted and misappropriated it."[30]. You may wonder, in the context of conversing with Hellenic Gentiles: What was wrong with using the Greek text? I believe that I answered that in Chapter 2-1. Secondly, even before becoming acquainted with Rabbi Tovia, I noticed how often Paul misquoted Scripture, and here let me give just one example, one that has led Christians ministers to develop the most bizarre doctrines. In Romans 3:10 we read: "As it is written, 'There is none righteous'" etc., supposedly quoting Psalm 14 and 53, and Ecclesiastes 7:20. He has omitted the opening words of the Psalms: *"The fool says in his heart, there is no God"*, thus removing a significant qualifier and entirely changing the meaning. Ecclesiastes makes the point that none are entirely righteous, for all have sinned, but how many Christians have understood this as it was intended by the author? Clearly not the ministers who preach that we are all evil and are deserving of eternal punishment! You may not have encountered such people, but believe me, they are out there, and in great numbers.

Rabbi Tovia continued:

> "In fact, Paul more accurately quoted Greek philosophers, playwrights and poets than the Jewish prophets. Moreover, if, as Christians insist, the writings of Paul were divinely inspired and Heaven-breathed, why would God quote from godless, Greek writers? Would God quote Voltaire or Russell?
>
> For example, Paul quoted Plato in 1 Cor 13:12; the Greek poets Epimenides of Crete, who worshipped Zeus; and Aratus of Cilicia in Acts 17:28. In 1 Cor 15:33, he quoted the comedy playwright Menander, who frequently used vulgarities in his plays. Would God quote from an off-colour playwright who oftentimes used the filthy phrase 'Sh... -eaters' in his plays?"[31]

Somewhat taken aback by these accusations, I decided to check them out for myself.

"For now we see in a mirror, dimly, but then face to face. Now I know in part, but then I shall know just as I also am known." (1 Cor 13:12. NKJV) Digging into the ancient literature of Plato, we find this: "For there is no light of justice or temperance or any of the higher ideas which are precious to souls in the early copies of them: they are seen through a glass dimly; and there are few who, going to the images, behold them in the realities, and these only with difficulty." (Phaedrus 250b)

"Do not be deceived: Evil company corrupts good habits." (1 Cor 15:33) This quote is from an ancient comedy play called *Thais*, written by Menander. He wrote plays, comedies and moral maxims, the latter collated into an anthology of moral teachings entitled, *"Meanders One Verse Maxims"*. Here are some examples:

- "He who labors diligently need never despair, for all things are accomplished by diligence and labor."
- "The chief beginning of evil is goodness in excess."
- "I call a fig a fig, a spade a spade."
- "Riches cover a multitude of woes."
- "Let the die be cast", quoted by Julius Cesar when he went to war.

I do wonder whether this is the source of the word, *meandering*, but I digress (or meander). Many philosophers, throughout the ages, have provided moral sayings, as did Confucius, Buddha, and so forth, but a question remains.

Here is another text: "*But we all, with unveiled face, beholding as in a mirror the glory of the Lord, are being transformed into the same image from glory to glory, just as by the Spirit of the Lord.*" (2 Cor 3:18) Compare that with: "And he who employs aright these memories is ever being initiated into perfect mysteries and along becomes perfect." (Phaedrus 249c) The wording is different, but the meaning is the same: the idea of aligning yourself to the divine allows you to attain that which is impossible without such aligning.

In Acts 17, Paul is addressing the men of Athens, and in verse 28 he says: "*for in Him we live and move and have our being, as also some of your own poets have said, 'For we are also His offspring'*". Note: Greek poets. I see nothing wrong in Paul quoting Greek poets to Greeks, but I am a little curious about Paul being so familiar with Greek poetry: what does that say about the way he thought? To what degree was Paul's theology influenced by Greek theology, especially as he considered it appropriate to equate Greek sayings with Jesus' Gospel.

Understand that I am not critical of Paul for his citing of Greek philosophers, playwrights and poets – how better to communicate with Greeks than by quoting the literature with which they were familiar? Thus, I do not entirely agree with Rabbi Tovia for his criticism – his is from an entirely Jewish-centric view. However, it does raise one or two questions. Firstly, how was it that Paul was so intimately familiar with Greek literature that he could so readily quote it? How was it that a Pharisee, the son of a Pharisee (Acts 23:6), well-schooled in Jewish Law, would have spent time studying Greek literature? Paul is said to have been born in Tarsus circa 5 CE, making him about the same age as Jesus. We do not know precisely when Jesus was born, opinions varying from 7 BCE to 2 BCE, but scholarly consensus has him starting his public ministry in 27-29 CE, and his death after 3 years at 30-32 CE. Thus, if we accept this dating, Paul was 25-27 years of age when Jesus died.

Why would God choose one so young? Why not, you may ask, for Jesus himself was of the same age when he began his public ministry?

In the culture of the times, the teachings of people of that age were not generally accepted: in many ways, they were still considered students of their rabbi. Whilst Paul may well have been able to convince the Gentiles, he would have had difficulty debating with the elders of Judaism.

Surveying the literature, I get a somewhat confused view of Paul's early life. Most accounts have him born in Tarsus, Cilicia, Anatolia, in what is now south-central Turkey near the border with Syria. It was an important city on the trade route, a Roman province heavily influenced by the Greeks, hence Paul's Roman citizenship. According to one source, Paul's claim that he was "a Hebrew born of Hebrews" (Phil. 3:5), "shows that his parents, though living in Diaspora among the Greeks, were far from being assimilationist Jews, but remained faithful to the language and customs of Palestinian Jewry."[32] According to some stories, Paul learned his trade as a tent-maker before being sent to study "at the feet" of Gamaliel in Jerusalem at the age of thirteen. Gamaliel was a highly respected, senior member of the Great Sanhedrin, and is also mentioned in Jewish literature. Of his teaching, only one saying is preserved in the Talmud: it enjoins the duties of study and scrupulous observance of religious ordinances. Gamaliel's renown is summed up in these words recorded in the Talmud: "When Rabban Gamaliel the Elder died, regard for the Torah [Jewish Law] ceased, and purity and piety died." Thus, one would expect that anyone who studied at the feet of Gamaliel would have the same view of Torah as King David (Psalm 113). Paul was not like that at all.

But again, we are back to the question: did Gamaliel teach children, or adults already well versed in Torah? I am inclined to accept the view of Jewish scholars, rather than Christian, and accept that as a highly respected sage, he would have left basic education to others.

But here is the question: If Paul did study under some other rabbi, was it perhaps for just a short period, or did he complete the full discipleship? The Hebrew word for "disciple" is *talmid*, and here note the similarity to the word *Talmud*. A disciple in those times was someone who dedicated his life to learning everything that his master (rabbi) had to teach. He memorised his teacher's explanations, interpretations, and exegesis of Scripture. He memorised the stories, parables, illustrations, and anecdotes his teacher told. He learned to practice Torah by imitating his teacher and incorporating his manner of observance into his own. Disciples kept the

Torah the way their teacher kept it. A disciple endeavoured to become like his teacher in every way, and it became a permanent imprint in their character. *"A disciple is not above his teacher, but everyone when he is fully trained will be like his teacher."* (Luke 6:40).

Was Paul fully trained?

We can conclude from this that Paul, had he completed his discipleship, would have been a devout follower of Judaism, just as he claimed. However, as we have already noted, Paul taught Greek philosophy, as a Greek would do, yet *the teaching of philosophy, that is, Greek thought, was shunned.* Similarly, the study of literature by the Pharisees was concentrated on Hebrew, with scant attention paid to Greek. Paul, and Luke, have played us as fools, for Paul was no more a Pharisee than Luke was – his Greekness, if I can use that word, gives him away.

My conclusions, are to a degree, confirmed by an article in the conservative Christian journal, Touchstone:

> "Second, there was Paul's inherited Hellenic culture, primarily manifest in his habit of citing the Bible in the Septuagint version. Greek was his native language. Though he pursued his rabbinic studies in Jerusalem, Paul had been raised in the pagan city of Tarsus, where he learned to be at home just about anywhere in the Mediterranean world, particularly in such cultural centres as Damascus, Antioch, Ephesus, and Athens."[33]

So, Paul, raised in a pagan, Hellenic culture, with Greek as his native language, is supposed to have pursued rabbinic studies in Jerusalem, where Hebrew was the sacred language of Scripture. Highly unlikely, I would have thought. How would Paul have conversed and debated with his teachers in Hebrew? How, and where, would he have learned the rabbinic method of argumentation? Rabbinic teaching in those times was conducted very differently to modern teaching methods.

As earlier contended, there is evidence that Paul was not who he, or Luke, claimed him to be. He wrote many allusions to the Old Testament, but only ever referred to the Septuagint, not the Hebrew Tanakh. For example, James Dunn notes: "Paul's Damascus experience must have led him immediately to Dan. 7:13 because he saw a heavenly figure 'like a son of man' just as Daniel did."[34] However, whilst the Greek Septuagint has "one like a son of man", most Hebrew versions, and I am given to believe, the original Hebrew version has: "one like a man". Thus, Dunn, perhaps unknowingly, is arguing against Paul being a Pharisee, one who learned (in Hebrew) at the feet of Gamaliel in Jerusalem. Gamaliel, as a disciple of Hillel, considered the Greek writings to be blasphemy, as did Judean Pharisees.

A Jew accustomed to the Hebrew scriptures would have considered those Greek citations erroneous, blasphemous even. Since Paul shows no evidence of knowing the Hebrew scriptures, there must be considerable doubt as to whether he was really educated in Jerusalem, by Gamaliel, or any other Jewish rabbi. We also have Paul's familiarity with Greek literature, and his quoting from Greek poets, which further deepens my suspicions about who he really was, and whether he lied to the churches he founded, attempting to establish his credibility.

However, I could be wrong, to some extent at least, if in truth, Paul was not born in Tarsus, but in Galilee, and thus not a Roman citizen:

> "Whether Paul was born in Tarsus, one has to doubt because Jerome, the fourth-century Christian writer, knew a different tradition. He says that Paul's parents were from Gischala, in Galilee, a Jewish town about twenty-five miles north of Nazareth, and that Paul was born there[35]. According to Jerome, when revolts broke out throughout Galilee following the death of Herod the Great in 4 B.C., Paul and his parents were rounded up and sent to Tarsus in Cilicia as part of a massive exile of the Jewish population by the Romans to rid the area of further potential trouble. Since Jerome certainly knew Paul's claim, according to the book of Acts, to have been born in Tarsus, it is very unlikely he would have contradicted that source without good evidence. Jerome's account also provides us with the only indication we have of Paul's approximate age. Like Jesus, he would have had to have been born before 4 B.C., though how many years earlier we cannot say. This fits rather nicely with Paul's statement in one of his last letters, to a Christian named Philemon, written around A.D. 60, where he refers to himself as an 'old man' (Greek *presbytes*)[36]."[37]

Well, that puts the cat amongst the pigeons. If Jerome was right, then Paul was unlikely to have been a Roman citizen, and the narratives in Acts where this is invoked, may well be entirely false. Likewise, the Christian claim that Paul was born circa 5 CE is refuted by the witness of Jerome. I cannot know – I must rely on the scholarly works of others. There are a lot of details about Paul which are not adding up.

If you are not already overwhelmed by this confusion, I have put these issues in a different context in an earlier work, *"Once A Christian"*[38]. For more on Paul, I would recommend *"Pauline Christianity"*[39], and the other works referenced in this chapter. Of particular interest is the following, extracted from here[40].

> "The quest for the historical Paul began almost simultaneously, inaugurated by the German scholar Ferdinand Christian Baur (1792-1860). Baur put his finger squarely on the problem: There are *four* different "Pauls" in the New Testament, not one, and each is quite distinct from the others. New Testament scholars today are generally agreed on this point. Thirteen of the New Testament's twenty-seven documents are letters with Paul's name as the author, and a fourteenth, the book of Acts, is mainly devoted to the story of Paul's life and career—making up over half the total text. The problem is, these fourteen texts fall into four distinct chronological tiers, giving us our four "Pauls":
>
> 1. *Authentic or Early Paul*: 1 Thessalonians, Galatians, 1 and 2 Corinthians, Romans, Philippians, and Philemon (50s-60s A.D.)
> 2. *Disputed Paul or Deutero-Pauline*: 2 Thessalonians, Ephesians, Colossians (80-100 A.D.)
> 3. *Pseudo–Paul or the Pastorals*: 1 and 2 Timothy, Titus (80-100 A.D.)
> 4. *Tendentious or Legendary Paul*: Acts of the Apostles (90-130 A.D.)
>
> Though scholars differ as to what historical use one might properly make of tiers 2, 3, or 4, there is almost universal agreement that a proper historical study of Paul should begin with the seven genuine letters, restricting one's analysis to what is most certainly coming

from Paul's own hand. This approach might sound restrictive but it is really the only proper way to begin. The Deutero-Pauline letters, and the Pastorals reflect a vocabulary, a development of ideas, and a social setting that belong to a later time. We are not getting Paul as he was, but Paul's name used to lend authority to the ideas of later authors who intend for readers to believe they come from Paul. In modern parlance we call such writings forgeries, but a more polite academic term is pseudonymous, meaning 'falsely named'."

As it has been for the historical Jesus, there has been a quest for the historical Paul over the past 175 years, by Christian, Jewish, and secular New Testament scholars. It is difficult to ignore a consensus across these three distinct groups.

Paul's Gospel

Even in my own early studies, I sensed that Paul's gospel was not the same as that of Jesus, most especially concerning Judaism and the Law. My initial reaction was that I had misunderstood Paul, and I sought to reconcile the two narratives. The further I progressed, the more convinced I became that they *were* different, especially when I noted Paul's attitude toward the original disciples chosen by Jesus. This raised the obvious question: did Paul really experience Jesus on the road to Damascus? The Christianity of the Roman church departed from Judaism in significant ways, and here I found Paul's gospel similarly departing from the teachings conveyed to the Apostles, at least in the mind of Paul.

What was going on?

In the *Introduction* to "*The Authentic Letters of Paul*"[41], we read:

"The letter of Paul delivered a distinct voice and universal vision to the first century Mediterranean world. From the outset they were complex transmissions of a complicated man addressing a variety of issues for some fledgling communities of Jesus the Anointed. Unfortunately, the distinctive sound of Paul's letters has been distorted by the cacophony of later voices that have attempted to speak in his name. Indeed, modern readers of Paul are often unsympathetic to the

'Paul' filtered by the tradition. *The Authentic Letters of Paul* attempts
to being the voiceprint of Paul back to the conversation.

Readers will find that the Paul of the letters is not synonymous
with the Lutheran Paul, nor the Augustinian Paul. He is neither
the professional theologian, nor the ecclesial misogynist. Rather,
the Paul who emerges is an extraordinarily zealous Pharisaic Jew
who experienced a paradigm shift so profound that it transformed
the way he saw the world and all in it. This man is a thinker and
rhetorician, a visionary and prophet, whose experience of God
was so profound that he reimagined the conditions of existence."

I have included this opinion to evidence that not everyone in the
theological ranks agree on just who Paul really was. He is as enigmatic as
Jesus himself. On the evidence, I do not believe that Paul was a Pharisaic
Jew, although he was certainly zealous. He was definitely a thinker, a
rhetorician, and a visionary, but whether a prophet of God is open to
debate: I do not believe that he was, because he led his followers away from
Judaism and the teachings of the Hebrew Scriptures. That the quotation
above states that Paul *reimagined the conditions of existence* affirms my belief
that that is just what he did – he reimagined all by himself.

Earlier we noted Luke's efforts *to enlist Paul in the ranks of the proto-
orthodox cause*, but why was that necessary if Paul was doing no more than
conveying the message of Jesus to the Gentiles? Certainly, there needed
to be additional elements for the non-Jews, but none of these should
contradict earlier elements from Jesus if, as Paul claimed: "For by one Spirit
we were all baptized into one body, whether Jews or Greeks, whether slaves
or free" (1 Cor 12:13)? Why did Paul appear to consider himself a greater
apostle than the others, even though he claimed otherwise?

In his essay on how the New Testament authors used Old Testament
verses as proof-texts for their theology, Albert Sundberg wrote:

"Our earliest evidences of Christianity were written against a
background of Jewish rejection as an accomplished fact. Only
the Gentile mission is treated seriously in the New Testament;
the Jewish mission is perfunctory, to fulfill the prediction of

rejection. But certainly the earliest Christian activity must have been preaching to Jewish hearers. Probably in the first instance this preaching did not presuppose rejection. The Jewish-Christian community that existed in Jerusalem until A.D. 68-70 probably did not regard themselves as a lost cause. If Acts (15:1-29) may be trusted, the Jewish-Christian community was cautious in its attitude toward the Gentile mission. And, yet, our earliest sources regard the Jewish rejection as a *fait accompli*, according to the Scriptures; and there are doubly attested Old Testament proof-texts attesting thereto. The conclusion that a process of development preceded this doubly attested tradition is inescapable."[42]

The author also noted: "Careful examination of doubly cited passages indicates that there is no uniformity of Old Testament interpretation" (p. 191). However, which *doubly attested Old Testament proof-texts would these be*? The author does not say, but I assume firstly, Psalm 118:22 relating to the cornerstone being rejected (Matthew 21:42, Luke 20:17, Acts 4:11). The second I am not so sure of, but likely Isaiah 53:3, Isaiah 53:5, Zechariah 12:10, Zechariah 13:7, and perhaps even Genesis 3:15. We will later discuss these in the appropriate New Testament citations. My point here though is the statement: "Only the Gentile mission is treated seriously in the New Testament." The first mission statement by Jesus was: "I was not sent except to the lost sheep of the house of Israel" (Matthew 15:24), so is it claimed that Jesus failed in that mission, and sent Paul off on an alternate mission to the Gentiles, one which was successful? Could Jesus be God, doing only what the Father told him to do, and yet fail? Is God that powerless? You see, this quote from Sundberg evidences that it truly was Paul who formed the new religion of Christianity, one which entirely rejected Judaism, because the Jews rejected Jesus. If "our earliest sources regard the Jewish rejection as a *fait accompli*", and thus "the Jewish mission is perfunctory", what was Jesus on about when he told his Apostles: "do not go into the way of the Gentiles" (Matthew 10:5)?

A Christian misinterpretation of Matthew 10:5 is to assert that "way" in this verse refers to the religious practices of the pagan Gentiles. Certainly, "the way of ..." often refers to behaviour, but it cannot in this context. The NKJV translation uses the preposition, *into*, which more likely refers to location, not behaviour. I would contend that this is the correct meaning, based on the next sentence which says: "do not enter a city". The next verse affirms it even more: "but go rather to the lost sheep of the house of Israel." If the context was truly *behaviour* and not *location*, then Jesus was saying that his disciples should emulate the behaviour of these lost sheep, which would be curious indeed. After all, Jesus earlier said in relation to eating with sinners, "Those who are well have no need of a physician, but those who are sick" (Matthew 9:12), meaning spiritually sick.

Some Scholarly Observations to Contemplate

A few more quotes on Paul, from the referenced book, *The Right Doctrine from the Wrong Texts?*, page numbers shown after the texts:

• "He tells the Corinthians that he wishes them to learn what this means: 'not beyond what is written.' Alas! If only I knew what it meant! The most ingenious theory is, of course, that the phrase is gloss, so that to ask what Paul meant by it is to chase a red herring ... But does Paul himself really stick to Scripture? Or can he in turn be accused of going beyond what is written? Does he not often use Scripture simply as a convenient peg on which to hang his arguments? Although he may frequently quote from Scripture, the interpretation he gives it often lies beyond the obvious meaning of the text. His somewhat artificial exegesis leaves one wondering whether there is anything which it would not be possible for him to argue on the basis of Scripture." (p. 280) This again, is where presupposition comes into play. If we believe that Paul was indeed, chosen by God to preach the gospel to the Gentiles, then we will look for reasons to justify why Paul used Scripture as he did. If, on the other hand, we have concluded that Paul was not whom he and Luke claimed he was, then we would be inclined to discount Paul's *artificial exegesis* of Scripture, and agree with Marcion's portrait of Paul[8] as a radical who was hostile to the Hebrew scriptures and the world of the flesh, and who introduced an alien god that is distinct from the earthly creator of Genesis. Thinking about this from the opposite perspective, with no presuppositions whatsoever, other than what is taught in the Hebrew Scriptures, what would we conclude about Paul from his writings alone?

- "If Paul uses the law to refute the law, is he not quite blatantly wishing to have his cake and eat it? Is he really following his own advice to 'keep to what is what is written', or is he twisting is meaning to make it mean whatever he wants?" (pp. 280-281)

- "Paul's metaphor – typically – becomes a mixed one … Paul has jumped from one image to another; put them together, and he is clearly in a mess, for while it is possible to speak metaphorically of the Spirit of God writing on men's hearts, it really is not much use trying to write on stone with ink!" (p. 281) In relation to mixed metaphors, one academic opined: "Thus, felicitous mixing is a natural by-product of the shifting logic of clauses in complex argumentation. In addition, I present a qualitative typology of how clustering metaphors interact in argumentation. It calls into question the view that conceptual metaphors are the coherence-maintaining device *par excellence*. While conceptual metaphors may create "internal binding" in ontologically coherent clusters, complementary "external binding" models are needed to explain the mixed clusters (and ultimately for a full explanation of all kinds of metaphor-based argumentation)."[43] In other words, we cannot be sure whether the author of mixed metaphors had a coherent train of thought, or was in truth confused. The issue here is understanding Paul's audience, and whether they would have been able to follow Paul's *complex argumentation*. As best as I can understand, his audience was not like that, and would have been confused, just as confessed in 2 Peter 3:16. So, Paul was either a brilliant orator and writer, who cared little about whether people understood him or not, or he himself was confused and struggling to articulate what was going on in his head.

- "We need to recognize that Paul has – typically – moved in the course of his argument from one interpretation of the Old Testament image to another … It is typical of Paul to explore an idea in this confusing but very rich way." (p. 283) Again we are back to presuppositions: was Paul truly exploring *an idea in this confusing but very rich way*, or did he have no firm idea of what he was talking about? If Paul was simply *exploring*, can it be said that his letters were the inerrant word of God? What was Paul's gospel if he was developing it as he went along, exploring the Scriptures, and the unreliable Greek scriptures at that, based on his obvious Hellenic mindset rather than Hebraic? Was that truly how God wanted His Word interpreted and communicated to the Gentiles?

- "In looking at this passage [Ed. chapters 3-4] in 2 Corinthians, we have noted several times that there are blatant contradictions and *non sequiturs* in Paul's argument. From our point of view, his exposition is inconsistent. His arguments do not stand up logically, and he juxtaposes conflicting images and interpretations of the biblical text. Yet I have no doubt whatever that from his point of view, Paul's argument seemed proper and acceptable." (p. 290) That Paul thought his arguments proper and acceptable is of no import in adjudicating the evidence. I believe my arguments to be proper and acceptable, otherwise I would not write what I do, but that is not evidence of their truth, just what I believe. On the other hand, I would contend that my arguments are not flawed with blatant contradictions, inconsistencies, conflicting images, interpretations, and *non sequiturs*, so on what basis does one evaluate my arguments against those of Paul?

- "For him it is axiomatic that the true meaning of Scripture has been hidden, and it is only now made plain in Christ ... What seemed to Paul to be the true interpretation often seems to us to be a bizarre reinterpretation." (p. 291) What if, in fact, Paul's interpretation was truly a *bizarre reinterpretation*? On what basis, or evidence, do we decide whether Paul had wandered off the reservation, or was truly divinely inspired in his reinterpretation?

I would point out that all of these quotations are from essays written by Christian New Testament scholars, not as it might appear, by authors opposed to Christianity. This is a complex issue, like so many others, and to do it justice, I have included a discussion on Paul's gospel in the section on the resurrection, for the two are inextricably linked. See Chapter 9-4. For alternative opinions on these issues, I would recommend this online article, "*Was Paul a True Apostle of Jesus Christ*"[44].

Summary

Continuing a commentary quoted at the beginning of this chapter:

> "Paul's literary victory rested upon three pillars: 1) the gospel of Mark, our earliest narrative of the career and death of Jesus, is heavily Pauline in its theological content; 2) the two-volume work of Luke-Acts vastly expand Mark's story to culminate with a final scene of Paul preaching his gospel in Rome; and 3) the six later letters written in Paul's name, but after Paul's lifetime offered a more domesticated Paul, which pleased the church and ensured the muting of his more radical message. (These six letters are Colossians, Ephesians, 2 Thessalonians, 1 and 2 Timothy, and Titus.)"[45]

Paul's literary victory. Why would it be a victory – victory over whom, or what? Who or what was the loser? Given that the Church of Rome sought to persecute the Nazarenes, and declare them heretics, I can only conclude that Paul was victorious over the original followers of Jesus, the *Followers of the Way.* If that be so, then it is the Church of Rome that is better described as heretical, at least insofar as the teachings of Jesus. Food for thought indeed.

I cannot be sure, but my suspicion is that Paul was either delusional, or someone simply seeking recognition and influence, or perhaps a combination. I am not alone in that thinking, for many New Testament scholars have offered a similar opinion. This is not the place for such a discussion, for we have ample literary evidence concerning our primary focus: prophecy fulfillment. We will have more to say about Paul's perspective, when we later discuss perhaps the most pivotal issue of all: the resurrection.

Lest I be hoist on my own petard, let me confess that the evidence against Paul's authenticity is mostly circumstantial. The other side of the coin is that the written evidence we have, of Paul's authenticity, is of questionable authority. But again, back to the context: prophecy fulfillment. If, as I believe, Paul was a fraud, then we can give his evidence no credence whatsoever. If later writings that we find in the Gospels, and the pseudo-Pauline Epistles, have been heavily influenced by Pauline Christianity, as many modern New Testament scholars attest, then their evidence should carry similar weight. That the Christianity that developed in Rome departed almost entirely from the theological foundations of Judaism, and the Nazarenes, with the Nazarenes branded as heretics, is further evidence to my mind that Christian claims of messianic prophecy fulfillment have been fabricated.

That is how I would evaluate the evidence.

REFERENCES:

1. Tabor, James D., *Paul and Jesus: How the Apostle Transformed Christianity*, Simon & Schuster Paperbacks, New York, NY, 2012, p. 7
2. MacCoby, Hyam, *The Mythmaker: Paul and the Invention of Christianity*, Barnes & Noble Books, San Francisco, CA, 1998, p. 18
3. Dunn, James D.G., *Christianity in the Making: Beginning from Jerusalem*, Wm. B. Eerdmans Publishing Co., Grand Rapids, MI, 2009, Chapters 6 & 7
4. Acts 9:2, 19:9, 19:23, 22:4, 24:14, 24:22
5. Dunn, James D.G., *Jesus, Paul, and the Gospels*, Wm. B. Eerdmans Publishing Co., Grand Rapids, MI, 2011, pp. 119-120
6. Tabor, *Ibid*, p. 6
7. Tyson, Joseph, *Marcion and Luke-Acts: A Defining Struggle*, University of South Carolina Press, USA, 2006
8. Dewey, Arthur J., *The Authentic Letters of Paul*, Polebridge Press, Salem, OR, 2010, p. 11
9. Dunn, *Ibid*
10. Dunn, James D.G., *Jesus, Paul and the Law*, Westminster / John Knox Press, Louisville, KY, 1990
11. Sheppard, J.D., *Jesus vs. Paul: Christianity's Greatest Lies Exposed*, Lamps With Oil, 2013
12. Tabor, *Ibid*
13. MacCoby, *Ibid*
14. Sheppard, *Ibid*, p. 11
15. *Ibid*, p. 14
16. https://readingacts.com/2011/09/07/paul-at-the-feet-of-gamaliel/
17. MacCoby, *Ibid*, p. 9
18. *Ibid*, p. 11
19. Flavius Josephus, *Antiquities* Book 18 Chapter 1
20. MacCoby, *Ibid*, p. 6

21. *Ibid*

22. *Ibid*, pp. 11-12

23. *Ibid*, p. 13

24. *Ibid*, p. 52

25. *Ibid*, p. 53

26. Talbot, Wayne, *Once a Christian*: How the Bible Convinced Me to Walk Away, Xlibris, Bloomington, IN, 2017

27. MacCoby, *Ibid*, p. 20

28. *Ibid*, p. 21, quoting the Babylonian Talmud, Bava Metzi'a, 59b.

29. Singer, Rabbi Tovia. *Let's Get Biblical* – Expanded Edition Volumes 1&2, Outreach Judaism, Jerusalem, Israel, 2015

30. Singer, *Ibid*, Vol. 1, p. 362

31. *Ibid*

32. F.F. Bruce, "Paul the Apostle", in *The International Standard Bible Encyclopedia. Vol. 3: K-P*, ed. by. G. Bromiley (Eerdmans, 1995), pages 709-710

33. Reardon, Patrick Henry, *As It Is Written: The World of Paul's Mind*, Touchstone, Jan/Feb 2018, p. 64

34. Dunn, *Jesus, Paul, and the Law*, p. 94, quoting S. Kim, *The Origin of Paul's Gospel*, Tubingen, 1981, p. 257

35. Jerome, *De Virus Illustribus* (PL 23, 646)

36. Murphy-O'Connor, *Jerome, Paul: A Critical Life*, Oxford University Press, Oxford, UK, 1997, pp. 1-5

37. Tabor, *Ibid*, p. 233

38. Talbot, *Ibid*, Chapter 7-3: Paul – Hero or Heretic

39. Ziesler, John, *Pauline Christianity*, Oxford University Press, Oxford, England, 1983

40. https://www.biblicalarchaeology.org/daily/people-cultures-in-the-bible/people-in-the-bible/the-quest-for-the-historical-paul/

41. http://www.jesuswordsonly.com/books/478-was-paul-a-true-apostle-of-jesus-christ.html

42. Beale, G.K., *The Right Doctrine from the Wrong Texts? Essays on the Use of the Old Testament in the New*, Baker Academic, Grand Rapids, MI, 1994, pp. 192-193

43. https://www.sciencedirect.com/science/article/pii/S0378216609001222

44. Dewey, Arthur J., *The Authentic Letters of Paul*, Polebridge Press, Salem, OR, 2010 (additional authors Roy W. Hoover, Lane C. McGaughy, Daryl D. Schmidt)

45. Tabor, *Ibid*, p. 7

CHAPTER 2-7

WHO WERE THE APOSTLES?

*"The ancient Apostles were common men, and
that was part of their credential."*
~ David A. Bednar (1952 -), Church of Jesus
Christ of the Latter-day Saints ~

From my perspective, that could be rationalisation after the event, but it prompts the question: Why would Jesus choose common men; why not scholars? Thus, it behoves us to appreciate the view of others. Google the question: "Why did Jesus choose fishermen as his immediate disciples", and you will find some interesting answers.

One commentary[1] opines that fishermen have the following traits, as required by their occupation: willingness to learn, patience, determination, instinct, and imagination. The commentary continues:

> "They were open to Jesus, who "baited" them with a simple invitation, "Come after me and I will make you fishers of men." Fishers of what!? Jesus spiked their curiosity, hence Andrew and

Peter left their equipment, followed by James and John. They wanted to know more. They were willing to follow Jesus in order to learn more. Their lives were transformed forever."

Another commentary[2] reads:

"We often lose our identity in our jobs, our titles, or position. But these things didn't appear to be significant to Jesus. The positions he does mention are those of common workers. They aren't the boss, the leader, or the priest. Just a corrupt tax collector and a few common fishermen. When Jesus looked for servants, he didn't only look at those who were climbing the corporate ladder, or those who were working in the synagogue. Jesus looked at common, hard-working people. He went to them; in their places of work. He didn't wait until they were done for the day and headed home, he met them in their workplace."

A third commentary[3] opines that fishermen have the following traits: patience, knowledge, compassion, and perspective. This is not the same set as in the first commentary, and I do wonder what knowledge fishermen could have had that would be of use to Jesus; what perspective they could have in relation to the prophesied Messiah; and why compassion would be unique to fishermen. Just one more:

"I believe Jesus chose mostly fisherman because they were everyday people just like you and me. They had the everyday cares of the world to deal with just like us. Jesus hung around with professionals too, CPAs and doctors, but mostly he hung with fisherman. They pretty much lived from day to day. If they didn't catch any fish, they didn't eat, so life could be stressful at times."[4]

I offer these four commentaries as evidence that the true answer to the question: Why did Jesus choose fishermen, is: *No-one knows!*

As we are dealing with opinions, I will offer this thought. Jesus chose them because of: (1), their lack of knowledge regarding Scripture and prophecy; and (2), likely gullibility on issues of a spiritual or theological nature. Ok, perhaps I am being unfair, particularly with the suggestion of gullibility, but let us address these points. On what basis would anyone suggest that Andrew, Peter, James, and John, would have anything but a rudimentary knowledge of the Hebrew Scriptures? No doubt they would have shared the Jewish anticipation of the *mashiach*, but what was it that they would have expected the *mashiach* to accomplish? We have ample evidence that the Jews of the Second Temple period expected the messiah to lead them to victory over the Romans, heralding the *End of Days* when God would redeem Israel. When Jesus invited them to follow him, and he would make them "fishers of men", what would they have understood in the context of their messianic expectations? Certainly they would have been curious, but to the extent that they would down tools, abandon their families, and head off into the unknown, to work at a calling hardly different to that offered by Doctor Who? Yes, Abraham did something similar, but he understood that he was called by God – not so these early followers of Jesus. When they accepted his invitation, did they have any inkling that he was the promised Messiah, let alone God? The Gospels give us no evidence that they did, but even if they did, they would not have expected to be invited to be *fishers of men*.

Put yourself in their position. There you are mending your nets, wondering what your next catch might be, if anything, wondering how you are going to feed you family, maybe your boat needs repairs, and along comes a stranger who says: "Come with me, and I will make you fishers of men". If you have seen the look Hawkeye exchanges with his mates in "M*A*S*H", that is what I would expect of the fishermen. You might contend that they were inspired by the Holy Spirit to accept the invitation of Jesus, but curiously, none of the opinions offered above mention that.

The first commentator expressed the view that fishermen back then, were not a lot different to fishermen of today. I have no reason to disagree. However, I have known professional fishermen, and yes, have watched some of those television series featuring fishermen in extremely harsh conditions. Of one thing I am certain: they are hard-headed, pragmatic people, highly unlikely to immediately abandon their livelihood on some mysterious promise. Fishers of men? Yeah, right, I can support myself and my family in that occupation! How much are you willing to pay? Again, put yourself in their position: What would convince you to respond as they are said to have responded? Is there any evidence that they were motivated by whatever is in *your* mind on the issue? If it is on your bucket list, wander Mediterranean seaports and observe the local fishermen: What do you notice about them? Do they seem the type of people who would jump to their feet on an invitation to be "fishers of men"?

Now back to the Scriptures.

What do we know of the Prophets, those men called by God to speak on His behalf? Do we have evidence that they were knowledgeable of the Scriptures? Were they conversant with Torah, and the Covenant agreed at Sinai? What characterised their response to their calling? In what way were they similar to, or dissimilar from, those chosen by Jesus? Why would God choose to start afresh, rather than build on what He had already conveyed via the Prophets, and had instructed His people to record in the Hebrew Scriptures? Why did Jesus spend time with Rabbis, learning the Scriptures, and what was God's purpose in having the Scriptures written?

A Christian friend, with whom I discuss such matters, is intent on asserting that God's revelations have been progressive, pointing to the inter-testamental (or deuterocanonical) period: the gap between the time covered by the Hebrew Bible, and that by the Christian New Testament. It covers about four hundred years, spanning the end of the ministry of Malachi (c. 420 BCE) to the appearance of John the Baptist in the early 1st century CE, almost the same duration as the Second Temple period (530 BCE to 70 CE). In principle, I entirely agree that God's revelations have been progressive over the centuries, as He has led mankind on the path of His Plan. However, I would offer that the Christian interpretation of the progress from the Hebrew Scriptures, to the message of Jesus, is one of *regression* and *abnegation*, not progression.

Curiously, Islam teaches that the Quran was written in stone before the world began, but then to justify the contrary teachings found therein, the doctrine of *abrogation* is introduced – it is said that God overrules some of His revelations by later revelations. The issue is complex, and I find some Islamic explanations unsatisfactory, for some verses have been retained while their meaning is superseded, while other verses have been removed from the Quran, but their meaning retained in teachings. Christianity offers the same justification for the abrogation of much of what was taught to the Children of Israel.

Quite simply, I do not believe that such is the path of an omniscient God whose plan was established before the world began, as Christianity teaches (1 Peter 1:20, Revelation 13:8).

Summary

Much more could be written on the subject of why Jesus chose the Apostles whom he did, but all such commentaries are based on speculation. All that I have read start with the presupposition that his choice favoured his mission, and the spread of the Gospel throughout the then known world. This sounds plausible, but then raises these questions:

1. What was Jesus' understanding of his mission in those early days?
2. What was the essence of his gospel at that time?
3. Was his choice really the wisest he could have made, considering that he was not the *mashiach* the Jews expected?
4. Why would anyone, Jew or Gentile, take the word of a bunch of fishermen, who in all likelihood, were poorly educated and quite possibly, illiterate?
5. Did Jesus not foresee the difficulty these men would have had, if they encountered trained rabbis in their travels?

Hence the essence of my doubts.

In Part 8, we review scholarly opinions on why and how the New Testament authors used the Old Testament in the ways that they did. Opinions vary, but all appear to presuppose that these ancient authors were scholarly, and well versed in rabbinic thinking and knowledge of the Scriptures. Compare that with the opinions expressed above. Clearly, we are faced with diametrically opposed opinions, which suggests to me that these opinions are more in the manner of hypotheses designed to support a theological view. Truth is seldom found that way.

Christianity has developed doctrine and theology over two millennia, with thousands of books written on Systematic Theology and related subjects. Even today, the debate continues. If the message of Jesus was so simple that even fishermen could understand, and convey to others, why has Christianity made it so complex? If the message really was that complex, then Jesus made a very poor choice of disciples. Why did Jesus choose disciples with little or no training by rabbis? If he intended to demonstrate that he was fulfilling the Law and the Prophets, why choose disciples who had so little understanding? From a pragmatic perspective, if you want to convince people of your message, it is common to preach to people who have no prior understanding: that way, you will not be debated. But debate is how Judaism has been taught to generations, getting students (disciples) to think and understand for themselves. That was not the path that Jesus took. Yes, Jesus did teach by example, and by signs and wonders, but as a matter of intellectual integrity, given all that God had revealed up until that time, I find it very suspicious that God would anoint agents, very unlike His earlier Prophets, who were incapable of assimilating a new message in the context of the old. If you want to start afresh, by all means choose those who have no loyalty to what they already know, but as with all progressive education, start with what your students already know, and build on that. Why would God choose otherwise?

I cannot know, but as my presuppositions are unlike those of Christian commentators, my interpretation of these events inevitably varies accordingly.

Another Aside

An error that I often encounter in Christian literature, is that Jesus was entirely opposed to the Pharisees, and that they were completely wrong in their teachings. This thought developed in the early church in Rome, to the extent that Christianity chose to abandon Torah, the Sabbath, and all God-ordained commemorations. If you research why this happened, you will learn that it has no basis in the teachings of Jesus. I would highly recommend *"From Sabbath to Sunday"*[5] by Samuele Bacchiocchi as a starting point, bearing in mind that this study was published by The Pontifical Gregorian University Press in Rome, with the imprimatur (approval) of the Catholic Church. It is difficult to doubt the truthfulness of such a book, given that the Chairman of the Church History Department, Vincenzo Monachino, S.J., noted in the Preface: "The abandonment of the Sabbath and the adoption of Sunday as the

Lord's Day, are the result of an interplay of Christian, Jewish, and pagan religious factors."[6] The last part hardly sounds like something of which Jesus, or God, would have approved. I have published my own study along similar lines, *Defending God's Sabbath*[7].

The contention between Jesus and the Pharisees was an internal Jewish debate on the right way to observe Torah – nothing more. In essence, it was no different to the Protestant Reformation of the 16th century. Jesus' arguments were no more a repudiation of Judaism, than Martin Luther's dispute with the Catholic Church was a repudiation of Christianity. As Catholic scholar, Bernard Lee ventured, *"there is little likelihood that Jesus had any conscious intention of founding a new religious institution either superseding Judaism or alongside it."*[8] It was Paul who chose to turn his back on Judaism, and establish a new religion based on "my gospel" (Romans 2:16, 16:25), a superior announcement, one that he alone possessed, having received it directly from the risen Christ (Galatians 1:11-12).

Even if it can be demonstrated that Jesus did fulfill the messianic prophecies in the Hebrew Scriptures, there is indisputable evidence that the Christianity that developed in Rome departed significantly from the path followed by the early "Christians", the Nazarenes.

REFERENCES:

1. https://evangcatbr.org/2016/12/01/why-did-jesus-choose-fishermen/
2. https://www.theologyofwork.org/the-high-calling/blog/why-fisherman
3. http://creelsandreels.com/jesus-chose-fisherman/
4. https://steveprice.wordpress.com/2010/09/13/so-why-did-he-choose-fisherman/
5. Bacchiocchi, Samuel, *From Sabbath to Sunday: A Historical Investigation on the Rise of Sunday Observance in Early Christianity*, The Pontifical Gregorian University Press, Rome, Italy, 1977
6. *Ibid*, pp. 7-8
7. Talbot, Wayne, *Defending God's Sabbath: Obeying God's Commandment to Safeguard the Sabbath*, Peshat Books, Kelso, NSW, 2013
8. Lee, Bernard J., *The Galilean Jewishness of Jesus*, Paulist Press, Mahwah, NJ, 1988, p. 17

CHAPTER 2-8

BIBLE INERRANCY

*"The inerrancy of Scripture is an essential and
not optional doctrine for the church"*
~ Paige Patterson, President of Southwestern
Baptist Theological Seminary ~

If ever there was an indictment of the Christian approach to Scripture, this is it. There is not a shred of substantive evidence for this belief, yet it underpins Christian dogma. One cannot undertake an objective study of Scripture, of any version or translation, when as Norman Geisler, Co-founder, Southern Evangelical Seminary and Veritas Evangelical Seminary puts it: "the inerrancy of Scripture is the foundational doctrine in which all other doctrines rest". Another typical argument is offered by David Limbaugh, Attorney, Author, and Social Commentator: "Christian Biblical inerrancy was not only affirmed unambiguously by Jesus Christ"[1]. The irony here is that an attorney, someone supposedly familiar with the laws of evidence, completely ignores his own training when it comes to his approach to religion. The fallacy is evident, or at least should be: biblical inerrancy is true because Jesus unambiguously says so, and he must be right because biblical inerrancy is true. This is termed *begging the question*, or *affirming the consequence*, and from the mouth of an attorney, is shameful. As a reminder, our task here is to evaluate claims of prophecy fulfillment using the rules of evidence as in a court of law.

If Muslims, Buddhists, Hindus, and proponents of all manner of religious persuasions make the same claims for their writings, how are we to know which is true?

So, here let me declare my own belief and presupposition: neither the Hebrew Scriptures, nor the Christian New Testament, are inerrant, despite the many Christian claims to the contrary. Scriptural inerrancy is not a tenet of belief in Judaism, which makes the Christian belief ludicrous. It is almost as if one group writes a fictional account, and then a later reader insists that it is factual: whom would you believe? I am reminded of a comment by that much-respected Christian apologist, C.S. Lewis, regarding a series of essays that he published. A reviewer commented that Lewis obviously had very little interest in one particular discussion, whereas Lewis explained that in truth, that was the subject in which he had the most interest. I wish I could quote where I read that, but I have a copy of most of Lewis' books, and struggle to remember from which volume such memories derived. Nevertheless, the Hebrew Scriptures are not inerrant, as this description attests: "*The Hebrew Bible is not a book, but a whole literature comprising history, myth, lyric poetry, and impassioned ideology.*"[2] Myth is an entirely different genre of literature to the inerrant word of God.

I have previously published a detailed exposition on this subject, *Bible Inerrancy: Fact or Fiction*[3], but here I will just present one or two examples much discussed by scholars.

There are two issues that I would highlight:

1. The authorship, and thus the authority, as representing the Word of God; and

2. Our interpretation of extant texts, given our lack of understanding of the autographs, the language in which they were written, and their revisions over the centuries as the language of Scripture itself evolved.

Who wrote the five books of Genesis? In truth, nobody knows. Neither do we know when they were written, or in what version of whatever language in which they were written. This online resource[4] provides a useful overview of the script of the Genesis autograph. The point to note is that the use of significant characters (pictographs) severely limits the vocabulary of the language, especially compared to the alphabet that I am using here. Interpretation was conveyed orally, as the written language itself was insufficiently detailed to be read without guidance. Over time, as the Hebrew Scriptures were rewritten in more recent evolutions of the language, and despite the best intentions of the scribes, it cannot be guaranteed that the interpretation and preferred meanings were the same as those of the original author(s). The same has happened with the New Testament writings.

Some traditions have Moses writing Genesis, but recent scholarship has opined at least two authors. The internal evidence can be found, for example, by closely comparing Genesis 1 and 2. Traditionalists attempt to synthesise the two, just as Christian scholars attempt to synthesise the four Gospels, but all such attempts fail on multiple points. The more logical conclusion is that these two chapters represent two different perspectives on how the world came about, neither being entirely accurate as nobody really knew back then, just as we do not know today, and we have no evidence that God has revealed these secrets to anyone. These narratives were not written as factual history, but as attempts to give meaning to existence.

In Hebrew, Genesis is known as *bereishis*, translated as *in the beginning*, answering the question of when God did what He did. Scholar Dr. Joel M. Hoffman offers that a better translation of the first verse might be: "It was in the beginning that God created", or "Let's talk about when God created heaven and earth. It was in the beginning."[5] The intent of the text is not to specify the *what* of creation, but the *when* and the *why*. The respected Jewish Sage, Rashi, also offers alternate translations / interpretations, such as "When God began to create". Approaching Genesis from that perspective, we can see that the Young Earth Creationists have drawn conclusions based on more modern reasoning, and even the arguments against evolution, of some form at least, lose their foundations. Dr. Hoffman's book explains the logic behind this.

An objective reading of Genesis 1 and 2 evidences contradictions which cannot be ignored. The same can be said of the contradictory narratives concerning Noah's Ark, and how David killed Goliath. Theological presuppositions put aside, the conclusion is that these are separate narratives of the same events, seen from different perspectives, none necessarily being entirely accurate.

Does God accept wilful ignorance?

If you have decided that despite the evidence, that whatever version of the bible that you have in your hands is the inerrant word of God, do you really expect that such is acceptable to God – that you have no interest in pursuing His Truth? Only you can decide on this issue.

REFERENCES:

1. http://defendinginerrancy.com/inerrancy-quotes/
2. MacCoby, Hyam, *Revolution in Judaea: Jesus & The Jewish Resistance*, Ocean Books, London, UK, 1973, p. 64
3. Talbot, Wayne, *Bible Inerrancy: Fact or Fiction? The Inerrancy of God's Word versus the Fallibility of Human Interpretation*, Peshat Books, Kelso, NSW, 2012
4. http://www.hebrew4christians.com/Grammar/Unit_One/History/history.html
5. Hoffman, Dr. Joel M., *The Bible Doesn't Say That: 40 Biblical Mistranslations, Misconceptions, and Other Misunderstandings*, Thomas Dunne Books, New York, NY, 2016, p. 11

PART 3

REVIEWING SOME COMMON THEMES

"God has always worked wonders through his prophets to increase the faith of His chosen people or to correct their disobedience."
~ Mother Mary Angelica (1923-2016), Catholic
American Franciscan Nun ~

I find it interesting how quotations can be understood differently, depending on one's presuppositions. As Mother Angelica was Catholic, then Christians would likely understand her to be referring to the prophecies concerning Jesus, and *His chosen people* being the followers of Jesus. If that be so, then they obviously missed the part about *correcting their disobedience*, but we can leave that for now. From an Old Testament perspective, however, and especially that of the Jews, *His chosen people* refers to the Children of Israel, and the role of the prophets was to increase their faith in Hashem (God), not Jesus. Time after time, the Prophets called upon the people to repent, i.e., to correct their disobedience. I cannot be sure of the good Mother

Angelica's intentions, when she said these words, but I would take them in the sense of the Hebrew Scriptures, not the Christian New Testament.

Because some sections of the Old Testament are fundamental to the Christian claims of prophecy fulfillment, I believe it useful to address these before we evaluate the New Testament quotation of them. That way, we can skip them when later often encountered. The four authors whom I will address individually are Isaiah, Daniel, Jeremiah, and David (Psalms).

Using the New King James Version (NKJV) of the Old Testament, there are 138 verses annotated with an *Outline Star* ☆, indicating that the text contains a prophecy to be fulfilled at a future time. I will use the Hebrew divisions of *Torah* (Law), *Neviim* (Prophets), and *Kesuvim* (Writings), to remain consonant with the Jewish traditions. Christians may not understand the significance of these divisions, but as it was Judaism that compiled the canon of the Hebrew Scriptures, I contend that it is incumbent upon us to honour both their understanding, and intent, rather than impose the Christian arrangement. I suspect that this rearrangement was not done innocently, but my point is that in the Jewish tradition, none of the authors in the Writings are considered Prophets, although some of their statements are considered prophetic. The question is: In what sense – general for Israel, or messianic? As the purpose of this study is to understand how well Jesus fulfilled *messianic* prophecies, it does seem logical to focus on prophetic statements in the *Prophets* primarily. If we find prophecy fulfillment from say, the Psalms, but not from the recognised Prophets, we would need to reconsider our analysis. One may claim that the Israelites did not understand their own literature, and communications with God, but that is not an hypothesis that I would accept.

Eleven (NKJV) flagged verses appear in Torah (Pentateuch), and of those, eight are in Genesis. Eighty-five are in the Prophets, and forty-two in the Writings. Given this total of 138, I wonder what the editors of the NKJV would make of the much larger numbers mentioned below? Whilst the total count is not of great significance to me, patterns are. 38% of the verses, that the NKJV claims are prophecies to be fulfilled by the Messiah, are not from the Prophets. The scattering of verses is also of concern to me. I find it implausible that God would have the Prophets sending messages to His people, concerning contemporary affairs, and every so often, throw in a non-sequitur concerning the Messiah. That is a pattern of human behaviour, not God's. Of course, it could be that the Prophets were manifesting their own humanity, when they put in the occasional aside to refer to the Messiah, and then returned to their main theme. I would not discount that possibility, but then I would need to question the degree of God's guidance. That said, we do find the prophets changing themes from the near term, to the *last days*, but no prophecy of the last days could have been fulfilled by Jesus in Second Temple times.

I am not confident that the count is that important, as overlap across the Prophets is evident, but when Christian apologists assert, e.g., "353 Prophecies Fulfilled in Jesus Christ"[1]; "What Are The Odds"[2], whilst at the same time acknowledging "According to the Hebrew requirement that a prophecy must have a 100 percent rate of accuracy, the true Messiah of Israel must fulfill them all or else he is not the Messiah"; and "400 Prophecies of Christ in the Old Testament"[3], it does appear that *quantity* has more significance than *quality* in the minds of some. I find it curious that depending on which resource you accept, there were 44, 59, 127, 353, 400, or whatever number one has determined. I would question what criteria the proponents chose to apply, if any. What does strike me is that there is far too little discrimination between *general* prophecy, and *messianic* prophecy, the latter being out primary concern in these pages.

For me, the issue is far too important, with such far-reaching consequences, to apply anything but the most stringent and rigorous criteria to this analysis. That, I shall do, and if I find anything less than the requisite *100 percent rate of accuracy*, I can only conclude that Jesus was not the prophesied Jewish *mashiach*.

REFERENCES:

1. http://www.accordingtothescriptures.org/prophecy/353prophecies.html
2. http://y-jesus.com/what-are-the-odds/
3. http://www.biblearchaeology.org/post/2012/07/27/400-Prophecies-of-Christ-in-the-Old-Testament.aspx

Chapter 3-1

ISAIAH 40 AND THE WILDERNESS

"The voice of one crying in the wilderness: Prepare the
way of the Lord; make His paths straight."
(Mark 1:3)

In the translation from the Hebrew, Isaiah 40:3 is rendered, in part: "A voice calls out, in the wilderness, clear the way of Hashem". Notice the positioning of the commas. We could remove one, with two options:

1. "A voice calls out in the wilderness, clear the way of Hashem"; or
2. "A voice call out, in the wilderness clear the way of Hashem".

Obviously, we have two different meanings, the first being the one that the evangelists appear to have chosen, and Christianity has accepted, but is that correct? The text continues: "make a straight path **in the desert**, a road for our God" [emphasis mine]. Given that qualification, I would contend that option (2) is correct, not (1). The voice is not in the wilderness (desert), the wilderness is where the path is to be made.

Whose voice is it?

In Isaiah 40:3, it is not explicitly stated, but it "proclaims that the return to Jerusalem is imminent and the road should be cleared and prepared. It is '*the way of Hashem*' that leads to His holy city'"[1], Jerusalem. Now the voice could be that of God Himself, or one of His angels speaking on His behalf, but the context is the return to Jerusalem after the period of exile has been completed (Isaiah 40:1).

In the Christian interpretation, it is the voice of John the Baptist calling people to repentance, which is almost antithetical to the message in Isaiah. In the Gospels of Mark, Luke, and John, it is John the Baptist who is in the wilderness, and only a misinterpretation of Isaiah 40:3 could cause the writers to make that link: in truth, the two circumstances do not match at all. Yes, there is a match with the prophecy in Malachi 3:1, but we will deal with that later. The point here is that the voice of John the Baptist, in the wilderness, is not fulfillment of an historical instruction to the Israelites, as narrated in Isaiah 40:3, to prepare a path in the wilderness, a path for God, concurrent with the return of the Jews to Jerusalem. The followers of John the Baptist may have thought so at the time, but history has proven them to be wrong.

Consider also that the following allegorical verses were not fulfilled: "*Every valley shall be exalted, and every mountain and hill brought low*", synonymous with "the first shall be last, and the last shall be first" (Matthew 20:16). Nor can it be claimed that "*the glory of the Lord shall be revealed, and all flesh shall see it together*". This prophecy is reminiscent of Jeremiah 31:34, "*for they all shall know Me. From the least of them to the greatest of them*", a prophecy regarding the End of Days.

Isaiah 40:3 is quoted, or annotated, on five separate occasions in the Gospels, as a prophecy fulfilled by John the Baptist.

None is correct.

REFERENCES:

1.   Scherman, Rabbi Nosson, *The Tanach*, Mesorah Publications, ArtScroll English Edition, Brooklyn, NY, 2011, p. 650

CHAPTER 3-2

ISAIAH 53 AND THE SUFFERING SERVANT

"And He said to me, thou art My servant, O Israel"
(Isaiah 49:3)

Isaiah 53 is one of the most disputed passages between Judaism and Christianity, and after having spent quite some time studying the arguments from both perspectives, I have come to accept the former over the latter. Christian apologetics quote Isaiah 53 as a prophecy of Jesus' first mission: *to bear the sins of many*, but I am convinced otherwise. If one reads from Isaiah 50 through 56, chapter 53 would be out of context if it was referring to Jesus, not Israel. Certainly, in isolation, chapter 53 could be read as referring to Jesus, but even then, the Christian interpretation can be self-contradictory.

Let us review an example.

Isaiah 53:9

I sometimes have difficulty knowing which translation of Scripture I should trust, especially where absent of explanation, the wording is obscure. This verse is just one example:

a.   "And I shall give the wicked for his burial, and the rich for his death. For lawlessness he did not commit, nor was treachery in his mouth" (Septuagint Old Testament).

b.   "And they made his grave with the wicked, but with the rich at his death, because he had done no violence, nor was any deceit in his mouth" (NKJV),

c.   "He submitted himself to his grave like wicked men; and the wealthy submitted to his executions, for committing no crime and with no deceit in his mouth" (TJB).

The primary question is this: who is the "he" referred to? Christianity says Jesus, but from the context of the surrounding chapters, "he" is most likely Israel, as we shall discuss in a moment. Would Isaiah change the context from one chapter to the next without explanation? Well, yes, he does so on more than one occasion, but I do not believe so in this case. Secondly, mention of the rich, or wealthy, is problematic in the context of Jesus' crucifixion, other than it contradicts what is said to have happened. According to the Gospels, Jesus died with the wicked (*two criminals*), and was buried with the rich (by *Joseph of Arimathea*), entirely contrary to the NKJV account which has him dying with the rich, and being buried with the wicked. Curious, is it not? The Jewish explanation of Isaiah 53:9 is that: "*his executions* indicates that many people were killed by various modes of murder. Ordinary Jews chose to die like common criminals, rather than renounce their faith; and wealthy Jews were killed for no reason other than to enable their wicked conquerors to confiscate their riches (*Radak*)."[1]

Whether that is true or not, it certainly makes a lot more sense than the self-contradictory explanation of Christian apologetics. Now, what about the explanatory cause? The NKJV renders this, in part, "he had done no violence", but I am confident that the money lenders in the Temple would disagree with that (John 2:15). The NT translators should have followed the Greek and Hebrew, referring to lawlessness or crime, not violence. This is another example of where Christian apologists fail to understand their own doctrine. If Jesus is God made flesh, then he always was, as understood by "the Father and I are one" (John 10:30). Thus, Jesus, as God, participated in the violence enacted by God when He caused the Flood, the ten plagues of Egypt, the drowning of the Egyptian army, and caused the earth to open up and swallow Korah and his followers who rebelled against Moses and Aaron (Numbers 16). You see, God is a God of violence when people rebel against Him, so if Jesus *had done no violence*, he was not one with God in Old Testament times. You can't have it both ways. I find it odd that Jesus as man was non-violent, but Jesus as God was.

The TJB commentary on the second part of this verse, "with no deceit in his mouth", refers us to Zephaniah 3:13 which reads: "The remnant of Israel shall do no unrighteousness and speak no lies, nor shall a deceitful tongue be found in their mouth". If you read from the beginning of Zephaniah Chapter 3, or even from just verse 8, you will understand that the prophecy concerns the *End of Days*, and the *remnant* of Israel are those who have remained faithful to God. In that context, in what sense does Jesus represent *the remnant of Israel*? Zephaniah prophesied in the synagogues during Josiah's reign, and was a contemporary of Jeremiah who prophesied in the public market place.

I would urge you to read Zephaniah in full, from beginning to end. Understand to whom he is referring, and why. Contemplate his urging of the people: "Improve yourselves and improve each other ... Seek Hashem, all you humble of the land who have fulfilled His law; seek righteousness, seek humility" (Zeph 2:1-3). Understand what he meant by: "they have robbed the Torah - Hashem, the Righteous One, is within it; He commits no corruption" (v. 3:4-5). God is within Torah: why would anyone reject it? And then the important verses:

> "And I will leave in your midst a humble and destitute people, and they will take shelter in the Name of Hashem. The remnant of Israel will not commit corruption [*Ed. as their forefathers had done*], they will not speak falsehood, and a deceitful tongue will not be found in their mouth; for they will graze and lie down

with none to make them afraid. Sing, O daughter of Zion! Sound the trumpet, O Israel! Be glad and exult with all your heart, O daughter of Jerusalem." (Zeph 3:12-14)

Does that sound like the times of Jesus, and shortly thereafter? You see, when one studies the context of these prophecies, and what was happening in the lives of the Israelites at the time, it is very difficult to equate those times, and sayings, with Jesus. Now, let us dig a little deeper into what Isaiah was prophesying.

Repentance, by itself, is accepted by God for deliberate sin – see, for example, Jonah 3:10. Without providing a long list of quotations, the books of Samuel, Psalms, Isaiah, Micah, Hosea, and Jeremiah all discourage sinners from relying on blood sacrifices to atone for their sins. See 2 Samuel 12:13, Psalm 51:16-19, Micah 6:6-8, 1 Kings 8:46-50, Deuteronomy 4:26-31, and 2 Chronicles 6:36-39 for a general overview of the connection between repentance and forgiveness. As discussed in the previous chapter, one of the most curious "misquotes" of the Gospels is using Isaiah 40:3 as a prophecy of John the Baptist. If John came to prepare the way of Jesus, who was to die for our sins, why would that be necessary when Isaiah 40:2 say that Israel's sins had already been forgiven her? If the Apostles truly believed that the prophecy of Isaiah 40:3 was fulfilled by John the Baptist, and they knew the full context of Isaiah 40, then it confirms my suspicion of their eschatological view: that they believed Jesus to be the Messiah - not that he was going to die on the cross and come back a second time, but that this was the *End of Days*. That notwithstanding, John the Baptist did not fulfill a prophecy in Isaiah 40, although it could be said that he actions did *match* those narrated in Isaiah.

A most curious aspect of this whole affair is why the followers of Jesus continued to believe in him even after his crucifixion. Even more curious is where Jesus got the idea of dying for the sins of the world, when that concept cannot be found in the Hebrew Scriptures. We will come back to that in a later chapter on the mission of Jesus (see Chapter 9-2).

Isaiah 53 in Context

My first observation is that most seem to read Isaiah 53 without reading the preceding or following chapters. This brings us to the very controversial subject: who was the *suffering servant* mentioned by Isaiah: Israel or Jesus? We can start with the following verses:

- Isaiah 41:8-9 "You, Israel, are My servant … I have chosen you and not cast you away"
- Isaiah 44:1-2 "Jacob My servant, and Israel whom I chose"
- Isaiah 44:21 "O Jacob and Israel, for thou art My servant"
- Isaiah 45:4 "My servant Jacob, and Israel My chosen one"
- Isaiah 48:20 "The Lord has redeemed His servant Jacob"
- Isaiah 49:3 "And He said to me, thou art My servant, O Israel"
- Psalm 136:22 "Even a heritage unto Israel His servant"
- Jeremiah 46:27-28 "Jacob my servant, do not be dismayed Israel"

As we discuss below, Isaiah 53 directly follows the theme of chapter 52, describing the exile and redemption of the Jewish people. The prophecies are written in the singular form because the Israelites ("Israel") are regarded as one unit. Throughout Jewish scripture, Israel is repeatedly called, in the singular, the servant of God (as above). Isaiah states no less than 11 times in the chapters prior to 53, that the Servant of God is *Israel*.

Let us spend a moment on Isaiah 52, which refers to the final redemption, not the time of Jesus. It begins with an exhortation for Zion to awaken and rejoice, for: *"O Jerusalem, the holy city, the uncircumcised and defiled people will no longer enter you."* (Isaiah 52:1) Obviously, that could not refer to a Jerusalem which was utterly destroyed by the uncircumcised shortly after the death of Jesus. Next is a very important point, refuting the Christian concept of redemption: *"For thus said Hashem: For naught were you sold, and without money will you be redeemed."* The word *money* is allegorical, for Zion was *sold* to its enemies only in punishment for its sins, and can only be redeemed from its subjugation through repentance[2]. Verse 7 continues with the theme of God returning to Zion, and redeeming Jerusalem, stressing that: *"Behold, My servant* [righteous members of Israel] *will succeed; he will be exalted and become high and exceedingly lofty."*

Collective Israel is often referred to in the singular. The "him" in verses 52:14-15 continues to be Israel, God's servant.

All this seems clear to me, according to the Scriptures, so why Jesus? Note that nowhere in Isaiah is THE Messiah explicitly mentioned, whereas an *anointed one* is mentioned numerous times and in other books. Even Cyrus is referred to as "His anointed" (Isaiah 45:1). Next, we need to consider the issue: Who is speaking? As I do as an author, you would understand the purpose of chapters, especially in non-fiction works: they are used to introduce new subjects or lines of thought. When the medieval publishers of the Old Testament added chapter numbering, the intention was not to separate the narrative into individual sections, but primarily to provide a method of indexing for easy reference (at least I hope so). The early texts were written on scrolls, and chapter or verse numbering was not a feature of such documents. We should keep this in mind. So now, consider removing "53" from the numbering, and continue reading from 52:15 onward: Who is speaking?

The "multitudes were astonished over you [Israel] … for they will see that which had never been told to them, and perceive things they never heard." This is where the chapter division is misleading; the speakers in 53:1 are the *kings* in 52:15.

Whom has the arm of Hashem revealed?

Who indeed. "Formerly he grew like a sapling, or like a root from arid ground … without such visage that we [the kings of the nation's] could desire him. He was despised and isolated from men, a man of pains and accustomed to illness … But in truth, it was our ills that he bore, and our pains that he carried – but we had regarded him diseased, stricken by God, and afflicted" (Isaiah 53:2-4). Isaiah was speaking of someone who from the very beginning, was despised and isolated, and accustomed to illness. He was regarded as diseased, stricken by God, and afflicted, whilst still a sapling. Nowhere in the New Testament is Jesus described in that manner, but it *is* a description of Israel as a young nation. Jesus was never regarded as diseased, even metaphorically, and was never isolated from men. He could not be said to have been stricken by God and afflicted, certainly not in his youth, but perhaps at the very end of his life if the New Testament is to be believed. He, whoever "he" was, was pained because of our rebellious sins: note *was*, not *will be*. It should be obvious that Isaiah was speaking of the Nation of Israel, not a future Messiah, which brings an entirely different meaning to what follows. No longer is it a prophecy of Jesus, but of the "servant" previously identified, i.e., Israel.

Note *"arm of the Lord"* (v. 53:1) is also referred to in Psalm 44:3, as is "sheep" (53:7, and Psalm 44:11). The Christian Old Testament reads "and by His **stripes** we **are** healed" (v. 53:5), but the Hebrew translation is "and with his **wounds** we **were** healed": note *stripes* versus *wounds* and the change in the verb tense. According to Strongs Hebrew Concordance 2250, *stripes* is a permissible translation, but *bruises* or *wounds* are more common. A more recent Jewish translation contends that the correct interpretation is "in fellowship with Him we were healed". The explanation is too lengthy to repeat here, but if it be correct, it entirely invalidates the use of Isaiah 53:5 as a fulfilled prophecy. That said, this latter interpretation is not widely accepted, as far as I can discern.

Even so, were we spiritually healed by the flogging of Jesus, or by his crucifixion? Christian doctrine is that Jesus accomplished substitutionary atonement by his death, not by his scourging at the hands of the Romans, so in what way can the prophecy in Isaiah be said to have been fulfilled? If Jesus was tortured, but not put to death, perhaps one could claim prophecy fulfillment, but the Christian doctrine of salvation is based on the crucifixion, and more especially the resurrection, not the torture of Jesus.

Moving on to verse 53:11 "By his knowledge My righteous servant shall justify many": does Christianity teach that Jesus justifies by *knowledge*? If anything, Christianity downplays knowledge in its teachings, other than when Jesus quotes Scripture, but as I argue in more than one instance, the Gospels have Jesus misquoting Scripture, so that invalidates any claim of teaching from knowledge. One should note that even Origen, the 3rd century Church Father, conceded that Isaiah 53 referred to the whole Jewish people[3]. If that was the understanding back then, what evidence does Christianity offer to justify a new understanding? Jesus did suffer, no question about that, but if Jesus is NOT the "suffering servant" of prophecy, then there is NO prophecy of the Messiah suffering and dying.

This is of the utmost significance: I do contend that the *Passion of Christ* has been read back into prophecy, in order to justify the claim that he was THE Messiah. Excuse me for shouting, but having examined the evidence, I can come to no other conclusion.

How would you reconcile "Therefore I will divide him a portion with the great" (Isaiah 53:12) with "All authority has been given to Me in heaven and on earth" (Matt 28:18)? Can these two verses be speaking of the same person? Dividing a portion has a different connotation from being given all.

Part of the problem I have is that according to Christian apologetics, the subject of Isaiah's discourse changes from chapter 52 to 53, and then back again in 54. Verses 54:6-8 can hardly refer to Jesus as the suffering servant. Looking further through the verses, one might ask: Who is spoken of in Isaiah 57:17? One might also wonder that if Jesus is the one spoken of as the servant in Isaiah 42, why does Christianity ignore: *"He will exalt the law and make it honourable"* (v. 21)? Does Christianity exalt the law and make it honourable? On the contrary, Christianity teaches that the Law is no longer operative, and Protestant denominations accept Luther's view, that "the law, when it is in his true sense, doth nothing else but reveal sin, engender wrath, accuse and terrify men"? How is that honourable? Then we have: "For My salvation is about to come ... blessed is the man ... who keeps from defiling the Sabbath" (Isaiah 56:1-2). Has Christianity not defiled the Sabbath by refusing to keep holy the Sabbath, and teaching generations to continue to not observe the Sabbath? Curiously, Christianity has had difficulty with how to view the traditional Sabbath. A typical assertion is this: "He [God] imposed it solely on the Jews as 'a mark to single them out for punishment they so well deserved for their infidelities'[4]."[5] Compare that with this extract from the current Catholic Catechism: "God entrusted the sabbath to Israel to keep as a sign of the irrevocable covenant" (2171). Obviously the story changes with the retelling, and I am ever perplexed regarding this paradox of an *irrevocable covenant* versus a *New* (Replacement*) Covenant.* Perhaps you can understand why I find Christian doctrine and theology to be incoherent.

Regarding the Christian teaching of contempt for the Jew, and a theology bound up in Supersessionism and the *New Israel,* what is one to make of "Do not let the son of the foreigner who has joined himself to the

Lord speak, saying, the Lord has utterly separated me from His people" (Isaiah 56:3)? Note how Isaiah emphasises keeping both the Sabbath and the covenant, which makes it difficult to interpret one part of his prophecy in the Christian sense, and the rest as taught in Judaism (see also 58:13-14). If you would like more on the consequences of desecrating the Sabbath, I would recommend Jeremiah 17:19-27

Isaiah 63:7-19 remembers God's mercy to Israel, and there is not a hint, anywhere in Isaiah, where God would forsake His people.

In researching this issue, I also found an opinion that attempts to overcome the difficulties by asserting that Isaiah identifies not one, but two servants: the unrighteous one (Israel) and the righteous one (Messiah Jesus). The role of the righteous is to bring the unrighteous back to God, just as Jesus declared: "I was sent only to the lost sheep of the house of Israel", but that doesn't quite work in Christian thought because that leaves the house of Judah (and Benjamin) as righteous, which is likely true in the thinking of Jesus, because he would have been well aware of the split under Jeroboam after the death of Solomon. However, that does not fit with Christian doctrine of Jesus inaugurating a *New Israel*, because such is antithetical to Judah being righteous. Other than the article in which I found this contention, I have been unable to find any other support for it. Note also how Zephaniah alludes to the remnant of Israel being righteous. That aside, go back to Isaiah 49:2 where Isaiah states that he was chosen to return the unrighteous (Jacob) to righteousness (Israel).

When we continue into Isaiah 54, we find some interesting passages. For example, "For your Maker is your *husband*" (v.5) – clearly Jesus is not the husband of his Father, so the focus in 54 is not Jesus. However, note that relationship in Jeremiah 31:32 "though I was a *husband* to them", which would tend to confirm Israel as the focus. Does Isaiah switch from the Messiah to Israel in these two chapters? Verse 10: "*But My kindness shall not depart from you, nor shall My covenant of peace be removed, says the Lord, who has mercy on you.*" If the servant is Israel, as I contend, then the ramifications for the new, replacement covenant should be considered. And if you wonder about righteousness, then consider Isaiah 51:7 "*Listen to Me, you who know righteousness, you people in whose heart is My law, do not fear the reproach of men, nor be afraid of their insults.*" Should I understand this verse as an exhortation to not fear the reproach of Paul, of Luther, and of all others who seek to insult those who hold in their hearts, God's Law? Is this not a clear refutation of those who do not value the Law and its observance? For those who believe that keeping holy the Sabbath is no longer required, read and ponder Isaiah 56:2.

The Christian interpretation of Isaiah 53 is entirely discordant with the preceding and following chapters. Could Isaiah have inserted a sidebar, as I and other authors do? Could he have written an aside, to record some issue that he thought that he had better note whilst he had it in mind, before returning to his main plot? Possible, I guess, for such a literary device is found elsewhere in Isaiah's writings, but the context thereof always clarifies the change of subject: from prophecy to historical narration, and back again.

This is not the case here.

Summary

Quoting from the series of essays on Old Testament usage in the New, one author wrote concerning the Suffering Servant in Isaiah 53:

> "Who the Servant was meant to be, whether an individual or a personified community, and if an individual, whether a historical character or an ideal figure of the future, is a point on which there seems to have been no agreement in antiquity, even as there is no agreement on the question among modern scholars. A similar doubt arises about certain psalms which have some affinity with the fifty third chapter of Isaiah. Their plot is similar, at least so far that they describe the troubles of someone who suffers undeservedly in unshaken loyalty to God, and is ultimately delivered and glorified through his grace and power. We may call them Psalms of the Righteous Sufferer, whether the sufferer is to be conceived individually or collectively."[6]

Taken as evidence offered by a bible scholar, one would have to conclude that the claim of Jesus being the Suffering Servant, in fulfillment of prophecy in Isaiah 53, is open to debate. I would remind the reader of the gravity of the case before us: Was Jesus the Messiah because he fulfilled messianic prophecies? If the evidence does not support the case, more serious questions come into play, especially concerning the deity of Jesus.

Having studied this issue at length, I remain perplexed. If the Hebrew Scriptures did not prophesy as Christianity claims, then from where did arise "a concept of 'catastrophic' messianism in which the suffering, humiliation, and death of the Messiah were regarded as an integral part of the redemptive process"[7]? Chapter 9-1 explores that question.

REFERENCES:

1. Scherman, Rabbi Nosson, *The Tanach*, Mesorah Publications, ArtScroll English Edition, Brooklyn, NY, 2011, p. 669
2. Ibid, p. 667
3. Chadwick, Henry, *Origen Contra Celsum*, Cambridge University Press, 1953, p.50
4. Justin Martyr, *Dialogue* 23, 3
5. Bacchiocchi, Samuele, *From Sabbath to Sunday, A Historical Investigation*, The Pontifical Gregorian University Press, Rome, 1977, p. 186
6. Beale, G.K., *The Right Doctrine from the Wrong Texts? Essays on the Use of the Old Testament in the New*, Baker Academic, Grand Rapids, MI, 1994, p. 172
7. Knohl, Israel, *The Messiah Before Jesus: The Suffering Servant of the Dead Sea Scrolls*, University of California Press, Berkeley, CA, 2000, inside front flap.

CHAPTER 3-3

DANIEL 7 AND THE
SON OF MAN

"Who do people say the Son of Man is? ...But what about you? Who do you say I am?' (Mt 16:13,15). In the end, people's answer to this question will be the only thing that matters; it alone will determine people's eternal destiny."
~ Andreas J. Kostenberger, Encountering John: The Gospel
in Historical, Literary, and Theological Perspective ~

Hmmm ... if Jesus is the prophesied Messiah, the Son of God, the Second Person of the Trinity, then the eternal destiny of those who reject him looks to be bleak. On the other hand, if he is none of those things, then the eternal destiny of those who worship him as God may be even bleaker. I cannot know, but I do wonder.

The New Testament translators render *Son of Man* with initial capitals, as if it were a royal title, rather than accepting the common representation in the Hebrew Scriptures, and even in the Christian Old Testament. This is obviously done to reinforce the belief that Jesus was the son of man referred to in Daniel 7; that the relevant verses in Daniel 7 prophesied the Messiah; and that the Messiah would be God incarnated. As this is foundational to the doctrine of the Trinity, and the authority of Jesus, it needs to be examined more closely.

Let me apologise in advance if there is some duplication in the explanations that follow: this is an inevitable consequence of quoting from multiple sources. However, as this issue is so central to Christian theology, we should leave no stone unturned in our search for truth. If, as I accept as a premise for this enquiry, we are exhorted: *the Gospels* [must be] *Examined by the Rules of Evidence Administered in Courts of Justice*[1], then we must likewise examine the Old Testament, and call as many witnesses as we believe can provide sound evidence.

The questions we must resolve are these:
1. Is there justification for the term, son of man, being rendered as "Son of Man", as if it were a royal title of a significant individual?
2. Should we accept the Greek rendering of Daniel 7:13, "one like a *son of man*" in favour of the more common in Hebrew, "one like a man"?
3. Is there evidence that this entity was accepted before the days of Jesus, as the prophesied *mashiach*, or was that a later interpretation?
4. Is there evidence that this entity was perceived, before the days of Jesus, as being co-equal with God, and thus a deity?

Old Testament Usage

The term "son of man", occurs 93 times in the Book of Ezekiel, mostly referring to Ezekiel himself, signifying the unbridgeable gap between God and mankind. The term occurs just once in the Hebrew version of Daniel, but twice in the Greek. The one occurrence in the Hebrew has the same connotation as in Ezekiel, so let us compare these two occurrences in Daniel:
a. "And behold, one like the Son of Man" (Dan 7:13, NKJV).
b. "Understand, son of man, that the vision refers to the time of the end" (Dan 8:17, NKJV).

I find it interesting that the KJV, NKJV, ISV, GOD's Word, Douay-Rheims, and Webster's versions of Daniel 7:13 prefix "son" with the definite article "the", whilst the other 16 translations listed (bible.cc) have the indefinite article "a". Even more intriguing, both the Douay and Webster's have "son of man", not "Son of Man". Some translations use an initial capital for "Son", but not for "man". So what meaning are these various translations intending to convey? Researching both the Hebrew and the Greek, the etymology of the word translated "son" does not specify whether a definite or indefinite article should be used – that is up to the reader based on context. In this instance, there is no preceding verse which identifies, or even mentions this son, in which case there is no exegetical basis for identifying "son" in Daniel 7:13 with the definite article "the" – "a" is more appropriate. We should not ignore opinions, old and new, that agree with this observation: "For the same things expressed in Hebrew have not an equal force when translated into another language [e.g. Greek]. Not only so, but even the Law and the prophecies and the rest of the books differ not a little as to the things said in them"[2]. On that basis, I contend that the right approach is to accept translations from the Hebrew, rather than the Greek, especially as I have demonstrated above, Christian translators have been unsure of how to render the Greek into English. There is a substantive difference in the connotation of the definite article, *the*, from the indefinite article, *a*. The same issue must be raised concerning the meaning of Isaiah 7:14, but we will come back to that.

We must ask: Why would the single occurrence in the Greek version of Daniel 7:13 be interpreted differently to the common interpretation in Daniel 8:17? Exegesis requires consistent interpretation of terms, unless the text provide substantive evidence to do otherwise. I find no such substantiation in either the Hebrew or the Greek.

One last point, easily overlooked: "*the vision refers to the time of the end*" (Dan 8:17). As the end is yet to occur, on what basis was Jesus identified with the man in Daniel 7:13?

Daniel 7 Overview

"In the seventh chapter of the Book of Daniel, written circa 161 B.C, we find a remarkable apocalyptic story ... one of the earliest apocalypses that was ever written ... and became one of the most influential books for latter-day Jewry, including, perhaps even especially, in its Christian branch."[3]

As an aside, when Christians attempt to justify their theology with Old Testament references, they should be wary of interpreting passages in a way that which would pre-date the Jewish understanding: in this case, let us follow the historical trail that led to the Book of Revelation, so that we can properly interpret the messages therein. Bible passages quoted here are from the Artscroll English Tanach[4].

"I watched as thrones were set up, and the One of Ancient Days sat ... the judgement was set, and the books were opened." (Daniel 7:9-1) To my knowledge, the identity of the *One of Ancient Days* is not disputed: it is God, or even God the Father. "I was watching in night visions and behold! with the clouds of heaven, **one like a man** came; he came up to the One of Ancient Days, and they brought him before Him. He was given dominion, honour, and kingship, so that all peoples, nations, and languages would serve him; his dominion would be an everlasting dominion that would never pass, and his kingship would never be destroyed." (Daniel 7:13-14) The NKJV renders this, in part: "One like **the** Son of Man" whilst other versions have "one like **a** son of man" [emphasis mine], so obviously there is some interpretation in these translations. The question now arises: where did the term "son" come from, when it is not in all versions of the Hebrew bible? We will dig a little deeper.

"The Aramaic phrase Bar 'ĕnoš 'son of man' is a Semitic expression denoting a single member of humanity, a certain human being, hence 'someone'."[5] The reference here is from the Greek Orthodox Archdiocese of America, hence the drawing on the earlier Aramaic rather than later Greek sources. The full text is worth reading, but I shall just extract a few relevant ideas. Continuing from this source:

> "The Aramaic phrase: bar 'ĕnoš may connote more than a mere human being. It may define a human being in its defining characteristics vis-à-vis God, namely, weakness and mortality. Thus, I would suggest rendering the phrase bar 'ĕnoš as 'son of weakness' or 'the weak one.' This semantic detail, absent in the New Testament Greek claque, *huios (tou) anthrōpou* 'son of man,' may help one better understand Jesus' references to himself as the humblest human being who came 'to seek and save the lost one' (Luke 19:10) and whose eternal glory, temporarily overshadowed

by incarnation, will be fully and publicly revealed at the end of time (Matthew 16:27).

At the first sight, the Aramaic expression *bar 'ĕnoš* 'Son of Man' seems to be a reiteration of the Hebrew phrase *ben 'ā d ā m*; if this is true, it may be read to designate any human being. This phrase, *ben' ā d ā m*, appears 14 times in poetic parallels and 93 times in the book of Ezekiel, where it points to man's humility versus God's majesty. Interestingly, it is found only once in the book of Daniel, and designates the prophet as humble receptacle of divine messages (Dan 8:17). If the Hebrew phrase itself was known to the author of the current form of the book of Daniel, we might wonder what was his intention when he chose rather to include the Aramaic phrase *bar 'ĕnoš* in Daniel 7:13? Perhaps the Aramaic phrase is not simply a claque of the Hebrew phrase. The Hebrew word *'ā d ā m* 'humanity' is connected to the word *'ád ā m ā* "ground" (Genesis 2:7; 3:19) and therefore the phrase *ben 'ā d ā m* underscores man's earthly origin.

On the other hand the etymology of the Aramaic word *'ĕnoš* 'human being, man' in the Aramaic phrase *bar 'ĕnoš*, is still debated. We suggest relating the Aramaic word *'ĕnoš* to a homonymous root *-n-š* I, meaning 'to be weak.' Relating human being, man, to weakness seems a reasonable and clear path toward solving the etymology of this word. Additionally, while the Hebrew phrase underscores human humility, the result of being taken from the earth, the Aramaic phrase underscores a novel element of this humility, namely, the weakness of the human person when meeting God.

If Daniel 7 deals with the relationship between God the Father and God the Son, as the ancient Christian interpreters argued, then we can assume that the latter has a certain propensity towards weakness, or sharing in human weakness. This is why he was designated to become one of us long before he took flesh and became man. Paul underscores Christ's willingness to share in our weakness, when he writes, 'For we do not have a high priest who is unable to sympathize with our weaknesses (*astheneias*), but we have one who in every respect has been tested as we are, yet without sin. Let us therefore approach the throne of grace with boldness, so that we may receive mercy and find grace to help in time of need' (Heb 4:15-16). (NRSV)"

As best as I can understand, the Book of Daniel was written in Hebrew, Aramaic, or even a combination of those languages, so it could be said that based on the discussion above, both the Christian inclusion of the word "son" and the Jewish omission of "son" are not contradictions of one another - it could simply be an issue of a literal translation into Greek becoming a misunderstanding in English. Note how some Christian translations have "**a** son of man", being a non-specific reference to a single member of humanity, just as the Aramaic phrase allows, whilst the NKJV and others use the definite article and capitalise the words: "**the** Son of Man", the latter representing a doctrinal presupposition. The Jewish Jesus would have spoken primarily in Aramaic and Hebrew, particularly when conversing with Pharisees, so I think it fair to question what words he used, and what he meant by the term, son of man.

If, as the discussion above leads us to believe, the term was used to denote weakness, and humility in the presence of God, then there can be no justification for rendering it as a royal title, as in *the Son of Man*. On the other hand, *son of man* can be understood as an <u>emphatic</u> reference: simply "man" is one thing, but perhaps the authors or translators were trying to emphasise the situation – a mere human before God. If we look at it that way, there is no true contradiction between the terms *man* and *son of man* - the second is simply the first preceded by an adjectival phrase: "son of", denoting the unbridgeable gap between man and God, and is consonant with the repeated use of the term in Ezekiel. The argument then resolves to the far too common issue of theological annotations being used to influence understanding. In this case, the preference for the definite article "the", and the initial capitals for *Son* and *Man*. Remove those, and the problem goes away insofar as understanding the text, but presents a problem for Christian doctrine.

New Testament References

Acknowledging the duplicate references to the same events in the Gospels and Book of Acts, *Son of Man* occurs 76 times. The question is: when Jesus used that term about himself, was he using it in the sense found in Ezekiel, or in the sense as imposed on Daniel 7:13 by Christian translators? If we accept the Ezekiel understanding of the term, then this Jewish man was NOT claiming to be a deity, *made flesh* or otherwise; on the contrary, perhaps his persistent use of *son of man* was to discourage anyone from thinking of him in as other than a mere human. This is worth considering. If the Jews of the time considered the term, *son of man*, as having the meaning in Ezekiel, was Jesus attempting to prevent anyone perceiving him as a deity? In the Jewish hierarchy of Scripture, Ezekiel was a major prophet, and Daniel, a minor one, if at all. As best I can understand of the original Hebrew, Daniel does not refer to "one like a son of man", but more simply, "one like a man". Later rendering of the Hebrew, influenced by the Masoretic texts, allowed "son of". Either way, as discussed above, it makes no difference in the Jewish understanding. If Jesus was conversant with the contemporary Hebrew Scriptures only, and on the evidence, I believe that to be the case, then most probably, his use of the term "son of man" would have been as learned from Ezekiel's usage.

The Gospel has Jesus saying: "Therefore I say to you, every sin and blasphemy will be forgiven men, but the blasphemy against the Spirit will not be forgiven men. Anyone who speaks a word against the Son of Man, it will be forgiven him; but whoever speaks against the Holy Spirit, it will not be forgiven him, either in this age or the age to come." (Matt 12:31-32) Why did Jesus differentiate himself from the Spirit of God (Holy Spirit)? Why is it blasphemy to speak against the Holy Spirit, but not blasphemy to speak against the Son of Man? Could it be because Jesus did not equate himself with God, as his frequent self-identification with the *son of man* would suggest? One should also note how Jesus uses the term in the third person, not the first. I have thought about this, but with nothing approaching a conclusion.

Investigating further

Jesus, without any explanation, used the term "son of man" almost exclusively when referring to himself, or at least it appears that way. Why was that? We can assume, that he assumed, that his listeners would understand his meaning, which would have been as the rabbis and Pharisees taught at the time. Therefore, we should turn to Jewish sources, not Christian, for the most plausible, historical, explanation of this term. I have researched numerous Jewish sources, and all substantively agree with the quotations given here:

> "Son of man is a common term in the Psalms, used to accentuate the difference between God and human beings. As in Ps. viii. 4 (A. V. 5), the phrase implies "mortality," "impotence," "transientness," as against the omnipotence and eternality of God. Yhwh looks down from His throne in heaven upon the "children," or "sons," of "man" (Ps. xi. 4, xxxiii. 13). Among Jews the term "son of man" was not used as the specific title of the Messiah. The New Testament expression ὅ υἱὸς τοῦ ἀνθρόπου is a translation of the Aramaic "bar nasha," and as such could have been understood only as the substitute for a personal pronoun, or as emphasizing the human qualities of those to whom it is applied. That the term does not appear in any of the epistles ascribed to Paul is significant. Psalm viii. 5-7 is quoted in Ḥeb. ii. 6 as referring to Jesus, but outside the Gospels, Acts vii. 56 is the only verse in the New Testament in which the title is employed; and here it may be a free translation of the Aramaic for "a man," or it may have been adopted from Luke xxii. 69."[6]

The most significant assertions here are: "Among Jews the term "son of man" was not used as the specific title of the Messiah", especially with initial capitals as a title as in *Son of Man*; and, Paul never used the term. Here is another Jewish opinion, but note that the works of the *Apocalyptic writers* referred to are not the apocalyptic verses in the New Testament:

"It is this double use of the term "son of man" in the New Testament time and in New Testament documents which has caused great confusion to the recorders and translators as well as to the exegetes of the New Testament. As is seen in Enoch and IV Esdras (*l.c.*), "son of man" was among the Apocalyptic writers a favourite term for the Messiah, and accordingly it occurs frequently in Messianic apocalypses embodied in the New Testament (Matt. xxiv.-xxv.; Mark xiii. 26; Luke xxi. 27, 36) and in Messianic prophecies which are ascribed to Jesus regarded, in accordance with this conception, as the "son of man" in the clouds (of glory) (Matt. xii. 40; xiii. 27, 41; xvi. 27; xix. 28; xxvi. 64; Mark viii. 38, xiv. 62; Luke xii. 40; xvii. 22-30; xviii. 8, 31; xxii. 69; John i. 51, iii. 13, v. 27, vi. 62).

The term "son of man" has a quite different meaning in such sayings as "the son of man is lord even of the Sabbath day" (Matt. xii. 8 and parallels). It denotes simply man as master over the Sabbath in the same sense given it in the saying of the Rabbis, "The Sabbath is given over unto you, but not you unto the Sabbath" (Mek., Ki Tissa, 1). In many passages, the expression "son of man" is used in the sense of "that person," or "myself," a use of it known to have been common in Talmudic times. Thus, when Jesus says, "the son of man hath not where to lay his head" (Matt. viii. 20), he means simply "myself"; and likewise, when he speaks of his future suffering and betrayal, the term "son of man" has nothing to do with the Messianic title (Matt. xvii. 22 and parallels). Afterward the records confounded the two usages, and consequently Matthew uses the term promiscuously in a manner which has to this day, puzzled most of the commentators (see Wellhausen, "Des Menschen Sohn," in "Skizzen und Vorarbeiten," 1899, pp. 187-215; and comp. Dalman, "Die Worte Jesu," 1898, pp. 191-218)."[7]

When, or if, Jesus says, *the son of man*, did he simply mean: *myself as a humble human*? I think it likely.

Even where "the 'son of man' is claimed to be, among the Apocalyptic writers, *a favourite term* for the Messiah", we should next ask: But did the

Old Testament Prophets believe that the Messiah would be a deity? I can find no support in the Hebrew Scriptures for such a belief. We need to step back for a moment, and understand who these Apocalyptic writers were, when they wrote, and the influence they had on the trajectory of Jewish theological development. As their writings were not included in the canon, we should not place too much credence upon them (or maybe we should?)

Finally, we might consider the understanding of this verse amongst Jewish believers: "God is not a man that He should be deceitful, nor a **son of man** that He should relent" (Num 23:19) [emphasis mine]. Why would Jesus, well versed in Torah, persist with a contradictory meaning? And if God is not a man, nor a son of man, how could the man, and son of man, Jesus, be God?

Daniel 7:13-14

I would like to start by repeating an interesting Jewish commentary on Daniel 7:14 that I quoted in Chapter 1-8, simply because on some days, I am more inclined to ruffle feathers than placate:

> *"In those times, many will rise up against the king of the South; and sons of the lawless men of your people will exalt themselves to establish a vision, but they will stumble."* (TJB)

> *"Rashi* and *Ramban* take this as an allusion to the Nazarene and his disciples. For is there a greater stumbling block than this? All the prophets foretold that the Messiah would redeem the Jews, help them, gather in the exiles, and support their observance of the commandments. But he caused Jewry to be put to the sword, to be scattered, and to be degraded; he tampered with the Torah and its laws; and he misled most of the world to serve something other than God. (Hil. Melachim 11:4)"[8]

Irrespective of one's religious beliefs, one would be hard-pressed to entirely disagree with these Jewish sages. Other than *serving something other than God*, what could you claim, from a Christian theological perspective, was untrue? As I am wont to contend, discarding Torah is synonymous with tampering, although I do not believe that is what Jesus advocated. Likewise, I am not confident that it was Jesus who misled most of the world: rather, it was Paul, and the Roman Church that arose from their interpretation of his teachings.

In this context, we need now to take a closer look at verses 7:13-14, as these verses are central to the Christian, and perhaps even Jesus' claim, that Jesus is/was the 'one like the son of man' spoken of by Daniel. We should note that in the *Tanakh* (Hebrew Bible), Daniel is not included in the Prophets (*Neviim*), but in the Writings (*Kesuvim*). This is because the Sages disagreed as to whether Daniel was a prophet or not, and the Talmud states that he was not[9]. We are often given to thinking of prophecy as a definitive statement of future events, but as Rabbi Tzvi Freeman describes it: "a prophecy is the state of matters in a higher realm, before it has reached our earthly plane. There, it is amorphous, not fully defined and can materialize in more than one way."[10] That being so, we should be wary of our interpretation of any prophecy, especially where there is considerable doubt as to it having been fulfilled in the way we have been taught. I am as guilty of misunderstanding as anyone.

I have found an interesting study by Benjamin E. Reynolds of King's College, University of Aberdeen from which I will quote some relevant extracts. The text can be found online here[11]. The author makes the point that "Studies of the 'one like a son of man' in Daniel 7 typically follow the description found in the Aramaic text of Daniel."[12] There are two other versions worthy of study, the Old Greek (OG) and the Theodotion. Commenting on where the various translations differ, he quotes the opinion of Jennifer Dines who states:

> "Even if it is unclear whether a divergence between the LXX and the MT (Masoretic Text) comes from a translator or from his source-text, a difference of interpretation between the two texts has significance. If nothing else, it shows that there were different streams of tradition, and if the LXX witnesses to some elements of interpretation which have not otherwise been preserved in the Hebrew [or Aramaic], it is a very important window onto a period of biblical interpretation before the MT emerged as dominant."[13]

What I wish to contrast here, is the approach to Scripture by many Christian commentators, and those more interested in a scholarly discovery of how Scripture interpretation arose. The fact that scholars acknowledge variations in interpretation, and all translations are interpretations, is evidence to my mind that no extant version of Scripture can be infallible or inerrant. Thus, to treat them as such could be considered wilful blindness, for whatever reason. It is not my intention to impugn the integrity of anyone, but simply to convey to the reader why I question as I do.

There is a difference of fact, perhaps subtle to some minds, which caught my eye in the translations. Compare these versions:

a. "I saw in a vision of the night and behold on the clouds of heaven there came like a son of man. And like the Ancient of Days he arrived, and those standing there came to him." (Old Greek LXX)

b. "I was watching in night visions and behold! With the clouds of heaven, one like a (son of) man came; he came up to the One of Ancient Days, and they brought him before Him." (The Jewish Bible); and

c. "I was watching in the night visions, and behold, One like the Son of Man, coming with the clouds of heaven! He came to the Ancient of Days, and they brought Him near before Him." (New King James Version)

In the OG, "they", whoever they were, came to the one like a (son of) man, whilst in the other two versions, it was the other way around: "they" brought him before the Ancient of Days. The variation raises a question regarding the status of this "one": was he higher or lower than the others there present? I have no answer, but contend that the texts do not allow us to conclude one way or another, and most certainly not that he was a deity. However, all versions state that God, the Ancient of Days, confers special authority upon this man, which to my mind clearly implies that the man was not God, for no deity confers power or authority upon another deity, except in pagan traditions.

The author discusses numerous other aspects of the text, but for my purposes here, it is sufficient to skip forward to this:

"Thus, the OG of Dan 7:13-14 depicts the 'one like a son of man' as similar to the Ancient of Days in four ways, (1) The son of man figure arrives like the Ancient of Days, (2) he appears on the clouds of heaven, (3) receives service that suggests cultic worship given to God, and (4) is approached by those who stood before the Ancient of Days."[14]

It is interesting to note that whilst the Aramaic version of Daniel has 'the one like a [son of] man' given *dominion, honour,* and *kingdom,* the Old Greek version says that he was only given *authority.* In some other Papyrus texts, he was given *kingly* or *royal authority.* I am not sure that the differences matter much, other than that it evidences variations in understanding, and a developing tradition. More importantly, the simple fact that the (son of) man was given authority or status of any form, is evidence that he was not a deity, and whilst *similar to the Ancient of Days,* could not be coequal with Him. If whatever was given was in perpetuity, the recipient would be man in perpetuity, not God. Remember, we too are similar to God, for we are made in His image.

However, and I want to stress this: Daniel himself was addressed as *son of man* (v. 8:17), and an angel appeared before Daniel having *the appearance of a man* (v. 8:15), and a man's voice was heard. The obvious exegetical question is this: by what logic should the reference in Daniel 7:13 be interpreted differently than 8:17? If Daniel intended a different meaning, why was he not more explicit? If we are to examine and interpret Daniel's writings logically, accepting that he understood what he was writing, and that he was competent as an author, there can be no case for claiming that *son of man* has any connotation of a deity.

Psalms of Solomon

This referenced study[15] attempts a parallel with the Psalms of Solomon:

"When viewed in relation to the portrait of the Davidic Messiah in Pss. Sol. 17, this implication becomes more convincing.

Pss. Sol. 17,21: 'See, Lord, and raise up for them their king, the son of David, to rule over your servant Israel in the time which is known to you, o God.'

Pss. Sol. 17,32: 'And he will be a righteous king over them, taught by God. And in his days, unrighteousness will not be among them, for all will be holy, and their king will be Lord Messiah'."

These verses contradict the claim of the Messiah being God. Firstly, the Messiah does not know the time of his coming, and secondly, he will be taught by God. If God, the Second Person of the Trinity, is in heaven with God, the First Person of the Trinity, I do not understand how there could be any differences in their knowledge. If both are not omniscient, then one of them is not God. It is as simple as that. That aside, note the reference to "servant Israel".

A little later, he draws our attention to 2 Samuel 7:12-13, to corroborate the narrative of a King Messiah, descended from David, but he (carefully?) avoids reference to verse 7:14, "so that when he sins I will chastise him". I am open to a King Messiah, of the line of David, being prophesied, but sinless? Again, note also the words: *taught by God*. If Jesus was already God, he would have had no need of teaching. Yes, I understand the argument, as much as anyone can, that the Second Person of the Trinity put aside his deity whilst on earth, but I simply do not accept it. If he put aside his deity, then he could not get it back again, unless God the Father gave it back, but that is getting silly. God-ness is not like a coat that one takes off, and puts on again at will. An infinitude cannot become finite, and then return to the infinite state. Yes, an infinitude can manifest itself in a finite form, but the manifestation is not the one manifesting. Remember that as we are made in the image of God, then in a sense, we all are manifestations of God.

One should note that the Psalms of Solomon have no connection with King Solomon of old. The authorship is unknown, but there is some agreement on them being written by Pharisees in the first century BCE. Another interpretation of Psalm 17, worthy of consideration, is this one by Professor Barry D. Smith of Crandall University, a small Christian Liberal Arts university located in Moncton, New Brunswick, Canada:

"In this composition, the author confesses God as king and confesses
that "the kingdom of God is over the nations in judgment" (17:3).
The psalmist asserts the biblical position that the kingship in
Israel belongs to David and his descendants, which is an implicit
criticism of its usurpation by the Hasmoneans (17:4-10, 18-20).
He then interprets the overthrow of the Hasmoneans by Pompey,
called the "lawless one" as judgment for their misappropriation
of power (17:11-17); God's punishment also included drought
(17:19). The author expresses his hope for the appearance of a
sinless Davidic king, the Messiah, who would purge Jerusalem of
gentiles, reassemble the dispersed Jews and judge the tribes of the
people (17:21-44). He concludes with a benediction (17:45-46)."

Purge Jerusalem of gentiles? Exactly the opposite happened: it was the
Jews who were purged by the Romans. Continuing:

"3.3. The Davidic Messiah and Eschatological Salvation

As already indicated, the author(s) of *Psalms of Solomon* see
Pompey's invasion as God's judgment and discipline of the nation.
Presumably, one of the reasons that God brought Jewish political
independence to an end was that the Hasmoneans had usurped the
kingship from the rightful heirs, the descendants of David. The
author of *Ps. Sol.* 17 speaks of how the Hasmoneans despoiled the
throne of David (17:6). In 17:21-25, he asks God to raise up for
Israel a king from the line of David ("son of David") to replace
the deposed Hasmoneans and to purge Jerusalem of its gentile
occupiers. It is said that the king of Israel will be Lord Messiah,
and will be a righteous king, taught by God (17:31-32). In 18:4-5,
the author asks God to purify the nation through discipline for the
appointed day when the Messiah will reign. Gentile nations will
serve under the yoke of the Messiah, and the Messiah will be free
from sin and powerful in the holy spirit (see Isa 11:2) (17:36-37).
The Messiah will also purge Jerusalem (including the Temple).
During the Messiah's reign, it seems that dispersed Israel will

return to the land (17:31; see 8:28; 11), which shall be divided according to the biblical tribal divisions (17:28)."[16]

Note that the idea of a sinless Messiah is but a "hope" in the Psalm of Solomon 17:36-37, not a prophecy of Isaiah. We might also consider whether the arrival of this Messiah is coincident with the prophecy in Jeremiah 31:33, which suggests that people having God's law in their hearts and minds, they will no longer sin.

It is interesting, to me at least, that the authors of these psalms were expressing a hope, rather than quoting a prophecy. In fact, not once in all eighteen psalms is there any mention of a prophecy or a promise, other than the covenant made with His "first-born, only begotten son" (PSS. Sol. 18:4). The relevance of these psalms, to my way of thinking, is that, having been written by Judean Pharisees in the first century BCE, they represented the apocalyptic thinking of the immediate generations to follow. It would seem probable that having been taught at the feet of Pharisaic rabbis, both Jesus and Paul (if he was) would have had some familiarity with the hope expressed in these psalms, if not the written psalms themselves.

If this be true, then we have an insight to the worldview of Jesus and his immediate followers, and their eschatological temper. There is no suggestion of a redeemer from sin: just rescue from the yoke of their enemies. The psalms also convey the Pharisaic understanding of sin and redemption.

Let me finish with Reynold's study by quoting his conclusion:

"Examining the portrait of the 'one like a son of man' in the OG has indicated some unique characteristics of the son of man figure. This figure is more closely aligned with the Ancient of Days. He is described as having arrived like the Ancient of Days, appearing with the clouds, receiving service due a divine figure, and having those standing before the Ancient of Days approach him. While the 'one like the son of man' is similar to the Ancient of Days, there is no indication of equivalency or identification. In fact, the giving of authority to the 'one like the son of man' implies that the son of man figure's status is different from the Ancient of Days.

The OG portrait of the son of man figure also suggests that the 'one like a son of man' has a messianic nature. This is most clearly seen in the kingly authority that the figure receives. Other indications include his kingdom that will not pass away and his distinction from the holy ones of the Most High.

It is possible, then, that the interpretation of the 'one like a son of man' in the OG may have provided a basis for the more openly messianic and heavenly interpretations of this figure that are found in later Jewish apocalyptic literature such as the Similitudes of Enoch and 4 Ezra."[17]

So, what do we make of all that?

There can be no doubt that the "one like a [son of] man", seen by Daniel in his vision, was considered a messianic figure, *by some*, but in the opinion of numerous scholars, especially Jewish, this was not necessarily so. His true nature is obscure, other than he was different from the others gathered there, and likely not of an equal status with the Ancient of Days (God). Daniel saw him being granted kingly status, but logically, he could not have been a deity. I accept that, if true, the Trinity is a mystery, not fathomable by us ordinary humans, but for one god to have authority over another god, there must be a form of hierarchical authority, with one at the top being GOD, and those beneath, demi-gods. This is consistent with the Greco-Roman view of the heavens, but not with that of the Children of Israel and their descendants. I am not contending that such a view could not have later developed somewhere, but I am confident that it did not exist in Daniel's mind, and in the mind of his contemporaries.

As it turns out, this hierarchical structure of authority, within the Trinity, did make its way into Christian theology at some point, evidenced by an article in Touchstone magazine. I will quote only the salient passages without detracting from the sense of the argument:

"Technically, hierarchy requires three things: sameness, differentiation, and connectedness. Because most would agree that the godhead represents complete connectedness, the questions that require our attention are the nature of its Persons' sameness and the nature of their differentiation. With regard to sameness, many will point to Philippians 2:6, which (in the KJV) says that Jesus 'being in the form of God, thought it not robbery to be equal with God.' I would propose that this rendering of the text is not conclusive. Another viable rendering is that of the ESV, which says, 'though he was in the form of God, did not count equality with God as a thing to be grasped.'

The image of robbery, or grasping, gives a picture not of ownership, but of acquisition. Paul underscores the unity of 'form' (morphe) shared by the Father and Son, but implies there was a kind of equality (isos) that the Son chose not to reach out for (harpazo). As Paul points out, beyond this relinquishment of possible positional equality with the Father, the Son also endured the Incarnation, his other extreme humiliations, and his sacrifice. It was because of the full range of his submissive obedience that he has been raised to a place of highest honor, second only to that of the Father (Phil. 2:9-11).

'I do not seek my own will but the will of the Father who sent me' (John 5:30). This, I believe, displays the nature of divine hierarchy coexisting with divine unity."[18]

Note how the author starts with the presupposition of the Trinity, and then seeks to impose a hierarchical structure upon it. I entirely agree with the stated technical nature of a hierarchy, which is why I disagree with the existence of a Trinity. If God is infinite in every conceivable way, then there can be no differentiation – that is the nature of an infinity. Of course, if that understanding of infinity is wrong, then God in the form of a Trinity is not infinite, which brings with it a multitude of other problems. The next point is the suggestion of "acquisition": if Jesus chose to not acquire the status of God, then he cannot be God. It is illogical to have Jesus saying: "I won't be God now, but I will be later when I choose to be"! God cannot relinquish His godly nature and then take it back whenever He so chooses, rather like switching between Clark Kent and Superman. Next, we have God being submissive to Himself, and then raising Himself up to only second place: a most unlikely occurrence for a God who is One.

The whole problem with this line of thinking is as earlier described: seeking an anthropomorphic description of God because in our finite world, everything is separately discernible. If things were not, then we could not discern them. Discernment occurs because every finite thing has boundaries, but God, being infinite, has no boundaries, by definition, and is thus not discernible by us finite beings. Putting boundaries, and thus limitations, around an infinite God is foolishness. I would emphasise that this view of a godly hierarchy, with a lower god being submissive to a higher god, is a product of Roman and Greek mythology, and had no place in Jewish thought of a God who is One. There can be no better illustration of the difference between the Hellenic mindset, and the Hebraic.

Now back to Daniel: it is unlikely that he, as a monotheistic Jew, would have considered this "one like a [son of] man" to be a god. Had he done so, it would be reasonable to expect him to have had more to say on the matter, but we find that the instigator of all activities, in the subsequent verses, to be God Himself. That this "one" disappears from Daniel's dream, never to be mentioned again, anywhere in later writings of the Hebrew Bible, suggests to me that he was not seen as being of great consequence. I would remind the reader that in Judaism, Daniel is not seen as a major prophet, or even a prophet at all (Talmud), which is why the Book of Daniel is included in the Writings, not the Prophets. The Christian Old Testament hides this distinction. The term, son of man, does appear in Daniel 8, but its meaning is clearly as in Ezekiel.

Another opinion is as here: "The Christological titles, 'Servant', 'Son of Man', and 'Son of God', were all representative titles that were applied to Israel first. Then Jesus took on these titles because he had taken on Israel's task."[19] I am not confident that the term, son of man, was applied to Israel, but it is not an important issue. What is important however, is the contention that Jesus took on Israel's task. If we study Israel's task according to the Hebrew Scriptures, it was never to die for the sins of others. You may recall that Moses was not allowed to take on the sins of others, but we will discuss that later.

Similitudes of Enoch

The *Book of Parables of Enoch* (1 Enoch 37-71) is quoted by some Christian apologists as the source of the term, *son of man*, and that Jesus, when describing himself thus, was taking Enoch's meaning rather than that found in Ezekiel. Enoch's portrayal of the son of man (remember that Hebrew and Aramaic do not have capital letters) is confusing: at one stage, he speaks of the son of man as the eschatological redeemer, but then later identifies himself as that person. Researching the *Similitudes*, I found the issue to be far more complex than I had anticipated, with far less consensus amongst scholars. There is debate about when this book was written, by whom, and whether Jesus would have had knowledge of these writings. The writings of Enoch are not considered canonical in either Judaism or Christianity, and some early Christian scholars contended that the Epistle of Jude should not be included in the canon either, because it referenced a non-canonical work (Jude 1:14). Some opinions date the writing of 1 Enoch 37-71 as first century CE, and thus highly unlikely to have been in circulation during the life of Jesus. If this be so, and Jesus did self-identify as the son of man, then it is improbable that Jesus could have used Enoch's meaning, although later writers / editors of the Gospels may have done so.

I find it interesting that Paul never uses the term, *son of man*, and the only occurrences outside the Gospels are in Acts 7:56 and Revelation 14:14, both paraphrases of Daniel 7:13. There does seem to be a transition from *son of man* in the Gospels, to *son of God* in other writings, which would suggest a change in the perception of Jesus' nature over time, or perhaps within a tradition. Why was it, that in Paul's writings, especially those which preceded the Gospels, the term *son of man* is never used in connection with Jesus? What does that tell us about Paul's perception of Jesus? In his conversations with Paul, did the risen Jesus not refer to himself as the son of man, or did Jesus never actually refer to himself that way, it being an embellishment by the authors of the Gospels?

My research into the *Similitudes of Enoch* has been less than comprehensive, due to the extensive and contradictory opinions of scholars, and my limited interest in the subject, other than seeking to understand the usage of the term, *son of man*. I have concluded that it is unlikely that Jesus would have used the term about himself in the sense that it appears in Enoch, that of an *eschatological redeemer*. Note also that in Enoch, the redemption is not from sin, but from the yoke of foreign governance. Thus, even if Jesus did use the term in the sense found in Enoch, it does not support the argument about Jesus seeing himself as one sent to die for our sins.

If you are interested in pursuing this subject for yourself, I have chosen this online article[20] from the University of St Andrews School of Divinity to demonstrate the complexity of the issue.

Conclusion

Accepting that Daniel did indeed write "one like the son of man", the obvious questions are: From where did he get that expression, and what would it have meant to him? Daniel was a contemporary of Ezekiel, so it is possible, even probable, that they had a common understanding. Ezekiel received his prophecies from God, and we can assume that Daniel's dreams were inspired by God. God consistently referred to Ezekiel as son of man, so if that same term occurred in Daniel's dream, why would it not mean the same as for Ezekiel? If God had wanted to avoid confusion, would He not have used a different term?

Jesus may have seen himself in terms of Daniel's reference, and Daniel's reference could relate to the Messiah, but the only logical path to infer a deity in Daniel, is to work backwards from a belief that Jesus was a deity – one cannot work forward from Daniel. The Gospel writers did use the Greek, so perhaps the interpretation expressed as "Son of Man" came from them, not from Jesus himself.

In the Book of Daniel 3:25, Christian translations, from the Greek, refer to the fourth being as son of God, like the son of God, and so forth. In the Hebrew, "and the appearance of the fourth [one] is like an angel's" (TJB). The two are not inconsistent, given similar expressions in Job and elsewhere – the term relates to a divinely appointed being. In Daniel 7:13, we have one like a man, or son of man, depending on the version. In Daniel 8:15-17, we read:

> "When I, Daniel, saw the vision I sought understanding, then behold! There stood before me the likeness of a man. I heard a human voice in the middle of the Ulai; he called out and said,

'Gabriel, explain the vision to that man.' So, he came to where I was standing. When he came I was terrified, and I fell face down. He said to me, 'Understand, son of man, that the vision concerns the time of the End.'" (TJB)

The term, son of man, occurs in Daniel twice in the Greek version, but only once in early Hebrew, although twice in later versions. No matter, one must ask why the sense in verse 7:13 should be different to that in verse 8:17? In verse 3:25, we saw the different translations of son of God, like son of God, angel, etc., demonstrating that the translations are less than rigorous, but none conveyed the sense of a deity. Similarly, the term son of man in later verses. It occurs frequently in Ezekiel, clearly distinguishing between the infinite God and mortal man. Jesus, as a Jew taught by the rabbis from the Hebrew Scriptures, would most likely have understood the term as in Ezekiel, and thus when he repeated referred to himself as son of man, he could only have been expressing his humanity. There is no licence to understand his usage of the term in any other sense, and no licence to render it in initial capitals: Son of Man.

I conclude that Jesus likely saw himself as a man, not as God. To my mind, this does contradict the Christian assertion that the Apostles perceived Jesus as God, even before the resurrection.

REFERENCES:

1. Greenleaf, Simon, *The Testimony of the Evangelists*, Kregel Classics, Grand Rapids, MI, 1995, sub-title
2. Brenton, Sir Lancelot Charles Lee (1807-1862), *An Historical Account of the Septuagint Version*, http://www.bible-researcher.com/brenton1.html
3. Boyarin, Daniel, *The Jewish Gospels: The Story of the Jewish Christ*, The New Press, New York, NY, 2012, p. 31
4. Scherman, Rabbi Nosson, *The Tanach*, Mesorah Publications, ArtScroll English Edition, Brooklyn, NY, 2011
5. Pentiuc, Rev. Dr. Eugen J., *The Aramaic Phrase Bar 'ĕnoš "Son of Man" (Daniel 7:13-14) Revisited*, http://www.goarch.org/ourfaith/bar-enosh
6. http://www.jewishencyclopedia.com/articles/13913-son-of-man
7. http://www.jewishencyclopedia.com/articles/10342-man-son-of
8. *The Tanach*, Scherman, Rabbi Nosson, Mesorah Publications, ArtScroll English Edition, Brooklyn, NY, 2011, p. 1186

9. http://www.chabad.org/library/article_cdo/aid/1735365/jewish/Why-Isnt-the-Book-of-Daniel-Part-of-the-Prophets.htm

10. http://www.chabad.org/library/article_cdo/aid/489751/jewish/Is-the-Book-of-Daniel-authentic.htm

11. Reynolds, https://www.bsw.org/biblica/vol-89-2008/the-one-like-a-son-of-man-according-to-the-old-greek-of-daniel-7-13-14/34/article-p79.html

12. *Ibid*, p. 70

13. *Ibid*

14. *Ibid*, p. 77

15. *Ibid*, p.78

16. http://www.mycrandall.ca/courses/ntintro/intest/PsalSolo.htm

17. Reynolds, *Ibid*, p.79

18. Woerner, Diane, *The Heart of Paradise*, Touchstone: A Journal of Mere Christianity, Jan/Feb 2017, pp. 48-49

19. Beale, G.K., *The Right Doctrine from the Wrong Texts? Essays on the Use of the Old Testament in the New*, Baker Academic, Grand Rapids, MI, 1994, p. 37

20. https://www.st-andrews.ac.uk/divinity/rt/otp/dmf/enoch/

CHAPTER 3-4

DANIEL 9 AND THE 70 WEEKS

"I, Daniel, contemplated the calculations ... the
seventy years since the ruin of Jerusalem"
(Daniel 9:2)

Why was Daniel *contemplating the calculations*? What prompted him to do
so: was something not happening as expected?

Interpretation Difficulties

Although both Judaism and Christianity accept the Book of Daniel as
canonical, secular historians consider Daniel to be a mythical, rather than
real, figure of history. Some of his narrative is inconsistent with history
from other sources; for example, Darius the Mede, in verses 9:1-2, cannot
be verified from any extra-biblical sources. That notwithstanding, I shall
attempt to demonstrate from the texts themselves, that the Christian
interpretation of Jeremiah's prophecies of seventy years, which are the basis
of Daniel's prophecies, is entirely incorrect.

A difficulty arises with fixing dates, because the Jewish calendar uses a cycle of 19 years, and the number of days between any two annual commemorations of the same event, may vary by up to three days. Jewish dates BCE are very difficult to line up with Gregorian or other dating systems; for example, secular texts date the destruction of the First Temple in Jerusalem as 586 BCE, whilst conversion of the Jewish calendar year 3320, dates it at 425 BCE. If we use the secular history dates for important figures such as Darius and Cyrus, it then becomes impossible to reconcile events. I shall attempt, as best I can, to avoid arguments that involve date clashes.

The Christian Argument

Daniel 9 is used by Christianity as a proof text, that the Old Testament **predicted the very day that Jesus presented Himself to Jerusalem as the prophesied Messiah**, but have these verses been misinterpreted, either inadvertently or deliberately? More importantly, is it even possible to be certain of dates to the accuracy of a "day"?

Let me firstly deal with an assertion, found in many Christian apologetics, concerning the Greek version of the Book of Daniel. The following is typical, although unusually, I have misplaced the online source. Nevertheless, I doubt whether any Christian would disagree with this interpretation, especially regarding the final statement of 173,880 days; this article[1] agrees:

> "To fully appreciate the remarkable significance of the following article, it is essential to realize that the Book of Daniel, as part of the Old Testament, was translated into Greek prior to 270 B.C., almost three centuries *before* Christ was born. This is a well-established fact of secular history.
>
> The Septuagint
>
> After his conquest of the Babylonian Empire, Alexander the Great promoted the Greek language throughout the known world, and thus almost everyone - including the Jews - spoke Greek. Hebrew

fell into disuse, being reserved primarily for ceremonial purposes (somewhat analogous to the use of Latin among Roman Catholics).

In order to make the Jewish Scriptures (what we call the Old Testament) available to the average Jewish reader, a project was undertaken under the sponsorship of Ptolemy II Philadelphus (285-246 B.C.) to translate the Hebrew Scriptures into Greek. Seventy scholars were commissioned to complete this work and their result is known as the "Septuagint" ("70") translation. (This is often abbreviated "LXX" and is so shown on the diagram.)

The Precision of Prophecy

When we examine the period between March 14, 445 B.C. and April 6, 32 A.D., and correct for leap years, we discover that it is 173,880 days exactly, *to the very day!*"

Sadly, this narrative is false on numerous points. As noted earlier, there is irrefutable evidence that Hebrew was in common usage amongst the Jews, especially in Judea. Secondly, the Greek translations ordered by Ptolemy were of the first five books only, Torah (Pentateuch), not the complete Hebrew Bible. There were numerous Greek translations of other books, by unknown authors, but there are no surviving copies. The earliest fragments of Daniel, in Greek, date from the mid-second century CE, and lack the majority of Chapter 9. Thirdly, I have been unable to find any reputable scholar of history, who claims to be able to calculate the exact number of days between any two dates in that period. Even Jewish texts disagree with one another on the year, let alone a day. To claim a calculation being exact *to the very day* is lamentable, and again shows ignorance, desperation, or both, on the part of many Christian apologists.

Investigating Further

As to dates, as best as I can discover, nobody knows with certainty, when Jesus, or other figures central to this history, were born, or appointed to their roles, and even our present calendar evidences our ignorance. For centuries, the annotation BC/AD, now secularised to BCE/CE, was used based on a belief of when Jesus was born, but it is now believed that he was born somewhere between 7 – 3 BCE. The uncertainty arises due to a lack of consensus amongst historians on key dates from the period. If we have no reliable dating of Jesus' life, or of other significant events, how can claims of accuracy to the day be made?

Another point: which was the day that *Jesus presented Himself to Jerusalem as the prophesied Messiah*? According to Chuck Missler, the author of the Koinonia House article[2], it was the day of his supposedly *triumphal* entry into Jerusalem. Supposed, you ask? We will come back to that.

> "On this particular day he rode into the city of Jerusalem riding on a donkey, deliberately fulfilling a prophecy by Zechariah that the Messiah would present Himself as king in just that way: *Rejoice greatly, O daughter of Zion; shout, O daughter of Jerusalem: behold, thy King cometh unto thee: he is just, and having salvation; lowly, and riding upon an ass, and upon a colt the foal of an ass.* (Zechariah 9:9) This is the only occasion that Jesus presented Himself as King. It occurred on April 6, 32 A.D."

According to Missler, this date is confirmed by "Luke 3:1: Tiberias appointed in A.D. 14; 15th year, A.D. 29; the 4th Passover occurred in A.D. 32." Unfortunately, Chuck Missler's understanding of mathematics needs correcting. If Tiberius was appointed in the year 14, then the first year of his reign is 14, and the 15th year (by adding 14) is 28, not 29. I shall put that down as an honest mistake, but a mistake it clearly is. One cannot assert precision in prophecy, whilst simultaneously demonstrating incompetence in simple arithmetic. How many Christians have accepted this explanation, without seeing the obvious flaw?

Deliberately fulfilling a prophecy by Zechariah? I would contend that prophecy fulfillment does not work that way, otherwise all and sundry could go about deliberately doing things to prove that they were the prophesied Messiah, but their actions would not be acceptable as evidence. The credibility of prophecy fulfillment can only be accepted when the person is involved in an activity in his normal course of events, preferably unaware that the activity matches a prophesied event.

Just briefly, to have a triumphal entry, one needs to have triumphed in some way - in what way did Jesus triumph? He may have triumphed over sin when he was crucified, but I am adamant that such was not what the people of Jerusalem, and elsewhere, had in mind, when "they began to rejoice and praise God with a loud voice for all the mighty works they had seen, saying: 'Blessed is the King who comes in the name of the Lord'" (Luke 19:37-38). The multitudes who followed Jesus to Jerusalem, were not following him to watch him be crucified by the Romans, I am quite sure of that. And if Rome's accusation of the Jews being "Christ Killers" is to be accepted, then not all of those in Jerusalem acknowledged Jesus as King. I find no hint of triumph in the Gospel accounts, and thus to label his arrival in Jerusalem, for the last time, as being triumphal, the Gospel writers must have had something else in mind. I would then question why, after decades of no triumph being achieved, those words still made their way into the Gospel narratives. Very curious indeed.

The Book of Daniel

Finally, I would remind readers that the Book of Daniel is found in the Hebrew Bible, not under the Prophets, but under *Kesuvim* (Writings). Not all sacred teachings were meant as Divine Messages to be conveyed to the people; these tracts were called Writings, because they were written, rather than proclaimed as "prophecies". In the case of Daniel, it was considered to allude to the future Redemption, but not in the form of a God-ordained prophecy.

The passage quoted above, from the Koinonia House website, is not authoritative in any sense: it contains basic errors of fact, which invalidate any claims of prophecy fulfillment.

Consider also these scholarly opinions quoted from here[3]:

> "Moreover, the Septuagint version of the book of Daniel, available in only two ancient manuscripts, is said to be periphrastic [use of many words] and expansionistic, containing considerably more material than the MT, aside from such deuterocanonical additions as the Story of Susanna, the Prayer of Azariah, and the Song of the Three Young Men (Moore 1977).

The official Greek translation of Daniel used in ancient times was that of Theodotion, an Ephesian (ca. 180 AD). His translation, which has antecedents (Schmitt 1966), has "the distinction of having supplanted the current version of the book of Daniel" (Jellicoe 1968:84). Further, around 400 AD Jerome ventured the opinion that the Septuagint 'differs widely from the original [Hebrew], and is rightly rejected.'

The Hebrew/Aramaic Masoretic text of the book of Daniel now has stronger support than at any other time in the history, of the interpretation of the book of Daniel."

I would encourage the reader to study this online reference. What is clear, is that there is no certainty regarding the authenticity of extant versions of Daniel, but scholarly opinion leans toward the Hebrew or Aramaic, over the Greek. Even Jerome considered the Greek version to be unreliable. Thus, the presuppositions in Christian apologetics should be considered as false. For that reason, I will prefer translations from the Hebrew Bible, over Christian translations which rely on the Greek. At this juncture, you might care to review the earlier discussion on the Septuagint in Chapter 2-1.

Reviewing the Text

The discussion and explanations that follow are based on the translation from the Hebrew, Daniel 9:1-2, 24-26. Ignoring the verse numbering, I shall number the individual points as I will discuss them. Due to an inability to reconcile Gregorian and Jewish calendars, I will use only the Jewish, which is what Daniel and the other prophets probably used any way.

1. In the first year of Darius son of Ahasuerus of the offspring of Media, who was made king over the kingdom of the Chaldeans.
2. In the first year of his reign, I, Daniel contemplated the calculations, the number of years about which the word of Hashem had come to the prophet Jeremiah, to complete the seventy years since the ruin of Jerusalem.

3. Seventy septets have been decreed upon your people and upon your holy city to terminate transgression, to end sin, to wipe away iniquity, to bring everlasting righteousness, to confirm the visions and the prophets, and to anoint the Holy of holies.

4. From the emergence of the word to return to Jerusalem until the appointment of the prince will be seven septets.

5. And for sixty-two septets it will be rebuilt, street and moat, but in troubled times.

6. Then after the sixty-two septets, an anointed one will be cut off and will exist no longer.

7. The people of the prince who comes will destroy the city and the Sanctuary; but his end will be [to be swept away as] in a flood.

8. Then, until the end of the war, desolation is decreed.

9. He will forge a strong covenant with the great ones for one septet.

Discussion and Explanation

As you doubtless already know, a *septet* is 7 years; seventy septets equals 490 years.

Daniel identifies King Darius [1], who was in the first year of his reign [2], which Jewish history records as the year, 3390. Daniel was contemplating the two prophecies in Jeremiah, which both referred to a period of seventy years. The relevant passages are:

a. "I shall eliminate from them [the tribes of Israel] the sound of joy and the sound of gladness, the sound of the groom and the sound of the bride, the sound of the mill and the light of the candle. This entire land will be a ruin and desolation, and these nations will serve the king of Babylonia for seventy years." (Jer 25:10-11)

b. "Then, upon the completion of seventy years, I shall make an account of their sin for the king of Babylonia and for that nation – the word of Hashem – and for the land of the Chaldeans; and I shall make it into eternal desolations." (Jer 25:12)

c. "And I shall bring upon that land all My words that I have spoken concerning it, all that is written in this book, which Jeremiah prophesied concerning all the nations. For many nations and great kings will enslave [Babylonia] also; I shall repay them according to their action and according to their handiwork." (Jer 25:13-14)

d. "For thus said Hashem: After seventy years for Babylonia have been completed I will attend to you and I will fulfill for you My favourable promise, to return you to this place." (Jer 29:10)

At first reading, these two prophecies of seventy years appear to relate to the same period, but there are differences, which is likely why Daniel was contemplating them, just as he wrote.

First Period of 70 Years

The prophecy In Jeremiah 25 speaks of the subjugation of the people under Nebuchadnezzar; this was to continue for a period of seventy years, during which other things would occur in the lands of the Jewish people. Babylon's subjugation of Jerusalem occurred in the year, 3320.

Jeremiah 29 begins with an address to "all the people whom Nebuchadnezzar had exiled from Jerusalem to Babylonia" (Jer 29:1). The people are exhorted to reproduce and prosper, seeking the peace of the city to which they had been exiled. Most significantly, they are warned against false prophets, and are assured that their period of exile is seventy years, after which, God would return them to Jerusalem.

There is no discernible difference between the periods mentioned in Jeremiah 25 and 29: they do appear to be the same period of seventy years. However, Daniel did not seem to think so. At the end of these seventy years, Daniel was contemplating the significance, but what was his concern? If the two prophecies in Jeremiah were of the same period of seventy years, then there should have been signs of the restoration of the Jewish people and the Temple, but such was not happening. Daniel must have then thought that there were two separate periods prophesied, no doubt starting on different dates. Was he wrong, or do we have evidence that he was right?

Second Period of 70 Years

We now return to [2], the significant words in Daniel 9:2 which are overlooked: "to complete the seventy years **since the ruin of Jerusalem**" [emphasis mine]. Although Jerusalem was subjugated in 3320, and the Jews began their seventy-year servitude under the king of Babylonia, the destruction of Jerusalem did not occur until the year 3338, eighteen years later. Thus, the second period of seventy years begins in 3338, not 3320.

Now we can place Daniel's prophecy in its proper perspective, as relating to the period between the destruction of the first and second Temples: 490 years (3338 – 3829). Attempts by Christianity to apply this prophecy of Daniel to the Messiah are entirely false, as is evidenced by the attempt to date the timeline from 3320 instead of 3338. Now, I don't know about you, but I get confused with this terminology of weeks, years, and septets, and the Gregorian versus the Jewish calendars, so rather than stumble, I will simply quote from this explanation[4] by Jewish scholar, Rabbi Tovia Singer. I have validated the explanation for myself, and I shall let you do the same, should you be so interested. Remember – I am not out to convince you, simply relating why I am convinced.

> "70 weeks (of years) – Gabriel begins his prophecy to Daniel (9:24) with the revelation that '70 weeks' (490 years) have been decreed upon the Jewish people and Jerusalem, after which the Messianic Age can commence. The verses that follow contain a detailed description of what would transpire during this time. This period spanned from the destruction of the First Temple until the destruction of the Second, exactly 490 years (3338-3829).
>
> 'Seven weeks' (of years) – Gabriel reassured Daniel that after a full '7 weeks' (49 years) passed, counting from 'the going forth of the WORD when Jerusalem was destroyed (9:2), an anointed ruler would command the Jewish people to return and rebuild Jerusalem (9:25). Indeed, after half a century passed, Cyrus, who God declared as His 'anointed one' (Isaiah 45:1), ordered the Jews to return and rebuild Jerusalem and the holy sanctuary (Isaiah 44:28-45:1, 13; Ezra 1:2-3; II Chronicles 36:22-23).

'Sixty-two weeks' (of years) – In verse 9:25, the angel reveals to Daniel how, for nearly four and a half centuries, Jerusalem would be 'rebuilt, street and moat'. Gabriel adds, however, that throughout these '62 weeks', the Holy City would endure 'troubled times'. Accordingly, the Second Temple period was filled with spiritual and political turbulence. In verse 9:26, the angel reveals that the '62 weeks" would tragically conclude with two watershed events. First, an anointed one (the high priest) would be cut off, and would cease his ecclesiastical functions. Second, the 'people of the prince' (the legions of Vespasian and Titus) would come to destroy the Holy City and its sanctuary. Both of these tragic events occurred simultaneously, shortly after the 434 years, or '62 weeks' were completed.

Seven years before the Second Temple was destroyed, Rome permitted the Jews to offer sacrifices. This agreement, however, was broken when Nero sent Vespasian to crush Jewish life in Jerusalem in 66 CE, 3½ years before Titus razed Herod's temple in the years 3829 (Daniel 9:27)."

Summary

When I compare the NKJV version of Daniel 9, with the translation from the Hebrew, I find significant differences in the wording, although perhaps "subtle" would be a more accurate description for some; e.g., *desolations* of Jerusalem, rather than *ruin* of Jerusalem. Desolations is a word more suggestive of people, as in exile and subjugation, whilst ruin generally relates to property and buildings. In verse 9:24, the NKJV says "to anoint the Most Holy", suggestive of the Messiah, whilst the Hebrew has "to anoint the Holy of Holies", meaning the Temple. In verse 9:25, the NKJV says "until Messiah the Prince", whilst in the Hebrew, simply "the prince". In 9:26, the Hebrew has: "an anointed one will be cut off and exist no longer", whilst the NKJV has the curious "Messiah shall be cut off but *not for Himself*" – what does that mean?

Understanding a transliteration from the Greek can be perplexing, even more so as the grammar is very different to English. Determining to which noun, or event, an adjectival phrase relates can be problematic, and can be influenced by a prior understanding. Consider this transliteration of Daniel 9:25-26 from the Greek[5]:

> "The prince the Messiah to Jerusalem times and even in troublous and the wall and the street and shall be built again and the city to but not Messiah shall be cut off and two sixty weeks and after and the end that shall come of the prince and the people."

Firstly, note how this rendering has *Messiah* with an initial capital, a theological annotation, when "anointed one" would be a more theologically neutral translation. The first words equate the prince with the Messiah, and so the end of the prince should also be the end of the Messiah. Clearly, that would be antithetical to Christian doctrine, having Jesus cut off, so the translators came up with the obscure: *"not for Himself"*. I would love to have been a fly on the wall when they decided that! Did they have a ballot, or just leave it to the last person out the door?

Conclusion

I am convinced that Christian translators deliberately, and likely sincerely, interpreted the translation of Daniel 9, to make it appear as if the prophecy concerned Jesus as Messiah, but they have done a very poor job of it. The obvious error is ignoring that David was perplexed as to why some things were not happening as prophesied, and the misunderstanding of the starting point for Daniel's prophecy: the exile of the people, versus the destruction of Jerusalem, eighteen years later. But, of course, the greatest howler is the claim that a prophecy fulfillment can be dated to an exact day and date, when the consensus of scholars and historians, Jewish, Christian, and secular, is that no such precision is possible. But then, a Christian apologist attempts to enforce precision by using faulty arithmetic. Really!

I believe, on the evidence, that there is no justification for associating Jesus with these prophecies in Daniel 9.

REFERENCES:

1. http://www.alphanewsdaily.com/mathprophecy1.html
2. http://www.khouse.org/articles/2004/552/#notes
3. http://www.biblearchaeology.org/post/2012/07/31/New-Light-on-the-Book-of-Daniel-from-the-Dead-Sea-Scrolls.aspx#Article
4. Singer, Rabbi Tovia, *Let's Get Biblical – Expanded Edition Volume 1*, Outreach Judaism, Jerusalem, Israel, 2015, pp. 224-225
5. http://biblehub.com/interlinear/daniel/9-26.htm

CHAPTER 3-5

JEREMIAH AND THE NEW COVENANT

"Finding fault with them, he says: Behold, the days are coming … when I will make a new covenant"
(Hebrews 8:8)

If it were not for this mention in the Book of Hebrews, and that falsely attributed to Paul as the author, I doubt that Christian theologians would have voluntarily wandered into this trap, for a trap it most surely is. The only direct mentions of Jeremiah, in the New Testament, are in Matthew 2:17, 16:14, and 27:9, none of which refer to a covenant.

Our first interrogation of the witness is to establish identity, and thus credibility. Who wrote the Book of Hebrews? In Chapter 2-3, we noted the opinion of scholars going all the way back to Origen, that Paul was not the author of this book. We also noted: "Further, around 400 AD Jerome ventured the opinion that the Septuagint 'differs widely from the original [Hebrew], and is rightly rejected'."[1] That being so, and Hebrews having referenced the Septuagint, I do wonder why Jerome argued not just for its authorship, but also its authenticity. Jerome seems to have wanted it both ways. Irrespective of the authorship, we can verify from the text of Jeremiah that his prophecy related to the End of Days, not the time of Jesus.

A ship's captain, docking his vessel, looks fore and aft to ensure that he is positioning his vessel correctly, as I would hope, a driver does when parallel parking. Similarly, when studying Scripture, in this case Jeremiah 31, we must consider the preceding and following chapters to ensure that we have positioned our minds correctly, lest we take verses out of context, which I contend, the author of Hebrews has done, and the Church has solemnly followed suit. Let us start with Jeremiah 30, the following copied from The Jewish Bible, a translation from the Hebrew into English.

> "This is the word that came to Jeremiah from Hashem ... thus said Hashem, God of Israel, saying: 'Write down for yourself all these things that I am telling you into a book. For behold, days are coming – the word of Hashem – when I will return the captivity [those in captivity] of My people Israel and Judah, said Hashem, and I will return them to the land that I gave their forefathers, and they will possess it'." (vv. 1-3)

Three points to note:
1. "Days are coming" refers to the *End of Days*, not the time of Jesus of Nazareth.
2. God is referring to the Twelve Tribes – the house of Israel [10], and the house of Judah [2]; and
3. God is promising to return His people to *Eretz Israel* – the land He gave to their forefathers. Remember that God promised Abraham: "I will give to you and to your offspring after you the land of your sojourns ... as an **everlasting** possession" (Genesis 17:8) [emphasis mine]. As an aside, even Muslim clerics quote from the Quran stating the same.

Note that later, Jeremiah 31:30 also begins with *days are coming*, thus placing the renewed covenant contemporary with the return of the Jews to Israel. God then speaks of the terror to come in those days, but comforts Israel:

"But as for you, do not fear, My servant Jacob, the word of Hashem, and do not be afraid, Israel, for behold, I am saving you from distant places, and your descendants from the land of their captivity, and Jacob will return and be at peace and tranquil, and none will make him afraid, for I am with you – the word of Hashem – to save you; for I will bring annihilation upon all the nations among whom I have dispersed you, but upon you I will not bring annihilation; I will chastise you with justice, but I will never eliminate you completely." (vv. 10-11)

God explains that Israel caused her own troubles:

"How can you cry out over your injury, over your pain that is grave? It is because of your many sins, your transgressions that were so numerous, that I inflicted these upon you! Nevertheless, all who devoured you shall themselves be devoured; all who oppressed you will all go into captivity; who trampled you will be trampled; and all who despoiled you, I shall deliver to become spoils." (vv. 15-16)

Earlier generations were warned similarly: "Those who bless you [Israel] are blessed, and those who curse you are accursed" (Numbers 24:9). This should give all Christians cause to reflect on the oppression (persecution) of the Jews, by the Church of Rome, continued by some factions of Christendom, e.g. the World Council of Churches, with their support of the anti-Israel declarations by the United Nations, and the BDS (Boycott, Divestment, and Sanctions) movement of recent times. It was the Catholic Church that taught contempt for the Jew, the writings of the Church Fathers confirming this. For an in-depth review of this evil history, I would recommend this book by Jules Isaac[2]. Israel shall be spared, and better:

"I will make a cure for you, and I will heal you from your wounds ... they called you 'Discarded'! Saying, 'She is Zion – no one cares about her!' Thus, said Hashem: Behold, I am returning the captivity of the tents of Jacob and I will have mercy on his abodes, and the City [Jerusalem] will be built upon its hill, and the Palace will sit in its proper place. The sound of thanksgiving and the sound of merrymakers will emanate from them; I will multiply them, and they will not be diminished; and I will make them numerous, and they will not dwindle." (vv. 17-19)

*They call you **discarded***: Is that not what the Church of Rome did in discarding the Jews, disenfranchising them from the Covenant, calling Judaism a blasphemy, and self-styling Christianity as the *New Israel*? *She is Zion – **no one cares** about her*: Is that not the attitude of the modern world, with the United Nations moving more resolutions against Israel than all other nations combined, and refusing to condemn the terrorist organisations for their wanton attacks on Israeli citizens?

God again affirms what He told the Children of Israel, after rescuing them from their slavery in Egypt: "You will be a people unto Me, and I will be a God unto you" (v. 22). Isaiah conveyed the same message:

> "But you, O Israel, My servant, Jacob, you whom I have chosen, offspring of Abraham who love Me – you whom I shall grasp from the ends of the earth and summon from among all its noblemen, and to whom I shall say, 'You are My servant' – I have chosen you and not rejected you. Fear not for I am with you; be not dismayed, for I am your God; I have strengthened you, even helped you, and even sustained you with My righteous right hand. Behold, all who become angry with you will be shamed and humiliated; those who fight with you, they shall be like nothingness and naught." (Isaiah 41:8-11)

Referring to this promise of God, of Israel's return to Jerusalem, consider what Jesus is reported to have said to the Samaritan: "Woman, believe me, the hour is coming when you will neither on this mountain [Gerizim], nor in Jerusalem, worship the Father" (John 4:21). Was Jesus contradicting the Father, or was he foretelling of the time when Christian heresy would take them to Rome? Jesus continued: "You worship what you do not know; we know what we worship, for salvation is of the Jews." Consider this:

"The Samaritans were a pagan sect that grew out of the tribes of Manasseh and Ephraim after their deportation in 723 BC into Assyria by Shalmaneser. After the return of Judah, the Samaritans ceased to worship idols, but they invented a brand new alternate religion where they chose Mt. Gerizim as their holy mountain in direct opposition to Jerusalem. This action was a continuation of Jeroboam's policy of separating the ten northern tribes from the one true God at Jerusalem. His famous quote: "It is too far for you to go up to Jerusalem... worship at Bethel or Dan" says it all. The Samaritans, therefore represented all the worst of the Jews in that they opposed God's choice of David, of Jerusalem, and polluted their bloodlines which forever disqualified them from producing Jesus, Jesus Christ."[3]

Curious, is it not? Has Christianity entirely misunderstood John in this context?

Continuing with Jeremiah 30: God warns Israel of impending troubles, tells the people that until the *End of Days*, they will not truly understand what is happening to them, but assures them that He will not abandon them:

"Behold, the storm of Hashem: A rage shall go forth, a tempest shall seek rest; it will rest upon the head of the wicked. Hashem's burning wrath will not recede until He has accomplished it, and until He has upheld the plans of His heart. In the end of days, you will be able to understand it. At that time – the word of Hashem – I will be a God for all the families of Israel, and they will be a people for Me." (vv. 23-25)

I will leave the reader to continue the narrative for themselves, until we reach the passages which I contend, has been misinterpreted in Christianity: Jeremiah 31:30-33.

"Behold, days are coming – the word of Hashem – when I will seal a renewed covenant with the House of Israel, and with the House of Judah."

All along, the context of the prophecy is Israel in the *End of Days* – no other interpretation is possible, other than if taken out of context. I do not intend to review the prophecy itself, my purpose being satisfied by demonstrating that, whatever the author of Hebrews had in mind, he was entirely wrong in linking the renewed covenant with the accomplishments of Jesus. In another study, *The New Covenant on Trial*[4], I investigate the Christian claim of a New (Replacement) Covenant, and conclude that on the evidence, Jesus expressed no such sentiment.

REFERENCES:

1. http://www.biblearchaeology.org/post/2012/07/31/New-Light-on-the-Book-of-Daniel-from-the-Dead-Sea-Scrolls.aspx#Article
2. Isaac, Jules, *The Teaching of Contempt: Christian Roots of Anti-Semitism*, Holt, Rinehart and Winston, Inc., New York, NY, 1964
3. http://www.bible.ca/archeology/bible-archeology-samaritans.htm
4. Talbot, Wayne, *The New Covenant on Trial: Examining the Evidence for a Replacement Covenant*, Xlibris, Bloomington, IN, 2016

CHAPTER 3-6

ISAIAH AND THE VIRGIN BIRTH

"Behold, the virgin shall be with child, and bear a son".
(Matthew 1:23, NKJV)

Let me apologise in advance for what is a lengthy discussion, but in the context of prophecy fulfillment, I believe it crucial to our understanding of Jesus being the prophesied Messiah. I have encountered numerous opinions on the proper interpretation of Isaiah 7:14, some complementary, others contradictory; thus in the interests of intellectual honesty, I shall do my best to give them a proper airing.

Christianity reads Mary's virgin birth back into Isaiah 7:14 as a prophecy, so let us have a brief look at that verse and those leading up to it. Starting in 7:1, we have the story of the warring Jewish tribes, with God instructing Ahaz to ask Him for a sign. Ahaz refused, but Isaiah insisted that there would be a sign, in the form of the birth of a boy who was to be called Immanuel. This is where the Christian translation departs from the Orthodox Jewish, with most Christian versions referring to "**a** virgin", but the Jewish, "**the** young woman".

The Isaiah 7 Interlinear[1] translates *harah ha-almah* as "shall conceive a virgin", but checking Strongs Concordance 2030[2], we find 16 occurrences of the term *harah*, with 15 of them interpreted as *being pregnant*, or *with child*. For example: Genesis 16:11, 38:24, 38:25, Exodus 21:22, 1 Samuel 4:19, and 2 Samuel 11:5. The one exception is Isaiah 7:14, and one has to ask: Why? Similarly, "ha", in *ha-almah*, is the definite article, not indefinite: thus, just as in Genesis 24:43, Exodus 2:8, and others, it should be translated as "the" not "a". Putting this together, we can legitimately paraphrase as: "the pregnant young woman shall deliver". Curiously, the NKJV version of Isaiah 7:14, and Matthew 1:23, does use the definite article, "the", rather than the indefinite "a", which as a prophecy, would make little sense without a prior identification of the woman.

The Hebrew word transliterated as *almah* means literally, young woman. *Virgin* can be inferred because most young women or maidens were virgins, but we must ask: is there a separate Hebrew word for virgin? Turns out that there is, *bethulah*, and it can be found in numerous places in the Tanakh, e.g. Jeremiah 31:13. This suggests to me that if Isaiah meant "virgin", he would have used that specific term. On the other hand, people will argue from the Septuagint that the word "alma" was translated as "parthenos" which, they claim, always meant "virgin". But that too is highly debatable because in the Septuagint version of Genesis 34, Dinah, who was raped by Shechem, is still referred to as *parthenos* even after the rape (Genesis 34:3). As best as I can understand, a raped woman is no longer a virgin, by definition. That aside, in the opinion of Jerome and other Christian scholars, as discussed earlier: the Septuagint "differs widely from the original [Hebrew], and is rightly rejected". Before arguing from the Greek, we need to assure ourselves that the source is reliable.

Delving further into scholarly opinion, Jacques Doukhan[3] offers a contrary explanation. As a Hebrew scholar, he analyses what he terms, the *poetic structure* of the text, to derive his understanding, a technique about which I cannot comment. He states:

> "The problem of this text is, first of all, a linguistic one and concerns the meaning of the Hebrew word '*almah*' ("virgin").

Does this word really mean virgin? This particular meaning has been challenged on the basis of the following argument: If Isaiah indeed meant "virgin", why did he choose the word *'almah'* which is used only nine times in the Hebrew Bible and carries an ambiguous meaning (virgin or young woman)? Why did he not use instead the technical word *bethulah*, which is used 51 times in the Hebrew Bible with the allegedly unambiguous meaning of "virgin"? First of all, it should be noticed that it is not correct to say that the word bethulah means unambiguously 'virgin'."[4]

The author then goes on to explain that *bethulah* can also refer to a non-virgin woman, quoting texts from Ugaritic literature. He notes that: "In the Hebrew Bible, only three of the 51 occurrences of *bethulah* mean unambiguously 'virgin' (Lev 21:13; Deut 22:19; Ezek 44:22) and once it clearly does not, in Joel 1:8, where the *bethulah* weeps about the husband of her youth."[5] Doukhan then states:

> "On the other hand, it is remarkable that in none of the passages where the word *almah* occurs is it applied to a married woman. The biblical evidence then suggests that the word *almah* more than the word *bethulah*, could be qualified to express the idea of virginity. Actually, it is only later, in the legal context of rabbinic literature, that the word *bethulah* acquires the technical meaning of 'virgin'. It is, therefore, a mistake to read the biblical word *bethulah* with the exclusive rabbinic meaning in mind. As we already indicated, the biblical document shows that at that time, the idea of virginity was expressed through the word *alma* rather than through the word *betulah*"[6]

The assertion: "none of the passages where the word *almah* occurs is it applied to a married woman" piqued my curiosity. Doukhan accepts that Isaiah used the word, *almah*, so is he now saying that whoever this woman was, she was not married? Was God saying that this young, unmarried woman, a virgin, would become pregnant and bear a son? Why is Ahaz's reaction not recorded: "Really? An unmarried virgin? Who is going to marry her ... me?" Later, Doukhan refers to Ahaz's wife, but does not clarify if this is the same woman. Something is awry with this argument. The long and the short of his discussion is that we cannot be certain of Isaiah's intentions when he used the word *almah*. Given these contrary scholarly opinions, I would conclude that indeed, we cannot be sure, and that we must look for other clues to help us in understanding Isaiah 7:14.

The definite article "the" as in "the young woman" suggests that the young woman in question was already known to both Isaiah and Ahaz. If Isaiah was intending a prophecy, he would most likely have used the indefinite article as in "a young woman". Doukhan begs to differ; he argues:

> "Actually, the use of the definite article with the word 'virgin' may support the interpretation of the virginity of the woman in question, since the definite article is often used in a generic sense to refer to 'classes or species' that 'are unique'. In this instance, the use of the definite article suggests the special and unique category the 'virgin' represents. Also, the fact that this future son was to be born from a particular virgin woman, fits quite well with the expressed intention to give this birth as a prophetic sign for the supernatural intervention of God. For, if the text did not intend a birth from a virgin woman, how could a natural birth from a regular woman such as Ahaz's wife or Isaiah's wife be then interpreted as a sign of the supernatural?"[7]

Do you see what he has done here? Despite accepting that there is a lack of consistency in the usages of the words, *almah* and *bethulah*, he has concluded that *almah* in Isaiah 7:14 does mean *virgin*. Why would he do that unless he has accepted the virgin birth by Mary *as fact*, and then used that to argue that Isaiah <u>must</u> have been prophesying of her. He rejects the notion of a natural birth, not because the text does not allow it, but because he already believes that Isaiah intended *to give this birth as a prophetic sign for the supernatural intervention of God*. Logically, he has put the cart before the horse, or in more formal terms, is begging the question. The question we are attempting to have answered is whether or not Isaiah 7:14 is a prophecy of a supernatural conception of Jesus by Mary. Logically, it cannot be answered by affirming the consequent, which is precisely what this scholar has done. Combined with this is his assertion that *almah* was never used in connection with a married woman, and therefore the woman could not have been married. But if we are exercise our imagination on this, when we are bereft of evidence, the woman may have been an unmarried virgin at the time of the prophecy, but was later married and conceived in the normal way. There is no suggestion in the narrative that this birth of Ahaz would be a miraculous virgin birth, or more, that the birth of Ahaz's mother would have been an *immaculate conception*, as was later claimed for Mary, the mother of Jesus.

So, who was this woman? Think on this for a moment. Why do we know so little about her, when so much theology is riding on her identity? Why would Isaiah, at a revelation from God, have so little to say on the matter? Would God have not foreseen the stumbling of generations over this issue, and sought to have clarified it? I cannot know, but I do wonder. That said, let us hear from the editors of The Jewish Bible:

> "Although Ahaz contemptuously refused to ask for a sign from God, Isaiah told him that there will be a sign, which will involve a young woman who will give birth to a son. Since the Hebrew uses the definite article *the* – ha'almah – *the* young woman, it is clear that her identity was known. Most classic commentators agree that she was either the young wife of Ahaz, or Isaiah's wife (see 8:3). The 'sign' is that she would be Divinely inspired to name her newborn child Immanuel, 'God is with us', implying an assurance to Ahaz that Rezin and Pekah will come to naught within a short time."[8]

Again, Doukhan has a contrary opinion as to the identity of the son. He states: "This son cannot be the prophet's son since the prophet's wife already had a son Shear-Jashub (Isa 7:3) and could, therefore, not qualify as a virgin."[9] Again, the presupposition of virgin. He argues that the child will be conceived without the help of Ahaz, or any male help: "the virgin shall conceive and bear a son", again begging the question before the question can be settled. Doukhan concludes, quite logically for him: "Ahaz is, therefore, naturally excluded as the father of that son."[10] We do know, however, from 2 Kings 18:1, that Hezekiah was the son of Ahaz, so the suggestion here is that the son referred to in Isaiah 7:14 is not Hezekiah. Effectively, the father of this "Immanuel" is not identified in Scripture. In isolation, this hypothesis is plausible, but does the wider context allow that hypothesis?

What do the following verses tell us? "He will eat cream and honey as soon as he knows to abhor evil and choose good" (v. 15). This is a recurring theme in the Hebrew Scriptures: there are rewards in this life for those who choose good. The source of these is explained in verses 21-22: "It shall be on that day (see verse 20) that each man will raise a heifer and two sheep, but it shall be that from the abundant production of milk he will eat cream, and whoever is left in the midst of the land will eat cream and honey." Now I ask you: How does this relate to the life of Jesus? If you answer: It does not, then the boy in question cannot be Jesus. However, before he can know these things, "the land of the two kings whom you fear will be abandoned" (v. 16). The military threat posed by the two kings, those of Damascus and Syria, ended just thirteen years later, some 700 years before the birth of Jesus. Using beautiful allegory, Isaiah explains: "On that day the Lord will shave with a large razor those who crossed the [Euphrates] river with the kings of Assyria; the head, the hair of the legs, and the beard, as well, will be destroyed." (v. 20)

Dr. Jacques Doukhan attempts to sidestep this issue by having us believe that Isaiah 7:14 is an aside, and not relevant to the preceding and subsequent texts. I do not, and cannot, accept his hypothesis, for it is stretching credibility too far to isolate verse 14, as if it were just an aside. Christianity, and some of Messianic Judaism, weave a web of intrigue, with many scholars accepting the plain meaning of the text, but also asserting that it is a prophecy of Jesus: Isaiah was speaking of two births – one then, and one later! But then one must ask, were there two virgin births, one in Isaiah's time, and one centuries later? Is the argument that Hezekiah's mother was also a virgin? It is obvious to me, and hopefully to you as well, that these attempts to read a messianic prophecy into Isaiah's foretelling of impending events, are both clumsy and at times, self-contradictory.

The issue becomes: whom should we believe – a modern Messianic Jewish scholar, or the Sages who have passed down their understanding from the earliest times? Even the text itself refutes messianic interpretation. If nothing else, the choice for me comes down to the source of the confusion:

the reliability of the Greek scriptures, which as we have seen, many do question, or that of the Hebrew Bible, which as far as I have been able to ascertain, nobody questions. Compare the translations of Isaiah 7:14,

a. Behold, the young woman will become pregnant and bear a son (TJB); versus
b. Behold, the virgin shall conceive and bear a Son (NKJV).

Quite obviously, if *the young woman will become pregnant*, then we should have no problem with her being a virgin *before* becoming pregnant. What else would we expect? In researching bible versions on Isaiah 7:14, I encountered these:

• "For this cause the Lord himself will give you a sign; a young woman is now with child, and she will give birth to a son, and she will give him the name Immanuel." (The Bible in Basic English)

• "For this cause the Lord himself will give you a sign; a young woman is now with child, and she will give birth to a son, and she will give him the name Immanuel." (Good News Bible)

Obviously, some Christian translators accept the Hebrew over the Greek Septuagint, or at least, convey the same meaning as I understand of this verse in Isaiah. "Is now with child" relates to a contemporary event, not one 700 years into the future. Another interesting article on this issue can be found online here[11]. Citing the relevant comments:

"It seems pretty clear to me that Isaiah 7:14 mentions a pregnant woman (who, at least as far as translation can take us, may or may not have been a virgin) and that the NT refers to the virgin birth of Jesus. It seems equally clear that the lack of perfect harmony between the texts is in keeping with other kinds of prophesy in the NT.

The issue is how to reconcile the virgin birth with Isaiah 7:14, which is cited in Matthew 1:23. The most straightforward way is to note that even though Isaiah 7:14 refers to a "young woman," not a "virgin," the text doesn't say that she wasn't a virgin. She could have been. (By comparison, the text also doesn't say that the woman had long hair, but she might have.) In other words, Isaiah 7:14, even with the better understanding of the original text, doesn't contradict anything in the NT.

The more nuanced way to reconcile the two texts is to recognize what the verb in Matthew 1:22, *plirow,* really indicates. Though the word is commonly translated "fulfill" (as in, "All this took place to fulfill what the Lord had said through the prophet [Isaiah]"), better is "match," as I describe here ("What Happens to Prophecies in the New Testament?"). I won't go through the whole explanation again, but for now I think it suffices to note that Matthew knew that the details in Isaiah 7:14 differed from those he was describing. After all, the name of the child in Isaiah 7:14 was Immanuel, not Jesus."

If Matthew knew that *the details in Isaiah 7:14 differed from those he was describing*, then Matthew was not claiming that the birth of Jesus *fulfilled* Scripture.

One last point: Why the conditional "Therefore" or "For this cause" in the Old Testament narrative, and how does that apply to Matthew's account? According to Matthew 1:22, it was done to fulfill (or match) the Scripture (not prophecy), but in the OT, it was done because Ahaz did not want a sign. It is illogical to have Ahaz refusing a sign, just so that there would be a sign prophesizing the birth of a messiah. Whilst this was clearly a prophecy, it was one concerning contemporary events, not centuries into the future.

The Name: Immanuel

Another oddity in the New Testament, easily explained by some, and we will come to that, is that despite being told to call the son, *Immanuel,* that name is never used: Why was that? Why did Joseph not understand the supposed prophecy fulfillment, but instead: "he called his name Jesus" (Matt 1:25)? If the name, Immanuel, means "God is with us", does it better fit Jesus, or the son of Ahaz, Hezekiah?

Continuing with Isaiah, "The Lord will bring the king of Assyria upon you and your people" (Isaiah 7:18), which occurred long before the days of Jesus, but the connection between the Hezekiah and this story begins in Isaiah 8, where we again find the term *Immanuel*. The NKJV reads: "He ... will fill the breadth of your land, O Immanuel" (Isaiah 8:8). In the Hebrew Bible, we find the following explanation:

> "The tribe of Judah, under righteous King Hezekiah, will miraculously be saved from the Assyrian invasion, as foretold by Isaiah (2 Kings 19:7, 35). This Divine assistance was foreshadowed by Isaiah's prophecy, that a child would be born to a woman known to King Ahaz, and that he would be named Immanuel, which means "God is with us" (7:14)."[12]

We then pick up the story in 2 Kings 16:1, with Ahaz becoming King, and his son Hezekiah following him (2 Kings 16:20, 18:1). Hezekiah fits the prophecy in Isaiah 9:6, "He trusted in the Lord God of Israel, so that after him was none like him among all the kings of Judah, nor who were before him" (v. 18:5). Where the text states of Hezekiah, "The Lord was with him" (v. 18:7), it suggests that the term, Immanuel, is appropriate. Isaiah and Ahaz were contemporaries, and Isaiah's prophecies (*forthtellings*) fit perfectly with what occurred in those times.

It may be claimed that Isaiah was prophesying of the future Messiah, but that would have to be in addition to the contemporary fulfillment. Is it valid to interpret a prophecy as referring to two different people, in two different circumstances, in two different times, hundreds of years apart? You decide.

As for *Jesus* versus *Immanuel*, the answer lies in our translation of the term, and for that we can turn to Isaiah 8:8-9, "*... and its wingspread will be the full breadth of your land, O Immanuel ... speak your piece and it shall not stand, for God is with us!*" We can see from this, as the term is used in Isaiah 7:14, and quoted in Matthew 1:23, that term is shorthand for "*God is with us*". Christian apologists attempt to render *Immanuel* as a title, implying that Jesus was God, but that interpretation does not fit the circumstances of Ahaz and Hezekiah, for Hezekiah clearly was not God. The term should be understood in its literal sense, meaning that the event confirms God's support. In the context of Isaiah 7, it was an assurance from God to Ahaz, that the efforts of Rezin and Pekah (v. 7-1) in waging war against Jerusalem, would come to naught. That was the sign that Ahaz resisted, but God insisted nonetheless.

And His Name will be called Wonderful, Counselor

A later verse in Isaiah, 9:6, is also quoted in this context. Compare these two versions:

a. TJB – "For a child has been born to us, a son has been given to us, and the dominion will rest on his shoulder; the Wondrous Advisor, Mighty God, Eternal Father, called his name Sar-shalom [Prince of Peace]."

b. NKJV - "For unto us a Child is born, unto us a Son is given; and the government will be upon His shoulder, and His name will be called Wonderful Counsellor, Mighty God, Everlasting Father, Prince of Peace."

Christian apologists attempt to identify this child as Jesus, but one must ask the question: Where in all of Scripture is Jesus referred to as *Everlasting Father*? He is consistently referred to as *one like the son of man*, *son of man*, or *son of God*, but never Father. The Hebrew has God, Eternal Father, calling the son, Prince of Peace, but in the clumsy attempt to have the verse refer to Jesus, Christian translators seemingly failed to notice the reference to Father (or just ignored it), and thus evidenced their duplicity, or to be fair, perhaps simple incompetence. That said, let us take another look at the context:

> "For the yoke of its burden and the staff on its shoulder, the rod that oppressed them, You smashed like the day of Midian. For all tumultuous battles are fought with an uproar, and the garments wallow in blood, but [Sennacherib] became a blaze and was consumed by fire. **For a child has been born to us**, a son has been given to us, and the dominion will rest on his shoulder" (Isaiah 9:4-5, TJB) [emphasis mine].

Why was Sennacherib defeated? Because a child, Hezekiah, was born to the people, leading to the miraculous end of Sennacherib's siege of Jerusalem (see Isaiah 36-37). In passing, reference to Midian recalls how God assisted Gideon in defeating the Midians (Judges 7-8).

Summary

Whilst I accept the validity of competing arguments concerning the correct interpretation of *almah* in Isaiah 7:14, in the larger context, they are irrelevant – a red herring in fact. Pragmatically, whether the woman in question is referred to as a young woman, or a virgin, is immaterial, because if the narrative intended to convey that a woman will become pregnant and give birth to a child, being a virgin beforehand would have been quite normal. Matthew's account is specific: Joseph *did not know* Mary until after she had birthed Jesus, but there is no similar wording in Isaiah – even the NKJV says simply: "the virgin shall conceive", and as far as we know, Hezekiah was his first, and perhaps, only son, we have no evidence one way or the other concerning the virginity of his wife, about whom we also know nothing. Perhaps Isaiah was simply stating no more than necessary, just as the narrative in Genesis 17:19 says simply: "your wife shall bear a son". In the absence of evidence, one ought to not come to conclusions simply to suit one's theology – such is not acceptable under the rules of evidence.

The verse taken in isolation, as translated from the Greek, does allow conjecture. However, from the Hebrew, it does not. Further, the context of the verses preceding and following verse 14, if we are to take verse 14 as part of the continuing narrative, disallow any suggestion of a messianic prophecy to be fulfilled seven centuries into the future.

Two other issues need to be considered as evidence:

1. The NKJV rendering of: "For unto us a Child is born … and His name will be called … Everlasting Father" is nonsensical, for nowhere is Jesus ever called Father, always Son; and

2. The sign in Isaiah 7:14 is not the child, but the calling his name *Immanuel*, meaning *God is with us* is the sign, for he was named Hezekiah. The same is true in Matthew's account: "and they

called his name Jesus" (v. 1:25), even though the earlier verse said
to call his name Immanuel. The significance for Matthew was the
same as for Ahaz – the child would have God with him.

In his book, *The Bible Doesn't Say That*, Dr. Hoffman explains that
the issue of virgin / young woman arose from a mistranslation from the
Hebrew to the Greek, and there the matter ends[13]. Whether or not Mary,
the mother of Jesus, conceived a child whilst still a virgin, is something for
Christians to debate, but what should be clear is there is no virgin birth
in Isaiah's narrative. As other scholars have done, Hoffman notes that
in places in the New Testament, and pointedly in Matthew 1:22, "that
we should replace the word *fulfill* here with the more accurate *match*."[14]
This is a recurring theme in many commentaries, and I have come to the
conclusion that it is likely the correct understanding: Matthew was saying
that the birth of Jesus was similar to that of Hezekiah because in both
cases, God would be with them ... *Immanuel*.

REFERENCES:

1. http://biblehub.com/interlinear/isaiah/7-14.htm
2. http://biblehub.com/hebrew/strongs_2030.htm
3. Doukhan, Jacques, *On the Way to Emmaus: Five Major Messianic Prophecies Explained*, Lederer Books, Clarksville, MD, 2012, Chapter 3
4. *Ibid*, p. 81
5. *Ibid*
6. *Ibid*, p. 82
7. *Ibid*, p. 83
8. Scherman, Rabbi Nosson, *The Tanach*, Mesorah Publications, ArtScroll English Edition, Brooklyn, NY, 2011, p. 611
9. Doukhan, *Ibid*, p. 85
10. *Ibid*, p. 86
11. https://goddidntsaythat.com/tag/isaiah-714/
12. Scherman, *Ibid*, p. 612
13. Hoffman, Dr. Joel M., *The Bible Doesn't Say That: 40 Biblical Mistranslations, Misconceptions, and Other Misunderstandings*, Thomas Dunne Books, New York, NY, 2016, pp. 151-156
14. *Ibid*, p. 153

THE CHIEF CORNERSTONE

"The stone which the builders rejected has become the chief cornerstone."
(Psalm 118:22)

Quoting from the TJB (Hebrew Scriptures), the Old Testament verses which provide the context, not all of which are referenced in the NKJV New Testament, are:

1. Job 38:4-6 – "Where were you when I laid the earth's foundation? Tell, if you know understanding! Who set its dimensions? – if you know – or who stretched a [surveyor's] line over it? Into what are its bases sunken, or who laid its cornerstone?"
2. Isaiah 19:13 – "The officers of Zoan have become foolish, the officers of Noph have become misguided. The cornerstones of her tribes have caused Egypt to stray."
3. Isaiah 28:16 – "Therefore, thus said my Lord Hashem / Elohim: Behold, I am laying a stone for a foundation in Zion; a sturdy stone, a precious cornerstone, a secure foundation. Let the believer not expect it soon."

4. Zechariah 10:4 – "From themselves the cornerstone; from themselves the peg; from themselves the bow of war; - from themselves all the leaders will come forth together."
5. Psalm 118:22 – "The stone the builders despised has become the cornerstone."

We can see from these that the cornerstone, other than in Job, refers to leaders who establish the foundations of their communities. In that sense, Jesus is justifiably seen as a cornerstone, certainly of the path of his followers, but was he the *chief cornerstone* of all that God would have us believe and do? That is the question, and does the Old Testament allow us to identify Jesus in that way. Clearly, Jesus, and thus his followers, believed so, but before accepting that as truth, we must examine the wider context of the Old Testament verses to determine whether Jesus accomplished what the *cornerstones* referenced accomplished.

The primary theme of this Christian theology is that the fact of Jesus being rejected by many, was prophesied in David's psalm, even though the psalm itself contains an historical account of David's own life. Jesus asked: "*Have you never read in the Scriptures: The stone which the builders rejected*" (Matt 21:42). The next verse is important for our understanding of what Jesus thought about himself, and where his mind was: "*Therefore I say to you, the kingdom of God will be taken from you and given to the nations bearing the fruit of it.*"

This statement of Jesus, is to my mind, suggestive that he was not speaking on behalf of God, and may well have abandoned his mission. Earlier he had declared: "*I was not sent except to the sheep of the house of Israel.*" (15:24), presumably because the house of Judah was not lost. Now, however, he now saying that because *he* was not accepted in Judah, God would take His kingdom away from them. Perhaps it was Jesus who had not read the Scriptures, wherein God had promised that such would never be the case (reread the section on Jeremiah, Chapter 3-5).

Backing up to Matthew 21:23-27, Jesus displayed arrogance when he was asked the reasonable question: "*By whose authority are you doing these things?*" His answer was too clever by half, and smacked of political evasiveness, this from a man of whom it was said, there was *no deceit in his mouth* (2 Peter 2:22, quoting Isaiah 53:9). Deceit can be by both commission and omission.

Irrespective of his feelings toward the chief priests and the elders, a true man of God would not have answered as he did. If the mission of Jesus, truly was, to save the people of Israel, why would he be so rude to them? How can it be claimed that there was "no deceit in his mouth", when he sought to hide the truth from those who enquired of him? These were not the actions of a righteous man, claiming to be doing the will of God.

When Jesus stated that the kingdom of God would be taken away from them, what did he mean? I cannot be sure, but Christianity has taken this verse to bolster its claim that the Sinaitic Covenant has been annulled, and that the Christian Church is the New Israel. Gill's Exposition notes:

> "Though God may take away the Gospel from a people, as he did from the Jews; yet he does not, nor will he, as yet, take it out of the world: he gives it to another "nation"; to the Gentiles, to all the nations of the world, whither he sent his apostles to preach and where it must be preached before the end of the world comes, in order to gather his elect out of them: for not one particular nation is meant, unless the nation of God's elect, among all nations, can be thought to be designed."[1]

The Hebrew Scriptures are very clear: God would never reject the Children of Israel, His First-Born Son. If Jesus was contradicting his Father, then he was not speaking the words of his Father, nor was he as conversant with the Hebrew Scriptures as he seemed to claim.

Now back to the cornerstone – In reference to David, there was **NO** stone which the builders **REJECTED**. Just how that mistranslation of Psalm 118:22 came about is lost to history, but the original wording from the Hebrew Scriptures is: "The stone the builders **despised**", semantically very different. It was Saul, the father of David, who was rejected by God: "I have rejected him from reigning over Israel" (1 Samuel 16:1). God sends Samuel to Jesse the Bethlehemite, "for I have seen a king for Myself among his sons." Jesse remains the reference point for Isaiah's later prophecy, that "A staff will emerge from the stump of Jesse, and a shoot will sprout from its roots" (Isaiah 11:1). The theological significance here is that despite the punishments that God brings down on the Israelites, a remnant always remains, and in the context of Isaiah's prophecy, the Ten Tribes of the house of Israel, which were exiled by the Assyrians, will also be redeemed by the future Messiah, who will descend from the son of Jesse, i.e., David. This, quite probably, was in the mind of Jesus when he declared that he was only sent to the house of Israel (Matthew 15:24). Isaiah directly refutes Jesus' assertion that "*the kingdom of God will be taken from you and given to the nations bearing the fruit of it.*" If Jesus truly believed that, he was badly mistaken. Again, reread Jeremiah 31:35-37.

When Samuel arrived in Bethlehem, he organised a feast and invited Jesse and his sons. Samuel first thought that Eliab would be the anointed one, but God advised: "Do not look at his appearance or at his tall stature, for I have rejected him" (vv. 6-7). Jesse presented all of his sons there present, but God reject each one of them. David, as the youngest of the clan, was tending the family's sheep, and was not invited by his father to the feast. Samuel enquired of him, and insisted that the feast would not begin until David arrived, whereupon God instructed Samuel to anoint him, which he did, and the Scriptures record that "the spirit of Hashem passed over David from that day on." When David was later crowned King, all were amazed, with David proclaiming "This has emanated from God" (Ps 118:23). Thus, that oft repeated refrain: "This is the day the Lord has made: let us be glad and rejoice in it" (v. 24).

So, who was the stone that the builder's rejected? Certainly not David. Yes, he was despised by his brothers, not unlike Joseph those many generations before, but he nevertheless became the cornerstone. There is no genuine parallel between the life and anointing of David, and the life of Jesus. In the main, Jesus was not despised, else how could he have had a triumphal entry into Jerusalem? Yes, he was despised by some, but they were in a minority. Christianity is trying to have it both ways: Jesus was rejected, but also accepted.

"The stone the builders despised" (Psalm 118:22) could not be a future Jesus, because of the tense of the verb: "**has** become the cornerstone". David pleads: "Please, Hashem, save now! Please, Hashem, bring success now!" (v. 25, TJB). This entreaty precedes the verse quoted in Matthew 21:9: "Blessed is he who comes in the name of the Lord" (v. 26). In the context of the Jesus in his last days, "save now" did not happen. Also note the difference in sense occasioned by the translations: "whoever believes will not act hastily" (NKJV), and ""Let the believer not expect it soon"

(TJB). Curiously, the TJB rendering supports the claim of messianic prophecy better than that of the NKJV.

Isaiah 28:16 is subject to a number of interpretations, with the Jewish sages not reaching a consensus. Radak said that it referred to Hezekiah, whilst Rashi said the Messiah. There is also the nature of this cornerstone: was it to be a person, or was it a metaphorical line in the sand? Read verse 17: "I shall use judgement as a measuring line, and righteousness as a plumb bob." How could that refer to a person? The cornerstone is not the instigator of the actions, it is God Himself. Subsequent verses also speak of what God will do, not the cornerstone. Thus, I am not inclined to understand it to be a person. Even so, even if this does refer to the future Messiah, the question arises: can self-referential statements be accepted as evidence? If an accused claims to be innocent, does a jury accept that as evidence, or just a plea? Similarly, if someone claims to be the Messiah, is that evidence, or just a plea?

<u>Matthew 21:44</u> – "*Whoever falls on this stone will be broken*", again annotated with a ☆, quoting Isaiah 8:14, 15; 60:12; and Daniel 2:44. Isaiah 8 begins with: "*Take a large scroll, and write on it in with a man's pen concerning Maher-Shal'al-Hash-Baz*" (NKJV). Who was that? The term translates from the Hebrew as: *Plunder Hastens, Spoil Quickens*, or as Christian texts render it: *Swift to the booty, speedy to the prey*. It refers to an unborn child of Isaiah and his wife, the prophetess, and warns that the newly emerging Assyria will plunder and conquer even before the boy learns to speak. I hope Isaiah understood that, because I would not have done so. My point is that this was a prophecy concerning the immediate future of Israel, although Christian theology wants it to be about Jesus, the Son of Man, returning in the End of Days.

Why write in *clear script*, or with *a man's pen*? The purpose was to strengthen the message of the prophecy so that it would be neither misunderstood, nor forgotten. The context was that Sennacherib's plunder of the Ten Tribes was at hand, and that Nebuchadnezzar's spoil of Jerusalem, though years away, was already approaching. Thus, mention of the "two houses of Israel". The message was that in the coming troubles, God would be a fortress of protection for those who were loyal to Him, and a stumbling rock for those who were not. Again, the issue is: Can a prophecy be for two events, in two separate time periods? If one believes this to be so, what evidence is there other than the claims of the Evangelists, whom we already understand, were confused about Jesus as Messiah, and what he was to accomplish, when?

Isaiah 60:12 does not refer to individuals who do not accept Jesus, but about kingdoms, specifically: "For the nation and kingdom that does not serve you (God) will perish, and those nations will be utterly destroyed." Likewise, Daniel 2:44 does not refer to individual people, but to kingdoms, and specifically to the four kingdoms that he mentions in verses 36-43, as he interprets Nebuchadnezzar's dreams. The New Testament attempts to make Isaiah and Daniel about individuals, but they are not. Just why the writer of Matthew's Gospel, or anyone for that matter, saw these writings as prophecies of those who do not accept Jesus in the End of Days, is quite beyond my imagining.

Apart from the above, I am suspicious of the NKJV rendering on Matthew 21:44, which is: "And whoever falls on this stone will be broken; but on whomever it falls, it will grind him to powder." Another translation is: "The one who falls on this stone will be broken to pieces; and it will crush anyone on whom it falls" (Jewish Annotated New Testament). The Aramaic New Testament renders this verse as: "And whoever falls upon this Stone, it will destroy", the theological annotation "**S**tone" linking it with Jesus, but no mention of the stone falling on anyone. Stern's Jewish New Testament omits verse 44 altogether, commenting "The manuscripts which have v. 44 probably borrowed it from Lk. 20:18"[2], which does indeed have the same wording. The Greek translation does have "grind him to powder", but other Christian bibles have crush, grind, scatter, shatter, and smash. Perhaps this indicates nothing other than attempting to not breach the copyright laws.

In summary, I find the arguments for Jesus being the *chief cornerstone* to not be supported by the Hebrew Scriptures, and thus there is no evidence of prophecy fulfillment.

REFERENCES:

1. http://biblehub.com/matthew/21-43.htm
2. Stern, David H., *Jewish New Testament Commentary*, Jewish New Testament Publications, Jerusalem, Israel, 1989, p. 64

CHAPTER 3-8

QUOTING THE PSALMS

"Foresight is better than hindsight, but insight is better than either of them."
~ Anonymous ~

This is but a brief overview; for a more extensive commentary, see Part 5.

There are 150 poems in the Book of Psalms, of which only 73 are attributed to King David. David is also mentioned, by writers in the New Testament, as the author of two additional psalms. Psalm 2 is attributed to David in Acts 4:25, and I can see no reason to disagree. Psalm 95 is attributed to David in Hebrews 4:7, but according to Jewish literature, this was written by Moses, and later incorporated into the Psalms by David. Numerous other authors contributed, and the completed book was not compiled for many years until after David's death. Thus, in the Hebrew Scriptures, the Book of Psalms is in the *Writings* and not the *Prophets*, simply because the writers were not recognised as prophets.

According to the Jewish Sages, the Psalms do contain some prophetic statements, even though in general, the poems are not meant as prophecy. It requires careful study to firstly, identify which verses are prophetic, and secondly, to understand what is being prophesied. Primarily, the foretelling is of the fate of Israel, and often in reference to the End of Days. Messianic prophecies can be found, but always in the context of the *eschaton*. There are no prophecies of a two-stage redemption, nor of an interim Messiah who comes twice.

Another issue is to differentiate between the guidance of God, and the wisdom of men. *Proverbs* and *Ecclesiastes* are also prophetic in a sense, and although we can rightly assert that such writings were likely inspired by God, their realisation was due to the insight of wise men, their purpose being to guide us in our personal lives, not to foretell of the future. I contend that, in the main, we should view the *Psalms* in a similar light, exceptions as noted above.

Who Wrote Psalm 110

Which brings us to Psalm 110: who wrote it? According to both Messianic Judaism and Christianity, it was written by David, and thus it is interpreted as containing messianic prophecies. Verse 110:1 is referenced just once in each of the Gospels of Matthew, Mark, and Luke, but in the other NT books, it is referenced 10 times as supporting prophecy fulfillment. However, in the Hebrew Scriptures, verse 1 is rendered: "Regarding David, a psalm"; i.e., it was written **about** David, not **by** David. So, who is right? In an interesting study[1] by a Messianic Jewish scholar, of impeccable credentials, I found that he often conflated the Septuagint with the Hebrew Scriptures, just as I have found in other Messianic Jewish commentaries (see Chapter 4-7). Given the earlier observations about the Greek Septuagint (see Chapter 2-1), it is entirely possible that this is another example of a mistranslation by the Hellenic Jews, or whoever did the translation from the Hebrew to the Greek. In passing, one should note that Messianic Jews fall into two categories: those who practice Judaism in a messianic context, much as the Nazarenes would have done, and those who are culturally Jews, but religiously Christian. I find it necessary to dig into the backgrounds of those claiming to be Messianic Jews, to understand their presuppositions – sometimes these people are more rightly, Jewish Christians, just as there are English, Italian, or American Christians. The identification of Messianic Jew can be misleading.

Now back to the Psalm - let us discover whether the text can clarify this for us; here I will quote from the Jewish translation from the Hebrew:

> "*Wait at My right hand, until I make your enemies a stool for your feet. Hashem will despatch the staff of your strength from Zion; rule amid your enemies! Your people volunteer on the day of your campaign; because of your majestic sanctity from the inception of your reign.*" (vv. 1-3)

Does this sound like the days of Jesus, or the days of King David? The commentary in the Jewish bible reads:

> "[110:3] When you do battle, your nation will be loyal to you, because you retained the pure, unselfish character of your humble shepherd youth."[2]

I cannot perceive any of the actions of Jesus as *waiting* at the right hand of God, certainly not during what is described as his *First Coming*. Likewise, Jesus did not rule amid his enemies – on the contrary, it was his enemies who ruled against him. At best, one might contend that this is a prophecy of his claimed *Second Coming*, but as we are considering evidence of Jesus being the prophesied Messiah, what might happen in the future is irrelevant.

Incidentally, the wording of Isaiah 41:10 has me wondering whether people have misunderstood references to *the right hand of God*: "Fear not for I am with you; be not dismayed, for I am your God; I have strengthened you, even helped you, and even sustained you with My righteous right hand." In common usage, being "at" a leader's right hand is understood as synonymous with "being" the right hand, as in a leader's right hand man. But contemplating Isaiah 41:10, and other mentions of the right hand of God, I am coming to see it meaning *the place in God's presence where the righteous sit*. Psalm 110:1 says *wait at My right hand*, which does not necessarily imply that David is God's right hand man. Rather, I believe that it means: *remain in righteousness*. God does not require assistance, but He does delegate activities to man, acting through man, but righteousness is a continuing theme throughout the Scriptures.

Verse 110:1

"*The Lord said to my Lord*": to which Lords was the author referring? Obviously, this depends on to whom authorship is attributed.

The point arises with Jesus asking the Pharisees: "*What do you think about the Christ? Whose Son is He?*" (Matt 22:42). The terminology, as written here, rings false to me – I cannot accept that Jesus would have used the term, *Christ*. The term derives from the Greek, *Christos*, and is synonymous with *anointed one*, or the Hebrew *mashiach* (messiah), but the latter is a matter of contention. In Second Temple Judaism, according to the Sages, there was no prophecy of a specific person coming as the *mashiach* – he could arise in any generation when God decided, based on the character of the person. There is no preamble in Matthew's account, and as the Pharisees had not accepted Jesus as the messiah, his wording would have needed to have been sufficiently precise to focus their attention. Thus, I believe that in asking his question, he was not directing their attention to himself, as the theological annotations in the NKJV would have you believe, but to the general topic of the messiah (anointed one). Reread from the beginning of Matthew 22, ignoring any theological annotations, and you will see the Pharisees asking questions, that "they might entangle him in his talk" (v. 15). They referred to him as "teacher", questioning him on the law, so it is illogical to interpret him as switching the topic to himself as messiah (Christ) in verse 42.

The Pharisees answered: "*The Son of David*" (NKJV); again, note the initial capital, which I am confident the Pharisees did not intend. Jesus responds with the question: "*How then does David in the Spirit call Him Lord?*" The question arises: Did Jesus learn his Scriptures from the Greek, or is this narrative fictional? I am inclined toward the latter, and suspect that although Jesus may well have discussed the identity and lineage of the *anointed* one (not the Greek *Christos*), the insertion of Psalm 110:1 was a theological addition. Consider this: if the current versions of the Hebrew Scriptures are correct, and that this psalm was not written by David, but about David, and Jesus learned his Scriptures from the Hebrew, not the Greek, then he would not have raised this issue. If he did, in truth, speak as the narrative would have us believe, then he could not have been learned in the Hebrew Scriptures.

Mark's account is in the same context, but the question is directed at the scribes, not the Pharisees, and is worded accordingly: *"How is it that the scribes say that the Christ is the Son of David"*, which of course, is not how the scribes would have said it. Luke's account agrees with that of Mark. The confusion no doubt arose because the Scribes and Pharisees, although being very different groups with different occupations, are often mentioned together. Could it be that Mark and Luke, not being from Jerusalem, were not aware of the difference? John, as we so often find, does not narrate this event at all.

My final point concerns the very different reactions of the listeners. Luke has them not daring to ask a question, even before this discourse. Mark narrates similarly, and then states that *"the common people heard him gladly."* With a different audience, the Pharisees, Matthew states: *"And no one was able to answer Him a word, nor from that day on did anyone dare question Him anymore."* I am not persuaded. The Pharisees, well versed in the Hebrew Scriptures, would have taken exception with Jesus' interpretation of the Psalm. They may not have answered Jesus, but it would not have been because they *could not*. Perhaps they did not question him further because they knew that such would be futile, we cannot know. The Pharisees were highly respected teachers of the law just as Jesus attested (Matthew 23:2): I strongly doubt that they would have been cowed by Jesus.

Returning to the topic of evidence, I find the Gospel case weak on this point. I accept that Jesus would have discussed the lineage of the Messiah, but I am not confident that the event has been narrated accurately. My primary issue is this: If the Hebrew Scriptures are right, in that David did not write this Psalm, and Jesus did interpret the Psalm as Christian bibles render it, then Jesus was not as familiar with the Hebrew Scriptures as is claimed. Every text that I have read, concerning the diligence of the Scribes in faithfully reproducing the Scriptures, convinces me that they would not have changed the authorship of Psalm 110. I can find no suggestion that later Scribes would have done so either, and given scholarly comments on the accuracy of the translations into Greek, I can only conclude that such was the source of this error.

Verse 110:4

Other wording in contention is found in verse 4; the Jewish Bible has: "Hashem has sworn and will not relent, *'You shall be a priest forever, because you are a king of **righteousness***'", [emphasis mine]. The NKJV renders this verse as: "You *are* a priest forever according to the order of Melchizedek" (italics in original).

Who was Melchizedek?

Melchizedek is mentioned only once in the Hebrew Scriptures, in Genesis 14:18. "But Malchizedek, the king of Salem, brought out bread and wine; he was a priest of God, the Most High." The notes read: "they were met by King Malchizedek, whom the Sages identify as Shem, son of Noah. He is called *priest of God, the Most High*, because unlike priests of other nations who served angels, Malchizedek served Hashem (Ramban)."[3] Given this single reference, it is highly unlikely the there was ever an "order of Melchizedek", in the sense of a priestly order like the Levites. There is no mention of this anywhere in Jewish literature.

As king of Salem, Melchizedek was the king of Gentiles, whereas David was the king of Israel, thus considered higher in the sense of spiritual obligations. A commentary reads:

> "[110:4] A Jewish king should be like a priest, drawing God's people closer to His service. It is the duty of everyone to sanctify himself and be an example of loyal service to God, as He said to the Children of Israel before giving the Ten Commandments, "You shall be to Me a kingdom of priests", meaning that the entire nation, not merely the priests, was commanded to dedicate itself to God's service. Furthermore, both the priests and the members of the royal family has a special obligation to serve God and uphold justice (see Deuteronomy 17:12, 2 Samuel 8:18, Jeremiah 21:12)."[4]

There is reason to believe that *Melchizedek* was originally not one word but two: *malki* (or Melchi) meaning king and *tzedek* meaning righteousness; in the *Chumash*[5] it is written as *Malchi-zedek*, king of Salem

(Gen 14:18). This is further supported by the Dead Sea Scrolls which refer to *Melchi-resha*, meaning king of evil (Satan). Given that this king of Salem is a rather obscure figure of history from the time of Abraham, I find it curious that the writer of the Book of Hebrews, dusted him off to make his point about Jesus being *a priest forever* (Hebrews 5:6, 7), when no other New Testament author saw fit to mention Melchizedek at all. Did the author of Hebrews, whomever he was (see Chapter 2-3), develop this theology on his own, or in concert with others with whom he may have collaborated? Was he misled by the wording in the Greek Septuagint, and if that was so, why did the Greek translation vary from the Hebrew? Could it be that the later Septuagint, adopted by the Church of Rome, was edited to agree with the theology offered in Hebrews?

Another thought occurs to me, consonant with Paul being the self-styled apostle to the Gentiles. As we discussed in Chapter 2-6, Paul's letters evidence that he saw no future in Judaism, instead, that all should be *one in Christ*, and that did not require any adherence to the practices and laws of Judaism. The direction of Christianity was increasingly away from the Jews, to the Gentiles, eventually resulting in the rejection of Judaism entirely. Now, what if the author of Hebrews, writing much later (67 CE at the earliest), correctly understood Melchizedek to be a king of the Gentiles, a priest in the general sense of the Jews being a kingdom of priests, and not of the order of the Levites? Was he suggesting that Jesus was, in truth, a king of the Gentiles, not of the Jews? We know that there was no *priestly order of Melchizedek*, as such, so this interpretation is plausible, to my mind at least.

We cannot know the answers to these questions, but as long as they remain, this narration in Hebrews must be treated with some scepticism, as evidence of prophecy fulfillment. Melchizedek is a minor figure in the story of Abraham, and is not mentioned further in either the Old or New Testaments, other than by the author of Hebrews, of whom we know nothing at all. Thus, in terms of authenticity and authority, it is lacking indeed.

In passing, note: *It is the duty of everyone to sanctify himself.* Where have we heard that before? Firstly, in Leviticus 20:7-8, but the Apostle John records Jesus telling his followers to sanctify themselves with *truth*. The term is bandied about quite a lot in the New Testament, having people sanctified by Jesus, by God, by faith, by the Holy Spirit, and so on. Many Christians denominations teach that we cannot sanctify ourselves, only God can do that, but consider this definition: to *set apart*, to *make holy*, to *consecrate*. These are things that we can do, and ought to do. Another definition is: to *purify*, or *free from sin*, but can we do that? Well, according to the New Testament, we can: "And everyone who has this hope in Him (Jesus) purifies himself, just as He is pure" (1 John 3:3). The following verses deal with sin and lawlessness, the same theme as in Leviticus: "You shall observe My decrees and perform them" (20:8). It would seem, from the mixture of sayings, that this is an issue on which no-one should be dogmatic. Rather than be legalistic on the matter, the simple message is to set ourselves apart from the lawless ones, to serve God, and be obedient.

Summary

The questions to be resolved are:
1. Did King David write Psalm 110?
2. Even if he did write this Psalm, is it truly prophetic of the Messiah?
3. Even if the Psalm does prophesy the Messiah, could Jesus have fulfilled it some two thousand years ago?
4. Was the author of Hebrews justified in drawing a parallel between Jesus and Melchizedek?

My own conclusion is that this Psalm was not written by King David, and makes no reference to a future Messiah. Even if David did write it, the internal evidence convinces me that it was not prophetic of the life and times of Jesus. The study by Jacques Doukhan is of immeasurable interest, especially in relation to the five prophecies that he examines, but as I argued in an earlier chapter, the choice of source language is crucial to how we understand what was written concerning the prophesied Messiah. Just why a scholar of Doukhan's ability and scholarly accomplishment chooses to place so much credence on the Greek is beyond my understanding, but perhaps I am entirely wrong, perhaps the Septuagint is more reliable than I have been led to believe. Nevertheless, we must take evidence where we find it, and evaluate it in competition with other evidence on the same subject. I must here declare what I have come to believe: the Greek scriptures are not reliable. Thus, the evidence of any scholar, no matter his/her credentials, who uses the Septuagint as the source of Scripture, I shall treat with reserve.

Mystery upon mystery, and I can only beg God's indulgence if my ear has not been turned to a credible source.

REFERENCES:

1. Doukhan, Jacques, *On the Way to Emmaus: Five Major Messianic Prophecies Explained*, Lederer Books, Clarksville, MD, 2012
2. Scherman, Rabbi Nosson, *The Tanach*, Mesorah Publications, ArtScroll English Edition, Brooklyn, NY, 2011, p. 998
3. *Ibid*, p. 20
4. *Ibid*, p. 998
5. *The Chumash*, Scherman, Rabbi Nosson, Mesorah Publications, ArtScroll English Edition, Brooklyn, NY, 2009, p. 65

PART 4

CLAIMED PROPHECY FULFILLMENT

"The Gospels Examined by the Rules of Evidence
Administered in Courts of Justice"
~ Simon Greenleaf (1783-1853), Professor of Law, Harvard University[1] ~

Let me contend that this is the most important evidence that we will ever have to examine and evaluate. If we are to believe in God, a God who is One, and Who has warned us against worshipping other gods, then we need to be very certain that we know whom we are worshipping. If Jesus, likely a pious and well-intentioned man, is not the Son, the Second Person of the Trinity, then all who worship him as God are guilty of idolatry. That is a grave charge, but one which all Christians must all consider: Have I done my utmost to ensure that I have not been misled into idolatry? Simon Greenleaf is right and has challenged us to evaluate the evidence as in a court of law, so let us be cognizant of the rules of evidence.

In Chapter 1-1, we reviewed the rules of evidence that we should apply, so let us consider some common errors.

Evidential Errors

Christian apologists make fundamental, evidential errors, when attempting to demonstrate from the Gospels, that Jesus fulfilled Old Testament prophecies.

The first, and one that underlies so many problems with Christianity, is the use of the Greek translations as the basis for their understanding of the Hebrew Scriptures. As we saw in Chapter 2-1, the sense of the Greek can be entirely different, and at times, contradictory, to what was originally committed by God to his oracles (Romans 3:1), the very advantage of the Jew. If even Christian scholars admit to "its **inadequate** renderings, its **departures** from the sense of the Hebrew, [and] its **doctrinal deficiencies** owing to the **limited apprehensions** of the translators"[2] [emphasis mine], why would anyone base their understanding of prophecy fulfillment on such documents?

The issue here is the reliability of the witnesses. Whilst the character of the evangelists might be beyond reproach, as Simon Greenleaf is wont to point out, the source of their understanding of the Scriptures is not. The Greek Septuagint is not authoritative, and in that sense, is an unreliable witness.

My second point is the presupposition that Jesus was the prophesied Jewish *mashiach*, and thus certain prophecies will be fulfilled in his Second Coming, but not just fulfilled, but will be fulfilled *by him*. Unless, and until, it can be reliably demonstrated that Jesus was/is *that* Messiah, evidenced by his fulfilling of prophecy during his lifetime on Earth, claims of what he may do in the future are inadmissible. Whatever **may** happen in the future is not evidence of what happened in the past, and is thus irrelevant to the case at hand.

The third exegetical error is to spiritualise the Old Testament in a way that none of the Jewish Sages would have understood, and many modern scholars now reject. I do not question the proposition that prophecies can have multiple levels of meaning: I will stipulate to that as being fact.

However, I can find no evidence in Jewish literature that a prophecy would be fulfilled twice, by two different people, in two different time periods, unless of course, two different interpretations were valid. Some Christian apologists attempt to rationalise prophecy fulfillment in that manner, but to me that is a sign of desperation.

A mistake, sometimes encountered, is where a prophecy which applies to the Children of Israel collectively, is claimed as a prophecy fulfillment of Jesus as Messiah. For example, Matthew 15:7-8 has Jesus saying: "Hypocrites! Well did Isaiah prophesy about you, saying: These people draw near to me with their mouth", quoting Isaiah 29:13. Isaiah's prophecy is true of untold numbers of people, and is not relevant as evidence of Jesus fulfilling messianic prophecies. Another example is found in John 7:5, "For even his brothers did not believe Him", referencing Psalm 69:8 and Micah 7:6. The Psalm reads: "I have become a stranger to my brothers", but that does not necessarily imply what in written in John's account. Micah reads: "For son dishonours father ... a man's enemies are the men of his own household", which again cannot be adjudged as prophecy of the Messiah. Common behaviour is just that, and it is unacceptable as evidence to extrapolate beyond the ordinary.

In saying that, there is the question of how much the evangelists saw in Jesus, not just the fulfillment of prophecy, but the climax of Israel's history. It is entirely valid to compare the life and experiences of Jesus in that light, if one already believes that Jesus is the Messiah. In a sense, the evangelists would have been using the Old Testament in hindsight, all of a sudden realising how all of Israel's history was pointing toward the momentous event of the arrival of the promised Messiah, one whose life reflected all of the triumphs and tragedies of the past fifteen hundred years. I suspect that this is one of the reasons why they found so much resonance in the Psalms – the life of King David, from whom Jesus was said to have descended, now being mirrored in the life of Jesus himself. In an allegorical way, it all makes sense. However, all of that was predicated on Jesus *being* the Messiah, but in this study, we are more concerned with whether or not he was the Messiah, because he fulfilled prophecy in its intended sense.

Another fudge is where an event happened in the past, with no indication of significance beyond the then contemporary circumstances; yet, it is quoted as prophetic because it happened again in the life of

Jesus. One needs to be confident that it is not simply coincidence, before assuming prophecy. We find something similar with attempting to make common events into prophecy fulfillment. For example, when Jesus was offered "sour wine mingled with gall" (Matthew); "wine mingled with myrrh" (Mark); or "sour wine" (Luke and John), this was common practice at crucifixions. From an evidentiary perspective, a common practice occurring in the life of Jesus cannot be declared as being in fulfillment of a messianic prophecy. To prove a case, one needs substantive evidence, demonstrating where that person, and that person alone, could have committed that action, or was subject to a specific experience. Even more, we need good reasons to believe that the occurrence in the Old Testament was intended as a *messianic* prophecy.

I accept that the rules of evidence for theological determinations can be very different to the rules of evidence in a court of law, but in this study, I am accepting the challenge of that eminent jurist, Simon Greenleaf. If I seem to be repeating myself, you are not mistaken; I am doing so deliberately to keep both myself, the author, and you, the reader, focused on the mission.

Context! Context! Context!

The most common mistake is to lift verses out of context, attempting to make them fit the circumstances of Jesus. If a prophecy states two or more actions, and Jesus' circumstances, at best, could fit just one of them, then he could not have fulfilled that prophecy. Further, if the prophecy states an outcome which is entirely the opposite of what Jesus accomplished, then such is substantive evidence that he did NOT fulfill that prophecy. For example, as we discussed in Chapter 3-1 regarding the prophecy in Isaiah 40:3, "*The voice of one crying in the wilderness, prepare the way of the Lord*", is claimed to have been fulfilled by John the Baptist. However, the subsequent allegorical verses were not fulfilled. Most especially, it cannot it be claimed that "*the glory of the Lord shall be revealed, and all flesh shall see it together*". This prophecy is reminiscent of Jeremiah 31:34, "*for they all shall know Me. From the least of them to the greatest of them*", a prophecy regarding the End of Days.

Dividing the Books of the bible into chapters and verses provided both a service, and a disservice, to biblical exegesis. Certainly, it provided a method of indexing for quick reference, but it also served to disguise context, allowing commentators to extract verses that suited their theological purpose, whilst ignoring those that did not. For example, the NKJV editors found fulfillment of Isaiah 50:5-6 in Mark 14:36, 14:55, and 15:19; and also, in Luke 22:42. However, let us examine the full context of Isaiah 50:5-9 from the NKJV:

> [5] The Lord God has opened My ear; and I was not rebellious, nor did I turn away.

> [6] I gave My back to those who struck Me, and My cheeks to those who plucked out My beard; I did not hide My face from shame and spitting.

> [7] For the Lord God will help Me; therefore, I will not be disgraced; therefore, I have set My face like a flint, and I know that I will not be ashamed.

> [8] He is near who justifies Me; who will contend with Me? Let us stand together; who is My adversary? Let him come near.

> [9] Surely the Lord God will help Me; who is he who will condemn Me? Indeed, they will all grow old like a garment; the moth will eat them up.

I have left the theological annotations in place, quite deliberately. Clearly, some of the statements in these verses can be applied to the suffering of Jesus, but not all. We have no record of Jesus having his beard plucked; his face was not like flint during his agonies in Gethsemane; he was disgraced, the very purpose of his public crucifixion; and he was condemned. Verses 8-9 contain a challenge to adversaries, with the suggestion that the challenge would not be taken up. We know, however, that the challenge was accepted by King David. I cannot be sure just why bible commentators are so prone to ignoring context, but being harsh, I would offer that the two probable causes are ignorance and dishonesty, driven by zeal for their faith. That is not the path to truth.

Here is another example. Remembering that Jeremiah did not include verse numbers in his prophecies, and the prophecies themselves were not by one verse alone, he wrote:

> "[5] Behold, the days are coming, says the Lord, that I will raise to David a Branch of righteousness; a King shall reign and prosper, and execute judgement and righteousness in the earth. [6] In His days Judah will be saved, and Israel will dwell safely; now this is His name by which He will be called: The Lord our Righteousness." (Jeremiah 23:5-6)

The NKJV editors, in Luke 3:31, managed to find a match with Jeremiah 23:5, but ignored the next verse, which had they considered it, would have demonstrated, beyond dispute, that verse 5 could not have referred to Jesus, because in his day, Israel did not dwell safely. In fact, Jesus as King did not reign and prosper, so even verse 5 doesn't fit. One could attempt to split the two verses to refer to two separate periods, but that would be eisegesis.

My point is simply this: Each Psalm, or narrative in the Prophets, must be taken as a whole, and understood in its entire context. Many narratives in, for example, Isaiah, extend across multiple chapters, much like a short story, and should be examined in that light, as one would an essay. It is evident, especially in the way that the NKJV editors have overlayed their theological annotations, that they have allowed the identification of who is speaking, or of whom is being spoken about, to change to suit their purposes, even when the context does not allow it. Most commonly, we find this in "he" and "He". Of course, these inconsistencies could represent little more than a lack of diligence, but if that be so, how do we determine when the editors have been diligent, and when they have not? More deliberate, I suspect, is the use of the ambiguous term, "Lord", where the Hebrew makes clear that *Hashem*, God, is the subject. The translation, Lord, allows the verse to refer to *Jesus*, as Lord, when that is not the meaning in the text. Similarly, translation of *Gentiles* in the NKJV, when the Hebrew refers to *nations*. Technically, from a Jewish perspective, this could be correct, but it also subliminally influences the reader to associate the text with Jesus saving the Gentiles, as distinct from the Jews. In several places, the term "nations" also includes the Ten Tribes of Israel, a distinction lost with the translation of "Gentile".

Much of the writings of the Evangelists represent *hearsay* evidence, and should be treated as such, especially when there is no evidence that the accounts narrated were witnessed by anyone, e.g. Jesus' temptations in the desert, and his agony in Gethsemane. Other narratives, such as the recording of the trial of Jesus, are suspect, because there is no evidentiary trail of how the Evangelists came to know of the details of the proceedings.

As we saw in Chapter 2-1, the Greek Septuagint, used by the Evangelists, was of an unknown version, and of unattributed provenance. It was not reliable in relation to prophecies, and subsequent English translations have perpetuated these errors. In cross-checking the Old Testament verses quoted in the New in support of prophecy fulfillment, I have often found that the Christian Old Testament wording differs significantly from translations from the Hebrew. Such mistranslations convey an entirely different sense. The frequency of this has me suspecting that this may have been deliberate at times, in an attempt to justify the assertion of Jesus being the prophesied Messiah. I may be unkind in my suspicions – perhaps the errors were innocent, being based on an unreliable Greek translation.

Finally, the error of omission. The prophets spoke of many things that the Messiah would accomplish, yet every Christian apologist whom I have read, blithely ignores that which was NOT accomplished; we deal with these in later sections. I am reminded on the oath witnesses are required to swear in a court of law: to tell the truth, AND the whole truth. When Christian theologians extract a verse from the Scriptures as evidence of Jesus fulfilling prophecy, yet ignore the subsequent verse which argues the opposite case, that is, to my mind, an egregious example of not telling the *whole* truth. Examples are omitting reference to "when he sins" in 2 Samuel 7:14, and "sacrificing to Baal" in Hosea 11:2.

If I put aside the Christian rejection of Torah, and the rejection of the Sabbath and other God-ordained commemorations, I would offer this as the primary reason why many Jews did not, and still do not, as I do not, accept Jesus as the Jewish *mashiach*. In short, he failed to deliver. Yes, many did initially accept him, but many later turned away. As I discuss in other works, and recognised scholars confirm, the early followers of Jesus believed that his return was imminent, even within their own lifetimes. As the years went by, the Temple destroyed, Jerusalem levelled, and the Jews expelled from their own lands, it became obvious that his return was not imminent, and the arguments for believing in him in the first place, were being increasingly refuted. Yes, Christianity did continue, but in an entirely different guise, as the centre shifted from Jewish Jerusalem, to Gentile Rome. But that is another story.

I know that many people accept the argument that Jesus *must be* the prophesied Messiah, because he fulfilled *so many* prophecies. Even if the evidence is circumstantial, surely only one person could fulfil so many, the probability of anyone else doing it decreases to zero. There is validity in that argument, but only if Jesus did fulfil so many. If he did not, then the argument ceases to have value. But once again, consider the stakes: How much of your future are you willing to gamble?

That is the question only you can answer.

The Lamb of God

Some Old Testament verses have been interpreted as prophecy because of references in the New Testament to the *Lamb of God*. It is my contention that this latter term arose through a misunderstanding of the lambs slain in Egypt immediately prior to the Exodus, and for this reason, I believe it useful, in relation to prophecy, to review the details.

Amongst the Gospels, it is only in John's account that we find Jesus associated with the Passover Lamb – the Synoptics do not make that connection. From the very beginning of John's Gospel, we have John the Baptist declaring: "Behold the Lamb of God" (John 1:36), but that narrative does not occur in the Synoptic versions. Backing up a tad, Mark has Jesus crucified on the third hour (Mark 15:25), that being 9:00 am. According to John, "it was the Preparation Day of the Passover, and about the sixth hour" (John 19:14), that is, midday. Jesus is said to have died before darkness fell, effectively dusk. Now, according to the Jewish custom, they would slaughter the lamb, the *pesach offering*, on Passover Eve. "You shall keep it (the lamb) until the fourteenth day of the same month (Nissan). Then the whole assembly of the congregation of Israel shall kill it at twilight." (Exodus 12:6).

I have been able to resolve, to my own satisfaction at least, the apparent disparity between the Synoptics' and John's version of events, whether Jesus was crucified on the 14th or 15th of Nisan. Thus, it is not an issue for me regarding the credibility of the narratives. However, there is an issue of even greater importance.

John attempts to relate the *pesach offering* with Jesus himself, thus creating the allusion of a Passover Lamb, just as he earlier stated in his Gospel: "Behold the Lamb of God who takes away the sins of the world" (John 1:29). The only problem is: nowhere in the Old Testament is there a prophecy of a lamb, of any relationship, taking away the sins of the world. We will come back to Guilt and Sin Offerings later. The lamb sacrificed at Passover had nothing at all to do with the forgiveness of sin, and the irony is that God chose a lamb to be slaughtered to test the faith of those to be rescued from Pharaoh, and possibly as an insult to the Egyptians. It is unlikely that any Jew familiar with the Hebrew Scriptures and their interpretation, or anybody familiar with the Jewish customs associated with Passover, would have made that connection at the time of Jesus' death. This suggests that the author of the Gospel of John developed that theology later. He certainly had time – over fifty years.

Let us review the relevant Old Testament passages.

We find a suggestion of a link to the pesach offering in Genesis 22:7-8. It is worth noting that even in those early days, a lamb was used as a burnt offering:

> "But Isaac spoke to Abraham his father and said, 'My father!' And he said, 'Here I am, my son.' Then he said, 'Look, the fire and the wood, but where is the lamb for a burnt offering?" And Abraham said, 'My son, God will provide for Himself the lamb for a burnt offering."

Curiously, God did not provide a lamb, but a ram. So why did Abraham say that God would provide a lamb (v. 22:13): Could it have been a prophecy of future times when God would specify a lamb, and the author of John was attempting to use this? Possibly, but a lamb as a burnt offering was a common practice for drawing closer to God, not intended as a messianic prophecy. The next relevant passages are found in Exodus, when Pharaoh tried to trick Moses.

That John wrote in his Gospel that Jesus was the Passover Lamb, simply demonstrates that whoever came up with that idea did not have the Jewish understanding of what occurred in Egypt at that time. There is no prophecy of a Passover lamb being sacrificed for the forgiveness of sin. The *pesach offering* is a commemoration of when God brought death to the firstborn of Egypt - *passing over* the homes of those whom He would redeem (rescue). The story begins in Exodus 8:25-26 with Pharaoh attempting to trick Moses into sacrificing a lamb before the people of Egypt. "Then Pharaoh called for Moses and Aaron and said, 'Go, sacrifice to your God in the land.' And Moses said, 'It is not right to do so, for we would be sacrificing the abomination of the Egyptians to the Lord our God. If we sacrifice the abomination of the Egyptians before their eyes, then will they not stone us?'" *Abomination of the Egyptians*? In Egypt at that time, the lamb was deified and worshipped as a god. By Egyptian law, it was therefore forbidden to harm a lamb in any way, such an act being considered a crime punishable by death. Pharaoh knew that the Hebrews sacrificed lambs, and so he cunningly invited Moses and Aaron to do so in front of his own people, knowing that consequently, they would be killed as punishment. Fortunately for Aaron, Moses had grown up in Egypt and knew the customs. He knew that the lamb was considered a god, and thus to him and his God, the lamb was an abomination (in Egypt at least).

Next, we have Exodus 10:25, with Moses asking for "sacrifices and burnt offerings that we may sacrifice to the Lord our God. Our livestock also shall go with us; not a hoof shall be left behind. For we must take some of them to serve the Lord our God." But God hardens Pharaoh's heart, and Pharaoh refuses Moses' request. Moses wanted to continue with the Hebrew practice of sacrificing lambs during their journeys ahead. Subsequently, when God later ordered Moses that the people must sacrifice a lamb, in the presence of Pharaoh in Egypt, at great risk to their lives, what message was He conveying?

Which brings us to the next point: the choice by God to have the Hebrews sacrifice a lamb and spread its blood on the lintels of their houses (Exodus 12:7). Because killing a lamb in Egypt was punishable by death, it is reasonable to assume that God was testing the faithfulness of those whom He was rescuing - only those who feared nothing, but the God Who Is One, were deemed worthy of being *passed over* by the tenth plague. No Egyptian would dare slaughter a lamb, and neither would those who feared Pharaoh more than God. One might also consider that God sought to deliberately add insult to injury to Pharaoh, asserting that He alone was God.

It is unlikely that an educated Judean Jew would have honestly written the passion narrative in the Gospel of John, because such a man would not have made the mistake of misunderstanding this ancient Jewish custom. Alternatively, a Jewish man was fiddling with the truth. The early Gentile Christians in Rome were similarly ignorant. Christianity attempts to draw a parallel between the *pesach offering*, commemorating being *passed over* in Egypt, and the subsequent rescue from slavery, with Jesus as the Lamb of God slain for our rescue from sin. But you see, there is no historical parallel, and no prophecy of such. The author of John crafted a narrative which Christians have bought into, without understanding that it was nonsense. The sacrifice of the Passover Lamb on the 14th of Nissan, Passover Eve, was in commemoration of the Exodus – there were no other theological implications.

Repeating: "And Moses said, '*It is not right to do so, for we would be sacrificing the abomination of the Egyptians to the Lord our God.*'" The Exodus did not begin with a sacrifice of a lamb to God, but with the killing of *the abomination of the Egyptians*. Subsequently, sacrificing lambs was in commemoration of the faithful people of God being *passed over*, avoiding the tenth plague.

REFERENCES:

1. Greenleaf, Simon, *The Testimony of the Evangelists*, Kregel Classics, Grand Rapids, MI, 1995, sub-title
2. Brenton, Sir Lancelot Charles Lee (1807-1862), *An Historical Account of the Septuagint Version*, http://www.bible-researcher.com/brenton1.html

CHAPTER 4-1

PROPHECY FULFILLMENT CONSPIRACY?

<u>Conspiracy:</u> a secret plan by a group to do
something unlawful or harmful.
*"Knowing this first, that no prophecy of Scripture
is of any private interpretation"*
(2 Peter 1:20)

In some ways, one must admire the persistence of the Christian scribes, who scoured the Scriptures for verses that they could represent as prophecies fulfilled by Jesus. I wonder what went through their minds, for how could they have not seen the obvious discrepancies and inconsistencies that I and others have unearthed? Did they not feel discomfort at misrepresenting the Word of God? Taking a term out of context, were they guilty of asserting a *private interpretation* of God's Word through the Prophets, whilst purporting to affirm and preach it? Did they pray for the guidance of the Holy Spirit, or were they under instruction from the clergy hierarchy to do as they did? Either way, I would contend that they did indeed corrupt the

Scriptures which they nevertheless maintained was holy, and the inerrant Word of God. Thus, in the context of a conspiracy, they sought to do something harmful, most especially toward the Jew.

Again, however, I must allow that the evangelists did so honestly, believing in their hearts that Jesus was the promised Messiah. It is said that the road to hell is paved with good intentions, and likewise, less perilous paths. We cannot condemn those who acted in good faith, even when they were wrong, for God judges us by what is in our hearts, and what we can reasonably be expected to know. That was then, but this is now.

Amongst the many perspectives on the New Testament authors usage of Old Testament texts, there are two that I would like to highlight. The first is that in the main, the text says no more that it initially appears to say, with no hidden meaning; the second is that there is indeed a hidden meaning, and that both may exist: something contemporary, and something for the future. In the context of prophecy, some scholars will refer to *pesher* as an interpretation of, or part of, the Hebrew scriptures in which a historical context is used, instead of allegory, to prophesy the *End of Days*. As you can imagine, this interpretive technique is interpreted in a number of ways, depending on what the commentator is intending to demonstrate. For example:

"The principles of 'pesher' interpretation cited by Stendahl (1968, 191) may be listed as follows:

1) What the prophets wrote has a veiled, eschatological meaning.
2) Since the meaning is veiled, the meaning may be discerned by what may appear to be a forced interpretation.
3) One may observe textual or orthographical peculiarities.
4) One may also make use of textual variants (for the light they shed on the text or to replace text).
5) One may note analogous circumstances.
6) The text may be allegorized in an appropriate manner.
7) One may find more than one meaning in the words. One may assume that the author has hidden the meaning he intended in various ways and 'undo' his techniques;
8) by substituting synonyms for the intended words,
9) by using anagrams,
10) by substituting similar letters for the ones he really intended,

11) by running words together, which must be split to get the meaning,

12) and by using abbreviations which must be spelled out in full.

13) One may find that other passages of Scripture illuminate the meaning of the text."[1]

Note how the first definition I quoted said *instead of allegory*, but the above list includes allegory. I am puzzled, almost to a state of disbelief, that scholars have concluded that the Old Testament writers wrote such complicated mysteries. If God is the author, why would he deliberately mislead those who would subsequently read His words? When God said, *"I did not speak in secrecy, some place in the land of darkness"* (Isaiah 45:19, TJB), meaning that He did not keep His prophecies a secret, but instead chose to reveal them to the peoples of the world through His Prophets, was He being mysterious, or did He mean what He plainly said? When modern scholars opine as in the list above, are they ascribing these considerations to the words of God, or only to the words of the Prophets, and if so, on what basis do they differentiate one from the other? Did God speak through His Prophets for them and others to understand, or did He speak with the deliberate intention that only centuries later could His meaning be discerned by those gifted in particularly scholarly ways? In short, have modern scholars created their own dilemma because believing in Jesus as Messiah, Son of God, Second Person of the Trinity, they needed to substantiate those beliefs when a plain reading of the Scriptures, as I am inclined to practice, would not allow them so to do? Are we seeing nothing but rationalisation after the fact, the informal fallacy of reasoning?

In his essay from which I have just quoted, Marshall notes two assumptions in the pesher techniques, the first being that "the prophets message has a meaning which is 'eschatological'", and:

> "the second assumption is that this eschatological meaning is often (but not always) 'hidden' and needs to be recovered by a suitable procedure which involves going beyond the apparent message of the text to a hidden meaning which can be detected by noting abnormalities in the text. In other words the abnormalities represent a deliberate coding of the message which must now be

decoded. Principles 3-13 are in effect methods for apprehending this hidden meaning."[2]

My question becomes: why the need for such assumptions, and on what basis have they been formulated?

My point here is simply this: I wish to acknowledge the extremes of the *pesher* methodologies, and to admit that in the next sections where I debate the numerous New Testament verses claimed as being in fulfillment of messianic prophecy, I attempt to follow the simplest understanding of the *pesher* technique – based simply on historical context, not the complicated structure as noted above.

My reasoning is that if, and that remains a big if, the books of the New Testament were authored by those to whom Christianity attributes them, then I believe it unlikely that these authors were sufficiently scholarly to depart from the *pesher* approach. Perhaps you could review the PaRDeS table illustrated in Chapter 1-6, noting that level 2 could only be accomplished by the Nobles: lawyers, judges, and scientists. None of the attributed authors of the New Testament could claim to be a *Noble* under that definition. Yes, I understand that Christianity claims that Paul was a lawyer, a trained Pharisee, but in Chapter 2-6, I offer the evidence that has convinced me that he was not. Luke may well have been a medical doctor, but such training would not qualify him as a Noble that Jewish scholars would accept.

On the other hand, if the New Testament evidences Old Testament interpretations of which only scholars would have been capable, then in all probability, it was not authored by those to whom Christianity attributes it. This is an important point from the perspective of evidence in a court of law. We have earlier discussed authenticity, authority, and chain of custody (Chapter 1-1), as essential considerations in the acceptance of written evidence. If Christianity is wrong about authorship, then it is unlikely that the true authors were firsthand witnesses of the life and times of Jesus, as is claimed. This casts a different light on the evidentiary value of the New Testament writings.

That said, I cannot know – I can only be guided by the works of those more qualified than I. Thus, my own interpretation of Old Testament verses quoted or annotated in the New, is from a rather simplistic *pesher* perspective, and my analysis of the validity of their usage is thus predicated. In Part 8, we will review what genuine scholars have to say, albeit, acknowledging their Christian presuppositions, and thus bias.

Now to the analysis.

Analysis Overview

The "★" count, that is, the number of times the NKJV annotates a Gospel verse as a prophecy fulfillment, is as follows:

1. Matthew: 40
2. Mark: 16
3. Luke: 19
4. John: 22

The total is 97, which even ignoring the duplications, and that some refer to John the Baptist, is far less than claimed by various commentators. Some say 44 Messianic prophecies were fulfilled; some say 100; some say over 300 prophecies; and others the more specific 353. One commentator resorted to mathematical probabilities to prove that Jesus must have been the Messiah, to have fulfilled whatever number of prophecies: "What are the odds?" he asked. Odds indeed: if you fudge the numbers, as any statistician knows, you can prove whatever your heart desires.

I contend, because I have proved it to myself, that the claims of prophecy fulfillment are false. Now I would not accuse all Christians of dishonesty, for I too believed what I had been taught, for a time at least. But there must have been a period, in the history of Christianity, where a conspiracy to deceive was concocted by persons unknown. No sincere scholar, on his or her own, could possibly have made so many mistakes in Scripture interpretation, especially as some are so easily refuted. It is also evident that Scripture has been tampered with, again by these unknown scribes under the direction of their clerical masters, to theologically annotate the translations of the Old Testament, in accordance with the goals of that conspiracy. I acknowledge the good intentions of some, but church history demonstrates that not all were so intentioned.

Why was such dishonesty necessary, other than that the truth would have told an entirely different story? Do the means justify the end? I know that you will think me harsh, but the behaviour, writings, anti-Jewishness, and compromise with pagans by the early church of Rome are what have promoted such suspicions that I entertain.

REFERENCES:

1. Beale, G.K., *The Right Doctrine from the Wrong Texts? Essays on the Use of the Old Testament in the New*, Baker Academic, Grand Rapids, MI, 1994, p. 207
2. *Ibid*

CHAPTER 4-2

GOSPEL OF MATTHEW

"The New Testament authors are not scholars but church leaders. They are interested in showing how the Old Testament passages apply to the New Testament situation."[1]

Matthew the Theologian

For a moment, ponder the import of that opinion by Christian scholar, Vern Sheridan Poythress, as expressed in his essay, *Divine Meaning of Scripture*. The Apostle Matthew was a tax collector, no doubt literate to a degree, but hardly likely to have been a scholar of the Hebrew Scriptures, or even the Greek. However, with that in mind, also consider this opinion on the dating and authorship of the Gospel attributed to Matthew:

> "Most scholars believe it was composed between AD 80 and 90, with a range of possibility between AD 70 to 110 (a pre-70 date remains a minority view). The anonymous author was probably a male Jew, standing on the margin between traditional and

non-traditional Jewish values, and familiar with technical legal aspects of scripture being debated in his time. Writing in a polished Semitic "synagogue Greek", he drew on three main sources: the Gospel of Mark, the hypothetical collection of sayings known as the Q source, and material unique to his own community, called the M source or 'Special Matthew'."[2]

No doubt, you are wondering where I am going with this, but bear with me: I am going to present more scholarly evidence that this Gospel could <u>not</u> have been written by Matthew, and indeed is a theological treatise, written by someone *familiar with technical legal aspects of scripture*, a competence likely well beyond Matthew the tax-collector. For this we turn to an essay entitled, *The Formula-Quotations of Matthew, and the Problem of Communication*[3], by R.T. France, a New Testament scholar and Anglican cleric, but before doing so, we must ask the question: If this Gospel was not written by Apostle Matthew, one of the original twelve disciples chosen by Jesus, on what basis can we accept that it is an authoritative account by a witness to the narratives therein? From an evidentiary perspective, we must consider it suspect.

I would recommend that you read this essay for yourself, but here I will just quote some passages to give you a sense, or rather, my sense, of how the author of the Gospel was perceived by R.T. France. Consider yourself a member of a jury, faced with reconciling these writings to what can be known of the Apostle Matthew, and tasked with offering a verdict on whether Matthew was the author. I would ask you to pay attention, not so much to the words themselves, but what they suggest about the scholarly credentials of "Matthew":

1.   "The complexity of allusion intelligible to a modern scholar with lots of books and little else to do is much greater that that accessible to any member of Jesus' audience. A civilization based on the printed book may be in danger of forgetting that a scroll of even one Old Testament book was in the first century an inconvenient and expensive luxury, and so of assuming an ease of reference which is more appropriate to the age of the 'pocket Bible' than to primitive Christianity." (p. 115)

2. "With the exception of the location of Jesus' birth in Bethlehem and his later residence in Nazareth, and of the bare historical datum of the death of Herod and the succession of Archelaus, these stories find no echo in any independent source, Christian or non-Christian." (p. 116)

3. "If the facts were negotiable, why need Matthew twist the wording of his chosen texts? Why not twist the facts to suit the wording? Micah 5:1 has undergone some careful surgery, and something so dreadful has apparently happened to whatever text lies behind [Matthew] 2:23 that no one can be sure of what it was." (p. 118)

4. "The freedom with which Matthew finds it necessary to adapt his chosen texts to the narrative strongly suggests that the narrative was there first. It was the fact of Jesus' residence at Nazareth that made it necessary to **concoct** the quotation 'He shall be called a Nazarene', and not vice versa." (p. 118) [emphasis mine]

5. "The Magi come 'from the East' are presumably Gentiles from Mesopotamia. Their involvement thus represents an ultimately wider role for Israel's Messiah, and the probable echoes of Psalm 72 and Isaiah 60 in the account of their 'worship' reinforce this theme of the homage of the Gentiles." (p. 121)

6. "Matthew's primary purpose in chapter 2 is to teach about the Messiah through his geographical movements and associations, with the scriptural texts which these bring to mind. This is not to deny that he is also developing a Moses and Exodus typology, but this forms only a sub-plot, less conspicuous and even capable of being missed completely by the casual reader." (p. 122)

7. "In any recoverable version Micah 5:1 clearly names Bethlehem as the place of origin of the future leader of Israel. Why then has Matthew found it necessary to introduce at least three deliberate changes into the wording?" (p. 124)

8. "All these three alterations, then, while not at all necessary for the surface meaning of the text, combine to convey a deliberate christological message to those who recognise them. The ordinary reader, who was not closely acquainted with the Old Testament text, might well miss them all, *as alterations*. In that case he might still notice the repeated word 'Judah', and be confirmed in his

belief that Jesus was the true king of Israel; this would be a small bonus for the 'sharp-eyed reader'." (p. 125) [italics in original]

9. "So here again, as in the use of Micah 5:1, we have both a surface meaning based on the central geographical term and also a variety of christological implications available to those with the scriptural knowledge and perceptiveness to dig deeper into Matthew's purpose." (p. 126)

10. "These geographical associations would be completely lost on the more naïve reader, but might well have provoked (and been intended to provoke) some fascinating lines of thought for those with the scriptural knowledge to discern them." (pp. 127-128)

11. "May we then believe that Matthew wanted his readers to summon up their knowledge of Jeremiah 31, and see in it not only a precedent for exile as a part of the purpose of God, but a pattern of exile *and return*, of loss and sorrow as a prelude to restoration and joy." (p. 128) [italics in original]

12. "He [Matthew] was a sufficiently sophisticated author and communicator not to aim only for the lowest common denominator in his readership, not to write an esoteric manual for initiates only, but to cater for the different levels of comprehension at the same time." (p. 133)

13. "It is evident that Matthew imposed an arbitrary pattern on the genealogy, and adjusted the Old Testament data to fit the pattern." (p. 147) So much for bible inerrancy, and proving the lineage of Jesus! We examine this in more detail a little later.

There are many other such observations by R.T. France, and others, that I could quote, but these should be sufficient for you to understand my point: if a reader is expected to be sharp-eyed, and have the scriptural knowledge and perceptiveness to discern the deeper meanings intended by the author of Matthew's Gospel, what does that say about the author himself? Authors, generally, cannot write more than they know, although they can sometimes reveal how little they know. How knowledgeable must he have been, to have him described as a "*sophisticated author and communicator*", and how gifted a writer must he have been to have embedded such deep, even esoteric meanings in the text? Does that really sound like Matthew the tax-collector, a disciple of Jesus chosen because he was, as described by one Christian apologist: "The ancient Apostles were common men, and that was part of their credential"? Not at all to my way of thinking.

Renowned Christian apologist, C.S. Lewis, wrote of the Gospels: "Of this [gospel] text there are only two possible views. Either this is reportage ... or else, some unknown [ancient] writer ... without known predecessors or successors suddenly anticipated the whole technique of modern novelistic, realistic narrative."[4] You may agree with him, but I cannot, although I once did before I undertook my studies. The extracts I have quoted above convince me that Lewis was wrong: this Gospel, at least, is not simply reportage, but a theological treatise, and that seems to be the understanding of numerous modern New Testament scholars.

So, let us keep that in mind when we review the claimed Old Testament prophecy fulfillments. R.T. France also observed: "That Matthew wrote these words rather than any others must tell us something about the man and his purpose"[5]. Professor C.F.D. Moule, Lady Margaret's Professor of Divinity at Cambridge University from 1951 to 1976, wrote of the use of the Old Testament by Matthew: "to our critical eyes, manifestly forced and artificial and unconvincing."[6] *To our critical eyes* – this is the way that evidence must be adjudged, if we are to be worthy of our calling.

Overview

"So all this was done that it might be fulfilled which
was spoken by the Lord through the prophet"
(Matthew 1:22)

Let us start with some statistics, which may or may not tell us anything. I have analysed the occurrences in the Gospel of Matthew where the NKJV flags a verse as prophecy fulfillment. These are the results, confusing as they are:

1. Old Testament verses referenced in the New in relation to prophecy.
   a. The NKJV editors reference 76 unique verses of the Old Testament.
   b. Of these 76, only 43 verses are flagged within the OT as being prophetic.

c. 9 of the OT verses are from the Psalms, all of which are flagged as prophetic.

2. New Testament
    a. 40 individual Gospel verses are flagged as being in fulfillment of prophecy, either by Jesus, or by John the Baptist.
    b. Of those 40, 14 refer to the same OT verse.
    c. Of the 40 verses referenced, where it is claimed prophecy had been fulfilled, in only 13 cases does the NT verse itself state explicitly that such was in fulfillment of a prophecy, although not clearly a *messianic prophecy*, in contrast to those verses simply flagged as such by the NKJV editors.
    d. 13 of these Gospel verses refer to a verse in the Psalms only, no other OT book.
    e. 9 verses are flagged as a prophecy yet to be fulfilled, either in the life or death of Jesus, or what could only be in the Second Coming.
    f. 3 verses flagged as prophecy fulfilled had no reference to an Old Testament verse.

Not much can be made from this data, other than it does evidence a lack of coherence. It is interesting that many OT verses, referenced in the Gospel prophecy verses, are not themselves flagged as prophetic: I have found no pattern to these, and do not know why the NKJV editors noted them.

The editors found more prophecy fulfillment in the Psalms (8), than did the Gospel's author, who quoted just two Psalm verses - 22:18 regarding casting lots for Jesus' clothing (Matt 27:35), and 78:2 regarding speaking a parable, uttering dark sayings of old (Matt 13:35). I am uncertain of why the author of Matthew considered King David to be a prophet (Psalm 22), especially as the Psalms are included in the Writings, and not the Prophets. Similarly, Asaph, the author of Psalm 78, was recognised as a "seer", one whose words were *forthtelling* - insight into the will of God; these words were exhortative, challenging men to obey. This was different to the words of the recognised Prophets, whose words were *foretelling*, predictive sayings entailing foresight into the plans of God.

Casting lots was a common practice: thus, it carries no weight as evidence of prophecy fulfillment. Curiously, though Matthew 13:35 explicitly states: *"that is might be fulfilled which was spoken by the prophet"*, the NKJV editors did not flag this verse as prophecy fulfillment. Perhaps we can adjudge this as merely an oversight, but to do it justice, it is discussed in detail in Part 5 on the Psalms.

Turning to the 13 cases where the NT verse itself states explicitly that such was in fulfillment of a messianic prophecy: one concerns the virgin birth; one about Judas; two about John the Baptist; one where Jesus spoke concerning himself; and eight that are entirely circumstantial. Other than these eight, six are misinterpretations, or mistranslations, of the Hebrew Scriptures.

Now think about that: Not one single verse that refers to what the Messiah would accomplish – not one! The very essence of the Messiah, whom the Jews believed would redeem them, was not who he was, but what he would accomplish. The Messiah would be recognised by his actions: the actions define the man, not the other way around. I would conclude from this that whilst the evangelists may well have thought Jesus to be the Messiah, fulfillment of his prophesied role would have to await his return, whenever that would be. Many would appear to be the Messiah, just as Theudas, Judas of Galilee, and later Simon bar Kokhba were initially perceived to be, but their failure to achieve what was expected of them, marked them as a false messiahs.

The Lineage of Jesus

Matthew 1:1 – *"The book of the genealogy of Jesus Christ, the Son of David, the Son of Abraham."* The Davidic Covenant was considered, by many, to be the most significant promise God ever made to His people. Under that covenant, according to the prophet Nathan, only the descendants of King David would rule over the Children of Israel:

> "When your days are complete, and you lie with your forefathers, I shall raise up after you your offspring who will issue from your loins, and I shall make his kingdom firm. He shall build a Temple

for My sake, and I shall make firm the throne of his kingdom forever. I shall be a Father unto him, and he shall be a son unto Me, so that **when he sins** I will chastise him with the rod of men and with afflictions of human beings" (2 Samuel 7:12-14, TJB) [emphasis mine].

According to the Torah, only the father conveys the tribal identity to the son: "and they established their genealogy according to their families, according to their fathers' household" (Num 1:18), which accords with *will issue from your loins*. One should note that the claimed sinless Jesus of Christianity does not meet the conditions of this prophecy in 2 Samuel, on three counts: (1) blood line, (2) building a Temple, and (3), sin. Keep that issue of sin in mind, and ponder it at length. Now let us investigate the blood line.

Matthew's Gospel starts with the genealogy of Joseph, in an attempt to authenticate the claim that Jesus was of the royal bloodline, a descendant of King David. The problem is, if the virgin birth is true, then Joseph is not the biological father, and his lineage is irrelevant. Christian apologetics gets around this as here, but please accept my apology that I cannot provide the reference, because in between originally finding this text on Catholic Answers, and including it in this chapter, it has disappeared from the internet. You will have to take me on trust.

> "Joseph ... was Jesus' legal father only; the reason is that according to ancient mentality legal paternity (adoption, levirate, etc.) is sufficient, by itself, to confer all hereditary rights: the rights here are of the messianic line. The main purpose of this first incident in Matthew is to show how Jesus came to be a member of the royal line of David, namely through the adoption by Joseph."

Notwithstanding my carelessness, we are fortunate that there are many similar articles available which make the same assumption of adoption, because in later narratives, Jesus is referred to as the son of Joseph:

> "the bemused citizens of Nazareth remark 'Is not this the carpenter's son? Is not his mother called Mary?' (Mt 13:55) ... In the Jewish

tradition, a person's lineage was determined by one's legal father. Joseph is called a son of David, and because he adopted Jesus, he too could claim lineage from David."[7]

However, consider this view:

"Adoption is not known as a legal institution in Jewish law. According to *halakhah,* the personal status of parent and child is based on the natural family relationship only, and there is no recognized way of creating this status artificially by a legal act or fiction. However, Jewish law does provide for consequences essentially similar to those caused by adoption to be created by legal means. These consequences are the right and obligation of a person to assume responsibility for a child."[8]

The text goes on to explain that an adopted child does have hereditary rights in terms of material welfare, but there is no suggestion of the adoption of titles or position. I have been unable to find a definitive statement in Jewish literature on this issue, but the general tone suggests that Jesus could not belong to the messianic line, by inheritance alone. The same text continues:

"The possibility that adoption was practiced in this period cannot be excluded, especially since contemporary legal documents are lacking. Nevertheless, it seems that if adoption played any role at all in Israelite family institutions, it was an insignificant one. It may be that the tribal consciousness of the Israelites did not favor the creation of artificial family ties, and that the practice of polygamy obviated some of the need for adoption. For the post-Exilic period in Palestine there is no reliable evidence for adoption at all."

The assertion, in the Catholic commentary, that the royal line of King David could be inherited by adoption, I would contend is false. It seems exceedingly unlikely that the judges of Judaism would ever contradict Torah on this matter. Reviewing British and European royal family tradition, we find that only biological children can inherit titles, or be in the line of succession. Adopted children, or those not of the biological royal line, can be given honorary titles, but no entitlement to succession. As best as I can discover, adoption was not common in ancient times, and neither was royal lineage inherited by those not of royal blood. There are many "just so" stories invented by supporters of the evolution narrative – I sense the same behaviour amongst theologians.

Now to be clear, I do not contend, categorically, that adoption never occurred in the history of the Jewish people prior to Jesus. There is some evidence that such may have occurred, and it is not a point that I am qualified to debate. I would encourage you to read the full text in the referenced Jewish article for yourself. The main point is that irrespective, adoption does not confer hereditary titles.

The other option is that the narrative of the virgin birth is false. If Joseph was the biological father of Jesus, then the royal line could be inherited, but only if the royal line was unbroken. The plot thickens.

Matthew's Account in Detail

Matthew notes: "So all the generations from Abraham to David are fourteen generations, from David to the captivity in Babylon are fourteen generations, and from the captivity in Babylon until Christ are fourteen generations" (Matt 1:17). Why the emphasis on three sets of fourteen? As far as I can determine, there is no prophecy concerning these numbers, so it would appear that Matthew is attempting to make a point that only Jews would understand, and likely only scholars. One commentator noted: "The evangelist Matthew … is interested in the run of generations from Abraham to David, from David to the Babylonian exile, from the exile to the birth of Christ. His chronology, indeed, is symbolic rather than exact, but it is clearly his intention to present the coming of Christ as the culmination of a real process in history."[9] I do wonder at such an opinion: why was the author of Matthew so specific about the number *fourteen* when the chronology was meant to be *symbolic rather than exact*? At least we have one suggestion for the three sets, representing three periods of history, but the essayist does not explain, in this essay at least, any meaning behind these three periods.

Fourteen is the numerical value of the Hebrew name, *David*. Fourteen, in Jewish numerology, also represents the number seven which symbolises perfection, so fourteen could be perfection doubled. Three is sometimes indicative of a spiritual struggle or journey, but it is unclear what the Jewish mind would have made of that. In passing, Luke tried a different tack, putting the genealogy into four groups, rather than three.

The genealogy given is questionable on a number of counts, and this can be demonstrated by studying 1 Chronicles. One commentary notes: "The genealogy is unusual in citing women, non-Jews, and morally questionable characters among the ancestors"[10]. Non-Jews? How can they be of the Davidic bloodline? When we compare the list given by Matthew, to the genealogies found in 1 Chronicles, we find numerous inconsistencies. In the second set, Matthew omits the kings Ahaziah, Joash, and Amaziah. Elsewhere, Matthew also omits the kings, Jehoiakin and Zedekiah. In the third set, only the names Jechoniah, Salathiel, and Zerubbabel are mentioned in the Tanakh, and the list of generations is only thirteen, not fourteen. The *Aramaic New Testament* offers that the Yosip (Joseph) in verse 16, was in fact the guardian or adopted father of Mary, not her husband, thus there were fourteen generations[11]. There is no scholarly support for that interpretation outside of scholars of the *Aramaic Peshitta*. A Catholic text states that it was common, when listing genealogies, to omit lesser persons, which would account for there being one short in the final group, but that argument is defeated by the observation above concerning women, non-Jews, and so on. Another apologetic is that Matthew only removed the wicked kings from Jesus' noble lineage, but what about Ahaz and Manasseh? The rule of Ahaz was marked by idolatry, and Manasseh murdered the Prophet Isaiah!

It is interesting that in the 14th century Hebrew version of Matthew, verse 1:5 records: "Salmon begot Boaz from Rahab the harlot". None of the Christian bibles I have surveyed contain that titbit, not surprisingly. Researching that issue, there is debate as to whether the source word should be translated as *harlot* or *innkeeper*, so I will leave that for you to ponder at your leisure.

Let us next focus on the third set beginning with Jeconiah, who was the king deposed in the Babylonian exile. According to Matthew 1:12, Jeconiah begot Shealtiel, and Shealtiel begot Zerubbalel. However, according to 1 Chronicles 3:17-19, it was Pedaiah who begot Zerubbalel, not Shealtiel. Jeconiah's children were born after the Babylonian captivity in 597 BCE.

Shealtiel is a significant but problematic member in the genealogies of the House of David, and of the genealogy of Jesus. There is conflicting text in the Hebrew Bible as to whether Zerubbabel is the son of Shealtiel, or of Shealtiel's brother, Pedaiah. However, though both genealogies of Jesus list Zerubbabel as the son of Shealtiel, they differ as to Shealtiel's paternity, with Matthew agreeing with 1 Chronicles that Jeconiah was Shealtiel's father, while Luke lists Shealtiel's father as an unknown man named Neri.

As an aside, Jesus is said to have been born circa 5 BCE, thus giving a time span of roughly 600 years which covered supposedly 14 generations. Some commentators argue that this would give an average life-span of over 50 years, when typically, in those days, the average life-span was just 30-35 years. These numbers ignore the high infant mortality rate, which skew the averages toward the low end. Those who survived into adulthood may well have had lifespans between 50 and 70 years, and some even more (or less, obviously). However, none of that is relevant. The reason is simple: the count of generations should be based on when the successive children, who fathered the next generations, were born, not when their parents died.

In my own family, counting from Alfred Gerald born in 1843, to the latest children born in 2016, there are 8 generations in 173 years. Thus, the *generation-turn-rate*, if I can coin that term, was 22 years. The average lifespan before the Common Era was 30-35, and we can assume that most families had children early in the marriage. Even allowing for variations, Matthew's account of just 14 generations does not ring true, because the *generation-turn-rate*, at 43 years, would have exceeded the average lifespan. Yes, I understand the lineages given in the Old Testament, but there is a certain implausibility regarding them being accurate, and one must presume that some generations were not listed for whatever reason. My contention is that whoever asserted 14 generations, for the sake of aligning with Jewish numerology, were not being entirely honest. To my mind, this is tampering with Scripture.

My final point is one found in Jeremiah 22. Depending on the translation, you may read *Coniah* or *Jeconiah*. In the NKJV, Coniah is used in Jeremiah, and Jeconiah in Matthew for the same person. According to

Jewish sources, Coniah was a derisive nickname, for his behaviour was so unsavoury that he was often referred to as the "Jewish Caligula". For this he was cursed by God:

> "Is this man Coniah a despised, shattered statue, or an unwanted vessel? Why have he and his descendants been displaced and thrown into a land they did not know? O land, land, land! Hear the word of Hashem! Thus, said Hashem: Inscribe this man to become childless, a man who will not succeed in his life; for none of his descendants will ever succeed in being a man who sits on the throne of David, and ever to rule over David." (Jeremiah 22:28-30, TJB)

So, according to the Prophet Jeremiah, no descendant of Jeconiah could be King David's successor, and that would include Jesus. From history, we learn that none of Jeconiah's lineage ever became king. Instead of his son, it was Jeconiah's uncle, Zedekiah, who inherited the throne. There are anomalies in Luke's version of the genealogy also, but here I will mention just one. We read: "the son of Zerubbabel, the son of Shealtiel, the son of Neri" (Luke 3:27). Who was Neri? There is no trace in the Tanakh of a person so named, so it is suggested that Luke was trying to hide the truth of Jeconiah's curse from his readers. There are numerous apologetics to get around this curse. Many offer, as here: "But, since Jesus was only an adopted son and not biological son of Joseph, the curse did not affect his right to the throne as he was not of Jeconiah's seed. This curse also indicates that the Messiah cannot have a human father since then the curse would pass onto him too."[12] Another is that Jeconiah repented in Babylon: God forgave him and lifted the curse, but if that were true, why did the lineage not continue? But also note the inadvertent admission: Jesus was not of Jeconiah's seed, and therefore not of David's lineage. Some arguments wind back on themselves.

If you read the Gospels carefully, you would note that Luke lists fifty-six generations, which is four times fourteen, not the three times fourteen in Matthew. Digging deeper, in his first group of fourteen, Matthew omits Ahaziah, Joash, Amaziah, and Jehoiakim from the kings of Judah. To "create" fourteen in the second and third groups, Matthew includes

Jeconiah in both groups. If that is not fiddling with Scripture to suit his own purposes, what is?

The issue of genealogy is of the most utmost importance, for in the eyes of the Jews, only a direct descendant, of the bloodline of King David, would qualify to be the Jewish *mashiach*. Christian scholars have acknowledged the difficulties associated with the genealogies given in Matthew and Luke, but there is no consensus on how to resolve them. Again, I go back to the Christian claim that the bible is inerrant, that every word is that of God, and that *God is not the author of confusion* (1 Cor 14:33). Really? I am confused, scholars are confused, so what does that say about Christian doctrine concerning the authenticity of the New Testament?

It is apparent to me that in recognising the importance of the Messiah being a direct descendant of King David, the authors of Matthew and Luke attempted to construct a genealogy that would qualify Jesus for that role. Unfortunately, they made quite a mess of it, for reasons unknown, but a mess it is. Unfortunately, Paul the Apostle made an even greater mess of it:

> "*Concerning his son Jesus Christ our Lord, who was born of the seed of David according to the flesh.*" (Romans 1:3)

According to the flesh: really? The "seed", in most usages, refers to the father, and irrespective of whether Joseph was truly of the seed of David, Jesus was not born according to the seed and flesh of Joseph (although he was born of the flesh of Mary). Had Paul not been told that Mary was supposed to have been a virgin?

Virgin Birth Prophesied?

Matthew 1:23 – "*Behold, the virgin shall be with child, and bear a son*".
See Chapter 3-6, and note that Matthew must have used a Greek translation which renders the original Hebrew *almah*, which normally means young woman but can also mean virgin, as *parthenos*, whose usual meaning *is* virgin. Another example of the unreliability of the Greek version of the Scriptures.

The Birth of Jesus

<u>Matthew 2:1</u> – *"But after Jesus was born in Bethlehem of Judea"*. I can understand why Jesus' birth in Bethlehem *could* have been prophesied in Micah 5:2, but then how do we account for the remainder of Micah 5, for Jesus did not accomplish any of those things? No point in arguing that he would do so in the Second Coming, it needs to have occurred in the First Coming. Note that according to Luke, Jesus was born in Nazareth, the family home of Jesus, before they made the journey to Bethlehem for the census. I can also understand why Herod would have been reminded of this, but it simply does not fit the circumstances. The prophecy speaks of Bethlehem, out of which would "come a Ruler, who will shepherd My people Israel."

A difficulty we have is with verse numbering, but that aside, consider the wording of the translations:

a. "Therefore, He shall **give them up**, until the time that she who is in labor has given birth; then the remnant of his brethren shall return to the children of Israel" (v. 5:3, NKJV).

b. "On account of this, he will **appoint them** unto a time of giving birth. She shall give birth and the remnants of their brethren shall return unto the sons of Israel" (v. 5:3, Septuagint Old Testament); and

c. Therefore, He will **deliver them** [to their enemies] until the time that a woman in childbirth gives birth; then the rest of his brothers will return with the Children of Israel" (v. 5:2, TJB) [emphases mine].

Which is right: give them up, appoint them, or deliver them, and what would that mean anyway? Who is "He"? The "He" cannot be Jesus, because "he" precedes the birth, and there is no return of the Jewish brethren. The Jewish explanation, consistent with similar allegories, is that "the hardships of exile will become as intense as labour pains, but it will end with the rebirth of the Jewish nation, and the return of their brethren."[13] That does fit better than the Christian interpretation, and I accept it as likely correct. This prophecy of Micah cannot have been fulfilled by Jesus, because Jesus did not accomplish the return of the Children of Israel – on the contrary, they were totally dispersed not long after. That Jesus was born in Bethlehem is but circumstantial evidence, and carries no evidentiary weight, given the other errors.

As for "*wise men from the East came to Jerusalem*" being a fulfillment of a prophecy in Genesis 25:6, or in any way being a related text, that is pure fantasy: "And Abraham gave all that he had to Isaac. But Abraham gave gifts to the sons of the concubines which Abraham had; and while he was still living, he sent them eastward away from Isaac, his son, to the country of the east" (Gen 25:5-6). Finding correlation between words in the Old and New Testaments, and then making them out to be prophecy fulfillment, is *eisegesis* not *exegesis*. I deal with this entire episode in greater detail here[14], demonstrating the improbability of the entire narrative of these "wise men", who in other and earlier translations, are identified as "Magi". *Magi* is a translation of the Assyrian, *magician* or *astrologer*, whose practices God forbade (Deut 18:10). I contend that it would be highly unlikely that God would choose to guide such people to the birth of His Son, and even more unlikely that God would want to warn Herod, resulting in the deaths of many infants. The scholars whom I have studied on this subject agree that these people were Gentiles. I wonder whether Matthew introduced this narrative to ascribe a wider role to Jesus, in contrast to him being "not sent except to the lost sheep of Israel" (Matthew 15:24)?

Matthew 2:15 - "*Out of Egypt I called My Son*", quoting Hosea 11:1. Again, circumstantial based on coincidence; this is hardly a specific identification of Jesus: many Jews came out of Egypt, all the way back to Exodus and before. What is the context of Hosea? "When Israel was a child, I loved him, and out of Egypt I called My son. As they called them, so they went from them; they sacrificed to the Baals, and burned incense to carved images." (NKJV) *When Israel was a child* refers to the infant nation of Israel; and *the son called out of Egypt* is the same son as identified in Exodus 4:22-23 – Israel. However, the Jewish rendering of this verse conveys a very different sense: "When Israel was a lad, I loved Him, and since Egypt **I have been calling out to My son**." [emphasis mine] (See also Exodus 4:22-23). So, rather than God calling Israel out *from* Egypt, He had been calling out *to* Israel ever since He rescued them from Egypt. Was the paraphrasing of the Hebrew Scriptures deliberate, in an attempt to backfill an event in Jesus' life into a prophecy fulfillment?

As Israel fell into error, the plural is used to identify those who succumbed to idolatry. Did Jesus, Mary, and Joseph succumb to idolatry, sacrificing to Baals, and burning incense to carved images? If not, then the passage cannot refer to Jesus: substantive evidence that this is NOT a prophecy fulfillment. Anglican cleric, and New Testament scholar, R.T. France observed: "The problem, so obvious to us, that the 'son of God' in Hosea was Israel, not the Messiah, would only occur to those with a reasonable acquaintance with Hosea."[15] Does this suggest that the editors of the NKJV do not have a reasonable acquaintance with Hosea?

Matthew 2:18 - *"Then was fulfilled what was spoken by Jeremiah the prophet saying*: [see Jeremiah 31:15]". Better still, start reading from the beginning of Jeremiah 31, and see how poorly the entire chapter fits with the life and times of Jesus. This is an example of taking verses out of context, and attempting to make them fit where they clearly do not, if that is, one bothers to read the full context. There is no prophecy in Jeremiah, or anywhere else, of Herod slaying the children in Bethlehem. The real meaning of these verses in Jeremiah is as here:

> "The verses relate that all the Patriarchs and Matriarchs attempted to appease God when King Manasseh introduced idolatry into the Temple (2 Kings 21:4-5). But He rejected all their pleas until Rachel recalled her own magnanimity to her sister Leah. When Leah was fraudulently married to Jacob in place of Rachel, Rachel did not let jealous resentment lead her to protest. Why, then, should God be so zealous in punishing His children for bringing idols into His Temple? God accepted her plea and promised that Israel would be redeemed eventually, in her merit (*Rashi*)."[16]

In a curious way, the author of Matthew might have been attempting to allude to the promise to Israel, as a result of Rachel's plea, but his quotation ended up in the wrong place. His allusion would make sense if the author was attempting to see the flight of Jesus (Redeemer) to Egypt, and his escape from Herod, in the context of Israel's redemption. But if so, the text is poorly structured, because verse 18 is clearly a *non-sequitur* - Jeremiah the Prophet had said nothing concerning the events in verse 17.

Matthew 2:23 - "*And he came and dwelt in a city called Nazareth, that it might be fulfilled which was spoken by the prophets, He shall be called a Nazarene*". The NKJV annotates this as fulfillment of a prophecy in Judges 13:5. That text reads: "For behold, you shall conceive and bear a son; and no razor shall come upon his head, for the child shall be a Nazirite to God from the womb; and he shall begin to deliver Israel out of the hands of the Philistines." Does that sound like Jesus of Nazareth? Of course not! Jesus was a Nazarene (from Nazareth), not a **Nazirite**. The requirements for a Nazirite were given in Numbers 6, amongst the strict requirements being no contact with the dead but Jesus raised people from the dead. The father of the child of Judges 13 was Manoah whose wife was barren, but not a virgin, for how could they have known she was barren? They were from the town of Zorah, about five miles south-west of Jerusalem. Nazareth is about seventy miles due north of Jerusalem. Did Jesus deliver Israel out of the hands of the Philistines? Nope. Who was the son? It was Samson, who was not of a type foreshadowing the Messiah – certainly not of the type that Jesus is said to have been. The truly sad aspect of this supposed prophecy fulfillment, is that the life and times of Jesus do not match those described in Judges 13 in any respect.

Perhaps the author of Matthew's Gospel had something in mind which we cannot properly discern. But even given that, the translators of the NKJV should not have flagged this as a fulfilled prophecy, perpetuating the error for generations to come. In the opinion of one scholar at least, the author was not attempting a direct quotation, but alluding to a theme of the prophets that the Messiah would come from a humble background. Nazareth is not mentioned in the Old Testament, so there can be no specific prophecy of Jesus coming from Nazareth. But by the time of Jesus, Nazareth "has clearly acquired this connotation [a sense of inferiority], and the remoteness of Nazareth would thus give it a derogatory sense of 'backwoodsman' particularly for the Judean whose view of Galilee in general was not flattering."[17] Hence the scorn, or perhaps just incredulity, in these words: "*Can anything good come out of Nazareth?*" (John 1:46) In passing, note that according to Matthew, Jesus was born in Bethlehem, fled to Egypt with his family, and on return settled in Nazareth, Joseph being warned by God to "turn aside into Galilee" (Matthew 2:1-23). Luke

tells it differently: Jesus was born in Nazareth, and the family went up to Bethlehem for the census (Luke 2:1-15).

In passing, note the NKJV rendering of Judges 13:6, "A Man of God came to me, and His countenance was like the countenance of the Angel of God." Note how initial capitals are used here and throughout the following verses. Why? What are the translators attempting to convey: that this Man of God was Jesus? Such theological annotations are rightfully considered as tampering with the Scriptures. I cannot be sure of how God views this practice, but I view it as disgraceful, at the very least.

Hmmm ... page after page, verse after verse, prophecy fulfillments that are not, I am reminded of the words of Shakespeare in Hamlet: "*The lady doth protest too much, methinks.*" Maybe I, too, doth protest too much, but what else can I do? In a diligent search for truth, should I just accept such poorly constructed arguments that these prophecy claims represent? Are these cries of desperation, by people wanting others to believe in Jesus, or are they justification after the fact, to comfort those who already believe? Is there not better, more substantive evidence, that could be offered?

I am often advised that the narratives must be true, because so many people are said to have believed, and the religion rapidly spread across the world. But that is no argument, for the same can be said for the religion of Islam. Did you know that in their respective first 100 years, it is said that more people joined the Mormon faith than the early Christian? Just why people are given to believe one religion over another is always a mystery to me, but what must be true is that the truth of the religion can have little to do with it.

Further Claims

<u>Matthew 3:1-3</u> – "*For this is who was spoken of by the Prophet Isaiah.*" This is one of the more curious "misquotes" of the Gospels, using Isaiah 40:3 as a prophecy of John the Baptist. If John came to prepare the way of Jesus, who was to die for our sins, why would that be necessary when Isaiah 40:2 say that Israel's sins had already forgiven her? If the Apostles truly believed that the prophecy of Isaiah 40:3 was fulfilled by John the Baptist, and they knew the full context of Isaiah 40, then it confirms

my suspicion of their eschatological view: that they believed Jesus to be the Messiah - not that he was going to die on the cross and come back a second time, but that this was the end of days. That the Gospel was written decades after the death of Jesus suggests that it was an oral tradition that had not been revised.

One should also note a similar prophecy in Malachi 3:1. Rather than "prepare the way" as in the NKJV, it is "clear a path", meaning eliminate the wicked. Malachi 4:4 (3:22 in the TJB) reminds the people: "Remember the Torah of Moses My servant, which I commanded him at Horeb (Sinai) for all of Israel – its decrees and its statutes." This is a problem for Christianity: If John the Baptist was doing the task assigned to Elijah, as Jesus asserted that he was (Matthew 11:14), why would Jesus later tell his followers to forget Torah? The prophecy continues: "Behold, I send you Elijah the prophet before the coming of the great and awesome day of Hashem." This refers to the End of Days, as in Isaiah, so if Jesus believed John was the fulfillment of the promised Elijah, he too must have believed that he was heralding the End of Days, which he clearly wasn't. The plot becomes a little confusing when Jesus later meets with Moses and Elijah (Matt 17:3): just what that is meant to signify is unclear.

Matthew 3:11 – "*He who is coming after me … he will baptise you with the Holy Spirit*". The NKJV annotates this verse with an *Outline Star* ☆, indicating that the text contains a prophecy that at the time of the action, had yet to be fulfilled. However, no Old Testament verse is referenced – the only references are to other NT texts. Thus, the claim is that the narrative in Matthew's Gospel is itself, a prophecy. From a logical perspective, a text written long after an event cannot be said to be prophetic: first the prophecy, then the fulfillment.

Matthew 3:16b – "*He saw the Spirit of God descending like a dove and alighting upon him.*" Isaiah 11:2 does state that the spirit of God will rest upon the "stump of Jesse", the prophesied Jewish *mashiach*, but the following verses deny that Jesus was that messiah, e.g. "It shall be on that day that the Lord will once again show His hand, to acquire the remnant of His people, who will have remained, from Assyria, and from Egypt, etc." (Isaiah 11:11). Neither on that day, nor the days after, did God show His hand. On the contrary, He continued to withhold His hand from the Children of Israel, and watched them be once again, dispersed from

Jerusalem. It will not do to say that Jesus will return and accomplish that, if these verses are to prove that Jesus was the Messiah back then. Promissory accomplishments are not yet accomplishments.

<u>Matthew 3:17</u> – "*This is My son, in whom I am well pleased*", quoting Psalm 2:7. Yes, God was well pleased with David, His son, as He was with many of His "sons". At best, this is circumstantial evidence.

<u>Matthew 4:12-15</u> – I will let you read this for yourself, but the referenced passage in Isaiah 9:1-2 is not a prophecy. In truth, Isaiah interrupts his prophesying to thank God for the miraculous end to the siege of Jerusalem by Sennacherib. Isaiah likens the route of the Assyrian army to the miracle granted Gideon, when with his small force, he defeated the Midianites (Judges, chapters 7-8). That too, might have been in the mind of the author of Matthew, but the relevance is obscure.

<u>Matthew 8:17</u> – "*He himself took our infirmities and bore our sicknesses*" quoting Isaiah 53:4. I discussed Isaiah 53 in the previous section, and here will simply restate that Jesus was NOT the suffering servant.

<u>Matthew 10:35</u> – "*For I have to set a man against his father, etc.*" ☆, referring to Micah 7:6. I have long had difficulty with Matthew 10:34-36. It is entirely natural that when a person espouses one philosophy, others will take exception, and conflict will arise even within a family. Evidence the American Civil War. However, I am unable to understand why Jesus would deliberately set out to cause disruption within families: is that an example that Christianity would champion? Certainly, disruption would arise *as a consequence*, but it should not be the goal. If Jesus did indeed intend as written, then he could not be a man of God, and not someone whose example I would wish to follow. Proverbs 6:12-19 has much to say about sowing discord, especially as it tends to arise from the sowers seeking to serve their own interests. Jesus claimed to be following the instructions of the Father: was that the intention of the Father? Did the Father really want Jesus to sow discord, or was the mission of Jesus as stated in the Gospels:

a. "For I did not come to call the righteous, but sinners, to repentance." (Matt 9:13)

b. "I was not sent except to the lost sheep of the house of Israel." (Matt 15:24)

If Jesus was describing his intention for coming to earth, when was this prophecy to be fulfilled: before his death, or after? Not that it was a prophecy of the Messiah anyway: Micah stated that despite the shortcomings of the people to whom he was speaking, he remained steadfast in his allegiance to God. For Micah, that meant abiding by the Covenant, and God's laws. If Jesus was quoting Micah, then we should expect that he also intended as Micah did – abide by the Covenant, and God's laws.

Matthew 11:5 – "*The blind see and the lame walk ... the poor have the gospel preached to them*", claimed as prophecy fulfillment of firstly, Isaiah 29:18 and 35:4-6; and then Psalm 22:26 and Isaiah 61:1. Isaiah 29:18 begins with the words: "In that day", so what day was that? The answer is in verse 29:2, "Yet I will distress Ariel". The explanation from the Hebrew Scriptures is:

> "Ariel is a name for the Temple Altar (see Ezekiel 43). Here it is used to symbolise the entire city of Jerusalem, saying that Assyria will besiege it (see 2 Kings Ch. 18, 19), and after that the multitudes of slain people will be reminiscent of the Altar, which is surrounded by slaughtered animals (Rashi)."[18]

Continuing with this explanation through to Isaiah 29:18,

> "Isaiah reprimands the people for rejecting the word of God and following false prophets (*Rashi*). Isaiah illustrates the futility of the situation: Intelligent people would not try to decipher the prophecy, saying that the message was sealed, i.e., too vague. Unintelligent people were truly incapable of understanding the message. Thus, no one paid attention to the prophecy (*Radak*). The Lebanon is a forest with great cedar trees. When God judges the people, the haughty will be brought down, and the meek elevated, all to their appropriate places. Then, those who had been blind and deaf to God's word will see and hear."[19]

Isaiah 35 then prophesies about the return to Jerusalem. Yes, "then the eyes of the blind will be opened, and the ears of the deaf will be unstopped" (v. 5), but what about: "the redeemed of Hashem will return and come to

Zion with glad song" (v.10)? Did that happen? No, exactly the opposite happened, so this could not be a prophecy fulfillment by Jesus. Isaiah 61:1 clearly refers to a time, very different to the time of Jesus. Where the NKJV has "Me", the TJB correctly renders it as "me", for the person referred to is Isaiah himself, not the future Messiah, Again, the claim of prophecy fulfillment is false. Quoting Psalm 22:26 is simply a case of mining the Scriptures for matching words, irrespective of context, and this reference should be ignored.

Matthew 11:10 – see Mark 1:2 (next chapter)

Matthew 11:13 – "*For all the prophets and the law prophesied until John*" referencing Malachi 4:4-6. I find this most odd, as fulfillment of a prophecy. Firstly, it is not a statement of prophecy: it is a statement of history that the Prophets prophesied. Secondly, verse 4 in Malachi begins with: "Remember the Law of Moses, My servant", yet Christianity chooses to discard it. That aside, if we look for an inferred prophecy, verse 5 says: "Behold I will send you Elijah the prophet", which we understand not as Elijah reincarnated, but one like Elijah. But this is where Christian theologians utilise circular logic: because John said that he came to *prepare the way of the Lord*, this is accepted as proof that Jesus was the Messiah. Jesus said: "But I say to you that Elijah has come already" (Matt 17:12), but first one must accept that Jesus was the Messiah, to accept that John fulfilled the Elijah prophecy. It is illogical to have person B testifying to the identity of person A, and relying on person A to testify to the identity of person B. I am reminded of Simon Greenleaf's book[20], wherein he urged Christians and others to investigate the evidence of the Evangelists as one would in a court of law. In a court of law, two witnesses corroborating the identity of each other would not be acceptable as evidence, due to the possibility of collusion. If we are to take Simon Greenleaf at his word, we should apply that evidence test here.

Matthew 12:18 – see Chapter 3-2 on the *suffering servant*.

Matthew 13:14 – see Mark 4-12

Matthew 13:35 – "that it might be fulfilled which was spoken by the prophet, saying: *I will open my mouth in parables; I will utter things kept secret from the foundation of the world*", quoting Psalm 78:2. We cover this in detail in Part 5, where we examine the Psalms that the evangelists quoted as specific prophecies, so I will leave a discussion on this until later.

Matthew 15:8 – *"These people draw near to me with their mouth"* quoting Isaiah 29:13 and Psalm 78:36. Isaiah's verse was explained earlier in the context of Mathew 11:5, and those comments are relevant in this context. We also find a difference in the wording between the TJB and the NKJV, which alters the meaning of the text:

    a. TJB – "their fear of me is like rote learning of human commands."

    b. NKJV - "And their fear toward me is taught by the commandment of men."

Subtle for some, I will admit, but the emphasis changes from "rote learning" to "commandments of men", perhaps again attempting a divide between Jesus and the Pharisees. Quoting Psalm 78:36 is another example of data mining, and its irrelevance is demonstrated in a subsequent verse: "But He, being full of compassion, forgave their iniquity" (v.38). Did Jesus forgive their iniquity? On the contrary, he condemned them by calling them hypocrites.

Matthew 16:27 – *"For the Son of Man will come in the glory of his Father"* quoting Daniel 7:10 (see Chapter 3-3).

Matthew 17:23 – *"they will kill him, and the third day he will be raised up"*, another prediction of a prophecy fulfillment, acceptable in the context, but curiously, the translators of the NKJV do not annotate any Old Testament verse, just corroboration in the New. There are two points to note: [1] there is no Old Testament prophecy of this; and [2], there is no evidence of Jesus being resurrected on the third day - only that the tomb was empty on the third day. Jesus may well have been long gone, shortly after his burial, for all the Apostles could have known. This has no evidentiary weight whatsoever.

Matthew 20:28 – *"Just as the Son of man did not come to be served, but to serve"* quoting Isaiah 53:10-12 and Daniel 9:24, 26. We have covered Isaiah 53 at some length, but here I will point out two issues concerning verse 53:10: [1] if the Hebrew translation is used, it uncovers an obvious fallacy in attempting to identify the suffering servant in Daniel, with Jesus; and [2], the Greek and English translations convey an entirely different sense, which has me suspecting that these later translations have been deliberately corrupted to justify Christian theology:

a. "Hashem desired to oppress him, and He afflicted him; if his soul would acknowledge his guilt, he would see offspring and live long days" (TJB). Did the sinless Jesus need to acknowledge his guilt? Did Jesus have offspring and live long days? One can attempt to spiritualise the latter, but that is eisegesis.

b. "Yet it pleased the Lord to bruise Him; He has put Him to grief. When You make His soul an offering for sin. He shall see His seed, He shall prolong His days" (NKJV)

The irony is that the translators did not know what to do with the last sentence, and thus left it as ambiguous. As for Daniel 9:24 & 26, we covered that in Chapter 3-4.

<u>Matthew 21:5</u> – *"Tell the daughter of Zion, Behold, your King is coming to you, lowly, and sitting on a donkey, a colt, the foal of a donkey"* quoting Isaiah 62:11 and Zechariah 9:9. We can excuse the author's absurdity in having Jesus riding on BOTH the donkey AND the colt, "they brought the donkey and the colt, laid their clothes on **them**, and set him on **them**" (v. 21:7), but it does demonstrate the author's unfamiliarity with the nature of Hebrew poetry, as used by Zechariah, and again raises the question of how familiar this author was with the Hebrew Scriptures at all. Putting that aside, the verse begs the question (affirms the consequent), because it assumes that Jesus was King. As evidence, it carries no weight whatsoever. One must first prove that Jesus was the prophesied King, before offering this as a prophecy fulfillment. That aside, read Isaiah 62 from the beginning, and ask yourself: Does this sound like the times of Jesus? Again, we must seek beyond the referenced verse to understand the context, and the full meaning of the prophecy; let us compare the translations of Isaiah 62:12:

a. NKJV – "And they shall call them The Holy People, the Redeemed of the Lord; and you shall be called Sought Out, A City Not Forgotten."

b. TJB - "People will call them, 'the Holy People, the Redeemed house of Hashem'; and you will be called, 'Sought After', 'The City Not Forsaken'."

You see, when the King arrives, riding on a donkey (if that is to be taken literally), the Children of Israel will be redeemed from their oppression, and Jerusalem will be a sought after city, one not forsaken by God. That is what the people of Jerusalem were expecting, and why they cried out: "Hosanna to the Son of David". Sadly for them, however, the outcome was not what they were anticipating.

As for Zechariah 9:9, again, read from the beginning: the prophecy concerned the land of Hadrach, and Damascus was where it would be fulfilled (its resting place). If you read through the following verses, Jesus does not accomplish what is prophesied there: "For I will bend Judah [as a bow] for Me; I will fill [the hand of] Ephraim with a bow; and I will stir up your children, O Zion, against your children, O Greece; and I will make you like the sword of a warrior" (Zech 9:13, TJB). Given that Jesus did none of these things, I would offer this passage in Zechariah as substantive evidence the Jesus did NOT fulfill the prophecy. You might also consider, allegorically, that rather than Israel overcoming Greece, Hellenism defeated Judaism in Rome and the Catholic Church.

Matthew 21:9 – "*Then the multitudes … cried out, saying: 'Hosanna to the Son of David etc.*" quoting Psalm 118:26. I have no doubt that if this narration is true, then the people did believe that Jesus was the promised Messiah. However, that they did so is not proof of prophetic fulfilment – people have believed many things that are untrue. In believing that Jesus was the Messiah, what were their expectations: that he would shortly be executed, or that he would restore Israel? There is no evidence that the people's expectation of the Messiah was that he would shortly die for their sins. If Jesus had publicly preached that, and he did not, then I doubt that the Jewish people would have hailed him as king – that is not what kings did back in those days (if ever). This verse cannot be offered as prophecy fulfillment.

Matthew 21:12 – "*Then Jesus went into the temple of God and drove out all those who bought and sold in the temple*", referencing Psalm 69:9, 119:139; Isaiah 56:7; Malachi 3:1; and Deuteronomy 14:25. Starting with Deuteronomy, this is not even remotely associated with a prophecy of the Messiah. Likewise, Isaiah 56:7, the irony here being that Christianity has *defiled the Sabbath*, contrary to the word of God (think on it). Malachi 3:1 has previously been used in relation to John the Baptist, so why try to squeeze it in here? Quoting Psalm 69:9 is also ironic, because David was speaking of his own sins. The point is that whilst there is some justification in finding a prophecy that people would abuse the sanctity of the Temple, there is no prophecy that Jesus would drive them from the Temple. It is absurd to attempt to make one possible prophecy to mean something entirely different.

Matthew 21:15 – "*But when the chief priests and scribes saw ... the children crying ... 'Hosanna to the Son of David!' they were indignant*", referencing Psalm 118:26. This attempt at correlation between the Son of David and coming in the name of the Lord is begging the question. That David opined: "*blessed is he who comes in the name of the Lord*", is not a prophecy of Jesus as Messiah – it could refer to anyone, including the later Prophets. To prove a case, using the rules of evidence, as exhorted by Simon Greenleaf, we need **substantive** evidence that supports just one proposition, not many. Quoting verses which can support numerous propositions, not just one, is circumstantial at best, and unconvincing.

Matthew 21:42 – "*Have you never read in the Scriptures: The stone which the builders rejected*", see Chapter 3-7.

Matthew 21:44 – "*Whoever falls on this stone will be broken*", see Chapter 3-7.

Matthew 22:44 – "*The Lord said to my Lord*" quoting Psalm 110:1. Here we have the dispute between Christianity and Judaism as to the author of this Psalm. Judaism teaches that this psalm was written *about* David, not *by* David. This changes the identification of each of the "Lords" spoken about. I have no path to resolution, other than believing those who were closest to the autograph, and conveyed the sense of the psalm for some one thousand years before the reinterpretation by Christianity. We do not know who translated the Hebrew/Assyrian psalms into Greek, and whether they truly understood the background. As we have discussed earlier, the Septuagint is not necessarily reliable. See Chapter 3-8.

Matthew 24:30 – "*Then the sign of the Son of Man will appear in heaven*" ☆, a prophecy of the future which on the rules of evidence, cannot authenticate Jesus as Messiah during his time two thousand years ago.

Matthew 26:14 – "*Then one of the twelve, called Judas Iscariot, went to the chief priests*", referencing Psalm 41:9. My initial reaction to this claim is firstly, the psalms are not truly prophetic; and secondly, I find the tale of betrayal by Judas to be implausible, as I wrote about in detail in *"Once A Christian"*[21]. Without repeating the detail, my question was: What did Judas know, that the chief priests could not have known, that was worth thirty pieces of silver (half a year's wages)? As to the Psalm itself, the message is: "By contemplating the experiences of the poor and the sick, one becomes aware of God's loving closeness to man, even in the most hopeless circumstances"[22]. It is a prayer, not a prophecy.

Matthew 26:67 – *"Then they spat on his face and beat him"* quoting Isaiah 50:6, 53:3. Isaiah 53 we have already reviewed in the context of the *suffering servant*. Isaiah 50 is about Isaiah himself, about how he took up the challenge of doing God's will, despite the opposition of his contemporaries. *"I gave My back to those who struck Me, and My cheeks to those who plucked out the beard; I did not hide My face from shame and spitting."* If this is considered a prophecy of Jesus, it should also be considered a prophecy of all those who have suffered in the name of God, although curiously, we have no record of Jesus having his beard plucked. At best, and a very slim best at that, it could be considered circumstantial evidence.

Matthew 27:9 – *"Then was fulfilled what was spoken **by Jeremiah** the prophet, and they took thirty pieces of silver, the value of him who was priced"* [emphasis mine]. Unsurprisingly, the NKJV annotates this not as a quotation from Jeremiah, but of Zechariah 11:12. There is a similar narrative in Jeremiah 32, but of very different circumstances, although it does relate to redemption. Jeremiah states: "The word of Hashem came to me, saying: 'Behold, Hanamel, the son of your uncle Shallum, is coming to you to say: Buy for yourself my field that is in Anathoth, for upon you is the law of redemption, to buy it'." (32:6-7) That law of redemption is stated in Leviticus 25:25, "If your brother becomes impoverished and sells part of his ancestral heritage, his redeemer who is closest to him shall come and redeem his brother's sale." The price is given in these terms: "I weighed out the money for him: seven shekels and ten silver pieces" (32:9). I find it absurd that a story of redemption, by law as stated in Leviticus, should be turned into a prophecy of betrayal! What was in Matthew's mind, or was that added by someone who had little or no understanding of the Hebrew Scriptures?

Now back to Matthew. Why thirty pieces of silver: on what basis was that price determined? There are two mentions of this amount in the Old Testament:

1. "If the ox gores a male or female servant, he shall give to their master thirty shekels of silver" (Exodus 21:32); and of more relevance in the context of Judas,

2. "Then I said to them, 'If it agreeable to you, give me my wages; and if not, refrain'. So, they weighed out for my wages thirty pieces of silver. And the Lord said to me, 'Throw it to the potter – that princely price they set on me. So, I took the thirty pieces of silver and threw them into the house of the Lord for the potter." (Zechariah 11:12-13, NKJV)

It is easy to see how Christian scholars latched onto Zechariah, as a prophecy of the betrayal by Judas, but unfortunately, they misunderstood the nature of the prophet's discourse: it is allegorical not literal. Without launching into a long explanation, which involves understanding the two staffs: *Hobelim* and *Noam*, the thirty pieces of silver in Zechariah are thirty righteous people. Of interest is that the Christian version of Zechariah, translated from the Greek, refers to a "potter", but the Hebrew does not; it reads: "Hashem said to me, 'Throw it to the **treasurer** of the Precious Stronghold, which I have divested from them.' So, I took (full amount of) thirty silver coins and threw it into the Temple of Hashem, to the **treasurer**." [emphasis mine] If one studies Zechariah 11 in full, it should be obvious that the Hebrew version makes far more sense than that derived from the Greek: reference to a *potter* is inconsistent with the overall theme. As per our earlier discussions on the Septuagint, I do wonder whether this is an example of the Greek being retrofitted to the Gospel to derive a prophecy.

As an aside, for it does not directly relate to claimed prophecy fulfillment, Matthew 27:6 has the chief priests saying: "It is not lawful to put them (30 pieces of silver) into the treasury, because they are the price of blood." This is further evidence that this episode cannot be a fulfillment of Zechariah 11:12-13, because in that narrative, the money was given to the treasurer of the Temple.

Matthew 27:10 – as above.

Matthew 27:14 – "*But he answered him not one word*", quoting Isaiah 53:7. Even if one were to accept Jesus as the *suffering servant*, Matthew's narrative is questionable, because the accounts of Mark, Luke, and John have Jesus answering in an ever-increasing number of words; see especially Luke 22:67-70 and John 18:19-37. Either they were wrong, or Matthew's claim is false.

Matthew 27:26 – "*And when he had scourged Jesus; he delivered him to be crucified*", quoting Isaiah 50:6 and 53:5. See the comments on Matthew 26:67.

Matthew 27:30 – "*Then they spat on him*": see above.

Matthew 27:34 – "*they gave him sour wine mingled with gall to drink*", quoting Psalm 69:21, which reads from the Hebrew: "But they put gall in my **meal**, and for my thirst they gave me vinegar to drink. May their **table** become a snare before them, and a trap to their peacefulness. Let their eyes be darkened so that they cannot see, and their loins falter continually. Pour your fury upon them, and let the fierceness of Your anger overtake them." (Psalm 69:22-25, TJB) [emphasis mine]. This is not a prophecy of the Messiah, but "a vivid prophetic portrayal of Israel's plight in its long and bitter exile, and an impassioned plea for its speedy deliverance"[23]. I am intrigued not a little as to how Matthew, or whoever, saw a parallel between this Psalm, and the impending death of Jesus, who clearly was not about to rescue anyone.

Matthew 27:35 – "*Then they crucified him, and divided his garments, casting lots*", quoting Psalm 22:18. This Psalm comes in for a lot of attention regarding Jesus' crucifixion, so let us step back and examine it in a broader context. I believe Christianity has misinterpreted, deliberately or otherwise, the relevant passages. *Gotquestions.org*[24] states that verse 22:16 prophecies that "Messiah will have His hands and His feet 'pierced' through, but compare these translations:

a. "For dogs have surrounded Me; the congregation of the wicked has enclosed Me. They pierced My hands and My feet" (NKJV).
b. "For dogs have surrounded me; a pack of evildoers has enclosed me, like a lion they attack my hands and my feet" (TJB).
c. "and my feet my hands dig have enclosed of evil doers the assembly for dogs have compassed for in stare they look my bones (Greek Interlinear).

Curious? It would seem that the Christian translation is an attempt at harmonising the Septuagint and Masoretic texts. To my mind, rendering "my" as "My" is a theological annotation intended to convey doctrine, not truth. In the Psalm, David is speaking of his own circumstances, not speaking of *a vision of the future* – the context does not allow that interpretation. Note that the metaphor of a lion is mentioned in an earlier verse, but more importantly, consider this verse: "and all my bones became disjointed" ("out of joint" in NKJV). So, here is the question: If verse 16 is a prophecy of Jesus' suffering, why not verse 14? Were the bones of Jesus out of joint, or disjointed, on the cross? If not, how can one honestly claim that verse 16 is a prophecy, but verse 14 is not? This persistent selective quoting of Scripture is not the way to determine truth.

Gotquestions.org also interprets "I can count all my bones" (v. 17) as meaning "The Messiah's bones will not be broken", but I do not accept that. It is far more logical to link that statement to verse 14: "all my bones became disjointed", because it would be far easier to count bones when they are disjointed, than when they are not (broken or otherwise). Casting lots for captured booty, or the clothing of condemned criminals (Psalm 22:18), was a common practice in ancient times, and we should not attempt to turn a common practice into the fulfillment of a prophecy.

Matthew 27:36 – "*Sitting down, they kept watch over him there*", quoting Psalm 22:17. The NKJV renders this verse as: "they look and stare at me", and the TJB: "they look on, and gloat over me". I cannot be sure of the connotation of Matthew 27:36, but it does not seem consonant with either version of the Psalm. This is very unconvincing as a prophecy fulfillment.

Matthew 27:39 – "*And those who passed by blasphemed him, wagging their heads*", quoting Psalm 22:7, 8. One needs to read the entire psalm to understand why none of it concerns a prophecy of the Messiah: it is all about David's plight. It may be said that the plight of Jesus parallels that of David, but it also parallels the plight of the Prophets, and many other Jewish people. Even if Jesus was a descendant of David, and that I question, so too were many other Jewish people who could write as David did, firstly noting: "Our fathers trusted in You; they trusted You, and You delivered them", but then: "I am a worm, and no man; a reproach of men, and despised by the people. All those who see me ridicule me." Firstly, that latter claim did not apply to Jesus. Secondly, I am tempted to ridicule

Christian translators, for every occurrence of "me" where David is referring to himself, they have rendered it as "Me", in an attempt to make it appear a prophecy of Jesus, rather than a recounting of David's life. This is nothing but a blatant corruption of Scripture. How can Christianity claim that "every word is the inerrant Word of God", when they have deliberately, and fraudulently, rewritten the text to have it say what they want it to say? It is one thing to claim that verses in a psalm are prophetic, but it is another entirely to rewrite it to make it appear so.

Matthew 27:43 – "*He trusted in God; let Him deliver him now if He will have him*", again quoting Psalm 22. No more need be said.

Matthew 27:46 – "*Jesus cried out … my God, why have you forsaken me?*", quoting Psalm 22:1. Enough has been said about the Christian corruption of Psalm 22, and so moving on, is it just me, or do others find this a curious thing to say, when Jesus is said to have voluntarily sacrificed himself, on the wishes of the Father, so that we may be saved from our sins? Was Jesus really saying: "Father, I believed myself to be the Messiah, sent to restore Israel, but how can I do that if You do not save me now?" I understand the stress of his persecution, as much as anyone can who has not experienced it, but his despair seems out of character with the Christian version of his mission. Peter is said to have suffered a gruesome death, but we have no witness, other than the claim that he took his persecution stoically. Many Christian martyrs faced a gruesome death, but with hope and joy, rather than despair, so why did Jesus despair in his claimed moment of triumph? This episode is inconsistent with the mission narrative, and as best as I can tell, out of character of a God incarnate who, foreknowing what was to occur, would have girded himself to endure, that which was needed to accomplish his mission. Heroes are like that. I cannot know the truth of this verse in Matthew, but I am not convinced of it.

Matthew 27:57 – "*Now when evening had come, there came a rich man … Joseph*", noting Isaiah 53:9. Again, we are back to the NKJV version of Isaiah 53:9, which demonstrates the clumsiness of the translators. Jesus died with the wicked (two robbers), and was buried with the rich (in a rich man's tomb), entirely contrary to the NKJV account which has him dying with the rich, and being buried with the wicked.

Matthew 27:60 – "*laid it* (Jesus' body) *in his new tomb which he* (Joseph of Arimathea) *had hewn out of the rock; and he rolled a large stone against the door of the tomb, and departed.*" I can find nothing in the wording of this verse which even approximates that in Isaiah 53:9, as discussed in Chapter 3-2, so why has it been flagged as a prophecy fulfillment? This is deceitful. Many Christians take the count of prophecy fulfillments as evidence that Jesus MUST have been the prophesied Messiah, but the numbers have been fudged: in any other circumstance, this would be labelled fraud, and maybe it should be here also.

Summary

I must admit to being perplexed, very perplexed, if I were to read Matthew's Gospel at a surface level only, expecting him (and the NKJV editors) to be honestly quoting the Old Testament in the belief that Jesus did indeed fulfill prophecy.

If I accept the Apostle Matthew, or whoever wrote the Greek version, as being honest, and attempting to write an authentic account, how was it that he got the prophecies so wrong? Likewise, the editors of the NKJV: how did they find prophetic statements in the Old Testament, when so obviously, they were not, and on occasions had little or nothing at all to do with the life of Jesus. What was in their minds that they saw correlations which I do not discern? They may well have seen events from a perspective which is obscure to me, and likely would have been misled by the unreliable Septuagint, as well as their eschatological view, but building an entire theology on such unstable grounds is unlikely to pass the test of a diligent observer. In Part 8, we review the essays of several Christian scholars who attempt to unravel the mysteries of how the authors of the New Testament used the Old Testament in their writings. Despite that study, I am still mystified.

As we saw at the beginning of this chapter, all is not necessarily as it seems, especially in the way that the author of Matthew's Gospel used Old Testament verses to substantiate his case. That notwithstanding, in the context of legal evidence, as espoused by Simon Greenleaf, Matthew's case, in the NKJV, for Jesus fulfilling messianic prophecies, fails miserably.

REFERENCES:

1. Beale, G.K., *The Right Doctrine from the Wrong Texts? Essays on the Use of the Old Testament in the New*, Baker Academic, Grand Rapids, MI, 1994, p. 111
2. Burkett, Delbert, *An introduction to the New Testament and the origins of Christianity*, Cambridge University Press, 2002
3. Beale, *Ibid*, pp. 114-134
4. Lewis, C.S., *Christian Reflections*, William B. Eerdmans Publishing Company, Grand Rapids, MI, p. 154-155
5. Beale, *Ibid*, p. 134
6. Moule, C.F.D., *The Origin of Christology*, Cambridge University Press, UK, 1977, p. 129
7. http://www.goodnews.ie/josephaccepts.shtml
8. http://www.jewishvirtuallibrary.org/adoption
9. Beale, *Ibid*, p. 169
10. *The Jewish Annotated New Testament*, Levine, Amy-Jill, and Brettler, Marc Zvi, Oxford University Press, New York, NY, 2011, p. 3
11. *Aramaic English New Testament*, Roth, Andrew Gabriel, Netzari Press, Jerusalem, Israel, 2012, p. 2
12. http://www.complete-bible-genealogy.com/genealogy_of_jesus.htm
13. Scherman, Rabbi Nosson, *The Tanach*, Mesorah Publications, ArtScroll English Edition, Brooklyn, NY, 2011, p. 893
14. Talbot, Wayne, *Once a Christian*: How the Bible Convinced Me to Walk Away, Xlibris, Bloomington, IN, 2017, Chapter 6-4 *Developing Anti-Jewishness*
15. Beale, *Ibid*, p. 126
16. *The Tanach, Ibid*, pp. 733-734
17. Beale, *Ibid*, p. 130
18. Scherman, *Ibid*, p. 636
19. *Ibid*, p. 637
20. Greenleaf, Simon, *The Testimony of the Evangelists*, Kregel Classics, Grand Rapids, MI, 1995
21. Talbot, *Ibid*, Chapter 6-7 *The Betrayal of Jesus*
22. Scherman, *Ibid*, p. 956
23. *Ibid*, p. 971
24. https://www.gotquestions.org/death-resurrection-Messiah.html

CHAPTER 4-3

GOSPEL OF MARK

"As it is written in the Prophets: Behold I send
My messenger before your face"
(Mark 1:2)

Overview

As with Matthew, we will start with some statistics. The occurrences in the Gospel of Mark, where the NKJV flags a verse as prophecy fulfillment, are as follows:

1. Old Testament referenced in the New in relation to prophecy.
    a. The NKJV editors reference 34 unique verses in the Old Testament.
    b. Of these 34, only 26 verses are flagged in the OT as prophetic.
    c. 9 of the OT verses are from the Psalms, 8 of which are flagged as prophetic.

2. New Testament
   a. 16 individual Gospel verses are flagged as being in fulfillment of prophecy, either by Jesus or by John the Baptist.
   b. Of those 16, 6 refer to the same OT verse.
   c. Of the 16 where it is claimed prophecy was fulfilled, in only 3 cases does the verse itself state explicitly that such was in fulfillment of a messianic prophecy, in contrast to those verses simply flagged as such by the NKJV editors.
   d. 9 of these Gospel verses refer to a verse in the Psalms only, no other OT book.
   e. 5 verses are flagged as a prophecy yet to be fulfilled, either in the life or death of Jesus, or what could only be in the Second Coming.
   f. 1 verse flagged as prophecy fulfilled had no reference to an Old Testament verse (Mark 10:45).

Not much can be made from this data, but it will be interesting to see it tabulated across all four Gospels, as we will do at the end of the section. Of interest is that in only three verses does the text explicitly state that the event was in fulfillment of prophecy (Mark 1:2-3, 15:28). The first two relate to John the Baptist; the other to Jesus being *numbered with the transgressors*. Put another way, not once does the author of the Gospel of Mark explicitly state that Jesus fulfilled messianic prophecies. As this Gospel was the first to be written, this omission should be considered significant.

Mark in Detail

Mark 1:2 - this Gospel starts with misquoting of the prophets, Malachi and Isaiah. Misquote: you ask? If Mark truly believed that John the Baptist was the person prophesied, then let me offer that he was badly mistaken. Let us take a look at the prophecies, and most particularly, the context. It is in three parts, covered under this verse and the next two. Mark 1:2 - "As it is written in the Prophets: *'Behold, I send My messenger before Your Face, who will prepare Your way before You'.*" Now compare this with the prophecy as rendered in the Old Testament of the same bible version (NKJV):

"Behold, I send My messenger, and he will prepare the way **before Me**. And the Lord, whom you seek, will suddenly come to His temple. Even the Messenger of the covenant, in whom you delight. Behold, He is coming, says the Lord of hosts. But who can endure the day of His coming? And who can stand when He appears?" (Mal 3:1-2, NKJV). [emphasis mine]

Notice how the wording is different, and has been altered in Mark to refer to Jesus not the Father (Me). Secondly, the prophecy clearly relates to the end times. The last two sentences cannot be said to have occurred in the time of Jesus: Could anybody endure the day of his coming? Actually, yes, practically everybody did, and it was Jesus who did not endure. If we turn to the end of Malachi, we find the prophet repeating his message, but with words clarifying the future time: see Mark 1:4.

Mark 1:3 - *"The voice of one crying in the wilderness: Prepare the way of the Lord; make His paths straight."* Again, compare with Isaiah's prophecy which is said to have been fulfilled:

"Comfort, yes, comfort My people! Says your God. Speak comfort to Jerusalem and cry out to her, that her warfare is ended, that her iniquity is pardoned; for she has received from the Lord's hand double for all her sins. The voice of one crying in the wilderness: Prepare the way of the Lord; make straight in the desert a highway for our God. Every valley shall be exalted and every mountain and hill brought low; the crooked places shall be made straight and the rough places smooth. The glory of the Lord shall be revealed, and all flesh shall see it together, for the mouth of the Lord has spoken." (Isaiah 40:1-5)

The wording is close to the Hebrew Scriptures, and is acceptable provided that one understands that the *Lord* in the last sentence is God (Hashem), not Jesus. With that understanding, it should be obvious that this passage in Isaiah does not refer to John the Baptist preparing the way for Jesus. Apart from that, consider the context. Comfort? That is hardly how we could describe the events of the time. There was no comfort for Jerusalem, and far from her warfare being ended, it was continuing and was about to get worse. The Temple was destroyed and shortly thereafter, Jerusalem itself was sacked, and the Jews banished from their ancestral home. Was the glory of the Lord revealed such that all flesh did see it together? Clearly not. Again, this prophecy concerns the end times, not the time of John the Baptist and Jesus.

Mark 1:4 - "*John came baptizing in the wilderness and preaching a baptism of repentance for the remission of sins*" referencing Malachi 4:5,6 which reads:

> "Remember the Law of Moses, My servant, which I commanded him in Horeb for all Israel, with the statutes and judgements. Behold, I will send you Elijah the prophet before the coming of the great and dreadful day of the Lord." (Mal 4:5-6 NKJV)

There are numerous things wrong here. Firstly, the wording of Mark doesn't begin to approximate the wording in Malachi. Secondly, Christianity teaches that Jesus repealed Mosaic Law, yet the prophecy refutes that notion, with God commanding that the Law be remembered. Thirdly, according to the Apostle John, John the Baptist denied that he was the Prophet Elijah (John 1:21), although Jesus stated that John the Baptist did fulfill what was prophesied of Elijah (Matt 11:14), or as Luke puts it: "*in the spirit and power of Elijah*" (Luke 1:17). Fourthly, nowhere in the Old Testament is there a prophecy concerning *preaching a baptism of repentance for the remission of sins*. The Prophets are clear: forgiveness is available to all those who repent, no additional baptism is required. Finally, the prophecy relates to "*the great and dreadful day of the Lord*": in other words, the End of Days. Two thousand years later, we are still waiting.

This is certainly a very strange beginning to a Gospel which is said to be inerrant, and which supposedly describes the events of the time. Did Mark truly believe that John the Baptist fulfilled those prophecies, and if so: Why? I suspect that if he did, his reasons tied in with the eschatological temper of the times, which we discuss in a later chapter.

Another explanation, by Christian apologists, not unexpectedly, is that there were to be two comings of Elijah, just as there were to be two comings of the Messiah. I have read numerous Christian commentaries where, in partial support of what I have been writing here (for they too had understood the problem), it is claimed that "Most of the prophecies recorded in the Bible have at least two fulfillments"[1]. Having pondered this at length, I disagree. If God intended such a pattern to His revelations through his Prophets, I believe that God would have made that clear. I cannot understand why God would deceive His Prophets, and those to whom the Prophets were to guide. Throughout the Hebrew Scriptures, the focus is on the trajectory of God's Chosen People, His First-Born Son, as He instructed Moses to tell Pharaoh. On several occasions, God tells His Prophets that what He had done, was for His Name's Sake, not for theirs. But now, Christian apologists, would have us believe that there was an undisclosed sub-plot running through the times of the Children of Israel, one not revealed until the coming of Jesus.

Quite frankly, I do not believe it, and see it as an attempt of justification after the event. Mark has attributed to Isaiah, words that appear to be a combination of Exodus 23:20, Malachi 3:1, and Isaiah 40:3. I have no objection to what is termed, *testimonia*, in an attempt to explain a circumstance, but I believe it wrong to combine verses from different periods to make it look like a prophecy. If the Prophets spoke the words of God, those words should be sufficient in adjudicating prophecy fulfillment.

Mark 3:6 – "*Then the Pharisees went out and immediately plotted with the Herodians against him, how they might destroy him*", referencing Psalm 2:2. King David is questioning why the nations rage, and why "the kings of the earth set themselves, and the rulers take counsel together, against the Lord and against His anointed". To whom was David referring in his time? The preceding psalm sets the context: "Praiseworthy is the man who walked not in the counsel of the wicked, and stood not in the path of the sinful, and sat not in the session of the scorners." Jewish sage, Rashi, commented that the psalm alludes to the encounter between the nations and the Messiah, but this does not fit the context of Jesus times. Jesus did not have an encounter with the nations, just the Romans and some of his own people. That the Pharisees and the Herodians plotted against Jesus is not evidence that he was the Messiah – plotting against one's enemies was normative in those times. To link this psalm with Jesus, one must first demonstrate that Jesus was the Messiah, not use a common practice for that purpose. See also Mark 9:7.

Mark 4:12 - "*Seeing they may see and not perceive, and hearing they may hear and not understand, lest they should turn and their sins be forgiven them*" supposedly quoting Isaiah 6:9-10, and 43:8, so let us compare the texts of Isaiah from two bibles:

1. TJB – "He said, go and say to this people: 'Surely you hear but you do not comprehend, and surely you see but fail to know.' This people is fattening its heart, hardening its ears, and sealing its eyes, lest it see with its eyes, hear with its ears, and understand with its heart, so that it will repent and be healed."

2. NKJV – "And He said, go and tell this people: Keep on hearing, but do not understand; Keep on seeing, but do not perceive. Make the heart of this people dull, and their ears heavy, and shut their eyes; lest they hear with their ears, and understand with their heart, and return and be healed."

Note the change in sense from the Jewish to the Christian versions of Isaiah. Now ask yourself: why would God send Isaiah *to make the heart of this people dull*? Why would God want to prevent these people from repenting, when the very mission of the Prophets was to exhort them to repentance, returning to God and the covenant? Who were these people? They were Israelites of Judah in the time of King Uzziah, and as with other events in the life of Isaiah, his task was to preach repentance to them. The Christian version of this text has God sending Isaiah not to preach repentance, but to deny them any chance of repentance. The more I contemplate this strange Christian distortion of the Hebrew Bible, the more I am inclined to believe that the meaning has been deliberately changed in the cause of anti-Jewishness. I do wonder whether this corruption of the Hebrew Scriptures began with Paul, for he wrote:

> "But their minds were blinded. For until this day the same veil remains unlifted in the reading of the Old Testament, because the veil is taken away in Christ. But even to this day, when Moses is read, a veil lies on their heart. Nevertheless, when one turns to the Lord, the veil is taken away." (2 Cor 3:14-16)

Again, note the difference in sense: the NKJV has God telling Isaiah to enforce dullness, heaviness, and blindness upon the people lest they understand, repent, and be healed. It is, as if, God did not want them to repent and be healed. The Hebrew version has the people themselves, deliberately doing those things. The context is Isaiah prophesying, and the people paying no attention. As I cannot imagine God not wanting the people to repent, and the Hebrew version better fitting the circumstances, I am confident that the NKJV version is incorrect. That being so, Paul was not correctly conveying a prophecy, and his accusation concerning the veil over the eyes of the people was false.

The logical conclusion from this is that the veil was never truly there, because the words of Isaiah were corrupted. Thus, the veil could not have been lifted by Christ, and Paul's gospel was false. Making up stories to suit one's argument is not something that I would expect from one claiming to be guided by the Holy Spirit. However, I would contend that in the transition from Jerusalem to Rome, a veil has descended upon Christians, and will only be taken away by returning to God.

The inclusion of the reference to Isaiah 43:8 is most odd, for the text speaks of people who were physically blind and deaf, not deliberately spiritually so. At best, this can be attributed to sloppy editing of the NKJV, selecting verses that might fit without first checking context.

Mark 6:6 – "*Well did Isaiah prophesy of you hypocrites*": see Matthew 15:8.

Mark 9:7 - "*And a cloud came and overshadowed them; and a voice came out of the cloud, saying: This is My beloved Son, Hear Him!*" This is claimed as a prophecy from three sources. Firstly, Exodus 30:44 referring to the cloud covering the Tent of Meeting – yes, the circumstances appear the same, if true, but Exodus is not a prophecy. John's account does not mention the cloud, so without corroboration, Mark's evidence carries little weight. Next, "*Behold! My Servant whom I uphold, My Elect One in whom My soul delights!*" (Isaiah 42:1, NKJV): at best, this is circumstantial evidence, as it could refer to any number of people. Jewish sources confirm that this passage in Isaiah does refer to the coming Messiah. However, the following verses speak of bringing justice to the Gentiles – more correctly, nations, as written in both the Greek and Hebrew. Did Jesus do that? Fulfillment of Psalm 2:7 is implausible, for the psalm is clearly related to King David. However, a French Rabbi of the 11th century, Solomon

ben Isaac (Shlomo Yitzhaki), known as Rashi, one of the most influential
Jewish commentators in history, commented that "the psalm alludes to the
encounter between the nations and the Messiah. From that perspective,
one could say that the psalm does relate to the Messiah, but it could not
relate to Jesus as Messiah, because Jesus had no such encounter: that will
occur in what Christians believe to be, the Second Coming. As the psalm
does not relate to the so-called First Coming, it cannot be said to be a
fulfilled prophecy."

Mark 11:7 – see Matthew 21:5

Mark 11:9-10 - "*Then those who went before and those that followed
cried out saying: 'Hosanna! Blessed is he who comes in the name of the Lord',*
etc.*". I covered this in the discussion of Jesus' triumphal entry to Jerusalem
(Chapter 3-4), so no need to discuss it further here. The point was this:
what triumph was being celebrated – his impending death, which nobody
was expecting? Whilst the crowd saw it as a triumphal entry, and Jesus
may have seen it as a triumphal entry, their respective understandings of
triumph were in no way similar.

Mark 14:36 - "*Abba, Father, all things are possible for You. Take this cup
away from me; nevertheless, not what I will, but what You will*" referencing
Isaiah 50:5. Here we have one of the worst examples of searching the
Old Testament, attempting to prove a prophecy fulfillment, but coming
up with a solution that is fanciful in the extreme. Firstly, this was not
witnessed by anyone, and it is drawing a very long bow indeed to suggest
that later, Jesus told his disciples of his agony and his prayers to the Father:
a most implausible story. Now the prophecy said to be fulfilled: "*The
Lord God has opened my ear; and I was not rebellious, nor did I turn away.*"
(Isaiah 50:5). Even if we are to accept Jesus' words as narrated, this is
but circumstantial evidence, as it is not inconsistent with the fulfillment
propositions, but can also be consistent with other propositions. Could this
not also apply to you, as I offer, it does to me: *not what I will, but what you
will*? Do we not find that in how we are taught to pray (Matthew 6:9-13)?
Incidentally, you may be interested in the "Hebrew Origins of the Lord's
Prayer"[2], evidencing that it was not an entirely new idea of Jesus.

In the verses, 4-9, it is Isaiah speaking about himself, of his readiness
to be God's spokesperson, and God's readiness to inspire him. A prophecy
cannot be capable of being fulfilled by multiple people, else we would have

all and sundry claiming to be the Messiah, as has happened. The test of prophecy is that it could only be fulfilled by just one person, not many. There is nothing in Isaiah 50:5 which can be said to be unique to Jesus, most especially when the link is to words of Jesus that no-one witnessed, nor can corroborate. One can only conclude that the entire scenario is implausible.

Mark 14:57 – "*Then some rose up and bore false witness against him*", quoting Psalm 35:11, which reads: "Fierce witnesses rise up; they ask me things that I do not know." Now, how does false witness against Jesus fulfill a prophecy, that he was asked questions that he could not answer? Witnessing involves making statements, not asking questions.

Mark 14:65 – "*Then some began to spit on him*": see Matthew 26:67.

Mark 15:1 – "*the chief priests held a consultation with the elders*", claimed to be fulfillment of a prophecy in Psalm 2:2 "*the rulers take counsel together*", for no reason other than the wording in one, approximates that in the other. That is nonsensical – rulers taking counsel together is normal, and is no cause for comment, let alone a claim of prophecy fulfillment. Christian apologists need to understand, that sometimes, more is less, and this is one of those times.

Mark 15:3 – "*And the chief priests accused him of many things, but he answered nothing*"; see Matthew 27:14 and Luke 23:9.

Mark 15:19 – "*Then they struck him on the head … and spat on him*"; see Matthew 26:67.

Mark 15:27 – "*With him they also crucified two robbers*", citing Isaiah 53:9, 12, which I suggest, the editors of the NKJV have not understood. See Matthew 27:57.

Mark 15:28 – "So the Scripture was fulfilled which says: *And he was numbered with the transgressors*" quoting Isaiah 53:12. We have dealt with that in detail in Chapter 3-2.

Mark 15:29 – "*And those who passed by blasphemed him, wagging their heads*"; see Matthew 27:39.

Mark 15:31 – "*Likewise the chief priests also, mocking among themselves … He saved others, himself he cannot save*", quoting Psalm 22:8. See Matthew 27:35 regarding the identity of the person in this psalm.

Mark 15:34 – "*My God, My God, why have you forsaken me?*"; see Matthew 27:46.

Mark 15:36 – "*Then someone ran and filled a sponge with sour wine*"; see Matthew 27:34.

Mark 15:45 – "*So when he found out from the centurion, he granted the body to Joseph*"; this is a duplicate of the claimed prophecy fulfillment in Mark 15:27.

Mark 16:19 – "*He was received up into heaven, and sat down at the right hand of God*", quoting Psalm 110:1. This is another psalm that Judaism asserts, was written *about* King David, not *by* David. If Judaism is right, this has no connection with Jesus or the Messiah.

Summary

So, not a single verse which qualifies as substantive evidence of prophecy fulfillment. There is plausible evidence, to my mind, that the Scriptures have been tampered with to align the prophecies with the life of Jesus. There is certainly, circumstantial evidence of prophecy fulfillment, but it largely relates to common practice of the time, and must carry no weight. If anything, Mark's account, and the annotations by the NKJV editors, demonstrate Jesus to be a prophet like any other, or at least, a Jew suffering at the hands of the Romans, at the instigation of the High priest, Caiaphas, for political reasons: "You know nothing at all, nor do you consider that it is expedient that one man should die for the people, and not that the whole nation should perish." (John 11:49-50)

Footnote: I was a little surprised that the NKJV editors did not find a prophecy fulfillment in Mark 16:18, which reads: "*they will take up serpents; and if they drink anything deadly, it will by no means hurt them*". I cannot know what the author meant, but I wonder whether this was an allusion to Numbers 21:6-9, where after "the Lord sent fiery serpents among the people … and many died", Moses was instructed to make a fiery (bronze) serpent and put it on a pole? Those who were bitten by the serpents, but looked upon the bronze serpent, lived. Alternatively, could the verse be attributed to post-editing after hearing of Paul's encounter with a serpent (Acts 28:3)?

The NKJV editors have made more of less.

REFERENCES:

1. http://www.herealittletherealittle.net/index.cfm?page_name=Elijah
2. Gordon, Nehemiah, and Johnson, Keith, *A Prayer to Our Father - Hebrew Origins of the Lord's Prayer*, Hilkiah Press, 2010

CHAPTER 4-4

GOSPEL OF LUKE

"And all things that are written by the prophets concerning
the Son of Man will be accomplished."
(Luke 18:31)

Overview

Continuing the data analyses, these are the results in the Gospel of Luke:

1. Old Testament referenced in the New in relation to prophecy
   a. The NKJV editors reference 50 verses in the Old Testament.
   b. Of these 50, only 31 verses are flagged in the OT as prophetic.
   c. 6 of the OT verses are from the Psalms, all of which are flagged as prophetic.

2. New Testament
   a. 19 individual Gospel verses are flagged as being in fulfillment of prophecy, either by Jesus or by John the Baptist.

b. Of those 19, 5 refer to the same OT verse.

c. Of the 19 where it is claimed prophecy was fulfilled, in only 2 cases does the verse itself state explicitly that such was in fulfillment of a messianic prophecy, in contrast to those verses simply flagged as such by the NKJV editors.

d. 6 of these Gospel verses refer to a verse in the Psalms only, no other OT book.

e. 10 verses are flagged as a prophecy yet to be fulfilled, either in the life or death of Jesus, or what could only be in the Second Coming.

f. 1 verse flagged as prophecy fulfilled had no reference to an Old Testament verse.

In reference to 2(c), the 2 cases where the text itself explicitly states messianic prophecy fulfillment, both relate to John the Baptist, not Jesus. What does that tell us about Luke's understanding of Jesus fulfilling messianic prophecies?

Luke in Detail

Responding to the quotation at the head of this chapter, I have diligently searched the Hebrew Scriptures for *things that are written by the prophets concerning the Son of Man*, but have come up empty. I wonder what Luke understood by the term, *son of man*, and why Jesus used that term almost exclusively about himself? I have no answer, so let us proceed with the claimed prophecy fulfillments.

Luke 1:17 – "*He will go before him in the spirit of Elijah*" ✩, quoting Malachi 4:5-6; see Mark 1:4.

Luke 1:27 – "*to a virgin ... the virgin's name was Mary*"; see Matthew 1:23.

Luke 1:31 – "*And behold you will conceive*"; duplicate of Luke 1:27.

Luke 1:33 – "*And he will reign over the house of Jacob forever*" ✩, quoting Daniel 2:44, Obadiah 21, and Micah 4:7. It is worth pondering the reference to *Jacob*, rather than *Israel*: are they considered one and the same in the Hebrew Scriptures, and why over *the house of Jacob*, when Jacob was not one of the names of the Twelve Tribes of Israel? Jacob was

Israel's former name, when he was still a compliant person easily swayed by stronger characters like his mother. God changed his name to Israel, "*for you have striven with God and men and have prevailed*" (Gen 32:28). Isaiah's mission was to return the people, from being like Jacob (unrighteous), to being like Israel (righteous) - see Isaiah 49:5. What did Luke have in mind? Was he alluding to the mission of Jesus, to recover the lost sheep, or did he simply not understand the significance of the two names, Jacob and Israel?

Daniel 2:44 does refer to the Messiah, but there is no evidentiary link with Jesus, nor does Daniel mention the house of Jacob. Obadiah does allude to the Messiah, but nothing more; curiously, the NKJV does not flag this verse in Obadiah as a prophecy to be fulfilled. Micah reads: "*I will make the lame one into a remnant, and the one forced to wander into a mighty nation.*" This is a curious way of referring to the Houses of Judah and Israel, if that is what is meant. Micah 4 begins: "It will be in the end of days that the mountain of the Temple of Hashem will be firmly established as the most prominent of the mountains, and it will be exalted up above the hills, and peoples will stream to it." Micah is clearly referring to Israel, yet Christianity denies Israel's future, positioning itself as the *New Israel*. If this is a prophecy to be fulfilled by Jesus in his Second Coming, the verse is a refutation of Christian theology. Note the prophecies following: "nation will not lift sword against nation, nor will they learn war anymore" (v. 4:3). None of this occurred during the life of Jesus, or at any time since – thus, as evidence of Jesus as Messiah, it is irrelevant.

Luke 1:79 – "*To give light to those who sit in darkness and the shadow of death*" ☆, quoting Isaiah 9:2. This passage in Isaiah is not prophetic, but refers to the miraculous end to the siege of Jerusalem by Sennacherib. Luke may be attempting to foretell the future, using the example of past miracles, but his usage of history does not qualify as prophecy.

Luke 2:4 – "*Joseph also went up from … Nazareth … to Bethlehem*", quoting 1 Samuel 16:1, and Micah 5:2. 1 Samuel tells the story of how God sent Samuel to Bethlehem, to anoint David as King of Israel – it is not prophetic of the Messiah. Micah is prophetic, but Jesus living in Bethlehem is but circumstantial evidence of him being the Messiah – far more substantive evidence is required, especially as Luke has Jesus born in Nazareth, whereas Christian apologetics favour the Messiah being born in Bethlehem, as was King David.

Luke 2:11 – *"For there is born to you this day in the city of David, a Saviour who is Christ the Lord"*, quoting Isaiah 9:6 and Micah 5:2. Apart from the mix-up over the birth city, here we have another identity conundrum, brought about by mistranslation from the Hebrew. Compare these two translations of Isaiah 9:6, noting the theological annotations and the change of verb tense:

c. TJB – "For a child has been born to us, a son has been given to us, and the dominion will rest on his shoulder; the Wondrous Advisor, Mighty God, Eternal Father, called his name Sarshalom [Prince of Peace]."

d. NKJV - "For unto us a Child is born, unto us a Son is given; and the government will be upon His shoulder, and His name will be called Wonderful Counsellor, Mighty God, Everlasting Father, Prince of Peace."

The context is as discussed earlier in Luke 1:79: the miraculous end to the siege by Sennacherib. The NKJV translators, and I assume, other Christian translators, have changed from the past tense used in the Hebrew, to the future tense, attempting to render these verses as prophecy. The TJB commentary notes: "This wondrous salvation took place in the days of the child of Ahaz, the righteous King Hezekiah whom God – the Wondrous Adviser, Mighty God, Eternal Father – called 'Prince of Peace' (Rashi)." Why would Jesus be called "Everlasting Father", when Jesus himself is reported to have said: "for One is your Father, He who is in heaven" (Matt 23:9), meaning God the Father, NOT God the Son? Indeed, how can Jesus be *Everlasting Father*?

Luke 2:32 – *"A light to bring revelation to the Gentiles, and the glory of Your people Israel"*, referencing Isaiah 42:6. This was a speech given by Simeon on the occasion of Jesus' circumcision. Luke's account has the Holy Spirit upon Simeon, who was thanking God: "my eyes have seen Your salvation". If the narrative is accurate, then Simeon believed that Jesus was the prophesied Messiah, and if, in stating that Jesus would bring light to the Gentiles, he was echoing Isaiah 42:6, his understanding would have been that redemption from oppression by the Romans was nigh, as was the End of Days. We know that Jesus did not fulfill that prophecy.

Isaiah 42 does refer to the Messiah, but note: "He will not shout, nor raise his voice, *nor make his voice heard in the street*" (v. 2) Was that true of Jesus? On the contrary, the voice of Jesus was heard in the streets as he preached far and wide. The TJB commentary reads: "He (Messiah) will be accepted by all and will have no need to proclaim his judgements". In other words, these verses refer to the *End Times*, not two thousand years ago. In passing, I wonder at the NKJV translation of *Gentiles*, whilst the TJB refers to the *nations* – is this a theological annotation intended to subliminally influence our thinking?

Finally on this verse, the mention of the Holy Spirit. Christian apologetics makes much of the narrative in Acts 2 with the Holy Spirit coming upon the Apostles. It is said to be in fulfillment of Jesus' promise to send a Helper, and I have often heard it said of people who do not believe in Jesus, that they do not have the guidance of the Holy Spirit. Early episodes in the Gospels, and in the Old Testament, demonstrate that God sent His Spirit to guide people long before the death of Jesus, and we have no reason to believe that He ever stopped doing so.

<u>Luke 3:4</u> – "*The voice of one crying in the wilderness*"; see Mark 1:2-3.

<u>Luke 3:31</u> – "*the son of Nathan, the son of David*", quoting Zechariah 12:12 and 2 Samuel 5:14. Here we have Luke attempting to prove that Jesus was of the line of King David – see Chapter 4-2 on *The Lineage of Jesus*. Luke's account of the lineage suffers from the same errors as that of Matthew, but Zechariah 12:12 does confirm that Nathan was the son of David. However, how is that fulfillment of prophecy? It is simply the recounting of history. 2 Samuel confirms Zechariah, but again, has nothing to do with prophecy fulfillment, unless one first assumes that Jesus is the Messiah, effectively begging the question.

<u>Luke 4:18</u> – "*The Spirit of the Lord is upon me*", quoting Isaiah 49:8-9, and 61:1-2. A reader not versed in the Old Testament might believe that Jesus opened to book to Isaiah and read the verses that Luke quotes, but Luke's story is false, if taken at face value that is. The practice in Judaism was to read what was written, from start to finish, but Luke has Jesus reading the beginning of Isaiah 61:1; substituting *poor* for *humbled*; inserting *recovery of sight to the blind* which is in neither the Hebrew nor Greek; and skips verses before the beginning of verse 61:2. I have no problem with Luke paraphrasing the Scriptures, for such was not an

uncommon practice, but we need to be careful with claiming the words to be a quotation of Scripture when strictly speaking, they were not. Even worse was the annotation by the NKJV editors of prophecy fulfillment. That error should have been obvious, because the *acceptable year of the Lord* refers to the last days, as it says: *the day of vengeance of our God*. That did not happen. Isaiah 49 starts with Isaiah confirming that he was chosen by God to be His prophet, and thus the references in verses 8-9 are to Isaiah, not to some future prophet, let alone the Messiah. The NKJV version of Isaiah 49 flags a number of verses as prophetic of the Messiah, but that is just not so. The Redeemer of Israel, in verse 7, is *Hashem* (God), not Jesus. I consider this corruption of Scripture scandalous. In Isaiah 61:1-2, Isaiah is speaking of himself, not a future Messiah.

Luke 7:22 – *"Go and tell John … the blind see, the lame walk"*; see Matthew 11:5.

Luke 7:27 – see Mark 1:2.

Luke 8:10 – *"To you it has been given to know the mysteries of God"*, quoting Isaiah 6:9. Not only is Isaiah 6:9 not a prophecy of any form, but the rendering in the NKJV: "Seeing they may not see, and hearing that may not understand", changes the sense of the Hebrew, which states: "Surely you hear, but you do not comprehend; and surely you see, but fail to know". Jesus may have decided to speak in parables, but that has nothing to do with Isaiah's account.

Luke 19:38 – *"Blessed is the King who comes in the name of the Lord"*, quoting Psalm 118:26. See Mark 11:9-10, and Chapter 3-4 concerning Jesus' supposed triumphal entry to Jerusalem.

Luke 20:17 – *"The stone which the builders rejected"* ☆; see Matthew 21:42.

Luke 20:42 – *"The Lord said to my Lord"* ☆; see Matthew 22:44.

Luke 20:27 – *"Then they will see the Son of Man"* ☆; reference to what will happen in the End of Days is irrelevant in the context of proving Jesus to be the Messiah.

Luke 22:37 – *"And he was numbered with the transgressors"* ☆; see Mark 15:28 and Chapter 3:1. It is interesting, to me at least, that this appears in Luke's narrative before the crucifixion, but Mark includes it after the crucifixion.

Luke 22:42 – *"Father, if it your will, take this cup away from me; nevertheless, not my will but Yours be done"*, quoting Isaiah 50:5; see Mark 14:36. Isaiah was speaking of his own tribulations, and was not making a prophetic statement concerning the future Messiah. That Isaiah suffered in the course of his duty to God, is no different to other prophets suffering, and indeed, the suffering of King David.

Luke 22:47 – *"Judas … went before … and drew near to Jesus to kiss him"*, quoting Palm 41:9. The first point to note is that Luke's narration agrees with that of Matthew and Mark, but neither is flagged in the NKJV as a prophecy fulfillment (lack of consistency by the editors?) Secondly, John's account differs, in that Judas does not kiss Jesus, but instead, John provides a more dramatic version, having Jesus steps forward to identify himself, whereupon "they drew back and fell to the ground" (John 18:6). This is not flagged as prophecy fulfillment either. Psalm 41 has David speaking of his own tribulations, not prophesying that the Messiah would suffer the same. It does speak of betrayal, but it cannot be extrapolated beyond David's context.

Luke 23:9 – *"Then he questioned him with many words, but he answered him nothing"*, quoting Isaiah 53:7 (see also Chapter 3-2). This is where the plot unravels. Luke has Jesus questioned by Herod, to whom *he answered him nothing*, but none of the other Gospels mention Jesus being before Herod. In John's account, Jesus has a great deal to say, and only when Pilate asks Jesus where he is from, did Jesus not answer (John 19:9). It is nonsense, in John's narrative, to have Jesus not answering just one question, as a prophecy fulfillment of Isaiah's words: "he did not open his mouth", when Jesus did open his mouth quite a lot. This is a contrived fulfillment, and likely a fabrication.

Luke 23:32 – *"There were also two others, criminals"*; see Matthew 27:57

Luke 23:35a – *"But the people stood looking on"*; see Matthew 27:36, and note the tone of the wording.

Luke 23:35b – *"He saved others, let him save himself"*; quoting Psalm 22:17. See Matthew 27:35 regarding the identity of the person in this psalm. As mentioned earlier, this psalm by David is about himself, as he tells God of his woes, not a prophecy of a Messiah in the future, and unlike the account in Luke, the account in the Psalm does not end badly as it did for Jesus. The NKJV also directs our attention to Zechariah 12:10 because therein are found the words: "then they will look upon Me whom they pierced". Sadly, the scribes omitted to read verse 12:9, "It shall be in that day that I will seek to destroy all the nations that come against Jerusalem." Did God do that? On the contrary, shortly thereafter, the nation of Rome came against Jerusalem and utterly destroyed it. What could be clearer evidence that the prophecy in Zechariah was NOT fulfilled?

Luke 23:36 – "*The soldiers ... offering him sour wine*"; see Matthew 27:34. Across the four Gospels, the accounts of Jesus crucifixion and his last words all vary, so all cannot be true, especially his <u>last</u> words. Jesus is offered sour wine mixed with stupefying drugs, a common practice of the time to help calm any remaining aggression, and in some cases, to relieve the pain. In Matthew (27:34), the wine is mixed with gall, Jesus tastes it, but chooses to not drink. In Mark (15:23), it is mixed with myrrh, Jesus does not drink, but there is no mention of him tasting it. In Luke (23:36), Jesus is offered the sour wine, but does not drink. John tells an entirely different story. In the Synoptics, it is the soldiers offering the sour wine, which at a stretch, could be said to accord with "But they put gall in my meal, and for my thirst they gave me vinegar to drink", if you ignore the context of the Psalm, but John's account cannot. According to the only Apostle who was present at the crucifixion, Jesus cried out: "I thirst!" (John 19:28). "Now a vessel full of sour wine was sitting there", which does accord with the practice of the time. However, in this account, the sponge filled with sour wine was put on hyssop. In Leviticus, God commanded His people to use hyssop in the ceremonial cleansing of people and houses. Was John making a point? Anyway, Jesus drank the wine, contrary to what was written in the Synoptics.

Luke 24:51 – "*Now it came to pass, while he blessed them, that he was parted from them and carried up into heaven*", quoting Psalm 68:18. Turning to that Psalm, the preceding verses 68:15-16 tell of the highest mountains having no cause for pride, for God had chosen Mount Zion over them for His abode on earth, even though Zion was not as high as Bashan. Micah 4 prophesies similarly. The verse, "you have ascended on high", is followed by: "you have taken captives" (TJB), although the NKJV renders this as "you have led captivity captive". Checking other Christian bible versions, there is no consensus on the proper translation of this verse. We have: "you took many captives" (NIV); "you led a crowd of captives" (NLT);

"You have led captive Your captives" (NASB); "you took captives" (ISV); "You took prisoners captive" (GOD'S WORD Translation); and so on. Evidently, the translators have struggled to understand the Greek, resulting in these different interpretations. On that basis alone, one should accept the translation from the Hebrew Bible.

Did Jesus take captives on his ascension into heaven? I can understand, in a mysterious way, that Jesus might have taken *captivity captive*, in that he is said to have released people from the captivity of Satan, or that he released us from the last enemy to be destroyed: *death* (1 Cor 15:26), but it is interesting that no other Gospel makes that connection, although we do find it again in Ephesians 4:8. Perhaps Luke, or whoever made that connection, has been influenced by Paul's letter to the Corinthians, I cannot know, but it does seem Pauline in origin. In any event, it is a stretch to claim that Luke 24:51 is a fulfillment of Psalm 68:18.

Turning to the TJB translation of the Hebrew Scriptures:

> "The mountain of God is a choice mountain. Why do you prance, O you mountains of majestic peaks? The mountain that God desired for His abode – Hashem will even dwell there forever! God's entourage is twice ten thousand, thousands of angels; the Lord is among them, at Sinai in holiness. You ascended on high, You have taken captives, You took gifts of man and even of rebels, to dwell with Yah, God. Blessed is the Lord, day by day He burdens us, the God of our salvation, Selah. God is for us, a God of salvations; and though Hashem/Elohim, the Lord, has many avenues toward death, God will cleave only the head of His foes, the hairy skull of him who saunters with his guilt." (Psalm 68:16-22) [emphasis mine]

King David frequently mixed his metaphors, and here we have more than one. The *mountains* are metaphors for *kingdoms*, and David was pointing out that God had chosen Israel over other more powerful kingdoms, from which He had taken both captives and even gifts. The *hairy skull* is a metaphor for the Edomite empire, descendants of the hairy Esau (see Genesis 25:25). I can understand that perhaps Luke was alluding to a theme of Jesus coming from humble beginnings, that the first shall be last, and similar ideas, in seeing this Psalm being fulfilled in Jesus. That much I would grant, but not that he fulfilled the prophecy, for he failed practically all of the details.

Summary

Luke's account has content not found in other Gospels. Repeating an observation from Chapter 2-5, whilst Luke may have had some knowledge of Judaism, it was likely Hellenic Judaism in the Diaspora, and any familiarity he would have had with the Scriptures, would have been of the Greek versions, rather than the Hebrew. I would assume that Luke believed what he wrote, and was seeking to convince others similarly. I do not understand why Luke believed that Jesus fulfilled prophecy – perhaps, as a disciple of Paul, he was convinced by Paul, and believed that Jesus must have been the prophesied Messiah. He then sought to spiritualise history, justifying this to himself, and perceiving links which convinced him of the truth of his beliefs. Remember that like Paul, Luke was Hellenic in his thinking, and some themes resonated with him more than they would a Hebrew. Nevertheless, it does appear that he developed his own theology from those beliefs, and perhaps sought Scripture passages to support it.

I cannot know.

That said, his Gospel, as evidence of Jesus fulfilling messianic prophecies, carries no weight whatsoever. Not one of his messianic prophecy claims are valid.

CHAPTER 4-5

GOSPEL OF JOHN

"In the beginning was the Word, and the Word
was with God, and the Word was God"
(John 1:1)

Overview

Continuing the data analyses, these are the results in the Gospel of John:
1. Old Testament referenced in the New in relation to prophecy.
   a. The NKJV editors reference 24 unique verses of the Old Testament.
   b. Of these 24, only 14 verses are flagged in the OT as prophetic.
   c. 6 of the OT verses are from the Psalms, all of which are flagged as prophetic.

2. New Testament
   a. 22 individual Gospel verses are flagged as being in fulfillment of prophecy, either by Jesus or by John the Baptist.

b. Of those 22, 6 refer to the same OT verse.

c. Of the 22 verses referenced, where it is claimed prophecy had been fulfilled, in only 5 cases does the NT verse itself state explicitly that such was in fulfillment of a *messianic prophecy*, in contrast to those verses stating general prophecy, and those simply flagged as such by the NKJV editors.

d. 6 of these Gospel verses refer to a verse in the Psalms only, no other OT book.

e. No verses are flagged as a prophecy yet to be fulfilled, either in the life or death of Jesus, or what could only be in the Second Coming.

f. No verses flagged as prophecy fulfilled had no reference to an Old Testament verse.

An oddity is than John 12:38 is not flagged as a prophecy fulfillment, even though the text explicitly states: "*that the word of Isaiah the prophet might be fulfilled*", referring to Isaiah 53:1. That aside, examined closely, this verse is Isaiah is commentary, not prophecy.

John in Detail

These opening words testify to the belief of the author of this Gospel, but it does not represent evidence in the case that we are examining. The *opinion* is based on the belief that Jesus was that prophesied Messiah, and that he was God incarnate, but is it substantiated? If Jesus was not the prophesied Messiah, would the second belief still be held? Probably not. Thus, if the prophetic case is not proven, then neither is the deity case. Thus, to be confident that Christianity is not preaching idolatry, the prophetic case must be proven beyond doubt, with rigorous examination of the proffered evidence.

The Prologue to John's Gospel, verses 1:1-14, is perhaps the best loved of Christianity, claiming as it does, that God became flesh and dwelt amongst us. The linking to Genesis 1 is an attempt to prove the pre-existence of Jesus, Son of God, Second Person of the Trinity. The capitalised *Spirit of God* (Gen 1:2) is claimed as the Third Person, the

Holy Spirit, and because God spoke the world into existence, then Jesus is the Word. It all makes sense, in a way, when translated into English, and annotated with initial capitals to make ordinary words into Royal Titles, but studied in the original languages, the case is not supported. Now to the claimed prophecy fulfillments.

John 1:11 – "*He came to his own, and his own did not receive him*", quoting Isaiah 53:3. We discussed Isaiah 53 in detail in Chapter 3-2, but from the Hebrew, this verse reads: "*He was despised and isolated from men, a man of pains and accustomed to illness*". Hosea, a contemporary of Isaiah, also used the singular when referring to Israel in this context. Was Jesus isolated? No, he preached to multitudes, and was followed by multitudes. Was Jesus accustomed to illness? We have no evidence that he was. Note also that in the NKJV, the tense of the verbs has been mixed, with the first sentence using the present, and the second, the past. In the Hebrew Scriptures, the past tense is used consistently.

John 1:23 - "*the voice of one crying in the wilderness*"; see Matthew 3:1-3.

John 1:33 – "*Upon whom you see the Spirit descending, and remaining on him, this is he who baptises with the Holy Spirit*", quoting Isaiah 42:1, 61:1. See Mark 9:7 (also Matthew 3:11). My first issue is that we have no evidence that this exchange was witnessed by any of the Evangelists, and John's account is far lengthier than given in the Synoptics. Isaiah 61:1, which is not quoted in Mark's account, is also quoted in support of Matthew 11:5, which has me wondering. John's account of the Spirit descending upon Jesus at his baptising fails the test of uniqueness, and is at best circumstantial evidence. There are numerous occurrences of the Spirit of God coming upon people, even upon Simeon (Luke 2:25), and thus there is nothing about this incident which can be claimed as fulfillment of a messianic prophecy. Linking John 2:14, where Jesus went into the Temple, with Malachi 3:1, evidences desire on the part of the translators. Read the subsequent verses in Malachi 3 and see how well they fit with the life and times of Jesus: they clearly do not. One cannot take coincidence as prophecy fulfillment – that is poor biblical exegesis, and cannot even be counted as correlating evidence.

John 2:14 – "*And he found in the Temple ... and the money changers doing business*", quoting Malachi 3:1. Anybody, and everybody, who walked into the Temple in those times, would have witnessed the same activities, so there is no uniqueness here. Linking John 2:14 with Malachi 3:1, again evidences desire on the part of the translators, at least, as far as I can understand it.

John 2:17 – "Then his disciples remembered that it was written, '*Zeal for Your house has eaten Me up*'", quoting Psalm 69:9. Really? These illiterate fishermen, and others, knew the Scriptures that well? But here is the irony: if they did indeed know the Psalms as claimed, they would have had no reason to associate those words of David with Jesus as later revealed. They would have understood them from the perspective of their contemporary rabbis, and the history of King David. The Jewish sages identify Psalm 69 as "a vivid prophetic portrayal of Israel's plight in its long and bitter exile, and an impassioned plea for its speedy deliverance". Now if the disciples did see Jesus in the light, they would soon know that he was not the expected deliverer, because he failed to deliver. Had John's Gospel been written before the death of Jesus, it might make some sense, but as it was a half-century later, when it was evident that Jesus did not deliver as David prayed, one would wonder why the author of this Gospel would include that episode.

John 3:34 - "*For He whom God has sent speaks the words of God, for God does not give the Spirit by measure*", quoting Deuteronomy 18:18. In logic, claiming this to be fulfillment of a prophecy, is begging the question. Firstly, it presupposes that the speaker was sent by God, but that is what claiming of a fulfillment of prophecy is intended to prove: affirming the consequent is not acceptable evidence. That notwithstanding, if John the Baptist did speak these words, his knowledge of God giving the Spirit, was not formed from Scripture, for a study reveals that God *does* give the Spirit by measure. Reading through the Old Testament up to the end of 2 Samuel (my diligence faltered at that point), I found 30 occurrences[1] where the Holy Spirit came upon people, and in each case, it was for a specific purpose, and was either temporary, or if continuing, in relation to a particular attribute only. For example: "*and it happened, when the Spirit rested upon them, that they prophesied although they never did so again*" (Num 11:25); "*Now Joshua the son of Nun was full of the Spirit of Wisdom*" (Deut 34:9); "*But the Spirit of the Lord came upon Gideon and he blew the Trumpet*" (Jud 6:34). Particularly interesting is this entry: "*the Spirit of the Lord came upon David from that day forward ... but the Spirit of the Lord departed from Saul*" (1 Sam 13-14): the context of the narrative reveals the purpose.

Without researching the rest of the Old Testament, it is apparent that there was a pattern to the visitations of the Holy Spirit upon people:

a.   It was for a specific purpose, most commonly to prophesy; and

b.   It was almost always for a special occasion and thus temporary.

This notion of singular assistance is confirmed here: "*But the Helper, the Holy Spirit, whom the Father will send in My name, He will teach you all things, and bring to your remembrance all things that I said to you*" (John 14:26). The audience for this dissertation by Jesus, was the eleven Apostles at the Last Supper, Judas having departed. The obvious question is whether, or not, we can extrapolate this promise to all people, not just the Apostles there present. I suspect not, for the "all things" that the Spirit would teach, could only be in relation to "the things that I said to you". There is no licence to take it beyond that because otherwise you could add anything your imagination desired: physics, chemistry, astronomy, and so forth.

Skipping forward to the Book of Acts, we read: "Then there appeared to them divided tongues, as of fire, and one sat upon each of them, and they were all filled with the Holy Spirit and began to speak with other tongues as the Spirit gave them utterance" (Acts 2:3-4). Again, we have this nexus between the visitation of the Holy Spirit and a specific purpose: "to speak with other tongues"; note that the text suggests that each of them may have been assigned specific tongues: "as the Spirit gave them utterance". As to whom "each of them" refers, it could only be the twelve Apostles - it makes no sense to suggest everyone there present because everyone would have been talking and no-one listening.

In summary, then, the statement that "*God does not give the Spirit by measure*" is demonstrably false, or else John had something in mind that I have not apprehended. Thus, the claimed fulfillment of prophecy fails on two counts: (1), the statement begs the question; and (2), the statement cannot be the word of a truthful God.

John 5:45 – "*For if you believed Moses, you would believe me, for he wrote about me*", referencing Deuteronomy 18:15, 18. This verse is not flagged as prophecy fulfillment, but as it relates to that subject, it is worthy of mention. Here, Jesus is claiming to be the promised prophet like Moses. We have no corroboration of this claim, and thus it must be treated with reserve.

John 7:5 - *"For even his brothers did not believe in him"*, quoting Psalm 69:8 and Micah 7:6. The Psalm refers to the episode in David's life where he was chosen before his brothers, even though he was the youngest (1 Samuel 16, and 1 Chronicles 2): it was a recording of history, not a prophecy. Micah 7:6 reads: *"For a son disparages his father; a daughter rises up against her mother*; etc.*"*, in other words, that is the way of the world. That Jesus encountered the world as everybody else does, is simply coincidence, not prophecy fulfillment, especially when the verses quoted are not prophetic, but more proverbial.

John 7:14 – *"Now about the middle of the feast, Jesus went up into the temple and taught"*, quoting Psalm 22:22. Again, this is nothing other than coincidence. The psalm reads: I will declare Your name to **My** brethren; in the midst of the assembly I will praise You" (NKJV) [emphasis mine]. Notice how the Christian scribes have used an initial capital to convince you that this was a prophecy of Jesus speaking, when in truth, it was simply David declaring his faith in God. What was special about Jesus, or any rabbi for that matter, going to teach in the temple? Nothing at all – it was common practice. One could claim this to be circumstantial evidence, but it is very weak, given the multitudes who, over time, must have gone up to the Temple and taught. But more to the point, in this psalm, there is no mention at all of the Temple, just a congregation or assembly – there is no justification of assuming the Temple.

John 12:13 – *"Blessed is he who comes in the name of the Lord"*; see Matthew 21:9.

John 12:15 – *"Behold, your King is coming, sitting on a donkey"*; see Matthew 21:5.

John 12:40 – *"He has blinded their eyes and hardened their hearts"*, quoting Isaiah 6:9-10; see Mark 4:12.

John 13:18 – *"He who eats bread with me, has lifted up his heel against me"*; see Matthew 26:14. There really is no prophecy of a person specifically betraying the Messiah. Betrayal was not uncommon in those days, especially in such politically charged circumstances as then existed with the Zealots and others attempting to overthrow the Romans. There is evidence that the competition for the role of High Priest, being an appointment by the Romans, also involved a level of betrayal, so at best, this could be circumstantial evidence.

I wonder whether in stating: "*has lifted up his heel against me*", John was alluding to Genesis 3:15, "*and you shall bruise (bite) his heel*"? Irrespective, using one's heel against another was long considered a metaphor for attacking. See Chapter 4-10 for an explanation of the meaning of "heel" in the Hebrew Scriptures.

I cannot fault Christian scholars finding a link between this verse in Genesis, and the events in the life of Jesus, as they understood them. However, the understanding of the Sages better fits the overall context, for it refers not to just a single, unique person, but to all generations (offspring). Finding the verse to be prophetic of the Messiah is understandable, but not acceptable as evidence.

John 17:8 – "*For I have given to them the words which You have given me*", quoting Deuteronomy 18:15, 18. This is claimed as the fulfillment of the promise made to Moses, as the Children of Israel were about to enter the Promised Land, because Moses was not permitted to go with them. God promised that he would raise up a prophet, like Moses, to accompany and guide them with His words, unlike the current occupiers of the land who relied on astrologers and diviners (Deut 18:14). This promise was specific to the circumstances of the time, and was not a prophesy of the Messiah. There are two verses worth noting in the context of this study:

1. "But the prophet who wilfully shall speak a word in My Name, that which I have not commanded him to speak … that prophet shall die" (Deut 18:20); and

2. "If the prophet shall speak in the Name of Hashem, and that thing will not occur, and not come about – that is the word that Hashem has not spoken; with wilfulness has the prophet spoken it; you should not fear him." (Deut 18:22)

I find it ironic that the editors of the New Testament have flagged a verse as fulfilling a prophecy, which was in truth, a contemporary promise, but the subsequent verses warn against doing so.

John 18:40 – "*Then they all cried again, saying, not this man, but Barabbas. Now Barabbas was a robber*", quoting Isaiah 53:3. Now even if

Isaiah 53 referred to the Messiah as the suffering servant, which it does not, verse 3 is not sufficiently specific to relate it to Barabbas being preferred to Jesus for release. Yes, the preference is indicative of Jesus being rejected, but we can make no more of it than that. It is illogical, and dare I say, duplicitous, to equate a generalisation with a specific case. Whilst the specific is consistent with the generalisation, the rules of evidence would disallow the equivalence. Substantive evidence is needed, and this is not even close.

John 19:9 – "*But Jesus gave him no answer*"; see Luke 23:9.

John 19:18 – "*They crucified him, and with two others*", quoting Isaiah 53:12. I suspect that the NKJV editors got a little muddled here, as the verse more closely relates to Isaiah 53:9 (see Chapter 3:1). John 19:18 has no connection with Isaiah 53:12, other than that perhaps the editors had in mind: "for he bore the sin of the multitudes, and prayed for the wicked." Let us put it down to poor editing.

John 19:24 – "*Let us not tear it, but cast lots for it*"; see Matthew 27:35. I am curious about the wording here: casting lots was a common practice, and I cannot conceive of the Roman soldiers having a discussion about it. The author of this Gospel does embellish his narratives far more than the Synoptic authors, which is suggestive of story-telling, rather than disciplined recital of facts.

John 19:29 – "*Now a vessel of sour wine was sitting there*"; see Matthew 27:34.

John 19:33 – "*they did not break his legs*"; see Matthew 27:35.

John 19:36 – "*None of his bones shall be broken*"; see Matthew 27:35.

John 19:37 – "*They shall look on him whom they pierced*", quoting Psalm 22:16-17, and Zechariah 12:10, 13:6. It is curious that where Matthew 27:36 is flagged as fulfilling the same Psalm 22 supposed prophecy, Zechariah is not noted. Turning to that reference, we do find matching words in Zechariah 12:10, but the context concerns God protecting the inhabitants of Jerusalem (v. 12:8), which did not apply to Jesus. Note also: "house of David". This term is used in connection with David's time only, and is not synonymous with Israel, house of Israel, or other groups. Zechariah 13:6 is not even remotely predictive of Jesus being pierced with a sword, especially as the wounds occurred "in the house of my friends". I suppose this could be allegorised to mean Jerusalem, that much we could allow.

<u>John 20:27</u> – "*Reach your finger here, and look at my hands; and reach your hand here, and put it into my side*", quoting the same references as in John 19:37. At a stretch, and a very long one at that, these Old Testament references could be associated with Jesus being pierced with a sword, but Jesus displaying his wounds, and Thomas touching them, is not a subject of prophecy. It might be associated with prophecy fulfillment, in which case, it can be considered corroborating evidence, but no more.

Summary

John's references to fulfillment of messianic prophecies primarily relate to John the Baptist, and Jesus' subsequent trial, torture, and crucifixion. My problem here is that the narrative in both Isaiah and Malachi, concerning the one who would "*clear the way of Hashem*" (Isaiah 40:3), sets the timing as being the End of Days:

> "Every valley will be raised, and every mountain and hill will be lowered; the crooked will become straight and heights will become valley. The glory of Hashem will be revealed, and all flesh together will see that the mouth of Hashem has spoken." (Isaiah 40:4-5)

The meanings in these verses are later encountered in: "*So the last shall be first, and the first last*" (Matthew 20:16), and "*for they shall all know Me, the least of them, to the greatest of them*" (Jeremiah 31:34). Any prophecy which is eschatological cannot be accepted as evidence that Jesus was the prophesied Messiah. Again, note that nothing in John provides evidence that Jesus accomplished what the Jews of Second Temple Judaism were expecting, based on their understanding of the prophesied Messiah: redemption from their oppressors, and a return of all Israel to Jerusalem.

REFERENCES:

1.   Ex 31:3, 36:31, Num 11:17, 25, 26, 29, 24:2, 27:18, Deut 34:9, Jud 3:10, 6:34, 11:29, 13:25, 14:6, 14:19, 15:14, 1 Sam 10:6, 10, 11:6, 16:13-16, 23, 18:10, 19:9, 20, 23, 2 Sam 23:2

CHAPTER 4-6

SUMMARY OF THE GOSPELS

"In examining the evidences of the Christian religion, it is essential to the discovery of truth that we bring to the investigation a mind freed, as far as possible, from existing prejudice, and open to conviction. There should be a readiness, on our part, to investigate with candour, to follow the truth wherever it may lead us, and to submit without reserve or objection, to all the teachings of this religion, if it be found to be of divine origin."
~ Simon Greenleaf[1] ~

That is the essence of it, is it not: *"to submit without reserve or objection …* **IF** *it be found to be of divine origin"*? If, on examination, with a mind freed, as far as possible, from existing prejudice, and open to conviction, we find insufficient evidence of divine inspiration, then we should have reservations about the Christian religion. I would refer you back to the discussion on "Tradition" in Chapter 1-1.

Reviewing the Count

As many Christian apologists are enamoured with the number of messianic prophecies that Jesus is claimed to have fulfilled, let us address that issue first. As can be seen below, 100 unique Old Testament verses are referenced by either/both the authors and/or the NKJV editors in relation to prophecy fulfillment, but only 61 of those verses are flagged as prophetic in the Old Testament itself.

The following table relates to the frequency of verses flagged in the NT as being in prophecy fulfillment. Note that the last column is not a sum of the Gospel counts, but refers to the count of unique verses referenced in the OT, for not unexpectedly, there is a great deal of duplication in the NT.

	Matt	Mark	Luke	John	Unique Count
OLD TESTAMENT					
Count of OT verses referenced in NT	76	34	50	24	100
Verses flagged as prophetic in OT	43	26	31	14	61
Psalm verses referenced	13	9	6	6	17
Psalm verses flagged as prophetic	13	8	6	6	16
NEW TESTAMENT					
Verses flagged as prophecy fulfilled	40	16	19	22	
Verses flagged as prophecy yet to be fulfilled	9	5	10	0	
Verses explicitly claiming prophecy fulfilled	13	3	2	5	-
Verses flagged as prophecy fulfilled, but no OT reference.	3	1	1	0	-
Prophecy verses referencing Psalms only	13	9	6	6	-

I was interested to note the frequency, across the Gospel accounts, of individual Old Testament verses being referenced:

a. Just once - 61 (53%)
b. Twice - 29 (25%)
c. Three times - 12 (10%)
d. Four times - 8 (7%)
e. Five times - 4 (3%)

f.   Six times - 2 (2%)

More than half of the verses were only referenced once, and a quarter, twice, which seems to indicate a different understanding of prophecy fulfillment in each Gospel. Whether that means anything significant, I cannot be sure, but it does lend credence to the contention that each of the Gospels developed through separate traditions, even though there is a degree of cross-fertilization.

The most popular verses (NKJV) were:

1.   Isaiah 53:12 [6 times] – "Because He poured out his soul unto death, and He was numbered with the transgressors, and He bore the sins of many, and He made intercession for the transgressors."
2.   Psalm 118:26 [6 times] – "Blessed is he who comes in the name of the Lord! We have blessed you from the house of the Lord."
3.   Isaiah 53:9 [5 times] – "And they made His grave with the wicked, but with the rich at His death, because He had done no violence, nor was any deceit in His mouth."
4.   Isaiah 50:6 [5 times] – "I gave My back to those who struck Me, and My cheeks to those who plucked out the beard; I did not hide My face from shame and spitting."
5.   Isaiah 40:3 [5 times] – "The voice of one crying in the wilderness; prepare the way of the Lord; make straight in the desert a highway for our God."
6.   Malachi 3:1 [5 times] – "Behold, I send My messenger, and he will prepare the way before Me, and the Lord whom you seek, will suddenly come to His temple, even the Messenger of the covenant, in whom you delight. Behold, He is coming, says the Lord of hosts."

Ignoring Psalm 118:26, which could refer to practically anyone, note the twin themes: the Messiah being persecuted and killed, and one like Elijah, John the Baptist, preparing his way. The condensed version is that Jesus was the Messiah because he died on the cross, but note that none of the Old Testament verses quoted explicitly claim *substitutionary atonement*, i.e., Jesus dying, taking our sins upon himself, so that we may be justified in the sight of God. But, you may argue, *he bore the sins of many*, so let us review the context of Isaiah 53:12. I have already contended, in Chapter 3-2, that Jesus was not the *suffering servant* of the Hebrew Scriptures. I acknowledge that verses 53:4-5 could be interpreted in the sense of substitutionary atonement, but we have earlier evidence that God does not accept that for the forgiveness of sin. The real meaning is that suffering was brought upon the suffering servant, whoever that was, because of the sins of others, not that the sins of others were forgiven through that suffering. It is not uncommon, in the history of mankind, that some suffer because of the sins of others; this is particularly evident in wars. The Christian interpretation of Isaiah 53 confuses *cause* with *consequence*.

Making *intercession* (Isaiah 53:12) could equate with Jesus as *Mediator*, but nothing more than that. However, the references in the New Testament to mediation, are not in connection with transgressions - Galatians 3:19-20 refers to the law; Hebrews 8:6, 9:15, and 12:24 refer to the new covenant; and 1 Timothy 2:5 is not specific about the role of the Mediator between God and men. We do have Jesus claiming that he would die for our sins, but our focus here is whether there is any Old Testament support, in the form of prophecy, to support that claim. I can find none.

This does bring us back to Isaiah 53, and the identity of the suffering servant, but we have discussed this adequately (I hope) in Chapter 3-2.

Prophecy in Overview

Coming back to the total number of prophecies fulfilled by Jesus as Messiah, which according to Christian commentators, varies from 33 to over 400, my analysis found just 100 Old Testament verses referenced in the NKJV, but of those, only 61 are flagged in the OT as prophetic. There are only 21 verses in the New Testament where the authors explicitly claimed an event, or saying, in fulfillment of prophecy, but 5 of those were duplicates within, or across, the Gospels. Eliminating those duplications, I have listed the 16 Old Testament verses in the NKJV sequence, and where there is a significant difference from the Hebrew Scriptures, I have shown those translations in *italics*:

1. Exodus 12:46 - [Regarding the Passover lamb] In one house it shall be eaten; you shall not carry any of the flesh outside the house, nor shall you break one of its bones. (Quoted in John 19:36)

2. Isaiah 6:9-10 - And He said, Go, and tell this people: Keep on hearing, but do not understand; keep on seeing, but do not perceive. Make the heart of this people dull, and their ears heavy, and shut their eyes; lest they see with their eyes, and hear with their ears, and understand with their heart, and return to be healed. (Quoted in John 12:40)

   Hebrew – *He said, "Go and say to this people, 'Surely you hear, but you do not comprehend, and surely you see, but you fail to know.' This people is fattening its heart, hardening its ears, and sealing its eyes, lets it see with its eyes, hear with its ears, and understand with its heart, so that it will repent and be healed."*

3. Isaiah 7:14 - Therefore, the Lord Himself will give you a sign: Behold, the virgin shall conceive and bear a Son, and you shall call His name Immanuel. (Quoted in Matt 1:23)

   Hebrew – *Therefore, my Lord Himself will give you a sign: Behold, the young woman will become pregnant and bear a son, and you will name him Immanuel.*

4. Isaiah 9:1 - Nevertheless, the gloom will not be upon her who is distressed, as when at first He lightly esteemed the land of Zebulun and the land of Naphtali, and afterwards more heavily oppressed her, by way of the sea beyond the Jordan, in Galilee of the Gentiles. (Quoted in Matt 4:15)

5. Isaiah 40:3 - The voice of one crying in the wilderness; prepare the way of the Lord; make straight in the desert a highway for our God. (Quoted in Matt 3:3, Mark 1:3, Luke 3:4, Luke 7:27)

   Hebrew – *A voice calls out, in the wilderness, clear the way of Hashem; make a straight path in the desert, a road for our God.* (See Chapter -1)

6. Isaiah 40:9 - O Zion, you who bring good tidings, go up into the high mountains of Jerusalem ... lift up your voice ... be not afraid, say to the cities of Judah: Behold your God. (quoted in John 12:15)

7. Isaiah 42:1-4 - Behold! My servant whom I uphold, My Elect One in whom My soul delights! I have put My Spirit upon Him; He will

bring forth justice to the Gentiles. He will not cry out, nor raise His voice, nor cause His voice to be heard in the street … He will bring forth justice for truth, He will not fail nor be discouraged, till He has established justice in the earth; and the coastlands shall wait His law. (Quoted in Matt 12:18)

8. <u>Isaiah 53:4</u> - Surely He has borne our griefs and carried our sorrows; Yet we esteemed Him stricken, smitten by God and afflicted. (Quoted in Matt 8:17)

9. <u>Jeremiah 31:15</u> - Thus, said the Lord: A voice was heard in Ramah, lamentation and bitter weeping, Rachel weeping for her children, refusing to be comforted for her children, because they are no more. (Quoted in Matt 2:18)

10. <u>Ezekiel 12:2</u> - Son of man, you dwell in a rebellious house, which has eyes to see but it does not see, and ears to hear but it does not hear; for they are a rebellious house. (Quoted in Matt 13:14)

11. <u>Micah 5:2</u> - But you, Bethlehem Ephrathah, though you are a little among the thousands of Judah, yet out of you shall come forth to Me the One to be Ruler in Israel, whose goings forth are from of old, from everlasting. (Quoted in Matt 2:6)
Hebrew – omits "*from everlasting*"

12. <u>Zechariah 11:12</u> - They I said to them, if it is agreeable to you, give me my wages; and if not, refrain. So they weighed out for my wages thirty pieces of silver. (Quoted in Matt 27:9)

13. <u>Zechariah 12:10</u> - And I will pour on the house of David and on the inhabitants of Jerusalem the spirit of grace and supplication; then they will look on Me whom they pierced. Yes, they will mourn for Him as one mourns for his only son, and grieve for Him as one grieves for a first-born. (Quoted in John 19:37)
Hebrew – *I will pour out upon the house of David and upon the inhabitants of Jerusalem a spirit of grace and supplication. They will look toward Me because of those whom they have stabbed; they will mourn over him as one mourns over an only child, and be embittered over him like the embitterment over a deceased firstborn.*

14. <u>Zechariah 13:7</u> - Awake, O sword, against my Shepherd, against the Man who is My Companion, says the Lord of hosts. Strike

the Shepherd, and the sheep will be scattered; then I will turn My hand against the little ones. (Quoted in Matt 26:31)

15. <u>Malachi 3:1</u> - Behold, I send My messenger, and he will prepare the way before Me, and the Lord whom you seek, will suddenly come to His temple, even the Messenger of the covenant, in whom you delight. Behold, He is coming, says the Lord of hosts. (Quoted in Matt 11:10, Mark 1:2)

16. <u>Psalm 22:18</u> - They divide My garments among them, and for My clothing they cast lots. (Quoted in Matt 27:35, John 19:24)

These are the sixteen Old Testament verses that the Evangelists themselves, believed to be prophetic of the Messiah, and which they asserted Jesus fulfilled. Note the imbalance across the Evangelists: Matthew (12), Mark (2), Luke (2), and John (5).

Certainly, some of these verses can be seen to be identifying Jesus as the Messiah, and descriptive of his tribulations, but are they evidence that it was prophesied that Jesus was the Son of God, Second Person of the Trinity, sent to earth to die for our sins, and subsequently be resurrected to the right hand of God? Even in overview, I would contend that they do not. More especially, when we examine each verse in its Old Testament context, the evidence is not at all convincing. Why the author of John thought that Exodus 12:46 was prophetic of Jesus is concerning, but as discussed earlier in the Part 4 introduction, there is no theological connection between the lamb offered for unintentional sins, the Passover lamb, and Jesus. The same author has twisted the meaning of Isaiah 6:9-10, having God enforcing deafness and blindness upon the people, as opposed to them deliberately choosing to neither hear, nor see.

If we take the Evangelists at their word, ignoring the annotations of the NKJV editors, there really is no substantive evidence of Jesus fulfilling messianic prophecy.

Daniel's One Like the Son of Man

Given the Christian theology developed upon Daniel 7:13 mentioning *"One like the Son of Man"* (theological annotations noted), I was surprised to find so little support in the Gospels. Neither Mark nor John have any reference at all, with Matthew and Luke as follows:

a. ☆ Matthew 16:27 – Daniel 7:10
b. ★ Matthew 20:28 – Daniel 9:24-26
c. ☆ Matthew 21:44 – Daniel 2:44
d. ☆ Matthew 24:30 – Daniel 7:13-14
e. ☆ Luke 1:33 – Daniel 2:44
f. ★ Luke 4:18 – Daniel 9:24
g. ☆ Luke 13:35 – Daniel 9:27
h. ☆ Luke 20:18 – Daniel 2:34-35, 2:44-45
i. ☆ Luke 21:27 – Daniel 7:13

Only two entries are flagged with a ★ indicating that the prophecy was fulfilled at that stage of the narrative. The other seven entries starting with ☆ are flagged in the NKJV as prophecies to be fulfilled in the future, and thus are not evidence of what was accomplished in the past. We must have substantive evidence of prophecy fulfillment by Jesus in his First Coming, before we can consider his hypothetical second. We are left with just two said to be fulfilled by Jesus in his First Coming.

Matthew 16:27 has Jesus declaring: "For the Son of Man will come in the glory of His Father … reward(ing) each according to his works", which the NKJV editors see a reference to Daniel 7:10 when the Ancient of Days comes to judge. That is a reasonable interpretation, but implies the assumption that Jesus will be seated at the right hand of God at that time.

Matthew 20:28 mentions "the Son of Man did not come to be served, but to serve", the NKJV referencing Daniel 9:24 and 26. Verse 24 does say "to make reconciliation for iniquity", which could be related with substitutionary atonement, but "to make an end of sins" cannot, so in combination, the context does not fit the supposed mission of Jesus. We also have the obscure "the Messiah shall be cut off, but not for Himself", but we discussed that earlier in Chapter 3-4, and is hardly a prophecy of the Messiah coming "to give His life a ransom for many". Finally, there is consensus across Christianity, as far as I can tell, that verse 7:27 refers to the End of Days, and thus the whole vision, verses 24-27, must also refer to the End of Days, and cannot offer any evidence that Jesus was the prophesied Messiah two thousand years ago.

Luke 4:18 is also annotated as Jesus fulfilling Daniel 9:24, but the connection is obscure, especially as the verses quoted are from Isaiah.

Both Matthew 21:44 and Luke 1:33 attempt to link Daniel's dream interpretation of the fate of kingdoms (Daniel 2:44) with the fate of individuals, who do not accept Jesus as their Saviour. Not exactly a strong argument, I would have thought, and referring to prophecy fulfillment at the End of Days adds no evidence of Jesus being Messiah in his own days, two thousand years ago.

From an evidentiary perspective, I would have expected a better argument for linking Jesus with David's "one like the son of man. The Christian doctrine relies heavily on this point, justifying Jesus' own use of the term, Son of Man, signifying that he was the promised Messiah. Without that link, the term *son of man* would be as found in Ezekiel, signifying a mortal human, way below the level of God. If Jesus saw himself as "one like the son of man", this suggests that he was likely using the Greek Scriptures, not the Hebrew, which raises many new questions, the implications of which cast Jesus in an entirely new light. Did Jesus not really study the Hebrew Scriptures, or have his words been reinterpreted to align with the Greek scriptures that the Evangelists used? Just what Jesus meant by that term is unclear, but the preponderance of evidence from the Old Testament would favour the understanding in Ezekiel, not a single occurrence in Daniel.

Quality of the Evidence – Evidentiary Weight

According to my assessment, there is not one, single, substantive, messianic prophecy fulfillment – not even one. There are a number of incidents which can be described as circumstantial, one or two are corroborating, and quite a number where there is correlation. However, I must come back to the gravity of the case, as Greenleaf describes it: *"a subject fraught with such momentous consequences to man"*[2]. I share that view, for no case ever tried in a human court can even approach the gravity of this one. At stake is the most grievous sin against God: idolatry. Each of us is entitled to evaluate the evidence for themselves, but herein has been my assessment so far, and my verdict on the evidence is that Jesus was not the prophesied Messiah, and could not be God incarnate.

My Quandary

If we are to believe the Gospel narratives, then at least some of the Apostles, early disciples, and even Jesus himself, believed Jesus to be the prophesied Messiah. Why else would there have been so many attempts to mine the Old Testament, in this case the Greek Septuagint, not the Hebrew Scriptures, to find passages that proved that he was? Prior to Jesus, two other Jews attempted to overthrow the Romans, with their followers believing them to be the promised Messiah, but their attempts ended in tragedy. About a hundred years later, many Jews thought that Simon bar Kokhba was the Messiah, because he was attempting to do what the Jews believed the Messiah was prophesied to do: overthrow the Romans and restore Israel. That didn't turn out so well either. Clearly, belief by people is not necessarily, evidence of truth.

I think that I have mentioned this before, but anyway, I would reiterate the words of Paul: "God is not the author of confusion" (1 Cor 14:33), for I entirely agree with him. Yet, according to the Christian scribes, He most certainly is. For example, in the narratives of Jesus' death, putting aside the variations and contradictions across the four accounts, all of which are said to be the inerrant word of God, we also have God speaking through Isaiah, Zechariah, and two separate Psalms of David, to convey one prophecy. Studying the Prophets, we do find more than one warning of the same future events, but when the context is considered, we find that the forewarned event is less specific than can reasonably be applied to the crucifixion of Jesus.

There are numerous examples in the Christian interpretation, or perhaps better, misrepresentation of the Gospels, where messianic prophecies are used in an attempt to prove that Jesus was the promised Messiah, but at the same time, ignoring the deliverance that he was expected to achieve, but did not. If Jesus did not deliver on the promise of a prophecy, that is substantive evidence that he did NOT fulfill that prophecy.

I have said it before, and I will say it again: this is the "bait and switch" technique so beloved of salespeople throughout the ages. Introduce a truth, get people to accept it because it *is* true, then apply just part of it to a fiction, so that the fiction also appears to be truth. In this case, a truth concerning a prophesied Messiah, who would deliver Israel from oppression, is partially applied to a Messiah who would deliver Gentiles from their sins. The trick is to firstly get people to accept Jesus as Messiah, ignoring the details of the prophesied mission, and then introduce a different mission, as if that was the one prophesied. This is the great sin of the early Catholic Church of Rome.

Jesus is said to have warned: "Take heed and beware of the leaven (yeast) of the Pharisees and the Sadducees" (Matthew 16:6), for "a little leaven leavens the whole lump" (1 Corinthians 5:6). That warning should more correctly be applied to much of Christian teaching, especially that based on the writings of Paul.

But .....

I remain perplexed.

For the Evangelists to have written as they did, claiming prophecy fulfillments, and quoting Greek Scripture verses in support of their contentions, what are we to make of their efforts? I would quote from C.S. Lewis, at one time, Professor of Medieval and Renaissance English at Cambridge University, and was a Fellow of Magdalene College. Lewis was a world-class literary critic, and was able to recognize the various genres of literature and their characteristics. He understood the content and structure of the many literary types, and was an expert in identifying them. When faced with the criticism that the Gospels were myths, legends, or fables, he had this to say,

> "First then, whatever these men may be as Biblical critics, I distrust them as critics ... If he tells me that something in a Gospel is legend or romance, I want to know how many legends and romances he has read, how well his palate is trained in detecting them by flavour ... I have been reading poems, romances, vision literature, legends and myths all my life. I know what they are like. I know none of them are like this. Of this [gospel] text there are only two possible views. Either this is reportage ... or else, some unknown [ancient] writer ... without known predecessors or successors suddenly anticipated the whole technique of modern novelistic, realistic narrative."[3]

It would be ambitious of me to contend with the scholarship of C.S. Lewis, but I am not about to suggest that the Gospels are *myths, legends, or fables* (well, ok, just a bit). On the contrary, I believe that, in the main, they are *reportage*, to use Lewis' word. However, I would contend that they are not reportage of substantiated fact, but of what the Evangelists came to believe over time to be true, which is an entirely different matter. Lewis has offered a false dichotomy, indeed a logical fallacy of the false alternative: a *modern novelistic, realistic narrative* is not the only alternative to reportage – there is also what the Gospels more truly represent: a theological discourse. The provenance of the Gospels is unknown, evidenced by the volumes written by scholars offering their opinions, sometimes in consensus, but mostly contentious. Thus, we are justified in having a lack of confidence in them, as being the genuine autographs of those who witnessed the life and times of Jesus. We know that even the attributed authors were not all eye-witnesses to events.

Were the Evangelists uneducated in the Hebrew Scriptures, and the teachings of the Jewish Sages, resulting in them doing the best they could from the unreliable Greek Septuagint (see Chapter 2-1)? Were they cleverer than we know, guided by the Holy Spirit, to interpret events with insights not previously given to their Jewish predecessors? If so, when God advised Isaiah: *"I have not spoken in secret … I did not say to the seed of Jacob, seek Me in vain"* (Isaiah 45:19), have I read too much into this verse, and rather than it being a statement on God's guidance to His people generally, its application was only specific to that conversation?

Fortunately for me, and you as well I hope, scholars have sought to address some of these issues, but unfortunately, they have not reached a consensus. No matter, what they have to say is interesting, and we must glean as best we can from their words. We do so later, in the section entitled: *The Right Doctrine, Wrong Text?*

Finally, back to the observation of C.S. Lewis, "Either this is reportage … or else, some unknown [ancient] writer … without known predecessors or successors suddenly anticipated the whole technique of modern novelistic, realistic narrative." With a degree of humility, as one who has read hundreds of modern novels, I cannot agree that the Gospels are like them. I have yet to read a novel whose plot is so full of improbable events, contradictions, and confusion, even in the genres of science fiction or horror. Lewis would have us believe that all four Gospels tell the same story, which they do in general, but not so in detail. Not that they just cover different details, but that they cover the same details in such varied, and even contradictory ways. Closely studied, and compared with one another, conducting a *forensic analysis* to use a modern term, these narrations are very poorly constructed, and far more incoherent than any *myths, legends, or fables* that I have read, let alone *modern novelistic, realistic narratives.*

I have great respect for C.S. Lewis, and have thoroughly enjoyed his writings, but on this one issue, I cannot agree.

REFERENCES:

1. Greenleaf, Simon, *The Testimony of the Evangelists*, Kregel Classics, Grand Rapids, MI, 1995, p. 11
2. *Ibid*, p. 12
3. Lewis, C.S., *Christian Reflections*, William B. Eerdmans Publishing Company, Grand Rapids, MI, p. 154-155

CHAPTER 4-7

JEWS FOR JESUS

"We exist to make the messiahship of Jesus an unavoidable issue to our Jewish people worldwide"
~ *Jews for Jesus* website homepage ~

I apologise for the duplications in this chapter, but as I was directed by a Christian to this website[1], *"Top 40 Most Helpful Messianic Prophecies"*, attempting to demonstrate that Jesus, as Messiah and Spiritual Redeemer, was prophesied in the Tanach (or Tanakh), I thought it useful to treat it on its own. That way, the chapter can then stand alone as a useful reference. As an earnest scholar, I reviewed the so-called "proof texts" and following are my comments, which I believe, effectively refute their contentions. You may conclude otherwise.

My first comment is that curiously, *Jews for Jesus* (JFJ) accept the Christian interpretation of these passages, rather than that of the Jewish Sages. If these *Jews for Jesus* showed respect for the Jewish Sages, they would refer to the commentary in the *Chumash*[2], or the Artscroll Tanach Commentary on *Bereishis* (Genesis)[3]. That they do not makes clear that they are Jewish Christians, and use their ethnicity in an attempt to give credibility to their opinions. Sadly, they are no more credible than Christians of any other ethnicity.

Now to the claimed **Top 40**.

1. Genesis 3:15 - *The Messiah would be the seed of the woman.*

   Both the Greek and Hebrew translate "offspring" not "seed". The context is God speaking to the serpent, and when God said that He would put enmity between the seed (offspring) of the woman, and that of the serpent, then it should be understood as a metaphor, for what offspring of the serpent would God be referring to: snakes? It is logically invalid to interpret seed of the woman as literally, descendants, and seed of the serpent as ... what exactly? In the opinion of the Sages, the serpent represents the evil inclination of man. Homiletically, the serpent seduces man to trample the commandments with his heel, but man can prevail using his head, meaning the study of Torah. See Chapter 4-10 for an explanation of the meaning of "heel" in the Hebrew Scriptures. This verse is not a prophecy of the Messiah.

2. Genesis 12:3 - *The Messiah would be the descendant of Abraham through whom all nations would be blessed.*

   At best, this can only be circumstantial evidence, as Abraham had millions of descendants. If there was substantive evidence, this could be considered corroborative, but without substantive evidence, it proves nothing.

3. Genesis 22:1-18 - *The Messiah would be a willing sacrifice.*

   By what *eisegesis* do people turn the lesson of Abraham's faith, into a prophecy of the Messiah? What I find interesting, reading the words that Jesus is said to have spoken on the cross, Jesus was not really that willing, certainly not as willing as Abraham appeared to have been. Abraham did not quibble with God at all, yet in the garden of Gethsemane, Jesus is said to have pleaded: "O, My Father, if it is possible let this cup pass from me; nevertheless, not as I will, but as You will." (Matthew 26:39) – this amounts to resignation and acceptance, not willingness.

4. Genesis 49:10 - *The Messiah would be the coming one to whom the sceptre belongs.*

In formal logic, this is begging the question, or affirming the consequent. The following sentence reads: "Until Shiloh comes", meaning the Messiah. Thus, to assert that this is a prophecy of the Messiah, you are saying that the Messiah is the Messiah because he is the Messiah! Hardly scholarly. Even so, we have no evidence that the sceptre belonged to Jesus, especially as his reign, if we could call it that, was so brief.

5. Exodus 12:1-51 - *The Messiah would be the Passover lamb.*

That John wrote in his Gospel that Jesus was the Passover Lamb, simply demonstrates that whoever came up with that idea, did not have the Jewish understanding of what occurred in Egypt at that time. There is no prophecy of a Passover lamb being sacrificed for the forgiveness of sin. The *pesach offering* is a commemoration of when God brought death to the firstborn of Egypt - *passing over* the homes of those who trusted in God. The story begins in Exodus 8:25-26 with Pharaoh attempting to trick Moses into sacrificing a lamb before the people of Egypt. "Then Pharaoh called for Moses and Aaron and said, 'Go, sacrifice to your God in the land.' And Moses said, 'It is not right to do so, for we would be sacrificing the abomination of the Egyptians to the Lord our God. If we sacrifice the abomination of the Egyptians before their eyes, then will they not stone us?'" *Abomination of the Egyptians*? In Egypt at that time, the lamb was deified and worshipped as a god. By Egyptian law, it was therefore forbidden to harm a lamb in any way, such an act being considered a crime punishable by death. Pharaoh knew that the Hebrews sacrificed lambs, and so he cunningly invited Moses and Aaron to do so in front of his own people, knowing that they would be killed as punishment for doing so. Fortunately for Aaron, Moses had grown up in Egypt and knew the customs. He knew that the lamb was considered a god, and thus to him and his God, the lamb was an abomination.

Next, we have Exodus 10:25, with Moses asking for "sacrifices and burnt offerings that we may sacrifice to the Lord our God. Our livestock also shall go with us; not a hoof shall be left behind. For we must take some of them to serve the Lord our God." But God hardens Pharaoh's heart, and Pharaoh refuses Moses' request. Moses wanted to continue with the Hebrew practice of sacrificing lambs, during their journeys ahead. Subsequently, when God ordered Moses that the people must sacrifice a lamb, in the presence of Pharaoh in Egypt, at great risk to their lives, what message was He conveying?

Which brings us to the next point: the choice by God to have the Hebrews sacrifice a lamb, and spread its blood on the lintels of their houses (Exodus 12:7). Because killing a lamb in Egypt was punishable by death, God was testing the faithfulness of those whom He was rescuing; only those who feared nothing but God Almighty, were deemed worthy of being *passed over* by the tenth plague. No Egyptian would dare slaughter a lamb, and neither would those who feared Pharaoh more than God. One might also consider that God sought to deliberately add insult to injury to Pharaoh, asserting that He alone was God.

6. Numbers 21:6-9- *The Messiah would be lifted up.*

    One cannot take the event of Jesus being lifted up onto the cross, search Scripture to find another event that seems to match, and then turn that into a prophecy. Besides, the circumstances do not match. A fiery serpent was placed on the pole, the snakes being considered a fitting agent of punishment because the serpent had slandered God to Eve. Thus, if Jesus is synonymous with the serpent, it could only be because he slandered God. Is that what is meant?

7. Numbers 24:17 - *The Messiah would be the star coming out of Jacob.*

    "Balaam spoke about the very distant future of the Jewish people, the time when the final Messianic redemption would come. Thus, his entire series of pronouncements encompassed four periods of Jewish history: in the Wilderness (23:7-10); their impending conquest of the land (23:18-24); their period of greatness after conquering the Land and their surrounding enemies (24:9); and now of the *End of Days* (Ramban)."⁴ Did Jesus *"pierce the nobles of Moab and undermine all the children of Seth"*? NO? Then this is not a prophecy of Jesus; rather, it is a prophecy of King David.

8. Deuteronomy 18:15-19 - *The Messiah would be a prophet like Moses.*

I would have thought this to be obvious to any thinking bible student, but perhaps not. If Jesus was like Moses, a prophet, then he was not the Messiah, the deified Son, the Second Person of the Trinity – Moses was just a human prophet.

9. Ruth 4:4-9 – *The Messiah would be our Kinsman-Redeemer.*

There is a certain irony in Christians, who reject Torah, quoting from the Book of Ruth. Jews read Ruth at *Shavuot*, the celebration of receiving the Law, because Ruth, a Moabite woman, converted to Judaism by accepting Torah in its entirety. If anything, the book of Ruth is an affirmation of the permanency of Torah, and God's covenant with the Children of Israel. That said, this is another case of mining Scripture to find events that match Christian theological development, and attempting to turn the results into a prophecy. It goes like this: we are kin to Jesus, Jesus is our redeemer, therefore we will create the notion of a Kinsman Redeemer, and massage the story of Ruth selling land to a redeemer into the Jesus narrative. Note from verse 4:12, that Boaz said that the privilege of redemption should be offered first to Elimelech's brother, a closer relative. Can that be massaged into the narrative as well? That notwithstanding, the redemption in the story of Ruth is in accordance with Leviticus 25:25, and has nothing to do with redemption from sin.

10. 2 Samuel 7:12-16 – *The Messiah would be a descendant of David.*

Well, yes, the Messiah would be a descendant of David, but David had many descendants. Even if Jesus was a descendant of David, as both Matthew and Luke ineptly attempted to prove, being a descendant is but circumstantial evidence. We need more, much more.

11. Psalm 2:1-12 - *The Messiah would be called God's Son.*

How many people, prior to Jesus, were called God's son (Gen 6:2, Ex 4:22, Deut 14:1, Job 1:6, 2:1, Ps 2:7, 2 Sam 7:12-14, Hos 11:1), and did any of those occurrences indicate a deity? Well, no, they did not. Certainly, there is no cause to turn it into a royal title, Son of God (emphasis mine). Biblically, the term generally related to a person anointed by God, and thus not God. Additionally, Jesus never referred to himself that way. Where we read: "The beginning of the gospel of Jesus Christ, the Son of God" (Mark 1:1, NKJV), it seems probable that as for most of his generation, and many previous, his reference was to the prophesied return to kingly rule. We also have: "'And the high priest said to him, 'I put you under oath by the living God: Tell us if you are the Christ, the Son of God!' Jesus said to him, 'It is as you said. Nevertheless, I say to you, hereafter you will see the Son of Man sitting at the right hand of the Power, and coming on the clouds of heaven." (Matt 26:63-64) The high priest, being Jewish and reader of the Hebrew Bible, would not have said "Christ", a translation of the Greek term "Christos" meaning anointed one. What he was really asking is whether Jesus was *God's Anointed King of Israel.* Jesus said he was, which could only have been interpreted in the contemporary Jewish understanding of the prophesied Davidic King, who would restore Israel. That is why Pilate had the words, *King of the Jews,* inscribed on the cross. Jesus must have thought he was, but then referred to a separate entity, the son of man. However, we know that Jesus, those two thousand years ago, did not restore Israel.

12. Psalm 16:8-11 - *The Messiah would be resurrected.*

Firstly, in Jewish tradition, King David is considered many things, but not a prophet. That is why the Psalms are included in the *Kesuvim* (Writings), so from an evidentiary perspective, quoting his words as messianic prophecies should be considered *unsafe* (to use a legal term). The NKJV reads: "For You shall not leave my soul in Sheol", whereas the Hebrew has: "Because you will not abandon my soul to the grave." I would offer that both are correct in a sense, except that the Christian version has overlaid the intent of David with an otherwise correct hope. We discuss the nature of Sheol in a later chapter, but it is not Hell in the Christian sense, but rather, a place where everyone goes until the final judgement. David's plea was concerning this life, not the next. David here is referring to an earlier event: "David said to Nathan, 'I have sinned to Hashem!' Nathan responded to David, 'So, too, Hashem has commuted your sin; you will not die.'" (2 Samuel 13:13) David's sin? "You have struck Uriah the Hittite with the sword; his wife you have taken to yourself for a wife, while him you have killed by the sword." (2 Samuel 12:9) Many of David's Psalms must be read in conjunction with the more complete narratives of his life, and this one is an exemplar: it has nothing to do with messianic prophecy.

13. Psalm 22:1-31 - *The Messiah would be forsaken and pierced, but vindicated.*

This is all about David himself, and has nothing to do with Jesus. Yes, I understand Systematic Theology, and the attempts to find "types" in the Old Testament to prophesy events in the New, but that is *eisegesis*, not *exegesis*. If Christian theologians and scholars spent as much time understanding the Scriptures, as trying to find passages to validate their theology, we may all get closer to the truth. One should understand that Christianity has ventured beyond theology into philosophy. We discussed Psalm 22 in the Gospel reviews, and demonstrated that it was not applicable.

14. Psalm 69 - *The Messiah would be the righteous sufferer.*

Quoting this psalm is an attempt to link it with the "suffering servant", but those doing so seem unaware of the trap that they have laid for themselves. See below.

15. Psalm 110:1-4 - *The Messiah would be greater than David.*

Yes, agreed, but who said Jesus was greater than David, other than Jesus' allusion about himself being so (Matt 22:42-45)? In the messianic sense, *mashiach* would be a King greater than King David, and Jesus was certainly not that, at least not on earth some two thousand years ago. However, this is a misrepresentation of Psalm 110. Christianity claims that this is a psalm, by David, about the Messiah, but in the Hebrew, it reads: "Regarding David, a psalm". The author is unknown, but it is about King David, and must be read as such. Once again, attempting to turn David into a prophet is deliberate twisting of Scripture, or more kindly, a result of using the unreliable Septuagint. Once again, however, Jews for Jesus are disingenuous when they claim evidence from the Tanach, a Jewish text in Hebrew, but appear to use the Greek Septuagint.

16. Psalm 118:22-24 - *The Messiah would be the rejected cornerstone.*

See Chapter 3-7.

17. Psalm 118:25-29 - *The Messiah would be acclaimed.*

Well, so what? Many are acclaimed, but that is not evidence that they were the Messiah. See notes to point (2).

18. Isaiah 7:14 - *The Messiah would be born of a virgin.*

Much disputed verse, and I agree with the Hebrew rendering of *the young woman*, not *a virgin*, not that it matters much, for the issue is a red herring. See Chapter 3-6.

19. Isaiah 9:1-2 (8:23 – 9:1) - *The Messiah would be the great light.*

Well, yes, but Jesus was hardly a great light in his time, being quickly extinguished. Any prophecy in the Tanach, referring to a *mashiach* (messiah), concerns a triumphant King who would bring peace and reign forever. Jesus failed that test, and instead of Jerusalem being restored and the Jews regathered, the exact opposite happened, and no, there is no prophecy concerning *Two Comings.*

20. Isaiah 9:6-7 (Hebrew 9:5-6) - *The Messiah would be the Wonderful Counsellor, Mighty God, Everlasting Father and Prince of Peace.*

This another disputed text where Christianity attempts to turn an historical account into a prophecy. The Hebrew reads: "the Wondrous Adviser, Mighty God, Eternal Father, called his name Sar-shalom [Prince of Peace]". If you read the history of King Hezekiah, this latter title fits him perfectly. So instead of the Christian misinterpretation that this is a prophecy of Jesus, the Jewish understanding has always been that the Wondrous Adviser is God, speaking about Hezekiah. As always, I go with the original, as should JFJ. The other point, which Christians seem to miss, is: when is Jesus ever referred to as *Everlasting Father?* Is he not the *Son*, and does not Jesus himself always refer to his, or our, Father? This contention is self-contradictory, and has no evidentiary weight whatsoever.

21. Isaiah 11:1, 53:3 - *The Messiah would be called a Nazarene.*

These references are *bogus*, which demonstrates the lack of scholarship of JFJ. Check them for yourself. Nowhere in the Hebrew Scriptures do the prophets refer to the Messiah as a Nazarene. The assertion of prophecy fulfilment in Matthew 2:23 is pure fantasy. There are numerous references to *Nazarites*, but that is an entirely different concept, and even Paul is said to have taken a Nazarite vow (Acts 18:18).

22. Isaiah 35:5-6 - *The Messiah would perform signs of healing.*

Peter, the Apostles, and other disciples did likewise, but they were not the Messiah. You might review the sense of Matthew 7:22.

23. Isaiah 40:3-5 - *The Messiah would be preceded by a forerunner.*

This *could* be a relevant prophecy, except that it relates to the *End Times*. Read verses 1-2. "Comfort, yes, comfort My people! Says your God. Speak comfort to Jerusalem, and cry out to her, that her warfare has ended. That her iniquity is pardoned; for she has received from the Lord's hand, double for all her sins." Did Jesus bring comfort to Jerusalem, or distress? Had Jerusalem's warfare ended, or only just begun? That the evangelists believed John the Baptist to be the one referred to in Isaiah, simply evidences that they thought Jesus to be King Messiah, who would rescue Israel from the Romans, and usher in the *End of Days*. Clearly, they were wrong.

24. Isaiah 42:1-6 - *The Messiah would be a light for the nations of the world.*

True, but the light is to be permanent for all the nations. The light of Jesus did initially spread, except in the Far East, and is now progressively diminishing in the glare of Islam.

25. Isaiah 52-13–53-12 - *The Suffering Servant, part 1.*

I shall start by referring to these verses, all of which identify Israel as the *suffering servant*:

    a.   Isaiah 41:8-9 "You, Israel, are My servant … I have chosen you and not cast you away"

    b.   Isaiah 44:1-2 "Jacob My servant, and Israel whom I chose"

    c.   Isaiah 44:21 "O Jacob and Israel, for thou art My servant"

    d.   Isaiah 45:4 "My servant Jacob, and Israel My chosen one"

    e.   Isaiah 48:20 "The Lord has redeemed His servant Jacob"

    f.   Isaiah 49:3 "And He said to me, thou art My servant, O Israel"

    g.   Psalm 136:22 "Even a heritage unto Israel His servant"

    h.   Jeremiah 46:27-28 "Jacob my servant, do not be dismayed Israel"

By being selective with verses, as they have, the Jesus apologists have twisted Scripture in an attempt to have it mean what they want it to mean, especially verse 52:3 "you shall be redeemed without money". Verses 53:2-3 have particular application, as they detail the sufferings of the suffering servant, which do parallel the sufferings of Jesus. If that was the only information we had, then it could be seen as a prophecy, but we have far greater information identifying the suffering servant as Israel. Some Christian scholars acknowledge this, but then attempt to spiritualise Jesus as Israel. I do not believe that works very well.

Other verses also prohibit the identification of Jesus as Israel, for example: "For the Lord has comforted His people, He has redeemed Jerusalem". We know that the exact opposite happened: the Jews became distressed and rather than Jerusalem being redeemed, it was devastated.

26. Isaiah 52:13-53-12 – *The Suffering Servant, part 2.*

See Chapter 3-2, but as the website from which this was extracted deals with the suffering servant in three parts, so as to quote NT passages that appeared to match, I will repeat the arguments here. Most do not match, in the sense of substantive evidence, for example: "So he opened not his mouth" (v. 53:7). The NKJV points us to John 19:9 "But Jesus gave him no answer" when before Pilate. The lack of consistency is evident when we also note in John 18:33-37, that Jesus was anything but silent before Pilate. The reference in Matthew 26:63 where "Jesus kept silent" was before the high priest, but he did answer the next question. In John's version, 18:19-23, Jesus was again outspoken, contrary to Matthew's account.

It is entirely illogical, and dare I say, disingenuous, to extract a verse from Isaiah, and try to make it match the Gospels, without also revealing where it does not match, and the clearly evident contradictions across the Gospels regarding Jesus' reactions when interviewed by Pilate and the high priest.

27. Isaiah 52:13-53-12 – *The Suffering Servant, part 3.*

As above, but reiterating that the *suffering servant* was, and still is in the opinion of numerous scholars, Israel, and any attempt to spiritualise Israel as a "type" of Jesus, or Jesus as Israel, is entirely fanciful.

28. Isaiah 61:1-2 - *The Messiah would do life-affirming, redemptive deeds.*

This could be a prophecy of Jesus, as Messiah, but did Jesus "proclaim … the day of vengeance of our God" (v. 61:2)? This refers to the *End of Days*, but Jesus said that he did not know when that was. If he did not know, then he could not so proclaim, and therefore this is not a prophecy referring to Jesus.

29. Jeremiah 31:15 - *The Messiah would be the object of a murderous plot.*

This is really stretching the truth. There is no mention of a murderous plot in Jeremiah 31 at all. The whole chapter is about the final redemption of Israel, not its downfall in the time of Jesus. Verse 15 refers to an attempt to appease God when King Menasseh introduced idolatry into the Temple (2 Kings 21:4-5). But he rejected all their pleas until Rachel recalled her own magnanimity to her sister, Leah. When Leah was fraudulently married to Jacob in place of Rachel, Rachel did not let jealous resentment lead her to protest. Why, then, should God be so zealous in punishing His children for bringing idols into His Temple? God accepted her plea and promised that Israel would be redeemed eventually, in her merit.

Try reading the passage in that light, instead of the non-existent *murderous plot*, or alternatively try to find the murderous plot in the text.

30. Jeremiah 31:31 - *The Messiah would bring in a new covenant.*

According to the Hebrew Scriptures, the Messiah would not bring in a *new* covenant, but a *renewed* covenant, and then with the ancient houses of Israel and Judah, not some spiritualised *New Israel*, and only in the last days, not over two thousand years before. But let us look at the conditions of this covenant: "I will put My law in their minds, and write it on their hearts". According to Christianity, Jesus did not do that, but rather, he erased it from their hearts and minds. "No more shall every man teach his neighbour": did Jesus do that? Nope! He instructed the opposite: that they should go out and preach the Gospel to all nations. "They shall all know Me": did that happen? Nope, new religions such as Islam arose which took people in a different direction. So, on the evidence, Jesus was not that Messiah.

31. Daniel 7:13-14 - *The Messiah would be the Son of Man.*

There is only one occasion where the term, *son of man* (without initial capitals) is associated with the Messiah. In Ezekiel, the term is used 93 times, but also once in Daniel 8:17, where indisputably, it is used to draw a clear distinction between our infinite God, and mortal man. It is very poor scholarship to extract a term from the Septuagint, with all its known deficiencies, to make a case that is contrary to the common usage of the term.

32. Daniel 9:24-27 - *The Messiah would come according to a timetable.*

Jesus himself stated that the date, or timetable, of the Messiah coming in the *End of Days*, was unknown to anyone except the Father, but most significantly, Jesus did not come according to the Father's timetable for the *eschaton*: he arrived at least 2000 years too early! This is another of those appeals to future comings as proof of an earlier coming, but it fails the test of logic. In respect of Jesus' arrival, the appeal to Daniel 9:24-27 regarding the 70 weeks fails to understand that there are two periods of 70 weeks, each with a different starting date, separated by 18 years. The first is based on the subjugation of the people under Nebuchadnezzar, in the Jewish year 3320. The second period of seventy years begins in

3338 with the destruction of Jerusalem (Daniel 9:2). These cannot be reconciled into one prophesied date (see Chapter 3-3).

33. Hosea 11:1 - *The Messiah would be called out of Egypt.*

This evidences laziness, ineptitude, or deceitfulness on the part of those offering this as a prophesy fulfilled by Jesus as Messiah. Read verse 11:2, "They sacrificed to the Baals, and burned incense to carved images". Did Jesus do that? NO? Then this cannot be a prophecy fulfilled by Jesus.

34. Micah 5:1 - *The Messiah would be born in Bethlehem.*

Yes, Jesus was born in Bethlehem according to the accounts, but is Jesus to whom Micah was referring? Both King David and Ruth (Ruth 4:11) were born in Bethlehem, and we can accept that Micah 5:1 is a prophecy of the Messiah coming from there, but we need more evidence that Jesus was that Messiah, before applying this prophecy to him. How many people were born in Bethlehem?

35. Zechariah 9:9 - *The Messiah would come riding on a colt.*

Again, I accept this to be a prophecy concerning the Messiah, but not that it was fulfilled by Jesus. Read the next verse: "I will cut off the [war] chariot from Ephraim, and the [battle] horse from Jerusalem, and the battle bow shall be cut off." Did that happen? Clearly not, so again, the attempt to reconcile this prophecy with Jesus fails. In passing, note the silliness in Matthew's account: "They bought the donkey and the colt, laid their clothes on **them**, and set him on **them**" (Matt 21:7) [emphasis mine] – can you imagine Jesus sitting on two animals (hopefully of the same size). The author of Matthew lacked the understanding of Zechariah, that he wrote of just one animal not two, and subsequent translators seem not to have noticed either.

36. Zechariah 11:12-13 - *The Messiah would be betrayed for thirty pieces of silver.*

It is easy to see how Christian scholars latched onto Zechariah as a prophecy of the betrayal by Judas, but unfortunately, they misunderstood the nature of the prophet's discourse: it is allegorical not literal. Without launching into a long explanation, the thirty pieces of silver in Zechariah are thirty righteous people. Of interest is that the Christian version of Zechariah, translated from the Greek, refers to a "potter", but the Hebrew does not; it reads: "Hashem said to me, 'Throw it to the **treasurer** of the Precious Stronghold, which I have divested from them.' So I took (full amount of) thirty silver coins and threw it into the Temple of Hashem, to the **treasurer**." [emphasis mine] If one studies Zechariah 11 in full, it should be obvious that the Hebrew version makes far more sense than that derived from the Greek: reference to a potter is inconsistent with the overall theme. I do wonder whether this is an example of the Greek being retrofitted to the Gospel to derive a prophecy. That said, I am not confident that Judas did betray Jesus for thirty pieces of silver. If you examine the circumstances closely, what did Judas know that the chief priest did not know, or could not have known, without spending a very large sum of money? In my considered opinion, nothing at all.

37. Zechariah 12:10 - *The Messiah would be pierced.*

This is another of those lamentable occasions where Christian theologians have scoured the Scriptures looking for words or events that match, irrespective of context. Back up to verse 7 and read through to 9, these providing the context. Was Jesus' day "the day that I [God] will seek to destroy all the nations that come against Jerusalem", or did the nations destroy Jerusalem? Christian scholars and apologist should hang their heads in shame at this twisting of the Scriptures they deem to be holy and inerrant.

38. Malachi 3:1 - *The Messiah would be preceded by a messenger.*

Same story, a verse taken out of context. Read verse 2: "But who can endure the day of his coming?" Well, everyone apparently, and it was Jesus who did not endure.

39. Malachi 4:5-6 - *The Messiah would be preceded by Elijah the prophet.*

As above, Malachi is speaking of the Messiah at the *End of Days*, and as we are not there yet, he could not have been speaking of Jesus.

40. Hebrew Bible - *The Messiah is spoken of throughout the Hebrew Bible.*

This one is duplicitous. Just because a Messiah is prophesied in the Hebrew Bible, is not evidence that Jesus fulfilled that prophecy. One must also understand that in the Hebrew Bible, it is not "the" Messiah, but "a" mashiach. There is a difference in understanding that Christianity does not comprehend, preferring instead to superimpose its own theology on an ancient text.

ONE Coming of the Messiah, not Two

I can understand the Apostles and immediate disciples of Jesus, believing him to be the prophesied Messiah, and even after he was put to death, believing that he would still fulfill the prophecies. It is evident from their writings that they expected him to return soon, perhaps even within their own lifetimes, but as time went on, hopes must have faded amongst many. When Jesus failed to save Jerusalem from destruction, many more must have concluded that he definitely was not their promised Saviour from the Romans, and later gave their loyalty to Simon bar Kokhba, believing him to be the Messiah. He too failed.

It was inevitable that having developed a theology, many would cling to it despite the contrary evidence – the more zealous people are for a cause, the more reluctant they are to admit that they were wrong, and abandon it. Later Christians, who died for their faith, were unlikely to know the full story, just as Christians today are similarly ignorant. Once you are told that it is the Holy Spirit within Who gives you faith in Jesus Christ, and if you do not believe, you have not the Spirit, and thus heading for damnation, it is difficult to walk away (I know from personal experience).

Christianity invented the idea of two comings, because Jesus did not fulfill the messianic expectations of the Jewish people, according to Scripture. Pondering this conundrum, I can only conclude that Christianity persists with these false claims of prophecy fulfillment because, having declared Jesus to be the Messiah, they would give the lie to their own beliefs if they admit that they were wrong concerning the prophecies.

Summary

I am deeply saddened that Christians are deluded in their own beliefs, which, when boiled down, evidence their primary faith as being *faith in their own faith*, as if they are afraid of losing it, lest they lose their salvation. Christians will boldly offer Scripture as evidence of the authenticity of Jesus as Messiah and Saviour, but when shown their error, rather than debate the facts of Scripture, they will retreat to the time-worn *Holy Spirit* defence – they have it and you don't. To their way of thinking, or rather in accord with their indoctrination, if you did have the Holy Spirit within you, you would believe in Jesus Christ.

But here is the dilemma from which Christians retreat: When they offer false evidence, were they guided by the Spirit when doing so? If they truly have the Holy Spirit within, how is it that they are so prone to error when attempting to interpret Scripture and prove their own case? Was the Church of Rome guided by the Spirit when they self-evidently did not understand the doctrine of *substitutionary atonement*, instead accusing the Jews of being *Christ Killers*? Were they guided by the Spirit when they taught hatred and contempt for the Jews, instead of loving them, enemy or not? Were they guided by the Spirit when they abandoned Torah, the Sabbath, and all God-ordained commemorations? Were they guided by the Spirit when, under the influence of Emperor Constantine, they compromised with the pagans, choosing the winter solstice for the date of Jesus' birth (Christmas), and the equinox to determine Easter replacing Passover. Were Christian artists being guided by the Holy Spirit when, following the influence of Constantine, the sun worshipper, Jesus, Mary, and the saints were pictured with the sun behind their heads, later reduced to a halo? How can Christianity claim Jesus as the Passover Lamb, entirely misinterpreting the Book of Exodus, but then reject Passover in favour of a pagan feast?

Objectively analysed, the matter of Christian doctrine and theology, concerning the fulfillment of prophecy, is utterly incoherent. That anyone would offer these Scripture passages as their *Top 40 Most Helpful Messianic Prophecies*, leaves me in utter bewilderment, and not a little saddened. At best, they disprove the Christian case.

REFERENCES:

1. https://jewsforjesus.org/answers/top-40-most-helpful-messianic-prophecies/
2. *The Chumash*, Scherman, Rabbi Nosson, Mesorah Publications, ArtScroll English Edition, Brooklyn, NY, 2009
3. Zlotowitz, Rabbi Meir, *Bereishis (Genesis) with Commentary Volumes I & II*, Mesorah Publications Ltd., Brooklyn, NY, 2009
4. *The Chumash*, p. 872

Chapter 4-8

ACTS AND EPISTLES

"Physician, heal thyself!"
(Luke 4:23)

I have approached this chapter, more with completeness in mind, rather than anticipating anything new, especially from the Pauline Epistles. With an issue as important as this one is, with such significant ramifications, I think it best to be thorough as we can be. The Book of Acts, *aka* The Acts of the Apostles, is generally considered the Gospel of Luke, Part 2, but I choose to deal with it separately from the Gospels so named. As for the heading quote, *"Physician, heal thyself"*, let me offer that this proverb extends beyond the physical, and even the spiritual, but also to the intellectual as well. A false belief can be considered a mental illness, and if we are suffering from that, we need to heal ourselves by finding the truth. That is what I am attempting to do in this study, by revealing what I believe to be, the faulty thinking that has led to false beliefs.

Preview of References

I have ignored verses where the author himself has made a prophetic statement; e.g. "This same Jesus who was taken up from you into heaven, will soon come in like manner as you saw Him go into heaven" (Acts 1:11). Not directly relevant in this study, but let me point out the irony that according to other New Testament texts, Luke's statement is untrue. Jesus ascended into heaven very quietly, with very few witnesses, but his return will be anything but quiet, and everyone will know about it: perhaps Luke had something else in mind, or had not read Matthew's account. For the record, let us review what the New Testament says about Jesus' Second Coming:

- Matthew 24:29-31 you can read for yourselves.
- "But the day of the Lord will come as a thief in the night, in which the heavens will pass away with a great noise" (2 Peter 3:10). The term, *thief in the night*, does not have the same connotation as in the modern vernacular: someone quietly sneaking in like a cat burglar. It does have the sense of not knowing when it will happen, but in the understanding of the time, when it does, it will be more like a Viking attack, scaring people to remain inside. That is what thieves in the night did back then, and why the text refers to *a great noise*. See also 1 Thessalonians 5:2-3
- "Behold, he is coming with clouds, and **every** eye shall see him" (Revelation 1:7) [emphasis mine].

Now back to the subject at hand, starting with some brief statistics from these books, remembering that we have already dealt with the Gospels. Because of the number of references, I will deal with the Psalms separately to the other Old Testament books. Let us start with the latter; we will come back to the Psalms after surveying the other OT books:

a. There are 55 unique NT verses quoting 77 unique OT verses, of which only 37 are flagged as prophetic.
b. In total, there are 54 references to the Prophets, and 23 references to other books of the Old Testament, especially Genesis.
c. Significantly, there is not a single reference to the Book of Daniel, the source of the "Son of Man" references in the Gospels.

d.   The Book of Isaiah is referenced 39 times, Genesis 13 times, and the other book counts are in single figures.

e.   The most commonly quoted, or annotated Prophecy verses are Genesis 12:3, 18:18, 22:18; Isaiah 8:14, 11:1, and 53:5-12.

Again, the counts themselves are not important: we are attempting to understand any patterns they may evidence.

Overviewing the most commonly referenced Prophets and other OT Books:

a.   Genesis 12:3 – *I will bless those who bless you, and I will curse him who curses you; and in you all the families of the earth will be blessed*; (Acts 3:25; Gal 3:8, 14, 16, 29), in validation of God's chosen people, which has me wondering why the later Gentile church became Jew-haters.

b.   Genesis 18:18 – *[17]And the Lord said, Shall I hide from Abraham what I am doing, [18]since Abraham shall surely become a great and mighty nation, and all the nations of the earth shall be blessed in him*; (Acts 3:25; Gal 3:8, 14), as above.

c.   Genesis 22:18 – *In your seed all the nations of the earth shall be blessed, because you have obeyed My voice*; (Acts 3:25; Gal 3:8, 14, 16), and again.

d.   Isaiah 8:14 – *He will be as a sanctuary, but a stone of stumbling and a rock of offense to both the houses of Israel, as a trap and a snare to the inhabitants of Jerusalem*; (Rom 9:32, 33; 1 Pet 2:8), attempting to find fault with those who did not accept Jesus as the prophesied Messiah.

e.   Isaiah 11:1 – *There shall come forth a Rod from the stem of Jesse, and a Branch shall grow out of his roots*; (Acts 13:23; Rom 1:3, 15:12; Heb 7:14), establishing the credibility of Jesus as descended from the line of David; and

f.   Isaiah 53:5-12 – References here are to Jesus as the suffering servant (see Chapter 3-2).

The most common references here relate to the descendants of Abraham being a blessing to the world, and to the suffering servant in Isaiah 53. The difficulty I have with the first theme is the apparent attempt to make this prophecy specific to Jesus as Messiah, when the texts make clear that it concerns the descendants of Abraham generally. Yes, if Jesus descended from Abraham through David, it allowed him to be included in the prophecy, but no more so than any other Jew: the prophecy concerns the nations of the earth to be blessed by the "mighty nation" of Abraham, not specifically by an individual, although that is undoubtedly true. That is the meaning of the prophecy, and it is invalid, as evidence, to co-opt it to refer to Jesus specifically. Even so, there is no correlation with what Jesus is said to have accomplished. If one follows the thread through the prophecies, it can be seen as leading to the Messiah who would rescue (redeem) Israel from its oppressors, something which Jesus failed to do.

Psalm References

Following is the frequency of references to verses in the Psalms:
a. There are 58 unique NT verses quoting 60 unique psalm verses, of which only 21 are flagged as prophetic.
b. Of the 58, 14 NT verses also reference one or more other OT books.
c. 43 NT verses claim prophecy fulfillment.
d. The most commonly referenced psalms are Psalm 110 [13] and 16 [13].
e. The most commonly quoted, or annotated psalm verses are Psalm 110:1 [10] and 68:18 [6].

The Gospel authors aside, the New Testament authors, and/or the NKJV editors, reference the Psalms more often than they do the recognised Prophets. I find that curious. Overviewing the most commonly referenced Psalms:
a. Psalm 16:10 - *For you will not leave my heart in Sheol ... You will not allow Your holy one to see corruption*; (Acts 2:25, 2:31, 13:35; Rom 1:4; 1 Cor 15:4; Heb 13:20), no doubt intending to find a prophecy of the resurrection.
b. Psalm 68:18 - *You have ascended on high, you have led captivity captive*; (Acts 2:34; 1 Co 14:4; Eph 4:8, 10; Phi 2:9; Col 3:1),

again related to the resurrection, but the last phrase is a clumsy translation of the Hebrew.

c.   Psalm 110:1 - *The Lord said to my lord, sit at my right hand, till I make your enemies your footstool*; (Acts 2:33, 34; 1 Cor 15:4; Phi 2:9; Col 3:1; Heb 1:3, 13, 10:12, 13, 12:2), another resurrection allusion; and

d.   Psalm 110:4 - *The Lord has sworn … you are a priest forever according to the order of Melchizedek*; (Heb 5:6, 7:17, 21), which we discussed in Chapter 3-8, and will review again little later.

What this suggests is that the Psalms were used in a prophetic sense of the resurrection, NOT the crucifixion in substitutionary atonement. I find that significant in the context of prophecy fulfillment, for you may recall, we found no prophecy of substitutionary atonement in the Gospels either. What does that tell us about the thinking and beliefs of the authors? Now to the detail of the NT verses.

Acts of the Apostles

As an aside, scholars have contended that this book might more properly be named, "The Acts of Paul", as it has little to say about the activities of the Jerusalem church under James, being mostly about Paul. Another title is: "The Great Cover Up", as it deliberately obscures the truth of Christianity in Jerusalem before Paul comes on the scene. More importantly, however, the author published his work anonymously, and even though the work is attributed to Luke, why would Luke appear to hide his authorship? Why does the author never directly quote any of Paul's writings?

Acts 1:16 – "*this Scripture had to be fulfilled, which the Holy Spirit spoke before by the mouth of David concerning Judas*", quoting Psalms 41:9, 55:12-14, 20. In 41:9, David is referring to his own illness; 55:12-14 speaks of Ahithophel, who had been his friend and adviser, but had betrayed him; and 55:20 refers to those who persist in their evil ways, and never repent and return to God. So, how does one manipulate those texts to have them read as a prophecy concerning Judas betraying Jesus, if he really did? The

Gospels quote Zechariah 11:12-13 as the prophecy fulfilled, so it would seem that Luke was scratching about, unaware of the Gospels, and settled on the Psalms which in Judaism of the time, nobody considered prophetic, other than in a general sense concerning the *End of Days*. That David was betrayed by a friend was not unusual, people are betrayed by friends on a sadly regular basis, but normal human behaviour cannot be considered a prophecy of something happening to Jesus.

Acts 1:20 – "For it is written in the Book of Psalms: *'Let his dwelling place be desolate, and let no-one live in it'*; and, *'Let another take his office'*." Quoting Psalm 69:25 and 109:8. Psalm 69 is a prophetic portrayal of Israel's plight in its long and bitter exile. It takes a very great stretch of the imagination to link this Psalm with the "Field of Blood". That Psalm 69 is not about Jesus, or any aspect of his life (or death), is clearly conveyed by verse 36: "For God shall save Zion and build the cities of Judah, and they shall settle there and possess it." According to Christian doctrine, God has wiped His hands of Zion, and passed the baton to some *New Israel*. One can find parallels between the trials of David (Psalm 109), and that of Jesus, but such is but correlation, and cannot be considered prophetic.

Acts 2:25 – "*For David says concerning him*", quoting Psalm 16:8-11. David said nothing of the sort, but was speaking of his own soul. Read the psalm in full to understand. Attributing this psalm, as one concerning Jesus, is a preposterous misrepresentation of Scripture.

Acts 2:30 – "*Therefore, being a prophet, and knowing that God had sworn with an oath … He would raise up the Christ to sit on his throne*", quoting Psalm 132:11. This Psalm refers to David's pledge to rebuild the Temple, and to not enjoy the comforts of his own home until he had done so. He pleads to God: "For the sake of David, Your servant, turn not away the face of Your anointed. Hashem has sworn to David, a truth from which He will never retreat: From the fruit of your [David's] issue, I will place upon your throne. If your sons keep My covenant, and this, My testament, that I shall teach them, then their sons, too, forever and ever, shall sit upon your throne." David didn't get to build the Temple, God gave that task to his son, Solomon, although the Scriptures are not clear as to why. The Sages venture that David, although righteous in the eyes of God, was not sufficiently righteous. Solomon did sit on David's throne, but as history teaches, because his descendants failed to keep God's covenant as required, the throne of David became empty, and the palace destroyed. There is no prophecy concerning an <u>interim</u> King, in this case Jesus (Christ), appearing and disappearing again before the *mashiach* at the End of Days. When the King returns, he will stay and reign in peace, something which Jesus did not achieve.

Acts 2:31 – "*he [David] foreseeing this, spoke concerning the resurrection of the Christ*", quoting Psalm 16:10 and Isaiah 53:10. Here we need to compare the Hebrew with the Greek. In the Hebrew, David is expressing his faith in God, and states:

> "I have set Hashem before me always; because He is at my right hand I shall not falter. For this reason, my heart rejoices, and my soul is elated; my flesh, too, rests in confidence; because You will not abandon my soul to the grave, You will not allow Your devout one to witness destruction. You will make known to me the path of life, the fullness of joys in Your Presence, the delights that are in Your right hand for eternity."

This Psalm is a poem composed for/as a *michtam*. Some commentators refer to this as a musical instrument, but Rashi opined that in this context, a *michtam* refers to a poetic style. The opening verse sets the context: "Protect me O God, for I have sought refuge in You." Apparently, Luke interpreted "For You will not leave my soul in Sheol, nor will you allow Your holy one to see corruption" (v. 10) as prophesying that the promised Messiah, a King of the line of David, would be resurrected bodily. However, the Hebrew reads: "Because you will not abandon my soul to the grave, You will not allow Your devout one to witness destruction". David here is referring to an earlier event: "David said to Nathan, 'I have sinned to Hashem!' Nathan responded to David, 'So, too, Hashem has commuted your sin; you will not die.'" (2 Samuel 13:13) David's sin? "You have struck Uriah the Hittite with the sword; his wife you have taken to yourself for a wife, while him you have killed by the sword." (2 Samuel 12:9) Many of David's Psalms must be read in conjunction with the more complete narratives of his life. See also Chapter 1-8 regarding the meaning of "soul" in the biblical context.

There was no "foreseeing" by David, just an entreaty for God's protection, and faith that it would be received. There is no reference to a resurrected messiah, especially not one who would be killed. We have discussed the misrepresentation of Isaiah 53 in an earlier chapter (3-1) and have no need to revisit it here.

Acts 2:33 – "*Therefore, being exalted to the right hand of God*", quoting Psalm 110:1. Seventy-three Psalms are attributed to David, but this is not one of them. Psalm 110 was written **about** David, not **by** David, which changes the context significantly. From the Hebrew, it begins: "Regarding David, a psalm." Where the NKJV reads: "*The Lord* [Father] *said to my Lord* [Son]", the TJB reads: "*The word of Hashem to my master* [King David]", so this is not a prophecy of Jesus being exalted to the right hand of God. That aside, "*sit at My right*" is not the same as being "*being exalted to the right hand of God*". More importantly, we need to understand what is meant by the term, *right hand of God*, in the context of this Psalm. The conditional term, *until*, establishes this as a temporary position, not a permanent one. Rashi, evaluating this term from multiple contexts, writes: "AT My Right Hand means: FOR deliverance by means of My Right Hand." This is consistent with both *sit* and *until*. If we review the Gospels, nowhere do we find Jesus being exalted as claimed here. Matthew 28:18 does have Jesus asserting: "All authority has been given to me in heaven and on earth", and if he was whom Christianity says he was, then it could be said that Jesus sits at his sovereign's right hand. However, Psalm 110 provides no evidence for this. John 14:28, 16:16,17, and 20:17 all have Jesus going to the Father, but with no mention of his position there. So, Luke has joined these two concepts and attempted to have David prophesying that event, which on the evidence, he did not.

Acts 2:34 – "*For David did not ascend into the heavens, etc.*", again quoting Psalm 110, and also 68:18, neither of which is a prophecy of an interim Messiah who failed to rescue Israel from its oppressors.

Acts 3:18 – "*But those things which God foretold by the mouth of all His prophets, that the Christ would suffer, He has thus fulfilled*", quoting Isaiah 53 (See Chapter 3-2).

Acts 3:22 – "*The Lord your God will raise up for you a Prophet like me from your midst*", quoting Deuteronomy 18:15-19. Certainly, a prophet like Moses was promised by God, but if Jesus fulfilled that prophecy, he could not have been the Messiah. The promised Messiah is to be the Redeemer of Israel, not a prophet speaking about Israel. Luke can't have it both ways.

Acts 3:25 – *"And in your* seed all the families of the earth shall be blessed"*, quoting Genesis 18:18, 22:18, 26:4, and 28:14. These Old Testament verses refer to the descendants of Abraham as being "a light unto the nations", and are not prophecies of the Messiah specifically. In a sense, Jesus could be said to have fulfilled that prophecy, but so did numerous other descendants of Abraham, so as evidence of Jesus being the Messiah, these verses are not relevant.

Acts 4:11 – "This is the *stone which was rejected by you builders, which has become the chief cornerstone"*, quoting Psalm 118:22 and Isaiah 28:16. We have adequately covered these two references in Chapter 3-7, so I will not trouble you with them again.

Acts 4:25-26 – *"Why did the nations rage, and the people plot vain things? The kings of the earth took their stand, and the rulers were gathered together against the Lord and against His Christ"*, mis-quoting Psalm 2:1-2. It is interesting that the Greek has *"Christou"*, whilst both the Hebrew and NKJV versions of the Psalm itself have simply: *"Anointed"*. Whilst semantically the NT could be acceptable, logically it is not, for it alludes to Jesus Christ, whilst the original Psalm was speaking of King David. The context was the attack by the Philistines. Luke was making the point that Jesus, as God's anointed, was attacked in the same manner as David, but from an evidentiary perspective, the attack on David was not prophetic of the same happening to Jesus, for many throughout the ages had been attacked similarly during the wars of the Children of Israel. This is not evidence of prophecy fulfillment.

Acts 7:37 – *"The Lord Your God will raise up for you a Prophet like me* [Moses] *from your brethren"*, quoting Deuteronomy 18:15-19. To qualify as evidence of prophecy fulfillment, it is required to show **how** Jesus was **that** promised prophet, not just make an unqualified assertion. God raised up many prophets after Moses: Isaiah, Jeremiah, Ezekiel, etc.; what evidence is offered that one of them was not to whom Moses was referring? In what way was Jesus more like Moses than these other Prophets, and was Jesus really *just* a Prophet? See the comments under John 17:8 in Chapter 4-5.

Acts 8:32 – *"He was led as a sheep to the slaughter"* quoting Isaiah 53:7-8. Matthew 27:14, Luke 23:9, 1 Peter 1:19, and 2:23, all try to make various cases from Isaiah 53:7, but all fail for much the same reasons.

Certainly, there are parallels, but they are too non-specific to be considered as prophecy fulfillments. As evidence, this verse carries no weight.

Acts 10:40 – *"Him God raised up on the third day, and showed him openly."* The NKJV references Hosea 6:2, but reading from the Hebrew: "[They will say] Come, and let us return to Hashem, for He has mangled [us] and He will heal us; He has smitten and He will bandage us. He will heal us after two days; on the third day He will raise us up and we will live before Him." (TJB) The commentary reads: "The Hebrew word *yom*, literally day, often is used for 'a long period of time'. Here the prophet refers to two exiles – in Egypt and in Babylonia. Both of those exiles were 'healed' in the form of the First and Second Temples. After the 'third day', i.e., the exile after the destruction of the Second Temple, God *will raise us up* with the final Redemption and the Third Temple."[1] This verse in Hosea is not prophetic of Jesus' death and resurrection.

Acts 13:23 – *"From this man's seed, according to the promise, God raised up for Israel a Saviour – Jesus"*, referencing Isaiah 11:1 and Psalm 132:11. Isaiah did prophesy that the Davidic Messiah would "emerge from the stump of Jesse", but his role would be that of *Redeemer*, not *Saviour*. In the prophetic sense, the Redeemer would rescue Israel from its oppressors, whereas Saviour, in the Christian sense, refers to justification and redemption from the penalty of sin. This is a case of *literary sleight of hand*. The sense of redemption is found further in Psalm 132, verses 13-14: *"For Hashem has chosen Zion; He has desired it for His habitation. This is My resting place forever and ever, here I will dwell, for I have desired it."* It should be obvious that Jesus did not accomplish what was promised regarding redemption, and thus these verses provide no evidence of prophecy fulfillment.

Acts 13:33 – "God has fulfilled this [the promise to the fathers, v. 32] for us their children, in that He has raised up Jesus. As it is also written in the second Psalm: *'You are My son, today I have begotten you'*", quoting Psalm 2:7. Who wrote the second Psalm, and who is "I" in verse 7? The answer to both questions is: King David. The verse is historical, not prophetic. The term, *you are My son*, is a statement identifying the head of Israel, as Israel itself was declared as "My First-born son" (Exodus 4:22). The term, *begotten*, is metaphorical for "fathered". David was recalling that God had appointed him as King over Israel (1 Chronicles 14:2). See also Psalm 89:27 – "Also I will make him My firstborn, the highest of the kings of the earth." I find it interesting that only in Revelation 1:5 do we find the NKJV referencing this Psalm verse, and even then, it is wrong: "the firstborn from the dead" can hardly be linked back to David being firstborn. Whilst the evangelists and other disciples may well have considered Jesus in the same light as David, this verse in Acts is evidence of that belief, not evidence that he was. Luke is *corroborating* the evidence of John and others, as to their beliefs, which could be considered *circumstantial* evidence that Jesus was as claimed, but nothing more. As evidence of prophecy fulfillment, it fails, primarily because Psalm 2 is not prophetic.

Acts 13:34 – "And that He raised him from the dead, no more to return to corruption, He has spoken thus: *'I will give you the sure mercies of David'*", quoting Isaiah 55:3 and Psalm 89:28. Isaiah 55:3 reads, in part: "And I will make an everlasting covenant with you – the sure mercies of David". What were they? According to Jewish commentaries, the promise (2 Samuel 7:11-16) that the Messiah will be David's descendant. How does that promise relate to *not returning to corruption*? Well, not at all. Luke then has Paul confirming that same misunderstanding in the next verse.

Acts 13:35 – "Therefore he also says in another Psalm: *'You will not allow Your Holy One to see corruption'*", quoting Psalm 16:10. This is a common theme in Christian theology, attempting to have the psalm accepted as a prophecy of the resurrection, but it is entirely false. See my comments on Acts 2:31. Earlier, we encountered this observation concerning Luke's writings: *"This account owes more to Luke's ability to compose an engagingly plausible tale, than to his access to historically reliable information about Paul's missionary experience ... Luke gives us historical fiction rather than an historical report."*[2] Luke's narration of Paul's speech to the synagogue, Acts 13:16-47, is one such account. In verse 36, we have Luke stating that David did see corruption, so what point was he attempting to make in quoting the Psalm, suggesting that it was a prophecy fulfilled by Jesus? It makes no sense, to me at least.

Acts 13:47 – For so the Lord has commanded us: *'I have set you as a light to the Gentiles'*", quoting Isaiah 42:6 and 49:6. A command from God is not a prophecy, and people obeying God's commands cannot be construed as prophecy fulfillment. Remember that it was the Children of Israel whom God called "*a nation of priests*" (Exodus 19:6), and "*a light unto the nations*" (Isaiah as above). If Paul was quoting the Hebrew Scriptures, he should have been affirming the role as given to the Israelites, not to a breakaway religion of Christianity. Paul, if he did say as recorded, was misappropriating Scripture for his own purposes, which is lamentable. Even more lamentable is the NKJV editors annotating obedience to a command of God, as prophecy fulfillment. I am ever perplexed by this type of thinking, but in brief, this is not evidence of prophecy fulfillment.

Acts 28:26 – "*Go to this people and say: Hearing you will not hear, and shall not understand*, etc." quoting Isaiah 6:9-10. Matthew 13:14, Mark 4:12, Luke 8:10, and John 12:40 all quote these sayings of Isaiah, but the wording varies, as do the application. The Synoptics use Isaiah in support of why Jesus spoke in parables, whereas John uses the verses to express Jesus' frustration at people not believing in him. Luke's account in Acts of Paul's experience is similar in sentiment to that in John. I would refer you to the discussion in Chapter 4-3, Mark 4:12, regarding how the original Hebrew wording has been corrupted to have Isaiah say what he did not, thus invalidating the NKJV claim of prophecy fulfillment.

Acts 28:28 – "*Therefore let it be known to you that salvation of God has been sent to the Gentiles, and they will hear it*", the NKJV again referencing Isaiah 6:9-10. The promised salvation of God, as conveyed in Isaiah, and all the Prophets, going all the way back to Abraham, was as expressed at Sinai: "I am the Lord your God … you shall have no other gods before Me" (Exodus 20:2-3). The message conveyed by the Children of Israel, as *a nation of priests*, and *a light unto the nations*, was one of monotheism, contrary to the polytheistic beliefs of the pagans. Paul, or the author of Acts, has attempted to misappropriate that message, using it to have the Gentiles believe that it was about Jesus dying for their sins. My question, as always, is: Why? If Jesus was the prophesied Messiah, and if his prophesied mission was to die and be resurrected, why did Paul, Luke, the NKJV editors, and other writers, all twist the Scriptures to their own purposes?

Summary of Acts

Luke continues to rely on the Psalms as prophetic, even though the Jewish Sages insist that David was not a prophet, which is why his writings are in the *Kesuvim* (Writings). I am not about to believe that the Jewish Sages, the recognised Prophets, and even David himself, did not understand the later view apparently held by the followers of Jesus, that David was a prophet in his own right, inspired by God to write about Jesus as *interim* Messiah. Wherever David alludes to the Messiah, it is always in the context of the *End of Days*, not the days when Jerusalem would be once again destroyed, and the Children of Israel not only dispersed to foreign lands, but disallowed to live in Israel.

Luke's attempts at prophecy fulfillment cannot be accepted under the rules of evidence, the standard that we are using in this study.

Pauline Epistles

Romans 1:3 – "*concerning His son Jesus Christ our Lord, who was born of the seed of David according to the flesh*", quoting numerous OT verses, none of which are relevant for a very simple reason: if Mary was a virgin, Jesus was not born of the seed of David. Apparently, Paul had not heard of the virgin birth. In Judaism, *seed … according to the flesh*, is a common expression relating to **paternity**, not maternity. The only way Paul could be right is if Mary was not a virgin, and Joseph was Jesus' biological father.

Romans 1:4 – "*declared to be the son of God*", referencing Psalm 2:7. David was declared the son of God, as were many OT people, the term conveying a special relationship which does not infer divinity, otherwise David too would be a deity.

Romans 5:8 – "*God demonstrates His own love toward us, in that while we were all sinners, Christ died for us*", referencing Isaiah 5:3 (suffering servant). See Chapter 3-2.

Romans 5:18 – "*so through one man's righteous act the free gift came to all men, resulting in justification of life*", again referencing Isaiah 5:3. If Paul meant that Jesus' crucifixion was the *righteous act*, then we must question the righteousness of God. God prohibits the spilling of innocent blood, and the sacrifice of humans, and thus in His righteousness, He could not have demanded the sacrifice of one who was without sin.

Romans 9:32 – "*Because they did not seek it by faith, but as it were, by the works of the law*", the NKJV referencing Isaiah 8:14-15. The text reads:

"**Hashem**, Master of Legions, **Him** shall you sanctify; **He** is your reverence and **He** is your strength. **He** shall be a sanctuary, but also a striking stone and a stumbling block, for the two houses of Israel" [emphasis mine]. It is God, not Jesus, who is the stumbling block, and specifically, in the circumstances related to Israel's failure to obey the covenant. I can understand Paul co-opting this verse to apply to Jesus, but it cannot be taken in a prophetic sense. As for "*works of the law*", this is not a reference to obedience to Mosaic Law, but to the identity markers of Judaism, e.g. circumcision, dietary laws, observing the Sabbath, etc. Having found this term in the Dead Sea Scrolls, scholars have come to understand the true significance of what Paul was saying, consistent with his view that the Gentiles need not convert to Judaism. For an indepth discussion, see *Jesus, Paul, and the Law*.[3]

Romans 9:33 – "*Behold I lay in Zion a stumbling stone*", as above. Note the subtle difference in wording between the translations from the Greek and Hebrew: "a sanctuary but a stone of offence" (NKJV), versus "a sanctuary but **also** a striking stone" (TJB) [emphasis mine]. The NKJV also references Isaiah 28:16, but if you study the context, you will understand that it refers to two possible periods, that of Hezekiah and/or the *End of Days*. God will weed out the wicked, and that certainly has not happened to date. Paul's *eschatological temper*, and that of the evangelists, has been well-recognised in modern scholarship, which is why I have included a separate section on that subject (Part 6).

Romans 10:11 – "For the Scripture says: *Whoever believes on him will not be put to shame*", quoting Isaiah 28:16. In truth, Isaiah 28:16 says nothing at all like that – check it for yourself.

Romans 10:16 – "For Isaiah says, *Lord, who has believed our report?*". Indeed, Isaiah 53:1 does say something similar, but let us back up a verse to understand who is speaking:

> "so will the many nations exclaim about him, and kings will shut their mouths [in amazement], for they will see that which had never been told to them, and will perceive things they had never heard. Who would believe what we have heard, for whom has the arm of Hashem been revealed?" (52:15 – 53:2).

Let us understand the context and flow of Isaiah's prophecies: "Up until this point [chapter 40], many of Isaiah's prophecies have been visions of retribution and destruction. From here [40:1] through to the end of Isaiah, the prophecies speak words of consolation and assurances of the future Messianic redemption. This passage [40:1] serves as a divider between the two types of prophecy (*Rashi*)"[4]. So, yes, Isaiah 53 is a Messianic prophecy, but it concerns Israel as the suffering servant, and their redemption is not from sin, but from their oppression in exile - the promise is of a return to *Eretz Israel*, with Jerusalem as their capitol. If you do not understand the eschatological of the times of Jesus, expecting his imminent return, you will not understand why the followers of Jesus mistook him for the prophesied Messiah. Romans 10:6 is not evidence of prophecy fulfillment.

Romans 11:9 – "*Let their table become a snare and a trap, a stumbling block and a recompense to them*", quoting Psalm 69:22-23. Again, the context of this Psalm is established in the opening plea by David: "*Save me, O God!*" (NKJV) Save from what? Not from the penalty of sin, but from the oppression of his enemies. If Paul viewed Jesus as the promised Messiah, sent to redeem Israel from its enemies, then this verse is relevant in that context, even though not intended as prophetic. If, on the other hand, Paul believed that Jesus was sent to die in *substitutionary atonement*, then this Psalm has no relevance whatsoever. As evidence, of prophecy fulfillment, it carries no weight.

Romans 15:3 – "For even Christ did not please himself; but as it is written, '*The reproaches of those who reproached You fell on me*'", quoting Psalm 69:9. I cannot be sure whether Paul actually meant this to be a fulfillment of prophecy, or whether it was the NKJV editors who decided that it was. Perhaps Paul was doing nothing more than comparing the experience of Jesus, with that of David, showing a similarity between the two as further evidence of Jesus' heritage. I have no problem with that – I believe it to be a perfectly acceptable method of conveying Paul's message. However, it is not evidence of prophecy fulfillment.

Romans 15:12 – "And again Isaiah says: '*There shall be a root of Jesse; and he who shall rise to reign over the Gentiles, in him the Gentiles shall hope*'", quoting Isaiah 11:1, 10. I am ever suspicious where the word, *Gentile*, is used when the Hebrew has "nations". There seems a subliminal suggestion of anti-Jewishness, or at least, divisiveness – why else Gentile versus Jew? That said, read the following verses: "It shall be on that day that the Lord will once again show His hand, to acquire the remnant of His people, who will have remained ... *and He will gather in the dispersed ones of Judah from the four corners of the earth.*" Did that occur in the life of Jesus? No? Then Paul was being duplicitous in quoting Isaiah, for he either knew that he was, or he was expecting Jesus to soon return and accomplish what was prophesied in Isaiah 11:11-16. Either way, this is not evidence of prophecy fulfillment: on the contrary, it is evidence that prophecy was NOT fulfilled, because far from the remnant of His people being regathered, they were dispersed.

First Corinthians

1 Cor 15:3 – "*Christ died for our sins, according to the Scriptures*", the NKJV referencing Isaiah 53:5-12 and Psalm 22:15. We have already covered Isaiah 53 sufficiently in Chapter 3-2, and Psalm 22 elsewhere, but it is interesting to note that verse 15 in the NKJV is not flagged as a prophecy to be fulfilled. Perhaps we can attribute that to an administrative oversight. In brief, the Scriptures do not prophesy Jesus dying for our sins in *substitutionary atonement*. The case could be made that if Jesus was the prophesied Messiah, he died for the sins of Israel as is suggested in Isaiah, but not in substitutionary atonement, which is the real issue here.

1 Cor 15:4 – "*and that he was buried, and that he rose again the third day according to the Scriptures*", citing Genesis 1:9-13; Psalms 16:9-11, 68:18, and 110:1; Isaiah 53:10; Hosea 6:2; and Jonah 1:17, and 2:10. Without commenting on whether the resurrection occurred or not, the question is: Was it prophesied in the Scriptures, as Paul claimed? I have no idea of why the NKJV cites Genesis 1, for I can find nothing relevant. The Psalms were reviewed earlier, as was Isaiah 53. See Acts 10:40 for commentary on Hosea 6:2. Answering my own question: No, the resurrection was not in accordance with the Scriptures. There is no prophecy fulfillment in this verse. One commentary reads: "Christ 'rose the third say', says the ancient formula quoted by Paul in his first epistle to the Corinthians, 'according to the scriptures.' But in the Scriptures – *videlicet* [Ed. viz], in Hosea 6:1-3 – it is Israel whom God will raise on the third day."[5]

Second Corinthians

2 Cor 3:14 – "*But their minds were blinded. For until this day the same veil remains unlifted in the reading of the Old Testament, because the veil is taken away in Christ*", the NKJV citing Isaiah 6:9-10. I would refer the reader back to my commentary on Mark 4:12 in Chapter 4-3. I can believe that Paul believed what he wrote, but he was twisting the Scriptures to justify his belief in Jesus, as Messiah, when so many Jews did not.

2 Cor 5:21 – "*For He made him who knew no sin to be sin for us, that we might become the righteousness of God in him*", citing Isaiah 53:6, 9. The contentious Isaiah 53 – the "him" in verse 6 is not "**H**im", aka Jesus, but the nations that inflicted punishment on Israel. The Christian interpretation of verse 9 is the opposite of what is written: according to the Gospels, Jesus died with the wicked, and was buried with the rich, entirely contrary to the NKJV version of Isaiah: they made his grave with the wicked, but with the rich at his death. As for Jesus knowing no sin, I disagree. I know from experience that my contention is not accepted by Christians, but the narrative of Luke 2:41-50 says to me that Jesus disobeyed his parents, and irrespective of why he did so, he nevertheless sinned. That aside, where in the Old Testament does it prophesy that *He made him who knew no sin to be sin for us*?

2 Cor 6:2 – "For He says: '*In an acceptable time I heard you, and in that day of salvation I have helped you*'. Behold, now is the accepted time; behold, now is the day of salvation", citing Isaiah 49:8. The wording of the quotation is acceptable, except for the tense of the verbs – it is future tense in Isaiah. Now let us read of God's promised help: "*I will protect you, and I will make you the people of the covenant, to **restore the land** and to cause you to **inherit desolate heritages**.*" [emphasis mine] Did that happen in Jesus' time, or that of Paul? On the contrary: thus, this cannot be prophecy fulfillment.

Galatians

Gal 2:20 – "I have been crucified with Christ … *who loved me and gave himself for me*", the NKJV citing Isaiah 53:12, which I have previously disputed.

Gal 3:8 – "And the Scripture, foreseeing that God would justify the Gentiles by faith, preached the gospel to Abraham beforehand, saying, '*In you all the nations shall be blessed*'". The NKJV cites five verses in Genesis regarding the nations being blessed, and I am pleased to see the word *nations*, not *Gentiles*, as in other places. There is no disputing this quotation, but connecting this verse to the previous statements is invalid. Firstly, nowhere in the Hebrew Scriptures is there any mention of God justifying the Gentiles by faith. I cannot know what Paul meant by "justify", but Strongs Concordance gives it as, *dikaioó*: to show to be righteous, declare righteous. No-one is righteous merely by faith, for as in the Gospel: "And they (Zacharias and Elizabeth) were both righteous before God, walking in all the commandments and ordinances of the Lord blameless" (Luke 1:6). Righteous means *right standing* before God, and faith alone cannot achieve that, for even Satan has faith in God (James 2:19). Secondly, the wording: "*the Scripture preached the Gospel to Abraham*", is decidedly odd. I will let it pass, as I do not believe that it is important in the context of prophecy fulfillment. In summary, the Hebrew Scriptures make clear that the blessings the nations would receive would be acceptance of God, as the one and only God.

Gal 4:4 – "*But when the fullness of time had come, God sent forth His son, born of a woman, born under the law*", the NKJV citing Genesis 49:10 and 3:15, and Isaiah 7:14. *Shiloh* in Genesis 49:10 is the Messiah in the *End of Days*, not an *interim* Messiah. We briefly reviewed Genesis 3:15 in John 13:18, Chapter 4-5. This passage deserves a far more comprehensive treatment, but is outside the scope of this study. We discussed Isaiah 7:14 in Chapter 4-2, Virgin Birth Prophesied? My conclusions, as before, were that there was no evidence of prophecy fulfillment.

Ephesians

Eph 2:20 – "*Having been built on the foundation of the apostles and prophets, Jesus Christ Himself being the chief cornerstone*", citing Psalm 118:22. I have no problem with Jesus being considered the chief cornerstone of the religion which developed from his teachings, but the prophets were not his foundation. Chapter 3-7 was devoted to this claim of prophecy fulfillment regarding the chief cornerstone.

Eph 4:8 – "*When he ascended on high, He led captivity captive, and gave gifts to men*", quoting Psalm 68:18. See the comments on Luke 24:51, Chapter 4-4.

Eph 4:10 – "*He who descended is also the one who ascended far above all the heavens, that he might fill all things*", the NKJV again citing Psalm 68:18. Making such statements is evidence of what the writer believed, but belief is not evidence of prophecy fulfillment.

Eph 5:14 – "Therefore He says: *Awake you who sleep, arise from the dead, and Christ will give you light*", the NKJV citing Isaiah 26:19 and 60:1. This is the only occasion where the NKJV cites these two verses in Isaiah. The first verse speaks of the revivification of the dead at the End of Days, and as the dead did not arise in Jesus' times, this prophecy cannot have been fulfilled. Verse 60:1 follows the theme of 59:20, "A redeemer will come to Zion", with Isaiah addressing Jerusalem, assuring her that the redemption is at hand, and that never again will she be deprived of her children. It is believed that Paul wrote this letter to the Ephesians from Rome, whilst in prison there, circa 62 CE. Had he waited a few years, he would have found himself in error, for far from being redeemed, Jerusalem was destroyed, and the children scattered or killed. As evidence of prophecy fulfillment, this is another fail.

Philippians

Phil 2:9 – "*Therefore God also has highly exalted him, and given him the name which is above every name*", citing Isaiah 52:13, and Psalms 68:18 and 110:1. We have been here before, see Luke 24:51, Chapter 4-4. A statement is evidence of what author believes, not evidence of a fact.

Colossians

Col 3:1 – "If then you were raised with Christ, seek those things which are above, where Christ is, *sitting at the right hand of God*", again citing Psalms 68:18 and 110:1.

First & Second Thessalonians

The NKJV does not annotate any verse as prophecy fulfillment.

First Timothy

1 Tim 1:15 – "This is a faithful saying and worthy of all acceptance, that *Christ Jesus came into the world to save sinners*, of whom I am chief", citing Isaiah 53:5 and 61:1, and Hosea 6:1-3. Putting aside the false modesty of the author, we have covered Isaiah 53 sufficiently in an earlier chapter. Isaiah 61:1 cannot be separated from the following verse: "to proclaim a year of favour unto Hashem, and a day of vengeance for our God, to comfort all mourners, to bring about for the mourners of Zion to give them splendour instead of ashes, oil of joy instead of mourning, a cloak of praise instead of a dim spirit" (v. 61:2, TJB) This refers to the *End of Days*, which we know, did not happen two thousand years ago. Also, Jesus said that he did not know when he would return: If he did not know, then he could not so proclaim, and therefore this is not a prophecy referring to Jesus. We can ignore Hosea 6:1-3 as superfluous in this context, besides which we have examined its relevance in earlier commentary.

There are no annotations of prophecy fulfillment in Second Timothy.

Titus

Tit 2:14 – "*who gave himself for us, that he might redeem us from every lawless deed and purify for himself his own special people, zealous for good works*", citing Isaiah 53:10-12, Ezekiel 37:23, and Exodus 15:16. Examining these in reverse order, "his own special people" is linked to Exodus 15 which speaks of the Children of Israel; there is nothing here concerning messianic prophecy. "Purify" is linked to Ezekiel 37:23, the context of which is God cleansing the Children of Israel by taking them from among the nations, gathering them in their own land, so that they would no longer defile themselves with their idols. This could be considered a "type", foretelling of a future cleansing, but it is far from a prophecy. Isaiah 53 we have covered before. Whilst Titus speaks of Jesus purifying his own special people, John tells us that we should purify ourselves (1 John 3:3), but perhaps they both meant something different. Even so, if Titus was referring to *justification* by *substitutionary atonement*, we have no substantive evidence of this being prophesied.

Hebrews

I would reiterate that as best as I can discern, Paul was not the author of this book. Therefore, from an evidentiary perspective, there being no confidence in its authorship, and no chain of custody, its authority and credibility must be in question. Nevertheless, as Christianity has offered it into evidence by declaring it to be part of the canon of Christian Scripture, it is incumbent upon us to examine its claims.

Heb 1:3 – "*sat down at the right hand of the Majesty on high*", citing Psalm 110:1. We have examined this Psalm before, but should note that we have no evidence of Jesus sitting at the right hand of the Father, other than that he said that was where he would go. We only have his word, but if the evidence of him being the prophesied Messiah is inadequate, then his word carries no weight as evidence.

Heb 1:5 – "For which of the angels did He ever say: '*You are My Son, today I have begotten you?*'", quoting Psalm 2:7 and 2 Samuel 7:14. Using the history of King David, to exalt Jesus above the angels, seems a very odd way of preaching. Though the NKJV does not annotate it as such, I strongly suspect that these were not the OT verses that the author of Hebrews had in mind. I suspect reference to statements in the Gospels.

Heb 1:6 – "But when He again brings the firstborn into the world, He says: '*Let all the angels of God worship Him*'", the NKJV citing Psalms 89:27 and 97:7, and Deuteronomy 32:43. You can read Deuteronomy for yourselves, but I am perplexed as to its relevance. Neither of the Psalms have anything to say about angels worshipping anyone, but the point is that the verse is referring to the Second Coming, and thus cannot be considered a prophecy fulfillment.

Heb 1:8 – "But to the Son He says: '*Your throne, O God, is forever and ever; a sceptre of righteousness is the sceptre of Your kingdom*'", accurately quoting Psalm 45:6. According to the Sages, this Psalm was written by the sons of Korah: Assir, Elkanah, and Abiasaph (see Exodus 6:24), so I am unsure of the origin of "to the Son He says". Rashi's commentary states:

> "They were originally part of their father's conspiracy, but at the time of the revolt they disassociated themselves. When all those who were around them were swallowed up when the earth opened its mouth, their place remained in the earth's mouth in accord with what is stated in the Bible, '*The sons of Korah did not die*' (Numbers 26:11). It was in the earth's mouth that they sang a hymn of thanksgiving and [from there that] they ascended, and it was there that they composed these [eleven] psalms [attributed to them: Pss.42; 44-49; 84; 85; 87; 88]. Divine inspiration rested upon them, and they prophesied concerning the Exiles and concerning the destruction of the Temple and concerning the kingship of the Davidic dynasty."[6]

Despite mention of prophecy, what part of Hebrew 1:8, as above, could be considered messianic prophecy fulfillment? One might also note: "A star shall come out of Jacob; a sceptre shall rise out of Israel, and batter the brow of Moab, and destroy all the sons of tumult." (Numbers 24:20) In the NKJV, this is flagged as a prophecy to be fulfilled, but by whom? *Star* and *sceptre* are metaphors for a leader, and must be understood in context. This prophecy relates to King David, although some Christian commentators interpret it as a prophecy of the Jewish *mashiach*, and thus Jesus, though obviously in his second coming.

Heb 1:9 - "*You have loved righteousness and hated lawlessness; therefore God, Your God, has anointed you with the oil of gladness more than your companions*", accurately quoting Psalm 45:7. Now, the tricky part of Psalm 45 is when you get to verses 9-15, with king's daughters, accompanied by the virgins, her companions, being brought to you. Who is "you", and for what purpose are these women brought to the king's palace? The wording is genteel, but the meaning is clear, except if you read the NKJV version, perhaps because the latter does not like the implications in the original Hebrew, which reads: "Succeeding your fathers will be your sons; you will appoint them leaders throughout the land" (v. 17, TJB). The verse numbering in the NKJV is a little different, with the corresponding verse rendered as "Instead of your fathers shall be your sons", which makes no sense at all. There is no point in being squeamish about this – the king's daughter was brought to the palace for the purpose of procreation, leading to the sons succeeding the fathers. With that in mind, this could not be a prophecy of Jesus, the virgin, with no sons of his own.

The NKJV also cites Isaiah 61:1, 3, which are slightly more relevant, but as we have seen before, Isaiah 61 is not prophetic of Jesus as Messiah (see Matthew 11:5 in Chapter 4-2).

Heb 1:13 – "But to which of the angels has He ever said: "*Sit at My right hand, till I make your enemies your footstool?*", quoting Psalm 110:1. Apart from this Psalm not being about Jesus, this passage in Hebrews is simply the author's method of convincing his audience that Jesus is higher than the angels, whilst man is lower, which could be true but is hardly prophetic. Notice that it is only in the Book of Hebrews that the issue of mankind being higher or lower than the angels is discussed, suggesting that this was a theological development of the author himself. Whilst both the Christian and some Jewish Scriptures speak of man being created lower, or a little less, than the angels (Psalm 8:5), some Jewish scholars question whether "angels" is the correct translation. I cannot know the truth, but pass on the following comments from Rashi for you to consider: "You have made him a little less than God, when You empowered Joshua to make the sun stand still (Joshua 10:12-14) and to dry up the Jordan (Joshua 3:9-17), and Moses to split the [Reed] Sea (Exodus 14:21), and to ascend to heaven (Exodus 19:3, 'Moses went up to God'), and Elijah to revive the dead (1 Kings 17:17-21)."[7]

An important point is mention of *son of man* (v. 4). Even the NKJV editors decided that initial capitals were not appropriate, accepting that the term conveyed the same sense as in Ezekiel – man is much lower than God. Now, when we read of the honours that God has bestowed upon mankind, crowning "him with glory and honour", and giving him "dominion over the works of Your hands" (v.6), in what way could mankind be lower than the angels, who are but servants of God, with no authority to act independently as man can do? Were the angels made in the image of God, as was man? I can understand why Rashi was not confident of the translation, *angels*.

<u>Heb 2:12</u> – *"I will declare Your name to my brethren; in the midst of the assembly I will sing praise to you"*, quoting Psalm 22:22. Allow me to contend that it is nonsensical to try to make this a prophecy of Jesus as Messiah. This is what happened in every synagogue, and every church to this day. If everybody does it, it cannot be prophetic of the Messiah, that much should be obvious. Under the rules of evidence, it would not even rate as circumstantial evidence.

<u>Heb 2:13</u> – *"I will put my trust in Him"*. I mean really, how can this be a specific prophecy of the Messiah, when people throughout the ages have put their trust in others, for a variety of reasons? You may recall that many Jews put their trust in Simon bar Kokhba as Messiah, leading up to the Jewish revolt against the Romans, 132-136 CE. At least he was attempting what the Jews believed the Messiah was expected to do. The NKJV cites 2 Samuel 22:3. 2 Samuel 22 begins: *"David spoke to Hashem the words of this song, on the day that Hashem delivered him from the hand of all his enemies and from the hand of Saul."* No wonder David would have said, *"I will put my trust in Him"*, and no, it is not prophetic of the Messiah.

As for the second part, *"Here am I and the children God has given me"*, quoting Isaiah 8:18, the full text reads: "Behold, I and the children whom Hashem has given me are signs and symbols for Israel, from Hashem, Master of Legions, Who dwells in Mount Zion." The children to whom Isaiah is referring are his two sons: *Shaerjashub* [A Remainder Will Return] (v. 7:3), and *Maher-shalal-hash-baz* [Plunder Hastens; Spoil Quickens] (v. 8:4). Their names were divinely ordained signs for events that will befall the people of Israel. I believe it to be twisting of Scripture to attempt to turn this into a messianic prophecy. Certainly, one can find parallels if one already believes Jesus to be the Messiah, but that is putting the cart before the horse so to speak, or more formally, affirming the consequent.

<u>Heb 5:6</u> – "As He also says in another place: *'You are a priest forever according to the order of Melchizedek'*", quoting Psalm 110:4. In Chapter 3-8, I explained that according to those who should know best, the Jewish scribes and Sages, David was not the author of Psalm 110: it was written **about** him, not **by** him. Thus, in verse 4, the Lord is God, and the priest is David. Neither Melchizedek nor David was a Levite, of the anointed priestly tribe; that was why David was a priest like Melchizedek, although not entirely – Melchizedek was the king of Gentiles (Salem), whilst David

was the anointed king of Israel. I wonder whether the author of Hebrews understood the distinction? Kings of Israel were expected to behave as priests in their example of service to God. That aside, the Book of Hebrews is the only place where we find this representation of Jesus, and given the dubious authority of the text, we cannot consider it as evidence of a messianic prophecy fulfilment.

Heb 7:14-16 – rather than quote the text in full, you can read it for yourselves, the author continues to attempt justification of why Jesus is *a priest forever according to the order of Melchizedek.* Little remains to be said: If you believe that Psalm 110 contains a prophecy of the Messiah, you can accept the contention, but if not, then all we are reading is one man's understanding, likely based on an unreliable Greek translation of the Hebrew Scriptures. I would recommend reading through the Psalm in full, and on the basis that it is prophetic, consider whether it relates to the First or Second Coming. If it is the Second, which is how I would read it, then it cannot be evidence that Jesus was the Messiah in his First Coming, and that is the real issue. Nothing of what the Messiah will do in the Last Days can be accepted as evidence that Jesus was the Messiah two thousand years ago. What may happen in the future is not evidence of prophecy fulfillment in the past.

Heb 6:17 – as above.

Heb 6:21 – as above.

Heb 8:8 – No doubt the reader is familiar with the subject matter here, the prophecy in Jeremiah 31:31. I would refer the reader back to Chapter 3-5, for the evidence that has convinced me that Jeremiah's prophecy concerns the *End of Days.*

Heb 10:5 – "Therefore when he came into the world, he said: '*Sacrifice and offering you did not desire, but a body you have prepared for Me*'", misquoting Psalm 40:6-8. I say, misquote, because the wording in the NKJV Old Testament reads: "Sacrifice and offering You did not desire; My ears you have opened." This agrees with the wording in the Hebrew Scriptures. Now read verse 7, and you will see that reference to ears is consonant with the theme of the Psalm. We need proceed no further with this claimed prophecy fulfillment, for the obvious reason that there was no prophecy of: *a body you have prepared for Me.*

Heb 10:12 – *"But this Man, after He had offered one sacrifice for sins forever, sat down at the right hand of God"*, the NKJV citing once again, Psalm 110:1. Methinks the NKJV editors had a rubber stamp, because this Psalm has nothing to say of a sacrifice for sins, and we have no evidence of Jesus sitting at the right hand of God, only numerous unsubstantiated claims of such.

Heb 10:13 – *"from that time waiting till his enemies are made his footstool"*, citing Psalm 110:1. The sense of future (waiting till) invalidates this as prophecy already fulfilled. See also Chapter 3-8.

Heb 10:16 – *"This is the covenant that I will make with them after those days"*, quoting Jeremiah 31:31. *Those days* are, as yet, future, so this cannot be prophecy already fulfilled. See also Chapter 3-5.

Heb 12:2 – "Looking unto Jesus, the author and finisher of our faith, who for the joy that was set before him *endured the cross*, despising shame, and has *sat down at the right hand of the throne of God"*, citing Psalms 69:7, 19, and 110:1. We have covered these adequately before, my conclusion being these are not evidence of prophecy fulfillment.

Heb 13:20 – "Now may the God of peace *who brought up our Lord Jesus from the dead*, that great *Shepherd of the sheep*, through the *blood of the everlasting covenant*." Taking the NKJV references in sequence, it is claimed that Jesus being *raised from the dead* was prophesied in Psalm 16:10-11 and Hosea 6:2. We have covered these earlier in this chapter, see Acts 2:3 and Acts 10:40. Jesus being *Shepherd of the sheep* is claimed to have been prophesied in Psalm 23:1, Isaiah 40:11, and Isaiah 63:11. Psalm 23, one of the best know poems of David, was referring to God as David understood Him, not Jesus. Using this as prophecy fulfillment evidence is begging the question (affirming the consequence) because it assumes that Jesus is God, and is thus unacceptable as evidence. Isaiah 40:2 refutes the claim of Jesus being the shepherd of verse 11: "Speak comfort to Jerusalem, and cry out to her, that her warfare is ended, that her iniquity is pardoned" – did these events accompany Jesus as shepherd? Isaiah 63:11 does refer to a single shepherd in the NKJV, but in the Hebrew, the full context reads: "They [then] remembered the days of old, of Moses [with] his people. Where is the One Who brought [the Israelites] out of the sea, together with the shepherds of His flock?" These shepherds were ordinary folk, not prophetic of the Messiah.

Finally, *blood of the everlasting covenant* is claimed as prophecy fulfillment of Zechariah 9:11, which reads: "Also you, through the blood of your covenant I will have released your prisoners from the pit in which there is no water." Note *blood of your covenant*, not *blood of the everlasting covenant*. We have visited Zechariah 9 before in a different context, but my previous remarks are relevant here also. Read from verse 1: the prophecy concerned the land of Hadrach, and Damascus was where it would be fulfilled (its resting place). If you read through the following verses, Jesus does not accomplish what is prophesied there: "For I will bend Judah [as a bow] for Me; I will fill [the hand of] Ephraim with a bow; and I will stir up your children, O Zion, against your children, O Greece; and I will make you like the sword of a warrior" (Zech 9:13, TJB). Given that Jesus did none of these things, the remarks concerning blood of covenant cannot relate to Jesus either. According to the Jewish Sage, Radak, the blood concerns the circumcision covenant.

James

James 1:1 – "*To the twelve tribes which are scattered abroad*." James is not writing to the Gentiles, and so his words must be understood as the Jews of his time would have understood them. When he spoke of God, he meant the God Who revealed Himself at Sinai, and spoke through His prophets. When he said: "*But be doers of the word, and not hearers only, deceiving yourselves*", which word is more likely: Torah, or the words of Jesus? "*Pure and undefiled religion before God and the Father is this … and to keep oneself unspotted from the world.*" Again, how does one do this, other than by being Torah observant? Yes, James does encourage his readers to have faith in Jesus, but faith in Jesus to accomplish what? James tells his readers how to "*really fulfill the royal law according to the Scripture*" (James 2:8) – again a reference to Mosaic Law. He follows this with quotations from Jesus, thereby demonstrating that the Law of Christ was no different to the Law of God, as spoken to the Israelites.

James contends with how Christianity has understood works of the law, clarifying that: "*faith by itself, if it does not have works, is dead.*" (v. 2:17) As he offered to demonstrate: "*Show me your faith without your works, and I will show you my faith by my works.*" (v. 2:18) Whom should we believe, Paul, who never met Jesus, or James, the brother of Jesus, who accompanied him throughout his public life? "*You see then that a man is justified by his works, and not by faith only.*" (v. 2:24) "*For as the body without the spirit is dead, so faith without works is dead.*" (v. 2:26) As an aside, Martin Luther, he who declared that "the law, when it is in his true sense, doth nothing else but reveal sin, engender wrath, accuse and terrify men", sought to have James' Epistle removed from the bible. His motivation should be obvious.

James 2:19 – "*You believe that there is one God. You do well. Even the demons believe – and tremble!*" James does not say: draw near to Jesus, but rather "*submit to God … draw near to God, and He will draw near to you.*" (v.4:7-8) The twelve tribes would have understood this to mean the God with whom their forefathers made the covenant at Sinai. Nowhere, in his letter to the twelve tribes, does James even suggest that Jesus was God, or that God was Triune. If that was a doctrine of James, or a doctrine current during his time as leader of the Christian congregation in Jerusalem, why did he make no mention of the Father, Son, and Holy Spirit? To my mind, there is only one logical answer: James was not aware of, and did not believe in, the doctrine of the Trinity. He believed that his brother, Jesus, was the Jewish *mashiach* foretold in the Hebrew Scriptures, but as understood by the Sages.

Summarising James, I would draw your attention to James' view of the Law, and his understanding, consonant with the Judaism of his time, that man is justified, or more accurately, is seen as righteous by God, by being obedient, just as Zacharias and Elizabeth were (Luke 1:6). Justification, as defined in Christianity, was never a concept in Judaism, and still is not. Righteousness is the issue – right standing with God, and that is achieved through obedience and repentance, nothing more is required.

Despite its position in the New Testament sequence, toward the very end, numerous scholars have opined that this was the earliest letter written, and thus represents the thinking in the Jerusalem congregation before Paul began spreading his gospel. This is significant, for it is the only written evidence of that period. Rather than reject James, as Martin Luther and others have done, it might be wiser to accept his writings as more representative of the teachings of Jesus, and reject those writings which are contrary to the message of James.

Peter

1 Peter 1:3 – "*Blessed be the God and Father of our Lord Jesus Christ*". The verse is not flagged as prophecy fulfillment, but I thought that, nevertheless, it was worthy of comment. Think about this: The God who announced Himself at Sinai is both the God, and Father, of Jesus. If the Father is the God of the son, how can the son be God? Was Peter telling his readers that Jesus was not God?

1 Peter 1:19 – "*with the precious blood of Christ, as of a lamb without blemish and without spot*", referencing Exodus 12:5 and Isaiah 53:7. Attempting to draw a parallel with Exodus is inappropriate: the lamb was always to be "of the first year". Equating an adult with a lamb, less than one year old, is irrational. Referencing Isaiah 53:7 is also inappropriate. Apart from Jesus not being the *suffering servant* (see Chapter 3-2), Isaiah 53:7 has nothing to say about *a lamb without blemish*. Isaiah employs a metaphor: "as a lamb to the slaughter … as a sheep before its shearers is silent, so he opened not his mouth." What has that to do with 1 Peter 1:19?

1 Peter 2:6 – "*Behold I lay in Zion a chief cornerstone*"; see Chapter 3-7.

1 Peter 2:7 – "*The stone which the builders rejected*"; as above.

1 Peter 2:8 – "*A stone of stumbling and a rock of offense*"; as above.

1 Peter 2:22 – "*Who committed no sin*"; see Chapter 3-2. Incidentally, I believe that Jesus did sin as a boy: see Luke 2:43-50.

1 Peter 2:23 – "*who, when he was reviled, did not revile in return*", quoting Isaiah 53:7. See Matthew 27:14, but that aside, note the change in wording that entirely changes the meaning. Not saying a word, is not synonymous with not reviling in return, although not reviling in return, could be the same as not saying a word. My point is: Why did the author choose to convey the intent of *revile*? When was that ever an issue?

1 Peter 2:24 – "*who bore our sins in his own body*", again a misinterpretation of the *suffering servant*.

1 Peter 2:25 – "*For you were like sheep going astray*", referencing Isaiah 53:5-6. As above.

2 Peter refers to prophecy, without mentioning any specific prophecy fulfillment.

Summarising these letters attributed to Peter the Apostle, his understanding of prophecy fulfillment is entirely contingent upon Jesus being the *suffering servant* of Isaiah 53. If this suffering servant is indeed Israel, as Judaism teaches, and I concur, then this Christian contention is without merit.

John

1-3 John - The letters attributed to John the Apostle, the "one whom Jesus loved", contain no references to specific prophecy fulfillments. This is not surprising, especially the second and third, as they are addressed to individual people and are pastoral in nature. First John is also pastoral, but addressed to a wider audience to encourage them in their faith, and commitment to God. Curiously, John seems to confirm Jewish teachings: "*If we confess our sins, He is faithful and just to forgive us our sins, and to cleanse us from all unrighteousness*" (1 John 1:9). That does seem to refute the necessity for substitutionary atonement.

Now ponder that for a moment: why would God be "*faithful*" in forgiving our sins when we repent? Even more, why would God be "*just*"? God would only be faithful, if He had promised to do so, which is what the Hebrew Scriptures teach. To be just, means to be fair, or in the administration of law, properly determining rights, and assigning rewards or punishments. That God forgives those who repent, rather than punishing sinners irrespective, means that in His sense of justice, that is the proper course of action. Now, the relevance of this is whether there was any need of a redeemer from sin. This verse in 1 John, accords with the Jewish understanding of the Hebrew Scriptures, that God wants us to do our best, but as we have been given the ability to sin, a decision of God from before Creation, God foreknew that we would, but declared it *just* that we should be forgiven, and cleansed of all unrighteousness, if we truly repent. Thus – no need for *substitutionary atonement*.

"*Now by this we know that we know Him, if we keep His* [the Father's] *commandments*" (1 John 2:3, also 3:24). "Brethren, I write no new commandment to you, but an old commandment which you had from the beginning" (v. 2:7) – I wonder which commandments John had in mind? We will come back to John's eschatological view, verses 2:17-18, in the next section. When John spoke of the *many antichrists ... who went out from us*, was he speaking of the Nazarenes, or was he referring to the Hellenic Christians, disciples of Paul, who were in truth teaching a different Gospel, teaching converts to not obey Torah? Verse 22 gives the answer, but only partially. The author then refutes Jesus (or Matthew); compare these two verses:

- o   "Anyone who speaks a word against the Son of Man, it will be forgiven him" (Matthew 12:32).
- o   "Whoever denies the Son does not have the Father either" (1 John 2:23).

Both statements cannot be true, so the suggestion is that John's statement represents a developed theology. Verses 3:1-2 suggests that John's perception of the lawless ones are those that do not know God, rather than those who do not acknowledge Jesus. Rather than continue analysing what is to me, a rather confusing exposition, let me finish with perhaps two of the most contentious verses in the entire New Testament:

> "For there are three that bear witness in heaven: the Father, the Word, and the Holy Spirit; and these three are one. And there are three that bear witness on earth: the Spirit, the water, and the blood; and these three agree as one." (1 John 7-8)

These verses are so contentious, that they have even been given a name:

> "The *Comma Johanneum*, also called the **Johannine Comma** or the **Heavenly Witnesses**, is a comma (a short clause) found in Latin manuscripts of the First Epistle of John at 5:7-8. The comma first appeared in the Vulgate manuscripts of the 9th century. The first Greek manuscript that contains the comma dates from the 15th century. The comma is absent from the Ethiopic, Aramaic, Syriac, Slavic, Armenian, Georgian, and Arabic translations of the Greek New Testament. The scholarly consensus is that that passage is a Latin corruption that entered the Greek manuscript tradition in some subsequent copies. As the comma does not appear in the manuscript tradition of other languages, the debate is mainly limited to the English-speaking world due to the King James Only movement."[8]

This is significant, because Christian apologists use these disputed verses as proof of the Trinity. When these verses are removed, the case is weakened significantly. The question becomes: Why were they added, and by whom? I have long argued against the bible, whatever version you favour, being the inerrant Word of God, because far too many hands have redacted it with theological annotations, as if God's Word was somehow inadequate, or insufficient for His purposes. If John's narrative in Revelations includes the warning: *"If anyone adds to these things … and if anyone takes away from the book of this prophecy"* (Revelation 22:18-19), why have Christian translators thought it acceptable to add to other writings of John, especially as they assert that such words were divinely inspired? Is the guidance of the Holy Spirit inadequate?

Deuteronomy 13:1 warns against anyone finding God's Word insufficient: *"The entire word that I command you, that shall you observe to do; you shall not add to it, and you shall not subtract from it"* (TJB). Thus, if Jesus did not fulfill the Law in the sense that Christianity asserts, perhaps heeding the words in Deuteronomy 13 is in order, lest God finds you guilty of doing what He said not to do. In the context of prophecy, and prophecy fulfillment, consider that if Jesus did change the Law, or someone said that he did, were these prophetic words fulfilled in Christianity?

> "If there should stand up in your midst a prophet, or a dreamer of a dream, and he will produce to you a sign or a wonder, and the sign or wonder comes about, of which he spoke saying. 'Let us follow gods of others that you did not know, and we shall worship them!' Do not hearken to the words of that prophet or to that dreamer of a dream, for Hashem, your God, is testing you to know whether you love Hashem, your God, with all your heart and with all your soul. Hashem, your God, shall you follow and Him shall you fear; His commandments shall you observe and to His voice shall you hearken; Him shall you serve, and to Him shall you cleave. And the prophet and that dreamer of a dream shall be put to death, for he had spoken perversion against Hashem, your God … and you shall destroy the evil from your midst." (Deuteronomy 13:2-6).

Sounds clear enough to me. This verse is also relevant: "*Accursed is the one who will not uphold the words of this Torah, to perform them; and the entire people shall say 'Amen'.*" (Deuteronomy 27:26). I say, *Amen*, but does Christianity?

Jude

<u>Jude 1:18</u> – "*who told you that there would be mockers in the last time*". Why was Jude referring the *last time*, i.e. the End of Days? What was in his mind? What was he expecting to happen?

Revelation

<u>Rev 1:5</u> – "And from Jesus Christ, *the faithful witness*, the *firstborn from the dead*", citing Isaiah 55:4 in support of *the faithful witness*, and Psalm 89:27 in support of *firstborn from the dead*. The entry in Isaiah does refer to the Messiah, but quoting the passage is not evidence that Jesus was the Messiah – again, begging the question. Psalm 89 was written by Ethan the Ezrahite; he begins: "Of Hashem's kindness I will sing forever; I will make Your faithfulness known to every generation with my mouth". If you read through from verse 20, you will see that Ethan was speaking of King David, with no suggestion of a messianic prophecy. Use of the term, *firstborn*, is intriguing, for Israel also was called by God, His firstborn son. For a commentary on the significance of this term, see here[9].

<u>Rev 3:7</u> – "These things says He who is holy, He who is true, *He who has the key of David, He who opens and no one shuts, and shuts and no one opens*", quoting Isaiah 9:7, 22:22, and Job 12:14. I find it interesting that these OT passages are mentioned nowhere else in the NT. I am unsure of how Isaiah 9:7 relates here, and even more unsure of how 22:22 applies, but as this is the Book of Revelation, I should not be surprised. There is an interesting Christian commentary online here[10], and if nothing else, it evidences the uncertainty of others. As best as I can determine, the argument goes that David was a *type* of Jesus Christ, and holding the key to House of David, Eliakim son of Hilkiah, is also seen as a *type* of Jesus who holds the key to Scripture, or to the kingdom of heaven. These

are allusions, rather than prophecies, so I would not accept the NKJV annotation of messianic prophecy fulfillment - it is just a stretch too far, one that would be unnecessary if there really was more substantive evidence.

Rev 5:12 – "*Worthy is the Lamb who was slain*", citing Isaiah 53:7. Verse 53:6 says "we have all strayed like sheep, each of us turning his own way, and Hashem inflicted upon him the iniquity of us all": Who was "him"? As I argued in Chapter 3-2, it was the Nation of Israel, not the future Messiah. That aside, Isaiah wrote of being silent "*like a sheep being led to the slaughter, or a ewe that is silent before her shearers*": these are metaphors, and are not prophecies of a *Lamb who was slain*. These were adult sheep, not lambs, and were not yet slain if before the shearers. This is not evidence of fulfillment of messianic prophecy, even though parallels can be found between Isaiah 53 and the final days of Jesus' life – note final days only.

Rev 19:13 – "*He was clothed with a robe dipped in blood*", citing Isaiah 63:2-3. The NKJV editors would have us believe … well, I am not sure. Isaiah 52 ends with God announcing to the ends of the earth, that the time of Israel's redemption had come. The Children of Israel will be called "the Holy People, the Redeemed of Hashem", and Jerusalem will be called, "Sought After", "The City Not Forsaken". Well, certainly, Jerusalem is well sought after, by Jews, Muslims, and Christians, but the Jews are not called by Christianity: "the Redeemed of Hashem". On the contrary, from the early days of the Church of Rome, the Jews have continued to be despised as "Christ Killers", accused of deicide, and of taking the blood of innocent children to make their Passover bread. Their redemption is still future.

Chapter 63 "is a description of God's vengeance for Edom's persecution of His people, described through a dialogue between an anonymous onlooker and God Himself, as if He were a warrior coming from a destructive attack on the Edomite city of Bozrah"[11]. Rather than see this as a prophecy of Jesus as Messiah, Christians should take this as a warning, that *those who curse Israel will be cursed*. Read the chapter in full. So then, we have the lifeblood of grapes, splattered on a man's clothing whilst he had trodden in a winepress, being a prophecy of Jesus being scourged and bloodied, represented as being *clothed with a robe dipped in blood*. I doubt that the Apostle John, whilst writing this verse, was connecting it to Isaiah 63:2-3.

Summary

As to whether Jesus fulfilled prophecies as claimed in these writings, certain things should be obvious, the most significant being: Was Jesus the *suffering servant* of Isaiah 53? Second in importance, to my mind at least, is the eschatological temper of the times. Jesus failed to fulfill the prophecies concerning the redemption of the Jewish people, the overthrow of their oppressors, and the return to Jerusalem, to live forever in peace under the rule of a king, of the line of David. No Jew could have missed that, and thus, it would appear that the followers of Jesus reconsidered their expectations of his First Coming, transferring them to an *imminent* Second. Later we shall explore the evidence for them having this expectation.

One common evidential error is *affirming the consequent.* On many occasions, fulfillment of a prophecy was dependent upon Jesus being the prophesied Messiah, or more, a deity, Second Person of the Trinity. Under the rules of evidence, and even common sense really, we must be presented with plausible evidence that these were so, before the prophecies concerning them can be said to have been fulfilled. The case before us, in this study, is to evaluate the evidence that Jesus fulfilled messianic prophecies – it is invalid to proceed with the presumption that he did, and then attempt to reinterpret the prophecies in that light.

REFERENCES:

1. Scherman, Rabbi Nosson, *The Tanach*, Mesorah Publications, ArtScroll English Edition, Brooklyn, NY, 2011, p. 861
2. Dewey, Arthur J., *The Authentic Letters of Paul*, Polebridge Press, Salem, OR, 2010, p. 166
3. Dunn, James D.G., *Jesus, Paul and the Law*, Westminster / John Knox Press, Louisville, KY, 1990, p. 11
4. Scherman, *Ibid*, p. 650
5. Beale, G.K., *The Right Doctrine from the Wrong Texts? Essays on the Use of the Old Testament in the New*, Baker Academic, Grand Rapids, MI, 1994, p. 180
6. Gruber, Mayer I., *Rashi's Commentary on Psalms*, The Jewish Publication Society, Philadelphia, PA, 2007, p. 335
7. *Ibid*, pp. 198-199

8. https://en.wikipedia.org/wiki/Comma_Johanneum
9. https://en.wikipedia.org/wiki/Firstborn_(Judaism)
10. http://biblehub.com/revelation/3-7.htm
11. Scherman, *Ibid*, pp. 678-679

CHAPTER 4-9

SUMMARY OF PART 4

*"One man's generalisation is another man's succinct yet
profound summation of a complex theory or argument."*
~ Stewart Stafford, American actor, journalist, and author ~

What are we to make of all this?

In reviewing the four Gospels, where the NKJV flags the verse in relation to prophecy fulfillment, we find the following statistics:

- 100 individual Old Testament verses quoted or annotated.
- 61 of these referenced verses are flagged as prophetic in Old Testament.
- 104 Gospel verses are annotated as prophecy being fulfilled.
- 22 Gospel verses where the author explicitly claimed prophecy fulfillment.
- 24 Gospel verses of prophecy future with Old Testament reference.
- 34 Gospel verses quoting only Psalms
- 5 Gospel verses without and Old Testament reference.

Firstly note the inconsistencies. 39 Old Testament verses are annotated in the Gospels as being prophetic, yet in the Old Testament itself, they are not so annotated. In only 22% of cases does the New Testament author explicitly claim prophecy fulfillment – the rest are annotations by the NKJV editors. 5 Gospel verses are annotated as being in fulfillment of prophecy, yet the NKJV editors could not find that prophesied event in the Old Testament.

In reviewing the Old Testament verses quoted, 34% were from Isaiah (8 from Ch. 53), 15% from the Psalms, and 11% from Daniel. Accepting Daniel as a prophet, to avoid argument, 17% of the verses quoted were from non-prophetic books.

In reviewing the other books of the New Testament, where the NKJV flags the verse in relation to prophecy fulfillment, we find the following statistics:

- 137 individual Old Testament verses quoted or annotated.
- 58 of these referenced verses are flagged as prophetic in Old Testament.
- 98 verses are annotated as prophecy being fulfilled.
- 5 verses where the author explicitly claimed prophecy fulfillment.
- 16 verses of prophecy future: 8 referring to the church, and 8 referring to the End of Days.
- 44 verses quoting only Psalms
- 33 verses without and Old Testament reference.

Again note the inconsistencies between what is flagged in the New Testament as prophecy fulfillment, versus the corresponding verses in the Old Testament not being so flagged. Whilst there are only 5 verses where the wording explicitly states fulfillment of prophecy, there are many more alluding to an Old Testament verse suggesting that such was a prophecy, which could be said to be a little disingenuous. However, I am probably being unfair if the author truly believed what he wrote – if he saw a match with the Old Testament, we can question his judgement, but not his integrity.

Some of the annotations by the NKJV editors are, how should I put it politely … ludicrous. For example, this verse has been flagged as in fulfillment of prophecy: "But their minds were blinded. For until this day the same veil remains unlifted in the reading of the Old Testament, because the veil is taken away by Christ." (2 Corinthians 3:14) The prophecy supposedly fulfilled? Isaiah 6:9-10, which relate God instructing Isaiah regarding the people who were refusing to listen to His words conveyed through His Prophet. One could claim that the experience of Jesus was similar to that of Isaiah, but not that Isaiah's experience was a prophecy of what Jesus would experience. If that were so, one could claim that Isaiah's experience prophesied the experience of the other prophets who succeeded him, and even of the Pharisees who sat in Moses' seat (Matthew 23:2). Even more, there is no prophecy of the veil being taken away by the Messiah. Similarly, 2 Corinthians 5:21; where in the Old Testament does it prophesy that "He made him who knew no sin to be sin for us"?

Summary and Conclusions

The editors of the NKJV found far more instances of prophecy fulfillment, than the authors of the New Testament seemed to have done. This is interesting to my mind, for it demonstrates considerable theological development subsequent to that which preceded the literary phase of the New Testament. Scholars have commented on the latter, noting the development which must have occurred, and in Part 8, we will review the evidence that modern New Testament scholars attribute far greater scholarly competence to the New Testament authors than is usually admitted concerning the ordinary men that Jesus recruited.

In brief, concerning messianic prophecy fulfillment by Jesus, there is precious little evidence that would carry evidentiary weight in a court of law. The written evidence, and the annotations by the NKJV editors, may constitute proof to individual Christians, but it behoves them to review their own *rules of evidence* to re-evaluate what they believe. If the Bereans searched the Scriptures to see if it was so (Acts 17:11), each generation should do the same, rather than accept without question, the beliefs of previous generations.

CHAPTER 4-10

AN ASIDE -
UNDERSTANDING "HEEL"

"I will put enmity between you and the woman, and between your offspring and her offspring. He will pound your head, and you will bite his heel."
(Genesis 3:15)

The Jewish commentary on this passage reads:

> "Homiletically, the Sages derive from this description the proper tactics in the eternal war between man and the evil inclination, which is symbolised by the serpent. The *serpent* seduces the Jew to trample the commandments with his heel, and the Jew can prevail by using his head, meaning the study of Torah (*Midrash HaNe'elam*)."[1]

It is useful to ponder this commentary by Rabbi Berel Wein, one of Jewry's foremost historians. As is my predilection, I turn to Jewish commentaries to obtain clarity regarding obscure allusions in the Hebrew

Scriptures, rather than give preference to Christological interpretations. The Torah reading referred to here is *Parashas Eikev* "parashas" meaning "reading":

> "The word *eikev*, which is the name of this week's Torah reading, and is translated as "since" or "because", is associated with another Hebrew word, *akeiv*, meaning "heel." Rashi, the foremost commentator, already comments that this association indicates the Torah's warning against treating any of the *mitzvos* (religious duties) lightly, stepping upon them with one's heel in disdain, so to speak.
>
> The word *akeiv* in the sense of "heel" previously appears in the Torah regarding the birth of Esau and Jacob. There, the Torah records that when the twins were born, Jacob grasped the heel of Esau as they emerged into the world. The symbolism there once again conforms to the idea that Rashi conveys to us in this week's Torah reading. Esau steps on things with his heel. He destroys people and civilizations, holiness and lofty spirituality, by denigrating them, treating them as being insignificant and inconsequential, grinding them into nothingness with his heel.
>
> Jacob's -- Jewry's -- task in life is to hold unto Esau's heel, preventing him by his efforts from accomplishing that destructive goal. Apparently, he who controls the "heel" controls the fate and destiny of humankind. This is also the implicit message of this week's Torah reading — that listening to The Divine's word and not treating it with scorn or indifference is the key to maintaining a more human and peaceful society. Stepping on any of the values of Torah, no matter what the seeming ideological justifications for such behaviour at that time, leads to untold societal and personal harm.
>
> Be careful what one steps upon. It eventually rises up to bite back in return."[2]

In *Parashas Eikev* [because], Moses continues his closing address to the children of Israel, promising them that if they will fulfill the commandments (*mitzvot*) of the Torah, they will prosper in the Land they are about to conquer and settle in keeping with God's promise to their forefathers: "And it will be that as a consequence [*Eikev*] of listening to these judgments, guarding and doing them, that Hashem your God will guard for you the Covenant and the kindness which He swore to your fathers." (Deuteronomy 7:12)

It is easy to overlook the significance of the narration of the birth of Esau and Jacob in Genesis 25:24, and the continuation of the imagery from Genesis 3:15., but it is a mistake to do so. Remember that traditionally, these writings are from the hand of a single author. Whether or not the birth narrative is true as stated, is not as important as understanding the message of the story. The Jewish commentaries say that Jacob grasped Esau's heel because he wanted to prevent him being born first, so that he, Jacob, as the firstborn, would continue the spiritual mission of Abraham and Isaac. The imagery here is of Jacob being righteous and Esau, evil. A further commentary reads: "By grasping Esau's heel, the infant Jacob portended that Esau's period of domination will barely be complete before Jacob wrests it from him (*Rashi*), so that Jacob's ascendancy will come on the heels of Esau's"[3].

As is common in Jewish hermeneutics, more than one message is found in one passage, or in passages linked by words (*midrash*). Unlike the Christian doctrine of The Fall, and consequently all humanity being fundamentally evil, Judaism teaches that all are born with two inclinations or drives: good (*yetzer hatov*) and evil (*yetzer hara*). Our task in this life, just as John wrote: "everyone who has this hope in him, purifies himself as he is pure" (1 John 3:3), is to not allow our *yetzer hara* to dominate our *yetzer hatov*. God gave us the Torah to show us how to accomplish that. Thus, the allusion in Genesis 3:15 contains the same meaning as in Genesis 25:24 – beating Satan and evil to accomplish righteousness, just as was written concerning Zacharias and Elizabeth: "they were both righteous before God walking in all the commandments and ordinances of the Lord blameless" (Luke 1:6).

Note how Paul appears to have some understanding of this, where he quoted the Prophet Malachi (1:2-3): "As it is written, '*Jacob I have loved, but Esau I have hated*'." (Romans 9:13) The author of the Book of Hebrews did similarly: "lest there be any fornicator or profane person like Esau" (Hebrews 12:16). Any determination of immorality, as in the case of Esau, could only be based on Torah.

REFERENCES:

1. Rabbi Nosson, *The Chumash*, Scherman, Mesorah Publications, ArtScroll English Edition, Brooklyn, NY, 2009, p. 17
2. http://www.jewishworldreview.com/wein/wein_eikev18.php3#26g5SywMM0H0IgiF.99
3. Rabbi Nosson, *Ibid*, p. 127

PART 5

THE PSALMS AND PROVERBS

"The Psalter is the prayer book of Jesus Christ in the truest sense of the word."
~ Dietrich Bonhoeffer ~

I believe that Bonhoeffer had it right. Reiterating what was quoted in an earlier chapter:

> "Not all sacred teachings were meant as Divine messages to be conveyed to the people. Those are the Writings – so-called because they were to be written, rather than proclaimed as 'prophecies', but God ordained that they be preserved as part of Scripture. The reasons vary ... Perhaps the best example of a non-prophetic work that has a profound effect on countless millions of people is the Book of *Psalms*. King David is more than the 'Sweet Singer of Israel'. He is a musician of the soul, who plucks at the heartstrings of every Jew, and makes sacred music of every life experience.

Whatever a Jew needs, he finds in his Book of Psalms – gratitude, hope, prayer, aspiration, courage, insight. Millions of *Tehillin'lech* (i.e., little Books of *Psalms*) have soaked up infinite numbers of tears – tears that God treasures in His own treasury."[1]

As this Jewish commentator noted, the book: "evokes the image of King David, the sweet singer of Israel, whose quill recorded the longings and achievements, the heartbreak and inspiration of countless millions of people, from shepherd tents in the desert to penthouse towers in teeming cities."[2] If the Psalms were the basis of Jesus' prayers, what could he have been praying for, if not the same as David, and the millions of Jews before and since? There is no prayer, in the history of the Children of Israel, that their *voluntary* or *intentional* sins would be forgiven through the actions of a *sacrificial lamb*: they knew, from the Scriptures, that their sins could only be forgiven when repented. There were sacrifices for *unintentional* sins, but we will come back to that later. The prayers, as expressed in the Psalms, were not for the release from sin, but for the permanent release from oppression. Their hope for Redemption concerned this world, not the next – a physical redemption, not a spiritual one.

Book of Psalms

In that light, I am curious to understand why the evangelists used the Psalms so extensively. Given that in Judaism, David is not seen as a prophet, although Judaism does consider some verses as prophetic, what was their intention in referencing the Psalms so often? I say, *reference*, because sometimes they are quoted verbatim (insofar as we are able to determine from translations); sometimes the psalm is paraphrased; and at other times the writer simply alludes to a psalm. Did the writers understand the referenced psalms to be prophetic of the Messiah specifically, or did they have something else in mind? At this point I would refer the reader back to Chapter 1-6 on the question of: *fulfill* or *match*. Were the Evangelists simply commenting on how well the life and experiences of Jesus matched those of their Jewish forefathers? Were they attempting to show how similar Jesus was to King David, further evidence in their minds that he was the prophesied Messiah

Perhaps it was because they identified with the Psalms as here:

> "The Jew opens his Book of Psalms and lets David become the harp upon which his own emotions sing or weep. Small wonder that when the *Chofetz Chaim*, as an old man, was presented with his mother's ancient Book of Psalms, its pages swollen with her lifetime of tears, he was overcome with emotion. Who can assess the worth of the little Book that has been the chariot bearing countless tears to the Heavenly Throne?
>
> Upon reading of King David's many ordeals, one can begin to understand how he could compose the psalms that capture every person's joy and grief, thanksgiving and remorse, cries from the heart and songs of happiness. He was the Sweet Singer of Israel; more than that, however, he experienced the travail of every person, and that is why everyone can see himself mirrored in David's psalms."[3]

In that sense, David's psalms could be seen as prophetic, for they mirror the experience of every Jew, including Jesus. Where the evangelists referred to the Psalms, were they simply recounting the Jewish experience throughout the ages, demonstrating the Jewishness of Jesus? Has Christianity entirely misunderstood this application of the psalms? I encountered another perspective in a thought-provoking book by Rabbi Nathan Lopes Cardozo, *"Jewish Law As Rebellion"*[4]. Referring to the footnotes to his essays:

> "It is important to make the reader aware of the fact that the many sources that are mentioned throughout the book do not always prove my point of view. I use them as points of departure; signposts to move beyond what the actual source states. Also note that sometimes the sources argue the opposite point of view. The sources are provided as a reference for further study and to highlight various viewpoints, some in support and some against the claims made in the text."[5]

Points of departure; signposts to move beyond what the actual source states: could this be the intent of the evangelists? Were they asking their readers to look beyond that one verse of the Psalm, and absorb the context that King David was alluding to, if not, directly recounting his personal experience? What was the message behind each verse? I would contend that, if anything, they were expressing the validity of the Jewish experience, and its future as the anointed Nation of God – *His First-Born Son* (Exodus 4:22-23). In this context, the *first-born* is not a reference to the first in a family to be born, but is a metaphor expressing the rights normally granted to a first-born son. If we accept God as faithful, He would never reject those that He had chosen "for **His Name's sake**", not for their sake (Ezekiel 36:21-24).

Attempts to equate Jesus with Israel are interesting, but unconvincing to my mind, even if that was in the minds of the evangelists. We have long known that they were wrong in their eschatological expectations, so it is illogical to be dogmatic concerning the validity of their other beliefs.

Rashi's Commentary on the Psalms

Shlomo Yitzchaki (1040-1105), today generally known by the acronym *Rashi*, was a medieval French rabbi and author of a comprehensive commentary on the Talmud and commentary on the Tanakh. Acclaimed for his ability to present the basic meaning of the text in a concise and lucid fashion, Rashi appeals to both learned scholars and beginner students, and his works remain a centrepiece of contemporary Jewish study. His commentary on the Talmud, which covers nearly the entire Babylonian Talmud, has been included in every edition of the Talmud since its first printing by Daniel Bomberg in the 1520s. His commentary on Tanakh—especially on the Chumash— serves as the basis for more than 300 "supercommentaries" which analyze Rashi's choice of language and citations, penned by some of the greatest names in rabbinic literature.

With that background, let us hear what he has to say about the Psalms:

"This Book is composed of ten poetic genres [each identifiable by a characteristic introductory expression]: leading, instrumental music, psalm, song, *hallel* [i.e., 'praise'], prayer, *berakah* [i.e., 'blessing'], thanksgiving, laudations, Hallelujah. These correspond numerically to the ten people who composed [the 150 compositions contained in] it: Adam, Melchizedek, Abraham, Moses, David, Solomon, Asaph, and three sons of Korah. Opinion is divided concerning Jeduthun. Some say that he [Jeduthun in the titles of Ps. 39:1; 62:1; 72:1] was a person such as was written about in 1 Chronicles 16:38, while others explain that Jeduthun in this book is only [an acronym] referring to the judgements [*haddatot wehaddinin*], i.e., the tribulations, which overtook him [King David] and Israel."[6]

Perhaps you are as surprised as I was to learn that ten authors contributed to the Book of Psalms. In the following discussions on individual Psalms, I shall be referring Rashi's commentary, endeavouring to understand how well the Evangelists', and NKJV editors', usage conforms to the Jewish understanding. Note, at this stage, that *prophecy* is not listed as one of the ten poetic genres.

Book of Proverbs

Of interest also is reference to the Book of Proverbs: the NKJV annotates 22 references to Proverbs across the four Gospels, and here I shall also mention the 7 from Ecclesiastes. As these are not considered prophetic, especially not messianic, is it possible that many references to the Psalms are in the same sense as the references to the Proverbs: providing Jewish context and coherence with Hebrew Scriptures? For example: "So Jesus said to him, '*Why do you call me good? No one is good but One, that is God*'." (Luke 18:19) The NKJV references Psalms 86:5 and 119:68, which confirm what Jesus was saying. Incidentally, this suggests to me that here, Jesus could have been denying that he was God. For Luke to have written this some 40 years after the crucifixion, one can reasonably question Luke's view of Jesus' deity.

Sometimes the annotation by the NKJV editors is dubious, as in Matthew 22:4. Jesus spoke a parable, that "the kingdom of heaven is like a certain king who arranged a marriage for his son". In the narrative, mention is made of preparations for the wedding feast, but incongruously to my mind, the editors found a link to Proverbs 9:2 which reads: "She prepared her meat, mixed her wine, and also set her table". Could this be correct? Time for an excerpt from the Tanakh:

> "When the wisest of all people shares his wisdom, one would expect his teachings to have more than one layer of meaning. Though they can be understood in their simplest, literal sense, they may also allude to much deeper ideas. So it is with King Solomon's Book of Proverbs. Few Books of Scripture are as widely quoted as proverbs, for its wise and pithy aphorisms are so readily applicable to many areas of life. Nevertheless, both the Sages of the Talmud and classic commentators say that the true meaning of these proverbs is allegorical, and that when we plumb their depths they allude to much more than their simplest meaning. Rashi begins his commentary by saying that all Solomon's words are allusions and parables. For example, when Solomon speaks of a good woman, he is alluding to Torah; and when he speaks of a promiscuous woman, he is alluding to idolatry."[7]

We shall not be further addressing the Gospel and NKJV references to Proverbs in subsequent chapters, as there is nothing prophetic in them concerning the Messiah. That said, they are in a sense, prophetic in our daily lives.

Data Mining

"Not everything that can be counted, should be counted; and
not everything that should be counted, can be counted."
~ Paraphrasing a quotation, attributed to Albert Einstein ~

Data Mining: a process of discovering patterns, the overall goal of which is to extract information from a data set and transform it into an understandable structure for further use.

The caveat here is that there may be <u>no</u> pattern to discover, and this I keep in mind as I extract and tabulate every annotation of the Psalms in the Gospels. The subsequent analysis is performed to determine, if possible, what we can learn from the evangelists' frequent reference to them: what was going through their minds? Data mining is neither a biblical nor hermeneutical term, to be sure, but in my experience as an analyst, I have found that, Einstein's warning notwithstanding, sometimes the numbers, without *themselves* being significant, can evidence patterns deserving of further enquiry. That said, I am ever mindful of the dangers of statistics, for some people use them as a drunk uses a lamppost: more for support than illumination.

Potential Areas of Interest

Studying the NKJV annotations of prophecy fulfillment, it is necessary to differentiate between general prophecies, and messianic prophecies. For example, *"The kings of the earth set themselves, and the rulers take counsel together, against the Lord, and against His anointed"* (Psalm 2:2). This is annotated in the Old Testament with an *Outline Star* ☆, indicating that the verse contains a prophecy of a future event, but of what specifically? The events described had been going on for centuries before the arrival of Jesus, and so cannot be ascribed to his life specifically. Yes, it can be applied to Jesus, but not necessarily as Messiah. Thus, whilst the verse can be said to be prophetic, it not a messianic prophecy.

Reiterating the issue of *substantive evidence*: for a prophecy to be fulfilled by the Messiah, it must be one that can only be fulfilled by the Messiah, and no-one else. If others can and have fulfilled a prophecy, it is but *circumstantial* evidence, and should carry little evidential weight in an issue with such far-reaching consequences. The overall goals of the analysis, in this and subsequent chapters, are to evaluate how well Jesus fulfilled messianic prophecies from the Psalms, not just general prophecies; what we can learn from the evangelists' references to the psalms; and to what extent Christianity has read prophecy back into the Psalms, quite possibly distorting the evangelists' intentions. To that end, I considered the following issues:

1. Gospel verses where the author clearly intended to claim prophecy fulfillment, using words such as: "that it might be fulfilled which was spoken by the prophet" (Matt 13:35).

2. Gospel verses which are annotated in the NKJV as prophecy fulfillment, even though it is not clear that the Gospel author had such in mind.

3. Gospel verses which NKJV editors have linked back to a Psalm, but the relevance is debatable.

4. Where the NKJV editors have annotated the Old Testament, to claim a verse in a Psalm in as being prophetic.

5. Incidence of (4) that have no later annotation in the Gospels.

As noted earlier, the statistics may tell us nothing at all – we cannot know until we have studied them in detail.

Due to wording variations, it is sometimes difficult to understand the intent of the evangelist. For example, where one verse has: "that it might be fulfilled", another has: "And again, another Scripture says" (John 19:37). The first clearly conveys the evangelist's understanding, but the second is not so clear. In this example, the Scripture is: "They shall look on him whom they pierced", with the NKJV referencing Zechariah 12:10, 13:6, and Psalm 22:16, 17. Zechariah's prophecy begins in verse 8: "In that day the Lord will defend the inhabitants of Jerusalem … I will seek to destroy all the nations that come against Jerusalem." Clearly, this relates to the End of Days, not to the days of Jesus, i.e., Second Temple Judaism. Psalm 22 has David recounting his own experiences, entreating God to "Deliver me from the sword, my precious life from the power of the dog", which is hardly reflective of the trials of Jesus. Thus, if the author of John's Gospel did intend to convey prophecy fulfillment, he was obviously mistaken, as events had proven. More likely, he was saying that the life of Jesus matched that of earlier prophets, in which case, was he suggesting that Jesus was a prophet?

In adjudicating this issue, where the intent is not clear, I have decided to find in favour of the evangelists indicating their belief in prophecy fulfillment. This is favouring the Christian view, but I am not confident that such accurately reflects the intention of the evangelists.

The most difficult question of all to resolve is that at (3) above: *relevance*. Part of the problem here is the variation in wording between the Hebrew Scriptures, and the NKJV translation that I am using, which likely reflects the evangelists' use of an unidentified Greek translation from the Hebrew. The question I posed to myself was this: Should I focus on what the evangelists believed, irrespective of whether, or not, they were mistaken, or should I, and to what extent, take account of the errors in the Greek translation (see Chapter 2-1)? I decided to do both, addressing each issue separately. Thus, my first analysis, under the heading of "relevance", was based on comparing the New Testament text with the corresponding NKJV Old Testament version of the Psalms.

A second analysis was to compare the rendering of the Psalms in the NKJV, with the wording in the TJB, noting only those which would lead to a substantive difference in interpretation, other than simply taking them out of context. In about twenty percent of cases, the NKJV wording was sufficiently different from that in the TJB as to lead to a difference in interpretation. These were as follows, the NKJV rendering first followed by the TJB:

1. Psalm 2:7 – "The Lord has said to Me, you are My Son; today I have begotten You" *versus* "I am obliged to proclaim that Hashem said to me, 'you are My son, I have begotten you this day'."

2. Psalm 16:10 – "For you will not leave my heart in Sheol … You will not allow Your holy one to see corruption" *versus* "You will not abandon my soul to the grave, You will not allow Your devout one to witness destruction."

3. Psalm 22:16 – "For dogs have surrounded me; the congregation of the wicked has enclosed me. They pierced my hands and my feet" *versus* "… like a lion they attack my hands and my feet."

4. Psalm 22:26 – "The poor shall eat and be satisfied" *versus* "The humble will eat and be satisfied".

5. Psalm 35:11 – "Fiery witnesses rise up; they ask me things that I do not know" *versus* "False witnesses rise up, for that of which I know nothing they call me to account".

6. Psalm 40:7 – "In the scroll of the book it is written of me" *versus* "that is written for me".

7. Psalm 68:18 – "You have ascended on high, you have led captivity captive" *versus* "You ascended on high, You have taken captives".

8. Psalm 78:2 – "I will utter dark sayings of old" *versus* "I will utter and explain riddles of old".
9. Psalm 89:27 – "I will make him My firstborn" *versus* "I will make him a firstborn".
10. Psalm 110:1 – "The Lord said to my Lord" *versus* "The word of Hashem to my master (David)".
11. Psalm 110:4 – "according to the order of Melchizedek" *versus* "because you are a king of righteousness".
12. Psalm 118:26 – "in the name of the Lord" *versus* "in the name of the Hashem".

On the surface, some of these differences in wording may not seem significant, but in the New Testament context that they are quoted, that is not so. For example, Psalm 118:26 has *Lord*, which can be thought of as Jesus, if Jesus is already the context, but *Hashem* does not allow that understanding. Psalm 89:27 has **My firstborn** versus **a firstborn**, the NKJV suggesting only one firstborn, but the TJB allows many which we know to be true. Psalm 22:26 is annotated against Matthew 11:6, and quite apart from the reference being mystical, there is a substantive difference between the poor eating, and the humble having the gospel preached to them. Words DO matter – the difference between a really clever author, and one not so accomplished, is that the former can influence the reader so much more.

Extracted Data

Using the annotations by the editors of the New King James Version (NKJV), without necessarily validating their usage of them, I have extracted the following statistics from the entire New Testament, where a Psalm verse was referenced in connection with a NT verse, irrespective of whether it was said to be in fulfillment of prophecy:

Entire New Testament:
a. Count of total times psalm verses were referenced: 124
b. Count of unique psalm verses referenced: 55
c. Count of those psalms flagged in OT as prophetic: 41

d. Count of unique NT verses flagged as in prophecy fulfillment: 87
e. Count of NT verses which explicitly claim prophecy fulfillment of a Psalm: 28
f. Occurrences of an individual Psalm verse being referenced: 13 times [1]; 7 times [2]; 6 times [1]; 4 times [4]; 3 times [9]; 2 times [10]; and only once [28].
g. Most frequently referenced psalms: Psalm 22 [23]; Psalm 69 [14]; Psalm 110 [16]; and Psalm 118 [13].

Gospels Only:
a. Count of total times psalm verses were referenced: 50
b. Count of unique psalm verses referenced: 28
c. Count of those psalms flagged in OT as prophetic: 25
d. Count of unique NT verses flagged as in prophecy fulfillment: 44
e. Count of NT verses which explicitly claim prophecy fulfillment of a Psalm: 6
f. Occurrences of an individual Psalm verse being referenced: 4 times [2]; 3 times [3]; 2 times [10]; and only once [13].
g. Most frequently referenced psalms: Psalm 22 [17]; Psalm 69 [8]; and Psalm 118 [10].
h. Occurrences of verses referenced by Gospel: Matthew [18]; Mark [11]; Luke [11]; and John [10].
i. Occurrences of a single verse uniquely referenced in only one Gospel: Matthew [5]; Mark [2]; Luke [2]; and John [4].
j. Verses flagged in OT Psalms as prophetic, but not flagged in the Gospels: John [1].
k. Verses flagged in the Gospels as prophetic, but not in the OT Psalms: Matt [7]; Mark [7]; Luke [8]; and John [3].

Caveat: I would recommend against trying to add some of these numbers together, as there is a degree of overlap in the way that they are collated and summed. That said, there is likely a degree of inaccuracy which, nevertheless, would not affect the overall patterns.

It is interesting to note the size of the Book of Psalms: 150 Psalms containing 2,461 verses. Of these, the NKJV annotates just 41 verses as being prophecy to be fulfilled, with 28 noted in the Gospels, and 12 in other writings. Statistics can be manipulated to prove whatever case one chooses, but nevertheless, I am curious to know the process by which the editors of the NKJV decided that such were prophecies fulfilled in the Gospels. In Judaism, as discussed earlier, the Psalms are not considered prophetic: these statistics would indicate that Christianity generally agrees, and thus has me further wondering whether the prophetic annotations are valid at all.

I found it interesting that the most occurrences occurred in the Gospel of Luke, although I came to no conclusion as to whether that was significant or not. Matthew was not far behind.

As I set out to list all verses that were referenced, I immediately encountered an obstacle: which bible translation should I use? What is it that I am attempting to understand? If the evangelists used the Greek version of the Psalms, then perhaps I should use the NKJV rendering, as it would, hopefully, better represent their thinking. If, on the other hand, I wanted to discover how faithfully the evangelists understood the Hebrew Scriptures, then I should use a version translated from the Hebrew. As noted above, I decided to use the NKJV, and as a separate exercise, highlight any significant differences. I also decided that I would not copy the theological annotations of the NKJV editors, as these may well represent theological development, unless it could be shown from the context of the Gospel verses. Of course, the trap here is that the NKJV versions of the Gospels also contain theological annotations and interpretations, limiting one's ability to truly understand what was in the minds of the evangelists when they referenced these psalms.

Sometimes, the literary debris of centuries, hinders, thwarts, and even precludes discovery of the truth. It has me wondering why so many believe that they know the truth, when I have such difficulty discerning it from the evidence available.

Finally, the task of researching the usage of the psalms in the Gospels particularly, has been far more complex than I imagined, due to the variety of inconsistencies that I discovered along the way. I had intended to present my findings in a concise manner, but the nature of the usage does not lend itself to such abridgement. The primary distinctions are where:

1. The Gospel text explicitly refers to a verse as fulfillment of prophecy.
2. The Gospel text does not, but the bible editors annotate it as prophecy fulfillment.
3. The Gospel text is annotated as being prophecy fulfillment, but the OT Psalm text is not.
4. The OT Psalm text is annotated as prophecy to be fulfilled, but the Gospel text does not.
5. The words of Jesus allude to him being in fulfillment of prophecy.
6. The NT text does not match the OT text of the same bible translation; and
7. The NT text does not match the translation from the Hebrew Scriptures.

I shall do my best to simplify the evidence that I have uncovered, but apologise in advance if it is not as coherent as you, or even I, would like.

Initial Thoughts

Firstly, I must point out that some of the apparent discrepancies could have arisen through the NKJV editors' processes, and therefore, we should be careful about placing too much emphasis on them. I am fortunate in having a tool like Microsoft Excel to record and tabulate the occurrences of the data to evaluate, as well as experience in that discipline. The NKJV editors, as diligent as I am certain they were, likely had no such facilities, and we must consider their efforts kindly.

Secondly, the statistics themselves are simply indicative of trends which may, or may not, actually be there. The data is used to suggest a departure point for further research, and for initial observations. For example, it is interesting to note the number of occurrences where a psalm verse is quoted in only one Gospel: 79 times. Does that tell us anything about the thinking of the evangelists, or perhaps the religious culture of the communities where the individual Jesus traditions developed? Is it evidence that, as claimed by some scholars, the four individual Gospels did develop as separate traditions, with more thoughts added in the retelling? Would an analysis of the subject matter, by Gospel, be indicative of how Jesus' mission was perceived?

Why does Luke's Gospel contain almost twice the number of Psalm references than the other Gospels? Less than 50% of the Psalm references in the Gospels are flagged as prophetic fulfillment. Significantly, only twice in Matthew, and four times in John, do the Evangelists themselves claim that an event, or saying, was in fulfillment of a prophecy in the Psalms. Put another way, of the 54 Gospel verses flagged by the NKJV editors as being in fulfillment of a prophecy in the Psalms, only 6 (11%) are referenced that way by the Evangelists themselves. Does this indicate that the NKJV editors have read prophecy back into the Psalms where none truly exist? Only an examination of the relevant Psalms can lead us to the truth there.

Psalm 119 is referenced 6 times, which I find interesting, as this Psalm by David is primarily about Law and Covenant being forever, yet Christianity has rejected both. Why would the evangelists have quoted these Psalms if they understood, well after the death of Jesus, that their Master had inaugurated a new covenant which required no further obedience to the law?

Before moving onto an analysis by Gospel, let us focus on the six occasions where the Gospel text, in Matthew and John only, explicitly claim Psalm prophecy fulfillment: there are no such claims in Mark and Luke.

Explicitly in Matthew's Gospel

"All these things Jesus spoke to the multitude in parables; and without a parable He did not speak to them, that it might be fulfilled which was spoken by the prophet, saying: 'I will open my mouth in parables; I will utter things kept secret from the foundation of the world'" (Matthew 13:35).

It is debatable that Jesus spoke to the multitudes in parables only, but we will let that pass for now. The important point to understand is that many of the parables that Jesus narrated were not about *things kept secret from the foundation of the world*. Some of his parables have parallels in ancient Jewish literature, and others were words of wisdom that were not unique to Jesus (the Book of Proverbs also contains parables). Turning to Psalm 78, it begins: "A Contemplation of Asaph", indicating that this was written by Asaph, not David. Asaph, a contemporary of David, is mentioned in 1 & 2 Chronicles, and is described as a *seer*, not a *prophet*. A key difference between the two is as described earlier in Chapter 1-4: a *seer* relates to *forthtelling* - insight into the will of God; it was exhortative, challenging men to obey, just as Asaph wrote: "Listen, my people, to my teaching, incline your ear to the words of my mouth. I will open my mouth with a parable. I will utter [and explain] riddles from antiquity. That which we have heard and know our fathers told us, we shall not withhold from their sons, recounting unto the final generation the praises of Hashem, His might and His wonders that He has wrought." (vv. 1-4, TJB) Compare that to the wording in the NKJV: "I will utter dark sayings of old, which we have heard and known", and significantly, to how it is rendered in Matthew: "things kept secret from the foundation of the world". Reading Psalm 78, we find that it reviews events of Israel's history, and are parables in the sense that they are object lessons for all time. The question becomes: In what sense can this Psalm be considered prophetic of the Messiah, and why did the author of Matthew entirely change the context? There was nothing dark or secret about the sayings of old, but for the less educated, they were riddles in the sense of things that were difficult to understand, not statements intentionally phrased so as to require ingenuity in ascertaining meaning.

As an aside, as it may be relevant to the question of authenticity, this section of Matthew opens with the disciples asking Jesus: "*Why do you speak to them in parables?*" (Matthew 13:10) My question is: Why did they ask that question? Speaking in parables was a common practice amongst the rabbis, so it does seem odd that the disciples, perceiving Jesus to be a rabbi, would query him on this point. Is this indicative of these disciples not being conversant with the Scriptures, not having been taught by rabbis? Or can it be that whoever wrote the Gospel of Matthew was not conversant with contemporary Jewish practice, and added to the narrative to suit his own purpose? I cannot know, but it does seem odd.

"*I will utter things kept secret from the foundation of the world*" could be an allusion to Daniel 2:22, where David was interpreting the dreams of

King Nebuchadnezzar: "He reveals deep and secret things; He knows what is in the darkness, and the light dwells in Him." What the future holds could be termed, *dark* secrets, because they are hidden until revealed by God. But these things are not what was being discussed in Psalm 78, and thus the Psalm cannot be said to be prophetic of Jesus revealing secrets, if he really did.

"Then they crucified Him, and divided His garments, casting lots, that it might be fulfilled which was spoken by the prophet: '*They divided My garments among them, and for My clothing they cast lots.*'" (Matthew 27:35), noting Psalm 22:18 [emphasis mine]. Firstly, David, who was not a prophet, did not write "**My**" (initial capital) as a reference to the future Messiah. Secondly, casting lots was an ancient custom (Jonah 1:7), and dividing garments was a common practice of crucifixions of the time, this method of execution dating back to 519 BCE. King David lived much earlier, 1040 – 970 BCE, and so could not have had crucifixion in mind. Turning to the Psalm, it relates to the time of Israel's long exile from its land and the Temple. Reading the Psalm, understanding the context, and David beseeching God to redeem Israel from its enemies, casting this as a prophecy of the Messiah is a stretch too far.

Just why the author of this version of the Gospel made these links is quite beyond my understanding. They can only be peripheral to the claim of Jesus as Messiah, quite unnecessary, and tend to weaken, rather than strengthen, the evidentiary case. Let me remind the reader of our purpose: to evaluate the evidence of prophecy fulfillment. These quotations of the Psalms contribute nothing.

Explicitly in John's Gospel

"They said therefore among themselves, 'let us not tear it, but cast lots for it, whose shall it be', that the Scripture might be fulfilled which says: '*They divided My garments among them; and for My clothing they cast lots*'." (John 19:24) quoting Psalm 22:18. As in Matthew, Psalm 22 contains no messianic, or any other prophecy, and casting lots for the clothing of criminals was common practice. I would contend that the statement: "let us not tear it", is an embellishment, as the suggestion of tearing clothing is not found in the Psalm, Matthew, or any literature that I can find on the subject.

"For these things were done that the Scripture should be fulfilled: *'Not one of His bones shall be broken.'* And another Scripture says, *'They shall look on Him whom they pierced'*." (John 19:36-37), quoting Psalms 22:16-17 and 34:20. The NKJV renders Psalm 22:16 as "They pierced My hands and My feet", whereas from the Hebrew it is "like a lion they attack my hands and my feet". Rashi comments: "[i.e., My enemies hurt my hands and feet] as though they had been crushed in the mouth of a lion. In the same vein, Hezekiah said, '... like a lion, thus did he shatter all my bones' (Isaiah 38:13)."[8] In both the Psalm and Isaiah, the writer is using a metaphor to describe the level of pain. Hezekiah's lament from the Tanakh: "He will end my life with sickness; from morning to night You will put an end to me. I waited until morning – as [if it] were a lion, so [my sickness] would shatter all my bones; from morning to night You will put an end to me … My Lord, snatch away my [illness], be my surety." (TJB)

Given the Jewish interpretation, that in Isaiah, Hezekiah, and the Psalm, the writer is using a metaphor to describe the level of pain, the Christian translation has seemingly been selected to match the crucifixion. Even so, "I can count all my bones" (Psalm 22:17) does not infer that no bones shall be broken. I strongly doubt that the OT verse is prophetic of the Messiah' crucifixion, for among a number of reasons, there is no prophecy of the Messiah being executed, let alone crucified.

"For as yet they did not know the Scripture, that He must rise again from the dead" (John 20:9). The explanation is simple: they did not know, nor did anyone else, for there is no ancient prophecy of the Messiah dying, and then rising again from the dead. Now, to be fair to the author, he may have been referring to an earlier Gospel, which he considered Scripture. What most intrigues me about the NKJV annotation is that it references just Psalm 16:10, and not the other Gospels which is the usual practice. The subject of John 20:9 is also found in Luke 24:45-46, where Jesus refers to the Scripture, but the NKJV there just annotates verses in Acts. So, what is this mysterious Scripture?

The NKJV version of Psalm 16:10 reads: "For You will not leave my soul in Sheol, nor will You allow Your Holy One to see corruption. From the Hebrew: "Because You will not abandon my soul to the grave, You will not allow Your devout one to witness destruction". In the context of the Psalm, the Hebrew gives no sense of David claiming that after death, his body would be raised from the grave to avoid corruption, and we know that David was interred and remains so even now. Back to verse 2: "O my soul, you have said to the Lord" (NKJV). David has his soul speaking to God, proclaiming that it has sought refuge in Him, and speaks of those who rush after other Gods. David's entreaty is twofold: one spiritual, the other physical. The physical relates to his time of earth, before death. In the case of Jesus, the physical relates to a body risen, uncorrupted. See also Chapter 1-8 for the ancient Hebrew understanding of the "soul".

That said, the authors of Luke and John both seem to have believed that Jesus' resurrection was prophesied in Scripture; Luke's version going so far as to put those words in the mouth of Jesus. Whilst the Evangelists may have made such a connection in their minds, I strongly doubt that Jesus would have done so, for in Judaism, Psalm 16 is not considered as containing messianic prophecy. If God wanted such a significant event to be known, it is reasonable to assume that He would have conveyed it through one of the major Prophets, e.g., Isaiah, Jeremiah, or Ezekiel. If God was guiding the writing and compilation of the Hebrew canon, why would He tuck away such a portentous prophecy in a Psalm of David, to be collected under the *Writings*, where it would never be seen as such by His Chosen People?

Did He not want them to know?

Summary

At this stage, I am not much closer to understanding why the Evangelists referenced the Psalms in their Gospels, and most particularly, why the evangelists concluded that some verses were prophetic of the Messiah. I can understand, to some degree, why the editors of the NKJV found prophecy in the Psalms, but I believe that they were in error. Whether they were just over zealous, or whether they knowingly "invented" prophecy, is something only they can know. However, I am far from convinced that God would effectively keep secret, that He planned for the Messiah to die, be raised from the dead uncorrupted, and then some thousands of years later, come back to accomplish all that the Prophets clearly stated that he would accomplish.

Aside from John 20:9, quoting Psalm 16:10, there is only one other instance where the NKJV annotates a prophecy of the resurrection, Matthew 17:23. Even there, the editors failed to find a single Scripture reference to support their annotation. I find that most curious. We do have Jesus prophesying of his being "three days and three nights in the heart of the earth" (Matthew 12:40), and both Matthew and Luke (11:30) narrating Jesus warning that the only sign to be given to the current generation would be that of *the prophet Jonah*. In Judaism, Jonah is considered a minor prophet, insofar as his *forthtelling* (not foretelling) related only to his place and times. What would be *the sign of Jonah the prophet*? Jonah disobeyed God, and to give him time to rethink, God arranged for him to spend time in the belly of a large fish. We have no evidence that the people of Nineveh, or anyone else at the time, knew of Jonah's adventure. For later Jewish generations, the message from Jonah's episode related to repentance to avoid Jonah's warning: "Forty days more and Nineveh shall be overturned" happening to them. "He who knows shall repent and God will relent; He will turn away from His burning wrath so that we not perish." (Jonah 3:9).

Commenting on how the New Testament authors used the Old Testament, S.V. McCaslan, a former Professor of Religion at Virginia University observed: "The application of the saying about Jonah's sojourn in the belly of the whale to the period during which Jesus lay in the grave between his death and resurrection, although it does not really fit the narrative of the resurrection, indicates how desperately early Christians searched the Scriptures to find proof for the things happening among them."[9] I believe that there is significance in the fact that this equivalence in only found in Matthew's Gospel, though quite what to make of that I cannot be sure.

This is a consistent message throughout the Book of Prophets. Repent, and God will relent from His wrath, but fail to do so and life on earth will not be pleasant. There is no connotation of the after-life. Stepping back, consider the importance of the Resurrection to Christian doctrine and theology. Now examine the Scriptural evidence that the resurrection was prophesied. It surprises even me that there is no substantive evidence of such a prophecy. Finally, ponder why that would be so: why would God be so secretive on this issue?

I do not believe that He would be, and conclude, tentatively at least, that the Psalms were referenced because that was the only place in the ancient Scriptures that even a hint of such a prophecy could be detected. From an evidential perspective, the case for the resurrection being prophesied is particularly weak and unconvincing. If God did not reveal the resurrection in advance to His prophets, we have reason to be suspicious of it actually happening.

The jury is still out on that one.

REFERENCES:

1. Scherman, Rabbi Nosson, *The Tanach*, Mesorah Publications, ArtScroll English Edition, Brooklyn, NY, 2011, p. xxi
2. *Ibid*, p. xv
3. *Ibid*, p. 933
4. Cardozo, Nathan Lopes, *Jewish Law as Rebellion: A Plea for Religious Authenticity and Halachic Courage*, Urim Publications, Jerusalem, Israel, 2018
5. *Ibid*, p. 23
6. Gruber, Mayer I., *Rashi's Commentary on Psalms*, The Jewish Publication Society, Philadelphia, PA, 2007, p. 165
7. Scherman, *Ibid*, p. 1020
8. Gruber, *Ibid*, p. 257
9. Beale, G.K., *The Right Doctrine from the Wrong Texts? Essays on the Use of the Old Testament in the New*, Baker Academic, Grand Rapids, MI, 1994, p. 149

CHAPTER 5-1

MATTHEW'S
PROPHETIC PSALMS

This chapter does not repeat the discussions found in Chapter 4-2: Gospel of Matthew, the purpose of which was to analyse the claimed prophetic fulfillment in detail. The purpose here is to review the occurrences of only the *Psalm* references claimed to be prophetic, attempting to understand what we may learn (if anything).

Overview

There are thirty-six verses in Matthew's Gospel, where the NKJV references one or more verse from the Psalms, both pastoral and prophetic. In total, there are forty-six references to psalms, thirty-eight of which are unique. Nine of the referenced psalm verses are said to have been fulfilled by the Gospel verses, and three where the prophecy is yet to be fulfilled. It is an interesting exercise to identify which verses would be naturally understood as messianic prophecies; which *might* be prophetic, but could be fulfilled by anyone; and which would likely be just pastoral: most of the psalm references are of that nature.

Gospel Verses annotated as Fulfilling a Psalm Prophecy

In the following table, the "OT" column shows where the Psalm is flagged in the Old Testament as a prophecy to be fulfilled. In the "NT" column, a ★ shows where according to the NKJV editors, the psalm is fulfilled in that verse, and a ☆ where it is yet to be fulfilled. The "★★" column shows where the Gospel's author *explicitly* states that the activity was in fulfillment of a prophecy from the Psalm.

In Matthew's Gospel, two of the verses referencing psalms are explicit claims of prophecy fulfillment.

Matt	Psalm	OT	NT	★★	Psalm Verse from the NKJV Old Testament
11:5	22:26		★		Those who seek Him will be satisfied.
13:35	78:2	☆	★	★★	I will open my mouth in a parable.
15:8	78:36		★		Nevertheless, they flattered him with their mouth.
21:9	118:26	☆	★		Blessed is he who comes in the name of the Lord.
21:12	69:9	☆	★		Because zeal for You house has eaten me up.
21:12	119:139		★		My zeal has consumed me, because my enemies have forgotten Your words.
21:15	118:26	☆	★		Blessed is he who comes in the name of the Lord.
21:42	118:22	☆	☆		The stone which the builders rejected has become the chief cornerstone.
21:42	118:23		☆		This was the Lord's doing; it is marvellous in our eyes.
22:44	110:1	☆	☆		The Lord said to my lord, sit at my right hand, till I make your enemies your footstool.
26:14	41:9	☆	★		Even my own familiar friend … has lifted up his heel against me.
27:34	69:21	☆	★		They also gave me gall for my food, and for my thirst … vinegar.

27:35	22:18	☆	★	★ ★	They divide my garments … for my clothing they cast lots.
27:36	22:17	☆	★		I can count all my bones
27:39	22:7	☆	★		All those who see me ridicule me.
27:39	22:8	☆	★		He trusted in the Lord, let Him rescue him.
27:43	22:8	☆	★		He trusted in the Lord, let Him rescue him.
27:46	22:1	☆	★		My God, my God, why have you forsaken me?
27:48	69:21	☆	★		They also gave me gall for my food, and for my thirst … vinegar.

There are two occasions where Matthew's narrative explicitly claims fulfillment of a prophetic verse from the Psalms:

1. Matt 13:35 in fulfillment of Psalm 78:2; and
2. Matt 27:35 in fulfillment of Psalm 22:18.

Aside from these two, there are seventeen instances that are interpretations by the NKJV editors, but curiously, four of those are not correspondingly flagged in the Old Testament. This raises the question: Did the NKJV editor of the Old Testament not recognise these as prophecy to be fulfilled, or have the editors of the New decided differently? Has Christianity imposed a meaning not intended by the Gospel author? Consider these seventeen verses: note that not one of them specifically relates to the Messiah – all were originally written about King David, and many could apply to numerous people throughout the history of the Children of Israel, from the time of their rescue from Egypt.

Gospel Verses NOT annotated as Prophecy Fulfilled

The *previous* list was of the Gospel verses flagged by the NKJV editors as prophecy fulfilled. The following list is where the Gospel verses were not so flagged, even though the referenced psalm verse is flagged in the OT as a prophecy to be fulfilled – there are six of them. In the context of the Gospel verses, I can think of no reason why the editors failed to flag each as prophecy fulfilled, other than being an oversight. To be fair, I doubt that the editors had access to the same computer tools with which I am familiar.

Matt	Psalm	OT	NT	★★	Psalm Verse from the NKJV Old Testament
3:17	2:7	☆			The Lord has said to me, you are My son; today I have begotten you.
14:33	2:7	☆			The Lord has said to me, you are My son; today I have begotten you.
23:39	118:26	☆			Blessed is he who comes in the name of the Lord!
26:23	41:9	☆			Even my own familiar friend … has lifted up his heel against me.
26:50	41:9	☆			Even my own familiar friend … has lifted up his heel against me.
26:59	35:11	☆			Fiery witnesses rise up; they ask me things I do not know.

Review

On review, there is not a single instance where it can reasonably be claimed that these psalm verses are specifically, messianic prophecies. Whilst Psalm 110:1 could be claimed in that sense, the difficulty is with the interpretation of the psalm based on who wrote it. Jewish tradition has it being written *about* King David, not *by* him, which has it conveying an entirely different meaning. Overall, from an evidentiary perspective, this section contributes nothing to the proposition that Jesus fulfilled messianic prophecies.

CHAPTER 5-2

MARK'S PROPHETIC PSALMS

This chapter does not repeat the discussions found in Chapter 4-3: Gospel of Mark, the purpose of which was to analyse the claimed prophetic fulfillment in detail. The purpose here is to review the occurrences of only the *Psalm* references claimed to be prophetic, attempting to understand what we may learn (if anything).

Overview

There are twenty-two verses in Mark's Gospel, where the NKJV references one or more verse from the Psalms, both pastoral and prophetic. In total, there are twenty-nine references to psalms, twenty-six of which are unique. Eight of the referenced psalm verses are said to have been fulfilled by the Gospel verses, but none where the prophecy is yet to be fulfilled. It is an interesting exercise to identify which verses would be naturally understood as messianic prophecies; which *might* be prophetic, but could be fulfilled by anyone; and which would likely be just pastoral: most of the psalm references are of that nature.

Gospel Verses annotated as Fulfilling a Psalm Prophecy

In the following table, the "OT" column shows where the Psalm is flagged in the Old Testament as a prophecy to be fulfilled. In the "NT" column, a ★ shows where according to the NKJV editors, the psalm is fulfilled in that verse, and a ☆ where it is yet to be fulfilled. The "★★" column shows where the Gospel's author explicitly states that the activity was in fulfillment of a prophecy from the Psalm.

In Mark's Gospel, none of the verses referencing psalms are explicit claims of prophecy fulfillment.

Mark	Psalm	OT	NT	★★	Psalm Verse from the NKJV Old Testament
3:6	2:2	☆	★		The Kings of the earth set themselves, and the rulers take counsel together.
9:7	2:7	☆	★		The Lord has said to me, you are My Son; today I have begotten you.
9:12	22:6		★		But I am a worm, and no man, a reproach of men, and despised by the people.
11:9	118:25		★		Save now, I pray, O Lord; O Lord, I pray, send now prosperity.
11:9	118:26	☆	★		Blessed is he who comes in the name of the Lord!
12:10	118:22	☆	★		The stone which the builders rejected has become the chief cornerstone.
12:10	118:23		★		This was the Lord's doing; it is marvellous in our eyes.
12:36	110:1	☆	★		The Lord said to my lord, sit at my right hand, till I make your enemies your footstool.
14:57	35:11	☆	★		Fiery witnesses rise up; they ask me things I do not know.
15:1	2:2	☆	★		The Kings of the earth set themselves, and the rulers take counsel together.
15:29	22:6		★		But I am a worm, and no man, a reproach of men, and despised by the people.
15:29	22:7	☆	★		All those who see me ridicule me.
15:31	22:8	☆	★		He trusted in the Lord, let Him rescue him.
15:34	22:1	☆	★		My God, my God, why have you forsaken me?

Note the three verses in Mark: 9:12, 12:10, and 15:29 where the verse claims prophecy fulfillment, but the referenced Psalm verse is not flagged as a prophecy to be fulfilled.

Gospel Verses NOT annotated as Prophecy Fulfilled

In Mark's Gospel, there are no anomalies of where a Gospel verse not flagged as prophecy fulfilled, references a Psalm verse which is flagged as a prophecy to be fulfilled.

Review

Psalm verses 2:7, 118:22, and 110:1 can be interpreted as being prophetic of the Messiah, but as we discuss elsewhere, those interpretations take the verses out of context.

CHAPTER 5-3

LUKE'S PROPHETIC PSALMS

This chapter does not repeat the discussions found in Chapter 4-4: Gospel of Luke, the purpose of which was to analyse the claimed prophetic fulfillment in detail. The purpose here is to review the occurrences of only the Psalm references claimed to be prophetic, attempting to understand what we may learn (if anything).

Overview

There are thirty-nine verses in Luke's Gospel, where the NKJV references one or more verse from the Psalms, both pastoral and prophetic. In total, there are fifty-two references to psalms, forty-eight of which are unique. Five of the referenced psalm verses are said to have been fulfilled by the Gospel verses, and four where the prophecy is yet to be fulfilled. It is an interesting exercise to identify which verses would be naturally understood as messianic prophecies; which *might* be prophetic, but could be fulfilled by anyone; and which would likely be just pastoral: most of the psalm references are of that nature.

Gospel Verses annotated as Fulfilling a Psalm Prophecy

In the following table, the "OT" column shows where the Psalm is flagged in the Old Testament as a prophecy to be fulfilled. In the "NT" column, a ★ shows where according to the NKJV editors, the psalm is fulfilled in that verse, and a ☆ where it is yet to be fulfilled. The "★★" column shows where the Gospel text explicitly states that the activity was in fulfillment of a prophecy from the Psalm.

In Luke's Gospel, none of the verses referencing psalms are explicit claims of prophecy fulfillment.

Gospel Verses annotated as Fulfilling Prophecy

Luke	Psalm	OT	NT	★★	Psalm Verse from the NKJV Old Testament
13:35	69:25	☆	☆		Let their dwelling place be desolate.
13:35	118:26	☆	☆		Blessed is he who comes in the name of the Lord.
19:38	118:26	☆	★		Blessed is he who comes in the name of the Lord.
20:17	118:22	☆	☆		The stone which the builders rejected has become the chief cornerstone.
20:42	110:1	☆	☆		The Lord said to my lord, sit at my right hand, till I make your enemies your footstool.
22:47	41:9	☆	★		Even my own familiar friend ... has lifted up his heel against me.
23:35	22:7	☆	★		All those who see me ridicule me.
23:35	22:8	☆	★		He trusted in the Lord, let Him rescue him.
23:35	22:17	☆	★		I can count all my bones
23:36	69:21	☆	★		They also gave me gall for my food, and for my thirst ... vinegar.
24:51	68:18	☆	★		You have ascended on high, you have led captivity captive.

There is an apparent anomaly where Luke 13:35 and 19:38 both reference Psalm 118:26, but one Gospel verse is annotated with ☆ and the other ★. This is due to the NKJV editors going to a greater level of detail in the verses, than I have in my analysis, and thus is not an anomaly at all.

Gospel Verses NOT annotated as Prophecy Fulfilled

In Luke's Gospel, there are no anomalies of where a Gospel verse not flagged as prophecy fulfilled, references a Psalm verse which is flagged as a prophecy to be fulfilled.

Review

As before, Psalm verses 118:22 and 110:1 can be interpreted as being prophetic of the Messiah, but as we discuss elsewhere, those interpretations take the verses out of context. Of interest is Luke 18:31, not noted in the tables, where it is annotated with Psalm 22, without a specific verse. The context is similar to Luke 24:27 and 24:44, where Jesus states that "all things that are written by the prophets concerning the Son of Man will be (or have been) accomplished." We discuss this later in Part 9.

CHAPTER 5-4

JOHN'S PROPHETIC PSALMS

This chapter does not repeat the discussions found in Chapter 4-5: Gospel of John, the purpose of which was to analyse the claimed prophetic fulfillment in detail. The purpose here is to review the occurrences of only the Psalm references claimed to be prophetic, attempting to understand what we may learn (if anything).

Overview

There are twenty-four verses in John's Gospel, where the NKJV references one or more verse from the Psalms, both pastoral and prophetic. In total, there are thirty-three references to psalms, thirty of which are unique. Nine of the referenced psalm verses are said to have been fulfilled by the Gospel verses, but none where the prophecy is yet to be fulfilled. It is an interesting exercise to identify which verses would be naturally understood as messianic prophecies; which *might* be prophetic, but could be fulfilled by anyone; and which would likely be just pastoral: most of the psalm references are of that nature.

Gospel Verses annotated as Fulfilling a Psalm Prophecy

In the following table, the "OT" column shows where the Psalm is flagged in the Old Testament as a prophecy to be fulfilled. In the "NT" column, a ★ shows where according to the NKJV editors, the psalm is fulfilled in that verse, and a ☆ where it is yet to be fulfilled. The "★★" column shows where the Gospel text explicitly states that the activity was in fulfillment of a prophecy from the Psalm.

In John's Gospel, one of the verses referencing psalms makes an explicit claim of prophecy fulfillment.

John	Psalm	OT	NT	★★	Psalm Verse from the NKJV Old Testament
2:17	69:9	☆	★		Because zeal for You house has eaten me up.
7:5	69:8	☆	★		I have become a stranger to my brothers.
7:14	22:22	☆	★		I will declare Your name to my brethren; in the midst of the assembly I will praise you.
12:13	118:25		★		Save now, I pray, O Lord.
12:13	118:26	☆	★		Blessed is he who comes in the name of the Lord!
19:24	22:18	☆	★	★★	They divide my garments … for my clothing they cast lots.
19:29	69:21	☆	★		They also gave me gall for my food, and for my thirst … vinegar.
19:36	34:20	☆	★		He guards all his bones, not one of them is broken.
19:37	22:16	☆	★		They pierced my hands and my feet.
19:37	22:17	☆	★		I can count all my bones
20:27	22:16	☆	★		They pierced my hands and my feet.

The only anomaly is where Psalm verse 118:25 is included as prophesied in John 12:13, but that psalm verse is not annotated in the OT as prophetic.

Gospel Verses NOT annotated as Prophecy Fulfilled

In John's Gospel, there are no anomalies of where a Gospel verse not flagged as prophecy fulfilled, references a Psalm verse which is flagged as a prophecy to be fulfilled.

Summary

It should be obvious that none of the Psalm verses listed above are specifically, messianic prophecies. Any, and all of them, could be fulfilled by any number of Jewish people over the centuries, so at best, they contribute circumstantial evidence, but nothing more.

CHAPTER 5-5

PSALMS IN ACTS
AND EPISTLES

I don't intend to review these Psalms in the same detail as for the Gospels, for in my analysis of their usage and frequency, I found nothing of any significance that varied from that found in the Gospels. However, let us have a look at the usage statistics:

a. 22 verses where the New Testament author explicitly claimed fulfillment of a prophecy in the Psalms.
b. A total of 43 verses annotated by the NKJV editors as prophecy fulfilled.
c. 27 unique Psalm verses were referenced.
d. 16 of these Psalm verses were flagged in the Old Testament as prophetic.
e. A total 74 Psalm verses were referenced by the NKJV editors.

In terms of frequency, verses referenced 10 times [1]; 6 times [2]; 4 times [1]; 3 times [2]; 2 times [7]; and just once [26].

The most frequently referenced verses were:

   a.   Psalm 110:1 [10 times] – "The Lord said to my lord, sit at my right hand, till I make your enemies your footstool."

   b.   Psalm 16:10 [6 times] – "For you will not leave my heart in Sheol … You will not allow Your holy one to see corruption."

   c.   Psalm 68:18 [6 times] – "You have ascended on high, you have led captivity captive."

Note that the primary theme relates to the resurrection. Psalm 16:10 is a mistranslation of the Hebrew, and refers not to the resurrection of the future Messiah, but to David not being killed, as previously discussed. Throughout this section of the New Testament, there is little support from the Old Testament relating to the death of Jesus, and most especially, to the subject of substitutionary atonement. Though Paul does make the claim that Jesus died *according to the Scriptures*, he does not state which Scriptures those were. From an evidentiary perspective, he provides no corroboration for his claims, and thus we can give very little weight to his arguments.

It is apparent that all New Testament authors rely heavily on the Old Testament, although their purpose in doing so is not so easily discerned. In some cases, they make explicit prophecy fulfillment claims, but far less often than the NKJV editors have done. Christian New Testament scholars have pondered this issue in depth, and have varied opinions, based largely on their own approach to hermeneutics. The question is, however: how can we be sure that the evangelists wrote in accordance with that method of interpretation? Were the evangelists scholars of substantial literary skill, or were they ordinary folk who simply wrote as they understood their own beliefs, with no hidden agenda or meaning?

We deal with this in some detail in Part 8.

PART 6

ESCHATOLOGY

*"The part of theology concerned with death, judgement,
and the final destiny of the soul and of humankind."*

Clearly, the Apostles, early disciples, the Nazarenes, the *Followers of the
Way*, did believe that Jesus was the prophesied Messiah - but why? What
did they know that I do not know? Or was it a case of them believing,
with all their hearts, something which has subsequently been proven to
be untrue? Were they mistaken, and if so why? If their misunderstanding
was later overtaken by events that proved that they were wrong, how,
or perhaps why, did Christianity continue as a religion based on those
mistaken beliefs?

As implausible as that scenario might sound, history has shown it to
be not that uncommon.

Religions in Denial

The Mormon religion[1], or to give it its full name: The Church of Jesus Christ of the Latter-Day Saints, was founded in the 1820's by one, Joseph Smith, who was later found in a court of law to be a fraud. His having "golden plates" has never been corroborated, or in any way authenticated, and we only have his word for the guidance by the Angel Moroni. He claimed that in 1829, May 15th to be precise, John the Baptist himself was sent by Peter, James, and John, to confer the "Aaronic Priesthood" on him, and a recent convert, Oliver Cowdrey, in Pennsylvania. There is more, but we need not pursue that avenue further.

All this is well known and comprehensively documented, but nevertheless, the Mormon religion is not only still with us, but has continued to thrive.

A similar case is that of the Jehovah's Witnesses, and the Watchtower Bible and Tract Society[2]. This, another modern sect, was founded circa 1880, by Charles Taze Russell, with the energetic support of Judge J.F. Rutherford. The two later split along theological grounds. Russell claimed to be conversant in Greek, but upon cross-examination, under oath, where he had been charged with perjury, he failed to even identify letters in the Greek alphabet. He was forced to confess that in truth, he was not familiar with the Greek language. There are other disturbing tales that could be narrated, but I am sure that you see where this is heading. Again, all this is well documented, but nevertheless, your front door is likely graced by adherents to this religion, as is mine.

The strangest religion is the Church of Scientology, founded by a science fiction writer, L. Ron Hubbard. Being a fan of science fiction, I quite enjoyed his books, but his religion is something else. Amongst its numerous claims, we find[3]:

- Scientology teaches that the bible is a by-product pf Hindu Scriptures.
- God, or gods, may exist, but the individual must decide for himself (promoting relative truth).
- Christ is a legend that pre-existed earth-life on other planets and was implanted into humans on earth. Jesus was just a shade above "clear" and was no greater than Buddha or Moses.

- Reincarnation sufficiently explains man's existence, but Scientology is the freedom from reincarnation.
- Man is basically good, and in his evolution, he will finally become a godlike being known as "*homo novis*".

You didn't believe me, did you, that it was started by a science fiction writer, until now that is. Unsurprisingly, the most prominent members of this religion are also amongst the A-Listers of Hollywood. I guess that if your occupation involves fantasy, fantasy becomes your reality. Incidentally, Scientology is the most litigious religion in modern times, but that could just be a function of American culture.

Finally, the religion of Islam, much in the news nowadays. Muslims assert that Islam is a religion of peace, and always has been, which is true if one denies the history of Islam, and ignores the Islamic fundamentalists who are intent on returning modern day Islam to its well-documented roots.

All religions, that I have studied, have much to commend them, as evidenced by the behaviour of most adherents. However, a view that I take, in seeking to understand their truth, is to examine the lives of their founders. From the history that I have read, the self-styled Prophet Mohammed is not a man whose life any person should emulate. Islam was spread by the sword, with hundreds of thousands slaughtered if they failed to convert; worse, millions of Hindus were slaughtered during the Moghul invasion. Unlike Islam, well, unlike if we ignore the persecution of the Jews and others described as heretics, Christianity was spread peacefully.

So, the founders: Smith, Russell, Hubbard, and Mohammed, men who thought they were whom they were not. History has found them out. But just as Simon bar Kokhba was considered the Messiah, but failed in his redemption of the Jewish people from their oppressors, could it be that Jesus, likewise having failed, was not whom he, and his followers, thought he was?

Eschatological Temper

"But the New Testament writers on the whole do not do the theorizing [Ed. on matters apocalyptic]. They are content to accept current speculations. What they are concerned with is the application to Christ."[4]

This is significant: they expected Jesus to fulfill the prophecies concerning the End of Days, and so saw Jesus in that messianic context. For those claiming that the Messianic Era has already begun, paying lip service to the prophecies that align that era with the *eschaton*, consider this: Abraham died circa 1985 BCE, about two thousand years before Jesus was born. It is now about two thousand years since Jesus died. Is there any indication, in any literature, that the Messianic Era would last longer than the whole previous history of monotheism? If not, and if that notion seems implausible, then there is little to no reason to believe that the Messianic Era began with Jesus.

Each of the religions mentioned above, like Judaism and Christianity, has their own version of eschatology, except the Jewish Sadducees, who did not believe in life after death. I believe it probable, that irrespective of what they thought Jesus achieved during his public life on Earth, his followers still expected him, as the prophesied Jewish *mashiach*, to accomplish what they believed had been prophesied about him, namely: the physical redemption of Israel. He did not manage it in his first appearance: in truth, quite the opposite occurred, so, they reasoned, he must be coming back again.

In his book, "*The Place of the Old Testament in the Formation of New Testament Theology*"[5], British New Testament scholar and Anglican priest, Barnabas Lindars, wrote of the belief current in Second Temple Judaism:

> "There is obviously the extremely important biblical exegesis of the Qumran sect. The significance of this, by comparison with the rabbinic literature, consists not primarily in rules of interpretation, which are often shared with rabbinic exegesis, but in the sect's conviction that it was living in the crucial time before the transition of the ages, to which all Scripture refers ... There are really two points at issue here. First, there is the conviction that all Scriptures, not only the Prophets and the Psalms, but even the Torah itself, have the end times as their proper point of reference. Secondly, there is the conviction that the present generation is actually the end time to which they refer."[6]

In the previous chapters, I have attempted to demonstrate that the prophecies of the Hebrew Scriptures point to the End Times, and that the expectations of the Messiah were in that context, and that context alone. There was no concept of a first and second coming. I offered that a likely reason for his disciples seeing Jesus as Messiah was because they believed that the eschaton was nigh, and many verses in the New Testament substantiate that understanding. That view is shared by many New Testament scholars, for example:

> "It remains true that the rapid expansion of Christianity would really be inexplicable except against the background of a widespread feeling amongst Jews of the day that they were living in the end time. For it is, as Holtz has pointed out[7], only because of the pre-understanding of the Bible in this eschatological sense, attested not only in Qumran and apocalyptic, but also to some extent in rabbinic sources, that the church's application of the whole range of the Old Testament to Jesus could be felt to be a plausible undertaking and find acceptance."[8]

It does seem a human trait, in times of extreme stress, to perceive that the end of the world is nigh. We have many examples in modern times, even in primarily secular societies. It should come as no surprise that in a society holding fiercely to its religion, under persecution from an occupying pagan power, and well aware of the prophecies of their redemption, should see their present distress in that light. Wishful thinking perhaps, but such is the outcome of hope. Christianity continues to urge hope in the Messiah, so we should not think worse of the ancients. Whilst this eschatological view is apparent in the Gospels, it is also apparent in the writings of Paul.

Author, James Dunn, who, at the time of his book, was Lightfoot Professor Emeritus of Divinity at the University of Durham in England, described Paul as the *Eschatological Apostle*. He wrote:

> "If we are to understand the first generation of Christianity adequately, it is of crucial importance that we take into account the eschatological temper and perspective of first believers. For they believed that in Jesus Messiah the new age had dawned – not

just a new age, but the final age, the *eschaton* (=last) in which the ultimate promises of God and hopes for Israel would be realised. This conviction focused on two features:

- Jesus' resurrection as the beginning of the general/final resurrection (Rom 1:4, 1 Cor 15:20, 23);
- The soon-coming return of Jesus as manifestly Messiah and Lord (Acts 3:19-21)."[9]

James Dunn wrote an entire chapter on *Paul the Apostle*, questioning: Apostle or Apostate?[10] He raises some interesting issues, especially regarding Paul's so-called conversion[11]: Conversion from what to what? That aside, he argues convincingly that Paul's view of the *eschaton* was that it was about to begin, and that meant that the promises of the redemption (restoration) of Israel would be fulfilled: the houses of Israel and Judah would be rescued from captivity; they would be reunited in the Land of Israel; Jerusalem would be forever the capital of Israel; and the promises in the prophecies of Jeremiah, chapters 30-31, would be soon honoured. This was the view of many of the first generation of Jesus' disciples.

The confusion was further compounded by what appeared to be, contradictory statements by Jesus concerning the *Kingdom of God*. Was it close, nearby, or future? Was it to be on earth, or in heaven? Was that to be the *new heaven and new earth* of Revelation of 21:1, or the restoration of Israel as it had been in its glory days? Modern scholars offer modern views, but what did the contemporaries of Jesus understand?

We shall deal with this in two parts: firstly the Kingdom of God, and then NT verses that evidence belief in the *eschaton* being imminent.

REFERENCES:

1. Zacharias, Ravi, *The Kingdom of the Cults*, Bethany House Publishers, Minneapolis, MI, 2003, p. 49
2. *Ibid*, p. 193
3. *Ibid*, p. 352
4. Beale, G.K., *The Right Doctrine from the Wrong Texts? Essays on the Use of the Old Testament in the New*, Baker Academic, Grand Rapids, MI, 1994, p. 142
5. Lindars, Barnabas, *The Place of the Old Testament in the Formation of New Testament Theology*, Cambridge University Press, UK, 1976

6. Beale, *Ibid*, p. 140, quoting Barnabas.
7. Holtz, T., *Untersuchungen uber die alttestamentischen Zitatw bei Lukas* (TU 104), Berlin, 1968, Sp. 25
8. Beale, *Ibid*, p. 141
9. Dunn, James D.G., *Jesus, Paul, and the Gospels*, Wm. B. Eerdmans Publishing Co., Grand Rapids, MI, 2011, p. 143
10. *Ibid*, pp. 133-147
11. *Ibid*, p, 153

CHAPTER 6-1

THE KINGDOM OF GOD

*"The law and the prophets were until John. Since that time the
kingdom of God has been preached, and everyone is pressing into it."*
(Luke 16:16)

I am somewhat puzzled as to why Luke wrote that *the law was until John*,
but in the very next verse, he wrote: *"And it is easier for heaven and earth
to pass away than for one tittle of the law to fail"* (see also Matthew 5:18).
Was he confused, did he express himself clumsily, or did he just lift these
phrases from elsewhere without understanding? Given that heaven and
earth are yet to pass away, should we understand that Mosaic Law is still
in force? This may seem irrelevant in a discussion on the Kingdom of God,
but depending on how you understand that term, it might have a direct
bearing on how we should *live* in that Kingdom.

So, what should we understand by the term, *Kingdom of God*, as
mentioned in the New Testament? Depending on which verse you read, it
is here, near, within you, yet to come, or somewhere else. It is as confusing
as the competing theologies of "pre", "a", and "post" millennialism. We

shall review every mention in both the Old and the New Testaments, in an endeavour to resolve the question, but first a <u>caveat</u>: our purpose, in the context of this study, is not to understand the kingdom in a Christological sense, but to discover whether the New Testament provides evidence of prophecy fulfillment. If we allow our thinking to be based on Christian commentaries, we are simply affirming the consequent – presuming messianic prophecy fulfillment. That will not do at all.

I wish to thank the compilers of *The Strongest NIV Exhaustive Concordance* for their diligence, facilitating my efforts to extract this sought-after term, even though I am using the NKJV rather than the NIV which was their source bible version.

Old Testament

The Kingdom of God (Heaven, Lord) gets so few mentions that we can list them:
- "Yours is the kingdom, O Lord" (1 Chronicles 29:11).
- "The kingdom of the Lord, which is in the hands of the sons of David" (2 Chronicles 13:8).
- "The Lord has established His throne in heaven, and His kingdom rules over all" (Psalm 103:119).
- "They shall speak of the glory of Your kingdom and talk of Your power" (Psalm 145:11).
- "Your kingdom is an everlasting kingdom" (Psalm 145:13)
- "And in the days of these kings the God of heaven will set up a kingdom which will never be destroyed; and the kingdom shall not be left to other people; it shall break in pieces and consume all these kingdoms, and it shall stand forever" (Daniel 2:44).
- "His kingdom is an everlasting kingdom" (Daniel 4:3).
- "His kingdom is an everlasting kingdom" (Daniel 7:27).

I believe it a logical inference that if the Israelites, at least as far back as King David, declared God's Kingdom to be an everlasting kingdom, then it would be the same kingdom spoken about in the time of Jesus. God being infinite, omnipotent, and omniscient, it is unlikely that the nature of

His Kingdom would ever change. I contend that such is the understanding that should be taken forward into the New Testament, and if the latter contains assertions to the contrary, then they could be wrong.

Psalm 103 places God's throne in heaven, but His Kingdom is overall, which would suggest both the heavenly realm and all of Creation. If the kingdom of the Lord is in the hands of the sons of David (2 Chronicles 13:8), it likely refers to that part of the kingdom that is on earth. If God's kingdom is an everlasting kingdom, I believe that we can assume that the kingdom referred to in 2 Chronicles is also an everlasting kingdom. But what of: "*in the days of these kings the God of heaven will set up a kingdom*" (Daniel 2:44)?

Given the contrast with the previous four earthly kingdoms, all of which would be destroyed, this new kingdom "*which shall never be destroyed*", is likely a kingdom on earth as well. If we link this to "The kingdom of the Lord" in 2 Chronicles 13:8, then it would refer to the promised kingdom of Zion, centred in Jerusalem - "*For Hashem has chosen Zion; He has desired it for His habitation. This is My resting place forever and ever, here I will dwell, for I have desired it.*" (Psalm 132:13-14)

Assuming that my understanding of the Old Testament references is correct, let us see how well that would fit with the preaching of the kingdom of God in the times of Jesus.

New Testament

The count of mentions of the Kingdom of God (heaven, Lord) are as follows: Matthew [54], Mark [20], Luke [43], John [4], and the total in the other books, [26].

The terms used to describe the Kingdom, with or without an initial capital, relative to the people are: would appear immediately, was going to appear, coming, has come, will come, would come, does not come, waiting for, until it comes, has been forcefully advancing, has come upon you, is conferred on you, has been given to you, belongs to, is yours, near, not far, and within you. People can receive, inherit, or enter the Kingdom of God; it can come to them, or they can be counted not worthy. If there is any other variation, I must have missed it, but clearly, one can evidence virtually any case by selecting the definition which best fits. There are certainly plenty to choose from.

Jesus' Kingdom is not of this world and is from another place. The Kingdom is not a matter of eating, drinking, or marriage, and flesh and blood cannot enter. God's Kingdom will never end.

The task of the disciples was to preach the *Good News* of the Kingdom of God, but I wonder about their understanding, as do I of mine, given the myriad descriptions. Putting aside the Pauline theology, which we will come back to, I sense that the message contains two elements:

1. The spiritual aspect of the kingdom, referring to our right standing before God; and
2. Our place in the future earthly kingdom, depending on how God evaluates our righteousness.

We have evidence of these two concepts in Matthew's Gospel:

a. "Whoever therefore breaks one of the least of the commandments, and teaches men so, shall be called least in the kingdom of heaven" (v. 5:19).
b. "For I say to you, that unless your righteousness exceeds the righteousness of the scribes and the Pharisees, you will by no means enter the kingdom of heaven" (v. 5:20).
c. "But many who are first will be last, and the last first" (v. 19:30).
d. "So the last will be first, and the first last" (v. 20:16)

Unless I have missed them, there are no other NT references to this concept, which I find a little curious. That aside, in Matthew 5:20, was Jesus condemning the scribes and Pharisees to hell, if they did not change their ways? Can it be true that self-righteous people cannot inherit the kingdom of God, even if in all other ways, they are like Zacharias and Elizabeth, "walking in all the commandments and ordinances of the Lord blameless"? (Luke 1:6) I strongly doubt that to be true. I suspect, without rightly knowing, that the righteousness of the scribes and Pharisees to which Jesus was referring, are as described in Matthew 23:5-7 and Luke 11:43. Yes, they loved the best places at the feasts, the best seats in the synagogues, the greetings in the marketplaces, and to be called by men, Rabbi, Rabbi. But who doesn't, even amongst Christians? (see Chapter 10-2).

Unfortunately, the New Testament authors were never explicit in what they meant by the kingdom of God (perhaps they weren't sure). With his parables, Jesus did attempt to tell us what it is "like", so let us turn to those parables, all ten of them. I am not going to reiterate the explanations found in many Christian commentaries, they would simply distract from the overarching theme of this book, but I will offer a summary for you to consider, and how that does fit in with the theme of prophecy fulfillment.

Reading Christian commentaries on these parables, I find that in the main, they are interpreted in a Christological sense. That may be correct, but again, it seems to me to be affirming the consequent: Jesus is the Christ, therefore he was speaking parables about himself. If we begin without that presupposition, the description of the kingdom can be quite different. How does that help us understand the kingdom of heaven? From an objective perspective, not at all, because we are unable to separate that kingdom from Jesus. Yet, we have a sense of that kingdom from the Old Testament, one which does not necessitate a Messiah dying for our sins. As this study seeks to determine, on the evidence, whether Jesus fulfilled messianic prophecies, it is illogical to assume, *a priori*, that he did.

Thus, what follows is my interpretation as if I had been hearing these parables from a Jewish rabbi, a prophet even. Given that Jesus was often referred to as rabbi, and conveying God's Word via parables was a common practice of the time, I contend that it is reasonable to adopt that perspective. I will attempt to treat like with like, as I understand them.

Heavenly Parables Interpretation - Matthew

Matthew's Gospel contains parables of what the Kingdom is like: sower (13:24), mustard seed (13:31), yeast (13:33), treasure (13:44), merchant (13:45), net (13:47), householder (13:52), king owed debts (18:23), landowner (20:1), and again king (22:2).

The parable of the sower (13:24) and that of the dragnet (13:47), are similar in that in both stories, the bad are finally separated from the good, and discarded. In the first case, the bad are deliberately mixed with the good, whereas in the latter, the mixing is a natural occurrence, as found in all societies. The message: the good will be welcomed by God in the kingdom, the bad will not.

The parable of the mustard seed (13:31), and that of the yeast (13:33), are similar in that they both refer to a single source developing into much more, influencing / encouraging others to share in the bounty. I believe that they echo an earlier saying: "But he who received seed on good ground is he who hears the word and understands it, who indeed bears fruit and produces some a hundredfold, some sixty, some thirty" (13:23). Both the mustard seed and the yeast bear multiplying fruit. That gets us no closer to identifying "*the word*".

The parable of the householder (13:52) seems to continue that theme in a sense, in that having been instructed concerning the kingdom of heaven, those so instructed can now add those new teachings to what they had previously learned, bearing fruit as it were. Again, we are no closer to understanding those new teachings.

Two more parallel parables are that of a man finding a treasure in a field (13:44), and the merchant finding a great pearl (13:45). In both cases, they are prepared to sell all they have, so they may acquire what they desire. Objectively, what they treasure, and desire, is the kingdom of heaven – why else is the kingdom of heaven like that? These parables link to an earlier response by Jesus: "If you want to be perfect, go sell what you have and give it to the poor, and you will have treasure in heaven" Matthew (19:21). Hopefully, Jesus did not intend that everyone should follow that advice, else everyone would be poor, unless the previously poor were then rich and continued the cycle of giving. This reminds of a saying about being so heavenly minded as to be of no earthly good.

The parable of king who was owed debts (18:23) echoes what Jesus taught his followers to pray: "*forgive us our debts as we forgive our debtors*" (Matt 6:12). As an aside, this prayer has Jewish roots, and is known in ancient Hebrew as the *Avinu* Prayer[1]. The origin can be found in the rejoicing of King David:

> "And David blessed Hashem in the presence of the entire congregation. David said, 'Blessed are You, Hashem, God of Israel our forefather, from This World to the Word to Come. Yours, Hashem, is the greatness, the strength, the splendour, the triumph,

and the glory, even everything in heaven and earth. Yours, Hashem, is the kingdom, and the sovereignty over every leader. Wealth and honour come from You and You rule everything – in your hand is power and strength and it is in Your hand to make anyone great or strong. So now, our god, we thank You and praise Your splendrous Name." (1 Chronicles 29:10-13, TJB)

I believe that in teaching people what to pray, Jesus was repeating what he would have already known from the traditions of the Jewish people. In relation to debtors, I see no logic to interpret beyond that ethic, absent of presuppositions of Jesus' sacrifice, as many Christian commentaries entail. Did Jesus intend that his disciples were not to understand until after his death?

The parable of the kingdom of Heaven being like the landowner (20:1) is somewhat confusing. If we accept continuity from chapters 19 to 20, it is bookended by verses 19:30 and 20:16, saying: "the first will be last, and the last first", although expressed in the opposite sequence (is that significant?) I am even more confused as to why "For many are called but few chosen" is tacked on the end, seemingly a *non-sequitur* in this context, unlike where it concludes the parable in verse 22:2. Christian commentaries offer that we should ignore the Chapter 20 division, and that appears logical given that the first word in that chapter is "For", signifying continuity. However, continuity is not necessarily a feature of Matthew's Gospel: see 5:1 through 7:29, where Jesus appears to preach numerous subjects in one session with no context whatsoever. I find it presumptuous to insist on continuity in this instance, and if I am right, the Christian contention regarding the chapter division may arise from a desire to emphasise a Christological interpretation. You might note my urging to ignore the division separating Isaiah chapters 52 and 53, as I believe that it introduces a discontinuity in the narrative.

If we accept that at this stage in his public life, Jesus had not declared his mission of dying for the forgiveness of sin, it is logical to expect his disciples to have understood this parable in its plain sense, not from a Christological perspective. It tells of labourers accepting unequal work, but being given equal reward. Those who worked longest made the quite reasonable claim, that those who worked least should not have been rewarded equally with them. You may recall that earlier, Jesus advised: "the Son of Man will come in the glory of His Father ... and then He will reward each according to his works" (Matthew 16:27). Again, "I am coming quickly, and My reward is with Me, to give everyone according to his work" (Revelation 22:12). Paul had the same sense of heaven: "and each one will receive his own reward according to his own labour" (1 Corinthians 3:8). If each is to be rewarded according to his works, why did Jesus say the opposite concerning the kingdom of heaven – that the reward is the same irrespective of our work? I will leave that for theologians to ponder, but perhaps I have misunderstood the parable; perhaps Jesus was simply saying that God can do what He likes, irrespective of whether it to be fair or not.

The parable concludes with: "I wish to give to this last man the same as you (the first man)", somehow in justification of "the last will be first, and the first last". Had I been the labourer, I would have been totally confused; had I been a disciple, I would have asked: "But what about what you said earlier, that we would be rewarded according to our works?" I can only assume that the author of this Gospel was even more confused in his recollection of that narrative, or in the translation from Hebrew Matthew into Greek. But then the really strange part: for many are called but few are chosen. What that has to do in this context is beyond my understanding.

Finally, in Matthew, the parable of the king arranging a marriage for his son (22:2). This was not an original parable of Jesus, but was traditional in Judaism. As I have studied parts of the *Talmud*, and other sources of wisdom of the Jewish sages, I have gained a greater appreciation of just how Jewish Jesus was. Scholars note how often Jesus quoted from the Old Testament, yet few have noted that many of His parables were not new, being variations of the parables of old. The practice of conveying wisdom and truth, via parables, is as ancient as the Jewish people themselves, which is why Jesus used that method of communication. Perhaps obvious when we think about it, but are we conscious of its significance?

Here is an example:

> "Rabban Yochanan ben Zakkai, apparently in connection with this teaching of Rabbi Eliezer, also told a parable that is recorded in the Talmud. It tells, in effect, how a king issued invitations to all his servants to attend a banquet but gave no time for the event. The wise servants hurried to prepare themselves and, dressed in

their finest clothes, they waited at the entrance to the palace. They knew the King had everything at his disposal and could announce the banquet at any time. The foolish ones went about their regular business thinking that a banquet would take lengthy preparation, and they would have plenty of time to get ready for it. Suddenly, the call went out, the palace doors opened, and the servants were summoned in. The wise ones entered his presence dressed for the occasion, while the foolish ones rushed in dirty, wearing grimy work clothes. The King then commanded, 'Let those who are dressed and prepared properly for the banquet sit and eat and drink; let those who did not, stand and look on!'"[2]

My question: Should this parable in Matthew 22:2-14 be interpreted in other than the original Jewish sense? If we are being told to prepare for the kingdom of God (or heaven), what form should that preparation take other than repentance, as John the Baptist preached? And if we are to repent, or what should we repent other than not observing God's law in Torah? Could John have meant any different, as his preaching preceded that of Jesus?

Heavenly Parables Interpretation – Mark

There is only one parable referencing the kingdom of God that is unique to Mark's Gospel: "The kingdom of God is as if a man should scatter seed on the ground" (v. 4:26-29). It speaks of man's efforts, but primarily that of God continuing to work through His creation – the seed germinates, sprouts, and yields crops without the further efforts of man. This parable must refer to the kingdom of God in the earthly, present sense, rather than a future spiritual sense. It confirms the concept of the kingdom has already come, is here, is near, or is within you.

Heavenly Parables Interpretation – Luke

None of the ten parables, unique to the Gospel of Luke, draw a comparison with the kingdom of heaven, and so are not of interest here.

In passing, however, I do have a question mark over them concerning their authenticity. Given that these parables do not appear in any of the other three Gospels, particularly the Synoptics, how did Luke hear of them? If Matthew, Mark, and John knew of them, why did they not record them? I have no answer, and I doubt whether anyone can know, but I am curious nonetheless.

Heavenly Parables Interpretation – John

Whilst John mentions the kingdom of God on four occasions, none are descriptive of what the kingdom is "like", other than that one cannot see it if not born again (3:3); cannot enter unless one is born of water and the Spirit (3:5); and Jesus' kingdom is not of this world, and not from here (18:36). That Jesus' kingdom is *not of this world* is somewhat confusing given that other statements about the kingdom of God / heaven do have an earthly, here and now, connotation.

Kingdom Discussion

If I had nothing but the Gospels to guide me, I would be more than a little confused about the kingdom of God. Is it on earth, in heaven, or both? Is it already here, not here but near, still coming, albeit forcefully advancing, or is it yet to be set up, awaiting the End of Days? The answer, apparently, is "yes" to all those questions.

What was the Gospel of Jesus, the *Good News* to be spread by all the disciples to all nations? In the context of the eschatological temper of the times, why would Jesus commission his disciples to "Go therefore and make disciples of all nations" (Matthew 28:19)? How could they have time for missionary journeys, if Jesus' return was imminent? Given that the subject matter of this verse is not found in the other Gospels, could this be a later addition when any hope of Jesus' imminent return was rapidly fading?

If the *Good News* was about the kingdom of God, why did the Gospel of John contain not a single parable or metaphor? Could it be that by the time John released his version of the Jesus story, about half a century later, events had caused him to reconsider? If we consider the broader context of the New Testament, we can find additional meaning, as Christian commentaries do, but again the logic trap: begging the question. I would ask you to recall the caveat at the beginning of this chapter: our purpose is to discover what evidence, mentions of the kingdom of God provide in relation to messianic prophecy fulfillment. If we assume Jesus as the Messiah, we assume his intentions as interpreted by Christianity, and simply affirm what it is that we are attempting to discover. Not helpful at all.

Of the some 150 mentions of the kingdom in the New Testament, I am going to choose just a few that reinforce one another. I have a sense that the message of Jesus changed during the course of his public life, although from a Christian point of view, it was perhaps refined and became more specific (the doctrine of progressive revelation). Alternatively, we can consider whether *"Jesus' proclamation that the kingdom of God was soon to be established on earth"*[3] was the understanding of the Apostles, and hence their eschatological temper, but that *"Paul's message of a heavenly Christ"*[4], wherein Jesus rose not with a body of flesh, but with an immortal spiritual body (1 Corinthians 15:42-52) influenced the writings of the Evangelists.

It started, consonant with the preaching of John the Baptist:

a. "Repent, for the kingdom of God is at hand" (Matthew 3:2).

b. And from that time Jesus began to preach and to say, "Repent, for the kingdom of God is at hand" (Matthew 4:17).

c. Jesus came to Galilee, preaching the gospel of the kingdom of God, and saying, "the time is fulfilled, and the kingdom of God is at hand. Repent and believe in the gospel" (Mark 1:14-15).

The time is fulfilled: what could that mean, other than the period of waiting for God to establish His kingdom on earth was over (Daniel 2:44)? You see, that was the *Good News* for the Jews - their time had come, and their enemies would be defeated. That was the Gospel of Jesus from the beginning, the rest was just commentary. To *repent* was the message of all the Prophets, going all the way back to Moses, and so with the kingdom of God being at hand, repentance became urgent. When Jesus asserted: *"I was not sent except to the lost sheep of Israel"* (Matthew 15:24), he was saying the same as earlier prophets, who had continued their attempts to rescue those who no longer kept the covenant agreed at Sinai. Of interest is that repentance is mention 55 times in the New Testament, 11 times in the Book of Acts alone.

I contend that John the Baptist, and then Jesus, set an expectation amongst his hearers: the promised Messiah had come, ushering in the new age, with the triumph of God's people over their enemies about to occur. Jesus confirmed this to the Samaritan woman:

> "The woman said to him, 'I know that Messiah is coming' (who is called Christ [anointed one]). Jesus said to her, *'I who speak to you am He'*" (John 4:25).

Jesus saw himself as Messiah, and whatever expectations that he set amongst the people, they could only have been as prophesied in the Hebrew Scriptures, not that a Samaritan woman would have known of them (that story doesn't quite ring true). The expectation of the Messiah was the *eschaton*, the time when God would end the world as we know it. They foresaw a new beginning, though not as John described in his vision: "Now I saw a new heaven and a new earth, for the first heaven and the first earth had passed away. Also, there was no more sea." (Revelation 21:1) The Jewish expectation of the new order was as described in Jeremiah 31:31-40, with the Third and Final Temple to be built. The prophesied Kingdom of God had arrived.

Paul's Kingdom of God

In Second Temple Judaism, the traditional understanding of the new world order, under the Messiah, was one here on Planet Earth. Paul's concept was very different: the Kingdom would be heavenly, populated by immortal spiritual beings, just as he perceived the risen Jesus to be. In 1 Corinthians 15:47-48, Paul tells us that the first man [Adam] was made of dust, but the heavenly man bears the image of the heavenly Man [Jesus]. There were clearly two different scenarios: that of Judaism, and that of Paul. By the end of the 1st century CE, attempts had been made to synthesize the two, but not very successfully. Either there will be a new heaven and a new earth, according to John, with bodies of flesh and blood like the Gospel version of the risen Jesus, or there will be a new heaven, but no new earth, because immortal spiritual bodies have no need of such habitation.

Summary

*"Now when Jesus saw that he answered wisely, he said to
him: You are not far from the kingdom of God."*
(Mark 12:34)

What was the scribes answer? "There is one God, and there is no other but He. And to love Him with all the heart, with all understanding, with all the soul, and with all the strength, and to love one's neighbour as oneself, is more than all the whole burnt offerings and sacrifices" (Mark 12:32-33), neatly encapsulating the message of Torah, and paraphrasing that most Jewish of prayers, the *Shema* (Deuteronomy 6:4-5). The kingdom of God is here, in the way we live our lives, according to the Scriptures. Mark's account accords with the duality of the Jewish view of the time, where he noted that Joseph "was himself waiting for the Kingdom of God" (v. 15:43).

Quoting from Hyam MacCoby's study:

"It should be noted, too, that Jesus' singling out of these two verses from the Hebrew Bible (one from Deuteronomy and the other from Leviticus) as the greatest of the commandments was not an original idea of his own, but as an established part of Pharisee thinking. The central feature of the liturgy created by the Pharisees (and still used by Jews today) is what is called the *Shema*, which is the very passage from Deuteronomy cited by Jesus ... This injunction was regarded by the Pharisees as so important that they declared that merely to recite these verses twice a day was sufficient to discharge the basic duty of prayer.[5] Interestingly, too, in view of Jesus' final comment to the 'lawyer', the rabbis regarded these verses as having a strong connection with the 'kingdom of God' (a phrase not coined by Jesus, but part of Pharisaic phraseology). They declared that to recite these verses comprised 'the acceptance of the yoke of the kingdom of God'. It should be noted that in Pharisaic thinking, 'the kingdom of God' had two meanings: it meant the *present* kingdom or reign of God, or it could mean the *future* reign of God over the whole world in the Messianic age. It is possible to discern in Jesus' frequent use of the same expression the same twofold meaning: sometimes he meant a future state of affairs which he has come to prophesy (e.g. 'Repent, for the kingdom of God is near'), and sometimes he is referring to the present kingship of God, which every mortal is obliged to acknowledge (e.g. 'the kingdom of God is among you')."[6]

I'm glad that we managed to clear that up! Incidentally, notice mention of *the yoke of the kingdom of God* – did Jesus intend the same message when he said: "For my yoke is easy and my burden is light" (Matthew 11:30)?

We know that, despite expectations, there was no Second Coming, which leaves us with a quandary concerning the kingdom under discussion. In whatever manner Christianity chooses to interpret, "*the kingdom of God is at hand*", those early followers of Jesus would have understood it in one, or both, of two ways: (1) the kingdom of God is always present; and/or, (2), the redemption of Israel was imminent, consistent with the eschatological view of the evangelists (see Chapter 6-2). Putting it together in terms of prophecy fulfillment, the essence of the Old Testament prophecy was the redemption (rescue) of Israel from its enemies. A new world order would ensue, the Temple restored, the covenant renewed, the Law of God in the minds and on the hearts of everyone, and everyone knowing God. Thus would be, the Kingdom of God. Jesus saw himself as that prophesied Messiah, and his disciples believed in him, and what he would accomplish. He failed to accomplish what was prophesied concerning the End of Days, and thus he could not have been the prophesied Messiah.

There is a kingdom of God present, just as there has always been. This kingdom is the rule of an eternal, sovereign God over all the universe. In the context of prophecy, however, that is not the kingdom yet to be ushered in by the Messiah, whatever that may be. I have no idea, so I will just have to wait.

REFERENCES:

1. Gordon, Nehemiah, and Johnson, Keith, *A Prayer to Our Father - Hebrew Origins of the Lord's Prayer*, Hilkiah Press, 2010

2. Hannah, Keren, Pirkei Avot, *Ethics Now and Then - 28 - Avot 2:15*, T.B. *Shabbat* 153a

3. Tabor, James D., *Paul and Jesus: How the Apostle Paul Transformed Christianity*, Simon & Schuster Paperbacks, New York, NY, 2012, p. 6

4. *Ibid*

5. Babylonian Talmud, Berakhot 13b.

6. MacCoby, Hyam, *The Mythmaker: Paul and the Invention of Christianity*, Barnes & Noble Books, San Francisco, CA, 1998, pp. 30-31

CHAPTER 6-2

ESCHATOLOGICAL TEMPER

"Little children, it is the last hour; and as you have heard
that the Antichrist is coming, even now many antichrists
have come, by which we know that it is the last hour."
(1 John 1:18)

And here we are, two thousand years later, and it still seems to be the *last hour*! Is that what John meant: that the last hour would last for millennia, or did he mistakenly believe that the return of the Messiah was imminent? Based on the evidence as provided in this chapter, I believe the latter to be true, and I am not alone in that understanding. Mind you, I am somewhat perplexed that after more than fifty years, with still no sign of the Second Coming, Christians were still believing in it, although perhaps the destruction of Jerusalem in 70 CE was seen as a fulfillment of Jesus' warning in Luke 21:8-36. Perhaps they thought: Jesus was right about that, so even if his return seems delayed, it is still about to happen. On the other hand, I have often wondered why none of the Gospels mention the destruction of Jerusalem. Christian apologetics use that fact as evidence that the Gospels were written prior to 70 CE, but an alternate explanation is that to mention it would lend doubt to Jesus being the Messiah: after all, he did not achieve what the Jews expected the Messiah to achieve.

We ended the previous chapter with the view, or at least, my view, that the term: *"the kingdom of God is at hand"*, arose from the acceptance of Jesus as Messiah, about to fulfill the prophecy of Daniel 2:44.

Gospel of Luke

We have confirmation of this understanding from Luke's account of the encounter with Jesus after the resurrection:

> "So they said to him, 'the things concerning Jesus of Nazareth, who was a Prophet mighty in deed and word before God and all the people, and how the chief priests and our rulers delivered him to be condemned to death, and crucified him. But we were **hoping** that it was he who was going to **redeem Israel**.'" (Luke 24:19-21) [emphasis mine]

So, even after the very end of Jesus' public life, and all his preaching about whatever, there were still some who anticipated whom he should have been, and what he should have achieved. The context of Luke 24:13, "Now behold, *two of them* were travelling that same day" [italics mine] would identify them as Apostles, or at least, disciples of Jesus. Some commentaries identify one of them as Peter; others that one of them was Luke; another that one was Nathaniel; and yet others that they were clearly disciples, but of no special significance. Could these have been the same people, or acquaintances of people, who just a short time earlier, had welcomed Jesus into Jerusalem, his so-called triumphal entry, even though up till that point, no recognisable triumph had been achieved: *"Blessed is the King who comes in the name of the Lord"* (Luke 19:38)? What else could have been in the minds of those people, and all those who had followed Jesus to Jerusalem, other than their belief in an imminent redemption from the oppression of the Romans?

What did Jesus mean when he said: *"The time has drawn near"* (Luke 21:8)? Yes, he did advise *"the end will not come immediately"* (21:9), but the terminology is not that used to allude to a time far into the future, but to a time near, albeit, not immediately. Why did Jesus warn his followers of impending wars and commotions (Luke 21:8-36)? Again, we come back to the question: To whom were these warnings directed – those then living, or those living far into the future?

Jesus foretold of when Jerusalem would be surrounded by armies, with its "*desolation near*" (21:20), but why frighten his listeners if such was not to happen in their lifetimes? What would be his purpose of highlighting the "*pregnant and to those who are nursing babies in those days*"? Was this why Paul later advised against marriage: because he was conscious of Jesus' warnings? Was Paul aware of Luke's narration of Jesus' saying: "Daughters of Jerusalem, do not weep for me, but for yourselves and your children. For indeed the days are coming in which they will say, 'Blessed are the barren, wombs that never bore, and breasts which never milked!'" (Luke 23:28-29) Given that this assertion is entirely contrary to the spirit of Genesis 9:7, it can only mean that something terrible was about to happen. Scholars generally agree that the authors of the New Testament were writing for a contemporary audience, not prophesying of events to occur at an unspecified time long into the future. We must, then, take them at their word, on this subject at least.

Gospel of John

"Most assuredly, I say to you, *the hour is coming, and now is, when the dead will hear the voice of the Son of God; and those who hear will live*" (John 5:25). This allusion to the resurrection of the dead can only relate to the End of Days, so effectively, Jesus was saying that the *eschaton* had arrived, although again, the timing of John's writing is mystifying. I must question my own understanding: John wrote a full half-century after these events were supposed to occur, so why did he chronicle these words, and why did he still believe? Perhaps he questioned his own understanding, but kept faith that Jesus would soon return. I cannot know.

> "You have heard me say to you, I am going away and coming back to you. If you loved me, you would rejoice because I said, I am going to the Father, for my Father is greater than I. And now I have

told you before it comes, that when it comes, you may believe."
(John 14:28-29)

Paraphrased: I am telling you now, so that when I do return, you will
believe that I am whom I claimed to be. Now think about this: Why would
Jesus say this to his followers, if his return was going to be long after they
were all dead and buried? Jesus understood that they were skeptical, and
so promised that he would return so that their doubts would be overcome.
The only problem was, and is, he has failed to return. Admittedly, another
Gospel records Jesus saying: "But of that day and hour no one knows,
not even the angels of heaven, but my Father only" (Matthew 24:36), but
that hardly answers my question. Another thought that comes to mind is:
why *day and hour*, why not just day? When being non-specific, the writers
usually used the term, day - when the term "hour" is added, it gives a sense
of immediacy, not some unspecified period long into the future. I have the
sense that Jesus thought that he would soon return, and that he conveyed
that understanding to his followers.

> "Peter, seeing him (John), said to Jesus, 'But Lord, what about *this*
> man?' Jesus said to him, 'If I will that he remain till I come, what
> is that to you? You follow me.' Then this saying went out among
> the brethren that this disciple would not die. Yet Jesus did not say
> to him that he would not die, but, 'If I will that he remain till I
> come, what is that to you?'" (John 21:21-23)

Undoubtedly, this narrative is open to interpretation, one of which is
that Jesus would return before John died. This would answer my concern
as to why John continued to believe in the Second Coming, long into his
old age. I wonder whether, on his death bed, John wondered about this,
and whether he had heard Jesus correctly? The structure and wording of
John 21:24 suggests that John was not the author of this section: "This is
the disciple who testifies of these things, and wrote these things; and **we**
know that **his** testimony is true." [emphasis mine] Most odd. Changing
from the *first* person to the *third* person in the one sentence, referring to
oneself, is most unusual, and I know not what to make of it. No matter, it
is not important in the context of *this study*.

Other Relevant Gospel Verses

Just briefly, consider these verses in the context of the expectations of the Apostles:

1. "Assuredly I say to you, there are some standing here who shall not taste death till they see the son of man coming in his kingdom" (Matt 16:28).
2. "Tell us when will these things be? And what will be the sign of your coming, and of the end of the age?" (Matt 24:3)
3. "Assuredly, I say to you, this generation will by no means pass away till all these things take place" (Matt 24:34).
4. "Assuredly, I say to you that there are some standing here who will not taste death till they see the kingdom of God present with power" (Mark 9:1).
5. Mark's account is similar, noting that Joseph "was himself waiting for the Kingdom of God" (Mark 15:43)
6. "Therefore, you also be ready, for the son of man is coming at an hour you do not expect" (Luke 12:40).
7. "Take heed that you not be deceived; for many will come in my name, saying 'I am he', and 'the time has drawn near'. Therefore, do not go after them" (Luke 21:8).
8. Foretelling the signs of the coming of the son of man (Luke 21:9-26).
9. "Then they will see the son of man coming in a cloud with power and great glory. Now when these things begin to happen, look up and lift up your heads, because your redemption draws near" (Luke 21:27-28).
10. Narrative of Jesus warning the women who followed him to his crucifixion (Luke 23:28-29).
11. "You also be patient; establish your hearts, for the coming of the Lord is at hand" (James 5:8).
12. "I suppose therefore that this is good because of the present distress (crisis, necessity)" (1 Cor 7:26).
13. "But this I say, brethren, the time is short" (1 Cor 7:29).
14. "For the form of this world is passing away" (1 Cor 7:31).

Jesus was not teaching theology to his disciples, to be passed down generation to generation: he was speaking to them of what was going to happen in their lifetimes.

Jesus' return was on the minds of the Apostles, and they had every reason to believe that it would be soon, even within the lifetimes of some of them. In hindsight, it is easy to allegorise these words of Jesus, but we must understand them in the same context as the immediate disciples would have understood them. Otherwise, one must accuse Jesus of deliberate deception. I find it curious that Luke's account, of Jesus conversing with the women on his way to the cross, is not found in either Matthew or Mark, and John has nothing to say on the matter either, even though that as far as we can ascertain, only John followed Jesus to his place of crucifixion. Similarly, Luke's recounting of Jesus' narrative, concerning the signs of the *End of Days*, is not found in the other Gospels in the same context. We can accept that Jesus conveyed these warnings, for they do appear in the other Gospels, though not in the same words or context, but this only lends weight to the contention that in the minds of Jesus' disciples, the *End of Days* were not far off.

I do not accept that Jesus was warning his disciples, so that they could warn future generations: we get no sense of this from New Testament writings – there is always a sense of immediacy. When the disciples wrote to the various followers of Jesus, the concern was for their immediate welfare, not for an unimaginable number of generations far into the future. We must always keep this in mind when we attempt to interpret both the Gospels and Epistles – the audience was contemporary, in contemporary circumstances.

Remaining as When Called

"Let each one remain in the same calling in which he was called."
(1 Corinthians 7:20)

In the minds of some commentators, this decree implies that Gentiles need not obey Mosaic Law, so it is worthwhile to review the context. 1 Corinthians 7 opens with: "Now concerning the things of which you wrote to me, it is good for a man not to touch a woman." From the commentaries that I have read, and drawing a logical inference, the question concerned the habits of Corinthian men who sought the pleasures of prostitutes, and Paul was advising against that practice. Paul recommended that each man have his own wife (1 Cor 7:2). But he deems marriage a "concession", saying that he would prefer it if all men were like himself: unmarried and celibate (1 Cor 7:6-7). This is a strange statement coming from a Jew, when the normal practice was for men to marry soon after their eighteenth birthday, honouring God's commandment to "be fruitful and multiply" (Gen 9:7). When did God ever proclaim that marriage was a "concession", or that its purpose was to avoid sexual immorality? Marriage was, and is, a commandment of God!

Paul also argued: "Do we have no right to take along a believing wife, as do also the other apostles, the brothers of the Lord, and Cephas" (1 Corinthians 9:5), so why would Paul have recommended against marriage, other than as a concession to avoid sexual immorality? What was on his mind? Curiously, Paul (or whoever) later appears to contradict his earlier advice: "Therefore I desire that the younger widows marry, bear children, manage the house, give no opportunity to the adversary to speak reproachfully" (1 Tim 5:14).

Paul next addresses the issue of divorce, particularly in marriages where one spouse is a believer, and the other not, Paul offering the possibility that one may save the other. Opening with: "as the Lord has called each one, so let him walk" (1 Cor 7:17), Paul then issues his controversial decree to all the churches: "let each one remain in the same calling in which he was called", neither circumcising nor uncircumcising [epispasm - reverse circumcision], because "circumcision is nothing and uncircumcision is nothing", but what truly matters is "keeping the commandments of God" (7:19). I find it impossible to interpret verse 7:20 to mean that the uncircumcised (Gentiles) are excused obedience to God's commandments, when Paul says precisely the opposite: that no matter whether you are circumcised (Jew) or uncircumcised (Gentile), keeping God's commandments is what matters.

Further on, Paul writes: "Brethren, let each one remain with God in that state in which he was called" (7:24). How do we understand state, in connection with God? If you were a pagan when called, should you remain a pagan? Obviously not! If you worshipped the Roman Emperor and observed the Roman festivals and rituals as dictated by Rome, should you continue in that observance? If you were a prostitute, or a priest of a pagan temple, should you remain so? Placed in its historical setting, there were only four theological groups of concern to Paul in his time: Jews, proselytes, God-fearers, and pagans. There was no such group as *Christian* - that was what you became *after* you answered the call, although more correctly, a Follower of the Way, a *Nazarene*. We know from Acts 21:17-24 that Paul, according to Luke at least, did not teach the Jews to "forsake Moses", so it is unlikely that there was any movement by Jews to become non-Jews, other than by those who sought to surgically reverse their circumcision (*epispasm*); usually to participate naked in the popular Greek games. From the perspective of *religious beliefs*, it should be clear that in his directive to remain as you were when called, Paul could only have been referring to Jewish proselytes and Gentile God-fearers, and most likely just the latter, making the point that there was no necessity to convert to Judaism.

As best as I can understand, the term "virgin" in verse 25 relates to both single men and women; in verse 28, the meaning changes to just the young women (the assumption being that all singles should be celibate). The recommendation against marriage seems based on the individual's ability to "care for the things of the Lord" (7:32), "that you may serve the Lord without distraction" (7:35). Again, why was Paul advocating that God's commission for His people (Gen 9:7) should now be ignored: what had changed?

Present Distress or Impending Crisis

Most bible translations of 1 Corinthians 7:26 use the term "present distress" or similar, whilst one Messianic Jewish version has "impending crisis": which is correct? I find little pattern in the commentaries, the persecutions by Nero being one theme, but two verses have me favouring the sense of an "impending crisis", for as one commentary puts it: "Paul believed that the last day was just around the corner. There was very little time left. To plan far ahead was pointless."[1] The relevant verses are as earlier: "But this I say, brethren, the time is short ... for the form of this world is passing away" (7:29 and 7:31). As many scholars have noted, Paul believed that the *eschaton* or *Last Days* was at hand.

Summary

I believe there to be three important understandings that we should take from 1 Corinthians 7. Firstly, Paul's eschatological view that the world in its then current form, was about to end, and that the return of the Messiah was imminent, perhaps even within Paul's own lifetime. As an aside, we should also consider whether this perception influenced what was written in Hebrews: "Now what is becoming obsolete and growing old is ready to vanish away" (8:13). My belief is that the scholars, long ago, who decided on the chapter and verse numbering got it wrong in this instance: chapter 8 should end with verse 12, and what is given as verse 13 should be verse 1 of chapter 9. I will leave you to ponder that for yourselves.

Whilst much of what Paul had to say about morality is true perpetually, some of his recommendations have no validity, because his underlying premise was wrong. This leads into my second point: the inerrancy of the New Testament must be in question because quite clearly, Paul misunderstood events and thus, one cannot claim that he was guided by the Holy Spirit in what he wrote in that chapter, most especially regarding the inadvisability of marriage. You may be aware that even in recent times, some Christian sects periodically proclaim: "the End is Nigh", and encourage others to give away all their possessions, echoing Jesus: "If you want to be perfect, go, sell what you have and give to the poor, and you will have treasure in heaven" (Matt 19:21). I would contend that Paul had a similar understanding of how to conduct oneself, with the coming of the Messiah just around the corner. This is the only context in which Paul's advice makes any sense.

Finally, the decree to *remain as when called* primarily concerned the issue of conversion to Judaism, as Paul was wont to emphasise:

- "There is neither Jew nor Greek" (Gal 3:28).
- "For in Christ Jess neither circumcision nor uncircumcision avails anything" (Gal 5:6)
- "For in Jesus Christ neither circumcision nor uncircumcision avails anything" (Gal 6:16).
- "circumcision is nothing and uncircumcision is nothing" (1 Cor 7:19).

Beyond that, we can include the advice against marriage and having children, but nothing else - there is no Scriptural warrant to extend beyond that context. Even more, one cannot argue from these verses that Christians are exempt from obeying the law as written in Torah. By the same token, there is no evidence therein as to which laws Christians are to obey, but I have discussed that in an earlier work, "Christians Too, Must Obey"[2].

The notion that the Son of Man would soon return, and that the *End of Days* was nigh, was put into the minds of the disciples by Jesus himself – either that, or the evangelists invented the words of Jesus. If Jesus did believe in the *eschaton* being imminent, and I am convinced (sort of) on the evidence that he did, then he was clearly wrong, and that thought could not have been put into his mind by the Father (God). This raises the question: If Jesus was wrong on that issue, and he claimed that he and the Father were one, by what logic do we accept his other pronouncements on his mission and accomplishments?

In his essay entitled, The Place of the Old Testament in the Formation of New Testament Theology, Barnabas Lindars commented: "It remains true that the rapid expansion of Christianity would really be inexplicable except against the background of a widespread feeling amongst Jews of the day that they were living in the end time. For it is, as Holtz pointed out, only because of the pre-understanding of the Bible in this eschatological sense, attested not only in Qumran and apocalyptic, but also to some extent in rabbinic sources, that the church's application of the whole range of Old Testament to Jesus could be felt to be a plausible undertaking and find acceptance."[3]

REFERENCES:

1. Murphy-O'Connor, Jerome, *1 Corinthians: A People's Bible Commentary*, The Bible Reading Fellowship, Oxford, England, 1999, p. 82
2. Talbot, Wayne, *Christians Too, Must Obey*: Putting a Fence Around Torah, Xlibris, Bloomington, IN, 2017
3. Beale, G.K., *The Right Doctrine from the Wrong Texts? Essays on the Use of the Old Testament in the New*, Baker Academic, Grand Rapids, MI, 1994, p. 141

PART 7

THE PROPHECY CONUNDRUM

"If there arises among you a prophet or a dreamer of dreams, and he gives you a sign or a wonder, and the sign or the wonder comes to pass, of which he spoke to you, saying, 'Let us go after other gods' – which you have not known – 'and let us serve them', you shall not listen to the words of that prophet or that dreamer of dreams, for the Lord your God is testing you to know whether you love the Lord your God with all your heart and with all your soul. You shall walk after the Lord your God and fear Him, and keep His commandments and obey His voice; you shall serve Him and hold fast to Him."
(Deuteronomy 13:1-5)

As best as I can understand from various Christian texts that I have studied, the messianic accomplishments of Jesus would fall under these headings:

a. Expiation.
b. Propitiation.

    c.   Reconciliation.

    d.   Redemption; and

    e.   Defeat of the Powers of Darkness.

In brief, *expiation* means the removal of our sin and guilt; *propitiation* refers to the removal of God's wrath; *reconciliation* refers to the removal of our alienation from God; *redemption* means that we are released from the curse of the law, the guilt of sin, and the power of sin; and finally, Jesus *defeated* the power of Satan over us. All of these are said to have been accomplished by Jesus dying on the cross, in *substitutionary atonement*. My first question is: Were any of these claimed triumphs prophesied, and if so, when and by whom? The simple answer is: No, none of these things were prophesied in the Hebrew Scriptures.

As we have discussed before, the Hebrew Scriptures make very clear that God forgives all those who love Him and sincerely repent. God holds everyone accountable for their own sins, and as He demonstrated to Moses, no-one can take accountability for the sins of others – substitutes are not allowed. Guilt remains only so long as either we do not love God, or do not repent of our sins. Similarly, we do not require reconciliation with God, as long as we continue on the path of righteousness. None can be fully righteous, for all sin, but the Scriptures make clear that we can achieve, and maintain, a level of righteousness acceptable to God. There was never *a curse of the law*: that is a nonsense perpetrated by Paul in his endeavour to justify his gospel. God gave us His law to guide us in how to live in harmony with Him and one another, and as God is ultimately wise and omniscient, His advice is for all time. Both Isaiah and Micah prophesied that Torah will go forth from Zion at the End of Days, meaning that all those who have ignored Torah will learn of the error of their ways.

In what way have we been released from the *power of sin*? Sin still holds as much power over all people, including Christians, as it ever did over the Children of Israel. Why do Catholics go to confession if the power of sin has been overcome? How can anyone claim that Satan has been defeated, even in the lives of Christians, when even the Christian clergy to the highest level continue to sin - some most egregiously? The sins of the early Catholic Church in relation to their persecution of the Jews is well documented. How can the power of Satan have been defeated when

Rome seemed to have misunderstood Jesus' supposed self-sacrifice, calling the Jews "Christ Killers". How could Rome have been guided by the Holy Spirit when it chose to abandon the Sabbath, which God said was forever, and abandoned the Law, which God said would be pronounced in the Last Days, to be written on the hearts and minds of everyone? Whom was Rome following when it was decided to compromise with the sun-worshipping, pagan Emperor Constantine, even adorning religious art with the sun behind the heads of the saints?

Now contrast those claimed achievements with what the Jews expected of the Messiah, their expectations built upon the words of the Prophets, and a degree of wishful thinking and hope. The Messiah was to bring about the political and spiritual redemption of the Jewish people by bringing them back to Israel, and restoring Jerusalem (Isaiah 11:11-12; Jeremiah 23:8; 30:3; Hosea 3:4-5). He would establish a government in Israel that would forever be the centre of all world government, both for Jews and Gentiles (Isaiah 2:2-4; 11:10; 42:1), and he would have the Temple rebuilt, re-establishing worship therein(Jeremiah 33:18). The Messiah would also restore the religious court system of Israel, and establish Jewish law as the law of the land (Jeremiah 33:15).

That is a very different set of achievements than those claimed for Jesus as Messiah; in truth, not only did he not accomplish any, but the opposite of all of them occurred within a few short years of his death.

Thus the conundrum: How can it be claimed that Jesus fulfilled Old Testament prophecies, when what it is claimed he accomplished was not prophesied, and what was prophesied was not accomplished? That said, let me repeat what I wrote earlier, regarding our understanding of prophecy.

We are often given to thinking of prophecy as a definitive statement of future events, but as Rabbi Tzvi Freeman describes it: "a prophecy is the state of matters in a higher realm, before it has reached our earthly plane. There, it is amorphous, not fully defined and can materialize in more than one way."[1] That being so, we should be wary of our interpretation of any prophecy, especially where there is considerable doubt as to it having been fulfilled in the way we have been taught. However, there is also a warning here for people like me, who reject a claimed prophecy fulfillment because events did not transpire in the way that I understood them - I have placed my own interpretation of what it would look like, and I could well be in error.

I am ever conscious of that intellectual trap … thus, even my conclusions above could well be suffering from a misunderstanding. However, I do not believe so, for there are far too many discrepancies, inconsistencies, and anomalies in the narratives, and in the resulting Christian theology.

REFERENCES:

1. http://www.chabad.org/library/article_cdo/aid/489751/jewish/Is-the-Book-of-Daniel-authentic.htm

CHAPTER 7-1

A NEW COVENANT?

"Behold, days are coming – the word of Hashem – when I will seal a renewed covenant with the House of Israel and with the House of Judah."
(Jeremiah 31:30)

Continuing our discussion from Chapter 3-5, or perhaps just reinforcing what I contend to be true, the TJB commentary on Jeremiah 31:30-32 reads:

> "After his lyrical portrayal of the redemption from exile of the newly unified nation, Jeremiah foretells the greatest aspect of the redemption: the renewal of the eternal covenant between God and Israel. In this context, the Hebrew word *chadashah* (which is usually rendered as 'new') should be rendered as *renewed*, which is how Jeremiah employs the word at the end of his *Book of Lamentations* (5:22): 'renew (Hebrew: *chadeish*) our days as of old.' The Sinaitic covenant delivered at Mount Horeb was renewed more than once in Israel's history (e.g., on the Plains of Moab,

Deuteronomy 29:9-13 and during the reign of Josiah, *II Chronicles 34:31*), but each time, Israel subsequently strayed from it.

Thus, *Radak* explains, the Hebrew *bris chadashah*, literally, *a new covenant*, is really a renewal of the original covenant at Sinai. It is new only in the sense that it will never again be violated by Israel, unlike in the past. Over the centuries of sinfulness and exile, Israel had seemed to abrogate its original covenant, but God declares that the covenant remains eternal. Chapter 26 of *Leviticus* foretells the grisly suffering that Israel would endure over the centuries of exile, but that chapter concludes with the Divine promise that god will never forget or annul the original covenant. Indeed, in the last book of prophecy (*Malachi 3:22*), the prophet exhorts, 'Remember the Torah of Moses My servant, which I commanded him at Horeb [i.e., Mt. Sinai] for all Israel – [its] decrees and [its] statutes'."1

How plausible is this explanation in The Jewish Bible?

Let us check the references given above. Firstly, Deuteronomy 29:9-13, "You are standing today, all of you, before Hashem, your God … for you to pass into the covenant of Hashem, your God, and into His imprecation that Hashem, your God, seals with your today, in order to establish you today as a people to Him and that He be a God to you … Not with you alone do I seal this covenant and this imprecation, but with whoever is here, standing with us today before Hashem, your God, and with whoever is not here with us today." This is Moses speaking, before the Children of Israel depart for the Promised Land, leaving Moses behind, as punishment for him not obeying God regarding speaking to the rock. So, yes, this is not God directly renewing the covenant, but if Jesus is claimed to be a prophet like Moses, and Jesus spoke only what the Father told him to speak, then it is reasonable to assume that Moses was speaking on behalf of God.

II Chronicles 34:30-31, "The king [Josiah] went up to the Temple of Hashem, [with] all the men of Judah and the inhabitants of Jerusalem and the *Kohanim* and the Levites and all the people from great to small, and he read in their ears all the words of the Book of the Covenant that had been found in the Temple of Hashem. The king then stood at his place and sealed the Covenant before Hashem, to follow Hashem and to observe

His commandments and His testimonies and His decrees with all his heart and with all his soul, to uphold the words of the Covenant written in this book." If you haven't read II Chronicles, I would recommend that you do, for this is an amazing story of intrigue, and how the kings of Israel dealt with the troubles that beset them. Despite the people straying from the Covenant, there were persistent attempts to return to it.

Another point that I would reiterate is this: the promises that God made with the Children of Israel, and the Covenant that He sealed with them, was not *for their sake*, but for **His Name's Sake** (see Deuteronomy 7:7-8, 9:4-6; Isaiah 43:25; Ezekiel 20:9, 20:44, and 36:22-23). The story of Israel, basically, is not about the people, but about God. This is why the final words of the last Prophet, Malachi, state:

> "Remember the Torah of Moses My servant, which I commanded him at Horeb for all Israel – [its] decrees and [its] statutes. Behold, I send you Elijah the prophet before the coming of the great and awesome day of Hashem. And he will turn back [to God] the hearts of the fathers with [their] sons and the hearts of sons with their fathers, lest I come and strike the land with utter destruction." (vv. 3:22-24)

This is why the disciples of Jesus, believing him to be the promised Messiah, thought that John the Baptist must be Elijah, but in doing so, also believed that *the great and awesome day of Hashem* was soon to occur. As events have proven, they were wrong. Similarly, the author of the Book of Hebrews had the same misconception when quoting Jeremiah 31:30-33, for this prophecy also related to the End of Days, although why he thought so over a half a century later, when the ingathering of the Jews did not occur, is quite beyond my imagining. The other aspect that has me wondering is how he missed the party of the second part: the Houses of Israel and Judah. I can think of no more precise way of defining with whom the covenant was to be renewed, or even made as a new covenant, if that is how one prefers to interpret the text, than was made in the phrasing of Jeremiah – it simply leaves no room for ambiguity, and no room for a claimed *New Israel* replacing the nation that God declared as His First Born.

Of one thing we can be sure, the prophecy in Jeremiah 31:31-38 has yet to come to pass.

CHAPTER 7-2

REDEMPTION

"I desire kindness, not sacrifice; and knowledge
of God more than burnt offerings."
(Hosea 6:6, TJB)

Immanence of God

A definition of the immanence of God is given here:

> "A belief in God's immanence holds that God is present in all
> of creation, while remaining distinct from it. In other words,
> there is no place where God is not. His sovereign control extends
> everywhere simultaneously."[1]

If God is immanent, is present in all of creation, then the natural
corollary is that we are always in the presence of God. As God is infinite,
there can be no difference to His presence, whether in this Earth, or in
heaven. Whether we are still in this life, or in the next, God's presence is

the same, and thus our being in His presence can be no different – God is the determinant in all circumstances. This raises the question: Why would we need to be perfect to be in God's presence in heaven, when we are nevertheless in God's presence in our imperfect state on Earth? There is undoubtedly a prerequisite for sharing in some future kingdom in a beneficial way, but that is an entirely different matter. If all souls are immortal, whether in heaven or hell, all souls must be in the presence of an infinite, immanent God, by definition.

A Jewish rabbi, David Aaron, whose teachings I study, reminded me of the following:

> A famous story tells about a man who dreamt that he saw his whole life's journey as footsteps in the sand. Sometimes there were two imprints — his and G-od's. But, during the parts of the trek that were most difficult he saw only one set of footprints. He complained to G-od, "G-od, you promised me that you would always accompany me in my journey. How is it that during the most difficult times in my life you disappeared?" G-od responded, "I have always been with you. The reason why you only see one set of footprints is because during your most difficult times I carried you. Those footprints our mine."

> It is especially helpful to remember this in the most challenging moments. During times of pain in your life have you ever asked, "Why is G-od doing this to me? Why is G-od hurting me?"

> There is no answer to that question because it is the wrong question.

> This question is based on a perception that there is a G-od, an invisible Being, floating out there in outer space, and you are down here on earth, separate and removed from Him. However, Kabbalah says that there is no such G-od and there is no such you. The true you is the soul and the soul is none other than a part of G-od.

> Therefore the real question is, "Why is G-od doing this to an aspect of Himself?"[2]

To my mind, God's immanence refutes the Christian notion of the need for substitutionary atonement, a process said to justify us in the sight of God, declaring us to be legally exonerated, and therefore sufficiently righteous to be in the presence of God. We are in God's presence, because God is in our presence, irrespective of our righteousness. I cannot see how God would need us to be declared exonerated from our sins, when the Hebrew Scriptures repeatedly tell us that God forgives those who repent. Our presence together is independent of our righteousness, because God is immanent, in our presence irrespective.

Mercy, not Sacrifice

"Go and learn what this means ...." (Matthew 9:13)

So, let us do that:

> "and the meaning is, that God takes more delight and pleasure, either in showing mercy himself to poor miserable sinners; or in acts of mercy, compassion, and beneficence done by men, to fallen creatures in distress, whether for the good of their bodies, or more especially for the welfare of their souls, than he does even in sacrifices, and in any of the rituals of the ceremonial law, though of his own appointing: and therefore must be supposed to have a less regard to sacrifices, which were offered, neither in a right manner, nor from a right principle, nor to a right end; and still less to human traditions, and customs, which were put upon a level, and even preferred to his institutions; such as these the Pharisees were so zealous of. The force of our Lord's reasoning is, that since his conversation, with publicans and sinners, was an act of mercy and compassion to their souls, and designed for their spiritual good; it must be much more pleasing to God, than had he attended to the traditions of the elders, they charge him with the breach of: besides, what he was now doing was the end [goal] of his coming into this world." (Gill's Exposition of the entire Bible)[3]

If we are to understand that "God takes more delight and pleasure in showing mercy ... than he does even in sacrifices, and in any of the rituals of the ceremonial law, though of his own appointing", why would He require human sacrifice and the spilling of innocent blood? Why would He not show mercy, even to one described as *His Only Begotten Son*? Why would God choose to not take delight and pleasure, but instead, require the very act that He Himself prohibited His creation from doing? God foreknew that the pagans would sacrifice humans to placate their false gods, which is likely why He prohibited His *Chosen People* from doing it. It was, and is, and abomination to Him, as it is to us. If placating false gods with human sacrifices is an abomination to God, why would He require it to placate Himself?

If we are to believe that God is the entirety of morality, and that His very existence defines morality, how could God contravene Himself? *"Burnt offering and **sin offering** You did **not require**"* (Psalm 40:6) [emphasis mine].

The Eucharist and Communion

I am aware of numerous texts which unfairly, and likely, ignorantly, condemn the Christian practice of taking communion in the form of bread and wine, so I shall do my best to not make that same mistake. Quoting from a Vatican online resource:

> "At the Last Supper, on the night he was betrayed, our Savior instituted the Eucharistic sacrifice of his Body and Blood. This he did in order to perpetuate the sacrifice of the cross throughout the ages until he should come again, and so to entrust to his beloved Spouse, the Church, a memorial of his death and resurrection: a sacrament of love, a sign of unity, a bond of charity, a Paschal banquet 'in which Christ is consumed, the mind is filled with grace, and a pledge of future glory is given to us'."[4]

Again, I ask: Why would God not only brutally sacrifice His son, but desire that those who love Him should *perpetuate the sacrifice of the cross throughout the ages*? This makes no sense to me, and is contrary to all that

I have read in the Hebrew Scriptures. There cannot be two Gods, with two disparate behaviours: God is either One, or He is not. As we shall see a little later, when God instructed the Israelites on sacrificial offerings, such offerings were always of a lower order than man, because man is made in the image of God. An assault on man is tantamount to an assault on God, and what He stands for.

Returning to the New Testament, The Book of Hebrews 10:5 states: "For it is not possible that the blood of bulls and goats could take away sins", with the next verse misquoting Psalm 40 in two ways:

1. "But a body you have prepared for Me", versus "My ears You have opened" (OT); and
2. "In burnt offering and sacrifices for sin you had no pleasure", versus "You did not desire" (OT).

The author then attempts to justify this in verse 8, saying that the will of God was that the first, animal sacrifice, was taken away and replaced by the second, human sacrifice, *once for all*. The original wording does not support the requirement for a sin offering, such as Jesus is said to have made of himself. The Hebrew Scriptures are clear: God does not require sin offerings, most especially the blood of an innocent man. Just why the author of Hebrews thought that he had licence to alter the words, and thus the meaning, of King David's writing is unclear to me, but to my mind, such distortion of Scripture is unconscionable. I am reminded of a passage in the Quran, where it states that Isa (Jesus) was given the Book by Allah (God), but that the Christians deliberately corrupted it. On the evidence as I have evaluated it, there is some truth to this.

The Book of Hebrews also presents a paradox: "For it is not possible that the blood of bulls and goats could take away sins" (10:5), versus "And according to the law almost all things are purified with blood, and without the shedding of blood there is no remission" (9:22). I will let you ponder that for yourselves.

Misrepresentation in the Book of Hebrews

There is a misunderstanding amongst Christians regarding the blood sacrifices in the Temple, and without indulging in an extensive discourse, the suggestion in Hebrews 9:22 that a blood sacrifice could atone for practically any sin is contrary to the teachings in the Tanakh. Likewise, the assertion that *"without shedding of blood there is no remission"* is false. I often wonder whether, when people read an OT quote in the NT, they bother to check whether the OT was quoted accurately, or whether the text has been deliberately altered, as was shown in the previous example. Why the difference, especially in the very same bible version? Check this for yourself. I may seem to be harping on the issue of *bible inerrancy*, but if one's faith is dependent upon that assumption, then such faith is on a very sandy foundation indeed.

You can perhaps understand why my suspicions are aroused, but continuing.

Firstly, read Leviticus 4:1-4 and Numbers 15:24-31, and then review Leviticus 17:10-11 in that light (*Derash*). The author of Hebrews, whoever he was (or they were), misunderstood the Judaic understanding of Leviticus 17:11, one of the reasons why so many scholars doubt that Paul was the author, not that I necessarily accept their reasoning for their doubts. Blood sacrifice for all Israel was only for *unintentional* sins, not for all sins: there were also special provisions for when the priest committed sins in the Temple. The two goats' scenario, when one is sacrificed, and the other set free to bear the sins, relates only to sins by the priest in the Temple – *no other*.

Biblical Blood Sacrifices

Yes, no debating it, the Children of Israel did practice blood sacrifice for the forgiveness of sin, because God so commanded it. However, three questions must be asked:

1. Was blood sacrifice alone, necessary for forgiveness, or were other practices acceptable to God.
2. Were such sacrifices for ALL sins, or only for some; and
3. Could the blood of mankind ever be sacrificed?

The first question is answered by God: "But if his means are insufficient for two turtledoves or for two young doves, then he shall bring, as his guilt offering for that which he sinned, a tenth-ephah of fine flour for a sin-offering" (Leviticus 5:11). Clearly then, God demanded a sin-offering, but not necessarily a blood offering. The issue of "why blood" is too lengthy to discuss in this study, but also irrelevant to the doctrine of substitutionary atonement. The point here is that whilst a blood sacrifice of an animal was preferred by God, He also accepted other sin-offerings.

Let me return to the issue of Hebrews 10:5 misquoting Psalm 40:6, to view it from another perspective: that of prophecy fulfillment. The Psalm states, in part: "sin offering You did not require", with the NKJV editors annotating related verses in Hebrews as prophecy fulfillment. Now, if the Psalm states that God did <u>not</u> require a sin offering, how could the very same Psalm be considered a prophecy of God requiring a sin offering that was fulfilled by Jesus? That makes no sense at all, to me at least. Jesus, by being a sin offering, could not fulfill a prophecy that stated that no sin offering was required.

Sacrificing Humans – Spilling Innocent Blood

Scripture makes clear that God hates human sacrifices, so why would He engage in that practice Himself? Consider these verses:

a. "Whoever sheds man's blood, by man his blood shall be shed; for in the image of God He made man." (Gen 9:6)

b. "Beware for yourself lest you be attracted after them, after they have been destroyed before you, and lest you seek out their gods, saying, 'How did these nations worship their gods, and even I will do the same'. You shall not do so to Hashem, your God, for everything that is **an abomination to Hashem**, that **He hates**, have they done to their gods; for **even their sons** and their daughters **have been burned in the fire** for their gods." (Deuteronomy 12:30-31, TJB)

c. "Because they forsook Me and estranged this place [from Me]; and they burned incense in it to the gods of other that they had not known – they and their forefathers and the kings of Judah; and they filled this place with the **blood of innocent people**; and they built the high places of Baal, [at which] to **burn their sons** in fire as burnt-offerings to the Baal, which **I never commanded, nor spoke of, nor even considered in My heart**." (Jeremiah 19:4-5, TJB)

d. "And they **sacrificed their sons** and daughters to the demons. They **spilled innocent blood**, the **blood of their sons** and daughters whom they sacrificed to the Canaanite idols; and the land was polluted by the blood-guilt." (Psalm 106:37-38, TJB)

e. "Then you took **your sons** and your daughters whom you begot for Me, and these **you slaughtered** for them [*as sacrifices for your deities*] to devour!" (Ezekiel 16:20, TJB)

Again, I find it incomprehensible that God would sacrifice "*His Only Begotten Son*" (John 1:18) to satisfy Himself, when He had earlier been unambiguously specific regarding the pagan practice of spilling innocent blood in the sacrifice of sons to the gods - He had not even considered it in His heart! How could there be a "*Lamb slain from the foundation of the world*" (Rev 13:8), when God proclaimed of old that human sacrifice was an abomination to Him? Is God a liar? If Christians believe in the inerrancy of the Old Testament, how can they explain God changing His mind about spilling the blood of an innocent?

I cannot believe that God ordered a human sacrifice, for any reason, when He had declared to the Children of Israel that such was an abomination to Him, and an action that He had not even considered in His heart.

Sin (Guilt) Offerings – Blood Sacrifice

That God commanded sin offerings at all, continues to be a mystery to me, although I have read some interesting commentary by both the ancient Sages and modern rabbis. However, He did so command, and thus we must be clear on the details, dispelling any Christian myths on the subject. The most common myth is this: that a blood sacrifice was necessary for the forgiveness of sin – no blood, no forgiveness. This theme is central to a book written by Joshua McClure, *The Crimson Thread of the Bible*[5], seeking to justify the spilling of innocent blood for the forgiveness of sin, but the narrative is false, for it ignores large tracts of the Old Testament, and God's instructions to the Children of Israel regarding blood sacrifice. Let us review what God did say on the subject.

We will start with an unambiguous example of where a blood sacrifice is *not* required:

> *"But if his means are insufficient for two turtledoves, then he shall bring as his guilt offering for that which he sinned, a tenth-epath of fine flour for a sin offering"* (Leviticus 5:11)

Quoting from this source[6]:

> "Those who believe in the efficacy of blood sacrifice look to Leviticus 17:11 for justification:
>
> > *'For the life of a creature is in the blood, and I have given it to you to make atonement for yourselves on the altar; it is the blood that makes atonement for one's life.'* [Leviticus 17:11]
>
> But if you read this verse in context, you will find that it refers to abstaining from eating or drinking the blood of a sacrifice, and nothing more. God commanded this prohibition in order to maintain the distinction between the Jewish people and the pagans. Most pagans ate the blood of their sacrifices as a means of incorporating their gods into their bodies and into their lives."

The concept of incorporating gods into their lives is why Jews reject the Christian practice of Communion. The entire quotation from Leviticus 17 reads:

> *Any Israelite or any alien living among them who eats any blood -- I will set my face against that person who eats blood and will cut him off from his people. For the life of a creature is in the blood, and I have given it to you to make atonement for yourselves on the altar; it is the blood that makes atonement for one's life. Therefore, I say to the Israelites, `None of you may eat blood, nor may an alien living among you eat blood. Any Israelite or any alien living among you who hunts any animal or bird that may be eaten must drain out the blood and cover it with earth, because the life of every creature is its blood.' That is why I have said to the Israelites, `You must not eat the blood*

of any creature, because the life of every creature is its blood; anyone who eats it must be cut off.'

As we saw in Leviticus 5:11, in the middle of the commandments concerning the sacrifices for sin, the Bible tells us we do not need any blood sacrifice – other means of forgiveness are provided, and preferred by God. There are examples in Scripture where forgiveness was granted by God without blood sacrifice, even to the Gentiles, or where God commanded what was especially important to Him: read Numbers 16:47, 31:50; Jonah 3:1-10; Isaiah 6:6-7; Jeremiah 7:22-23; and so on. Even in the New Testament, as we saw earlier, Hebrews 10:8 misquotes Psalm 40:6, echoing the sentiment in 1 Samuel 15:22-23, that offerings and contributions are no substitute for obedience to God: *"Does Hashem delight in elevation-offerings and feast-offerings as in obedience to the voice of Hashem?"*

But as emphasised in the Hebrew Scriptures, the ultimate and primary method of procuring forgiveness is repentance; for example:

- Let the wicked one forsake his way and the iniquitous man his thoughts; let him return to Hashem and He will show mercy … for He is abundantly forgiving." (Isaiah 55:7)
- As I live – the word of the Lord Hashem/Elohim – [I swear] that I do not desire the death of a wicked one, but rather the wicked one's return from his way, that he may live. Repent, repent from your evil ways! Why should you die?" (Ezekiel 33:11).

If God does not even require the death of a wicked one, why would He require the death of an innocent one? Next, when was a sin / guilt offering required, what did it accomplish, and for what type(s) of sin? The Book of Leviticus expounds on this across several chapters, which you should read for yourself, but here I will just summarise the details. We should note that there are five types of sacrifice stipulated in Torah[7]:

1. *Olah* (Burnt Offering) - Leviticus 1:1-17; 6:8-13
2. *Minchah* (Grain Offering) - Leviticus 2:1-16; 6:14-23
3. *Shelami* (Peace Offering) - Leviticus 3:1-17; 7:11-36
4. *Chatat* (Sin Offering) - Leviticus 4:1-5:13; 6:24-5:7
5. *Asham* (Guilt Offering) - Leviticus 5:14-6:7; 7:1-7

The explanation above is by a popular Messianic Jewish author, D. Thomas Lancaster, who has published numerous books which seek to explain Jesus in the context of Judaism. He notes: "Christians often think that in the Old Testament times, people had to bring sacrifices to pay for their sins. The sacrifices, for the most part, are not about paying for sin. In Torah, the death of the animal does not substitute for the death of the sinner. Instead, the death of the animal provides a proxy to bring the worshipper near to God. It does not appease an angry God. It provides a method by which God might be approached."[8] That said, the only sins of the Israelites which were forgiven by an offering, or sacrifice, were those committed unintentionally, even unknowingly – all others required confession and repentance.

If you think about that, it makes a lot of sense, at least it does to me. There is something quite hollow, insincere even, about someone confessing: "If I have offended you in any way, and I am sure that I have because I am not perfect, then forgive me, for I did not intend to." It is one thing for Jesus, or anyone, to pray to God saying: "Forgive them, for they know not what they do", but I believe that God does want us to know what we do that offends Him, and wants us to improve. If our confession of non-specific sins becomes a habit, it reminds me of another practice that Jesus also noted: *"And when you pray, do not use vain repetitions as the heathens do; for they think that they will be heard for their many words."* (Matthew 6:7) Jesus, being Jewish, and trained in the teachings of Torah, understood such things. Non-specific confessions, and expressions of repentance, quickly become vain repetitions. Thinking back to my Catholic school days, and the number of rosaries that I was given to say for penance, I am quite certain that, as said by me, they were nothing other than vain repetitions, and I wonder why Catholic priests did not understand that. Perhaps they did, and were just carrying out the traditions of their fathers. Either way, if you do not bring to mind the details of your transgressions, then how can you commit to not doing them again, the very essence of repentance?

In a later chapter entitled "Necessity of a Redeemer", Chapter 9-5, I give further details of ritual offerings for sin, and so I will bore you no longer on that subject here. I simply ask that you study the Book of Leviticus to understand the subject properly, and to dispel any misunderstandings that you may have on the subject.

The Purpose of Sacrifice

As I stated earlier, that God commanded sin offerings at all, continued to be a mystery to me, until I began studying Jewish literature on the subject which opened my eyes somewhat. In an essay by Nathan Lopes Cardozo, perhaps my favourite contemporary Jewish commentator, where his topic concerns the building of the Third Temple, he also offered some wisdom concerning the sacrifices. Asking why the sacrifices, he comments:

> "Perhaps the answer to this is found in a profound statement made by Rabbi Eliezer Ashkenazi in his work *Ma'asei Hashem* (*The Works of God*), chapter 27. He draws our attention to a strange but repeated commandment in the Torah concerning the sacrifices: They must be brought as a *"re'ach nichoach LaShem"* normally translated as "a pleasant aroma to the Lord" (for example, *Vayikra* 1:9). This is a rather strange expression, as if God is in need of some aroma to please Him.

Here are his words:

The phrase 'a pleasant aroma to the Lord' does not reflect the absolute quality of the sacrifices; on the contrary, it conveys a possible flaw in their nature. In case the worshipers imagine that they indeed have achieved atonement for their sins by just offering a sacrifice, the Torah tells them that this is far from true. The sacrifice is only 'a pleasant aroma,' *a foretaste of what is yet to come.* If the worshiper does not repent, the Almighty will then say (*Yeshayahu* 1:11): 'Of what use are your many sacrifices to Me?' The concept of aroma is attributed to the Almighty because of its metaphoric connotation. Just as a pleasant aroma coming from afar bears witness to something good in the offing, so every time the Torah uses the phrase 'a pleasant aroma' in connection with the sacrifices, [the meaning is that] it should be to the Almighty as a foretaste of the good deeds that the worshiper is planning to perform. It is called a 'pleasant aroma' because anything that can be detected by the senses before it actually reaches the person is called a smell, as is written in the Book of Iyov (39:25): 'He smells war from afar,' which implies that he sensed the battle even before he actually reached it. Every human being who wants to bring a sacrifice must know that it should be done for the purpose of reconciling with God. Consequently, the sacrifice is to be brought as a foretaste of good deeds that are yet to come."[9]

This is consonant with the earlier expressed idea of bringing one closer to God, and highlights what is perhaps, the most important aspect of repentance: a commitment to doing better in the future. Without such commitment, evidence by behaviour, our repentance may not be acceptable to God. The Apostle James confirmed this: "What does it profit, my brethren, if someone says he has faith but does not have works? Can faith save him? ... faith by itself, if it does not have works, is dead." (James 2:14-17) In this context, faith in the efficacy of repentance is futile, if repentance is not followed by good works, works in the form of obedience to God's commandments. We should remember that these words of James may well be the first letter (Epistle) written, even earlier than the letters of Paul, and best represent the thinking of the early church in Jerusalem. This would confirm that Judaism was still at the heart of their religious thinking and practices.

Understanding Sin

I fear that the Christian understanding of sin, and its relationship to God's commandments, has been far too influenced by the thinking of people such as Martin Luther: "the law, when it is in its true sense, doth nothing else but reveal sin, engender wrath, accuse and terrify men, so that it bringeth them to the very brink of desperation. This is the proper use of the law, and here it hath an end, and it ought to go no further." We all know that according to Jesus, the greatest commandment is: "*You shall love the Lord your God with all your heart, with all your soul, and with all your might*" (Matthew 22:36). What Jesus does not say, here at least, is how to do that. Imagine that you are facing your Final Judgement, and you are accused of NOT loving God. Your response could likely be: "What do you mean? In what way did I not love God?"

If I may, I will use an example from my own experience to illustrate my point. During my time as a serving office in the RAAF (Royal Australian Air Force), I was required to know Air Force Law, and apply it where necessary. There was a law which in some respects, echoes the law to love God. This law specified the requirement to maintain good order and discipline, in the interests of smooth running of the Service. If someone contravened that order, the charge was framed as: "[name and rank of accused] is charged under Section xx of Air Force Law for failing to maintain good order and discipline." If that charge was levelled at you, what would be your response? I know mine: "What do you mean? What did I do, or not do?" You would want to know the specifics of the offence. Thus, such a charge would always have additional wording to substantiate the charge, e.g., "In that he attended parade with dirty boots, crumpled clothing, and a generally dishevelled appearance." A failure to maintain good order and discipline is a sign of disrespect for the Service, and thus in some ways, akin to not loving. A failure to obey God's commandments is also a failure to maintain good order and discipline as prescribed by God, and thus akin to not loving God.

The Air Force Law (AFL) Manual was comprised of multiple sections, the first being general, applying to the Service as a whole; followed by others which were specific to musterings, duties, and so on. Not all AFL applied to all personnel: thus, people were only required to know, and obey, those laws applicable to their position in the Service.

Facing your Final Judgement, and accused of not loving God, you would similarly want to know the details of your offence. Perhaps: had sexual relations with your mother / father / brother / sister. You see, the essence of the sin is that you failed to love God: you failed to keep the first, and most important, commandment. The detail of what you did, or did not do, is the specifics of the offence, these being documented in Torah (God's Law). Now imagine if the RAAF Legal Department decided to amend the AFL Manual, keeping just the first section, and discarding the rest: how would personnel know what constituted *good order and discipline*?

Curiously, this is what Christianity claimed God did through Jesus – He kept the *loving God* section, but threw out the rest. The inevitable result was that ever since, Christians do not know HOW to love God, in the way that God told them. Without Torah, we do not have the sections that are specific to each of us in our circumstances. Even more curiously, Christianity has ignored, or misconstrued, the teachings of the Apostle John on that issue:

1. "If you love Me, keep My commandments" (John 14:15).
2. "He who has My commandments and keeps them, it is he who loves Me" (John 14:21).
3. "If anyone love me, he will keep my word … and the word which you hear is not mine but the Father's who sent me" (John 14:23-24).
4. "If you keep my commandments, you will abide in my love, just as I have kept my Father's commandments and abide in His love" (John 15:10).
5. "Now by this we know that we love Him, if we keep His commandments. He who says, 'I know Him', and does not keep His commandments, is a liar, and the truth is not in him" (1 John 2:2-3).
6. "For this is the love of God, that we keep His commandments; and His commandments are not burdensome" (1 John 5:3), echoing Moses (Deuteronomy 30:11-14).
7. "This is love, that we walk according to His commandments" (2 John 1:6).

I do not intend to argue the continuance of Mosaic Law here, having already done so in an earlier work, "*Christians Too, Must Obey*"[10]. My point is primarily this: If we discard Torah, how do we know how to keep the first commandment – to love God?

The essence of sin is not that we break a commandment, *per se*, but that in doing so, we have failed to love God.

REFERENCES:

1. https://www.gotquestions.org/immanence-of-God.html

2. http://www.jewishworldreview.com/david/aaron_Devarim18.php3#44BFKxRTfsEKA5Ky.99
3. http://biblehub.com/matthew/9-13.htm
4. http://www.vatican.va/archive/ccc_css/archive/catechism/p2s2c1a3.htm
5. McClure, Joshua A., *The Crimson Thread of the Bible*, Deep River Books, Sisters, OR, 2011
6. http://whatjewsbelieve.org/explanation2.html
7. Lancaster, D. Thomas, *What About the Sacrifices?* First Fruits of Zion, Marshfield, MO, 2011, p. 9
8. *Ibid*, p. 8
9. Ashkenazi, Rabbi Eliezer, *Ma'asei Hashem* (The Works of God), Chapter 27, as quoted by Nathan Lopes Cardozo, July 19, 2018
10. Talbot, Wayne, *Christians Too, Must Obey: Putting A Fence Around Torah*, Xlibris, Bloomington, IN, 2017

PART 8

RIGHT DOCTRINE, WRONG TEXT?

"Were the New Testament writers so immersed in Jewish interpretive methods that they employed both the contextual and non-contextual? If they sometimes employed non-contextual interpretive procedures in using the Old Testament, did they err in doing so, or did the Holy Spirit guarantee the truth of their doctrinal conclusions for the church of following generations?"[1]

It is always reassuring when you find a book that asks the same questions that have been troubling you, especially when it contains diverse opinions on the same subject. That the opinions, are diverse, from scholars well versed in both Old and New Testament studies, testifies to the truth, that the truth of the matter is indeed difficult to discern. I am comforted by the fact that some scholars agree with me, even whilst others do not, for I find myself in good company.

The book, from which the above quotation is taken, on the back cover asks the question: "If Paul and other New Testament authors were publishing today, would scholars accept their exegetical method?" Some do, and some do not, as I do not, evidenced by the preceding chapters. The book is described thus:

> "This collection of essays presents various perspectives concerning the hermeneutical issue of whether Jesus and the Apostles quoted Old Testament texts with respect for their broader Old Testament context. Each of the contributors debates the interpretive understandings by which Old Testament texts are quoted and applied in the New Testament. Were New Testament teachers and authors simply children of rabbinic midrashic scholarship? Did they revere the original context of passages they quoted, or fill them with different meaning? What presuppositions about the Old Testament guided their approach?"[2]

I took heed of the context of the book under review, and did not expect it to answer questions that were beyond its purview. The questions to which I had hoped to find answers were:

1. How did the evangelists get the prophecy fulfillment issue so wrong, as I have analysed the texts?
2. How did they interpret the Old Testament in such a way as to find correspondence with the accomplishments of Jesus?
3. Why did they find so many prophetic statements in the Psalms of King David, when the Sages insisted that David was not a prophet?
4. Why did they find Jesus to be the suffering servant of Isaiah 53, when the Sages did not?
5. Why did they identify *one like a son of man* in Daniel 7 as a deity, when over ninety other usages of that term clearly identified the enormous chasm between the reality of finite man and an infinite God?
6. Why, in accepting Jesus as Messiah, did they pay so little attention to what he failed to accomplish?

It is not my intention here to attempt a comprehensive critique, or even review, of this scholarly work – such is well beyond my competence or remit. However, in addition to seeking answers to the questions listed above, I paid attention to certain themes which, if not consciously treated, would serve to diminish the credibility of the essays, in my mind at least. I have discussed these in earlier chapters, but list them here as I did before reading the book, if for no other reason than to remind myself of their importance, in objectively evaluating the essays:

1. Credibility of the contributing authors as **objective** (disinterested) "experts" in this field of biblical commentary.
2. The theological presuppositions evident in the arguments of the essayists.
3. Attention to the rules of evidence pertaining to ancient documents, and their present-day copies.
4. Language, and versions, of the Old Testament source texts used by the New Testament authors.
5. Authentication of the attributed NT authors.
6. Presuppositions regarding the learning and literary competence of the attributed NT authors.
7. Consideration of rabbinic teachings in the Second Temple period.
8. Consideration of the Jewish literature of that period[3].
9. Recognition of the change of perceived mission of Jesus, from the recording of his earliest statements, to the subsequent theology that developed.
10. Evidence of the probability of guidance of the Holy Spirit.
11. Presupposition that the Holy Spirit did guide the writings of the evangelists, despite the evidence that makes such a proposition unlikely.

As you can see, the evaluation of essays, even by recognised scholars, is more complication than it might at first appear. I am no longer one to succumb to the *Cult of Authority*, even though I once did, which has people believing whatever is said by persons in authority. Of interest is that the Royal Society chose an expression of similar meaning for their motto: *Nullius in verba* (Latin for "on the word of no one" or "Take nobody's word for it"). It is an expression of the determination of Fellows to withstand the domination of authority and to verify all statements by an appeal to facts determined by experiment. I skip the experiment bit, but nevertheless appeal to the evidence, rather than just opinion, although opinion is always evidence of some fact. The trick is discerning it.

This is one of the reasons why we must authenticate written evidence, for the authors may be lacking in authority, to conclude on the subjects that they have, due to their presuppositions. And of course, that includes myself, but on that issue, you will have to decide for yourselves. My point is that the credibility of scholarly writings often suffer due to unstated presuppositions which one can discern from reading between the lines. If an essayist offers an opinion as to why an evangelist, believing Jesus to be the Messiah, wrote what he did, that is one thing; but to offer an opinion based on the essayist himself believing Jesus to be the Messiah, that is a different kettle of fish altogether. Objectivity has gone out the window.

From the outset, let me highlight a possible presupposition, one to which I succumbed by not paying sufficient attention to the title. At first I thought it a statement, and then realised my error: I had missed the question mark at the end! Foolishness. Each of the essays in the book respond to the question: Did early Christian doctrine develop from the NT writers utilising the wrong OT texts, and if so, why? Very satisfyingly, for me at least, the contributing essayists say both yes and no, and explain why they so conclude. In some essays, the usually unstated presupposition underlying the essayists' analysis, is that the entire New Testament is the inspired word of God, conveyed through chosen men, and inerrant in expressing God's intentions for the writings. In other essays, this belief is not so evident. All essays have been written by Christian New Testament scholars, and at no stage did I sense that any considered Christian doctrine to be in error. Thus I concluded that the presupposition of all the scholars was that fundamental Christian doctrine follows the teachings of Jesus, and has the *imprimatur* of God. However they got there, the New Testament writers still managed to get it right in the end.

However, in contrast to the suggestion in the title of the book, I have been arguing from the opposite perspective: that it is the doctrine itself which is wrong, derived by improper use of the right texts, following a poorly reasoned belief in Jesus as Messiah. We shall attempt to discover the truth. That said, the editor of the book did explain:

"The uniqueness of the book especially lies in its unswerving focus on exegetical methodology rather than theology, as this pertains to the use of the Old Testament in the New. In this respect, the presuppositions and assumptions which underlie Jesus' and the apostles' exegetical method will be examined and compared with the presuppositions underlying typical twentieth-century methods of exegesis."[4]

Whilst I will review the first two essays in some detail, I will not separately review them all. I have sprinkled a great number of their thoughts amongst previous chapters where relevant. Rather, I will treat them on their subject matter, and on the general thrust of their arguments, as I am confident that there will be a large degree of commonality and overlap. Following the review of the first essays, I will present my overall impressions.

Just how relevant this is to a study of prophecy fulfillment I cannot be sure, but the fact that numerous scholars debate how the evangelists used the Old Testament is evidence, albeit circumstantial, that the claims of prophecy fulfillment may be in error, due to the NT authors misinterpreting their source texts. Whether this was inadvertent, due to ignorance, or whether they sought to justify their beliefs by quarrying the Scriptures is open to debate, but I have a sense of the latter. It might also be said these scholarly essayists corroborate my own observations, and thus lend weight to them. You will have to decide that for yourselves.

REFERENCES:

1. Beale, G.K., *The Right Doctrine from the Wrong Texts?* Essays on the Use of the Old Testament in the New, Baker Academic, Grand Rapids, MI, 1994, p. 8
2. *Ibid*, back cover (paperback)
3. Helyer, Larry R., *Exploring Jewish Literature of the Second Temple Period*, IVP Academic, Downers Grove, IL, 2002
4. Beale, *Ibid*, p. 9

CHAPTER 8-1

THEOLOGICAL
PRESUPPOSITIONS

*"There is a consensus among a significant group of New
Testament scholars, if not a majority, that the New Testament
uses the Old without regard for its original meaning."*[1]

That is a curious proposition to consider in the context of my study on
prophecy fulfillment. If this *significant group of New Testament scholars*
are correct, then we can rightly question any claims which contain
words such as "but this is done that the Scriptures might be fulfilled"
(Mark 14:49, ASV). Was this the opinion of the author of Mark, or was
he divinely guided to write as he did?

None of the essayists declare the version of the bible that they use. As
I have contended in Part 2, this has greater significance than Christian
apologists are wont to admit. The presupposition that all versions are
authored by God is false: if I were to cross-examine a scholar on a quoted
verse, I would ask from which bible version he/she was quoting, and then

offer a different rendering of that same verse to evidence variations in meaning. (Then the fighting begins!)

"But I also hold that the words of Scripture were intended to have one definite sense, and that our first object should be to discover that sense, and adhere rigidly to it."[2] This would appear to invalidate the approach taken by the NT authors, as opined in the opening quotation, but let me admit that I have taken this slightly out of context. The author prefaced his remark with: "I hold undoubtedly that there is a mighty depth to all of Scripture, and in this respect it stands alone." My point here is not to argue over meaning, but to point out how often Christian apologists ignore their own arguments, especially in relation to explicit statements in the Hebrew Scriptures, even where correctly rendered in the Old Testament. For example, references to *failing to observe* the Sabbath, to the *everlasting* covenant with the Children of Israel, and to the *perpetual* authority of the Law. In the words of the essayist being quoted: these verses *have one definite sense*, and we rightly ought to *adhere rigidly to it*. However, that is not what has been done, from the earliest days of the church in Rome. This is foundational to understanding whether Christianity is preaching the <u>right doctrine</u> from the <u>right text</u>.

Authority of the NT Authors

"The New Testament authors are not scholars but church leaders. They are interested in showing how the Old Testament passages apply to the New Testament situation."[3]

I find this to be a fascinating admission, especially from a scholar: *they were not scholars*. In Chapter 5-2, we reviewed what can be known about these NT authors, and pondered their academic credentials. Unlike today, where bibles are everywhere, even in motel drawers, the disciples of Jesus did not have ready access to written versions of Scripture. In Judaism generally, after the canon of Scripture was finalised, only accredited scribes were permitted to copy the sacred scrolls, and even then under supervision. Before that point, scribes were also editors, and would impart their own understanding to a narrative, much as happened when Hebrew writings were translated into Greek. Parchment and ink were expensive, and even lower quality writing materials were primarily used in commerce – the general population were not literate in the sense of being able to write a lengthy discourse, such as we find in the Gospels and Epistles.

The Hebrew Scriptures are now held on sixteen scrolls, most scrolls containing more than one of the twenty-four books in the Jewish canon. We can be confident that before the finalisation of the canon, more than sixteen scrolls were extant. The question becomes: did any of the NT writers have access to the full canon, whether in Hebrew or Greek? In all likelihood, they did not – they could hardly just wander off to the local library to have a read. Even in the synagogue, only nominated people could unroll a scroll to read from it, because apart from being sacred texts, they were also relatively fragile, and repeated handling would only cause them to deteriorate more quickly.

We must admit to the ancient reality of access to biblical scrolls – it was just not that common, and so when we ponder how the NT authors would have interpreted the Scriptures, we must also ponder the process by which they did so. I have no verifiable information on that process, but I am reasonably confident that these authors would have had great difficulty in accessing authoritative texts. Earlier, I observed the frequency of reference to the Psalms. Could it be that because the psalms were so integral to the lives of the Jewish people back then, that it was their familiarity with these writings that caused them to so often quote them in relation to the life of Jesus?

In three of the essays, firstly by C.H. Dodd (pp. 167-181); secondly, by Albert C. Sundberg, Jr. contending with Dodd (pp. 182-194); and thirdly, by I. Howard Marshall contending with Sundberg's contentions and supporting Dodd (pp. 195-216), the primary theme concerns the documentary sources of the New Testament authors, a subject which has long intrigued me. It is a lengthy discourse, with many scholarly references, so I will not attempt a synopsis of the essays. Let me begin by stating that I could find little consensus on the subject, and even less clarity. If there is any consensus, it is that none of the NT authors had access to a full copy of the Scriptures, either in Hebrew or Greek. There is evidence suggesting that some early Christians had "collections" of writings, which may have contributed to one author quoting one source more than another. For example, "Daniel is the most important book to Mark and Matthew. But Exodus ranks first in Luke-Acts. Daniel does not even appear among the five most important [OT] books for this author. Isaiah is almost twice as frequently cited in Matthew as in Mark, moving from fifth in importance in Mark to second in Matthew." (p. 188) One suggestion is that these authors chose their sources based on the theme of their writings; another is that their writings were influenced by the sources they had available.

Sundberg performed an analysis of Old Testament usage in the New, much as I have done with prophecy related verses, and he tabulates this on pages 186-7. He states:

> "Forty-two percent of the four hundred twenty-three Old Testament chapters cited in the New Testament are cited by more than one New Testament writer. Fifty-six of Isaiah's sixty-six chapters are cited, seventy-one percent doubly. Of the one hundred one Psalms cited, more than a third are doubly cited." (p. 185)

Note that his analysis is at the chapter level, whereas mine is primarily at the verse level. Whether the granularity of my analysis provides greater clarity is open to debate, for there is the suggestion that where a verse is cited, the author's intention was to point the reader to the whole chapter. There could be truth in this, remembering that verse and chapter numbering was not introduced until the mid-fifteenth century. Just how portions of a Book were referenced back then is beyond my understanding, but I suspect it was based on episodes within the narrative, as that seems to me to be the most logical. In a sense, this invalidates Sundberg's analysis by chapter, because some episodes span more than one chapter, as I have argued in relation to Isaiah 52-54, where the chapter 53 division interrupts the natural flow of the narrative, leading to a false interpretation of what follows.

Reviewing the skills of the NT authors, Matthew, the tax collector, was likely sufficiently literate to read and write, but what of the fishermen? What was the source of their biblical learning? How familiar were they with the Scriptures that they were able to show *how the Old Testament passages apply to the New Testament situation*? My sense of this is that one would have needed to be a rabbi, or similarly learned, to do as this essayist claims. They did not need to be scholars, just as I am not a scholar, but I have a studied appreciation of the effort needed to comprehend and apply Old Testament passages. I do wonder how these gentlemen could have acquired a knowledge even to my level.

But then the conundrum.

Why would we consider the interests of the New Testament authors, if their writings were divinely inspired, as Chuck Colson asserted: "*The Bible's power rests upon the fact that it is the reliable, errorless, and infallible Word of God*"? We could contend that Chuck Colson was a pastor, a church leader, not a scholar, but I would contend that we need scholars to determine the truth of Scripture, as the series of essays we are examining attests. So now, we are back to intentionality, so let us go there.

Intentionality of Scripture

> "*Ultimately God is the author of Scripture, and it is his intention alone that exhaustively determines its meanings.*"[4]

We can note two issues from this statement: (1), the essayist's belief in the divine inspiration and authority of whatever bible version he/she is using; and (2), we may never be able to fully determine the meaning of the texts because we do not have the mind of God. I can agree with the second, but not with the first. The process by which the canon of the Hebrew Scriptures was derived and documented, likely from fragmented sources by different authors and editors over centuries, means that God would have been supervising and guiding not just the attributed authors, but a multitude of other unidentified writers and collectors. With God, such things are possible, but Christianity seldom reflects on this, preferring instead to take a more naïve approach, which leaves authority and credibility open to question, at least at the pastoral level.

At the scholarly level, we have numerous contrasting opinions, all honestly acknowledged as considered *opinions* rather than unassailable fact, which is refreshing to say the least. In an essay by Vern Sheridan Poythress, a scholar entirely unknown to me, he discusses the issue under the headings of Divine Meaning and Human Meaning, Interpreting

Human Discourse, Interpreting Divine Speech, Divine Speech as Propositional and Personal, Speech with Two Authors [God and the NT author], Personal Communication of Authors, Christological Fullness in Interpretation, Progressive Understanding, Progressive Revelation, and so forth. It is an absorbing read, and I would challenge very little, apart from the underlying assumptions that form the foundation of the Christian religion. The author argues from within that paradigm, but the purpose of my study is to question the validity of that paradigm. Nevertheless, much of what Poythress wrote is revealing, in that he exposes the lack of consensus on numerous issues concerning biblical exegesis, and why no-one should be dogmatic on what is prophesied in the Old Testament, or how it has been interpreted in the New.

I keep that in mind for myself. Now to review the first two contributors to this collection of essays.

REFERENCES:

1. Beale, G.K., *The Right Doctrine from the Wrong Texts*? Essays on the Use of the Old Testament in the New, Baker Academic, Grand Rapids, MI, 1994, p. 9
2. *Ibid*, p. 56
3. *Ibid*, p. 111
4. *Ibid*, p. 70

CHAPTER 8-2

ESSAY BY ROGER NICOLE

"Can we use their (the NT authors) techniques to find
significance in the Old Testament texts, or were they operating
from a revelatory stance in ways that we cannot?"[1]

This essay by Roger Nicole, entitled, *The New Testament Use of the Old Testament*, is an extract from the book, *Revelation and the Bible*[2].

The author begins, much as I have in previous chapters, with a count of Old Testament references in the New, encountering issues with which I became familiar – accurate identification. As a guide, accepting his protocol and purpose being different to mine, he found 224 direct citations, and 71 others. Further, he found that "these occupy some 352 verses of the New Testament, or more than 4.4 percent. Therefore one verse in 22.5 verses of the New Testament is a quotation." (p. 13) He then notes that if allusions are taken into consideration, as they have been by other scholars, then the count is much higher. Unfortunately, he does not specify which version of the bible he was using, and what notice he took of annotations by that version's editors.

He notes that, "From beginning to end, the New Testament authors ascribe unqualified authority to Old Testament Scripture. Whenever advanced, a quotation is viewed as normative. Nowhere do we find a tendency to question, argue, or repudiate the truth of any Scripture utterance." (p. 14) I must disagree with him in part: if the NT authors ascribed unqualified authority to OT texts, why did they so often misquote or paraphrase? A quotation at the beginning of Chapter 8-1 stated, in part, *"that the New Testament uses the Old without regard for its original meaning."* If that be so, how can it be claimed that the authors ascribe unqualified authority to Old Testament Scripture? I would have thought, quite the opposite in fact.

Further comments as follows:

(p. 17) - Referring to Jesus' quoting the Old Testament: *"he referred to it in his prayers, when alone in the presence of the Father"*; how could anyone know, if Jesus was alone? Scholar or no, the author has taken leave of his senses.

(p. 18) - *"The New Testament writers had to translate their quotations. They wrote in Greek and their source of quotations was in Hebrew ... When the New Testament writers wrote, there was one Greek version of the Old Testament, the Septuagint"*. I believe that both of these statements are incorrect. Neither Luke not Mark were likely competent in Hebrew, and the opinion of other scholars is that their OT source was the Greek. There was not "one Greek version": there were at least three, although there may have been just one in the region where the authors resided when they wrote. Even then, there is considerable debate over the competence of the translators, and we have no chain of custody as to how any one version was compiled.

(p. 19) - Concerning errors in translation: *"no blame can be laid on them as long as they base no argument on what is mistaken in the translation"*. As I have shown, a great deal of Christian theology is based on mistakes in translations, and note the earlier comments regarding the Septuagint (Chapter 2-1). I am curious to understand how the NT writers could have erred in their translation, but not based their argument on that translation. If not that translation, then on what did they base their argument?

(p. 19) - *"We do not find any example of a New Testament deduction or application logically inferred from the Septuagint and which cannot be maintained on the basis of the Hebrew text.*" I am already doubting this author's scholarship, and thus credibility, for I have documented many such cases, and there are many more which do not fall within the scope of prophecies. The author then appears to retract this assertion: "It would be precarious, however, to rest an argument on any part of the Septuagint quotations which appears not to be conformed to the Hebrew original": why mention this if there are no such occurrences?

(p. 20) - "*In the quotations made from the Septuagint, we have indeed God's seal of approval upon the contents of the Old Testament passage, but the form of the citation is affected by the language and conditions of those to whom the New Testament was addressed.*" The supposition here is that the effect of the *language and conditions* is not sufficient to significantly alter the original meaning. We have evidence of the opposite, and besides, on what evidence can it be asserted that we have God's imprimatur on the faulty Greek translation? Other scholars as far back as Jerome ventured the opinion that the Septuagint 'differs widely from the original [Hebrew], and is rightly rejected'."[3]

(p. 20) - "*But we cannot admit to an accommodation in which inspired writers would give formal assent to error.*" Again, the presupposition that the writers were inspired by the Holy Spirit. If errors can be shown, and they have been, the obvious deduction is that the writers were not divinely inspired.

(p. 20) - "*The frequent use of the Septuagint*"; has the author just refuted what he wrote earlier: "their source of quotations was in Hebrew" (p. 18)?

(p. 21) - "*The New Testament writers sometimes paraphrased their quotations. Such a procedure certainly needs no justification, since a free translation sometimes renders the sense and impression of the original better than a more literal one.*" Indeed, it does, but just as often, it leads to error. The author again reveals his presuppositions concerning the authors: that they were competent scholars of the Hebrew Scriptures. We have no evidence of that, especially if their primary reference was some unknown version of the Septuagint. My studies of Jewish commentaries have revealed a lack of consensus amongst both the ancient Sages, and more modern rabbis, as to the meaning of the Hebrew Scriptures. According to the Sages, there are 70 valid explanations to every part of the Torah (*Bamidbar Rabbah* 13:15).

On what basis, then, can we trust the paraphrasing by people of unknown training and competence?

(p. 24) – "*It is an unsearchable mystery that the Holy Spirit could inspire the sacred writings so as to communicate his inerrancy to their very words and, at the same time, respect the freedom and personality of the writers so that we might easily recognize their style and their characteristics.*" Unsearchable indeed, likely because the mystery stems from the imagination of the author. Again, that unsubstantiated presupposition of divine inspiration, and no acknowledgement that in many cases, there is very little verbal agreement on the same subject. I cannot believe that the Holy Spirit would *communicate his inerrancy to their very words*, when the words written about a given event, convey an entirely different sense, e.g. the last words of Jesus before he died.

(p. 25) – "*The Spirit of God was free to modify the expressions that he inspired in the Old Testament.*" Once again, we have Christian commentators ignoring the meaning of "omniscience". Being omniscient, God has no reason to change His mind, and would have no occasion to modify the meaning of earlier expressions or inspirations. Certainly, God would give *new* inspirations, but not *altered* inspirations.

(p. 25) – "*It has been urged at times that the New Testament writers have flouted the proper laws of hermeneutics, have been guilty of artificial and rabbinical exegesis, and thus have repeatedly distorted the meaning of the Old Testament passages which they quote.*" I mostly agree with this, except the assertion that the writers were "guilty of rabbinical exegesis". If the author is equating rabbinical exegesis with artificial exegesis, he is entirely wrong. Having studied the rabbinical exegesis of passages in the Hebrew Scriptures, and compared that with the exegesis of the NT writers on problematic passages from the Septuagint, I can assure the reader that the two are not at all the same.

(p. 26) – "*Few Christians, it is hoped, will have the presumption of setting forth their own interpretation as normative, when it runs directly counter to that of the Lord Jesus or of his apostles.*" I find it appalling that a scholar would venture such a proposition, for it does nothing but beg the question. It suffers from the same logical fallacy as found in the use of 2 Timothy 3:16. This says that all Scripture is given by the inspiration of God; this letter is Scripture; therefore, this letter is given by the inspiration of God; therefore, what it says is inerrant. I expect better of Christian scholars.

(p. 26) – "*In general … the writers of the New Testament, in making use of passages from the Old Testament, remain true to the intention of their writers.*" A very bold assertion, especially as Jewish scholars, and even Christian scholars, wholeheartedly disagree. I would refer you again to the quotation at the beginning of the previous chapter. Should we believe Christian scholars, who demonstrably evidence presuppositions to support their theology, or the Jewish Sages and commentators, when it was the Jews to whom were trusted the very words of God (Romans 3:2)? The other question that we must continue to ask is: How well trained were the NT writers in the Hebrew Scriptures?

(p. 27) – "*Not all the passages quoted in the New Testament are necessarily to be considered as definite prophecies, but many are cited as simply characterizing in a striking way the New Testament situation.*" I wholeheartedly agree: it is the bible translators / editors who must be held to account for not having this understanding. That said, putting aside the notion of divine inspiration, that the NT writers, having accepted Jesus as Messiah, perceived parallels between his life and the Scriptures, is not evidence that such parallels were evidence of prophecy fulfillment. Confirmation bias comes into play, and I am confident that many such parallels would have come naturally to the evangelists. However, I am still troubled by their failure to address the very obvious lack of parallels relating to the primary mission of the prophesied Jewish *mashiach*.

(p. 27) – "*The student of Scripture is not bound to provide the solution of all the difficulties which he encounters in the Bible. It is better to leave matters unharmonized than to have recourse to strained or artificial exegesis.*" Again, I agree, but would emphasize that this burden falls even more heavily on the shoulders of scholars, who ought to understand that presuppositions of the nature discussed in these pages, do in truth lead to artificial exegesis.

(p. 28) – The author, noting plenary inspiration benefitting the authors, refers to "*the judgement of men who can surely be quoted as impartial witnesses*". Well, the truth is, mostly there were no witnesses to the events they recorded. As for being impartial, that is nonsense. These men sought to spread the Gospel in which they had come to believe, often learned third hand from others. They were no more impartial than the Catholic Pope.

Summary

The author of this chapter, the late Roger Nicole, is described thus[4]:

"Roger Nicole (b. 1915) is visiting Professor of Theology at
Reformed Theological Seminary in Orlando and professor
emeritus of Gordon-Conwell Seminary. A native Swiss Reformed
theologian and a Baptist, Dr. Nicole is regarded as one of the
preeminent theologians in America. He was an associate editor
for the New Geneva Study Bible and assisted in the translation of
the NIV Bible. He is a past president and founding member of the
Evangelical Theological Society, and a founding member of the
International Council on Biblical Inerrancy. He has written over
one hundred articles and contributed to more than fifty books
and reference works.

Nicole received S.T.M. and Th.D. degrees from Gordon Divinity
School, a Ph.D. from Harvard University, and D.D. from Wheaton
College."

One cannot minimise his scholarship, nor his devotion to his religion,
but from the perspective of my study into prophecy fulfillment, his essay
adds no value, for his presuppositions have diluted his evidence. Nicole
has assumed that either: the evangelists were competent scholars in their
own right, and/or, the Holy Spirit guided their writings in such a way as
to overcome any scholarly deficiencies. He could be right in his acceptance
of these as brute facts, but I am not convinced. Whilst there may be no
explanations for them, them are numerous explanations to counter them,
as I have attempted to outline.

Nicole has a lot more to say in his essay, but his presuppositions persist,
and curiously, his essay hardly addresses at all, the issues implied in the
title of the book. He talks around them, and has much of interest to say,
but offers nothing that could be interpreted as a conclusion. Nevertheless,
a very informative discussion.

REFERENCES:

1. Beale, G.K., *The Right Doctrine from the Wrong Texts?* Essays on the Use of the Old Testament in the New, Baker Academic, Grand Rapids, MI, 1994, p. 49
2. Henry, Carl F.H., *Revelation and the Bible: contemporary evangelical thought*, Baker Books, Grand Rapids, MI, 1958, pp. 135-151
3. Simon, Marcel, *Verus Israel: A Study of the Relations between Christian and Jews in the Roman Empire AD 135-425*, Schoen Books, South Deerfield, MA, 1986, p. 59
4. https://www.theopedia.com/roger-nicole

ESSAY BY KLYNE SNODGRASS

"The Hebrew and Aramaic Scriptures were, of course, the only Bible the early Christian thinkers and writers had."[1]

Well, that is not a very good start.

Klyne Snodgrass (PhD, University of St. Andrews) is a professor of biblical literature, and served as the Paul W. Brandel Chair of New Testament Studies at North Park Theological Seminary. He is a well-published author and winner of a Christian Book award. It is well to accept his credentials. This essay, entitled *The Use of the Old Testament in the New*, has been taken, with permission, from the book, *New Testament Criticism and Interpretation*[2].

The author's supposition is contested by numerous authors, including the one discussed in the previous chapter. There is incontrovertible evidence that many of the quotations in the New Testament, as we have the versions today, were taken from the Greek Septuagint, not the Hebrew or Aramaic Scriptures. I have a copy of the Aramaic English New Testament[3], and can demonstrate many discrepancies between that, and for example, the

NKJV. One also has to wonder why, for centuries, Christian apologists insisted as here: "The simple fact is that **the Jews lost their facility in Hebrew.** That is why the Old Testament had to be translated into the Greek language (this translation is known as the Septuagint)."[4] [emphasis mine] If Snodgrass was giving oral testimony in a court of law, cross-examination by competent authorities would quickly undermine his credibility.

(p. 29) - As the previous author did, he then seemingly refutes his own assertion: "Many of these Christians were transformed Jews and would have known Hebrew. Other early Christians would have known the Jewish Scriptures only in the Greek translations." To put this in the context of the New Testament authors, which of them would have been conversant with the Hebrew, and which with the Greek? Matthew is the most likely conversant in Hebrew, but canonical Matthew is in Greek, though translated by whom, we know not. John may have been conversant with the Hebrew Scriptures, but maybe not. He was the youngest of the original twelve, eight to ten years younger than Jesus, and was a fisherman. He may have been taught from the Hebrew Scriptures, but it is doubtful that he would have been any more knowledgeable of the Old Testament, than a modern Christian middle-school student would be of the New. If John spoke Aramaic, which is likely, this further diminishes his credibility in Hebrew, despite them being closely related languages. Those from Galilee were more likely to speak Aramaic, with some understanding of Greek – competence in Hebrew was more likely centred in Judah.

Jewish tradition in Second Temple Judaism, was that disciples would learn at the feet of a rabbi. As is said in another context: "Many were called, but few were chosen". The same applied here, for to be a student of the Hebrew Scriptures, one had to dedicate oneself to the profession. It is unlikely that a fisherman, whose livelihood came from the Sea of Galilee, undertook such studies. I believe it implausible to attribute scholarship of the Hebrew Scriptures, to any of the twelve Apostles. I am reminded of another Christian apologetic: that Jesus chose simple, uneducated people, rather than scholars, because their faith should be that of a child. You cannot have it both ways, to suit whatever line of argument you are pursuing.

Both Mark and Luke were likely Gentile, whose *lingua franca* was Greek. Luke claimed that Paul had been trained at the feet of Gamaliel in

Jerusalem, but Paul's actions and writings provide evidence that such was not so (see Chapters 2-5 & 6). And then we have the claims of the Eastern churches that the autographs were in Aramaic (see Chapter 2-1). With so many opinions, scholarly or otherwise, on the language of the autographs, and what happened to these manuscripts (scrolls) subsequently, I find it difficult to accept the assertions of anyone on this subject. I contend that all should admit: we simply do not know.

(p. 30) – *"There is both continuity and discontinuity between the Old Testament and the New Testament. That is, while some parts of the New Testament are direct extensions of the Old Testament message, some parts of the Old Testament message have been superseded."* This is not an assertion that I would make to God's Face: did God change His mind? Is God not omniscient? *"The New Testament writers have been disturbingly creative in their use of the Old Testament. Not only do New Testament quotations of the Old Testament sometimes differ from the Hebrew and Aramaic Scriptures on which our translations are based, the New Testament writers also have applied texts in surprising ways."* I am not confident that our New Testament translations are based on the Hebrew and Aramaic Scriptures – there is substantive evidence that they are based on the Greek. That aside, what should we conclude from the evidence given here? Let us consider this from an academic perspective. If this were said of a first-year student, a professor would likely counsel the student regarding his/her lack of education, training, and knowledge of the subject at hand. If this was the work of a tenured professor, one would expect greater explanation. Again, the presupposition seems to be that the New Testament writers were highly educated, and/or, they were writing under the guidance of the Holy Spirit. There is no substantiation in favour of the first assumption, and substantive evidence against the second.

(p. 31) – I was delighted to read the following, for it agreed with what I have long contended, contrary to traditional Christian teaching: *"He (Jesus) argued that sin defiled a person, not eating with unclean hands (Matt 15:10-20)."* But then I was disappointed with the next assertion: *"Mark 7:19 extends Jesus' teaching so that all foods are clean[5]. So much for dietary laws!"* Jewish dietary and purity laws have been a particular study of mine, and I disagree entirely with the conclusions of Snodgrass, and Robert Banks as referenced below. If you should be so interested, I would refer you to my own analysis of the texts[6]. Curiously, the author then states: *"Jesus focused on the intent of the law in the love commands and on the theme of mercy. Still, he claimed that none of the Scripture was set aside (Matt 5:17-20)"*, with no further explication on that last sentence. Is Snodgrass contending with the traditional Christian view that Jesus fulfilled the Law in such a way that effectively, it was voided thereafter?

(p. 32) – *"Most Christians ... sought to extend the interpretive practices of the New Testament writers and appropriate the Old Testament for Christian purposes in new ways. The Old Testament was combed for passages that could be understood of Christ and his church. Christians used the Old Testament to teach morality, to explain who Jesus was, and to provide illustrations of Christian thought. Unfortunately, however, usually there was little historical sensitivity or treatment of extended texts. Instead, the Old Testament was viewed as prophecy about Christ, as providing types of Christ, or as holding hidden ideas and symbols that may be spiritually understood through allegory."* This is very thought provoking: I have the impression that these early Christians paid no heed to the teachings of the Jewish Sages, and sought their own interpretation of the Greek texts based on the premise that Jesus was the prophesied Messiah. In a way, this is like people ascribing meaning to a work of Shakespeare based on a translation of an essay written by a scholar giving his/her own interpretation of what Shakespeare really meant. From an evidentiary perspective, these later Christian writings are too far removed from their original source to be given credibility.

(p. 34) – *"[exegetical] solutions ... vary in the degree to which they see the Old Testament as Christological, how they deal with Old Testament history, and how they balance continuity and discontinuity. The main problem for modern readers in the New Testament use of the Old Testament is the tendency of New Testament writers to use Old Testament texts in ways different from their original intention."* Now, if the latter be true, then it behoves us to consider how well Jesus could have fulfilled prophecy, if the intention of the Prophets has not been honoured. Did the Prophets not understand what they were told by God, or did they not document His words correctly?

(p. 37) – *"The christological titles 'Servant', 'Son of man', and 'Son of God' were all representative titles that were applied to Israel first. Jesus took on these titles because he had taken Israel's task. He was representative of Israel and in solidarity with her. God's purposes for Israel were now taken up in his ministry. If this were true, what had been used to describe Israel could legitimately be used of him.*" Indeed, IF it were true, but that is a big "if". Jesus may have considered himself in that light, and his followers likewise, but did he really accomplish what was prophesied? In truth, what he is said to have accomplished was not prophesied, even though the New Testament writers found allusions in the Old Testament. The primary theme of messianic prophecy was the ingathering of the Children of Israel, defeat of their enemies, and as was prophesied: "*From Zion will the Torah come forth, and the word of Hashem from Jerusalem*" (Isaiah 2:3, TJB). We know from history that since the second century, the word has come from Rome, not Jerusalem, and Torah has been hidden. I can understand why the early disciples misunderstood prophecy, but not why that misunderstanding has been perpetuated for centuries.

(p. 40) – "*The application of Isaiah 6:9-10 to the ministry of Jesus is another example of correspondence in history. This Old Testament text was spoken specifically to Isaiah about the hardness of heart of his hearers. Other Old Testament prophets picked up the language of Isaiah 6:9-10 so that these words became the classic expression of hardness of heart (cf. Jer 5:21; Ezek. 12:2). In the synoptic Gospels the words were applied to Jesus' ministry as evidence of the hardness of heart of Jews in not responding to the teaching in parables (Matt 13:14-15 / Mark 4:12 / Luke 8:10). They applied in a similar way in John 12:39-40 as a summary statement marking the rejection of Jesus by the Jews. Interestingly. These words are also addressed to the disciples in Mark 8:18 to ask whether they have hardened hearts. Isaiah 6:9-10 finds further correspondence as a description of the rejection of the Jews in Paul's ministry (Acts 28:26-27)*"

In case my taking this out of context has the reader misinterpreting the essayist's meaning, he was not asserting the truth of the historical correspondence, but simply the fact of it (although I sense that he did accept it as true). But let us put that to the test. Firstly, and it is not that important, mention of *hardness of heart* did not originate with Isaiah, but can be found as far back as Exodus, with God hardening the heart of Pharaoh. Secondly, when quoting Isaiah 6:9-10, the New Testament authors twisted the original meaning of the Prophet. Let us compare the texts of Isaiah from two bibles:

1. TJB – "He said, go and say to this people: 'Surely you hear but you do not comprehend, and surely you see but fail to know.' This people is fattening its heart, hardening its ears, and sealing its eyes, lest it see with its eyes, hear with its ears, and understand with its heart, so that it will repent and be healed."

2. NKJV – "And He said, go and tell this people: Keep on hearing, but do not understand; Keep on seeing, but do not perceive. Make the heart of this people dull, and their ears heavy, and shut their eyes; lest they hear with their ears, and understand with their heart, and return and be healed." (Mark 4:12)

Note the change in sense from the Jewish to the Christian versions of Isaiah. Isaiah was issuing a warning to the Israelites, but in the New Testament, the authors have rejected the original meaning to have it say that God is hardening their hearts, *lest they return and be healed*! It is as if God did not want the people to repent, which is sheer nonsense. This echoes modern Christian apologetics which declare that if we do not accept Jesus, we have not the Holy Spirit. The presumption of Jesus as the Messiah, and a deity at that, has people misquoting Scripture to suit their own purposes.

(p. 44) – "*There are a few places where Old Testament texts seem to have been joined in unexpected ways. For example, Mark 1:2-3 attributes to Isaiah words that appear to be a combination of Exodus 23:20, Malachi 3:1, and Isaiah 40:3. An attractive explanation of these phenomena is the argument that early Christians used* testimonia. *That is, they used collections of Old Testament texts that have been grouped thematically for apologetic, liturgical, and catechetical purposes.*" I have no issue with this approach for teaching purposes – I, and even the essayists, do the very same, but in the context of my study, I must ask: Is this practice appropriate for determining prophecy fulfillment? Mark prefaces his remarks with: "As it is written in the Prophets", having his readers believe that what follows are prophecies being fulfilled, and whilst he may have believed so, careful analysis shows it to be not so. There is a degree of historical correspondence, that much can be said, but such is not sufficient from an evidentiary perspective.

(p. 45) – "*Testimonia provide a window into the way the early church did its theology and ministry. They also provide insight into Old testament quotations that are otherwise anomalies. Therefore, when an Old Testament quotation occurs, one must inquire about its use and textual form elsewhere in the New Testament and, if possible, in Judaism and the patristic period as well."* This is a wise observation, one which I believe that the editors of the NKJV have failed to appreciate in their multitudinous annotations of prophecy fulfillment. A study of Jewish commentaries on the Hebrew Scriptures reveals that almost without exception, the Old Testament verses that the NKJV flags as prophetic were not considered prophetic by the Jewish Sages. Although it cannot be accurately determined just when these Jewish perceptions were determined, I believe we can be confident that they were extant in Second Temple Judaism, for they appear in the Talmud, a composition of contemporary and later writings. In determining the truth of prophecy fulfillment, I am not inclined to accept conclusions from New Testament writers and commentators who have paid inadequate attention to the centuries of Jewish scholarship. Tested in a court of law, as Simon Greenleaf urges us to do, one would be hard pressed to accept nascent Christian theologians over the Jewish scholars they have rejected.

(p. 47) – *"When people heard Isaiah 61, they understood it as a classic text describing end-time salvation. In effect, Jesus proclaimed to his hearers that God's end-time salvation had been fulfilled in their hearing. Their surprise is understandable."* So is mine – I wonder whether this Christian scholar appreciates what he has just admitted: that Jesus was NOT the Messiah. Follow me on this. The context is Luke 4:17-19 where Jesus unrolled the scroll of Isaiah and read Isaiah 61:1-2. When he had finished and sat down, he said: *"Today this Scripture is fulfilled in your hearing"* (Luke 4:21). If these verses refer to the *eschaton*, then clearly Jesus was wrong, as we can attest two thousand years later. If John was right quoting Jesus as saying: *"For I have not spoken on my own authority; but the Father who sent me gave me a command what I should say and what I should speak"* (John 12:49), then Jesus was again wrong, for the Father would not have told him to claim that the day of the Lord was fulfilled – God is not a liar. With such evident errors in the New Testament, the whole plot begins to unravel, and it is asking too much to claim as many do, that every word is the inerrant word of God. God is better than that. So, back to the courtroom and the adjudication of evidence: this claim of Jesus in Luke 4:21 is not credible, for the truth has overtaken it.

(p. 50) – *"The Scriptures were the frame of reference for their [Christian] theology and provided many of the tools for their thinking. The same should be true of us.*" So true, and all should say, *Amen*. Undoubtedly, the Scriptures provided many of the tools for the thinking of the New Testament authors, but they misused them. Metaphorically, they used hammers to crack eggshells, and cross-saws for delicate surgery. Where their tools should have been honed before use, they considered a blunt edge acceptable. The Scriptures were the frame, but they failed to look deeply through the window. What they saw was not truly there.

Summary

I am ever curious as to why well-educated scholars make such fundamental mistakes in their literature. Beginning with the erroneous heading quotation, "*The Hebrew and Aramaic Scriptures were, of course, the only Bible the early Christian thinkers and writers had*", the author took me further into confusion over what it was that he really believed. Later, he admitted that other Christians would have only used the Greek, which is the truth of the matter for all of the New Testament authors. Perhaps getting too immersed in his subject, analysing Old Testament usage in the New, he seems to not have reflected on what he was saying in the context of Christian orthodoxy. Whilst he did not explicitly assert the inerrancy of the New Testament, as many Christian apologists, I sense that he did so believe, to a significant extent at least. However, what he demonstrated to my mind was that such could not be true, any more than it could be true of a weekly sermon in a parish church.

Again, whilst not explicitly stated, he conveyed the impression that the New Testament authors appropriated Old Testament verses to suit their purposes, with often little regard for the intentions of the original authors. I do not have an issue with that when used as a teaching tool, but it does confirm human intent, not Divine, and argues against inerrancy. Which brings us back to the primary topic of prophecy fulfillment: yes, the early disciples could be forgiven for mistaking Jesus as Messiah, but I am not confident that the same could be said for later writers. If the eschaton loomed large in their thinking, how could they have continued to believe that way after the destruction of Jerusalem, and the banishment of the Jews from *Eretz* Israel, entirely contrary to messianic prophecy?

REFERENCES:

1. Beale, G.K., *The Right Doctrine from the Wrong Texts?* Essays on the Use of the Old Testament in the New, Baker Academic, Grand Rapids, MI, 1994, p. 29

2. Black, David A., and Dockery, David S., *New Testament Criticism and Interpretation*, Zondervan, Grand Rapids, MI, 1991

3. Roth, Andrew Gabriel, *Aramaic English New Testament*, Netzari Press, Jerusalem, Israel, 2012

4. *The History of the Septuagint*, http://www.kalvesmaki.com/lxx/

5. The author's footnote says: See Roberts Banks, *Jesus and the Law in the Synoptic Tradition* (Cambridge: Cambridge University Press, 1975), 132-46. Is Jesus' thought from Prov. 4:23? See also Acts 10:9-16; Rom. 14:14; 1 Cor 10:26-27; and 1 Tim 4:4, which place Christian conclusions in opposition with dietary restrictions in the Old Testament.

6. Talbot, Wayne, *Christians Too, Must Obey: Putting a Fence Around Torah*, Xlibris, Bloomington, IN, 2017, Chapter 5-11: *God's Dietary Laws*

CHAPTER 8-4

THE ESSAYS IN REVIEW

"Not everything in the Old Testament is brought into the new faith. There is both continuity and discontinuity between the Old Testament and the New Testament. That is, while some parts of the New testament are direct extensions of the Old Testament message, some parts of the Old Testament message have been superseded. Even so, none of the New Testament writers ever suggests that the Old Testament is less than fully the Word of God."[1]

I must contend that if that latter assertion is true, then it could only have been later Christian theologians who considered that indeed, *the Old Testament is less than fully the Word of God*. If God is accepted as being immutable and omniscient, which parts of His message would be superseded? I can accept that some would be, just as some prophecies by the Prophets Isaiah, Ezekiel, and others, were messages for their times, and superseded by the passing of time and fulfillment of the events. But Christian doctrine has also seen as superseded, some messages of God which He described using terms such as *eternal* and *forever*. Consider the Law and the Sabbath. I agree, that apart from Paul and others writing under his name, none of the other evangelists disputed the ongoing application of the Law, and need to forever keep holy the Sabbath, but that is not how later Christianity interpreted the Gospels. Is it now to be admitted that Christianity has indeed departed from the message of the evangelists, just as I have elsewhere claimed?

If there was but one conclusion that I would take away from this series of essays, it would be this: the assertion of C.S. Lewis that the Gospels are "reportage"[2] cannot be substantiated by the evidence, and is not supported by modern, Christian, scholarly opinion. The repeated references to early and later development of theology, and statements such as: "what Dodd was discussing was the fields used in the *earliest* stage of the church's study of the Old Testament. It is reasonable to assume that at the literary stage of composition of the New Testament the writers would not be tied to the specific fields and would be free to explore more widely." (p. 201, italics in original). Mention of the *literary stage of composition of the New Testament* would also suggest that claims of an earlier dating of the writings are likely untrue, and that the much later dates are more plausible. Do you see what the author seems to have unwittingly admitted? He lends support to the argument that the New Testament was written later than Christianity admits, and not by the original witnesses of the life and times of Jesus. Either that, or he is claiming that after the death of Jesus, these witnesses went away to study the Scriptures (in Greek), and other sources (?), to understand what they had seen, and what it meant. That hardly seems likely, if it be true, as one Christian commentator observed, and many agree, that *"The ancient Apostles were common men, and that was part of their credential"*. That is simply not what common men do – not now, and not then.

This also questions the attribution of authorship, especially that of Paul who died circa 65 CE. To my mind, it is too much to ask that Paul both travelled and preached widely (which would have been very time consuming), supported himself through tent making or other means, and also studied the Scriptures to develop his theology. It is only scholars who have the time, and the inclination, to *explore more widely*, to develop and document a theology, and none of these could have been first generation witnesses to the life and times of Jesus. If Paul was, as claimed, a Pharisee, the son of a Pharisee, trained at the feet of Gamaliel in Jerusalem, there would be reason to accept that he studied the Scriptures to develop his theology, but there are sound reasons for rejecting this description of his education and background (see Chapter 2-6).

Another general observation is that none of the essays questioned the truth of the New Testament – all discussed various hypotheses on how the Old Testament was used in the New. That is not a criticism, as Beale quite deliberately collected essays on a particular theme, and all essays were true to that theme as you would expect. I point this out, however, to underline the presuppositions behind many, if not all, of the hypotheses, and how that relates to evidence. Let me use evolution as an example. In recent years, the Neo-Darwinism Synthesis has come in for substantial criticism as being inadequate to explain what is now known about the complexity of life. Evolutionists have been offering numerous hypotheses for the true mechanisms, but all based on the belief that *microbes-to-man* narrative is true. Hypotheses within a paradigm only have validity if the paradigm itself has validity. So it is with hypotheses within the paradigm that Jesus was the prophesied Messiah, and that the New Testament narrative is true. The hypotheses themselves cannot offer evidence of the truth of the paradigm. Arguing consistently within a paradigm is logical, but it does not necessarily lead to truth.

Accepting the theme of the book, "*The Right Doctrine from the Wrong Texts?*", and the constraints such a theme placed upon the authors of the essays, I was nevertheless interested to find any unintentional admissions, *Freudian slips* as it were. The collection of essays is a literary record of Christian scholars debating amongst themselves: one offering an opinion, a second refuting it, and a third refuting the second, and so on, all in the interests of healthy intellectual debate. As with most such debates, however, proponents often say more than they intended. What follows in this review, in no particular order, are issues which were of particular interest to me in the context of my study into prophecy fulfillment.

Scholarship of the New Testament Authors

With a few exceptions, I consistently gained the impression that the essayists considered the New Testament authors to be peers of modern scholars, equalling or perhaps even exceeding their own scholarly insights and achievements. Two thoughts occur to me:

1. If the essayists are right, then the New Testament is not the product of first generation witnesses of the life and times of Jesus, but the result of much later theological development, likely at least into the second century CE; and/or

2. The essayists have read far too much into the New Testament, likely in an attempt to understand, or perhaps even justify, how far Christianity has departed from the Jewishness of Jesus and his early followers.

In no particular order, following are quotes from the essays to illustrate what I believe to issues of significance. Page numbers in the book are shown at the end of the quotations.

"I have here only hinted at the significance for Christian theology of a right understanding of the treatment of the Old Testament in the New. I believe it represents an intellectual achievement of remarkable originality, displaying penetration into the meaning that lies beneath the surface of biblical text, and a power of synthesis which gathers apparently disparate elements into a many-sided whole, not unsuitable to convey some idea of the 'manifold wisdom of God'." (pp. 180-181) Are we to believe that the initial disciples of Jesus, including Paul, were capable of such an intellectual achievement, men who were chosen because of their ordinariness? By apparently attributing this achievement to men, does it not argue against divine inspiration? If the New Testament represents the inerrant word of God, why would anyone comment on them being an intellectual achievement? This, to my mind, is another example of where scholars offer opinions that are contrary to the preachings of the clergy, the latter being the truth to which Christians should adhere. Why do the Christian clergy not teach what the scholars claim to know?

"Any New Testament scholar who is in any way interested in the problem of hermeneutics is well aware of the dichotomy between the approach of New Testament authors to 'Scripture' and our own. A study of their methods of exegesis must surely make any twentieth-century preacher uncomfortable, for they tear passages out of context, use allegory or typology to give old stories new meanings, contradict the plain meaning of the text, find references to Christ in passages where the original authors certainly never intended any, and adapt or even alter the wording in order to make it yield the meaning they require." (p. 279) No arguing with that, for it is precisely what I have experienced in my own studies, especially evidenced in my analysis of prophecy fulfillment. The essayist continues, "Yet we cannot simply dismiss their interpretation as false, for they were certainly being true to the exegetical methods of their day." (p. 280) I could agree with the essayist, but only if I were convinced that the exegetical methods of their day represented a valid interpretation of the Scriptures, but we have no evidence of that, and numerous scholarly opinions to the contrary. No doubt, it is a valuable scholarly exercise to study and comment on such things, but in the context of evidence, as in a court of law, it carries little weight. For one thing, we do not know which "Scriptures" the New Testament authors exegeted. We know that multiple versions of the Greek translations were then extant, but we do not know who performed those translations; their competence in the performance of those translations; to what extent they represented accurate translations of the Hebrew; nor to what extent they agreed with one another. We do not have copies of those early documents, even though we can, to some extent, reconstruct verses from the quotation of them, bearing in mind that as acknowledged, the New Testament authors do not always accurately quote them. The New Testament authors may well have been true to their exegetical methods, even if we could be confident of reverse engineering them from the New Testament writings, but so what? What does that offer us in terms of truth?

"Did the early church go to the Scriptures to find evidence that he [Jesus] died 'for our sins' or was it a study of the Scriptures that led to the realisation that he died 'for our sins'?" (p. 198) If it was the latter, how does that square with the reportage assertion by C.S. Lewis?

"It is true that the theology of the New Testament approaches the Old Testament wearing the spectacles of Judaism, but this does not affect the basic fact that it was to the Old Testament and to the traditions inspired by it that the church turned when it began to do its theology." (p. 199) If that be true, and I am not confident that it is, why did the Church of Rome utterly reject the traditions of Judaism? You cannot have it both ways: you cannot claim that New Testament theology used Judaic perspectives and traditions in its development, and then have the Church later reject that very foundation. Actually, I suppose that you can, which is why I often contend that Christian theology is incoherent, and does not follow in the footsteps of Jesus.

"Certainly Dodd did not deny that there was what he called 'a certain shift, nearly always an expansion, of the original scope of the passage' (Dodd 1952, 130), and he argued that great literature contains the potential of more meaning than the author explicitly intended ... He argued that the finding of an appropriate text in part of the Old Testament led the Christians to look in the same context for further appropriate texts, and that in some cases the choice of a text was dependent upon the assumption that the larger passage is christologically oriented." (p. 202) I would again remind the reader of the assertion by C.S. Lewis, that "Either this is reportage ... or else, some unknown [ancient] writer ... without known predecessors or successors suddenly anticipated the whole technique of modern novelistic, realistic narrative"[3], but I would substitute for his modern novelistic, realistic narrative - a "modern theological treatise". I may seem to be harping on this, and perhaps I am, but as so many Christian apologetics appeal to the opinions of Lewis and his Mere Christianity, I feel it necessary to demonstrate the incoherence of these divergent opinions.

"The point may be made that the New Testament authors thought that they were respecting the context and original meaning, since they would have argued that the meaning which they found was the meaning which God intended" (p. 203). Thought indeed. This admission is tantamount to saying that the words in the New Testament were not necessarily God inspired. From an evidentiary perspective, they are the opinions of men who were not, to our knowledge, experts in the field in which they wrote. That being so, their evidentiary weight is minimal to none at all.

"We can trace shifts in the application of the Old Testament passages in different parts of the New Testament ... and the starting point of this process lies in the apologetic activity of the early church. The early church was particularly concerned to answer Jewish objections to the messiahship of Jesus." (p. 203) Rereading the essay, I can find no reference point for "early", and so cannot be sure of to which specific period the essayist was referring. In my own usage of the term, I attempt to locate the period with the words "in Rome" or similar, although I will not claim one hundred percent compliance. There were two periods during which there may have been structured Jewish objections: (1), from sometime after the claimed resurrection of Jesus until the destruction of the Temple, the period thereafter when Christianity and Judaism split; and (2), decades later when the Jews, under the School of Hillel at Yavneh, started to formalise their own theology in defence against the incursions of Christianity. Again, this suggests that the literary stage of composition was later than Christianity traditionally claims.

There is a certain irony here when you compare one essayist's opinion against another. Earlier we noted: "It is true that the theology of the New Testament approaches the Old Testament wearing the **spectacles of Judaism**", but then we read: "The early church was particularly concerned to answer **Jewish objections** to the messiahship of Jesus" [emphasis mine]. The two statements do not necessarily contradict one another, but having studied both the Jewish and Christian messianic interpretations, I believe that in this context, they most certainly do. We cannot know how many scripturally literate Jews accepted Jesus as Messiah after his death, and how many remained loyal to the cause after the destruction of Jerusalem. Acts 21:20 tells of "many thousands of Jews ... who have believed, and they are all zealous for the law", but I have discussed my reasons for doubting the accuracy of Luke's narratives, and here he might well have been exaggerating – I cannot know. One essayist commented: "Our earliest evidences of Christianity were written against a background of Jewish rejection as an accomplished fact. Only the Gentile mission is treated seriously in the New Testament; the Jewish mission is perfunctory." (p. 192) Measured against the other quotations, how concerned really, was *the early church particularly concerned to answer Jewish objections*? If Paul, according to some writings, was the most active evangelist during the first decades, it is plausible that the Gentile mission overshadowed the mission to the Jewish community. The Epistle of James evidences that those in Jerusalem had a different emphasis in their evangelising, one that remained true to the Judaism of the time.

Ignoring his context, David Seccombe noted: "Luke's concern was not just to establish the *bona fides* of the founder of Christianity" (p. 255). There is considerable agreement amongst New Testament scholars that Jesus was not the founder of Christianity: it was more probably Paul. The clearest evidence is Rome's rejection of Jesus' initial followers, the

Nazarenes, whom Rome described as heretics. I find this and the anti-Jewishness of early Christianity to be irreconcilable with the claim that Jesus founded the religion of Christianity, with its rejection of Torah, the Sabbath, the God-ordained commemorations, and everything Jewish.

A doubt cast upon the integrity of the New Testament authors is found in this comment: "The recent study of B. Lindars ("The Place of the Old Testament in the Formation of New Testament Theology: Prolegomena," *N.T.S.* 23 (1977): 59-66) argues that New Testament writers had no interest in the meaning of the Old Testament for its own sake, but simply quarried texts to support and illustrate a pre-existing New Testament theology." (p. 248) I am sympathetic to that view, which also suggests a later date of writing following a period of theological development. Another comment, along similar lines, although with a twist in the tail, is this:

> "Professor Lindars and Professor Borgen have suggested that the Old Testament may be regarded in some ways as servant and in some ways as master in the process of formation of New Testament theology. The paradox emerges that the Scriptures 'have an authority which is unquestioned', and yet 'the place of the Old Testament in the formation of New Testament theology is that of a servant, ready to run to the aid of the gospel whenever it is required' (Lindars 1976, 59, 66). Granted that Jesus Christ is the new master, we may perhaps remind ourselves that to be 'a slave of Jesus Christ', as Paul so frequently called himself, is to occupy a position of humble service which is at the same time one of authority and dignity." (p. 214)

The indecision about whether the Old Testament is the servant or the master is evident, although perhaps context is absent. It could be that where the Old Testament is valuable to the New Testament authors, for example, in matters of undisputed history, it is the master, but where interpretation is possible, such as in the writings of Isaiah and Daniel, it becomes the servant. I have noticed this trend myself. This is not an uncommon literary device, practised especially by modern fiction writers: add fact to fiction to make the whole narrative more plausible. Some ancient Greek writers did similarly. The sting in the tail is the brute fact of Jesus as master, as if that is sufficient evidence to put an end to the discussion.

"Research has been done on the way in which Jewish midrashic material, especially in the form of synagogue sermons, was structured in terms of its relation to the *seder* and *haftarah*, and it has been claimed that similar structures can be found in the New Testament." (p. 213) I found this suggestion to be most thought provoking. If true, it suggests that the New Testament authors either remembered the lessons of old, or continued to attend Jewish synagogues conducted by rabbis, well versed in the Hebrew Scriptures and the teachings of the Sages. Compare that with a later scathing outburst by so-called *Golden Mouth*, St. John Chrysostom:

> "The synagogue is worse than a brothel ... it is the den of scoundrels and the repair of wild beasts ... the temple of demons devoted to idolatrous cults ... the refuge of brigands and debauchees, and the cavern of devils. [It is] a criminal assembly of Jews ... a place of meeting for assassins of Christ ... a house worse than a drinking shop ... a den of thieves; a house of ill fame, a dwelling of iniquity, the refuge of devils, a gulf and abyss of perdition."[4]

If the New Testament authors still had a theological or religious link to the synagogue, then later Church Fathers repudiated that link, and in effect, repudiated the source of their own religion.

"The use of ... methods helps to draw out the continuity felt by the New Testament writers between the work of God in their own day and in Old Testament times and hence between themselves and the ancient people of God. But there is also the consciousness of differences, and it may be interesting to work out how far the early Christian uses of the Old Testament as a court of appeal was affected by their readiness to do away with some of its teaching. Did they see themselves as abrogating it or rather as reinterpreting it to suit their own situations?" (p. 210) Again, this reflects the *servant* and *master* approach: master when it suits, servant when it does not. Why were the New Testament writers so ready to *do away with some of its teaching*, a practice which could be considered a *type* for later Christian theological development?

What is particularly interesting here is the contrast of these scholarly opinions, with the pastoral message that the New Testament is the inerrant word of God. I often wonder whether when attending Bible or Theological college, trainee pastors are exposed to this level of scholarly opinion. If so, why is it so seldom manifest in their preaching, and if not, why not?

Typology

"Typology in Christian theology and Biblical exegesis is a doctrine or theory concerning the relationship of the Old Testament to the New Testament. Events, persons, or statements in the Old Testament are seen as types pre-figuring or superseded by antitypes, events or aspects of Christ or his revelation described in the New Testament."[5] Admittedly a quotation from Wikipedia, but I doubt whether there is cause to disagree with this definition. Typology is a regular theme in Christian apologetics, at times employed with validity, and at other times with lesser authority. Some quotations to ponder:

1. "Typology may be defined as the study which traces parallels or correspondences between incidents recorded in the Old Testament and their counterparts in the New Testament such that the latter can be seen to resemble the former in notable aspects and yet go beyond them." (p. 211)

2. "What remains uncertain is whether the Old Testament incident was thought to have been deliberately planned as a type for its antitype, so that a full exposition of the Old Testament passage recording it would have to say 'and God did this *in order that* it would serve as a type for his later redemption of the world in Christ'." (p. 212, italics in original)

3. "A major element in Paul's interpretation of the Old Testament was typology, where a comparison is made between events in the New Testament an events in the Old Testament which are historical, which happened in accordance with the divine plea and which may have 'a dispensational or economic relationship to the New Testament fact' (Ellis 1957, 128)." (p. 211)

4. "Typology begins and ends with the present salvation. NT typology is not trying to find the meaning of some OT story or institution. It compares Jesus and the salvation which he has brought with the OT parallels in order to discover what can be learned from this about the new and then perhaps, what can be learned also about the old. (Goppelt 1982, 201)" (p. 212)

Notice the subtle differences in the wording of the Wikipedia entry and that in quotation (1). The first speaks of *prefiguring* or *superseding*, whereas the second has the milder *parallels* or *correspondence*. In my studies of Christian apologetics, I have found the Wikipedia definition to be more representative. Point (2) questions an important issue: Did God deliberately do something as a forerunner of a subsequent event, a stage in His overall plan as it were, or did the New Testament authors discover the type themselves, making more of it than originally intended? I believe both answers to be true, depending on context. This brings us to the question of redemption and/or salvation, depending on what those terms mean to the reader.

Salvation / Redemption

"Luke's characterization of the salvation which becomes present with the coming of Jesus is largely Isaianic." (p. 251) Luke does reference Isaiah more often that other Old Testament books: out of 54 prophetic references in his Gospel, 22 are from Isaiah, 11 from the Psalms, 7 from Daniel, and a sprinkling from other books. However, as deal I with in Chapter 4-4, none of these prophecy fulfillment claims can be substantiated in the light of history. A point to note regarding Isaiah's prophecies is that where the Messiah is suggested, they are always in the context of the End of Days – there is no suggestion of an interim messianic mission, which in the words of the author of Hebrews, "was offered once to bear the sins of many ... he will appear a second time, apart from sin, for salvation" (v. 9:28). It is clear, to my mind at least, that when Jesus failed in the mission of redemption of Israel from Roman oppression, it became necessary to find an interim mission for him.

Redemption for the Jews, as understood from the Hebrew Scriptures, was rescue from exile and from oppression of other cultures – in the

Second Temple period, primarily Greek and Roman. They understood that their periodic exiles were the result of their own turning from God and the Covenant, and that God would redeem them when they repented. There was no concept of spiritual redemption from the penalty of sin; no concept of escaping the power of Satan; no concept of substitutionary atonement. Reconciliation with God occurred when they approached God with repentance in their heart. To convince them otherwise, in terms of Christian theology, would have been a very hard sell, which is why I can believe the earlier observation: "Only the Gentile mission is treated seriously in the New Testament."

Eschatology

"The New Testament writers share the view that at least some prophecy looks forward to the last days and that the coming of Jesus and the establishment of the church are parts of the events of the last days (indeed the most significant events) and are the object of prophecy. This means that both groups [Ed. Qumran sect and NT writers] regarded themselves as having a 'key' to understanding the Old Testament: they 'know' that the text *must* apply to their own situation in the last days, and therefore they use their techniques to get at this meaning." (pp. 209-210) Well, it was the last days for the Qumran sect, and close to the last days of the true followers of Jesus, the Nazarenes, but not for the world in general.

I believe that we sufficiently covered the subject of eschatology in Chapter 6-2.

REFERENCES:

1. Beale, G.K., *The Right Doctrine from the Wrong Texts? Essays on the Use of the Old Testament in the New*, Baker Academic, Grand Rapids, MI, 1994, p. 30
2. Lewis, C.S., *Christian Reflections*, William B. Eerdmans Publishing Company, Grand Rapids, MI, p. 154-155
3. *Ibid*
4. Brown, Michael L., *Our Hands Are Stained With Blood*, Destiny Image Publishers Inc., Shippensburg, PA, 1990, p. 10
5. https://en.wikipedia.org/wiki/Typology_%28theology%29

PART 9

UNDERSTANDING JESUS

"Why do you call me good? No one is good but One, that is, God."
(Mark 10:18)

If we were to take this verse in isolation, we could understand Jesus to be making one thing clear: He was NOT God! Therein the danger of quoting verses out of context. On the other hand, given that many of the sayings of Jesus, as recorded in the Gospels, are entirely lacking in context, perhaps the mistake is expecting context when there isn't any, and Jesus was just making a clear, self-contained, unequivocal statement, so that no-one could misunderstand. Would this be the right approach to exegesis?

Caveat

From the outset, let me assure the reader that I do NOT understand who Jesus was, who he thought he was, or who his disciples thought he was, at least up until the time of the resurrection, and probably even

WAYNE TALBOT

much later as Christian theology developed under the influence of Paul. Speaking of the resurrection, we have no evidence that Jesus rose on the third day, only that the tomb was empty on the third day, but we have evidence that according to one of the evangelists, Jesus rose, spiritually at least, on the same day as the crucifixion: *"Assuredly, I say to you, today you will be with me in Paradise"* (Luke 23:43). Very curious, but of course, the editors of the NKJV simply made a mistake in how they punctuated this sentence: perhaps the comma should have been after the word, *today*, not before. That raises another question: how scholarly were the NKJV editors, and to what extent should we trust how they have punctuated the texts. Punctuation does matter, as evidenced by these alternate punctuations of lyrics from the musical, Jesus Christ Superstar:

1.   I have known so many men before, in so many ways he is just one more; or

2.   I have known so many men before in so many ways – he is just one more.

That aside, whilst we have the documentary witness of the Gospels and Epistles, we also know from an evidentiary perspective, that we cannot ascribe 100% credence to them in the form that we have them today. How much of the Gospels, in particular, faithfully record the events and sayings of the time, and how much is a product of a developed tradition and theology, is a question subject to much contention.

The Gospel of Jesus

If we were to summarise the Gospel of Jesus succinctly, which explanation should we use?

One source answers the question this way: "The word gospel means "good news," so the gospel of Christ is the good news of His coming to provide forgiveness of sins for all who will believe (Colossians 1:14; Romans 10:9)."[1] Another says: "The gospel of Jesus Christ is the summary explanation of who he is and what he accomplished for you. The word gospel literally means "good news". It's good news because it's an answer to a problem. So...what's the problem? The problem is no one deserves to go to heaven."[2] Yet another: "The gospel of Jesus Christ is our Heavenly Father's plan for the happiness and salvation of His children. It is called the gospel of Jesus Christ because the Atonement of Jesus Christ is central to this plan."[3] Another: "It's a message from God saying, "Good news! Here is how you can be saved from my judgment!" That's an announcement you can't afford to ignore."[4] And finally, a slightly longer, and more imaginative explanation: "The word *gospel* means "good news" and is explained by the following six key truths of the GOSPEL Journey:

1.	**G**od created us to be with Him. (Genesis 1-2)
2.	**O**ur sins separate us from God. (Genesis 3)
3.	**S**ins cannot be removed by good deeds. (Genesis 4 – Malachi 4)
4.	**P**aying the price for sin, Jesus died and rose again. (Matthew – Luke)
5.	**E**veryone who trusts in Him alone has eternal life. (John); and
6.	**L**ife with Jesus starts now and lasts forever. (Acts – Revelation)."[5] [emphasis in original]

I have no quibble with (1) and (2), but (3) is straw man argument: sins <u>can</u> be removed by *repentance*; good deeds are what you do because you love God, as Luke put it regarding Zacharias and Elizabeth, "they were both righteous before God walking in all the commandments and ordinances of the Lord blameless" (Luke 1:6). This did not mean that they never sinned, but because they repented as the Hebrew Scriptures teach, they were both righteous before God, and had no need of substitutionary atonement. Nevertheless, from the five opinions quoted, the Gospel of Jesus was the good news that by his dying on the cross, he paid the price for our sins, so that we do not have to. Accompanying the good news was bad news: if you do not believe in Jesus, you don't get to go to heaven, even if you are also told that "anyone who speaks a word against the Son of Man it will be forgiven him" (Matthew 12:32). Just how that works is quite beyond me, but I can only take the Christian view of the gospel of the man whom they believe is their saviour.

However, how does that fit with Old Testament prophecy? Well, as best as I can determine from the Hebrew Scriptures, not at all. In Part 8, we reviewed some scholarly opinions of how the New Testament authors used the Old Testament in developing their theology. I have expressed my conclusions, and no doubt, God will hold me accountable. Your conclusions are between yourself and God.

The Accomplishments of Jesus

The only rational approach to a review of the accomplishments of Jesus, is to accept that he accomplished what the Gospel said was his good news. According to Luke, "all things that are written by the prophets concerning the Son of Man will be accomplished" (Luke 18:31; also 24:27, 24:44). Notably, the Prophets had very little to say about what the *Son of Man* would accomplish: Luke must have decided that Jesus, as the Son of Man, was the prophesied Messiah mentioned or alluded to, but at no time did the Prophets even hint at the Messiah dying for our sins. Nor is there any mention that the Children of Israel were forever separated from God because of their sins. On the contrary, they were quite specific about how they could be reconciled to God, and that without some future Messiah dying for them.

The big question remains: If the accomplishments of Jesus were as pronounced in his good news, was that prophesied?

REFERENCES:

1. https://www.gotquestions.org/gospel-of-Jesus-Christ.html
2. http://www.provethebible.net/T2-Hist/TheGospel.htm
3. https://www.lds.org/manual/the-gospel/the-gospel?lang=eng
4. https://www.crossway.org/articles/what-is-the-gospel-2/
5. https://www.lifein6words.com/the-g-o-s-p-e-l-message-explained/

CHAPTER 9-1

DEFEAT INTO VICTORY

"We are not interested in the possibilities of defeat. They do not exist."
~ Queen Victoria ~

An issue which has long mystified me is this: if Jesus was not fulfilling Old Testament prophecies, as I am convinced he was not, where did he, or his disciples, get the idea of the Messiah dying for the sins of the people? There is something missing from the plot. As we discuss in the next chapter, Jesus started his public mission with the words: *"I was not sent except to the lost sheep of the house of Israel"* (Matthew 15:24), which is entirely consistent with the mission of the Prophets of old. John the Baptist preached the same message: "Repent, return to God", meaning return to Torah and the Covenant. All that seems entirely plausible with Jesus seeing himself acting in concert with those who had gone before. However, toward the end of Jesus' public life, he announced that he was about to die. Not only that, but he was to die for the sins of the world. What caused him to see a change in his mission, or if it not him, who was it? What was the motivation for turning an Old Testament style prophet into someone entirely different?

According to the evidence: "*it is expedient for us that one man should die for the people, and not that the whole nation should perish*" (John 11:50), Jesus was to be executed for being a threat to the political stability of Judea. If the latter is true, why is there so little in the Gospels about Jesus' subversive activities? In the Book of Acts, we read of Gamaliel cautioning against persecution of Peter and others, because previous subversives like Theudas, Judas of Galilee, and Zadok were all sorted by the Romans themselves. If the Nazarenes were not from God, then they would get their comeuppance just as previous subversives did. It is significant that Gamaliel, a highly respected Pharisee and senior member of the Sanhedrin, made no mention of the religious beliefs of the disciples of Jesus, which is circumstantial evidence that his concern was political, rather than religious. So to the conundrum: on the evidence from both the Gospels and the Book of Acts, the conflict between the Jews and Jesus was political, with occasional skirmishes over minor religious interpretations. On the other hand, the conflict between the Jews and Christians is entirely religious, with the Gentile Church of Rome seeking to entirely eradicate any and all traces of Judaism.

How did this state of affairs come about?

I had no idea, and remain uncertain, but this book[1] which we are about to discuss provides much food for thought. In some ways, it provides answers, but at the same time, raises even more questions concerning gaps in the Gospel accounts, and the process of turning a political defeat into a spiritual triumph. C.S. Lewis claimed that this was neither myth nor legend, but *snatching victory from documented defeat* certainly reads as such, to me at least.

The Messiah Before Jesus

In a previous work[2], I commented on how secretive Jesus was about various events during his public life, and who he was, notably that no-one should reveal that he was "Jesus the Christ" (Matthew 16:20). Others have commented similarly[3]. Israel Knohl, Chair of the Bible Department at Hebrew University, asks, much as I have:

"How can we solve the riddle of Jesus' personality and messianic self-understanding? Did he regard himself as the Messiah? If so, why did he not say so plainly, and why did he forbid his disciples to make his messianic identity known to the public, thus creating a 'messianic secret'? Did Jesus really foresee his own suffering, death, and resurrection? If he did, why did he not refer to himself directly in this context, but only indirectly as the 'son of man'? Did Jesus see himself as a divine redeemer? If so, why is this not reflected in the Synoptic Gospels"[4].

That others ask these same questions goes some way to justifying my conclusion that the New Testament narrative, and the Christian theology that has developed therefrom, to be entirely incoherent. Judaism neatly flows from the Hebrew Scriptures, whereas Christianity owes very little to the evidence provided in the New Testament. Quoting from the synopsis of the book:

"In a work that challenges notions that have dominated New Testament scholarship for more than a hundred years, Israel Knohl gives startling evidence for a messianic precursor to Jesus who is described as the Suffering Servant in recently published fragments of the Dead Sea Scrolls. The Messiah before Jesus clarifies many formerly incomprehensible aspects of Jesus life and confirms the story in the New Testament about his messianic awareness. The book shows that, around the time of Jesus birth, there came into being a conception of catastrophic messianism in which the suffering, humiliation, and death of the messiah were regarded as an integral part of the redemptive process. Scholars have long argued that Jesus could not have foreseen his suffering, death, and resurrection because the concept of a slain savior who rises from the dead was alien to the Judaism of his time. But, on the basis of hymns found at Qumran among the Dead Sea Scrolls, Knohl argues that, one generation before Jesus, a messianic leader arose in the Qumran sect who was regarded by his followers as ushering in an era of redemption and forgiveness. This messianic leader was killed by Roman soldiers in the course of a revolt that broke out in

Jerusalem in 4 B.C.E. The Romans forbade his body to be buried and after the third day his disciples believed that he was resurrected and rose to heaven. This formed the basis for Jesus messianic consciousness, Knohl argues; it was because of this model that Jesus anticipated he would suffer, die, and be resurrected after three days. Knohl takes his fascinating inquiry one step further by suggesting that this messiah was a figure known to us from historical sources of the period. This identification may shed new light on the mystery of the Paraclete in the Gospel of John. A pathbreaking study, The Messiah before Jesus, will reshape our understanding of Christianity and its relationship to Judaism."[5]

Could this be true? Did Jesus change from an old style prophet to a messiah modelled on a previous claimant to the title. Was his entombment and resurrection written back into the narratives because that was what was supposed to happen to this form of messiah, one who died for the sins of others?

Messianic Fervour

First, some history, which incidentally provides further evidence against the inerrancy of the New Testament, and the lack of accuracy in the Book of Acts. Luke had Gamaliel referring to Theudas (Acts 5:36), and Judas of Galilee (v. 37), but we have reason to believe that this was Luke embellishing his tale. The problem is that according to Josephus, the revolt by Theudas was circa 45 CE, long after that of Judas of Galilee, which was before the census in 6 BCE. Luke puts them in the reverse order, ignoring that his narrative of Gamaliel would have occurred circa 37 CE. There were other false messiahs after Jesus, besides Theudas. Though the New Testament has little, if anything, to say about the friction between the Jews and the Romans, Josephus has much to say, as it was the defining issue in the region ever since the Roman general, Pompey, captured Jerusalem in 63 BCE. "Rome did allow the Jews to practice their religion, but Roman paganism and Caesar worship were constantly encroaching upon Jewish beliefs. Herod once had a huge golden eagle, the symbol of Rome, placed atop the great gate to the temple and the priesthood enacted a daily sacrifice for Caesar. The Romans also placed an unbearable tax burden upon the Jews. All this combined with Roman brutality made Jewish rebellion inevitable."[6]

Thus, the rise of the Zealots with the intention of overthrowing the Romans.

It was likewise inevitable that many Jews saw in this state of affairs, signs that redemption by the prophesied Messiah was at hand. Likely it was more in hope than anything, but hope is often all that people can cling to. There were other false messiahs after Jesus: Menahem, the son of Judas the Galilee in 67 CE, who took his father's subversion to new heights; John of Gischala, contemporary of Menahem, and even worse, and much later, Simon bar Kokhba in 132 CE. One reason to doubt the New Testament accounts is how it entirely ignores the fact of the conflict between the Jews and the Romans, the persistent subversive activities by the Zealots, and the armed rebellions that led firstly to the destruction of Jerusalem, and finally the expulsion of the Jews from their homeland. If one studies the history of these conflicts, which surely dominated the lives of the Judeans, much as the lives of Jews were dominated in Europe during the Second World War, one gets the sense that the New Testament was written in a political vacuum.

Of note is the conciliatory tone to not just the Zealots, e.g. Simon the Zealot (Luke 6:15); the corrupt tax collectors, e.g. Matthew; but also to the Romans, e.g. Matthew 8:5-13, Matthew 27:54, Mark 12:17, and Luke 7:1-10. How do we reconcile this evidence with the evidence of Jesus' political execution? Even more, how do we reconcile this evidence with the historical evidence of the simmering tensions between the Jews and the Romans? It is almost as if the authors of the New Testament went out of their way to not further antagonise the Romans, who were already furious with Jewish revolutionary activities. The literary period of the New Testament occurred contemporaneously with the Jewish revolts, and outside Jewish lands. I find it entirely plausible that the New Testament writers chose a conciliatory tone toward the conquering Romans, and wrote primarily for a Gentile audience already subjected to Roman influence.

Which brings us back to Jesus as Messiah. Clearly, he could not be portrayed as a messiah like those who openly opposed the Roman oppressors, and thus there could be no emphasis on the redemptive role of the messiah in restoring the Israelites to occupy the land promised to them by God. This was what the Hebrew Scriptures prophesied, but obviously, political correctness was in vogue even back then. So ... we have a messiah, but accomplishing what exactly? Enter the influence of the Qumran sect.

The Essenes

In some ways, the Essenes can be compared to the modern phenomenon of ISIS, a fanatical sect of Islam that accuses both Shia and Sunni members of being too lax in their following of Allah. The Jews had progressively succumbed to Hellenism in the Diaspora, inter-marrying with Gentiles, and the Sanhedrin has acquiesced to Roman control in Judea. In modern times, Muslims have become more conservative, inter-marrying with infidels, and acquiescing with the demands of Western culture. It was, perhaps, inevitable, given the influence of the Ayatollahs in Iran, that fundamentalism would arise with proponents seeking a return to the strictures of earlier days, and outright warfare with the infidels. The Essenes represented the most fanatical form of Judaism, partly in reaction to the corruption of the Levites, and their acceptance of the High Priest being a Roman appointee rather than a descendant of Aaron, as required by the Scriptures. Their antipathy is evidenced by this example from the Dead Sea Scrolls:

> "And the Levites shall curse all the men of the lot of Belial, saying: 'Be cursed because of all your guilty wickedness! May He deliver you up for torture at the hands of the vengeful Avengers! May He visit you with destruction by the hand of all the Wreakers of Revenge! Be cursed without mercy because of the darkness of your deeds! Be damned in the shadowy place of everlasting fire! May God not heed when you call on Him, nor pardon you by blotting out your sin! May He raise His angry face towards you for vengeance! May there be no "Peace" for you in the mouth of those who hold fast to the Fathers! And after the blessing and the cursing, all those entering the Covenant shall say, Amen, Amen." (1QS II 5-12)

Note the tacit acceptance of the Hebrew Scriptures concerning the forgiveness of sin. Israel Knohl comments:

> "The people of Qumran expected the coming of a Messiah who would bring them atonement for their sins. In one of the Qumranic scrolls, the Damascus Covenant, we read that the laws it contains would be valid until the advent of the Messiah. The Messiah would bring members of the sect an atonement superior to that which could be obtained through meal or sin offerings:
>
> *'And this is the explication of the rules by which they shall be governed until the rise of the anointed of Aaron and Israel, and he will atone for their iniquity better than through meal and sin offerings'."*[8]

Laws valid until the advent of the Messiah: is that not how Christianity has interpreted Matthew 5:17-20, the rationale behind the subsequent abandonment of Torah? A *superior atonement*: is that not what Christianity teaches, a doctrine not found in the Hebrew Scriptures, one that makes God to be a liar? Perhaps, to be kind, not a liar, but misunderstood by the Jews, ironically their *advantage* being that to them were committed the oracles of God (Romans 3:1-2). It is not unreasonable to believe that the Jesus narrative was a continuation of this story from Qumran. Whether Jesus believed himself to be that Messiah from the beginning of his public life; whether he developed that belief later on; or whether his biographers simply wrote of him that way, is something that we cannot know. However, it is stretching credibility to assert that there was no interaction between this Qumranic story, and that of Jesus, especially as I contend, it has no foundation in the Hebrew Scriptures. The New Testament authors must have realised that for Jesus to be accepted as the prophesied Messiah, they needed to scour the Scriptures to find justification for that claim. It is not surprising that their efforts were so unconvincing.

Summary

There is a great deal more to this story, which provides evidence from the Dead Sea Scrolls that the belief in messianic redemption from sin did not originate with Jesus, but in the Qumran sect many years before. There is opinion, from numerous New Testament scholars, that Jesus had some association with the Essenes, which would suggest that quite possibly, he obtained the idea for his own messianic mission from them, one that was different to the one he expressed in Matthew 15:24. Whilst investigating the claim that Jesus "declared all foods to be clean" (Matthew 15:1-20, Mark 7:14-23), which was entirely contrary to the view of the Essenes, I encountered in 1 Timothy 4:1-6, a suggestion that the influence of the Essenes was still in the minds of New Testament writers as late as the mid-60's CE. I concluded at the time that the words, "speaking lies in hypocrisy ... forbidding to marry and commanding to abstain from foods which God created to be received with thanksgiving", had been misinterpreted in Christian theology, because the only community forbidding marriage was the cloistered Essenes, who also abstained from eating any meat at all, contrary to the restrictions in Torah[9]. We cannot be sure who authored 1 Timothy, but whether Paul or one of his disciples, he must have had some knowledge of the disciplines of the Essenes.

I would highly recommend Israel Knohl's book, for it provides many more insights to the world of Second Temple Judaism, and especially what can be learned from the Dead Sea Scrolls. Knohl is not the only scholar to write on this subject; another is "The First Messiah: Investigating the Savior Before Christ" by Michael Wise[10]. The synopsis reads:

"In *The First Messiah* renowned Dead Sea Scrolls scholar Michael O. Wise brings to light the life of Judah, a forgotten prophet who predated Jesus as a messianic figure by a century and has had a profound impact on the course of Christianity and Western civilization.

Although Judah, known in the Dead Sea Scrolls as the Teacher of Righteousness, preached a message distinctly different from that of Jesus, the parallels between their lives are striking. Sharing with his successor a strong foundation in earlier written revelation, Judah came to believe--through meditation on Holy Writ--that he brought a divine message from God; like Christ, Judah's claims to messianic status led to his arrest and condemnation. Judah's warnings of Jewish apostasy and his apocalyptic prophecies, combined with powerful personal charisma, also built a movement that survived his death and even grew into an institution comprising bishops, priests, and laity.

Unlike Jesus, Judah left behind a personal testament, in his own words, of his relationship with God. By analyzing the Thanksgiving Hymns discovered among the Dead Sea Scrolls, Wise uncovers the basis of a ground breaking understanding of the prophetic mind. In so doing, Wise deepens our understanding of Christ, his impact on the Jewish community of his time, and even his interpretation of his own messianic role.

The parallels between Judah and Jesus blaze forth in sharp relief:
- Both declared themselves prophets.
- Both were hailed by followers as He Who Is to Come and worked attendant wonders.
- Both founded vital and long-lasting movements before leaving this world.

In all these things, Judah was first, anticipating the far more famous prophet from Galilee. How can these similarities be explained?

A century before Christ, a man came to Jerusalem who became known as the Teacher of Righteousness. In *The First Messiah,* distinguished Dead Sea Scrolls scholar Michael O. Wise provides a detailed examination of Judah, a figure whose life and prophecies helped lay the foundation for the acceptance of Jesus as the savior. Drawing on ancient texts as well as contemporary anthropological thought, Wise reveals compelling parallels between early prophets such as Judah and Jesus, and messianic figures who have emerged through the ages to the current day in cultures around the world."

There is overlap across these two studies, which is why I have quoted from only one, but reading both provides a greater understanding of how Jesus came to be seen as he is in Christianity.

The evidence of a messiah, one intriguingly like Jesus, but predating him by a century, should be added to our considerations on how well Jesus fulfilled prophecy. It does not contribute as substantial evidence in itself, but by offering an alternative explanation, it does corroborate the testimony of those who reject the Christian claims. Remember that in the study so far, the evidence offered for prophecy fulfillment has been circumstantial. In the language of evidence, *circumstantial* evidence exists where the data is consistent with the proposition in question, but may or may not itself directly contribute to the proof. At best, it shows that the proposition *may* be true because it is not inconsistent with the proposition, but if other evidence is available which is equally consistent with the proposition, then further investigations must be pursued.

This is the case here. In my evaluation of the source of Jesus' claimed messianic credentials, the testimony from the Dead Sea Scrolls is more plausible than any texts found in the Hebrew Scriptures, or even the Greek variants.

REFERENCES:

1. Knohl, Israel, *The Messiah Before Jesus: The Suffering Servant of the Dead Sea Scrolls*, University of California Press, Berkeley, CA, 2000
2. Talbot, Wayne, *Once A Christian, How the Bible Convinced Me to Walk Away*, Xlibris, Bloomington, IN, 2017, *Chapter 6-5: Why Was Jesus Secretive?*
3. Knohl, *Ibid*, p. 1
4. *Ibid*, p. 2
5. *Ibid*, inside flap
6. https://www.thorncrownjournal.com/timeofchrist/zealots.html
7. The translation given here is based on a combination of text CD 14:18-19 and the fragment from cave four. See J.M. Baumgarten "Messianic Forgiveness of Sin in CD 14:19 ($_4$Q$_2$66 frg. 10, col.I:12-13)"
8. Knohl, *Ibid*, pp. 22-23
9. Talbot, Wayne, *Christians Too, Must Obey: Putting a Fence Around Torah*, Xlibris, Bloomington, IN, 2017, *Chapter 5-11: God's Dietary Laws*
10. Wise, Michael O., *The First Messiah: Investigating the Savior Before Christ*, HarperOne, San Francisco, CA, 1999

CHAPTER 9-2

THE MISSION OF JESUS

"I was not sent except to the lost sheep of the house of Israel."
(Matthew 15:24)

When, Where, and How Lost?

On the surface, this mission statement seems straightforward, but when examined in detail, in conjunction with the overall Jesus narrative, it tells us too little. To understand this, we first need a little geography, and then some history.

In ancient times, Jerusalem was at the most northern point of the Kingdom of Judah, with Galilee the southern-most province of Israel. According to Matthew's Gospel, Jesus was born in Bethlehem, to the south of Jerusalem, but after the sojourn in Egypt, his family settled in Nazareth in Galilee (Israel), about 120 kms to the north. According to Luke, Jesus was born in Nazareth, and later went up to Bethlehem for the census, but for now, we can ignore that discrepancy. Now for the history:

"Around 926 BCE, the kingdom of Israel split in two. Up to that point, all twelve tribes of Israel (plus the priestly tribe of Levi) had been united under the monarchies of Saul, David, and Solomon. But when Solomon's son Rehoboam ascended to the throne, the ten Northern tribes rebelled and seceded from the union. This left only two tribes—Judah and Benjamin (plus much of Levi)—under the control of the king in Jerusalem. From that time on, the tribes were divided into two nations, which came to be called the House of Israel (the Northern ten tribes) and the House of Judah (the Southern two tribes).

This situation continued until around 723 BCE, when the Assyrians conquered the Northern kingdom. To keep conquered nations in subjection, it was Assyrian policy to break them up by deporting their native populations to other areas and resettling the land with newcomers. When the House of Israel was conquered, most people belonging to the ten Northern tribes were deported and settled elsewhere in the Assyrian kingdom, including places near Nineveh, Haran, and on what is now the Iran-Iraq border. They were replaced by settlers from locations in or near Babylon and Syria."[1]

The first issue that scholars debate is the identity of the group referred to as lost sheep *of the house* of Israel, or more simply, lost sheep of Israel. The two are, perhaps, not synonymous. The house of Israel is quite specific: it refers to the ten tribes, whereas "lost sheep of Israel" could simply refer to people of Israel who were lost spiritually, and needed to return to God. Alternatively, Jesus residing in Israel, initially saw his mission as being to the ten lost tribes of Israel that had been assimilated into the Gentile world, which has me wondering why he later spent so much time in Jerusalem (House of Judah).

As best as we can discover, the ten tribes of Israel were gradually assimilated by other peoples and thus effectively disappeared from history as separately identifiable communities. Jesus travelled to Tyre, in the biblical region of the tribe of Asher, and to Sidon further north, both in what is now southern Lebanon (Matt 15:21). The area was populated by the Canaanites, though whether people of Hebrew extraction also lived there is open to question. If members of the house of Israel were in that region, they were likely indistinguishable from the Canaanites with whom they intermarried. Departing there, he returned to the Sea of Galilee via the region of Decapolis, populated by Hellenistic pagans (Mark 7:31). Such travels would have been in keeping with his mission to the lost tribes of [the house of] Israel, Israel being the northern kingdom, culturally and geographically distinct from the Kingdom of Judah in Judea.

Acknowledging that the Gospels are not necessarily, internally chronological, it is difficult to trace the movements of Jesus sequentially through his public life. I get the sense that he initially focused on the northern kingdom, consonant with his publicly stated mission, but then later preached further south. Jesus spent some of his time in Judea, where few of the lost tribes were likely to be found, other than some Hellenic Jews. Earlier, in Matthew 10:5, Jesus told his disciples to not go amongst the Gentiles, which was curious, as he himself later (or earlier) did just that. But he was specific: "go rather to the lost sheep of the house of Israel" (v. 10:6). Good, but where were they to be found, if not amongst the Gentiles? On what basis were the Apostles to identify these *lost sheep*, and where did Jesus expect them to be found?

In another episode, Jesus berates the people of Chorazin and Bethsaida, in Israel to the north of the Sea of Galilee, "in which most of his mighty works had been done" (Matt 11:20), because they had failed to repent, asserting that had such works been done in Tyre and Sidon, they would have repented long ago. I find it confusing that this event is reported in Matthew 11, but in Matthew 15:21 Jesus "departed to the region of Tyre and Sidon": was this a second trip to that region? Where he departed from is also not clear, as later we read that he departed from "there" (wherever that was), and skirted the Sea of Galilee. Another issue that I find intriguing is his dispute with the Pharisees during this period, because I do wonder how many Pharisees he would have encountered in that region. Pharisaism, though not confined to Judah, was where he would have encountered most of his opposition.

We know little of what Jesus did in Tyre and Sidon, how much time he spent in the two cities, or of how his influence spread there. Early in Mark's

Gospel, we read of a great multitude from Galilee, Judea, Jerusalem, Idumea (far to the south of Jerusalem), Tyre, Sidon, and people from beyond the Jordan (Mark 3:7-8). This, according to Mark, was before he appointed his twelve apostles. I find this a little difficult to accept, that his influence had spread all the way from Idumea in the south, to Sidon in the far north, when he was without his support team. It could be true, but it does not ring true.

I can come to no conclusion, other than that some confusion reigns somewhere, either in the narrative or our understanding of it. I suspect that somewhere along the line, Jesus' perception of his mission changed from calling the *geographically* lost tribes back to God, to calling the *spiritually* lost back to God. Certainly, those geographically lost would also have been spiritually lost, having largely assimilated with the pagan Greeks, and indeed we later find references to the Hellenistic Jews. Maybe the different rendering of 'house of Israel" and simply "Israel" evidence this confusion. There is no doubt that Jesus was calling those Israelites, irrespective of where they lived, who were lost from God, to repentance, a theme which runs throughout the Prophets, Gospels and Acts. We have a sense of this in Luke (5:32), "I have not come to call the righteous, but sinners, to repentance." Some scholars suggest that initially, Jesus was a disciple of John the Baptist, who likewise called people to repentance.

There are numerous mentions in the Gospels of Jesus preaching in the cities, going to one place and not another, working miracles, and so forth, e.g., "I must preach the kingdom of God to the other cities also, because for this purpose I have been sent" (Luke 4:43), but the specifics of that are not my interest here. The conundrum that I am seeking to resolve, concerns the nature of Jesus' messianic mission: from the Gospels, what can we learn of what he taught his disciples to believe, and what he may have believed of his mission in that context?

Did Jesus initially see himself as prophet, like those of old, calling the people to repentance, and only later develop the notion of being the Jewish *mashiach*, the prophesied Davidic King?

Prophesied Mission

In any appraisal of prophecy fulfillment, we need to understand the prophecies in the Hebrew Scriptures: which prophecies were fulfilled; which were unfulfilled; and which events in the life of Jesus can, and cannot, legitimately be claimed as prophecy fulfillment. We need to understand how Jesus perceived his mission in relation to those prophecies, how well acquainted his disciples were with prophecy, what they may have read into Jesus' life and death, and what may have been later added by various writers in the decades following the death of Jesus.

Chronology

It is difficult to be certain of the chronology of the events in the life of Jesus, so I beg your indulgence should my understanding vary from yours. Many events are presented in a different sequence across the four Gospels, and many sayings are associated with different events. It is reasonable to assume that in his years of public life, Jesus delivered the same message to different people, in different places, at different times, in different words, so I place little significance in these variations. However, what is interesting is the period covered by the Synoptics, versus that covered by John. It seems odd that the last Gospel to be published, anything up to half a century later, would have so much more detail than those published earlier. Also, the focus of the Synoptics is Jesus' Galilean experiences, whereas John primarily records events in Judea. In that sense, the Gospels are complementary, but I doubt that such was intentional. As Dunn observes: "Since the leadership of the earliest Jerusalem community of believers in Messiah Jesus were all Galileans, one could understand why the tradition which they began and taught focused on the Galilean mission."[2]

John's Gospel was written after the destruction of Jerusalem, 70 CE, when the Pharisees and others decamped to Yavneh, and the split between messianic and rabbinical Judaism was well underway. This is why we find what appears to be, anti-Jewishness in John's Gospel, for the tension between the two groups was palpable, with blame on both sides. Nevertheless, let us see what we can find in the Gospels.

The first event is found in Luke' account of the family visit to Jerusalem, with Jesus responding to his parents: "*Why did you seek me? Did you not know that I must be about my Father's business?*" (Luke 2:49) Just what Jesus meant by that is unclear to us, and I do wonder what did Jesus thought this business was? We cannot know. Incidentally, whilst it is claimed that Jesus was sinless, his disobedience in failing to follow his parents back to Nazareth evidences otherwise, in that he failed to honour his father and mother. Like it not, irrespective of any rationalisation, such failure is sin.

Beginning Jesus' Public Mission

I found the following discussion to be quite thought provoking:

> "All the Christian sources are agreed that Jesus is first remembered as having been baptised by John the Baptist – a baptising mission attested also by Josephus (*Antiquities* 18.116-119). It would not be an unfair evaluation of the evidence available to say that Jesus began as a disciple of John the Baptist. The testimony is all the more secure, since we can detect a clear sense of embarrassment in the Gospel accounts of this beginning. The first three Gospels begin their account of Jesus' mission after the Baptist had been imprisoned; they draw a veil over the period of overlap between John and Jesus which the Fourth Gospel briefly describes. Moreover, the fact that Jesus had undergone a 'baptism of repentance' (Mark 1:4) is a matter of some embarrassment in Matthew's account of the encounter between Jesus and John (Matt 3:14-15). And the Fourth Gospel avoids mentioning the fact that Jesus was actually baptised by John. So, we can conclude that the memory of Jesus' emergence from the ranks of the Baptist's followers was too firmly rooted in history for it to be ignored or omitted. The Gospels also indicate that Jesus probably experienced something equivalent to a prophetic calling when he was baptised by John."[3]

A *baptism of repentance* is indeed curious for someone said to be sinless. The argument that Jesus was simply complying with tradition, or was setting an example, is weak, for why did Mark use the words, *of repentance*?

The episode in Luke 2:41-48 is evidence, to my mind, that Jesus was not sinless, and likely just as rebellious toward his parents as any Jewish youngster.

So, we have the encounter with John the Baptist, with the latter perceiving himself as fulfilling Isaiah's prophecy concerning one *preparing the way of the Lord* (Isaiah 40:3). I am suspicious of the Apostle John's narrative here, because of the declaration: "Behold! The Lamb of God who takes away the sins of the world" (John 1:29). There is nothing in the Hebrew Scriptures prophesying such a mission, Abraham's near-miss with his son notwithstanding, and nothing even suggesting that the Redeemer was to be concerned with *taking away the sins of the world*. Secondly, the term, *Lamb of God*, is a misrepresentation of the function of the lamb sacrificed as a prelude to the Exodus (see Part 4). This narrative of John evidences theological development which has been written back into the life of Jesus. Matthew's narrative of the same event is sufficiently dissimilar to suggest that whilst Jesus did have an encounter with John the Baptist, the details were embellished with the retelling. Mark's Gospel begins with this event, and Luke presents it in a different context, with John the Baptist "preaching a baptism of repentance for the remission of sins" (Luke 3:3), which is more in accordance with Judaism of the time.

John's account of the wedding feast of Cana, just days later, has Jesus answering his mother: "*Woman, what does your concern have to do with Me? My hour has not yet come*" (John 2:4). This can be read two ways: [1], as a non-respectful rebuke of his mother, or [2], an innocent response - I will leave the reader to adjudge for themselves. As to his "hour", what was that? According to Luke, Jesus had been about his Father's business since an early age, so what was different now? One commentary reads: "The 'hour' for Christ to tell the world all that Mary knew had not come. The hour of the full revelation of his Messianic claims had not come", and another: "the hour for My being openly manifested as the Messiah"[4]. I find this most curious, given the public revelation by John the Baptist, and Nathanael's declaration: "*You are the Son of God! You are the King of Israel!*" As to what Mary knew of Jesus' mission, we can only guess, but various narratives in the Gospels suggest that Mary had not a clue, other than what we can believe in Luke's account of her pregnancy, and Jesus' birth. For me, the truth of this "hour" remains shrouded in mystery.

John's account has Jesus recruiting his Apostles the day after his baptism at the Jordan, but Matthew interposes Jesus' forty days in the desert, before Jesus meets them by the Sea of Galilee, some distance away judging by other data. John does not mention the temptations in the desert, which no-one could have witnessed, and it is unlikely that Jesus would have told them about. I would offer that this story is apocryphal.

Jesus chose twelve men to follow him: why twelve? That number has no significance in Judaism, other than that there were twelve tribes of Israel. James Dunn comments:

> "The most significant feature of this group was that it was *twelve* in number. No one doubts the obvious significance of this number: that it reflects the historic character of the twelve tribes of Israel. But this must mean that Jesus intended the group around him to somehow represent Israel, the twelve tribes of Israel. This in turn strongly suggests what many recent studies of the life and mission of Jesus have argued: that Jesus saw his mission in terms of *the restoration of Israel*. The twelve symbolised eschatological Israel, the renewed Israel of the end-time."[5] (italics in original)

This is evidence, to my mind, that in choosing his Apostles, Jesus was not considering dying for our sins, but saw his mission as commented above.

Following the recruitment of the twelve, the next mission statement is found after what has become known as the Beatitudes, or Sermon on the Mount, with Jesus declaring: *"Do not think that I came to destroy the Law or the Prophets. I did not come to destroy, but to fulfill"* (Matt 5:17). I have not found a satisfactory answer as to why Jesus began with: "Do not think", but there is the suggestion that he was refuting what some unidentified persons were saying about him, even so early in his public life. As an aside (yet again), we have another example of an unexplained comment here: *"You have heard that it was said, you shall love your neighbour and hate your enemy"* (Matthew 5:43). The NKJV annotates this as quoting Deuteronomy 23:3-6, but a review of those verses reveal that this was a prohibition specific to certain tribes, not a general call to hate your enemies. Studying Torah, and some relevant sections in the Talmud, there is not a hint that Judaism ever taught that the Jews should hate their enemies. On the contrary, there are numerous passages in Torah expressing the opposite, so where did Jesus get that idea, or was it in truth, not something that was said by him, but added by whomever?

It is curious that in their open, and well documented hatred of the Jews, the Church of Rome seemed blissfully unaware of this teaching of Jesus.

Mission Statements

Was Jesus' "coming", his coming into the world, coming down from heaven, or more simply, into public life? We cannot know. There is considerable debate on what Jesus meant by destroy and fulfill, and I have weighed in with my own considered opinion in another work, *"Christians Too, Must Obey"*[6]. Here is a representative opinion, with which I only partially agree, for I disagree with any suggestion that Jesus' fulfillment of the Law related only to the *moral law*, for who decides which is moral and which is ceremonial or civil? Is obedience to the Sabbath just moral? Nevertheless, for what it is worth:

> "Christ came not to abrogate the Law or the Prophets, but to satisfy them - to bring about in his own Person, and ultimately in the persons of his followers, that righteousness of life which, however limited by the historical conditions under which the Divine oracles had been delivered, was the sum and substance of their teaching. The fulfilment of the Law and the Prophets 'is the perfect development of their ideal reality out of the positive form, in which the same is historically apprehended and limited' (Meyer); and "I am not come to destroy, but to fulfil. By "the law" is meant the moral law, as appears from the whole discourse following: this he came not to "destroy", or loose men's obligations to, as a rule of walk and conversation, but "to fulfil" it; which he did doctrinally, by setting it forth fully, and giving the true sense and meaning of it; and practically, by yielding perfect obedience to all its commands, whereby he became "the end", the fulfilling end of it."[7]

The Gospel of Matthew records Jesus as saying: "I was not sent except to the sheep of the house of Israel." (15:24), and "Do not go into the way of the Gentiles, and do not enter a city of the Samaritans, but go rather to the lost sheep of the house of Israel; and as you go, preach saying, the kingdom of heaven is at hand." (10:5-7). What did he mean by *the lost sheep of Israel*? Likely he meant that they were unrighteous, because they had abandoned Torah and the Covenant. That is an uncomfortable thought for Christian theology, because that leaves the house of Judah as righteous. However, this is likely true in the thinking of Jesus. After the death of Solomon, his kingdom split. Only Judah and Benjamin remained loyal to the Davidic dynasty, while the other ten tribes broke away under King Jeroboam. Jeroboam's wickedness is well attested in 1 & 2 Kings, his successors imitating his evil ways, and at times surpassing them. Although the Kingdom of Judah remained relatively loyal to God and the Torah, though with frequent lapses, the Kingdom of the Ten Tribes (Israel) fell into a downward spiritual spiral. This was a history known to Jesus, I would assume, and the view that these tribes were lost was also held by the Pharisees.

From this I would conclude that in the early days of his public life, Jesus saw his mission as bringing these ten lost tribes of Israel, those under Jeroboam that rejected the Davidic dynasty, back into the fold represented by the tribes that had remained loyal, those of Judah and Benjamin. By that thinking, Jesus had no intention of creating a *New Israel*.

Continuing in Matthew, we find:

a. "Go and learn what this means: I desire mercy and not sacrifice." (9:13)

b. "For I did not come to call the righteous, but sinners, to repentance." (9:13)

c. "Do not go into the way of the Gentiles, and do not enter a city of the Samaritans, but go rather to the lost sheep of the house of Israel; and as you go, preach saying, the kingdom of heaven is at hand." (10:5-7) See also Matt 3:2.

d. "Do not think that I came to bring peace on earth. I did not come to bring peace but a sword." (10:34) According to the Hebrew Scriptures, and the beliefs of the Jews of Second Temple Judaism, the role of the Messiah was to bring ultimate peace, so here Jesus seems to be denying that he was fulfilling that prophecy.

e. "I was not sent except to the sheep of the house of Israel." (15:24)

f. "I will build my church." (16:18)

g. "Tell the vision to no one until the Son of Man is risen from the dead." (17:9) This is clearly a forthtelling by Jesus, but can this be considered part of Jesus' mission statement?

h. "Likewise, the Son of Man is also about to suffer at their hands." (17:12) As above.

i. "The Son of Man is about to be betrayed into the hands of men, and they will kill him, and the third day he will be raised up." (17:22) Again, a forthtelling, but did Jesus know of his impending execution because it fulfilled his mission, or because he had heard of the plot to kill him? We cannot ignore the likelihood that he would have heard about any conspiracy against him, although the question of his prediction of the resurrection remains unresolved.

j. "the Son of Man will be betrayed … they will condemn him to death." (20:18) As above. Having studied the nature of betrayals generally, and closely examined the narrative of the betrayal by Judas, I have earlier concluded that this is an implausible story. Should you be so interested, it is the subject of a chapter in an earlier work, *Once a Christian*[8].

k. "the Son of Man did not come to be served, but to serve, and to give his life a ransom for many." (20:28)

l. "You know that after two days is the Passover, and the Son of Man will be delivered up to be crucified." (26:2)

m. "For this is my blood of the new covenant, which is shed for many for the remission of sins." (26:28)

n. "Are you the King of the Jews? Jesus said to him: It is as you say." (27:11)

o. "My God, my God, why have you forsaken me?" (27:46)

Turning to Marks's Gospel, and omitting any duplications from Matthew's account:

a. "Follow me, and I will make you fishers of men." (1:17)

    b.   "Let us go into the next towns, that I may preach there also, because for this purpose I have come forth (was sent)." (1:38)

    c.   "He called the twelve to himself, and began to send them out two by two ... so they went out and preached that people should repent." (6:7-12)

    d.   "I was daily teaching with you in the temple, teaching, and you did not seize me; but the Scripture must be fulfilled." (14:49)

Luke's account contains details of Jesus' birth not found in the other Gospels:

    a.   "He will be great, and will be called the Son of the Highest; and the Lord God will give him the throne of his father David, and he will reign over the house of Jacob forever, and of his kingdom there will be no end." (1:32-33). It is interesting that this was written in retrospect, even after it was known that Jesus did not accomplish these things in his lifetime. See also Chapter 4-4 for further commentary on this claimed prophecy fulfillment.

    b.   "Did you not know that I must be about my Father's business." (2:49)

    c.   "The Spirit of the Lord is upon me, because he has anointed me to preach the gospel to the poor ... to set at liberty those who are oppressed; to proclaim the acceptable year of the Lord" (4:18-19), quoting Isaiah. Note that there is no mention here of dying for our sins – the mission is the same as that of the earlier Prophets. As to the gospel that Jesus was anointed to preach, read Luke 6:20-49; I would contend that such is what he had in mind at that time.

    d.   "Today, this Scripture is fulfilled in your hearing." (4:21) This suggests that Jesus saw himself as a prophet in the same circumstance as others before him, and could partially explain why he expected to die at the hands of those who rejected him.

    e.   "For the Son of Man did not come to destroy men's lives but to save them." (9:56) Why "lives" and not "souls"? Jesus was responding to James and John wanting Jesus to call down fire from heaven, so clearly, he must have meant physical, not spiritual life. The goal of the prophets' missions was redemption from oppression through repentance, and the restoration of the kingdom of Israel. Here, Jesus appears to be confirming that mission.

f. "but you go and preach the kingdom of God". (9:60) At this point in Luke's narrative, there is no mention of preaching the resurrection; thus, the kingdom of God could only be as taught in the Hebrew Scriptures, for the disciples of Jesus could know nothing else, especially after Jesus' speech in Luke 6:20-49.

g. Sending out the seventy, say to them: "the kingdom of God has come near to you" (10.9) This is another contentious topic, but I won't deal with that here. However, note the reference to repentance in Luke 10:13. As an aside, whilst we are in this part of Luke, verses 10:18-20 offer reason for disagreement, firstly because whilst Jesus said that he "saw Satan fall like lightning from heaven", Satan is still influencing the world as much as any time in history. Secondly, despite Jesus giving them authority "over all the power of the enemy (Satan?)", his promise that "nothing shall by any means hurt you" was hollow, as they were later much persecuted, even, reportedly, by Paul.

h. Luke 10:25-28 has implications for the mission of Jesus, as he understood it (at that time at least). The lawyer asked: "*What shall I do to inherit eternal life?*". Jesus answered: "*What is written in the law? What is your reading of it?*" The lawyer answered by reciting the Shema, the prayer of Deuteronomy 6:4-9. Jesus, no doubt pleased, commended the lawyer: "*you have answered rightly, do this and you will live.*" My interpretation of this incident is that Jesus was confirming the Law and Covenant, and had no sense that for the lawyer, or anybody else, to inherit eternal life, Jesus had first to die in substitutionary atonement for sin. "I, only I, am He Who wipes away your wilful sins for My Sake, and I shall not recall your sins" (Isaiah 43:25). Did Jesus, at the time of this incident, believe as written in Isaiah? Finally, note that in Mark's account, it is Jesus reciting the Shema, not the lawyer, and the context was the greatest commandment. These are contradictory, not complementary, accounts, and testify to the development of separate traditions based on poorly recalled events.

i.   The question of Jesus foreknowing that he was to die for our sins, is further deepened in Luke 11:4, where Jesus instructs his disciples on how to pray: *"Forgive us our sins"*. Why would he teach that, in the spirit of Isaiah 43:25, if he knew of what he later claimed his mission to be?

j.   *"Blessed are those who hear the word of God and keep it"* (11:28). So far in Luke's narrative, Jesus had spoken nothing different than is found in the Hebrew Scriptures, which suggests to me that again, he is confirming the Law and Covenant.

k.   *"I came to send fire on the earth, and how I wish it were already kindled"* (12:49). I cannot be certain of the meaning here, but I am inclined to go with Jeremiah 20:9, *"His [God's] word would be like a burning fire in my heart."* There are more Christological interpretations, but this is at least consistent with the message of the Prophets.

l.   *"For the Son of Man has come to seek and to save that which was lost"* (19:10). An ambiguous statement, but possibly consonant with Matthew 15:24.

m.   *"But we were hoping that it was he who was going to redeem Israel"* (24:21). Here we have evidence of some people, at least, believing that the mission of Jesus, as Messiah, was to redeem them from the oppression of other nations.

n.   *"That all things must be fulfilled which were written in the Law of Moses and the Prophets and the **Psalms** concerning me"* (24:44) [emphasis mine]. I find this inclusion of the Psalms quite debatable, especially as it comes from Luke, and such a reference is not found in the other Gospels. We discussed this more fully in Part 5.

o.   *"Thus it is written, and thus it was necessary for the Christ to suffer and to rise from the dead the third day, and that repentance and remission of sins should be preached in his name, to all nations, beginning at Jerusalem"* (24:46-47). The NKJV fails to annotate a single OT verse in support, other than Jeremiah 31:34 in relation to all nations. Could the editors not find any prophecies? Jeremiah's prophecy is specifically about the *End of Days*, not the days of Jesus. If we ignore the apocryphal story of Jesus at the age of twelve (Luke 2:49), Jesus began his ministry in Bethabara, Peraea (John

1:28), then in Galilee (John 1:43), and only later in Jerusalem for Passover (John 2:13).

Finally, we turn to the account in the Gospel of John, to understand the mission of Jesus as he appeared to understand it. I will try to avoid duplications in the accounts, but sometimes further comments come to mind.

a. *"For the law was given through Moses, but grace and truth came through Jesus Christ"* (1:17). So, part of the mission of Jesus was to bring grace and truth.

b. *"And as Moses lifted up the serpent in the wilderness, even so must the Son of Man be lifted up"* (3:14). Studying both Jewish and Christian interpretations of this reference to Number 21:8, I am undecided of what it means, but would recommend reading the Pulpit Commentary, online here[9].

c. *"For God did not send His son into the world to condemn the world, but that the world through him might be saved"* (3:17).

d. *"The (Samaritan) woman said to him, I know that the Messiah is coming (who is called Christ), when he comes he will tell us all things. Jesus said to her: I who speak to you am he"* (4:25). Here, Jesus declares himself to be the anointed Messiah. I find this narrative unlikely to be true. The Samaritans rejected David and Jerusalem in their eschatology, so how could Samaritans have so readily accepted Jesus as Messiah? The argument in the Synoptics was that Jesus was of the kingly line of David, and the Prophets always stated that the End of Days was to occur with Jerusalem as God's capital. I find it entirely implausible that the Samaritans would overnight abandon their religious beliefs, accepting Jesus as the prophesied Davidic King who would restore Jerusalem. For a more detailed description of the theology of the Samaritans, see here[10].

e. *"Jesus said to them, I am the bread of life. He who comes to me shall never hunger, and he who believes in me shall never thirst"* (6:35).

f. *"I am the light of the world"* (8:12).

g. *"I am the door"* (10:9).

h. *"I am the good shepherd"* (10:11).

i. *"I am the resurrection and the life"* (11:25).

j. *"the Son of Man should be glorified"* (12:23).

k. *"My soul is troubled, and what shall I say? Father, save me from this hour? But for this purpose I came to this hour"* (12:27).

l. *"I am the way, the truth, and the light"* (14:6).

m. *"I am the true vine"* (15:1).

n. *"You say rightly that I am a king. For this cause I was born, and for this cause I came into the world, that I should bear witness to the truth"* (18:37)

o. *"You could have no power at all against me unless it had been given to you from above. Therefore, the one who delivered me to you has the greater sin"* (19:11). This is a very ambiguous verse, and I shall add to that ambiguity. From the various commentaries I have read, the consensus seems to be that "the one who delivered" is not Judas, but the Sanhedrin. Perhaps that is what Jesus meant, but let us look a little deeper: Who was it that required that Jesus should die? Who was it that should take ultimate responsibility for Jesus being sacrificed? A Christian response would be: us, sinners of the world, but God had a choice of how He would deal with our sin. It would not be our choice that Jesus should die for our sins – surely there could be a better way than spilling of innocent blood in a human sacrifice? Did Jesus not say: *"Shall I not drink the cup which my Father has given me"*? I don't expect you to agree with me, but it is worth considering.

p. John 20:17 seems to contradict Luke 23:43, but perhaps we are not expected to take the latter as written.

Another Perspective

To be fair, one should examine what Christian sources have to say on this matter, and I have chosen the following for its brevity and ease of access, in this case, an online entry from Bible.org[11]. Following is a summary of the Gospel passages relating to the mission of Jesus:

"His Mission:

*   The theme and reality of glory in Jesus' ministry is stated (Matt. 17:1-8; Mark 9:2-8; Lk. 2:32; 9:31-32; Jn. 1:14; 2:11; 11:4, 40; 12:28, 41; 17:24).

- There is the right time or hour in his life (Matt. 9:15; 26:18; Mark 1:15; 14:35, 41; Lk. 19:44; 22:14; Jn. 2:4; 7:6; 8:20; 12:23).
- He enjoys the company of wine drinkers (Lk. 5:29-30; 7:34; 15:1-2; Jn. 2:1-11).
- He has authority and power, which opponents sometimes question (Matt. 7:29; 8:9; 21:23-27; 28:18; Mark 1:22, 27; 11:28-33; Lk. 4:32; 5:24; 20:1-8; Jn 2:18; 5:27; 10:18; 13:3; 17:2).
- He will "go up" or "be taken up" into heaven (Lk. 9:51; Jn. 3:14; 8:28; 12:32).
- He came to save people (Matt. 1:21; 10:22; 16:25; 19:25-26; Mark 8:35-36; 10:26-27; 13:13; Lk. 2:11, 30; 9:24; 18:26-27; 19:9; Jn. 3:17; 4:42; 5:34; 10:9; 12:47).
- He has come or been sent by God (Matt. 9:13; 10:34; Mark 1:38; 2:17; Lk. 5:32; 7:16-20; 12:49; Jn. 3:19; 5:43; 6:38).
- Salvation is from the Jews (Matt. 1:1-17, 21; Lk. 2:30; Jn. 3:23-38; 4:22).
- Jesus came not to do his own will, but the will of the one who sent him (Matt. 26:39-42; Mark 14:36; Lk. 22:42; Jn. 4:34; 6:38).
- He is greater than Old Testament prophets (Abraham, Solomon, and Jonah) and the temple (Matt. 12:6, 39-42; Lk. 11:29-32; Jn. 8:52-58).
- He lays down his life (Matt. 20:28; Mark 10:45; Jn. 10:11, 15, 17-18).
- He predicts his own death (Matt. 12:39-41; 16:21-28; 20:17-19; Mark 8:31; 9:44; 10:32-34; Lk. 9:22-27; 11:29:30; 18:31-33; Jn. 12:20-26).
- He successfully resists Satan during Jesus' lifetime (Matt. 4:11; Lk. 4:13; Jn. 12:31; 14:30)."

A useful feature of this list is that one can quickly review the individual aspects of Jesus' mission, as he declared them to be, but more importantly in the context of this study, what Jesus does NOT say. Reviewing his mission *to save people*, in what manner was he intending to do that? What was he intending to do that would accomplish this "saving", and would that be physical or spiritual? This is an arduous task, but it must be done in the interests of intellectual integrity, so here we go.

a. Matt 1:21 has: "for he will save his people from their sins". This is reportedly during a conversation between Joseph and an angel of the Lord, but being a third (or worse) hand account, without corroboration, we are entitled to question its authenticity. That notwithstanding, these words are not from the mouth of Jesus, and are thus irrelevant in this context.

b. Matt 10:22 is a stretch as a statement of mission.

c. Matt 16:25 again says nothing concrete about how Jesus will save.

d. Matt 19:25-26 is not relevant.

e. Mark 8:35-36 again says nothing concrete about how Jesus will save.

f. Mark 10:26-27 echoes Matt 19:25-26 and is not relevant.

g. Mark 13:13 again says nothing concrete about how Jesus will save.

h. Luke 2:11 echoes Matt 1:21.

i. Luke 2:30 is a quotation taken out of context from Isaiah 52:10, and like Luke 2:11 before it, was not spoken by Jesus.

j. Luke 9:24 echoes previous authors and again, says nothing concrete about how Jesus will save.

k. Luke 18:26-27 is not relevant.

l. Luke 19:9 can be interpreted in numerous ways, but cannot be said to be an exposition on how Jesus will save his people.

m. John 3:17 says that God sent His son that the world may be saved, but not how.

n. John 4:42 mentions "Christ, the Saviour of the world", but as the Samaritan theology had no concept of *substitutionary atonement*, this verse offers no useful evidence. The Samaritans rejected the notion of a Davidic King, and did not believe that Jerusalem would be destroyed, so it is illogical to claim that they would accept Jesus as their saviour.

o. John 5:34 writes of Jesus *saying things that we may be saved*, but that was true of the Prophets before him also, so again no useful evidence.

p. John 10:9 gives us a metaphor of Jesus' being a door, but nothing specific as to the process of saving.

q. John 12:47 writes of Jesus saying: "I did not come to judge the world but to save the world", which tells us nothing of the *how* or *why*.

Now, here's the thing: we have seventeen references, from an article on the *Historical Reliability of the Gospels*, concerning Jesus coming to save his people, yet not one offers any evidence of the *substitutionary atonement* doctrine of Christianity. Let us accept that Jesus believed that he had been sent by the Father to save the people, but wherein the evidence for him understanding that by dying, he would atone for the sins of the world, and earn remission for all those who believed? Quite simply, there isn't any. If Jesus did not know, and I cannot be certain that he did not, where did the idea come from? From an evidentiary perspective, this list of accomplishments of Jesus' mission offers us nothing in terms of fulfillment of prophecy.

Analysis

What a task!

So much of what is written about Jesus, what he said of himself, and what others said of him, tend to confuse rather than clarify. Analysing the Gospel statements regarding the mission of Jesus, I can find no consistent, coherent thread: on the contrary, all I find is confusion and a sense of development throughout the public life of Jesus, and the subsequent writings about him extending over more than seventy years. On the evidence, I do not believe that even Jesus had a clear idea of who he was, or the mission on which he believed he had been sent. If he saw himself as the prophesied Messiah, one who would restore Israel at the *End of Days*, he was indisputably wrong. We have evidence, discussed elsewhere, that his immediate disciples believed that the *End of Days* was near, but they too were mistaken, as history has proven.

There are but two statements regarding Jesus dying for the remission of sins, but they are tacked on almost as an afterthought. Developing the doctrine of substitutionary atonement from these, when it was never a theme of the Gospels, is adding to Scripture in my view, a practice proscribed in Scripture itself. For these reasons, among others, I find the evidence to be inconclusive.

What I find particularly curious, and have written about before[12], is how secretive Jesus was in the early part of his public life. Time and again, he instructed his disciples to not tell anyone of what he had said, or the miracles that he had performed. Why was that? Was it because he believed that his time (of his crucifixion) had not yet come, or was he simply afraid of the likely consequences of his actions, i.e., being seen as rebellious and a threat to the political stability of Jerusalem, just as Caiaphas warned: "Nor do you consider that it is expedient for us that one man should die for the people, and not that the whole nation should perish" (John 11:50)? There was an uneasy peace between the Jews and their Roman oppressors, with periodic threats from the Zealots, that finally erupted in open conflict in 70 CE with the destruction of the Temple. Jesus would have been aware of the politics of the time, including that the high priest was a Roman appointee, not as before, a successor to Aaron of the Tribe of Levi. Jesus, as a Torah observant Jew, had every reason to criticize the Temple Establishment, for they were more political than religious, and he knew the fate of prophets before him. I cannot know, but I think it plausible that Jesus had a justifiable fear of the political forces within the Sanhedrin. When Jesus warned of the "leaven of the Pharisees", and especially of the "leaven of Herod" (Mark 8:15), his disciples did not understand. I am not confident that I do either, but as he mentioned Herod, he may well have been referring to political, rather than just spiritual corruption.

Despite Jesus' attempts at secrecy, his public teachings and performance of miracles in the view of thousands, would foil any desires in that regard. Perhaps the paradox is due to poor narrating of events, but Jesus had as much chance of keeping his activities secret as would Billy Graham. These contradictions in intent have me suspicious of the truth of the narratives, and from an evidentiary perspective, I must treat them accordingly.

On many occasions, Jesus spoke of both repentance, and observing the commandments, including confirming that the Pharisees sat in Moses' seat, and thus they should be obeyed (Matthew 23:2-3). These themes represent part of the substance of Jesus' mission, the same as the mission of the Prophets.

What was the "gospel"?

When Jesus recited the parable of the sower (Luke 8:5-18), he clarified that "the seed is the word of God" (v. 11). What words did Jesus speak in Luke 6:20-49, or Matthew 5:2 to 7:27, if not the word of God? Jesus also asserted: "My mother and my brothers are those who hear the word of God, and do it" (Luke 8:21). In Matthew and Mark, this is stated as "doing the will of God", making the word of God synonymous with the will of God, affirming Jesus' statement that "man shall not live by bread alone, but by every word that proceeds from the mouth of God" (Matthew 4:4). Given the timing of these speeches, it is reasonable to conclude that such was the message that Jesus believed he was sent to deliver, one that was no different than as taught in the Hebrew Scriptures, most especially, in Torah. It is noteworthy that in Luke 8:4, Jesus commanded the cleansed leper to abide by Deuteronomy 24:8, an action that refutes those who claim that Jesus abrogated the Law, other than the moral. Adopting the Jewish practice of *midrash aggadah*, interpreting biblical narratives to seek the answer to theological questions, the preponderance of evidence leads me to conclude that at this stage of Jesus' public life, his preaching (and mission) was no different to that of the prophets, and that he likely saw himself in that role.

If that be true, then at best, one could claim that Jesus fulfilled the prophecy in Deuteronomy 18:18, *"I will establish a prophet for them from among their brethren, like you, and I will place My words in his mouth; He shall speak to them everything that I will command him."* Many have attempted to demonstrate that Jesus was the prophesied prophet, this being but one example[13]:

"Let's look at Yeshua's qualifications – is He really the "Prophet Like Moses"?

1. First off, He's definitely from "among the brothers" of Israel, so that's a good start. The Prophet must be Jewish, and Jesus' heritage was from the tribe of Judah.
2. Both were shepherds – Yeshua said, "I am the good shepherd", and Moses also tended sheep – figuratively and literally.
3. Both were sent to bring salvation after 400 years of apparent inactivity from God – the Israelites had been enslaved for 400 years in Egypt, and the 400 years before Yeshua came had been notably silent years from God.

4. Both fasted for 40 days and nights – Moses while on Mount Sinai, and Yeshua in the Judean desert, when being tempted by Satan

5. Both spent time in Egypt as children (as Yeshua had to be hidden there for a while as a baby to escape Herod)

6. Both were born at a time when evil kings pronounced death to all Jewish baby boys in the area – Pharaoh had commanded all Hebrew baby boys to be drowned at birth, and Herod had issued a command to kill all baby boys under the age of two. Both were miraculously rescued from that threat

7. Both were called by God to lead and save

8. Both did miracles to testify to their God-given authority

9. Both instituted a covenant of blood that brought salvation for many – Moses with the Passover lamb's blood on the doorposts, Yeshua, Lamb of God, brought in the new covenant in his blood on the beams of the cross

10. Both were given God's public stamp of approval with an audible voice from heaven, heard by the crowd – Moses at Sinai, and Yeshua at his baptism

11. Both gave up great riches to lead a humble life of service and poverty – Moses from the palace of the King of Egypt, Yeshua from the heights of heaven. Both were noted for their great humility (Numbers 12:3, Hebrews 11:26-27, Philippians 2)

12. Both were initially rejected by the Jews when the foretold salvation didn't seem as if it was going to happen. When Moses first challenged Pharaoh, things got a lot worse for the Israelites, leading to despair and anger. Yeshua's crucifixion looked like a hopeless defeat. Both salvation situations initially looked like the promises were not going to come true. But they did.

13. Both were criticized by their own families – Mary and Yeshua's brothers in Mark 3:20-21, and Moses' sister and brother in Numbers 12:1.

14. Both were willing to sacrifice their own lives for the sake of those they were leading, and to pay for the sins of their people – Moses in Exodus 32, and Yeshua's own readiness to die on our behalf is evident in the Garden of Gethsemane

15. Both miraculously provided the people with bread to eat – manna was sent from heaven for the Israelites and Yeshua famously fed the multitudes. Twice.

16. Both were accepted by Gentiles – Moses' father in law, a Midianite, instantly believed (Exodus 18:10-11) The Egyptians too came to believe that the God of Israel was real and true. And the non-Jews readily accepted Yeshua's message of salvation.

17. Under Moses, all those who believed him, those who followed the instructions and put the sacrificial blood on their doors, were saved from death. This means that all those who left Egypt had taken a step of faith and been saved. They were no longer just Hebrews ethnically, they had become a faith community. Similarly, under Yeshua, all those who appropriate his sacrificial blood, shed for us to save us from the power of death have entered into the faith community of those who follow Him.

18. Seven weeks (50 days) after the Exodus, the Israelites waited upon God to receive the Torah – now that they had been saved, how then should they live? God gave Moses His covenant and instructions on how to live as a faith community. Seven weeks (50 days) after the resurrection, the disciples waited as Yeshua instructed them to receive the Holy Spirit, and the church was born – a new faith community, and a new way to live as believers.

19. Both of their faces shone with the glory of heaven, as was noted by people who saw them – Moses had to wear a veil over his face because it was beaming so much, and Yeshua's disciples saw His glory on the Mount of Transfiguration.

20. Moses chose 12 spies to explore Canaan, and Yeshua chose 12 disciples. Moses appointed 70 rulers over Israel, and Yeshua sent 70 disciples out to share the gospel.

21. Moses led the people out from slavery into... the wilderness. 40 years of wandering, hardship, and a lot of lessons learned the hard way – but all with God's help and presence. The promised land would come only later. Yeshua has redeemed us into... life with Him, still on this fallen earth. A limited time not without pain and struggle, and many lessons learned the hard way – but all

with God's help and presence. The life we were created for with no sickness, pain or death is yet to come."

I will let readers ponder these so-called "proofs" for themselves, as some of the issues raised have already been covered elsewhere. Let me just comment that from an evidentiary perspective, these are not convincing. For example, point (4) regarding Jesus' temptations in the desert relies on events not witnessed nor corroborated. Point (11) regarding Jesus being from heaven is begging the question. Point (21) regarding Jesus redeeming us is again begging the question, as is not supported by prophecies in the Hebrew Scriptures. These are not *21 Proofs that Yeshua is the "Prophet Like Moses"*, as the author claims, these represent an attempted justification after the fact, relying on the authenticity and authority of the New Testament accounts, which as we have already seen, fail to pass the test of accepted literary evidence.

Yet Another Perspective

If one believes Jesus to be the Messiah, they will read the Gospel narratives from that perspective. If one believes Jesus to be simply an apocalyptic prophet, then the Gospels will be understood in a different sense. If one perceives Jesus as one who sympathized with the Zealots, or perhaps, belonged to the sect of the Essenes, another story emerges. However,

> "If we stand back from the Gospel narrative and concentrate on the bare bones of the story, we see the four following stages in Jesus' life:
> 1. Jesus began his public career by proclaiming the coming of 'the kingdom of God'.
> 2. Later, he claimed the title of 'Messiah' and was saluted as such by his followers.
> 3. He entered Jerusalem to the acclamation of the people and took violent action in 'the Cleansing of the Temple'.
> 4. He was arrested, became a prisoner of Pilate the Roman Governor, and was crucified by Roman soldiers.

We can understand what it meant in first-century Palestine to proclaim the 'kingdom of God' and to assume the title of 'Messiah'. These were not (as they later became in the Gentile-Christian Church) purely 'spiritual' expressions. They were political slogans which put those who used them in danger of their lives from the Roman and pro-Roman authorities, just as the use of expression such as 'the dictatorship of the proletariat' would attract police attention in Tsarist Russia. They were expression of revolutionary content. Time and again, as we see from the pages of Josephus, these watchwords were raised in the trouble period with which we are concerned; and those who used these phrases became the targets of the Roman occupying forces and the native quislings and in many cases died by crucifixion. If we fix our attention on the *facts* of Jesus' life and death (as opposed to the interpretations of the facts added by the Gospels) we shall see that Jesus was a Jewish Resistance leader of a type not unique to this period."[14]

Do we have biblical evidence for this perspective, as well as the extra-biblical? Yes, we do. Firstly, "If we let him alone like this, everyone will believe in him, and the Romans will come and take away both our place and nation" (John 11:48). That is unambiguous, and brooks no misunderstanding: they were afraid that Jesus was seen by the Romans as a Jewish Resistance leader, perhaps aligned with the Zealots, and so being afraid for their very existence, Caiaphas declared: "it is expedient for us that one man should die for the people, and not that the whole nation should perish" (John 11:50). Who was Caiaphas? "Caiaphas was high priest that year" (John 18:13). That year? Did not the High Priest, a descendant of Aaron, serve for life? Not under the Romans, and not since before the Greek occupation. The Romans decided that the Jews could manage their own religious affairs, but that they would maintain control over the religious hierarchy, i.e. the office of the high priest, and many members of the Sanhedrin. Thus, the high priest came and went at the whim of the Roman Governor, depending on how well he bowed to the will of his political master.

When Jesus made his "triumphal" entry into Jerusalem, how did the Jewish people perceive this *triumph*? He hadn't told them that he was going to die for their sins, so in his role as Messiah, they could only have expected him to overthrow the Romans. This understanding is consistent with John's account of the reaction of Caiaphas, and the agreement of the Sanhedrin. The political nature of the perception of Jewish leaders is clear from the Gospel accounts themselves. On that basis, this contention by MacCoby, as just quoted, carries a great deal of evidentiary weight, most especially because the witness is firsthand, if we are to believe that John is the author. That aside, others witnessed the so-called triumphal entry of Jesus into Jerusalem: it is highly unlikely that this episode is entirely fictional. I find it highly improbable that *"as they went out of Jericho, a great multitude followed him"* (Matthew 20:29), just to watch him be crucified. They were expecting triumph from him, for he said, *"the Son of Man has come to seek and save that which was lost"*, and *"they thought the kingdom of God would appear immediately"* (Luke 19:1-11). The people in Jerusalem, "the whole multitude of disciples, began to rejoice and praise God with a loud voice … *Blessed is the King who comes in the name of the Lord"* (Luke 19:37-38), and then *"took branches of palm trees and went out to meet him"* (John 12:13). Remember that at this stage in Jesus' life, these disciples had no idea that Jesus was to die. The only rational conclusion is that those who followed Jesus to Jerusalem, and those present who welcomed him with palm leaves and cries of "Blessed is the King", believed that he was the Messiah who had come to redeem them from Roman oppression. No other interpretation is plausible.

Whilst I have admitted my skepticism concerning some narratives in the Gospels, some parts actually argue against Christian theology, and according to historians, such texts are the most likely to be true. Even Christian apologists will argue similarly; for example, that the women were the first to declare the tomb empty. The argument goes that as Jewish women at that time could not be witnesses, that the Gospels record their witness must be true, for no author would have made up that story given the likelihood of it not being accepted. Applying that logic to the narrative that we have just been discussing, it seems likely to be true, thus verifying the perception by the leaders in Jerusalem that Jesus was a threat to their physical security.

Conclusion

I still do not know who Jesus truly was, although I am convinced of who he wasn't. Likewise, I still am unsure of how Jesus perceived his mission, although I sense that it either changed over time, or that the New Testament authors wrote the story that way, quite clumsily if they did. We do know, from the Gospel accounts themselves, that it was only at the very end of his life that he privately made known to his Apostles, that he must die for our sins. There is no evidence that he made it known publicly. We also know, again from the Gospels, that the high priest and members of the Sanhedrin saw Jesus as a threat to the political stability of Judea, and that the people of Jerusalem welcomed him as the promised Messiah, about to deliver them from the Romans. Beyond that, we can "know" very little, for a great deal of what is taught in Christian theology does not accord with those facts, always provided, of course, that those are indeed facts.

Returning to the issue of prophecy fulfillment, and the evidence for it, my understanding of the mission of Jesus argues against the Christian case. The evidence we have reviewed tends to support the case that Jesus saw himself as the prophesied Messiah, a human who would lead the Jews to victory against the Romans. He clearly failed in that mission. The evidence that, from the outset, he saw his mission as one who would die for our sins, is flimsy and unconvincing. Even if he later came to that belief, nobody at the time understood messianic prophecy in that sense, and even today, few if any outside Christianity can understand prophecy that way.

Thus, from the stance of an impartial jury, the case for prophecy fulfillment fails.

In passing, have you ever noticed that in the Gospels, Jesus never criticizes the Romans? This would argue against him being a revolutionary, but then again, any omission could simply be in accordance with the focus on his supposed mission to the Gentiles, the Jews having rejected him. Remember too, that in all likelihood, the Gospels were written, or at least redacted and circulated, after the fall of Jerusalem. They were written outside Palestine, in the Greek language, by writers who can be seen to be more Hellenistic in outlook rather than Hebraic, in a community that was pro-Roman and anti-Jewish. Again, circumstantial evidence, but in truth, that is largely all we have.

REFERENCES:

1. MacCoby, Hyam, *Revolution in Judaea: Jesus & The Jewish Resistance*, Ocean Books, London, UK, 1973

2. Dunn, James D.G., *Jesus, Paul, and the Gospels*, Wm. B. Eerdmans Publishing Co., Grand Rapids, MI, 2011,

3. *Ibid*, p. 12

4. http://biblehub.com/john/2-4.htm

5. Dunn, *Ibid*, p. 18

6. Talbot, Wayne, *Christians Too, Must Obey – Putting a Fence Around Torah*, Xlibris, Bloomington, IN, 2017

7. http://biblehub.com/matthew/5-17.htm

8. Talbot, Wayne, *Once a Christian – How the Bible Convinced Me to Walk Away*, Xlibris, Bloomington, IN, 2017, Chapter 6-7: The Betrayal of Jesus, pp. 397-402

9. http://biblehub.com/john/3-14.htm

10. Talbot, *Ibid*, Chapter 6-4, pp. 372-373

11. https://bible.org/seriespage/13-similarities-among-johns-gospel-and-synoptic-gospels

12. Talbot, *Ibid*, Chapter 6-5: Why Was Jesus Secretive? pp. 378-384

13. https://www.oneforisrael.org/bible-based-teaching-from-israel/21-ways-yeshua-is-a-prophet-like-moses/

14. MacCoby, Ibid, pp. 123-124

CHAPTER 9-3

GOD AND/OR MAN

"And he said to them: What things? So they said to him: The
things concerning Jesus of Nazareth, who was a Prophet mighty
in deed and word before God and all the people ... And
beginning at Moses and all the Prophets, he expounded to them
in all the Scriptures the things concerning himself."
(Luke 24:19-27)

Having studied the Hebrew Scriptures in detail, most especially relating to the subject of this chapter, I am entirely convinced that Jesus would not have expounded to them in all the Scriptures, things concerning his "deity". That Luke's Gospel records no reaction from Jesus' audience, is circumstantial evidence that the subject was not raised. You see, this is all too ordinary, far too ordinary for an encounter with Almighty God. *"Hello, this chap is God, ho hum!"* I cannot believe it to be true, because the evidence is to the contrary. Go back and review what happened at Sinai when God made His presence felt.

Son of Man

This is a very complex subject, on which I have written extensively in another work[1]. In reference to the Son of Man, we discussed the detail of this in Chapter 3-3, so I do not intend to reiterate the detail here. As for whether Daniel 7:13 should read "one like the *son of* man" or "one like a man", I concluded that it really doesn't matter, and is perhaps a red herring. The longer term, *son of man*, can be understood as an emphatic reference: simply "man" is one thing, but perhaps the authors or translators of Daniel were trying to emphasise the situation – a mere human before God. If we look at it that way, there is no true contradiction between the terms *man* and *son of man* - the second is simply the first preceded by an adjectival phrase: "son of", denoting the unbridgeable gap between man and God, and is consonant with the repeated use of the term in Ezekiel.

What does matter, however, is the theological annotation of initial capitals: **S**on of **M**an. Such denotes a royal or divine title, and is intended to convey a meaning which, I believe, was not intended by the original users of the term.

Son of God

As for the term *son of God*, it occurs numerous times in the Hebrew Scriptures, and it refers to a close relationship between God and the entity called "son". Here a just a few examples:

a. *"Now there was a day when the sons of God came to present themselves before the Lord"* (Job 1:6).

b. "You shall say to Pharaoh, so said HASHEM, *My firstborn son is Israel. So, I say to you, send out My son that he may serve Me*" (Ex 4:22-23, TJB).

c. In the Psalms, we have David saying: "I am obliged to proclaim that Hashem said to me, '*You are My son, I have begotten you this day*'" (Psalm 2:7, TJB).

If we assume, as I believe we must, that the Jews of Jesus' time would have understood the term *son of God* as conveyed historically in the Hebrew

Scriptures, then we have no plausible reason for asserting that it would have meant something different when applied to Jesus. If the evangelists did want to convey a different meaning other than the traditional, then more likely, or at least hopefully, they would have used a different, and more specific, term. If Scripture interprets Scripture, and is our guide to understanding, then the term, *son of God*, can have no connotation of deity or messiahship.

In the Gospels, it occurs 22 times. In one instance, Jesus describes himself that way: "This sickness is not unto death, but for the glory of God, that the son of God may be glorified through it" (John 11:4). In another instance, Jesus accept does that term about himself, and then only in response to a question about making himself a God (John 10:33-36); in all other cases, it is other people referring to him that way. In a particularly interesting instance, the high priest asks Jesus if he is "the Christ, the Son of God" and in reply He states: "It is as you said. Nevertheless, I say to you, hereafter you will see the Son of Man sitting at the right hand of the Power, and coming on the clouds of heaven." (Matt 26:63-64) The account in Mark 14:62 is similar, whilst that in Luke 22:67-70 seems to be an improvisation.

Again, the high priest not being Greek, his question should be rendered as: "are you the anointed one, the son of God", meaning the one anointed as the Davidic King of Israel. Jesus seemed to have believed that he was. That said, what did Jesus have in mind when perceiving himself as both the son of man, and the son of God? Could he have understood himself as one anointed by God (son of God), but nevertheless still a man (son of man) as King David was?

Using the Hebrew Scriptures as my guide, I can find no justification for the use of initial capitals in these terms, and nothing to suggest that either refers to the Jewish *mashiach*, or establishes Jesus as God. One last observation; where we read: *"He made himself the Son of God"* (John 19:7), was the emphasis on him being Son of God, or, that he made himself? If the Jews were conversant with the Hebrew Scriptures, and understood the term as used therein, i.e., denoting a close relationship, established by God, between Himself and the entity called "son", then I would offer that this statement could be paraphrased as: "God anoints those whom He calls His son, but you have anointed yourself".

We must always consider these issues in the contemporary, cultural and religious context.

God Incarnate

"And the Word became flesh and dwelt among us"
(John 1:14)

In the context of this book, the question becomes: Is there any Old Testament prophecy that even suggests that the promised *mashiach*, the prophet like Moses, the *one like a man* in Daniel 7, would be God incarnate? Search the Hebrew Scriptures as diligently as you should, and I contend that you will not find any such suggestion - not even a hint. From a philosophical perspective, is it even possible that God who is spirit (John 4:24) could become flesh? You might answer that anything is possible with God, but that is not true – God cannot be anything other than God. God, as spirit, can influence the material world, even causing it to exist, and can create humans in *His Own Image*, but we really do not know what that means – He hasn't told us. We can infer some things, but always, whatever attributes we have that are in God's image, are severely limited in comparison with His. In truth, we are more *unlike* God, than like.

If the Old and New Testaments are truthful, we know that one does not need to be God to "work" miracles, even raising the dead. Peter is said to have raised Dorcas from the dead (Acts 9:36-42). We should understand that no-one actually works miracles - it is God working through His chosen people that this occurs. Thus, from an evidentiary perspective, Jesus working miracles is not proof that he was God. When Jesus claimed to forgive sins (Matthew 9:1-8), we cannot know that the person's sins were forgiven him without repentance: even the Catholic "sacrament" of confession requires sincere repentance before the priest can announce that the penitent's sins are forgiven. Jesus used his ability to perform miracles, to evidence his claimed authority to forgive sins, and this certainly gives credence to his claim. Why would God allow participation in one, and not the other? I have no answer, other than to weakly offer: God works in mysterious ways. However, we do have a warning from Scripture:

> "If there arises among you a prophet or a dreamer of dreams, and he gives you a sign or a wonder, and the sign or the wonder comes to pass, of which he spoke to you, saying, 'Let us go after other

gods' – which you have not known – 'and let us serve them', you shall not listen to the words of that prophet or that dreamer of dreams, for the Lord your God is testing you to know whether you love the Lord your God with all your heart and with all your soul. You shall walk after the Lord your God and fear Him, and keep His commandments and obey His voice; you shall serve Him and hold fast to Him." (Deuteronomy 13:1-5)

If Jesus claimed to be God, this warning seems noticeably apt, especially in view of the Christian doctrine that we need not obey God's commandments as given at Mt Sinai. For the Jew, Christianity's Triune God is a god "which you have not known", and thus, it is reasonable that they do not go after that god. I am inclined similarly.

Now let us review the data in the New Testament, which is offered as evidence of the deity of Jesus, Christ the *anointed one* according to the Gospels. To start, the term, "God is with us" (Matt 1:23), quoting Isaiah 7:14, should not be interpreted as Jesus is God, but more simply, that the child provided by God is evidence that God is with us. There are precedents in the Scriptures for this understanding.

If we are to believe John's account, Nathanael, when first meeting Jesus, declared: "Rabbi, You are the Son of God! You are the King of Israel" (John 1:49). If Nathaniel was versed in the Hebrew Scriptures, there is nothing in his declaration that can be construed as him perceiving Jesus to be God, although the use of the term, *King of Israel*, is evidence that Nathaniel believed Jesus to be the promised Messiah. I wonder what he later thought after Jesus was executed, because most certainly at this stage of Jesus' public life, Nathaniel would not have expected the Messiah to die, rather than save his people from the oppression of the Romans. I have listened to an interesting discussion, led by Catholic Bishop, Robert Barron, asking the question: Is the Resurrection of Jesus Credible?[2] We will come back to that later, but one point that he stressed is relevant here: the strongest possible evidence for the Jews, that Jesus was NOT the *mashiach*, was that he failed to rescue them from the Romans.

That aside, I do not intend to discuss every verse that suggests the deity of Jesus, but list most of them here for the sake of completeness, omitting Mark as mostly duplicating Matthew:

a. Matthew 4:7; 9:2-6; 10:32-33; 12:6-8; 12:41-42; 14:27-33; 26:63-
    64; 28:18
b. Luke 11:32; 18:19, 22:69, 23:3
c. John 1:1–12; 1:14; 1:49; 3:13; 5:18; 6:38; 8:23; 8:40; 8:57-59; 9:35-
    37; 10:30-36; 14:8–11; 16:15; 17:3-5; 17:24; 18:35-36; 18:37; 19:7;
    10:30-33; 20:28-29

Certainly, there are one or two verses, of which the most reasonable interpretation is that Jesus, or somebody, did perceive him as God, but the preponderance of evidence, considering the cultural context of the time, says that Jesus was seen as the *anointed* of God, as the promised *mashiach*, but not that he was God.

Consider the episode where Jesus was asked: "Which is the first commandment of all?" (Mark 12:28) In reply, Jesus recited the *Shema*, the prayer that the Jewish people recited morning and night: "Hear, O Israel: Hashem is our God, Hashem is the One and Only. You shall love Hashem, your God, with all your heart, with all your soul, and with all your resources"; quoting the *Hebrew* version of Deuteronomy 6:4-5, as I am sure that Jesus would have done. He was answering a question by the scribes. The scribe responded: "Well said, Teacher. You have spoken the truth, for there is one God, and there is no other but He" (Mark 12:32). Mark's account continues: "Jesus saw that he answered wisely" (v. 34), which would suggest that Jesus agreed – there is but one God, the entity he referred to as his Father.

What is apparent to me, and many others, is that the New Testament evidences confusion in the minds of Jesus' disciples concerning his return, and thus his mission. I would also contend that there is a lack of honesty in these accounts, although perhaps *honesty* is too strong a term. Look at it this way. There is nothing in the Hebrew Bible which in any way suggests the sacrifice of the Messiah for the forgiveness of sin. Yes, Christianity does try to read this back into the Scripture, but does a very poor job of it. The common belief, concerning a Messiah, was of one triumphing over Israel's enemies, and bringing peace to the world.

Jesus failed to triumph in that manner.

It is reasonable to assume that such was the view of the Apostles, being as they were, fishermen, tradesmen, and the like, and unlikely to be well versed in the vagaries of prophecy. When Jesus began telling them that he was to die, and then return to fulfill the expected Messianic mission, what was in their minds regarding why he was there in the first place? I am curious as to why there is no record of the disciples questioning Jesus on this issue. If you had been one of his disciples, would you have followed Jesus around with no curiosity as to why? I know that I wouldn't: I why want to ask: "Jesus, why are you here, if not to fulfill the messianic mission?" When Jesus informed his disciples that he would be arrested and killed, why is there no record of his disciples wanting to know why that was to happen, and even more, why Jesus insisted that it must happen? The same occurred when Jesus is said to have announced a new (replacement) covenant at the Last Supper. Loyalty to the Covenant was central to the life of the Jew, and the most discussed issue by the Prophets, as failure to adhere to the Covenant was the cause of their exiles and misery. Yet supposedly, when Jesus put that aside with a replacement, we have not a murmur from the Apostles, and no later reaction from the Sanhedrin or anyone questioning Jesus' authority. In a court of law, a lack of reaction by witnesses, to a claimed event or saying, is circumstantial evidence that it did not occur.

In fiction stories, a good author portrays the characters as real people, with real feelings and behaviours. What intrigues me about the Gospels is that this happens sometimes, but hardly at all on the most important issues of Christian theology, and what Jesus is said to have achieved. The Apostles did not question Jesus on the supposedly new covenant. They did not question him on his mission, especially regarding two comings. They did not question him on why he had to die, and why he voluntarily accepted an early death at the hands of the Romans. If you think deeply on the question, as I attempt to do, none of the most significant precepts of Christian doctrine are ever answered directly by the Synoptic Gospels, nor are the appropriate questions asked by Jesus' disciples.

I want to know why.

A Poached Egg?

Christian apologist, C.S. Lewis, in *Surprised by Joy*, made this observation regarding Jesus as God:

"I am trying here to prevent anyone saying the really foolish thing that people often say about Him: I'm ready to accept Jesus as a great moral teacher, but I don't accept his claim to be God. That is the one thing we must not say. A man who was merely a man and said the sort of things Jesus said would not be a great moral teacher. He would either be a lunatic — on the level with the man who says he is a poached egg or else he would be the Devil of Hell. You must make your choice. Either this man was, and is, the Son of God or else a madman or something worse. You can shut him up for a fool, you can spit at him and kill him as a demon or you can fall at his feet and call him Lord and God, but let us not come with any patronising nonsense about his being a great human teacher. He has not left that open to us. He did not intend to."[3]

My point is: did Jesus really claim to be God? I am not confident, as discussed earlier in this chapter, that Jesus did see himself as God. Certainly, he believed himself to be the promised *mashiach*, but God? If he did so believe and claim, then I am inclined to agree with Lewis on his description of Jesus being *on the level with the man who says he is a poached egg*.

The Man Who Never Was?

I would not contend for a moment, that Jesus did not exist: the evidence of his existence is far too compelling to even contemplate such a thing. However, the question, largely unresolved in my mind, is how closely the Jesus of Christianity matches the contemporary Jesus of Second Temple Judaism. I have many reasons for the suggestion in the heading above, but here I will just outline a few salient points.

Firstly, that ugly accusation by the Church of Rome, a seed that grew into universal anti-Jewishness: the Jews were *"Christ Killers"* and guilty of *deicide*, as if such were even possible. Killing gods was very much a concept beloved of pagan cultures, and could never have arisen within a Jewish culture. Why did the church of Rome not understand?

"Therefore, my Father loves me, because I lay down my life that I may take it again. No one takes it from me, but I lay it down of myself. I have power to lay it down, and I have power to take it again. This command I have received from my Father." (John 10:17-18)

Three explanations occur to me: [1], that the church in Rome so hated the Jews, for whatever reason, that they would say, or do, anything in their pursuit of the persecution of the Jews; [2], John's Gospel was written later than claimed, and Rome did not receive the message of these verses until after the persecutions had begun; or [3], this was a later redaction of John's Gospel. Either way, this contradiction between John's Gospel and Church behaviour is very suspicious.

The Church of Rome rejected Torah, the Sabbath, all God-ordained commemorations of the Hebrew Scriptures, and even accused the original follows of Jesus, Followers of the Way, the Nazarenes, of heresy. In other words, Christianity refused to follow in the footsteps of Jesus, as his Apostles and early disciples did. Which Jesus were they following? It is clear to me, and many others, that whilst the Church of Rome claimed to have established its religion **IN** Jesus, it was not the religion **OF** Jesus. Hence my suspicion that the Jesus of Christianity was not, and continues to not be, the Jesus of the Nazarenes, the people who were closest to his message and understood him best.

The parable of the sower comes to mind: *"And some (seeds) fell among thorns, and the thorns sprang up and choked them."* (Matthew 13:7) I would highly recommend a study by Jules Isaac, entitled *The Teaching of Contempt*[4]. After reading it, you may well need a cup of tea, a Valium, and a good lie down, for it will (or should) leave you as disgusted as reading about the Holocaust.

Finally, I am utterly convinced that the Apostles of Jesus, and the disciples that travelled with him, did not believe he was God, certainly not before the claimed resurrection.

Why?

Simply because they **did not treat him as God.**

Consider these verses:

a. "For it is written, 'As I live says the Lord, every knee shall bow to Me, and every tongue shall confess to God'" (Romans 14:11 quoting Isaiah 45:23)

b. "Therefore, God also has highly exalted Him and given Him the name which is above every name, that at the name of Jesus every knee should bow, of those in heaven, and of those on earth, and that every tongue should confess that Jesus Christ is Lord, to the glory of God the Father." (Philippians 2:9-11)

The letter to the Romans was written circa 58 CE, and to the Philippians four years later. The context of the quote from Isaiah is given starting in verse 22, "Look to Me and be saved, all you ends of the earth, for I am God and there is no other". In Philippians, Paul does not say that Jesus was God, but merely that Jesus had been exalted by God, and was Lord. So clearly, Paul was in no doubt that Jesus was Lord, but when, and in what sense? In his pronouncements, did Paul understand Jesus, as Lord, to be a special appointee of God, or as being coequal with God? Note that in Romans 1:4, Paul states of Jesus: "declared to be the son of God with power according to the Spirit of holiness, by the resurrection from the dead." Many were declared to be the sons of God, but Jesus was granted special powers. In 2 Corinthians 1:3, Paul writes: "Blessed be the God and Father of the Lord Jesus Christ." *God of the Lord Jesus Christ* – if the Father is the God of the son, then the son cannot be God. Examining the numerous references to *God our Father*, and the *Lord Jesus Christ*, as separate entities in Paul's writings, I am convinced that Paul did not view Jesus as God, Second Person of the Trinity.

As an aside regarding Paul's so-called "conversion", this is where the narrative is unclear. Paul mention this event in Galatians 1:15-16, "But when it pleased God, who separated me from my mother's womb and called me through His grace, to reveal His son in me, that I might preach Him among the Gentiles, I did not immediately confer with flesh and blood." He also wrote in 1 Corinthians 15:6-8 that Jesus appeared to him last. The three accounts in Acts all have Jesus appearing to Paul, but with extended narratives on the conversation between Jesus and Paul. If this is what really happened, why did Paul not mention it himself? We have earlier encountered opinions of the author of the Book of Acts embellishing tales to suit the developing theology, and this seems a case in point. Paul claimed that the risen Jesus had appeared before him, but only much later in his letter to the Corinthians and Galatians – he made no mention of this in his earlier letters to the Thessalonians, and I wonder why. Could it be that Paul included this in his narratives, following learning of the resurrection during his visits to Jerusalem? That aside, I strongly suspect that the expanded narrative in Acts is a fabrication.

I would have expected Paul to worship Jesus as God, had he met him earlier, and had that belief, but none of the Apostles or early disciples did so. Why did the Apostles blithely continue their relationship with Jesus as if he were just another man, a prophet perhaps, but not God? Even when after the resurrection, doubting Thomas was invited to put his hand in Jesus' wounded side (John 20:27), the narrative just doesn't ring true to me, because I cannot imagine anyone reacting to God as Thomas is said to have done. No other evangelist mentions this event, which has me wondering. If God appeared before me, I would be on the floor in an instant, and would be unable to gaze upon Him. That the Gospel narratives have people reacting to Jesus after the resurrection, no different to than before, is evidence to me that either they did not perceive him as God, or that their understanding of God was very different to the God who spoke to Moses at Sinai.

How do you think that you would react in the presence of the Almighty?

When people were in the presence of a king, or Caesar, or Pharaoh, they behaved in a certain way: in obeisance, in reverence even, yet how were the Apostles in the presence of Jesus? Did they treat him as God, or even as a king, or did they behave toward him as a man? How did Moses react in the presence of God? How would you react in the presence of God: would you dialogue with Him as an ordinary man, or perhaps a great teacher? One can talk about a *High Christology*, but it by no means approaches the awe in which the Jews held God. "Now there was leaning on Jesus' bosom one of his disciples, whom Jesus loved … then leaning back on Jesus' breast, he said to him" (John 13:23, 25). Really? Would, whoever this disciple was, really lean on the bosom of someone he believed to be God?

The God of Christianity is far too small for me, if they would have me believe that Jesus was God as presented in the Gospels. That is simply not the way that the Jews would have behaved in the presence of God. Yes, you might argue, but he had the appearance of a man. To Moses, God had the appearance of a burning bush, yet Moses was afraid to look upon God (Ex 3:6). Should I really be expected to believe that the Apostles, knowing of Moses' encounter with God, would nevertheless simply treat God as a man?

The gulf between God and man is unimaginable, just as the Old Testament attests. I am not about to believe that the Jews of Jesus' time saw Jesus as God, but treated him as simply a man: it is unbelievably implausible. I would not treat God that way: would you? If Jesus appeared in your church tomorrow, would you treat him as just a man, or as God? Would you invite Jesus to pray with you to God, believing him to be God? Why would you believe that it was any different in his day if people did believe him to be God?

The words in Luke 24:19, as quoted at the head of this chapter, evidence that the wider population saw Jesus not as God, but as a Prophet, one whom they were hoping was the Messiah who would rescue them from the Romans, as promised by God. That can say nothing about the view of his immediate disciples, but that may have changed after the resurrection. Let us examine the events surrounding this claimed miracle.

The Burial … and Empty Tomb

I am uncertain of on which day Jesus was crucified, for the day is disputed. The traditional view is that he died on Friday afternoon, and the tomb was found empty early Sunday morning. However, as that doesn't quite fit with "three days and nights in the tomb", some have proposed that there was a High-Day Sabbath on the Thursday, and it was that Sabbath, not the weekly, that determined the day of Jesus' crucifixion, i.e., Wednesday, not Friday. The problem with that idea is that if true, there was no reason why the women would have to wait until Sunday to complete the burial process – they could have done that on the Friday. That hypothesis fails on the evidence.

We have the gospel narratives of the empty tomb, but we have no extra-biblical evidence of what then happened to his body. From an historical perspective, we simply cannot say. What we can say, however, from historical evidence, is that the common practice of the time was to throw the bodies of criminals into a common grave, where decomposition would quickly occur. Perhaps the body of Jesus was saved from that fate, but we cannot be sure either way. I have already expressed my doubts concerning the authenticity of other tracts in the New Testament, so one should allow me this one as well.

This brings us to the discovery of the empty tomb, narrated in all four Gospels, but with very little agreement across the accounts. In brief:

a. Mark 16:1-14 – Mary Magdalene, Mary the mother of James, and Salome, went to the tomb very early on Sunday morning, when the sun had risen, and saw that the very large stone had been rolled away. They saw a young man, clothed in white, who instructed them to tell Peter, and the disciples, that Jesus was going to Galilee and they would see him there. But the women were afraid and said nothing to anyone. Early on that same day, Jesus appeared to Mary Magdalene, she told the disciples that she had seen him, but they did not believe her. After that, he appeared to "another two of them", who told this to the rest, but they still did not believe. Later he appeared to the eleven, but no mention of what "later" meant, or where the eleven were at the time.

b. Matthew 27:62 – 28:17 – The chief priests and Pharisees were concerned over Jesus' claim that he would rise from the dead after three days, so Pilate instructed the Jews to seal the tomb and set a guard. Contrary to some opinions, I believe this to be the Temple guard, not a Roman guard, for Pilate said: "You have a guard" (of your own?). Mary Magdalene and the other Mary watched as Joseph prepared the body, and the stone was rolled across the door of the tomb, and then came again to the tomb at dawn on the Sunday, and there was a great earthquake. An angel descended from heaven and rolled back the stone in their presence. The angel told them the same as in Mark's account, and they ran to the disciples, contrary to Mark. As they went, Jesus appeared to them, telling them to tell his brethren to go to Galilee where he would meet them. The soldiers reported back to the chief priests to report what had happened, and they were given money to keep quiet (I doubt that Roman soldiers would not have done that). Then the eleven disciples headed off to Galilee, about a four-day walk, and there Jesus met them. They worshipped him, but some doubted.

c. <u>Luke 24:1-53</u> – Very early on Sunday morning, "they" [the women who had come with Jesus from Galilee] and "certain other women" came to the tomb and found the stone rolled away. They entered the tomb, noticed the body of Jesus was missing, but "two men stood by them in shining garments". The men reminded the women of how Jesus spoke of his own crucifixion and resurrection, and the women, remembering these words, returned to the eleven in Jerusalem and told them of what had occurred. The women are then identified as Mary Magdalene, Joanna, Mary the mother of James, and others. The disciples were not convinced, so Peter ran to the tomb to see for himself. On the same day, "two of them", presumably of the eleven, but apparently not, were on their way to Emmaus when Jesus appeared to them and engaged them in conversation. The two returned to the eleven in Jerusalem and reported their experience. Whilst they were doing so, Jesus appeared in their midst, ate with them, and gave them further instructions.

d. <u>John 20:1 – 21:25</u> – Mary Magdalene went to the tomb early Sunday morning, "while it was still dark", found the tomb empty, and ran back to tell Peter and the "other disciple whom Jesus loved", i.e. John, whereupon both men ran back to the tomb, John getting there first. There was no-one there: not Jesus, not an angel, not a man in white, not two men in shining robes, no-one. Then we have the very curious wording: "*he saw and believed, for as yet they did not know the Scriptures, that he must rise again from the dead.*" Apparently, John had not read Luke, for Luke narrated almost the opposite: that the apostles and the women remembered what Jesus had told them. So, what did he believe, and what Scriptures were those? I can find no Scriptures of the Jewish *mashiach* dying and rising from the dead. The disciples went away to their own homes, but where were they: Jerusalem or

Galilee? Mary Magdalene remained and looking into the tomb, saw two angels; then turning around she saw another man whom she thought was the gardener, but was in fact, Jesus. After a brief conversation, she went and told the disciples, but just which ones we cannot be sure, because they had all gone, but whether to Jerusalem or their homes in Galilee depends on which account one believes. That evening, they were all assembled (which would have been difficult), *for fear of the Jews*, when Jesus appeared to them. John's account adds more details, not found in the other accounts, but these are of no interest in the context of my enquiry here.

During my career as an analyst, I developed a technique that I termed, the *Contribution of Implied Agreement*. In brief, if there were numerous witnesses to an event, even though their accounts varied, this was circumstantial evidence that the event occurred, but *only circumstantial*: substantive evidence was still required to confirm the occurrence. For example, if four witnesses gave varying accounts of a car crash, and the crashed car was in evidence, we could accept that the crash did occur. If, however, the crashed car could not be found, one would be justified in doubting all accounts. In the case of the empty tomb, all four accounts agree that the tomb was empty, but the accounts vary considerably in the detail. The question becomes: Is the variation *insufficient* to doubt the event, or *sufficient* to doubt it? The differences are not trivial: it was still dark, or the sun had already risen; the stone was already rolled away, or it wasn't; there was an earthquake, or there wasn't; only Mary Magdalene went to the tomb, or there were more women present; there was no-one there at first visit, or there was one in white, two in shiny robes, or angel, perhaps in white; the women told the disciples, or they didn't; the disciples believed the account, or they didn't; only Peter ran to the tomb, or both Peter and John ran to the tomb; Jesus was to meet them in Galilee, or in Jerusalem; Jesus had previously told them that he would die and rise again, or he didn't; and so it goes on.

If the four accounts agree that the tomb was empty, then under the rules of evidence, we should accept that the tomb was indeed, empty. The question arises: could they have been looking in the wrong tomb? James Tabor has offered that as probable, based on contemporary Jewish customs, and the evidence in the reports themselves. I was introduced to the "two-tombs" hypothesis (see below) by New Testament scholar, James Tabor, and have added some thoughts of my own: I would recommend that you read them for yourself (his, not mine). My intent here is add to my earlier contention that the Messiah dying and rising from the dead was NOT according to the Scriptures, and we have reason to question whether Jesus did rise from the dead. The existence of "an" empty tomb is not evidence that the tomb in which Jesus was buried was in fact empty.

Matthew has the chief priests and Pharisees gathering to meet Pilate, requesting that the tomb be made secure so that the body of Jesus would not be stolen, so off someone went to seal the tomb and a guard was posted. This suggests that perhaps sealing the tomb at that stage was not the norm, and that the tomb would only be sealed after all rituals were performed. Was this added to Matthew's account to substantiate the claim of the stone being rolled away? Mark's account makes no mention of the meeting, and is unclear as to who sealed the tomb: Joseph or a guard. Luke has the women following Joseph, "and they observed the tomb and how his body was laid", but no mention of the stone being rolled across to seal the tomb. John has Nicodemus accompanying Joseph, no women, and no mention of the stone. Given the lack of corroboration on the detail, is it possible that there was no stone rolled across to seal the tomb, and that mention of finding the stone rolled away was added, along with Matthew's specifics, to substantiate the claim of resurrection?

Of course, we now have to understand what happened to the guards. Were they bribed to look the other way, to go home, or were they never there? Matthew tells a story, verses 28:11-15, but the truth of this cannot be verified. If Jesus rose whilst they were still on guard, would they not have noticed the stone being rolled away, as the other three Gospels attest? Perhaps the author of Matthew, recognising the inconsistency in his account, added the story of the earthquake and the angel rolling back the stone whilst the women were there. On that subject, one commentator noted: "There is no question of a literal 'fulfillment' of apocalyptic traits such as darkening of the sun and the shaking of the earth. This is well understood imagery suggesting the magnitude and horror of the situation; and all that horror is present in the events of Christ's conflict and death. The Gospels may be thought to hint as much when they say that at the crucifixion of Christ the sun was darkened and the earth quaked."[5] What is being suggested here is that the Gospels are not strictly reportage, to use Lewis' term, but contain embellishments to emphasise the gravity of a situation.

These variations in the narrative are not inconsequential: they are substantive evidence that the narratives arose out of tradition, with embellishments. For an interesting discussion on the number of guards, see this online article[6].

The Two Tombs Hypothesis

Jesus died in the late afternoon, just hours before the Passover Seder, and in accordance with Jewish customs, it was necessary to recover his body and bury it before sunset. Haste was necessary, so where to bury him? The full burial rites involved washing the body, anointing with oil and spices, respectfully wrapping in clean linen, etc., but could that be accomplished in time, or would it have to wait until Saturday evening at the earliest? The Apostles, except perhaps for John, had fled to Galilee (Matthew 28:10), but this is where again, the narratives contradict one another.

Traditionally, it was the women who performed the role of the undertaker - a dead body was considered unclean (Numbers 19:11-13). Let us review the four Gospels. In Matthew's account, Joseph of Arimathea took down the body, "wrapped it in a clean linen cloth, and laid it in his new tomb which he had hewn out of the rock" (v. 27:59-60), and the women came after the Sabbath to complete the burial. Mark's account is similar, noting that Joseph "was himself waiting for the Kingdom of God" (v. 15:43), and adding that when the women came, "they brought spices that they might come and anoint him" (v. 16:2). Luke agrees with Mark regarding Joseph, and notes that the "tomb that was hewn out of the rock, where no-one had ever lain before" (v. 23:53). The women prepared spices and fragrant oils, otherwise resting on the Sabbath. John has a very different account, one which does not ring true, as not only does it contradict the Synoptics on an important issue, but is also contrary to contemporary Jewish practice. John's account has Nicodemus accompanying Joseph, bringing with him "a mixture of myrrh and aloes, about a hundred pounds" (v. 19:39), and together they "bound it [the body of Jesus] in strips of linen with the spices, as the custom of the Jews is to bury" (v. 19:39-40). Yes, it was customary for that to be done, but by women, not by men. As for the hundred pounds, forty-five kilograms, that is a lot for one man to carry, and from where did he carry it? If the time between Jesus being taken down from the cross, and being taken to the tomb was short, was Nicodemus already waiting in the expectation, however unlikely, that Pilate would grant permission? And from where would Nicodemus get such a large quantity of myrrh and aloes?

"Now when the Sabbath was past, Mary Magdalene and Mary the mother of James, and Salome bought spices that they might come and anoint him" (Mark 16:1), but that would have been unnecessary if Nicodemus had already done that, and remember that according to Matthew, two of these women were present when Joseph closed the tomb, so if Nicodemus had anointed Jesus' body, they would have known that. Likewise, according to Luke, "The women who had come with him from Galilee followed after, and they observed the tomb and how his body was laid. Then they returned and prepared spices and fragrant oils, and rested on the Sabbath according to the commandment." (vv. 23:55-56). It was after the Sabbath that the women returned to anoint Jesus, and found the stone already rolled away. These are not just *inconsistencies* in the narratives, these are *contradictions* of fact, which places suspicion on the credibility of all four accounts.

Nicodemus is said to have been a Pharisee, and a member of the Sanhedrin. You may recall the incidents narrated in Matthew and Mark where Jesus' disciples were criticised by the Pharisees for their failure to observe the purification laws. The Pharisees were very strict on that issue, and were aware of these strictures in Torah:

> "He who touches the dead body of anyone shall be unclean seven days. He shall purify himself with the water on the third day and on the seventh day; then he will be clean. But if he does not purify himself on the third day and on the seventh day he will not be clean. Whoever touches the body of anyone who has died, and does not purify himself, defiles the tabernacle of the Lord. That

person shall be cut off from Israel. He shall be unclean, because the water of purification was not sprinkled on him: his uncleanness is still on him." (Numbers 19:11-13, NKJV)

So, I ask myself, would Nicodemus, a high-ranking Pharisee, deliberately cause himself to be unclean and unable to participate in the Passover Seder? I do not believe so. There are other narratives in the gospel attributed to John, that have me doubting that it was written, in the form we have it at least, by the Apostle John. In an earlier chapter, I discussed similar doubts concerning the term, Lamb of God. Joseph of Arimathea is also said to have been a high-ranking member of the Sanhedrin, but whether a Pharisee or Sadducee is unknown. As a secret disciple of Jesus, believing in the resurrection of the dead, he could not have been a Sadducee, which brings us back to the question of being unclean by handling a dead body?

According to John, "in the place where he was crucified there was a garden, and in the garden a new tomb in which no-one had yet been laid." Studying maps said to represent the locations of Jesus' crucifixion and burial, I find that there are two possible sites for the crucifixion: one very close to the tomb, and the other about 500 metres away. What is interesting is that the closer one, in the garden, is inside the city walls, and the one further away is near the road outside the gate. Given the Roman propensity for leaving crucified bodies hanging as a warning to others, my sense of the times is that the site outside the walls is more likely, so that those about to enter Jerusalem knew what to expect. However, according to Jewish custom, the crucified were not to be left overnight during the Sabbath, so we can accept that the body of Jesus might well have been taken down if Pilate did give permission, but we cannot know about the other two. The Romans, including Pilate, were not known to be sensitive to Jewish religious customs, especially when such would override the message they intended to send when crucifying criminals.

John's Gospel tells us of a garden nearby with an unused tomb (John 19:41-42), but did it belong to Joseph? *"Based on Jewish law, he would not have placed Jesus in his [Nicodemus] own family tomb, but would have provided a separate tomb for Jesus."*[7] If you are of a mind, the publications referenced here provide the necessary explanation for this statement, and more, that Jesus would likely have been finally interred in his family tomb. The point here is that Matthew's embellished account notwithstanding, the initial burial of Jesus was necessarily rushed, so that he was interred before sunset, but the full burial process would not have been completed until sometime later, after the Sabbath. The suggestion is that Joseph returned on the Saturday evening to complete the task, and in doing so, removed the body of Jesus from its initial tomb to a permanent location somewhere else. Thus, when the women returned some twelve hours later, the tomb they went to was indeed empty, because the body of Jesus had been removed.

Returning to John's version of events, when Mary Magdalene found the tomb empty, she ran to Peter and the other Apostles to inform them: "They have taken away the Lord out of the tomb, and we do not know where they have laid him" (John 20:2). This is consistent with the two-tomb hypothesis. Mary's first reaction was not that Jesus had been resurrected, but that someone had removed his body. There is nothing in the reactions of Peter and the others that they thought otherwise, and as John explains it: "For as yet they did not know the Scripture that he must rise again from the dead." (John 20:9) We will come back to that contradiction, but for now, all I want to convey is the possibility, backed up by scholarly and archaeological research, that the body of Jesus was moved from its initial place of burial, to another site, and if the women were present at the initial interment, then it was inevitable that they would find the tomb empty. Note also that contrary to the Synoptic accounts, there was no angel or young man present.

The Resurrection

As this issue is both central to Christian doctrine, and also one of the most mysterious, I have chosen to discuss it on its own. See Chapter 9-4.

Summary and Conclusions

The first point that comes to mind is this: I do not understand how anyone can claim that the New Testament writings were inspired by the

Holy Spirit, such that every word is that of God, and inerrant. That claim must be seen for what it is: little more than desperation to have the New Testament accepted as authoritative.

The second point is that there is no evidence of *when* Jesus rose from the dead, if he did. As mentioned earlier, the Gospel of Luke records Jesus saying: "Assuredly, I say to you, today you will be with me in Paradise." (Luke 23:34) If that were true, then Jesus ascended into heaven that day, not on the third day. Otherwise. all we know from the Gospels is that on the Sunday morning, the tomb was empty, but which tomb? Jesus could have risen at any time between the stone being rolled across the tomb, and when the women arrived. Thus, the claim of having *risen on the third day* is a theological construct after the event, not a verifiable fact. I should repeat that for emphasis – it is a *theological construct*, not a piece of historical information.

The third point is the whereabouts of the eleven Apostles. Mark says that when Jesus was captured, "they all forsook him and fled" (Mark 14:50). Matthew agrees, but Luke does not corroborate that. Curiously, whilst ALL fled, the three Gospels nevertheless have Peter following Jesus at a distance. John is silent on them all fleeing, but has both Peter and one other disciple following Jesus. Presumably this was the Apostle John. After that, we have various conflicting accounts of where the eleven went, and where they were to meet Jesus. Both Matthew and Mark have them being told that they were to meet Jesus in Galilee, Luke has two of them meeting Jesus on the way to Galilee, yet apparently Jesus also met them in Jerusalem.

The fourth point is the source of the narratives themselves. Jesus' words in the garden, prior to his capture, were not witnessed by anyone (they were all asleep), yet we have these accounts. The trial of Jesus was not witnessed by any of the eleven, although Peter, and perhaps John, were nearby. The crucifixion was not witnessed by any of the eleven, although the author of John's Gospel does put John there with Mary, the mother of Jesus: none of the Synoptics make similar mention. There is a great deal of narrative in the four Gospels, with very little verbal agreement, that was not witnessed by any of four disciples to whom the Gospels are attributed. This is not to argue that the events narrated, or the words spoken, did not happen, but to point out that we have no reliable evidence of the source of the accounts. In legal terms, these accounts would be unlikely to even qualify for the common-law *hearsay rule* - the evidence is simply not that strong, and has very little corroboration, if any.

The narratives of the crucifixion, and the discovery of the empty tomb, evidence little agreement on the details, leaving substantial doubt, in my mind, as to whether the latter occurred at all. When combined with the historical evidence of how crucifixions were conducted, the disposal of the bodies, and the character of Pontius Pilate, I find it difficult to believe that Pilate would have allowed the body of Jesus to have been taken down from the cross, to respect Jewish religious sensitivities. Most especially, Passover was a time of nervousness amongst the Establishment in Jerusalem, as the Jews were commemorating their escape from the bondage of the Egyptians, with the ever-present desire to escape from the bondage of the Romans. Would Pilate have consented under those circumstances? I am not confident that he would have done so, but I would not be dogmatic on that point.

If the body of Jesus was not taken down that evening, he was not buried in the tomb. If he was not buried in the tomb, this would be consistent with the women finding the stone rolled away, and the tomb empty, although that hypothesis is inconsistent with the women witnessing the burial. Alternatively, Jesus was taken down from the cross, his body being laid in a temporary tomb, and then Joseph removed it to a permanent burial place on the Saturday evening. Perhaps this accounts for why three of the four Gospels recording that the stone was already rolled away, and the fourth writer understanding that issue, decided to the contrary that the tomb was still closed. If Jesus was not left in the tomb that the women first observed, there was no *physical* resurrection. That is not to say that Jesus could not have been spiritually raised, as some Gnostic groups later claimed, but that is not the issue here.

Many Christian books have been written contending for the historical accuracy of the resurrection itself, but all start their defence based on the acceptance of Jesus being taken down from the cross, entombed, and an empty tomb being subsequently discovered. I believe there to be sufficient evidence regarding the lead-up events to cast considerable doubt. Let me remind the reader that I am not claiming that I can know these things:

clearly, I cannot. This narrative is not about disproving the resurrection, but about adjudging the narratives under the *rules of evidence*.

That said, I have no explanation for the account of the subsequent appearance of Jesus to his disciples and others. I am not persuaded by Paul's claim that "he was seen by over five hundred brethren at once, of whom the greater part remain to the present" (1 Cor 15:6): he may well have been bluffing. Consider this: his letter was written circa 57 CE, and as best we can understand, children who lived past 10 managed to live until the ripe old age of 40-50 years, but many succumbed earlier. If we date the crucifixion to 30 CE, and "the brethren" were adults born perhaps circa the time of Jesus and Paul, i.e., 6-3 BCE, then Paul would have us believe that the greater part of the 500 lived into their late fifties or sixties. Possible, yes, but probable?

Even if the resurrection did occur as narrated, and I am willing to grant that it may well have done, there is insufficient evidence to support the Christian interpretation of that event, and the theology built up around it. The evidence of Jesus planning to die for our sins is paltry at best, and it is not supported by Old Testament prophecies. There is no evidence that Jesus arose on the third day, and a suggestion in the crucifixion narrative that he rose earlier, spiritually at least. The evidence points to Jesus believing himself to be the Messiah heralding the *eschaton*, but history proves him to have been wrong. Jesus is said to have been raised by the Father, he didn't raise himself, but God can raise anyone He so chooses, and it offers no evidence that Jesus was God, just that he was "special". If the Christian interpretation of the New Testament is right, we all shall be so raised!

Just where the resurrection fits in, I cannot be sure, but even if true, it provides insufficient evidence to support Christian doctrine. Finally, we have Paul's version, which is the first written account, and in the opinion of some scholars, his was the only eye-witness account, none of the Gospels having been written by those to whom they are traditionally attributed. That aside, Paul's risen Jesus was not flesh and blood, as the Gospels claim, but an immortal spiritual being. Both cannot be right, but both could be wrong, little more than traditions interpreted in the light of doctrine.

I cannot know.

It may surprise you, and maybe it is due to most of my life believing in Jesus as the Son of God, Second Person of the Trinity, and my redeemer from sin, but I continue to feel nervous in rejecting those earlier beliefs. I have argued myself back and forth, reviewed the evidence, reviewed my thoughts, reviewed my conclusions, and have no reason to change my mind, but still the doubts linger, still the uncertainty, still the concern that I may be offending God. I hope, and pray, not, but if nothing else, I can find comfort in these words:

"Anyone who speaks a word against the Son of Man, it will be forgiven him" (Matt 12:32).

REFERENCES:

1. Talbot, Wayne, *Once a Christian – How the Bible Convinced Me to Walk Away*, Xlibris, Bloomington, IN, 2017, Part 3: Son of God … or Man? pp. 123-214
2. https://www.youtube.com/watch?v=NEs3es9WyIg
3. Lewis, C.S., *The Case for Christianity*, Collier Books, New York, 1989, p. 52
4. Isaac, Jules, *The Teaching of Contempt: Christian Roots of Anti-Semitism*, Holt, Rinehart and Winston, Inc., New York, NY, 1964
5. Beale, G.K., *The Right Doctrine from the Wrong Texts? Essays on the Use of the Old Testament in the New*, Baker Academic, Grand Rapids, MI, 1994, p. p. 178
6. http://sntjohnny.com/front/how-many-guards-at-the-tomb-of-jesus/485.html
7. Tabor, James D., *Paul and Jesus: How the Apostle Paul Transformed Christianity*, Simon & Schuster Paperbacks, New York, NY, 2012, p. 77; referencing *The Jesus Dynasty*, pp. 22-33; Simcha Jacobovici and Charles Pellegrino, *The Jesus Family Tomb: The Evidence Behind the Discovery No-One Wanted to Find* (New York: HarperOne, 2008); and James D. Tabor and Simcha Jacobovici, *The Jesus Discovery: New Archaeological That Reveals the Birth of Christianity* (New York: Simon & Schuster, 2012).

CHAPTER 9-4

THE RESURRECTION

"The reality is that there is no historical explanation for the empty tomb, other than if we adopt a theological one, i.e. the resurrection. I leave it up to the reader to make up his own mind."
~ Shimon Gibson - *The Final Days of Jesus*[1] ~

I believe that it can be said, with great confidence, that at the earliest, if even then, the belief by his followers, that Jesus was God, stemmed from their belief in the resurrection. Without this belief, Jesus was just an apocalyptic prophet, whose preachings unsettled the Sanhedrin establishment regarding the political situation with Rome, leading to the call for his execution. Is there any extra-biblical evidence for the resurrection? Well, sadly not, and thus the event cannot be subjected to historical enquiry. We are limited to the New Testament narratives, with most of the writings on that subject being rightly classified as hearsay. We can be certain that when examined objectively, the writings of Paul, Luke, and Mark fall into that category. I have already detailed the variations and inconsistencies in the Gospel narratives, but it is worth considering the opinion of a Professor of Religious Studies whom we met previously, Bart D. Erhman:

> "We have already seen why the Gospels are so problematic for historians who want to know what really happened. This is especially true for the Gospel accounts of Jesus' resurrection. Are these the *sorts* of sources that historians would look for when examining a past event? Even apart from the fact that they were written forty to sixty-five years after the facts, by people who were not there to see these things happen, who were living in different parts of the world, at different times, and speaking different languages – apart from all this, they are filled with discrepancies, some of which cannot be reconciled. In fact, the Gospels disagree on nearly every detail in their resurrection narratives."[2]

We also must consider this opinion:

> "Placing the Gospels after Paul makes it clear that as written documents they are not the source of early Christianity but its product. The Gospel — the good news — of and about Jesus existed before the Gospels. They are the products of early Christian communities several decades after Jesus' historical life and tell us how those communities saw his significance in their historical context."[3]

My concerns neatly explained. The New Testament is my only source of historical evidence, but given the discrepancies, it is difficult to reconstruct a plausible narrative of what actually occurred. I cannot trust Paul's confirmation of the event, for his narrative is incoherent. Apart from the fact that there is no evidence of Jesus rising on the third day, just an empty tomb, none of these events were according to the Scriptures as claimed, and Paul, if he was the learned Pharisee that he claimed to have been, should have known that. Even the editors of the NKJV were unable to annotate the appropriate prophecies in their version of the New Testament! Note that at this point in history, none of the Gospels had been written, and thus when Paul referred to the Scriptures, he could only have meant the Old Testament.

Professor Erhman has a lot more to say, from an historian's perspective, on the burial and resurrection of Jesus, and I would recommend it as a worthwhile study, irrespective of one's beliefs. However, let me end this in what I believe to be an apt comment:

"Belief or unbelief in Jesus' resurrection is a matter of faith, not of historical knowledge."[4]

Ancient Hebrew View of Death

It is claimed that the resurrection was in accordance with the Scriptures, but if that be so, the nature of Christian claims about the bodily resurrection of Jesus should align with the Hebrew view of death. It makes no sense to argue that the two could be substantially different. It is widely known that whilst the Pharisees believed in an afterlife, the Sadducees did not, and we should seek to understand why they believed as they did. In case you are suspecting that I have wandered from the plot (again?), the issue is prophecy fulfillment, and if there was no prophecy of bodily resurrection from the dead, it could not have been fulfilled. I can find no such prophecy, and this brief section is to lend evidentiary weight as to why there would not have been anyway, at least, not in the form of a physical body of bones, flesh, and blood.

Adam was told: "You are dust, and to dust you shall return" (Genesis 3:19), which clearly means that our dead bodies will decay back into the ground. History has proven this to be so. The Hebrew Bible goes further:

> "For the fate of men and the fate of beast – they have one and the same fate: As one dies, so dies the other, and they all have the same spirit. Man has no superiority over beast, for all is futile. All go to the same place; all originate from dust and all return to dust. Who perceives that the spirit of man is the one who ascends on high while the spirit of the beast is the one that descends down into the earth? I therefore observed that there is nothing better for man than to be happy in what he is doing, for that is his lot. For who can enable him to see what will be after him?" (Ecclesiastes 3:19-22, TJB)

These words of King Solomon, if taken out of context, would substantiate the Sadducees view of the afterlife: there is no afterlife. On the other hand, the final verses of this book of wisdom provide the reasoning behind the counsel about being happy with our lot: "The sum of the matter, when all has been considered: Fear God and keep His commandments, for that is man's whole duty. For God will judge every deed – even everything hidden – whether good or evil" (vv. 12:13-14) One could reasonably infer from this that there will be an afterlife, for why else the judgement?

Another Old Testament view is here:

> "A man, born of a woman, has a short life span … he emerges like a blossom, and is then cut down; he flees like a shadow, and does not endure … You have made his limit which he cannot surpass … a man dies; he becomes feeble; a person perishes, and then where is he? As water flows from the sea, as the river becomes arid and dry, so a man lies down and does not rise. They do not awaken until the heavens are no more; they will not be roused from their slumber." (Job 14:1-12, TJB)

They do not awaken until the heavens are no more – that surely gives us hope of an afterlife. And one more, this from King David:

> "As for the heavens, the heavens are Hashem's; but the earth He has given to mankind. Neither the dead can praise God, nor any who descend into silence; but we will bless God from this time and forever. Halleluyah!" (Psalm 115:16-17, TJB)

The TJB notes: "Man need not perfect heaven because it is already dedicated to the holiness of God. But the earth is man's province, and he is bidden to perfect it. Indeed, mankind was created to elevate the earth to a heavenly state."[5] Why? "Not for our sake, Hashem, not for our sake, but for Your Name's sake give glory, for Your kindness and Your truth!" (Psalm 115:1) If all that be so, from where could any resurrection come, and in what form? James Tabor writes:

> "Like the Greeks, the Hebrews had a concept of an underworld of the dead that they called Sheol, somewhat akin to Hades, but it

was primarily a metaphor for the grave, and was often referred to as the 'pit'. Sheol is described as a land of silence and forgetfulness, a region gloomy, dark, and deep (Psalms 115:17; 6:5; 88:3-12; Isaiah 38:18). All the dead go down to Sheol, and there they make their bed together – whether good or evil, rich or poor, slave or free (Job 3:11-19). The dead in Sheol are mere shadows of their former embodied selves; lacking substance they are called shades (Psalm 88:10) … Death is a one-way street; it is the land of no return."[6]

So, we have all the dead in Sheol, awaiting the final Judgement, after which they will rise when *the heavens are no more*. This brings us to the question: If the dead shall rise in the Last Days, in what form will they rise? Both the Old and New Testaments have stories of people, like Lazarus, being "resurrected", but that was before they were in the grave: in each case, they eventually died like everyone else, and returned to dust.

Hebrew View of Resurrection

James Tabor notes, in relation to these miracles of dead people being revived:

> "The descriptive language in each of these cases is noteworthy: 'He lived', 'she got up', he sat up', or 'he came out'. These are verbal expressions of what took place, not conceptual terms about life after death more generally. In that sense the English term 'resurrection from the dead' is misleading. In the Hebrew Bible there is no noun for 'resurrection', just verbs describing the dead being revived. Even in the New Testament the Greek word *anastasis*, translated 'resurrection', occurs forty-two times; it literally means 'a standing up'."[7]

If you Google the etymology of "stasis", you will confirm this for yourself. Tabor continues: "Most scholars agree that there is only one unambiguous reference to a general resurrection of the dead in the entire Hebrew Bible", and for this we turn to the Book of Daniel:

"At that time [the End of Days] Michael will stand, the great heavenly prince who stands in support of the members of your people, and there will be a time of trouble such as there has never been since there was a nation until that time. But at that time your people will escape; everything that is found written in this book will occur. Many of those who sleep in the dusty earth will awaken: these for everlasting life and these for shame, for everlasting abhorrence. The wise will shine like the radiance of the firmament, and those who teach righteousness to the multitudes will shine like the stars, forever and ever. And as for you, Daniel, obscure the matters and seal the book until the time of the End; let many muse and let knowledge increase." (Daniel 12:1-4, TJB)

Wait a minute, you protest, what about Ezekiel? I was coming to that. Again quoting from James Tabor:

"Ezekiel's vision of the valley of dry bones is usually understood to be metaphorical, symbolizing the national regeneration of the people of Israel from Exile (Ezekiel 37:1-14). Isaiah 26:19 is sometimes cited as an early reference to a general resurrection but properly translated it says, 'Your dead shall live, my carcass shall arise', so the referents are unclear and the context suggests a symbolic rather than a literal meaning. There are a number of 'near death' references, but in each case they refer to escaping death by being rescued from Sheol (Jonah 2:2-6; Psalm 88:1-6). For a thorough discussion on these and related passages in the Hebrew Bible see Segal, *Life After Death*, pp. 255-61."[8]

I shall forego the thorough discussion, for now anyway, and simply accept this New Testament scholar at his word. Jewish commentators offer:

"There are two points of view in the Talmud as to whether this prophecy is a parable or whether the bones in the valley actually come to life (*Sanhedrin* 92b). In either case, it is understood by the commentators as a source of hope for Israel in its exile and as a reinforcement of the principle that the dead will come to life again in Messianic times."[9]

So far, from the Hebrew Scriptures, the evidence we have of a bodily resurrection is one which will occur only in the last days, or put another way, in Messianic times. If we have scant credible evidence of Jesus being the prophesied Messiah, the Christian case for Jesus' resurrection being prophesied, as Paul claimed, is insupportable. Remember that there are two issues: (1), did the resurrection actually occur; and (2), was it prophesied? Our focus in this study is primarily on the latter.

That notwithstanding, if there is to be such a resurrection, what would it look like, apart from what we have gleaned from the Book of Daniel? In short, the dead have been in Sheol, their former bodies turned to dust, and rather than being reconstituted, recreated, or whatever, into new bodies of flesh and blood, they will be transformed into a state of glorified immortal existence. It is of interest that two Gospel writers, and Paul, expressed views aligned with this. As Paul was the first witness, in terms of expressing his views in writing to the churches he founded, it is worth carefully noting what he has to say. Firstly, though, what does Jesus have to say in the Gospels, before we get to the later resurrection narratives? I would remind the reader that Mark's was the first Gospel to be written, and scholars opine that he was heavily influenced by Paul, as was Luke, so it should come as no surprise that they had a common view. Concerning the resurrection, Jesus said:

a. "Are you not therefore mistaken, because you do not know the Scriptures nor the power of God? For when they rise from the dead, they neither marry nor are given in marriage, but are like angels in heaven" (Mark 12:24-25); and

b. "The sons of this age marry and are given in marriage. But those who are counted worthy to attain that age, and the resurrection from the dead, neither marry nor are given in marriage; nor can they die anymore, for they are equal to the angels and are sons of God, being sons of the resurrection" [Ed. no doubt meaning his] Luke 20:34-36).

Jesus mentioned marriage specifically, for that was the context of the question he was asked, but if the resurrected are to be *like angels in heaven*, and will not marry, then inarguably, they will not have bodies similar to the one in which it was claimed, Jesus was raised. Angels are spiritual beings: no flesh, no bone, no blood.

Revisiting the Timeline

It is prudent to revisit the timeline of relevant events in the life of Paul, and his interaction with the Nazarene congregation in Jerusalem. We cannot be certain of the exact year of Jesus' death, but the New Testament does provide details of the length of periods between significant events, and it is these that we shall use. You may or may not accept the following dates which I have extracted from James Tabor's book, but I shall be using them as my guide. The exactitude of the dates is not that important – it is the sequence and intervening periods which are of major significance. Understanding the sequence of events helps us to understand how the resurrection narrative may have developed; and in highlighting the disparity between Paul's version and the later Christian interpretation, we get a glimpse of what may have happened, i.e., the post-resurrection narratives in the Gospels, which contradict Paul's theology, may well be fiction derived from traditions.

- 5 BCE – Birth of John the Baptist, Jesus, and Paul
- 30 CE – Execution of Jesus
- 37 CE – Paul's visionary experience on the road to Damascus
- 40 CE – Paul's first trip to Jerusalem; meets only Peter and James
- 50 CE – Paul's second trip to Jerusalem; Jerusalem conference
- 50 CE - James' Epistle
- 52-53 CE – First Thessalonians
- 55 CE – Letter to Galatians
- 56 CE – Paul's third and final trip to Jerusalem; confrontation with James
- 57 CE – First & Second Corinthians
- 56-58 CE – Letter to the Romans
- 62 CE – Execution of James

- 62-63 CE – Philemon
- 66-70 CE – First Jewish revolt against Rome
- 64-67 CE – Paul's imprisonment in Rome and his execution
- 66 CE – Gospel of Mark
- 67 CE – Gospel of Matthew
- 70 CE – Destruction of Jerusalem
- 90-95 CE – Luke and Acts

The first questions for which we seek answers are: (1), where was Paul between the death of Jesus, and his visionary appearance; (2), where was Paul between his visionary appearance and his first trip to Jerusalem; (3), where was Paul between his first and second visits to Jerusalem, and how long was that interval; and (4), what was happening in Jerusalem in the twenty years between the death of Jesus, and the Jerusalem conference?

(1) – The only evidence we have is from Acts 8:1-3, which suggests that Paul persecuted the Nazarenes who "were all scattered throughout the regions of Judea and Samaria, except the apostles". Just why Paul did not start with the Apostles is open to conjecture, and lends doubt that he persecuted anyone at all. If your goal is to suppress an uprising, where do you start: with the tail or with the head? That Paul took no action against the Apostles is circumstantial evidence that his story of persecuting the Nazarenes is false. We note from the interaction of Pilate with Jesus that the Romans had no interest in the religious affairs of the Jews: they were to sort that out for themselves. The Jews did not have prisons – they had other methods of punishment, in accordance with Torah. Thus, when Luke writes that Saul entered every house and dragged the men and women into prison, which prisons would those have been? The only prisons were Roman, and it is stretching credibility to believe that the Romans would have accepted Paul's prisoners. This story does not ring true. If Paul was not out and about persecuting the followers of Jesus, where was he? We have no way of knowing.

(2) - On the available evidence, after his visionary experience, Paul spent the period 37-40 CE firstly in Arabia, and then in Damascus (Galatians 1:17). His trip to Jerusalem in 40 CE seems to have been prompted because "the Jews plotted to kill him" (Acts 9:23) – a good reason to get out of town. According to Luke, he wanted to join the disciples in Jerusalem,

but due to his previous antagonism toward them, they were afraid of him. Instead, Barnabas took him to the Apostles, who for whatever reason, were not afraid of him (had they not heard of the previous persecutions?) According to Paul himself, he went up to Jerusalem to see Peter, not to join the disciples, remained with him for fifteen days, and also saw James, but none of the others (Galatians 1:18). According to Luke, Paul was banished back to Tarsus, and peace reigned in all the churches Judea, Galilee, and Samaria (Acts 9:31). According to Paul, he went into the regions of Syria and Cilicia, though whether under duress or not, he does not say.

(3) - "Then after fourteen years I went up again to Jerusalem" (Galatians 2:1). If the fourteen years started after Paul's first visit to Jerusalem, this could place our timeline into disarray, but the consensus of scholars is that it was fourteen years after his conversion. That leaves only ten years to be accounted. This online reference[10] is generally representative of most sources I have researched. As for the *Council of Jerusalem*, there is contention over the format that it took: a general council, or a private meeting as Paul describes: "privately to those who were of reputation" (Galatians 2:1). Luke portrays the meeting as amicable, whereas Paul's account, where he references false brethren secretly brought in to spy, seems less so. Paul later berated Peter, and seemed less than impressed with James (Galatians 2:11-12); in the opinion of many scholars, the relationship between Paul and the church under James in Jerusalem was far more strained than either Luke or Paul lets on.

(4) – The Book of Acts really says little about the Apostles, but mostly champions the activities of Paul. We have precious little literary evidence covering the activities in Jerusalem during the first twenty years after the crucifixion. We can get a sense of it from Paul's accounts, insofar as his gospel differs from that of the Apostles, and the religious traditions followed by the church under James, and the only writings of James that we have. Where Luke records "dissention among all the Jews throughout the world", because Paul was "a ringleader of the sect of the Nazarenes" (Acts 24:5), I contend that such was never the case, and that Luke was attempting to smooth over the differences between Paul and the Nazarenes. Paul was never a Nazarene, for they were a sect within Judaism, practising traditional customs which Paul opposed and preached against. I believe that we can discount Luke's attempts at reconciliation, and take Paul at

his word in his authentic letters to his churches. By inference then, the Nazarene church in those first twenty-plus years after the crucifixion, were the same Nazarenes that Rome later declared as heretics: a messianic sect within Judaism.

Paul's Gospel

I know, I appear to have wandered off-track again, but if we are to understand the mystery of the resurrection, and by that I do not mean the resurrection itself, but the competing narratives surrounding it, we need to investigate the background to those narratives. It is obvious, to me at least, that from the very beginning of Paul's missionary work, his gospel and his "Christianity" were very different to that of the early church in Jerusalem under James. Yes, some elements of a proclamation to the Gentiles would necessarily be different to a proclamation to the Jews, but that was not what Paul was preaching: he was preaching that his gospel was superior to that preached by the Apostles. Let us consider the evidence for this.

Quoting James Tabor: "There is good evidence that the two great apostles of Christianity, Peter and Paul, ended up bitter rivals. They seem to inseparably tied together, in later Christian history and tradition, that the idea of a severe quarrel between them seems inconceivable."[11] Tabor devotes an entire chapter of twenty four pages, entitled, "The Battle of The Apostles", to this issue, but here I shall just recount the bare bones of his argument.

> "Most scholars, including leading Roman Catholic ones, are agreed that given such sparse evidence, the tradition of Peter and Paul as founders of the Roman church, much less Peter as first bishop of Rome, is more likely a fourth-century tradition overlaid on a very flimsy factual foundation."[12]

Backtracking, John the Baptist has been described as "a fiery apocalyptic preacher, zealous for Israel's messianic redemption, and a strict adherent to the Torah". Peter, his brother Andrew, and Phillip, were disciples of John, when Jesus recruited them (John 1:37-44); thus, they were likely as zealous for the Torah and their ancestral traditions as John, and would probably not have followed Jesus if he preached differently. During his public life, Jesus treats Peter as the leader of the Apostles, but after the crucifixion, Peter appears to cede the leadership to James, with Peter seemingly acting as his emissary. During his visit to Jerusalem, Paul met with James and the elders, where he was accused that "you teach all the Jews who are among the Gentiles to forsake Moses, saying that they ought not to circumcise their children nor to walk according to the customs" (Acts 21:21). Luke does not record Paul denying the charge: I wonder why – would that not have been an opportune moment to deny the charge? The elders appear to compromise, instructing Paul to demonstrate "that you yourself also walk orderly and keep the law" (v. 21:24), and stating that the Gentiles "must keep themselves from things offered to idols, from blood, from things strangled, and from sexual immorality" (v. 25). Examined closely, these prohibitions relate to the idolatrous practices of the Romans and Greeks, and as I argue in another study[13], we cannot extrapolate this to mean that the Jerusalem church agreed to the Gentiles not following Torah. In Judaism, the general rule for Gentiles was, and is, that they must follow the Noahide Laws, but the overlap between these two legal systems is extensive.

Though Paul was initially comfortable with Barnabas, who for years had worked alongside him as a missionary partner, the incident at Antioch (Galatians 2:11-20) caused a rift between them, ending with a parting of the ways (Acts 15:39). The issue was Torah observance, with Paul accusing Peter and Barnabas of hypocrisy. It is obvious that Paul holds the Jerusalem leadership in contempt, referring to them in a sarcastic and dismissive manner: "But from those who seemed to be something – whatever they were, it makes no difference to me; God shows personal favouritism to no man – for those who seemed to be something added nothing to me." (Galatians 2:6) *Those who seemed to be something* were the men that Jesus chose as his Apostles; thus, Paul is refuting himself when he says that *God shows personal favouritism to no man*, for he clearly believes he is favoured. Why else would he be so dismissive of the chosen of Jesus? In dismissing them, he is dismissing the Gospel that they preached, the one they learned personally from three years as Jesus' disciples. Why did Paul describe James, Cephas, and John, to the Galatians as "seemed to be pillars"? (v. 2:9) If Paul's Gospel is different, and even superior, was the Jesus he experienced the same Jesus that the Apostles knew? Paul suggested as much: "For if he who comes preaches another Jesus whom we have not preached, or if you ... received a different gospel" (2 Corinthians 11:4). Who were these others preaching differently, if not those sent out from Jerusalem? Paul seems to confirm this: "For I consider that I am not at all inferior to the most eminent apostles" (v. 11:5). Paul claims that "the truth of Christ is in me" (v. 10), dismissing those who disagree as "false apostles, deceitful workers ... from Satan himself" (vv. 13-14). Paul again identifies these *others*: "Are they Hebrews? So am I. Are they Israelites? So am I. Are they the seed of Abraham? So am I." (v. 22) But then the boasting: "Are they ministers of Christ? – I speak as a fool [in indignant irony] – I am more." (v. 23) Christian apologetics interpret these verses to mean that Paul is simply defending himself against those who claim to be superior to him, but where is the evidence? Certainly, we can accept that those from James in Jerusalem disagreed with Paul, but on what basis can we accept that they claimed superior knowledge as Paul suggests? Borrowing from Shakespeare: *methinks he protests too much.*

"I know a man in Christ" (2 Cor 12:2) likely refers to Paul himself, using a way of speaking connected with the thought that "if any man be in Christ he is a new creature" (2 Corinthians 5:17; Galatians 6:15). *Fourteen years ago* would date the experience circa 43 CE, just prior to his long journey from Antioch before his second visit to Jerusalem. We only have Paul's word that he was caught up to the third heaven, and given what else I have discerned about Paul, I strongly doubt that it ever happened. There is much more than could be said on this subject, but I do not want to distract too much from my primary theme: prophecy fulfillment. What I wanted to demonstrate here, regarding Paul's Gospel, is that it departed from the teachings of Jesus as understood by the Apostles, and what was taught in Jerusalem under James. Despite the attempts of Luke in Acts to cover over the cracks, they are far too evident to ignore. Paul had his own Gospel, one not just specific to the Gentiles, but one which contradicted that to the Jews. It should come as no surprise then, that if Paul perceived a different Jesus, he should perceive a different resurrection. If he was not the trained Pharisee that he claimed to have been, an opinion I share, and thus his knowledge of the Hebrew Scriptures was suspect, this would explain why he claimed that the resurrection was according to the Scriptures (1 Corinthians 15:4). His audience would likely have been ignorant of such matters.

Paul's Version of the Resurrection

"If Christ is not risen, then our preaching is
empty and your faith is also empty."
(1 Corinthians 15:14)

What if Paul's understanding of the resurrection is not the same as we find in the resurrection narratives in the Gospels? If his resurrected Christ is a different Christ, should it not be said that the faith he preached was also different, and that our own "resurrection" would be different? It is not immediately obvious, and I did not notice until it was pointed out to me, but this seems to be the case. We noted earlier that we are wont to read the New Testament backwards, starting with the Gospels, thus falling into the natural trap of understanding Paul in the Gospel context. However, if we read Paul first, because he wrote first, and was first to document his encounter with the risen Jesus, we may be able to overcome our Gospel derived presuppositions. Of course, like me, you probably require the guidance of New Testament scholars: what follows is mostly their work, and for this particular exercise, as before, I have been primarily using "Paul and Jesus"[14] by James Tabor.

The four Gospels narrate finding the empty tomb, and then we have varying accounts of Jesus appearing to his disciples, sharing a meal with them, and even doubting Thomas being invited to put his hand into the spear wound in Jesus' side. All of this is to substantiate the claim that Jesus rose from the dead with the same wounded body that was entombed. The NKJV even claims this to be prophecy fulfillment of Isaiah 53:9. However, if we closely study 1 & 2 Corinthians, Paul seemingly does not agree; consider these words:

> "So also is the resurrection of the dead. The body is sown in corruption, it is raised in incorruption. It is sown in dishonour, it is raised in glory. It is sown in weakness, it is raised in power. It is sown a natural body, it is raised a spiritual body. There is a natural body, and there is a spiritual body … Now this I say, brethren, that flesh and blood cannot inherit the kingdom of God, nor does corruption inherit incorruption. Behold I tell you a mystery:

> We shall not all sleep, but we shall all be changed – in a moment, in the twinkling of an eye at the last trumpet." (1 Corinthians 15:42-52)

Now, pretend for the moment that this was the first that you were hearing of Jesus' resurrection: There is a natural body, and there is a spiritual body; the natural body will be raised as a spiritual body, because flesh and blood cannot inherit the kingdom of God. Would you think that the body in which you will be raised, will be the same body as the one you were then inhabiting? Paul states further: "So when this corruptible has put on incorruption, and this mortal has put on immortality, then shall be brought to pass the saying that is written: *Death is swallowed up in victory.*" (1 Cor 15:53-54) Paul has just told you the mystery that not all shall sleep, but all will be changed: why would you, being still alive, need to be changed at the Second Coming? If you and your fellow believers will be taken up to heaven in your existing bodies, very much as portrayed in Tim LaHaye's story, *Left Behind,* just disappearing from Earth from wherever you were at the time of the impending Rapture, why would Paul have preached that your resurrection will involve a metamorphosis from your mortal body of flesh and blood, into an immortal spiritual body?

Even more to the point, why was Paul's understanding, which according to him, he received directly from Jesus in heaven, be different to the later accounts of the disciples who encountered a risen Christ of flesh and blood, still scarred (corrupted) from his ordeal? This raises the question: If Paul had seen the risen Christ as he claimed (1 Cor 15:8), did Jesus appear as he is said to have appeared to the Apostles, scars and all, or did Paul see a Jesus in a different form? What was it that convinced Paul that he was seeing the risen Jesus, when according to most opinions, Paul had never met Jesus, and therefore could not have recognised him?

The Rapture aside, if you are to be raised as Jesus was raised, it will be in a body reconstituted from the dust of the body in which you lived, although I am unsure of from what age, not that it will matter. The point is, we have two versions of the resurrection: (1) Paul's version of an immortal spiritual body; and (2), the Gospel's version of a body of flesh and blood, but nevertheless immortal. If Paul was right, the resurrection narrative in the Gospels is largely false, and if the Gospels were right, then

Paul was not informed directly by Jesus, unless God deliberately sought to have two versions, which I would think unlikely.

Paul's letter to the Romans also gives us an insight to his thinking. Paul wrote: "… concerning His son Jesus Christ our Lord, who was born of the seed of David according to the flesh, and declared to be the Son of God with power according to the Spirit of holiness, by the resurrection of the dead" (Romans 1:3-4). *Born of the seed of David according to the flesh* means that Jesus had a natural birth, and that Joseph was his biological father, a descendant of King David. "Seed" cannot be allegorised to mean the "egg" of his mother, Mary - the contemporary language does not allow it, so Paul was unaware of the claim of a virgin birth, and would not have made the link with Isaiah 7:14 as others later attempted to do. Next, "**declared to be** the Son of God with power … **by the resurrection** of the dead" [emphasis mine]: a natural reading of this assertion is that Jesus was not declared the Son of God until God had raised him from the dead. This suggests to me that Paul saw Jesus as a natural man, as Paul himself was, but one anointed by God for a special mission, and it was only after successful completion of his mission that Jesus was raised from the dead in glory, in a new spiritual body, and declared to be the Son of God. At this point, you might care to refresh your mind with the discussion in Chapter 9-3 regarding the term, son of God, not being unique to Jesus.

This brings us to Colossians and the concept of Jesus being "the image of the invisible God, the firstborn of over all creation" (Colossians 1:15). We can be confident that Paul did not write this letter, but if he did, he should have known of Genesis 1:27, that "God created man in His own image, in the image of God", so it is reasonable to assume that he would have meant something different here, but what? To my mind, this confirms my earlier contention that for Paul, and presumably whoever wrote in his name, the risen Jesus was not as per the later Gospels, but as an immortal spiritual being. This is where I sense that the author of Colossians, whilst attempting to invoke the authority of Paul by writing under his name, nevertheless was influenced by others, for verses 16-17 represent a later theological development, with concepts that do not appear in authentic Pauline writings. As I contended earlier, Paul saw Jesus as a man of flesh and blood, only later glorified in a spiritual body when raised from the dead. Colossians echoes the first chapter in John's Gospel, which has me wondering about the date of authorship, and who was being influenced by whom. A consensus has Colossians written circa 60-65, with John some twenty to thirty years later, so how did Johannine theology make its way into Colossians? Could the author have been a disciple of John, or was there later additions to the original work?

The Appearances of the Risen Jesus

I am always curious of Paul's understanding when he wrote: "He was seen by Cephas and then by the twelve" (1 Cor 15:5): who were these other twelve? Judas was gone, and Matthias was yet to be appointed. It becomes even more confusing when he adds: "After that he was seen by James, then by all the apostles" (1 Cor 15:7): were Peter and James not one of the twelve, nor Apostles? Had Paul not learned of the betrayal by Judas, and his subsequent suicide? Another issue is Paul's claim that there are two types of body, the natural and the spiritual, and what is raised is not the natural body, but the spiritual body (1 Cor 15:42-44). This does not argue against a physical body, but that the spiritual body is a transformation of the natural body, one that is imperishable and immortal. I wonder whether those who were made aware of the empty tomb had that same understanding?

The variations in the accounts suggest to me that their origins were from four separate traditions. It is plausible that the tomb, where they thought that Jesus was buried, was empty on the Sunday, but that aside, the rules of evidence preclude the acceptance of what followed. A good story, but was it true?

A Recent Discovery

We have no literary or historical evidence of the source of Paul's knowledge of Jesus' resurrection. If he did persecute early Christians, which I doubt, he could have learned from them, giving him cause to persecute them. If he learned it directly from Jesus, he heard a different account, as discussed above. Another hypothesis has arisen following an archaeological find in 2000, known as *Gabriel's Revelation*. If you Google this title, you will be presented with numerous online entries. What follows is extracted from a document available online here[15]. The article is entitled, *A New Dead Sea Scroll in Stone? Bible-like Prophecy Was Mounted in a Wall 2,000 Years Ago*, by Ada Yardeni.

No-one is sure of the provenance of the stones - "Chances are it came from Jordan. It simply appeared on the antiquities market, however, and was acquired by Zurich collector David Jeselsohn, who has kindly permitted me to publish it. At one point, it apparently broke in three pieces, which still have not yet been glued together. Alas, the text bears another resemblance to the famous Dead Sea Scrolls. It is very badly preserved, with *lacunae* all over." The text is written in ancient Hebrew, eighty seven lines written in ink on stone, with twelve lines unintelligible. None of the lines are complete. If you download the pdf file for yourself, you will see the attempts at translation in both Hebrew and English. As it is so fragmented, I will quote directly from the article comments, rather than attempt to reproduce the writing itself:

> "The text has not been identified, but it is clearly a literary composition, similar to Biblical prophecies. It is written in the first person, perhaps by someone named Gabriel ("I Gabriel," line 77), so I have named the text "Gabriel's Vision." It is apparently a collection of short prophecies addressed to someone in the second person. Like the prophets of old, whoever wrote this composition proclaims the "word of Yahweh," the personal name of the Hebrew God. And, again like the Bible, many of the prophecies open with the words "Thus (or therefore) said the Lord [that is, *Yahweh* and sometimes the more generic *Elohim*] of Hosts." Sometimes the text uses *Elohei Yisrael*, "God of Israel." There are also numerous references to Yahweh's *kavod*, or glory, familiar to all students of the Hebrew Bible.

> The text also mentions "My servant David." Elsewhere it refers to "David the servant of Yahweh." Jerusalem is also mentioned several times. Apparently the composer of this texts supports the Davidic dynasty. And God "shows mercy to thousands," the same expression used in Exodus 20:6, Deuteronomy 5:10 and Jeremiah

32:18. "And I will shake the heaven and the earth" (lines 24–25) is a direct quote from the prophet Haggai (2:6). The text also includes expressions from books of the Biblical prophets Zechariah and Daniel. But the composition also includes expressions that do not seem to have parallels elsewhere. The text as a whole is not known from any other Jewish source.

In addition to the name Gabriel, the composition refers to the "messenger (or angel) Michael," who is mentioned in Daniel 10:13, in the New Testament (Revelation 12:7 and Jude 9) and in extra-Biblical sources like Enoch and the Dead Sea Scroll known as the War Scroll (1QM). In these extra-Biblical sources Michael is frequently mentioned together with Gabriel. It is difficult to be more specific, but it does suggest that the text as a whole is apocalyptic (referring to the end of days), as these are clearly apocalyptic figures. We may conjecture that a rivalry between two messianic groups is involved. There seems to be no doubt that the composer of this text belongs to the group supporting the Davidic messiah. It is difficult to say more.

Perhaps this intriguing text only emphasizes the variety of Jewish movements at the turn of the era—and how much about them we don't yet know."

You can make of that what you will, but if it is *clearly apocalyptic*, and suggests *a rivalry between two messianic groups*, the dating of the writing is significant. The article further states:

"Knohl's translation of the first-century B.C. "Gabriel's Revelation" inscription—and its revelations on Jewish messianism—pre-date the life of Jesus. What does "Gabriel's Revelation" tell us about the Jewish concept of a messiah leading up to the life of Jesus? Ada Yardeni's analysis of the artefact and Israel Knohl's discussion of the Jewish origins of a suffering Messiah and resurrection on the third day put "Gabriel's Revelation" in its ancient context while highlighting its significance in the latest theological debates."

You may wonder where I am going with this, but bear with me, this is important in the context of Paul's understanding of the resurrection of Jesus. Returning to James Tabor:

> "Experts date it to the end of the first century B.C., so it is definitely pre-Christian. The text purports to be a revelation of the angel Gabriel about the final apocalyptic battles between the forces of good and evil. We have various texts from this period dealing with this theme, including some of the Dead Sea scrolls, but the second half of the text contains something entirely new. According to Israel Knohl of Hebrew University, the final section of the text focuses on the death and resurrection of a messianic leader, most likely Simon of Perea, who led a revolt in Judea in 4 B.C. following the death of Herod the Great.[16] Josephus reports that Simon's followers crowned him … king of the Jews … What is fascinating and new about this text is that the slain leader, who has, according to the text, become 'dung of the rocky crevices', his body decayed in the desert heat, is nonetheless addressed by the angel Gabriel: 'I command you, prince of princes in three days you shall live!'".[17]

Curious, is it not? We have pre-Christian writings which describe a messianic leader slain in battle, and later instructed to rise again in three days. The similarities between this and the story of Jesus are too amazing to ignore. Reference (16) above is a magazine article by Israel Knohl, dated April 2007, and his conclusions are worth considering:

> The first mention of the "slain Messiah" called Mashiah ben Yosef (Messiah Son of Joseph) is in the Talmud (Sukkah 52a). In my book "The Messiah Before Jesus" (University of California Press, 2000), I argue that the story of this slain messiah is based on historical fact. I believe it is connected to the Jewish revolt in the Land of Israel following the death of King Herod in 4 B.C.E. This Jewish insurrection was brutally suppressed by the armies of Herod and the Roman emperor Augustus, and the messianic leaders of the revolt were killed. These events set the

slain Messiah Son of Joseph tradition into motion and paved the way for the emergence of the concept of "catastrophic messianism." Interpretations of biblical text helped to shape the belief that the death of the messiah was a necessary and indivisible component of salvation. My conclusion, based on apocalyptic writings dating to this period, was that certain groups believed the messiah would die, be resurrected in three days, and ascend to heaven (see "The Messiah Before Jesus," 27-42).

So, here is my question: Did Paul, believing that Jesus was the prophesied Messiah, and anticipating the End of Days as his writings clearly show, appropriate this story and apply it to Jesus? Did subsequent writers of the Gospels, taking their lead from Paul, then include that story in their version of the Jesus narrative? Such is entirely plausible, if we accept the scholarly opinion that the Gospels are the product of a developed tradition is correct.

Summary

There are so many inconsistencies and outright contradictions in the burial and resurrection narratives, that one is entitled to question the veracity of the entire episode. There is no need to recap, in truth, the recap would be almost as long as the original discussion, so let us attempt but a brief summary. There is no agreement on who was present when the body of Jesus was taken from the cross; none on the anointing; none on the circumstances surrounding the discovery of an empty tomb; the possibility that the body was removed to a different, permanent tomb; and two versions of the form of the risen Jesus. Paul's account more closely follows the ancient Hebrew understanding, but that understanding, except from the discovery of the recording of *Gabriel's Revelation*, is accompanied by the belief that the dead would rise only in the Last Days. There is no prophecy in the Hebrew Scriptures of the Jewish *mashiach* dying and rising again from the dead, and no prophecy, or even theology, about being resurrected body, bones, flesh and blood.

Revisiting Paul's claim, *"and that he was buried, and that he rose again the third day according to the Scriptures"* (1 Corinthians 15:4), Christian bible scholar, C.H. Dodd wrote: "Christ 'rose the third say', says the ancient formula quoted by Paul in his first epistle to the Corinthians, 'according to the scriptures.' But in the Scriptures – *videlicet* [Ed. viz], in Hosea 6:1-3 – it is Israel whom God will raise on the third day."[18] Repeating what was written earlier, Hosea 6:2 states: "He will heal us after two days; on the third day He will raise us up and we will live before Him." In this context, *yom* refers to *a long period of time*, in this case, the two days are the two exiles in Egypt and Babylonia, both of which were *healed* in the form of the First and Second Temples, but at the end of the third day, following the destruction of the Second Temple in 70 CE, God will raise up the people of Israel with the final redemption and the Third Temple.

In short, there is nothing in the Hebrew Scriptures which squares with the Christian understanding. Even if Jesus was resurrected, body and all, after his crucifixion and entombment, it has nothing at all to do with prophecy. Despite my continuing fascination with the resurrection narrative, I am confident that I can put it aside in the context of this study into prophecy fulfillment. On the other hand, serious students of this topic ought to consider the evidence that I have presented, based on the thoughtful work of scholars.

REFERENCES:

1. Gibson, Shimon, *The Final Days of Jesus: The Archaeological Evidence*, HarperOne, New York, NY, 2009, p. 165
2. Ehrman, Bart D., *How Jesus Became God: The Exaltation of a Jewish Preacher from Galilee*, Harper One, New York, NY, 2014, p. 133
3. https://www.huffingtonpost.com/marcus-borg/a-chronological-new-testament_b_1823018.html
4. Ehrman, *Ibid*, p. 143
5. Scherman, Rabbi Nosson, *The Tanach*, Mesorah Publications, ArtScroll English Edition, Brooklyn, NY, 2011, p. 1000
6. Tabor, James D., *Paul and Jesus: How the Apostle Paul Transformed Christianity*, Simon & Schuster Paperbacks, New York, NY, 2012, p. 53
7. *Ibid*, p. 56
8. *Ibid*, p. 250

9. Scherman, *Ibid*, p. 833

10. http://matthewmcgee.org/paultime.html

11. Tabor, *Ibid*, p. 203

12. *Ibid*, p. 205, citing Raymond E. Brown and John P. Meier, *Antioch and Rome: New Testament Cradles of Catholic Christianity* (New York, Paulist Press 2004), p. 98

13. Talbot, Wayne, *Christians Too, Must Obey*: Putting A Fence Around Torah, Xlibris, Bloomington, IN, 2017, pp. 472-473

14. Tabor, *Ibid*

15. https://www.biblicalarchaeology.org/get-ebook/thank-you/?freemium_id=24196

16. http://www.haaretz.com/magazine/week-s-end/in-three-days-you-shall-live-1.218552

17. Tabor, *Ibid*, pp. 65-66

18. Beale, G.K., *The Right Doctrine from the Wrong Texts? Essays on the Use of the Old Testament in the New*, Baker Academic, Grand Rapids, MI, 1994, p. 180

CHAPTER 9-5

NECESSITY FOR A REDEEMER

"It is written in the Book of Torah of Moses, which Hashem has commanded saying, 'Fathers shall not be put to death because of sons, and sons shall not be put to death because of fathers; rather a man should be put to death for his own sin."
(2 Kings 14:6, TJB)

If God commanded that a man should be put to death for his own sin, and for no other, how could God require an innocent man to be put to death for the sins of all? Isaiah was instructed to prophesy:

> "A redeemer will come to Zion, and to those of Jacob who repent from willful sin – the word of Hashem. And as for Me, this is My covenant with them, said Hashem: My spirit which is upon you and My words that I have placed in your mouth will not be withdrawn from your mouth not from the mouth of your offspring nor from the mouth of your offspring's offspring, said Hashem, from this moment and forever." (Isaiah 59:20-21)

According to this prophecy, the Redeemer will come to those who repent from willful sin, yet Jesus said that he came to those who do not repent, i.e. the lost (Matthew 15:24), and to the sick (Mark 2:17). In the Hebrew Scriptures, those who repent are considered righteous, even though they sin (Ecclesiastes 7:20), but Jesus said that "I did not come to call the righteous, but sinners to repentance". Whatever Jesus had in mind for his mission, it could not have been the same as that of the Redeemer in Isaiah 59. Throughout the Hebrew Scriptures, redemption concerns not spiritual rescue, but a physical rescue of the Children of Israel and their descendants, from those who would oppress them, culminating in the restoration of Jerusalem and the presence therein of God forever.

Substitutionary Atonement

"This people have committed a grievous sin and made themselves a god of gold. And now, if You would but forgive their sin! - but if not, erase me now from Your book that You have written. Hashem said to Moses, 'Whoever has sinned against Me, I shall erase him from My book."
(Exodus 32:32-33, TJB)

My contention here is that Moses offered himself in *substitutionary atonement*, but God said "No", everyone is responsible for their own sin, and no-one else can atone on their behalf. "The Lord your God will raise up for you a Prophet like me from your midst, from your brethren, him you shall hear." (Deut 18:15). Acts 3:22 attempts to link this passage to Jesus, saying that Jesus is the prophesied prophet, like Moses, whom God will raise up. But if God refused Moses his offer to die for the sins of the idolators, affirming that we each must be held responsible for our own sins, why would He later change His mind and appoint a subsequent prophet to die for our sins instead?

The Christian Doctrine

Christianity teaches the doctrine of *Substitutionary Atonement*, i.e., that Jesus was substituted for humanity and punished for our faults, to pay for the sins that we had committed, and reconcile us to God. The problem is this: there is no such doctrine in the Old Testament, and no prophecy of such an event. There are several references in the New Testament:

a. "For even the Son of Man did not come to be served, but to serve, and to give his life a ransom for many." (Mark 10:45)
b. "For you were brought at a price" (1 Cor 6:20).
c. "For He made him who knew no sin to be sin for us, that we might become the righteousness of God in him." (2 Cor 5:21)
d. "For Christ also suffered once for sins, the just for the unjust, that he might bring us to God" (1 Peter 3:18).

Christian apologists attempt to claim that this was prophesied in Isaiah 53:5, but a closer examination of the text reveals that to be not so. Firstly, consider Isaiah 45:12-13, where God explicitly states that what He did for His people, He did "not with a price and not with a bribe". Now if God is consistent, predictable, and thus *faithful* in the way that He deals with His creation, we cannot have Him changing His mind, as 1 Corinthians 6:20 asserts with the claim of us being bought with a price. One would have to admit that as far as proof texts go, those stated above are rather feeble. We know from history that during the first hundred years after the death of Jesus, far more Gentiles than Jews joined this new church, and even some unspecified number of Jewish followers fell away. By the time that the church became established in Rome, hardly any Jews were joining the cause. Rome had departed from *The Way*, the path followed by the *Nazarenes*, a Jewish sect of Judaism believing Jesus to be the Messiah, and in truth, the original *Christians*. Over time, Rome sought to persecute these people as heretics, and by the end of the fourth century, this sect had practically ceased to exist.

Why was this, apart from the anti-Jewishness of the early church? Quite simply, those Jews, learned in the Scriptures, did not believe in the necessity for a redeemer, one who had to die for their sins. Following is my reasoning based on what I believe about God, and what I have read in the Hebrew Scriptures.

As we learn from *epistemology*, all knowledge is built on prior knowledge, so let us start with a familiar scenario to establish context.

Scenario

You are a member of a jury with the responsibility of deciding liability for an accidental death. The plaintiff argues that the death was caused by a defect in the product, which the manufacturer knew about before releasing it for sale. Evidence was presented of internal discussions, resulting in the decision to release the product, without mentioning the defect specifically, but with the common warning that misuse of the product could result in injury or death. The manufacturer also provided detailed instructions on proper use of the product. The defendant (the manufacturer) argued that he could not be held liable for misuse of the product, and suggested that the user had either failed to read the instructions, or had read them but ignored them. The plaintiff argued that such was an acceptable defence if, and only if, there were no known defects in the product. Further, the plaintiff argued, that the manufacturer knew, or should have known, that misuse of the product was probable, and that serious injury or death would result.

How would you decide the case?

Would you find in favour of the manufacturer, on the basis that the death was caused by misuse of the product; would you find in favour of the plaintiff, because the product should not have been released with a known defect; or would you attribute blame to both parties in varying degrees?

What is your sense of justice in this case?

The Case Now Before You

Who is ultimately responsible for our sin?

It may seem the most outrageous blasphemy, but as I see it, God is ultimately responsible for the sins of the world. If you manufacture a faulty device and it causes harm to others, you, the manufacturer, are held responsible. If, as a pregnant woman, you drink, smoke, and indulge in other behaviours harmful to your unborn child, you are morally responsible for any defects the baby may suffer as a result. Now, I am not for a moment suggesting that we are not responsible for our own sins: on the contrary, I exhort everybody to take full responsibility for their actions and/or omissions. The issue here is entirely different.

Christianity teaches that God sent His Son to die for us, to make reparations for our sins, because no level of repentance, by a finite human, could ever satisfy an infinite God's requirement for justice. To sin against God is to cause infinite offence, because God is infinite: thus, reparation for our sins must match the nature of the offence, and the one offended. The only acceptable solution, therefore, would be a sacrifice by an entity who could match the degree of offence: an infinite offence requires an infinite reparation by a sinless entity.

That sounds logical, so far as it goes, but it misses an essential truth: it was God who created the conditions that led inevitably to Him being offended. In a sense, the offences that God has endured have been His Own fault – had He not created imperfect, fallible humans with free will, the problem would never have arisen.

Believing God to be omniscient, I assume that God knew what He was doing when He created humankind with free will, thus foreknowing that we would sin against Him. If God foreknew that in creating humankind, He would also create the circumstances whereby sin became inevitable, then being infinitely responsible, He would take ultimate responsibility for our transgressions against Him, our Creator. You may argue that this was the reason that He sent His son to die for us, but I contend otherwise.

In human affairs, we have concepts of "due care" and "do no harm". If this is an expression of morality, and all morality comes from God, then we must accept that these concepts come from God. Did God cause Creation with *due care* and an intention to *do no harm*? If we accept the Christian narrative, then no, He did not: He released an imperfect product with knowledge aforethought. But such accusations cannot be levelled against God – for God is perfectly moral and good in every sense that we can think about Him. Thus logically, God did exercise infinitely perfect, due care, and any harm that He allowed to occur in His Creation had to have been seen by God, as necessary in the accomplishment of His Plan.

We know from Isaiah 45:7 and Amos 3:6 that God is responsible for so-called natural phenomena (sun, light, dark, earthquakes, storms, floods, rain) that can cause both well-being and calamity, but theologians argue that these passages cannot be interpreted in a moral sense. I disagree. If it is God who caused it, then God is morally responsible, for God had a choice in the design of His Creation. I have contended elsewhere that the common perception of "natural" is arbitrarily restrictive – why are animals natural but humans not? Why is not all of Creation "natural" from God's perspective? I will not argue this point to a conclusion here, but mention it in passing in case these passages are in the minds of the readers.

Now back to the main theme: if God accepts the ultimate responsibility for our sins, and I believe that He does, then why would He demand of Himself the most excruciating sacrifice – the torture and crucifixion of His Son (or more specifically, a human incarnation of Himself)? If we take responsibility for an offence, do we set out to cruelly punish ourselves? There is an irksome practice in some Christian communities where on Good Friday, people whip themselves - mortification of the flesh by self-flagellation. From my reading of Torah, not only does God not desire such sacrifice, but He has specifically prohibited it. *"You are the children of the Lord your God: you shall not cut yourselves"* (Deut 14:1). That seems unambiguous to me: why would anyone ignore God on that issue?

If we create the circumstances, either deliberately, by omission, or by carelessness, whereby others are harmed, the civil judicial system may rightly hold us accountable, and even impose a penalty, but would we impose a penalty upon ourselves, other than to make reparation? Well, yes, we might, for we are human and fallible, and may well feel compelled to take further actions to appease our guilt. Guilt has been known to drive people to all sorts of behaviours, even suicide, but understand that guilt is a human feeling, and does not apply to God. If God does no wrong, as I here contend, then He would never have occasion to feel guilty, punish Himself, or cause others to suffer on His behalf. Can we say that God did do wrong in creating us with free will, such that we would offend Him? Of course not!

When we have children, we do so with the foreknowledge (hopefully) that from time to time, or even more often, our offspring will offend us, sometimes to the extent of outright rebellion. Do we seek reparation from *ourselves*, as parents, for having children in the first place? Of course not. We will hold our children accountable to the extent that is reasonable, given their maturity and circumstances, but at the same time, we will accept our complicity, at least I hope so, in creating the circumstances whereby we placed ourselves in harm's way. We cannot blame children for being children, for it is we, their parents, who caused their existence. We can, and should, expect a level of behaviour, but ultimately, it is we who must acknowledge that offence against us was our choice. Why would God be any different? Does God condemn us for having the ability to sin, and being imperfect, commit sin? Yes, on the latter, but as He is responsible for the former, He accepts sincere repentance, as is only just and fair.

Remember the guilt expressed by the creators of the atom bomb, when it was dropped on Japan? As they were developing the technology, they knew the harm it would cause when used, but they went ahead anyway. After the bomb was used, their consciences recognised their complicity in the death and destruction that followed. Would God not recognise, and accept, His complicity in the offences against Himself, when He created human kind with free will? Because I believe in His omniscience and infinitely perfect sense of responsibility, I believe that He does accept ultimate responsibility for His creative actions.

Now, that is not to suggest that we are not held accountable for our sins – that is an entirely separate issue. The issue here is whether God would require of Himself to be accountable for His Creation. As God can do no wrong, for what should He hold Himself accountable? Why would God insist, of Himself, that He must make reparations to Himself, for His own actions? But such is essence of what Christianity unknowingly teaches: that because God created the circumstances whereby His creation would offend Him, God is somehow obliged by His Justice to make reparation to Himself by sacrificing Himself. We find an interesting perspective in Jewish commentaries on Genesis. When we read of God saying: "Let us make man in Our image" (Gen 1:26), Christians imagine the Trinity, but in Judaism, it is aspects of God's nature in view. Firstly, we find the use of *pluralis majestatis* (the royal "we") in many other parts of Scripture, so we should not discount that possibility. Another explanation offered, is that before God decided to create humankind with free will, the opportunity to offend, and thus the necessity for punishment, God's Wisdom debated with His Justice as to the fairness of such a course of action. How could God justify to Himself, a creation that inevitably resulted in such misery and death? God's Justice was satisfied by His Grace, and Love for those who were obedient to His Will: it was considered fair that all should be given the opportunity. Thus, God's Justice was satisfied even before Creation.

The Christian theology concerning the need for a divine sacrifice, for the forgiveness of sins, clearly makes sense to many people, but to me it denies the infinitude of God. I cannot conceive of an omnipotent, omniscient God saying to Himself:

> "Hmmm. I will create some angels with a degree of free will, such that some will rebel; and then I can use one of these fallen angels to pretend to be a serpent, and tempt Eve in the Garden, knowing full well that she will succumb; and then tempt Adam who will also succumb; and then I will kick them out of the Garden (which I planned to be only temporary anyway) because they sinned against Me, even though I always knew they would; and then I won't be satisfied with any act of repentance on their part, but will send a part of Me, aka the Son (Second Person of the Trinity), to suffer a gruesome death, just so that I can satisfy My Own Sense of Justice, even though the whole chain of events was My Fault in the first place."

I accept that some would view this narrative as blasphemy and sacrilegious, but in essence, *that* is the Christian doctrine when it fails to acknowledge that behind the whole plot, is an infinite God who knows what He is doing and why. The Christian narrative has God, from Genesis onward, saying: "Oops, I didn't see that coming, we will have to resort to Plan B", and then C, and D, and so forth. At the same time, Christianity says that God did foresee how His Plan would unfold as testified in 1 Peter 1:2 and Revelation 13:8. We cannot have it both ways: either God foreknew all that would happen, and willed it so, accepting responsibility for the chain of events, or He did not, in which case He is neither omniscient nor infinitely responsible.

Finally, there is no prophecy of the Messiah being sacrificed for the forgiveness of sin, and those verses which might seem to suggest so have been deliberately mistranslated, or taken out of context. We have already reviewed those prophecies in a separate section.

Forgiveness Without Sacrifice

Christianity teaches that the sins of man cannot be forgiven without blood sacrifice, and point to various Old Testament passages to support that claim. Sadly, those passages concerning sacrifices have been misunderstood, or perhaps even misrepresented, and the many passages to the contrary have been simply ignored. We will address both issues, starting with the second as it is easier to demonstrate.

Earlier, I referred to human fears, in that case guilt, not being an aspect of God's existence, for God never has anything to feel guilty about. Next, we come to another fear based on human experience: forgiveness. We all know that there are instances in our lives where although we try to forgive, antipathy continues to linger. In our hearts, forgiveness is often not total, and whereas God says: *"I will forgive their iniquity, and their sin I will remember no more"* (Jeremiah 31:34), this is not something to which we can relate – remember no more? I am occasionally offended, sometimes inadvertently, other times spitefully, but try as I may, I just cannot completely expunge the memory, and with the memory comes a mixture of negative emotions. Not good, as you all well know. God went further in explaining that we are not like Him when it comes to forgiveness:

> "Let the wicked man forsake his way, and the unrighteous man his thoughts; let him return to the Lord, and He will have mercy on him, for He will abundantly pardon. For My thoughts are not your thoughts, nor are your ways not My ways, says the Lord. (Isaiah 55:7-8, NKJV).

See: repent, and God will abundantly pardon, unlike us who have trouble doing so.

Christian apologetics often quote a partial verse of Isaiah 55 to assert that we cannot know God: *"For My thoughts are not your thoughts, and your ways are not My ways"*. Extracted from its context, it can be used to support a variety of doctrines, but we must put it back where it belongs, as above, as inconvenient as that may be. What is it about God's thoughts and ways that are different and higher than our ways? He is abundantly forgiving! We are not, but He is. If that be true, how can anyone claim that the repentant are not forgiven, and need a redeemer to pay for their sins? It is insulting to God, blasphemous even, to say that He is abundantly forgiving, but leaves a penalty hanging over our heads. When God forgives, no reparation is needed.

The question becomes: Does God forgive and forget on a regular basis, or does He require some special event to accomplish the cleansing of our sins? Did Jesus accomplish that when he was crucified, or do we have to wait until the fulfillment of Jeremiah 31? What does Scripture say on the matter? Fortunately, we find statements in Scripture that confirm a simple truth: all that is needed for forgiveness is repentance. Sounds too easy, doesn't it, but that is what the good book says. Let us have a look, but before doing so, we should review how God described Himself to Moses, and clarify a Christian misconception:

> "Hashem passed before him and proclaimed: Hashem, Hashem, God, Compassionate and Gracious, Slow to Anger, and Abundant in Kindness and Truth; Preserver of Kindness for thousands of generations, Forgiver of Iniquity, Willful Sin, and Error, and Who Cleanses – but does not cleanse completely, recalling the iniquity of parents upon children and grandchildren, to the third and fourth generations." (Exodus 34:6-7, TJB)

I have quoted from the Jewish Bible because that is where I turn for an explanation (remember the advantage of the Jew?) According to the Sages, this passage reveals the Thirteen Attributes of God, and I will discuss just some, as written in the Chumash[1]. The repetition: "Hashem, Hashem, God" reveals three attributes: (1), God's mercy even before one sins, even though God knows that evil lies dormant in the person; (2), God's mercy in that even after a person sins, God mercifully accepts his repentance; and (3), the name, God, denotes power; in the context of His Attributes, it implies a degree of mercy that surpasses even that indicated by the name, Hashem.

Three kinds of sin are noted:

1. Iniquity – an intentional sin, which God forgives if the sinner repents.

2. Willful Sin – a sin that is committed with the intention of angering God. Even so serious a transgression will be forgiven, with repentance; and

3. Error – a sin committed unintentionally, out of apathy or carelessness.

Take note of the third type, because this is singled out in the discussion on ritual sacrifice a little later. The main point to note, however, is that God forgives sin when repented – there is no need of substitutional atonement.

Let us review some other texts that relate to forgiveness:

a. "As for the wicked man, if he repents from all his sins that he committed, and he observes all My decrees, and practices justice and righteousness, he shall surely live, he shall not die. All his transgressions that he committed will not be remembered against him; he shall live because of the righteousness that he did. Do I desire at all the death of the wicked man? - the word of the Lord Hashem / Elohim. Is it not rather his return from his ways, that he might live?" (Ezekiel 18:21-23, TJB)

b. "Seek Hashem when He can be found; call upon Him when He is near. Let the wicked one forsake his way and the iniquitous man his thoughts; let him return to Hashem and He will show mercy; to our God, for He is abundantly forgiving. For My thoughts are not your thoughts and your ways are not My ways – the word of Hashem. As high as the heavens over the earth, so are My ways higher than your ways, and My thoughts than your thoughts." (Isaiah 55:6-9)

c. "With what shall I approach Hashem, humble myself before God on high? Shall I approach Him with burnt offerings ... **shall I give over my firstborn** [to atone for] my transgressions, or the fruit of my belly for the sin of my soul? **He has told you, O man, what is good! What does Hashem require of you but to do justice, to love kindness, and to walk humbly with your God?** ... As for me, I put my hope in Hashem and await the God of my salvation; my God will hear me ... Who is a God like You, Who pardons iniquity and overlooks transgression for the remnant of His heritage? He does not maintain His wrath forever, for He desires kindness. He will once again show us mercy, He will suppress our iniquities. You will cast all our sins into the depths of the sea. Grant truth to Jacob, kindness to Abraham, as you swore to our forefathers in days of old." (Micah 6-7) [emphasis mine]

Micah was the last Prophet, so it is reasonable to assume that his words best represented the future that God wanted His people to know. Contemplate his words: "Shall I give over my firstborn [to atone for] my transgressions." The answer is clearly: NO! God has told you what He wants of you, and sacrifice of the firstborn is not it. If we are to accept the Christian practice of exegesis, reading more into the text that the immediate context suggests, then we should read that God would not give over His firstborn to atone for sin. *"For God so loved the world that He gave His only begotten Son* [firstborn]" (John 3:16) directly contradicts Micah 6:7. Whom should I believe: the Prophet Micah, or some unknown author of the Gospel attributed to John?

Winding back a bit, Exodus 34:6-7 is very comforting, until one gets to the last part: *"does not cleanse completely"*. What does that mean? Christian apologists use this passage to assert that one's sins are just "covered", but not fully forgiven and forgotten - the Sages say otherwise. However, in that context, it can only mean for the next three to four generations: there is clearly a specified limit. Why the limit, and why be so specific about the third and fourth generations?

But Does Not Cleanse Completely

Christian theologians extract this phrase from Exodus 34:7 to assert that God just hides our sins from sight, so that He pays them no mind, but that we still need the atonement of Jesus, so that our sins are forgiven and remembered no more. Let me correct that error.

Firstly, read through the various Christian translations on bible hub[2] to understand the common Christian interpretation, as exemplified here: "He never lets the guilty go unpunished, punishing children and grandchildren for their parents' sins to the third and fourth generation" (GOD'S WORD Translation). The Sages of Judaism offer a different interpretation, based on their understanding of the preceding verses, as they describe them: God's 13 Attributes of Mercy. These are enumerated in the Chumash[3] as: (1) Hashem; (2) Hashem; (3) God; (4) Compassionate; (5) and Gracious; (6) Slow to Anger; (7) and Abundant in Kindness; (8) and Truth; (9) Preserver of Kindness for Thousands of Generations. God forgives three categories of sin, and each forgiveness is reckoned as a separate Attribute: (10) Iniquity (intentional sin); (11) Willful sin (committed with the intention of angering God); (12) and error (sin committed out of apathy or carelessness); (13) and who cleanses.

I shall leave the reader to research these further, if of interest, but here I will elaborate on (13) only. Of course, you may not accept the Jewish Sages on this issue, but I would ask why you would accept a later Christian interpretation. My distrust of Christian doctrine leaves me with no choice but to accept the writings of the Sages.

The Chumash commentary reads: "When someone repents, God cleanses his sin, so that the effect of the sin vanishes. However, if one does not repent, He does not cleanse." The confusion in the Christian commentary arises from a mistranslation of Hebrew phraseology into Greek, and then a preferred interpretation of the Greek. I always find it challenging to interpret the Greek, but I assume that Greek scholars have figured it out, without bias (hopefully). Here is a transliteration:

"iniquity forgiving for thousands covenant loyalty keeping clear not will clear and sin and transgression and on the children on of the fathers the iniquity visiting and to the third to of their children the children the fourth."[4]

I have no idea, so I will go with those to whom were gifted the original writings, because their interpretation is consistent with the message of repentance throughout the Hebrew Scriptures: repent and God forgives. But of course, that is not the whole story, what is meant by reference to generations?

To the Third and Fourth Generation

Let us turn to an earlier passage in Exodus, concerning idol worship:

"You shall not prostrate yourself to them nor worship them, for I am Hashem, your God – a jealous God, Who visits the sin of the fathers upon children to the third and fourth generations, **for My enemies**; but who shows kindness for thousands of generations to those who love Me, and observe My commandments." (Exodus 20:5-6, TJB) [emphasis mine]

Note how sins are visited to the third and fourth generations, "*for My enemies*", or "*those who hate Me*" in the NKJV; they are not visited upon those who love God and observe His commandments. Idol worship is the greatest sin against God: the rejection of Him as the One and Only God, as proscribed in the First Commandment. One would think that if the sin of idolatry is not visited upon generations of those who love God, then neither should we think that other sins are necessarily visited upon them. We have an example of where the idolatrous worship of a father was not followed by the son. "*Your forefathers – Terah, the father of Abraham and the father of Nahor – always dwelt beyond the [Euphrates] river and they served gods of others*" (Joshua 24:2). Abraham's father was idolatrous, but God did not visit the father's sin upon Abraham, nor on his children, for Abraham loved God. God subsequently rescued Abraham and the rest is history, so to speak.

So, what does it mean to *visit the sin of the father* to subsequent generations?

Visiting Sins of the Father

"*Fathers shall not be put to death because of sons, and sons
shall not be put to death because of their fathers; rather,
a man should be put to death for his own sin.*"
(Deuteronomy 24:16)

It is a general rule that if Torah prohibits an action in an extreme circumstance, then the same principle applies in lesser circumstances. Next I shall quote directly from the *Chumash* (the Torah in printed form as opposed to a *Torah Scroll*):

"In response to the question of how children can be punished for sins they did not commit, the Sages explain that children are punished only if they carry on the sinful legacy of their parents as their own, or if it was in their power to protest, but they acquiesced to the life-style that was shown them. If so, they show that they ratify the deeds of the parents and adopt them as their own (*Sanhedrin 27b*). History shows that when sins are repeated over the course of generations, they become legitimated as a 'culture' or an independent 'life-style', so that they become regarded as a way of life and a new set of values. Thus, children who consciously accept and continue the ways of their iniquitous parents are forging a pattern of behaviour that has much more force than the deeds of only one errant generation. Thus, children who adopt the ways of their parents are, in a sense, committing more virulent sins than they would be if they acted only on their own. God refers to such people as *My enemies*.

In line with the Talmudic dictum that a child who had been kidnapped and raised by non-Jews is not responsible for sins that he never knew were wrong, a Jew educated in an assimilationist manner would also not fall under the category of this verse.

Even in such a case, the punishment for the sins of the parents does not go beyond the fourth generation. However, the next verse states that God *shows kindness for thousands of generations*, meaning at least two thousand generations into the future. Thus, the reward for good deeds is five hundred times as great as the punishment for sin (*Tosefta, Sotah 3:4*)."[5]

The Jewish teaching is clear: If children beyond the third and fourth generations do not know that they are doing wrong, because that is the culture into which they were born, then God does not hold them accountable on that issue. An interesting aspect of this explanation is in relation to people of other religions. Accepting the view of the Sages, these people are not held accountable for their idolatrous ways if such come from their culture, and they know no better. This explanation is consistent with my view of God: His expectations of His creation are reasonable, responsible, and most especially, fair and just. None of us can be held accountable for the circumstances in which we are born and nurtured, for that was God's choice.

Understanding Sacrifice

Let us again turn to the Jewish view of their own practices.

"In the lexicon of the Talmudic Sages, the Book of Leviticus is called *Torah Kohanim*. The Torah of Kohanim, or priest, because most of the Book deals with the laws of Temple service and other laws relating to the priests and their responsibilities.

> The opening chapters of the Book deal almost exclusively with animal '*korbanos*', a word that is commonly translated as either sacrifices or offerings, but the truth is that the English language does not have a word that accurately expresses the concept of a *korban*. The word 'sacrifice' implies that a person bringing it is expected to deprive himself of something valuable - but God finds no joy in His children's anguish or deprivation. 'Offering' is more positive and closer to the mark - indeed, we use it in our translation - but it too falls far short of the Hebrew '*korban*'. Does God require our gifts to appease Him or assuage His anger? And if He did, of what significance is a bull or a lamb to Him? 'If you have acted righteously, what have you given Him?' (Job 35:7); God does not become enriched by man's largess.
>
> The root of the word '*korban*' is '*karov*', to come near. The person bringing an offering comes closer to God; he elevates his level of spirituality. That is the true meaning of the word and the significance of the act."[6]

I thought it worth sharing this explanation because so many Christian translations use the word "sacrifice", when the context would deem the word "offering", or even "korban", as more appropriate. Another Hebrew word for this is "*qorbanot*". The NKJV renders Psalm 40:6 as "Sacrifice and offering You did not desire", whilst the Hebrew Bible renders more accurately, "Neither feast nor meal-offering did you desire." Skipping forward to Matthew 9:13 we read: "But go and learn what this means: '*I desire mercy and not sacrifice.*' I did not come to call the righteous, but sinners to repentance." There are many dimensions to this understanding. some of which can be found in Isaiah 1:11-17 and Hosea 6:6, but again it requires an accurate translation of "*sacrifice*" to understand fully. In passing, note that in Hosea 5:25, God reminded the Israelites that during the forty years they spent wandering in the desert, they brought neither sacrifices nor meal-offerings to Him, noting the exception in Numbers chapter 9.

My point here is this: If we accept the meaning in Psalm 40:6 and Matthew 9:13, and the Sages' explanation of offerings as bringing one closer to God, where is the logic in God sending His Divine Son, the Second Person of the Trinity, and thus effectively Himself, to elevate His own level of spirituality to bring Himself closer to Himself, when He has neither desire nor need to do so? And even if one asserts that it was Jesus, as man, his deity set aside, representing all mankind, who was elevating our spirituality: Why, when even Jesus said that God did not desire sacrifice, especially one as savage as the crucifixion?

Ritual Offerings for the Forgiveness of Sin

Yes, there were offerings for sin, but let us properly understand that ancient practice. As mentioned above, three types of sin are identified. There is an excellent article in Judaism 101 which explains the issue and I would highly recommend that you read it in full. Here I will just quote the text relevant to our discussion.

> "The atoning aspect of these offerings (qorbanot) is limited. For the most part, qorbanot only expiate unintentional sins, that is, sins committed because a person forgot that this thing was a sin. No atonement is needed for violations committed under duress or through lack of knowledge, and for the most part, qorbanot cannot atone for a malicious, deliberate sin. In addition, qorbanot

have no expiating effect unless the person making the offering sincerely repents his or her actions before making the offering, and makes restitution to any person who was harmed by the violation."[7]

Repentance requires that you specifically identify the sin you are repenting - asking for forgiveness of your sins in general is, in a sense, inadequate, for you cannot commit to not re-offending, if you have not specified the offence. One cannot say, with sincerity: "I won't do that again, whatever that was." Similarly, you cannot make reparation for an unknown offence. The practice of *qorbanot* is only for those sins which you have been unaware of committing, and no other.

In passing, note that in the discussion in the Judaism 101 article, there is reference to the idea of *substitution*, but it is peripheral to the main theme, not the theme itself. One cannot extrapolate this incidental aspect of *qorbanot* into a doctrine of *substitutionary atonement*.

Wilful Sin

> "*A redeemer will come to Zion, and to those of*
> *Jacob who repent from wilful sin*"
> (Isaiah 59:20)

Quoting from the notes to Isaiah 59:20,

> "Redemption depends on repentance. This verse testifies not only to the eventual redemption, but also man's capacity to elevate himself from sinfulness to goodness, for it states that even wilful sinners will be worthy of redemption when they repent. (*Yoma* 86b)".[8]

Note how this explanation echoes that of God in Genesis 4:7. Wilful sin is defined as rebellion against God, or sins committed with the intention of angering God. It should not be confused with deliberate sin. In case you were curious, *Yoma* (above) is the fifth tractate of Seder Moed ("Order of Festivals") of the Mishnah and of the Talmud.

Shedding Innocent Blood

God hates "*hands that shed innocent blood*" (Proverbs 6:17), so why would He soil His own hands? Why did God "bring such a catastrophe on this place [Jerusalem], that whoever hears it his ears will tingle" (Jer 19:3)? Because, as it says in the next verse, they "*have filled this place with the blood of the innocents*"! Would God seek to once more fill Jerusalem with the blood of an innocent? In addition to this verse in Proverbs, consider also these twelve verses: Deut 19:10; 1 Sam 19:5; 1 Kings 2:31; 2 Kings 21:16; Psalm 94:21; Isa 59:7; Lam 4:13; Joel 3:19; Jonah 1:14; Matt 27:4; Jer 22:17; and Psalm 106:38. If we are to learn nothing else from Scripture, it should be this: God does not shed innocent blood.

In the Epistle to the Hebrews, we read: "And according to the law almost all things are purified with blood, and **without shedding of blood there is no remission**" (Heb 9:22) [emphasis mine]. Firstly, note that there is no such statement anywhere in the Old Testament – this is purely the opinion of the author, and is not supported by Scripture. The NKJV refers us back to Leviticus 17:11, so let us go there; wisely though, we shall read from 17:10 to 17:12 so that we reveal the context. Before doing so, let us understand what we are reading, as before: "In the lexicon of the Talmudic sages, the Book of Leviticus is called *Toras Kohanim*, the Torah of the *Kohanim*, or priests, because most of the Book deals with the laws of the Temple service and other laws relating to the priests and their responsibilities."[6] Therefore, one must understand that there are strict procedural rules for every activity, and that such activities can only be performed by priests in accordance with Torah. Torah does not condone performance of such acts outside the scope and context of the Book of Leviticus, and there is no scope for Christian theologians to remove any verse from its context.

> "Any man of the House of Israel, and of the proselyte who dwells among them, who will consume any blood – I shall concentrate My attention upon the soul consuming the blood, and I will cut it off from its people. For the soul of the flesh is in the blood, and I have assigned it for you upon the Altar to provide atonement for your souls; for it is the blood that atones for the soul. Therefore,

I have said to the Children of Israel: Any person among you may not consume blood; and the proselyte who dwells among you may not consume blood."

Now firstly, how could the author of Hebrews derive "without shedding of blood there is no remission" from these verses in Leviticus? Yes, the soul of the flesh is in the blood, BUT, God has assigned it *upon the Altar* for atonement – nowhere else. And what does Scripture tell us about this atonement? The answer is found in Leviticus 4:1-2 and Numbers 15:24-31. I will let you look it up for yourself, but in brief, it relates to offerings on the altar for unintentional, or accidental sins only – NO OTHER.

Human Sacrifice

God hates the ritual sacrifice of human beings, and specifically forbids it. How, then, does Christianity rationalise the sacrifice of Jesus? Christian apologetics cover this in numerous ways, but as this resource[9] is representative of the genre, and is readily available online, I will quote from it. It starts with a presupposition with which I entirely disagree, for the reasons discussed above.

"There is no doubt that a sacrifice for sin was necessary if people are to have any hope of eternal life. God established the necessity of the shedding of blood to cover sin (Hebrews 9:22). In fact, God Himself performed the very first animal sacrifice to cover, temporarily, the sin of Adam and Eve. After He pronounced curses upon the first couple, He killed an animal, shedding its blood, and made from it a covering for Adam and Eve (Genesis 3:21), thereby instituting the principle of animal sacrifice for sin. When God gave the Law to Moses, there were extensive instructions on how, when, and under what circumstances animal sacrifices were to be offered to Him. This was to continue until Christ came to offer the ultimate, perfect sacrifice, which made animal sacrifice no longer necessary. "But those sacrifices are an annual reminder of sins, because it is impossible for the blood of bulls and goats to take away sins" (Hebrews 10:3–4)."

The first sentence is an invalid inference from God's instructions regarding the sacrifice of animals: Scripture clearly states that forgiveness is achieved by repentance. To assert that in killing an animal for a covering for Adam and Eve, God was "thereby instituting the principle of animal sacrifice for sin", is *eisegesis* – there is no Scriptural justification for such a claim. Quotations from the Book of Hebrews do nothing but *beg the question*, or affirm the consequent: they are statements of a developed theology and carry no more evidentiary weight that the article being quoted. As we noted above, there is no Scriptural support for that statement in Hebrews 9:22. The Christian interpretation is that if *it is impossible for the blood of bulls and goats to take away sins*, then it requires the blood of someone higher to take away sins. In formal terms, this is the logical fallacy of the false alternative. The Hebrew Scriptures make clear that the alternative is not the blood of a human, but repentance: without repentance, there is no forgiveness.

Next, in a spiritual sense, there is an unbridgeable chasm between animals and humans: to suggest any transition in practice from animals to humans, smacks of evolution theory, and in my view, it is blasphemous.

"*God said, let us make man in Our image, after Our likeness. They shall rule over the fish of the sea, the birds of the sky, and over the animal, the whole earth, and every creeping thing that creeps upon the earth … and Hashem God formed the man of dust from the ground, and He blew into his nostrils the soul of life, and man became a living being.*" (Genesis 1:26, 2:7). Humans have souls unlike the being of animals. Humans are living beings in the spiritual sense, animals are not. Humans have dominion over animals, but not over other humans. Animals are food for humans, but never humans for humans. There can be no valid, spiritual parallel, between animals and humans – none, and any so made is an insult to our Creator. Continuing from the article on the *Got Questions* website:

> "There are several reasons why the sacrifice of Christ on the cross does not violate the prohibition against human sacrifice. First, Jesus wasn't merely human. If He were, then His sacrifice would have also been a temporary one because one human life couldn't possibly cover the sins of the multitudes who ever existed. Neither could one finite human life atone for sin against an infinite God.

The only viable sacrifice must be an infinite one, which means only God Himself could atone for the sins of mankind. Only God Himself, an infinite Being, could pay the penalty owed to Himself. This is why God had to become a Man and dwell among men (John 1:14). No other sacrifice would suffice.

Second, God didn't sacrifice Jesus. Rather, Jesus, as God incarnate, sacrificed Himself. No one forced Him. He laid down His life willingly, as He made clear speaking about His life: "No one takes it from me, but I lay it down of my own accord. I have authority to lay it down and authority to take it up again" (John 10:18). God the Son sacrificed Himself to God the Father and thereby fulfilled all the requirements of the Law. Unlike the temporary sacrifices, Jesus' once-for-all-time sacrifice was followed by His resurrection. He laid down His life and took it up again, thereby providing eternal life for all who would ever believe in Him and accept His sacrifice for their sins. He did this out of love for the Father and for all those the Father has given Him (John 6:37–40)."

The argument that "Jesus wasn't merely human" is facile: consider the hierarchy of existence. It is acceptable to kill plants and animals, but not acceptable to kill humans. One cannot reverse the hierarchy and say: but it is ok to kill gods! God is higher than humans, who are higher than animals, which are, in a sense, higher than plants. Early Christianity would have recognised the paucity of this argument, for they accused the Jews of deicide. Notice again how this argument begs the question: presuming that a human sacrifice would be inadequate and temporary, and therefore a greater sacrifice was needed. I disagree: no sacrifice was needed, and there is no Scriptural justification for that claim. As I argued earlier, it is illogical to contend that "only an infinite being could pay the penalty owed to Himself" – no penalty is owed.

The argument that "God didn't sacrifice Jesus" is refuted by the Gospel of Luke: "Father, if it is Your will, take this cup away from me; nevertheless, not my will, but Yours, be done." (Luke 22:42) Not my will, but Your will: could that be any clearer? Mark's Gospel agrees, and later quotes Jesus as crying out: "My God, My God, why have You forsaken Me?" (Mark 15:34)

Are they the words of someone voluntarily sacrificing himself? According to the Gospels, Jesus acceded to the will of the Father, and accepted the fate that the Father ordained for him. To say that no-one forced him is facile. The Gospel of John may have put a different spin on it, but which is right? Given the general plot of the Gospels, if I were to believe anything, I would be inclined to accept the version in the Synoptics, rather than the later theological development in John.

To say that "God the Son sacrificed Himself to God the Father and **thereby fulfilled all the requirements of the Law**" [emphasis mine] is the most outrageous nonsense: in what way does self-sacrifice fulfill the Law? Where in the Law is that requirement specified? There is no doubt, in my mind at least, that Christian commentators get so carried away with their own sanctimonious prose, that they entirely lose the plot, the logical one that is. Where in Scripture, or even in logic, can there be found a relationship between Torah and self-sacrifice?

Again, one of the reasons that Christian doctrine and theology disappoint me is as evidenced here: the apologetics are not only weak and implausible, but they contradict the original Scriptures.

Summary

Relating back to opening scenario, we have God releasing a product (human kind) with a known defect (free will), but also with detailed instructions on proper use (Torah) and warnings concerning the dangers of improper use. Many fail to read the instructions (Torah), or believe that they can operate independently of those instructions (sin), and in consequence suffer spiritual death. Is God responsible for creating a fallible product; are we responsible for ignoring His instructions; or do we both share a degree of responsibility? We must hold ourselves accountable for our own actions: no responsible person would argue against that. But similarly, God must hold Himself accountable for His Own actions, lest He is less responsible than we are. Is God not responsible? If not, how can we trust any promise that He has made? Even if you believe in a Divine Redeemer dying for our sins, if God is not responsible, why would you trust in the promise of forgiveness?

That is my view, and I pray God's indulgence if I have it totally wrong, which I may do, but it does seem more logical, and more respectful of an infinite God, than the Christian narrative.

An infinite God has no need of apologising to Himself, nor of making reparation to Himself for the consequences of His Own actions. That is my understanding on this issue. Scripture bears witness, to the Jewish teachings, that sincere repentance is all that God requires of us – why would we choose to believe any differently? Let me finish by repeating a passage from Ezekiel that we encountered earlier:

> "Now you, Son of Man, say to the children of your people: ... If I say of a righteous person that he shall surely live, and he relies on his righteousness yet practices corruption, all his righteousness will not be recalled, rather because of his corruption that he practiced, for that he will die. And if I say to a wicked person, 'You shall surely die', and he repents from his sin and acts with justice and righteousness – the wicked person returns a pledge, repays for his theft, follows the life-giving decrees, without practicing corruption – he will surely live; he will not die. All his sins that he had committed will not be remembered for him; he has practiced justice and righteousness, he shall surely live ... If a righteous person turns back from his righteousness and practices corruption, he shall die for [his acts]; and if a wicked person turns back from his wickedness and acts with justice and righteousness, he shall live for [his acts]. Yet you say, 'The way of the Lord is not proper!' I shall judge you, each man according to his ways, O House of Israel." (Ezekiel 33:12-20)

It really could not be clearer than that: God judges each person according to his ways, and if one lives righteously, bearing in mind that none is perfectly righteous, God will forgive and remember his sins no more. If that was true in the time of Ezekiel, why would it not be true forever? I can find no evidence in the Hebrew Scriptures that God ever revoked that promise, or altered the conditions of forgiveness. If Jesus preached otherwise, then he was not one with the Father as he claimed.

REFERENCES:

1. *The Chumash*, Scherman, Rabbi Nosson, Mesorah Publications, ArtScroll English Edition, Brooklyn, NY, 2009, pp. 509-510
2. http://biblehub.com/exodus/34-7.htm
3. The *Chumash, Ibid*, p. 509
4. http://biblehub.com/interlinear/exodus/34-7.htm
5. The *Chumash, Ibid*, p. 409
6. *The Tanach*, Scherman, Rabbi Nosson, Mesorah Publications, ArtScroll English Edition, Brooklyn, NY, 2011, p. 159
7. http://www.jewfaq.org/qorbanot.htm
8. The Tanach, Ibid, p. 159
9. https://www.gotquestions.org/human-sacrifice.html

PART 10

SUMMARY & CONCLUSIONS

> The Bereans *"searched the Scriptures daily to*
> *find out whether these things were so."*
> (Acts 17:11)

These words appear convincing of the truth of Christianity, but let us cross-examine this evidence. Was Luke bluffing, attempting to lend credibility to Paul's gospel, or did this really happen, leading to "therefore many of them believed, and also not a few of the Greeks" (v. 12)? Who were the Bereans anyway? Berea was a city in south-western Macedonia (northern Greece), and was subjugated by the Romans circa 168 BCE. The city was populated by Greeks, Hellenic Jews, and no doubt, people of other cultures. The Jews had long been separated from the Jews in Judea, and were part of the lost tribes of Israel to whom Jesus, by his own admission, was only sent (Matthew 15:24). It is probable that the Scriptures to which they had access were in Greek, but improbable that they had a complete set.

Even if they did, the writings they had were unreliable translations, as we have already discussed. We cannot even be sure that their version matched the version that Paul and/or Luke used. Given what we have learned of how the New Testament authors used the Old Testament (see Part 8), I can understand how Paul may well have convinced his audience, if he did.

The Bereans "were more fair-minded than those in Thessalonica" (v. 17:11). What prompted that comment? Quite simply, because Paul and Silas were kicked out of Thessalonica. Possibly, it was not so much Paul's gospel to which the Hellenic Jews objected, but as with the problem for Jesus in Jerusalem, it was a political issue, for they were afraid of the Romans (John 11:50, 18:14). However, the narrative does mention "the Jews who were not persuaded" (v. 5), so we cannot rule out their theological resistance to Paul's message. If these Hellenic Jews had knowledge of the Scriptures, it would argue against Paul's claim to the Corinthians that "Christ died for our sins according to the Scriptures" (1 Corinthians 15:3). Whilst "a great multitude of devout Greeks … joined Paul and Silas" (v. 4) in Thessalonica, and likewise in Berea, it was not until the Jews of Thessalonica came and stirred up the people in Berea that once more, Paul felt the need to depart. I am curious as to why Silas and Timothy felt safe to remain in Berea – would the agitators from Thessalonica not have caused them grief also? I also wonder how many agitators there were. The distance is 75 kms, at least a 15 hour journey on foot, though fortunately, over mostly flat terrain. Would the non-believers have really been that upset that they would have pursued Paul that distance? We cannot know, but I do wonder.

My mind is uncomfortable with the thought that in just two short weeks, *devout Greeks* abandoned their previous pagan beliefs, and accepted the monotheism as preached by Paul, whilst Hellenic Jews in Thessalonica did not. What did Luke mean by "devout" in the context of pagan Greeks? What did Paul tell them that so easily convinced them? It could not have been the same Gospel as preached by James and his fellows in Jerusalem – I struggle to believe that pagan Greeks in Macedonia would have accepted the teachings of Messianic Judaism. IF Luke's story is true, it is circumstantial evidence that Paul was preaching a different gospel. Circumstantial, but powerfully so.

I am baffled as to why the Bereans would have accepted Paul's message, for having diligently searched the Scriptures myself, and likely in far more detail than the Bereans could have accomplished. Thus, I have concluded, that *these things were NOT so.*

Quoting from another reference source:

> "In Jesus' day, the idea of a *divine* Messiah was unknown. Those who believed that deliverance would come through a Messiah, 'the King of the Jews', thought of him as a human being, the next occupant of the Jewish throne. Those who believed that deliverance would come by entirely supernatural means thought of the deliverer as God Himself, or as an angel. The idea of a human being who was also divine was unthinkable. The whole of Jewish history cried out against such a concept. The first of the Ten Commandments forbade the worship of a human being. It was precisely because of their refusal to worship human-divine figures which filled the Ancient World, from Pharaoh to Caligula, that the Jews had undergone their long history of suffering."[1]

I find it entirely unlikely that God would have never told His First Born Son, Israel, of His Triune nature, if such were the truth of it. God told the Children of Israel that He was One, and the Only One, and He was persistent in His punishment of the Jews for their idolatry. The more I have studied the timeline of the New Testament writings, with even Christian scholars acknowledging how the evangelism of the time was focused more on the Gentiles than the Jews, the more I am persuaded that the notion of a human-divine messiah had a Gentile, or at least Hellenic, origin. Paul was an Hellenic Jew, well versed in Hellenic poetry and other Greek literature, and his writings evidence Hellenic thought patterns. As the original followers of Jesus, the Nazarenes, were what we would describe today as Messianic Jews, still practising the Judaism of their time, I strongly doubt that they saw Jesus as God, and it was only the influence of Paul that saw the concept appearing in later New Testament writings. Referring back to Chapter 9-1, whilst there was a recent culture of accepting a messiah who would die for sin, there was no suggestion in the Qumranic sect that the messiah would be an incarnated deity.

I have come to agree with New Testament scholar, James Dunn:

> "Without Paul this messianic sect might have remained a renewal movement with Second Temple Judaism and never become anything more than that ... Paul's mission and the teaching transmitted through his letters did more than anything else to transform embryonic Christianity from a messianic sect, quite at home within Second Temple Judaism, into a religion hospitable to the Greeks, increasingly Gentile in composition, and less and less comfortable with the kind of Judaism which was to survive the ruinous failure of the two Jewish revolts against Rome (66-73, 132-135 CE)."[2]

If I am right, then it argues strongly against the Christian claim of prophecy fulfillment.

A Summary

To put my argument as concisely as I can, these are the points that I would emphasize:

1. I do not accept the New Testament, in whatever version one prefers in this modern age, to be an authentic, and thus authoritative, account of the Word of God.
2. Christianity attempts to bolster its claims of authenticity by asserting that the bible is inerrant, but the evidence is to the contrary: Judaism does not teach inerrancy of the Hebrew Scriptures, and God cannot be the author of the incoherence and contradictions within the New Testament – He is better than that.
3. I can find no evidence in the Hebrew Scriptures of prophecies concerning a two-stage redemptive process, as claimed in the New Testament (Hebrews 9:28).
4. I can find no evidence in the Hebrew Scriptures that "redemption" referred to anything other than the ingathering of the Children of Israel, with their enemies defeated, and Torah going forth from Jerusalem.

5. *Catastrophic messianism*, such as claimed for Jesus, was a late theological development amongst the Qumran community, and cannot be claimed as deriving from the Prophets of old.

6. There was a false messiah before Jesus, who made the same claims, with the same fate as Jesus – a political assassination dressed up as the will of God.

7. Christianity, as it developed amongst the Gentile community in Rome, departed entirely from Judaism, contrary to what I believe Jesus taught in regard to Torah, the Sabbath, and the God-ordained commemorations.

8. I accept the following as God's truth refuting Christian theology: "Shall I approach Him with burnt offerings ... **shall I give over my firstborn** [to atone for] my transgressions, or the fruit of my belly for the sin of my soul? He has told you, O man, what is good! (Micah 6:6); and finally,

9. I do not accept that God, Who forbade the spilling of innocent blood and human sacrifice, would act contrary to His Own Morality and require that a man, supposedly God incarnate, would voluntarily act contrary to that morality.

REFERENCES:

1. MacCoby, Hyam, *Revolution in Judaea: Jesus & The Jewish Resistance*, Ocean Books, London, UK, 1973, p. 102

2. Dunn, James D.G., *Jesus, Paul, and the Gospels*, Wm. B. Eerdmans Publishing Co., Grand Rapids, MI, 2011, pp. 119-120

CHAPTER 10-1

PROPHECY VERSUS CREED

*"It is a truism that almost any sect, cult, or religion will legislate
its creed into law if it acquires the political power to do so."*
~ Robert Heinlein – American science-fiction writer (1907-1988) ~

Yes, ok, I am much given to quoting science-fiction writers, for I often find that they will express a truth that others are afraid to utter; George Orwell's *1984* is an exemplar, as is *Animal Farm*. However, back to the main theme. A critical issue that we have not so far examined, is to compare the claimed prophecy fulfillments of Jesus, with the creeds that express the centrality of Christian doctrine. For the religion to be coherent, the two should closely match. Let us review what these tell us.

The Creeds

Firstly we have the Apostles' Creed, which was not devised by the Apostles themselves, but is said to be a summary of what the Apostles taught. "Ancient theory or legend adopted the belief that the 12 <u>apostles</u>

were the authors of the Apostles' Creed. Today biblical scholars agree
that the creed was developed sometime between the second and ninth
centuries, and most likely, the creed in its fullest form came into being
around 700 AD. The creed was used to summarize Christian doctrine
and as a baptismal confession in the churches of Rome. It is believed
that the Apostles' Creed was originally formulated to refute the claims of
Gnosticism and protect the church from early heresies and deviations from
orthodox Christian doctrine. The creed took on two forms: one short,
known as the Old Roman Form, and the longer enlargement of the Old
Roman Creed called the Received Form."[1] It reads as follows:

> I believe in God, the Father Almighty, Creator of heaven and
> earth, and in Jesus Christ, His only Son, our Lord, who was
> conceived by the Holy Spirit, born of the Virgin Mary, suffered
> under Pontius Pilate, was crucified, died and was buried; He
> descended into hell; on the third day He rose again from the
> dead; He ascended into heaven, and is seated at the right hand of
> God the Father Almighty; from there He will come to judge the
> living and the dead. I believe in the Holy Spirit, the Holy Catholic
> Church, the communion of Saints, the forgiveness of sins, the
> resurrection of the body, and life everlasting.

Note the absence of the Trinity. We also have the *Nicene Creed*. "In its
present form, this creed goes back partially to the Council of Nicea (A.D.
325), with additions by the Council of Constantinople (A.D. 381). It was
accepted in its present form at the Council of Chalcedon in 451, but the
"filioque" phrase [Ed. *and the Son*] was not added until 589. However, the
creed is in substance an accurate and majestic formulation of the Nicene
faith. This translation of the Greek text was approved by the CRC Synod
of 1988."[2]

> We believe in one God, the Father almighty, maker of heaven and
> earth, of all things visible and invisible. And in one Lord Jesus
> Christ, the only Son of God, begotten from the Father before all
> ages, God from God, Light from Light, true God from true God,
> begotten, not made; of the same essence as the Father. Through

him all things were made. For us and for our salvation he came down from heaven; he became incarnate by the Holy Spirit and the virgin Mary, and was made human. He was crucified for us under Pontius Pilate; he suffered and was buried. The third day he rose again, according to the Scriptures. He ascended to heaven and is seated at the right hand of the Father. He will come again with glory to judge the living and the dead. His kingdom will never end. And we believe in the Holy Spirit, the Lord, the giver of life. He proceeds from the Father and the Son, and with the Father and the Son is worshipped and glorified. He spoke through the prophets. We believe in one holy catholic and apostolic church. We affirm one baptism for the forgiveness of sins. We look forward to the resurrection of the dead, and to life in the world to come. Amen.

I am not sure why two creeds are necessary to express virtually the same beliefs, but that there are two perhaps suggests theological development. I acknowledge that publication of a document does not necessarily indicate the date of the origination of a belief, just as the date of publication of the Gospels does not align with the events described. Nevertheless, there are other reasons in documented Church history which support the notion of a developed theology, and thus doctrine, leading to dogma. I find it interesting that the Nicene Creed omits the phrase, "He descended into hell" which is found in the Apostles Creed. No doubt, someone realised that such was antithetical to the nature of a man claimed to be God, and likely arose from a misinterpretation of Psalm 16:10. Once again, evidence of doctrinal development.

I would summarise these creeds, in the context of claimed Old Testament prophecy, and New Testament evidence, as follows:

1. Jesus, an eternal deity, the Son of God, taking on human form.
2. Incarnated for the purpose of dying for the sins of the world.
3. Conceived by the Holy Spirit, and born of a virgin.
4. Was crucified (and was somewhere spiritually for a while).
5. Rose again on the third day, according to the Scriptures.
6. Ascended into heaven to sit at the Father's right hand.

7. Will come again to judge the living and the dead, heralding the End of Days.

Examining the Evidence

Concerning the first credal tenet, there is no Old Testament evidence that would suggest a triune God, at least nothing substantive that has convinced the majority of learned rabbis of Judaism (nor me). Even the evidence in the New Testament is of doubtful weight, as demonstrated in Chapter 1-1 where we evaluated the authenticity and authority of these writings. Given the date of writing of the Gospels in particular, we have no evidence that the Apostles believed in a triune God in the early years immediately following the death of Jesus. A Google search on the Trinity reveals numerous college courses on Systematic Theology, teaching the basis of the development of this concept. That there are such courses suggests to me that the evidence for a Triune God is far from compelling. If God had wanted us to know of His triune nature, I doubt that He would have required academics to expound on the subject; after all, the twelve that Jesus chose, on the instructions of the Father, were just ordinary men of limited education.

As an analyst, I am forced to ask: If in the Hebrew Scriptures, God repeatedly insists that He is the God Who is One, why would He not have revealed His trinitarian nature to His Firstborn Son, Israel? The doctrine of the Trinity is cobbled together from multiple New Testament verses, the authenticity of some having long been refuted. I cannot find sufficient evidence to believe that God is other than One, especially as logically, I cannot comprehend multiple, individual, infinites, stated to be *one in all else, co-equal, co-eternal and consubstantial, and each is God, whole and entire*, yet separately discernible. I would recommend contemplating the *Identity of Indiscernibles*[3], and its natural corollary, the indiscernibility of identicals.

Point 2 – there is insufficient evidence in the Hebrew Scriptures to claim that there is a prophecy of anyone dying for the sins of the world in substitutionary atonement, let alone an incarnate, separately discernible, person of a Triune God. As we reviewed earlier, God has been very specific: Forgiveness is available to all those who sincerely repent, and as God told Moses, one cannot take on the sins of another. The evidence in the Dead Sea Scrolls, of a messianic figure upon whom the New Testament portrayal of Jesus may well have been modelled, seems more plausible to my mind.

Point 3 – We only have the New Testament texts, specifically Matthew 1:18-25 and Luke 1:26-38, that Jesus was conceived by the Holy Spirit, and the much disputed verse in Isaiah 7:14 that Mary was a virgin when she conceived. As one commentator wrote, and I largely agree:

> "Matthew's Gospel was written in about AD 80-90 for Christians who were not of Jewish provenance - that is, Gentiles who had no knowledge of Isaiah's original Hebrew. For them, the passage announced, unambiguously, the fulfillment of an ancient prophecy: the miraculous birth of a divine being. But the prophet himself and readers of his original Hebrew sentence regarded it as a quite specific allusion to the historical circumstances of Isaiah's age, and would have found its mutation in Greek into one of the foundations of Christian doctrine quite baffling."[4]

Irrespective of when Matthew's Gospel was presented in Greek, and whether or not it was for Gentiles or Hellenic Jews, I am convinced that Isaiah's prophecy was contemporary, and did not prophesy a virgin birth of an incarnated deity. One might also review Greek legends, and why the idea of a virgin giving birth to a god would have been acceptable to the Greeks.

Point 4 – Except for Islam and a few sceptics, no-one denies that Jesus died the horrible death of crucifixion. Was it prophesied? No, and the best that Christian apologetics can do is to arrogate the role of the *suffering servant* to Jesus, supplanting the true role of Israel (see Chapter 3-2). We also have the evidence of a precursor to Jesus (see Chapter 9-1). As for Jesus descending into hell (Apostles Creed), I am surprised that this tenet of belief remains in modern versions of the creed. This is one of those translation issues where nobody can be sure of an original meaning, and Christian apologists then offer reasoning for what was really meant. It is not a major issue, but my understanding is that the modern interpretation is that Jesus did not go to Hell reigned over by Satan, but went to the grave.

Point 5 – There is no evidence that Jesus rose on the third day: the Gospels only relate that the tomb, where Jesus was believed to have been buried, was empty on the third day. Chapter 9-3 discussed this issue in detail. The Resurrection narrative is questionable, although there is no substantive evidence that Jesus was <u>not</u> resurrected from the dead. The Gospel wording of both Jesus' prophecy, and the event, leaves one wondering whether Jesus thought that he would raise himself, or whether he would be raised by the Father. I guess that in a Trinitarian world, it is but a matter of semantics, but I am curious nonetheless, because it may tell us something of how Jesus perceived himself. It is invalid to claim that Jonah's experience was also a prophecy for Jesus, although the events do match, almost. Chapter 9-4 discussed the resurrection in more detail, but again, on the preponderance of evidence, or the lack thereof, I remain unconvinced that these events were prophesied. Whether they actually occurred or not is irrelevant to this study.

Point 6 – covers two events, the resurrection, and where Jesus went when resurrected. There is no prophecy in the Hebrew Scriptures that the Messiah would spend countless years at the right hand of God awaiting the End of Days. All prophecies of the Messiah relate <u>only</u> to the *eschaton*, with no intervening period. I would offer that such thoughts of the early Christians were based on the expectation that the Second Coming of Jesus was imminent, and that without such a belief, people would have quickly lost interest in Jesus as Messiah, just as they did with Theudas, Judas of Galilee, and later, Simon bar Kokhba. Chapter 6-2 discussed the evidence for the eschatological temper of the early Christians.

Point 7 – the belief that Jesus, as Messiah, will come again, is founded on the realisation that he failed to accomplish the prophesied messianic accomplishments in his claimed first coming. That he did so fail is evidence that he was not the prophesied messiah, which is why so many Jews did not believe in him, even though many did originally, if the Book of Acts is to believed. Personally, I tend to accept the scholarly opinion in Westar's Acts Seminar, which has concluded that Acts best fits the historical context of the early second century battle between proto-orthodox and gnostic Christians over the legacy of Paul.[5] Judaism exists today, because by and large, the Jews who fled to Yavneh following the destruction of Jerusalem, were led by Pharisees who had rejected Jesus. Perhaps that is why we can detect acrimony toward them, even though extra-biblical evidence presents them in a very different light.

Hebrew Scripture does support a messiah in the Last Days, but whether that is a matter of his coming *again*, rather than for the *first time*, is the primary issue in dispute.

REFERENCES:

1. https://www.thoughtco.com/the-apostles-creed-p2-700364
2. https://www.crcna.org/welcome/beliefs/creeds/nicene-creed
3. https://plato.stanford.edu/entries/identity-indiscernible/
4. Geza Vermes, "Matthew's Nativity is charming and frightening... but it's a Jewish myth," Telegraph, 2004-DEC-19, at: http://www.telegraph.co.uk/
5. Tyson, Joseph, *Marcion and Luke-Acts: A Defining Struggle*, University of South Carolina Press, USA, 2006

THE MODERN
CHRISTIAN CHURCH

*"Beware of the scribes, who desire to go around in long
robes, love greetings in the market places, the best seats
in the synagogues, and the best places at feasts."*
(Luke 20:46)

As a former Catholic, raised in an extended Catholic family, and having
spent eight years being taught in a Catholic Boys Boarding School, I am
conversant with the ways of the Church, at least as it was in the 1950's. I do
not know how much it has changed, but I do know that many Protestant
offshoots, especially American Evangelicals, do not follow the rituals and
works of the law of the Catholic Church. However, that the Church of
Rome developed such traditions, and prescribes such behaviours, allows us
to compare that religion with what was believed by the Apostles of Jesus.
We should not forget that before the Protestant Reformation beginning
in the early sixteenth century, Catholicism was the religion *de jour* – the
foundation of all later Christian sects, with the exception of the Eastern

Churches, which nevertheless practice rituals that are very similar to those of Catholicism. Protestantism can claim to be reformed Catholicism, but in my view, such reformation was incomplete, merely nibbling around the edges, being more concerned with overthrowing the authority of Rome than re-examining the fundamentals.

My question then is: How closely do the beliefs, behaviours, clerical dress, clerical hierarchy, works of the law, and liturgical calendar of the Catholic Church, match what we can learn of Jesus teachings in the Gospels? If there is significant divergence, then we are right to question whether Christianity is truly a religion of God, founded on the teachings and example of Jesus in Second Temple Judaism.

Beware the scribes … hmmm.

Is this warning in Luke prophetic? All warnings are, in a sense, prophetic, because they make us aware of behaviours, activities, or events where we should exercise caution, and if they were never going to occur, then there would be no need for us to be warned about them. The major prophets of old: Isaiah, Jeremiah, and Ezekiel, all warned the Israelites of behaviours that offended God, and of the consequences of not heeding the warnings. Further, they prophesied that the Israelites would not so heed, and that they were about to suffer. So back to Luke. If you have ever witnessed events at the Vatican, participated at High Mass, or supped with clerics, you would have noticed the clerical hierarchy, where they went about in long robes, accepted greetings on bended knee including the kissing of rings, had the front seats in the church, and sat at the head of the table at feasts, all activities of which Luke warned.

Consider the Pope, who seems to enjoy being called "Il Papa", despite Jesus warning: "Do not call anyone on earth father" (Matthew 23:9), meaning in the spiritual sense. The Catholic Church may well object, contending that the term refers to the Pope's secular role as father of his flock, but the looks on the faces of his flock tell me that they perceive him in a spiritual sense as well – no girlfriend ever looked at me with such adoration (I probably didn't deserve it). If you have attended a High Mass, or equivalent in the Anglican profession, you would have noticed that all the best seats are taken in the order of clerical hierarchy – cardinals, bishops, priests, nuns, and so on. Notice also their robes and adornments:

most colourful at the top, descending to the bland at the bottom. So, in the kingdom of Heaven, shall the Pope be last, and the deacons first?

Whilst at school, we were frequently reminded that we must *keep holy the Sabbath Day*, and that failing to do so was a mortal sin, meaning that hell was your likely final destination. I managed to beat the system by earning a plenary indulgence to be applied at the hour of death. This meant that because of my good deeds, specifically, attending Confession, Mass, and Holy Communion, on nine successive first Fridays, I would be forgiven my sins and bypassing Purgatory, go straight to heaven. Who said that good deeds do not earn forgiveness? Sometime in the late nineteenth century, Protestants started to drop mention of the Sabbath, and referred to Sunday as the Lord's Day. That term had been around for centuries, but civil law in Western countries evidence that it was the Sabbath which drove legislation forbidding work on Sundays, not the Lord's Day. Theology and doctrine continue to evolve, even to this day.

I mention this to show how far Christianity has wandered from the footsteps of Jesus, a Jewish man who practised the religion of Second Temple Judaism, who affirmed that the Pharisees sat in Moses' seat, confirming the continuity of the Law, and never spoke against the Sabbath. If Jesus was the prophesied Messiah, why has Christianity eschewed his basic teachings, consistent with the Hebrew Scriptures that he learned from an early age? Why did the Church Fathers in Rome condemn the Jew, the Synagogue, and all the practices of Judaism, and compromise with the sun-worshipping pagan emperor, Constantine? Why were the original *Followers of the Way*, the Nazarenes, a congregation in Jerusalem that included the original Apostles and disciples, condemned as heretics? The evidence of the pagan compromise remains today, especially in the Eastern Church, where religious icons still embrace the pagan practice of displaying the sun behind the heads of people, including Jesus, Mary, and the saints. The halo, introduced later, is just a stylised version of the sun.

Jesus warned concerning the Pharisees: "whatever they tell you to observe, that observe and do, but do not do according to their works; for they say and do not do" (Matthew 23:3). I entirely agree with the first part, but would offer that Catholicism has also accepted the second part as well, but you have probably already guessed that.

CHAPTER 10-3

A FINAL WORD

"The purely righteous do not complain about evil, rather they add justice. They do not complain about heresy, rather they add faith. They do not complain about ignorance, rather they add wisdom."
~ Rabbi Abraham Isaac Kook ~

You may wonder why I have chosen this quotation as my final word, and what relevance it has to the subject of Jesus fulfilling prophecy. I sometimes find it a little obscure myself, but for me it represents a truth that is antithetical to the Christian claim that we are a fallen race, evil even, and in need of rescuing from our sinful selves. As I have written about in other works, most noticeably *"Once a Christian"*[1], I entirely reject the Christian interpretation of the sin of Adam and Eve, and the consequences thereof. To my way of thinking, it makes God too small, not omniscient, not even aware of the consequences of His creating humanity the way that He did. I believe in a God whose infinitude is beyond our comprehension, as expressed in that Jewish appellation, *Ein Sof*: the Infinite and [thus] Unknowable God.

Because I am confident that God knew what He was doing, and the implications of His design decisions, it seems logical to me that God gave us free will so that we had the choice of whether or not to accept Him as our God, to love Him, and to obey Him as He directed Moses to convey to the Children of Israel, His firstborn son. He knew that we would disobey, but He told the Israelites that He would forgive those who repented. At no stage in His guidance to His Prophets, did He speak of the need for substitutionary atonement, by the shedding innocent blood in a human sacrifice. On the contrary, He advised against such evil. Repeatedly, however, God told us of His grace, His mercy, His sense of Justice, and His readiness to forgive, so long as we repented and showed our love for Him by keeping His commandments (John 14:15, 21, 23-24, 15:10, 1 John 2:3-5, 5:3, 2 John 1:6).

It was this belief system, my theological worldview, that drove me to investigate the claims of Jesus fulfilling prophecy in the way that Christianity teaches that he did. Without question, such investigations did begin with pre-existing doubts. However, as best I could, I proceeded with the words of Simon Greenleaf fresh in my mind:

> "Let (the Gospel's) testimony be sifted, as it were given in a court of justice on the side of the adverse party, the witness being subjected to a rigorous cross-examination ... it is essential to the discovery of truth that we bring to the investigation a mind freed, as far as possible, from existing prejudice, and open to conviction ... to explore the maze of falsehood, to detect its artifices, to pierce its thickest veils, to follow and expose its sophistries, to compare the statements of different witnesses with severity, to discover truth and separate it from error."[2]

This, I believe, I have done, committed to intellectual integrity, evaluating the evidence with all the objectivity of which I am capable.

REFERENCES:

1. Talbot, Wayne, *Once a Christian: How the Bible Convinced Me to Walk Away*, Xlibris, Bloomington, IN, 2017
2. Greenleaf, Simon, *The Testimony of the Evangelists*, Kregel Classics, Grand Rapids, MI, 1995

Postscript – Torah, the Portable Homeland

"It will be in the end of days that the mountain of the Temple of Hashem will be firmly established as the most prominent of the mountains ... from Zion shall go forth the Torah, and the word of God from Jerusalem."
(Micah 4:1-3)

I have included this article because I am firmly convicted of the need for Torah in the lives of everyone, Jew, Christian, and Gentile. The Sages observed, wisely I believe, that God would not have created humanity without giving them instructions on how to live. Having given those instructions, God being omniscient, He would not have occasion to change His mind – the Wisest of All knows how to formulate His instructions for all time. We also have the words of the Prophet as above, and I am compelled to ask in the context of prophecy fulfillment: Why has Christianity, following the lead of how the authors of the New Testament used the Old Testament in quite a dubious fashion, convinced itself of Jesus fulfilling prophecy, yet has ignored the very clear prophecy concerning Torah? Even the Book of Revelation, reminds us of the perpetual Covenant that God made with His firstborn, the Children of Israel, yet Christianity insists that Jesus gave them a new, *replacement* covenant, and appropriated for itself, the identity of a *New Israel*. In his vision, John saw "the temple of God was opened in heaven, and the ark of His Covenant was seen in His temple" (Revelation 11:19). Mentioning the ark, what Covenant could that be if not the Covenant that God made with the Children of Israel? Revelation 22:18-19 warns of taking from, or adding to, the words recorded therein, and whilst arguably, Christianity has done neither, it most certainly has detracted from the meaning and spirit of Revelation, by retiring the Covenant safeguarded in the Ark, and abrogating Torah, God's expression of that Covenant.

Unlike any culture before or since, the Jews have persisted throughout history, despite the repeated attempts to eradicate them from the face of the earth. Deep down, I agree with the Rabbi, that Torah, the Portable Homeland of the Jews, is what has kept them safe from annihilation.

Yom HaShoah – Holocaust Remembrance Day

Jewish Life or Merely Israeli Life?
~ Rabbi Yochanan ben Zakkai or A.B. Yehoshua?[1] ~

In one of its most dramatic texts, the Talmud discusses an episode that was perhaps the most decisive moment in Jewish history prior to the Holocaust. It took place in the first century C.E. just as the Second Temple was to be destroyed by the Romans, who were then occupying the land. Tens of thousands of Jews were killed and there was no longer any food. A widespread sense of despair pervaded the community, and it seemed as if there would be no future for the Jewish people, as the Romans had decided on a "final solution."

There were only two choices: to surrender and live, or to fight and surely die. Defeating the Romans was no longer an option. Their numbers and their determination to end all Jewish life were too much for the weak and exhausted Jews.

It was left to one man to decide their fate. Rabbi Yochanan ben Zakkai, the Sage and unchallenged Jewish leader of his day, was fully aware that surrender would save many lives, but at the same time would be the end of the Jewish nation. The Romans would force the Jews to assimilate and adopt their way of living. The Chosen People and its unique mission would cease to exist, causing not only the Jews to pay a heavy price but also the world at large. There would no longer be anyone around to stand up and fight for moral values, human dignity, and the knowledge of God. In his eyes, the world would become a place of immense moral pain, destruction, and ongoing disaster.

At that crucial hour, Rabbi Yochanan ben Zakkai made a decision that was as risky as it was courageous. That decision, against all logic, led to an unparalleled victory, which miraculously saved the Jews and consequently the moral fiber of mankind. Rabbi Yochanan instructed his pupils to smuggle him out of Yerushalayim in a coffin and bring him to the soon-to-be Roman emperor, Vespasian. When asked by the despot why he came to see him, Rabbi Yochanan, realizing that any major request would fall on deaf ears, asked him for one favor: "Give me Yavne and its Sages." Vespasian, not realizing that the town of Yavne held the core of the Jewish Sages of its time, and therefore the vitality of Judaism's spiritual power, readily agreed to this plea. And it was this minor request that saved Judaism from oblivion. Because Judaism had been rescued, Christianity was later able to bring some of the major Jewish and monotheistic values to the Roman Empire. This was probably one of the main causes of Rome's downfall.

What made Rabbi Yochanan believe that the Jews and Judaism would survive once he guaranteed the continuous existence of Yavne and its Sages? It was his realization that the Jews possessed a religious tradition that, if necessary, would function beyond time and space. He understood that even if the Jews were robbed of their homeland, they would still be able to continue living as Jews and somehow, by the skin of their teeth, keep Judaism alive. But only as long as Jewish learning would continue to flourish and the study of Torah would be emphasized. It would be very risky and the price would be enormous, but it would work.

Almost 1900 years later, Heinrich Heine powerfully expressed this idea when he claimed that the secret to Jewish survival is found in the concept of their "portable homeland"—the Torah—which they carry with them, inhabiting it when the physical homeland is lost. Many years later, George Steiner made a similar observation when he called the Torah "our homeland, the text."

Rabbi Yochanan was convinced that interaction with this divine text would enable the Jewish people to continue, while any other nation would capitulate under similar circumstances. If necessary, it would carry the Jewish people beyond the physical need for a homeland.

In May 2006, giving a highly controversial talk at the American Jewish Committee's Centennial Symposium in Washington, A.B. Yehoshua, one of Israel's most celebrated authors, made some important remarks about the contemporary Jewish scene. However, he also made some extremely dubious statements about Jewish life in Israel and the Diaspora.

He reminded his audience that "the Zionist solution, which was proven as the best solution to the Jewish problem before the Holocaust, was tragically missed by the Jewish people." He pointed out that after the Balfour Declaration of 1917, "if during the 1920s, when the country's gates were open wide, just a half-million Jews had come (less than 5 percent of the Jewish People at that time) instead of the tiny number that actually did come, it certainly would have been possible to establish a Jewish state before the Holocaust....This state not only would have ended the Israeli-Arab conflict at an earlier stage and with less bloodshed—it also could have provided refuge in the 1930s to hundreds of thousands of Eastern European Jews who sensed the gathering storm."

While this opinion could be challenged as wishful thinking, there is much truth in Yehoshua's belief that if the Jews had taken the threat of radical anti-Semitism more seriously, and if a more determined effort had been made to establish the State of Israel at an earlier time, many Jews would have been saved.

But Yehoshua did not leave it at that. He continued and said, "For me, Avraham Yehoshua, there is no alternative. I cannot keep my identity outside Israel... [Being] Israeli is my skin, not my jacket. You [Diaspora Jews] are changing jackets; you are changing countries like changing jackets. I have my skin, the territory [of Israel]." He then continued to claim that outside of Israel one cannot live a full Jewish life, and implied that the most secular Israeli in Israel was living a more Jewish life than his Orthodox brothers in Toronto or Brooklyn.

While I definitely agree that Israel is the only place in the world where one can live a full Jewish life, it is extremely naïve, and even ludicrous, to claim that secular Israelis are living a more Jewish life purely because they live in the State of Israel, surrounded by fellow Jews, governed by a Jewish Government, and protected by a Jewish army. It is true that in Israel, Jewish culture is not a subculture, and Judaism can flourish more in this country than in any other. But that does not mean that Israel is a Jewish country simply because the majority of its residents are Israelis.

Yehoshua is confusing two things. Being Israeli is not identical to being Jewish. Indeed, to be an Israeli one needs to live in the land, and when the land ceases to exist, being Israeli no longer has any meaning.

But, as Rabbi Yochanan ben Zakkai correctly understood, if need be, it is possible to remain a Jew—although surely not a complete one—without living in Israel. Yehoshua does not seem to understand that there would never have been a State of Israel if not for the fact that his own grandparents continued to live a Jewish life in the Diaspora. Had they and their contemporaries lived an exclusively non-Jewish life, there would no longer have been any Jews and no State of Israel would ever have been established.

What Rabbi Yochanan taught us is that Jews will survive without Israel, as long as there is Torah, the portable homeland; but Jews will not survive solely because of the existence of Israel—however powerful it may be—if Israel does not incorporate a large percentage of Jewish traditional resources. To believe that Jews will survive only because of Israel is an absurd claim that has no foundation in Jewish history or reality. The famous Jewish philosopher Eliezer Berkovits made this extremely clear when he said, "There is no Israeli claim to the land; there can only be a Jewish claim. Where there is no continuity, there can be no return."

Happily, a large number of Israelis realize this, and although many of them are not Orthodox or even religious, they try hard to bring some inner Jewishness to their lives and observe some traditions, because they know that Rabbi Yochanan ben Zakkai was right and A.B. Yehoshua is wrong.

REFERENCES:

1. https://www.cardozoacademy.org/thoughts-to-ponder/yom-hashoah-jewish-life-or-just-israeli-life/?utm_source=Subscribers&utm_campaign=7608304389-Weekly_Thoughts_to_Ponder_campaign_TTP_548&utm_medium=email&utm_term=0_dd05790c6d-7608304389-242339045

BIBLIOGRAPHY

1. Andrews, Professor E.H., *Who Made God? Searching for a Theory of Everything*, EP Books, Darlington, England, 2009
2. Bacchiocchi, Samuel, *From Sabbath to Sunday*, The Pontifical Gregorian University Press, Rome, Italy, 1977
3. Beale, G.K., *The Right Doctrine from the Wrong Texts?* Essays on the Use of the Old Testament in the New, Baker Academic, Grand Rapids, MI, 1994
4. Black, David A., and Dockery, David S., *New Testament Criticism and Interpretation*, Zondervan, Grand Rapids, MI, 1991
5. Boyarin, Daniel, *The Jewish Gospels: The Story of the Jewish Christ*, The New Press, New York, NY, 2012
6. Brown, Michael L., *Our Hands Are Stained With Blood*, Destiny Image Publishers Inc., Shippensburg, PA, 1990
7. Burkett, Delbert, *An introduction to the New Testament and the origins of Christianity*, Cambridge University Press, 2002
8. Cardozo, Nathan Lopes, *Jewish Law as Rebellion: A Plea for Religious Authenticity and Halachic Courage*, Urim Publications, Jerusalem, Israel, 2018
9. Chambers, Oswald, *My Utmost For His Highest*, Barbour Publishing Inc., Ulhrichville, OH, 1963

10. Dewey, Arthur J., *The Authentic Letters of Paul*, Polebridge Press, Salem, OR, 2010 (additional authors Roy W. Hoover, Lane C. McGaughy, Daryl D. Schmidt)

11. Doukhan, Jacques, *On the Way to Emmaus: Five Major Messianic Prophecies Explained*, Lederer Books, Clarksville, MD, 2012

12. Dunn, James D.G., *Christianity in the Making: Beginning from Jerusalem*, Wm. B. Eerdmans Publishing Co., Grand Rapids, MI, 2009

13. Dunn, James D.G., *Jesus, Paul and the Law*, Westminster / John Knox Press, Louisville, KY, 1990

14. Dunn, James D.G., *Jesus, Paul, and the Gospels*, Wm. B. Eerdmans Publishing Co., Grand Rapids, MI, 2011

15. Ehrman, Bart D., *How Jesus Became God: The Exaltation of a Jewish Preacher from Galilee*, Harper One, New York, NY, 2014

16. Feser, Edward, *Five Proofs of the Existence of God*, Ignatius Press, San Francisco, CA, 2017

17. Friedman, David, *They Loved the Torah – What Jesus' First Followers Really Thought About the Law*, Lederer Books, Clarksville, MD, 2001

18. Gibson, Shimon, *The Final Days of Jesus: The Archaeological Evidence*, HarperOne, New York, NY, 2009

19. Gordon, Nehemiah, and Johnson, Keith, *A Prayer to Our Father - Hebrew Origins of the Lord's Prayer*, Hilkiah Press, 2010

20. Greenleaf, Simon, *The Testimony of the Evangelists*, Kregel Classics, Grand Rapids, MI, 1995

21. Gruber, Mayer I., *Rashi's Commentary on Psalms*, The Jewish Publication Society, Philadelphia, PA, 2007

22. Haynes, Carlyle B., *From Sabbath to Sunday*, Review and Herald Publishing Association, Washington, DC, 1928

23. Helyer, Larry R., *Exploring Jewish Literature of the Second Temple Period*, IVP Academic, Downers Grove, IL, 2002

24. Henry, Carl F.H., *Revelation and the Bible: contemporary evangelical thought*, Baker Books, Grand Rapids, MI, 1958

25. Hitchens, Christopher and Wilson, Douglas, *Is Christianity Good for the World*, Canon Press, Moscow, Indiana, 2009

26. Hoffman, Joel M., *The Bible Doesn't Say That: 40 Biblical Mistranslations, Misconceptions, and Other Misunderstandings*, Thomas Dunne Books, New York, NY, 2016

27. Howard, George, *Hebrew Gospel of Matthew*, Mercer University Press, Macon, GA, 2002

28. Howard, George, *Hebrew Gospel of Matthew*, Mercer University Press, Macon, GA, 2002

29. Isaac, Jules, *The Teaching of Contempt: Christian Roots of Anti-Semitism*, Holt, Rinehart and Winston, Inc., New York, NY, 1964

30. Kaplan, Aryek, *The Real Messiah - A Jewish Response to Missionaries*, National Conference of Synagogue Youth, New York, 1995

31. Knohl, Israel, *The Messiah Before Jesus: The Suffering Servant of the Dead Sea Scrolls*, University of California Press, Berkeley, CA, 2000

32. Kramer, Chaim, *Mashiach: Who, What, Why, How, Where and When?* Breslov Research Institute, Jerusalem, Israel, 2013

33. Lancaster, D. Thomas, *What About the Sacrifices?* First Fruits of Zion, Marshfield, MO, 2011

34. Lee, Bernard J., *The Galilean Jewishness of Jesus*, Paulist Press, Mahwah, NJ, 1988

35. *Levine, Amy-Jill, and Brettler, Marc Zvi, The Jewish Annotated New Testament*, Oxford University Press, New York, NY, 2011

36. Lewis, C.S., *Christian Reflections*, William B. Eerdmans Publishing Company, Grand Rapids, Michigan

37. Lewis, C.S., *The Case for Christianity*, Collier Books, New York, NY, 1989

38. Lindars, Barnabas, *The Place of the Old Testament in the Formation of New Testament Theology*, Cambridge University Press, UK, 1976

39. MacCoby, Hyam, *Revolution in Judaea: Jesus & The Jewish Resistance*, Ocean Books, London, UK, 1973

40. MacCoby, Hyam, *The Mythmaker: Paul and the Invention of Christianity*, Barnes & Noble Books, San Francisco, CA, 1998

41. Marcus, Rabbi Yosef, *Pirkei Avot: The Ethics of the Fathers*, Kehot Publication Society, Brooklyn, NY, 2011

42. McClure, Joshua A., *The Crimson Thread of the Bible*, Deep River Books, Sisters, OR, 2011

43. Moule, C.F.D., *The Origin of Christology*, Cambridge University Press, UK, 1977

44. Murphy-O'Connor, Jerome, *1 Corinthians: A People's Bible Commentary*, The Bible Reading Fellowship, Oxford, England, 1999

45. Naylor, Carma, *A Mormon's Unexpected Journey - Volume I*, WinePress Publishing, Enumclaw, WA, 2006

46. Naylor, Carma, *A Mormon's Unexpected Journey - Volume II*, WinePress Publishing, Enumclaw, WA, 2006

47. Pritz, Ray A., *Nazarene Jewish Christianity: From the End of the New Testament Period until Its Disappearance in the Fourth Century*, Magnes Press, Hebrew University, 1992

48. *Roth, Andrew Gabriel, Aramaic English New Testament*, Netzari Press, Jerusalem, Israel, 2012

49. *Scherman, Rabbi Nosson, The Chumash*, Mesorah Publications, ArtScroll English Edition, Brooklyn, NY, 2009

50. *Scherman, Rabbi Nosson, The Tanach*, Mesorah Publications, ArtScroll English Edition, Brooklyn, NY, 2011

51. Sheppard, J.D., *Jesus vs. Paul: Christianity's Greatest Lies Exposed*, Lamps With Oil, 2013

52. Simon, Marcel, *Verus Israel: A Study of the Relations between Christian and Jews in the Roman Empire AD 135-425*, Schoen Books, South Deerfield, MA, 1986

53. Simon, Marcel, *Verus Israel: A Study of the Relations between Christian and Jews in the Roman Empire AD 135-425*, Schoen Books, South Deerfield, MA, 1986

54. Singer, Rabbi Tovia, *Let's Get Biblical – Expanded Edition Volume 1*, Outreach Judaism, Jerusalem, Israel, 2015

55. Singer, Rabbi Tovia, *Let's Get Biblical – Expanded Edition Volume 2*, Outreach Judaism, Jerusalem, Israel, 2015

56. Smith, Nehemiah, and Johnson, Keith, *A Prayer To Our Father: Hebrew Origins of the Lord's Prayer*, Hilkiah Press, 2009

57. Spangler, Ann, and Tverberg, Lois, *Sitting at the Feet of Rabbi Yeshua*, Zondervan, Grand Rapids, MI, 2009

58. Stern, David H., *Messianic Judaism - A Modern Movement with an Ancient Past*, Lederer Books, Clarksville, MD, 2007

59. Tabor, James D., *Paul and Jesus: How the Apostle Paul Transformed Christianity*, Simon & Schuster Paperbacks, New York, NY, 2012

60. Talbot, Wayne, *Bible Inerrancy: Fact or Fiction? The Inerrancy of God's Word versus the Fallibility of Human Interpretation*, Peshat Books, Kelso, NSW, 2012

61. Talbot, Wayne, *Christians Too, Must Obey: Putting a Fence Around Torah*, Xlibris, Bloomington, IN, 2017

62. Talbot, Wayne, *Defending God's Sabbath: Obeying God's Commandment to Safeguard the Sabbath*, Peshat Books, Kelso, NSW, 2013

63. Talbot, Wayne, *If Not God What? On Being an Intellectually Fulfilled Theist*, Peshat Books, Kelso, NSW, 2012

64. Talbot, Wayne, *Once A Christian, How the Bible Convinced Me to Walk Away*, Xlibris, Bloomington, IN, 2017

65. Talbot, Wayne, *The New Covenant on Trial: Examining the Evidence for a Replacement Covenant*, Xlibris, Bloomington, IN, 2016

66. Truss, Lynne, *Eats, Shoots & Leaves: The Zero Tolerance Approach to Punctuation*, Gotham Books, New York, NY, 2003

67. Tyson, Joseph B., *Marcion and Luke-Acts: A Defining Struggle*, University of South Carolina Press, Columbia, SC, 2006

68. Unger, Merrill F., *Unger's Commentary on the Old Testament*, Vol. 1, Moody Press, Chicago, 1981

69. Willis, Norman B., *Nazarene Israel: The Original Faith of the Apostles*, Custom Book Publishing, 2012

70. Wise, Michael O., *The First Messiah: Investigating the Savior Before Christ*, HarperOne, San Francisco, CA, 1999

71. Zacharias, Ravi, *The Kingdom of the Cults*, Bethany House Publishers, Minneapolis, MI, 2003

72. Zlotowitz, Rabbi Meir, *Bereishis (Genesis) with Commentary Volumes I & II*, Mesorah Publications Ltd., Brooklyn, NY, 2009

CPSIA information can be obtained
at www.ICGtesting.com
Printed in the USA
BVHW03*0839180918
527708BV00023B/106/P

9 781984 501684